The three children of Daniel and Serena Farman had left their ancestral New England home to live their own very different and venturesome lives. And then came December 1941.

JEROME, an Army Reserve Officer, was sent to Fort Bragg. There he met and married the lovely, spirited Creole, Alix St. Cyr, before he was sent overseas into the frenzy of desert battle.

JENNESS, a Washington Congressman's confidential secretary, became implicated in grave indiscretions both political and personal. And the outcome would only be known after a scandalous courtroom battle.

JUDITH, a nurse, was torn between her allegiance to her faithful suitor, Dexter Abbott, and her intense yearning to take a dramatic part in the war effort.

The story of these fascinating people is one of Miss Keyes's most engrossing. "One will hardly lay the book down until she discovers just how each life is 'coming out.' "

—*Springfield Republican*

S0-AQP-500

ALSO THE HILLS
was originally published by Julian Messner.

*Are there paperbound books you want
            but cannot find in your retail stores?*

Also the Hills

By

Frances Parkinson Keyes

PUBLISHED BY POCKET BOOKS NEW YORK

ALSO THE HILLS

Julian Messner edition published 1943

POCKET BOOK edition published August, 1976

This POCKET BOOK edition includes every word contained in
the original, higher-priced edition. It is printed from brand-
new plates made from completely reset, clear, easy-to-read type.
POCKET BOOK editions are published by
POCKET BOOKS,
a division of Simon & Schuster, Inc.,
A GULF+WESTERN COMPANY
630 Fifth Avenue,
New York, N.Y. 10020.
Trademarks registered in the United States
and other countries.

TO DORIS FLEESON

of whom I am very fond

NEW ENGLAND VILLAGE, 1942

Here are the hills, the river and the school,
   The grange, the stores, three churches. Down a way
You'll find the drowsing station, where the rule
   Is two trains up, and two trains down, each day.

St. Andrew's churchyard rests an ancient guild
   Of Howlands, Wathleys, Winegars and Lains
Who, by their way of living, helped to build
   The mood of peace the village still retains.

Yet look again, lest you conclude the world
   Spins past these homes. No leafy street but one
Bright window has a little flag unfurled,
   With every star of blue an absent son.

Loving its own, but loving freedom more
   This tiny village, too, has gone to war.

MILTON BRACKER.

New York Times
August 11, 1942

Contents

PART   PAGE

I. FARMAN HILL
      DECEMBER 1941-JANUARY 1942 1

II. WASHINGTON, D. C.
      JANUARY-FEBRUARY 1942 147

III. RAEFORD, NORTH CAROLINA
      MARCH 1942 341

IV. FARMAN HILL
      MARCH-SEPTEMBER 1942 367

V. ARZEU, NORTH AFRICA
      DECEMBER 1942-JANUARY 1943 501

VI. "THE RED PAVILION"
      JANUARY-JULY 1943 547

      AUTHOR'S NOTE 685

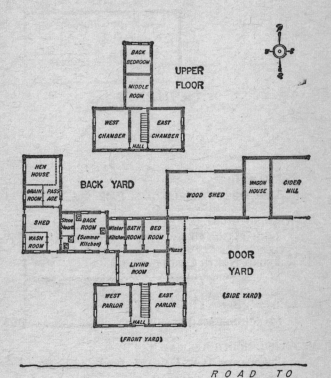

UPPER FLOOR

BACK BEDROOM

MIDDLE ROOM

WEST CHAMBER

EAST CHAMBER

HALL

HEN HOUSE

BACK YARD

GRAIN ROOM

PASS AGE

SHED

Stone Hearth

BACK ROOM (Summer Kitchen)

WASH ROOM

Winter Kitchen

BATH ROOM

BED ROOM

WOOD SHED

WAGON HOUSE

CIDER MILL

Piazza

DOOR YARD

(SIDE YARD)

LIVING ROOM

WEST PARLOR

EAST PARLOR

HALL

(FRONT YARD)

ROAD TO

PLAN OF THE HOMESTEAD
on
FARMAN HILL

━━ ━ ━━ DOOR   ━━━ ━ ━━━ WINDOW
C CUPBOARD

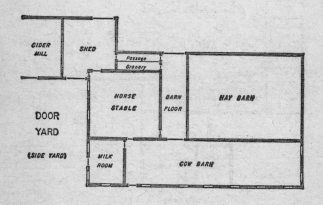

CIDER MILL

SHED

Passage

Granary

HORSE STABLE

BARN FLOOR

HAY BARN

DOOR YARD

(SIDE YARD)

MILK ROOM

COW BARN

VILLAGE

PART I

Farman Hill

December 1941–January 1942

CHAPTER 1

"IT'S BEEN a grand day, hasn't it, Dexter?"

"Grand, hell! It would be perfect, Judy, if you'd promise me just one thing."

"I might, at that. I'm in a pretty mellow mood."

"Then promise me you won't put me off again."

"I haven't the least idea of putting you off again. What made you think I had?"

"Nothing special. Except that you have done it, twice already."

"It isn't fair to blame the first time on me. Dad and Mom thought we were too young to get married then. And they thought I ought to see a few other places, besides this one little hick town, before I decided I wanted to spend my whole life in it."

"They were darn young themselves when they got married, weren't they? And they seem to have been happy enough living in a little hick town. But we'll let that pass. You can't blame the second time on them."

"No, I can't. But I've tried to explain before, Dexter, and I never could make you understand. It wasn't that I didn't want to marry you then, that I haven't always wanted to. But first I had to take that nursing course. I didn't *want* to, exactly, not nearly as much as I wanted to marry you. But there was something inside of me . . ."

The girl had met her companion's sober gray eyes, squarely, as she began to speak. Now she turned away from him, and gazed out over the silent countryside, almost as if she were seeking in it the answer she was trying to give him. The scene was one of boundless beauty and infinite peace. Not only the distant mountains, but the hills which clustered closer, were covered with smooth snow, and this also lay lightly on the branches of the firs and pines which bordered the road and prevailed in the timber lots. Between the evergreens, the silver birches rose in slim white formations, and the elms and maples were etched in skeletal outlines. The river, winding away in the distance between the twin meadows on either side of it, was calm and gray; but like the snowy mountains, it caught the reflection of the sun, sinking so riotously in the west, and a shimmer of rose spread over it, as this did over them. Judith, suddenly pressing Dexter's arm, turned back to him again with smiling lips and eyes.

"My, look at that color!" she said. "Did you ever see anything to beat it, anywhere? I don't understand how anyone who can live here, and see things like that, and lots of others just as lovely, all the time, would ever go away, if they could help it. I could never make out why Jenny was so restless, or why Jerome was—well, whatever it was that made him want to work in a Boston bank instead of staying on the farm with Dad. But anyway, I'm going to stop trying to explain about myself and the way I feel. And I am going to marry you."

"When?"

"Why, in the spring, I suppose. Wouldn't that be as good a time as any?"

"No. I think Christmas would be a darn sight better."

"Well, I don't. Jenny'll be back from Washington then, and there's even a chance Jerome might get leave. The house will be in enough of an uproar without trying to have a wedding there."

"I should think you'd like to have one when your brother and sister could be home for it."

"Well, I would, if that were all there was to think of. But Jenny can get away almost anytime, I guess, for a wedding in the immediate family. And there's no use counting on Jerome. That's just a chance."

She looked away again, and Dexter, watching her expression attentively, realized there would be no use in saying anything more about a Christmas wedding just then. He and Judith Farman had been friends and neighbors all their lives, and they had been sweethearts ever since they stopped being playmates; he recognized all her moods, and he had learned long before that all of them were not "mellow," by any means. The streak of hardness in her did not show at all. Her pleasant face, with its clear skin and candid eyes, was almost as gentle as her mother's, and the whole countryside said that if ever a woman were well named, it was Serena Farman. At the same time, it was almost as merry as the face of Judith's sister, Jenness, who had left an aching void behind her when she deserted the village to attend a business college. The void had never been filled, for after graduating with flying colors, she had been offered a splendid position in Washington, and she had been there ever since, doing better and better for herself all the time, until now she had become the valued private secretary of a prominent congressman named Horace Vaughn. There were any number of young masculine hearts which still ached because of her willing absence from her birthplace. Indeed, Dexter Abbott was almost the only unattached male in its vicinity who admired Judith more than he did Jenness. There was a dazzling quality about Jenness which Judith lacked, and it was not ephemeral, like so many dazzling things; it lasted. But Judith had an indefinable quality of her own which took the place of this, at least as far as Dexter was concerned, though for all his admiration he knew only too well that Judith was not as lighthearted as Jenness, really, any more than she was really as tranquil as Serena. Basically she was serious, more serious than he was himself, which was saying a good deal. One of the reasons they had always understood each other so well was because of this basic gravity they both possessed. But she was much the more stubborn of the two, and on occasion she could also be very stormy. Dexter was a peace-loving person, whose kindliness showed in his face as plainly as his strength. He desired nothing less than to stir up a storm at the end of a day which, as he and Judith agreed, had been practically perfect. But he pushed his luck to the point of asking one more question.

"You won't insist on going on with your nursing after we're married, will you, Judy?"

"I won't take any cases out of the village. You know I

don't now. I figure, with Jenny and Jerome both so far away, Dad and Mom aren't unreasonable, wanting to have me right near them. Besides there's plenty here to keep me busy. And what's more, I love this place better than any other in the world. I keep telling you that."

"Yes, you do keep telling me that. But there's something else I'd rather you'd tell me."

"All right, you persistent pest. I love you better than any other *person* in the world, even if you are a nagging old sobersides! I wish you'd brighten up a little, but I'm going to take a chance on you anyway. And if it's any satisfaction to you to hear me say it, well, I don't see how I'll have time to do much nursing after I marry you. I think you'll keep me too busy coddling you. I'm afraid you've made up your mind to. For such a swell guy as you really are, you've got some terribly obsolete ideas. You not only believe woman's place is in the home; I wouldn't put it past you to believe wives ought to obey their husbands."

She laughed, so iovously that it took most of the sting from her words. Most of it, but not quite all. Dexter winced a little, wishing she had not used the word "coddling," or inferred that the main reasons she would give up nursing after they were married lay with him and not with her. Although he was very strong, he had always been extremely sensitive about the lameness which had kept him out of sports, first at the local high school and later at the State University, and which, more recently, had been the cause of his rejection by the draft board. He had never found any consolation in the fact that he had led all his classes and been voted the best liked man on the campus, and now he found none in the fact that nearly all his neighbors believed there would not be a war anyway, and that even if there were, Dexter Abbott would be much more useful right where he was than in some outlandish place on the other side of the world. He not only ran his farm and mill with marked efficiency; he was a selectman, and a director in the bank, and the Master of the Lodge. Such activities as these the village understood and appreciated. It had never approved Jerome Farman's course in going to

Norwich Military Academy, instead of Dartmouth, which was his father's college, apparently for no better reason than because he had been intrigued with the cadets' uniforms when they came to play football at Hanover. Now the village said it "served him right" because, as a Reserve Officer, he had been wrested from the Boston bank where he was doing so well, and sent to Fort Bragg, before the new Defense Program was half under way. Except for his parents and sisters and Dexter Abbott, no one even said it was greatly to his credit that he had gone to Fort Bragg as a First Lieutenant instead of a Second Lieutenant, because he had boned up on Army paper work in Boston, nights, after his day's work was done. It was really all the more so, because his natural inclination would have been to go out and paint the town red. But everyone said that Jerome, like his sister Jenness, had an "itching foot," and that someday Daniel and Serena Farman would be sorry they hadn't put a little more money into their rundown old place and a little less into fancy schooling for their children . . .

Dexter was still thinking about his future brother-in-law, and trying to do so without envy, when Judith put her face against his, effectually banishing all thoughts of Jerome, though Dexter guessed the gesture was one of contrition rather than yearning. Her rosy cheeks were very cold, for they had been riding all afternoon in an old-fashioned open sleigh. After snow-balling each other in the back yard to "work off" Serena's ample Sunday dinner, they had gone exploring in the "cider mill," as the long shed, between the house and the barn, with a carpentry shop in its loft, was still called, though no cider had been made there for years. There they had found this old yellow sleigh shoved into a dusty cobwebby corner, as Judith's father had told them they might, and had merrily dragged it out. They had been sleighing ever since, and that was three hours ago; now the frostiness of the air had become a part of Judith's glowing skin, and Dexter was conscious of its freshness as his lips moved over her face. But her mouth was still miraculously warm, and it grew warmer as his kisses gained intensity. She did not draw away from him, either,

this time, as she so often had done in the past, and presently he leaned forward and twisted his reins around the
dashboard. Then he put his arms about her and held her
fast, kissing her harder and harder. Meanwhile the wise old
horse plodded patiently up the hill without guidance, as he
had done under similar circumstances, hundreds of times
before.

Long ago, as a colt, he had been so frisky that it had
been almost impossible to break him and in those days he
had never been used by courting couples. That was a com-
pensation which had come to him with advancing years.
He came of a breed from which, in bygone days, the Farmans had taken pride in supplying the leads for the mountain coaches which required a six-horse hitch. It was need-
ful that these leads, being far from the driver's reach,
should be spirited by nature, and none of the Farman
horses had ever been found wanting in this essential quality.
There were no coaches rattling through the passes of the
White Mountains anymore, but there were still horses on
Farman Hill, though it was a long time since there had
been any new colts. Unlike most of his neighbors, Daniel
Farman did not depend wholly on machinery to do his
work, but he had not kept up the stud farm which his forefathers had run so successfully. Gypsy, the old white horse
now patiently plodding up the hill, and his mate, Nell,
were the last of their line.

The rising stretch of road was a lonely one, only two or
three small abandoned homesteads, with pitiful blank windows and moss-grown sagging roofs being visible for more
than a mile. There was no one to see them or sneer at
them as Judith and Dexter rode along, and they were still
locked in each other's arms when the house towards which
they were heading loomed into sight at the top of Farman
Hill. Inside, it was always bright and cheerful, since Serena
Farman had a positive genius for homemaking, even
though she had so little to "do with"; and quite apart from
its livable qualities it had dignity and distinction. The
great panelled living room, which stretched straight across
it from east to west, back of the entrance hall dividing
the two parlors; the curious mural designs with which this

entrance hall and these parlors were painted; and the unimpeachable antiques with which the entire house was furnished, all combined to make it noteworthy. But outside,
especially on a midwinter day, its aspect was rather gaunt
and forbidding. There was nothing to relieve its rectangular
outline except the twin elms, now bare and black themselves, which stood on either side of it. The green shutters,
which in summertime had a softening effect on its façade,
were regularly removed in the Fall when the double windows were put on; and the white clapboards, on which the
paint had not been renewed in many years, looked soiled
and dingy against the brilliance of the snow. Only the
smoke, curling reassuringly up from the chimneys, gave a
promise of warmth and welcome within. Jenness, who was
not above poking fun at her birthplace and her family,
had remarked, the first time she came home from Washington, that the Farman place was a good deal like some
of the Farmans themselves: pretty grim until you got underneath the surface. Judith recalled this comment now, as
she detached herself, more lingeringly than she had ever
done before, from Dexter's arms.

"I'll tell the world that was quite a kiss!" she said, laughing again. But there was a little catch in her voice as she
laughed, and a new softness in her bright eyes. "I guess
Jenness wouldn't have thought I was so grim, after all, if
she'd caught me then! It's just as well we came out of our
clinch when we did. The next thing we knew, we'd have
been right in the yard, and Mom would have had to step
out in the snow and pry us apart."

"Your mother's never tried to separate us, Judy,"
Dexter said slowly. There was no levity in his voice as he
spoke. The embrace had exhilarated Judith; but it had
meant much more to him than awakened desire or satisfied
senses. He knew now that he would not let Judith put him
off anymore with one excuse after another. He would
give her until spring, since that was the breathing space
for which she herself had asked. But he would marry her
then, no matter what she said or did. No matter what he
had to say or do himself to make her. "Rhoda, maybe,"
he went on still more slowly. "But not your mother. Even

that time when she said we were too young, she was nice
about it. She said she hoped I'd understand it wasn't that
she had any objection to me for a son-in-law. And I did.
I've always felt towards her like I would have toward my
own mother, I guess, if she'd lived. A lot more than I ever
did towards Rhoda. It's mean to say so, because Rhoda's
been awfully good to me. But it's true."

"Oh, Rhoda!" Judith said, almost impatiently. She had
never bothered to conceal her contempt for the "old maid"
sister, nearly twenty years his senior, who had sacrificed
her school teaching to bring Dexter up and who still shared
the Abbott homestead with him. "Dexter—I don't know
why I've never asked you before—Rhoda doesn't expect to
go on living with you after you're married, does she?"

"Why I never asked *her!* But I took it for granted, myself, that she would. I never thought of her leaving her
home. Where would she live, if she didn't live there? She
couldn't take up teaching again now. She doesn't know
modern methods."

Gypsy was already turning into the yard. Dexter told
himself that it was because they were practically up to the
side porch that Judith did not answer. In another minute,
despite the cold, Serena Farman would come out to welcome them back, according to her habit. No matter how
busy she was, she always managed to watch from the east
window of the living room for Judith's homecoming, and
to open the east door, which led to the side porch, letting
the warmth and light and cheer which were her natural
elements stream forth into the chill outer air. No one who
went to the Farman house ever thought of using the front
door, which led into the frescoed hallway between the two
frescoed parlors. Even comparative strangers, who were
eventually taken into one of these, when it was not too
cold, made their entrance from the rear, through the living
room. In wintertime the snow was not shovelled away from
the front path, and grass had grown up so thickly between
its cobblestones that these were almost obscured; so it did
not show much in summertime either. But no one ever
missed it. The frescoed parlors were the pride of the Farman house, the feature that antiquarians and "summer

people" raved about. But the long panelled living room was its heart, and the entrance into this was the only one that counted.

The living room door opened now, before the yellow sleigh was actually at a standstill, as Judith and Dexter had both known it would, and Serena Farman came out on the side porch. Her head was bare, but she was wearing a little circular crocheted shawl over her print dress to protect her briefly from the cold. The dress and the shawl were both gray, but her apron was as white as the smooth snow, and her hair was very white too. She was only in her later forties now, and her hair had already been white a long time. Most women would have resented having it turn so early, especially as it had been such a beautiful bright brown when she was a girl. But Serena Farman did not resent it. If she had any vanity at all, it was centered in her white hair, and she dressed it in a careful and elaborate way, which, on anyone else, would have been almost incongruous with her simple homemade clothes. But somehow her clothes suited her too, possibly because they were always so spotless and because she wore them so well. She was, as the village said, a "fine figure of a woman," which meant that she had gained a certain amount of weight with the years, in spite of the active life she led. But she was very erect, and there was no clumsiness in her movements, only an effect of beautiful amplitude in her bearing.

"Well, I guess you've had an enjoyable ride," she said pleasantly. "I'm glad of it. I want you should come in, Dexter, after you've put the team up. Rhoda won't be expecting you until she sees you. And I've got a nice supper started. A corn chowder. I had good luck with my canning this year. You can't hardly tell the corn from fresh. We can kind of talk things over while we eat. It looks as if we might have quite a lot to say to each other."

"What's happened?" Judith asked quickly.

"Why your father turned the radio on just after you and Dexter left," Serena Farman said, still pleasantly. "I hadn't quite finished doing the dishes. Seems there's been some trouble over in Hawaii. Looks as if we hadn't come out of it any too well, either."

"Trouble? What kind of trouble?" Judith said, speaking more sharply.

"Some kind of a surprise attack. Your father can tell you, maybe, better than I can. It was the Japs did it. They surprised our fleet. It looks as if they'd done considerable damage. Yes, I'm afraid things look pretty bad. Jenness says war'll be declared tomorrow after all and——"

"Jenness?" repeated Dexter, his kindly voice suddenly as sharp as Judith's.

"Yes, Jenness telephoned from Washington. Of course she put in a station-to-station call. But she said she felt as if she'd got to talk with us. She'd been standing in a big crowd outside the Japanese Embassy and she was all excited. There were police patrols, and reporters kept dashing up, and lots of diplomats were strolling by, pretending they were just taking their dogs out for a nice Sunday walk, but all the time not missing a single trick. Jenness says the Embassy is a big blank-looking building, but smoke was pouring out of all the chimneys in big black puffs, and the crowds began to shout, 'They must be burning their records!' Of course no one knew for sure though, because no one could get in. The iron gates leading into the grounds were locked, and Western Union boys were shaking the grill work, bound and determined to get through, and the police were shoving them aside. No one could understand why there should have been so many messages to deliver just then and the crowd muttered about that too. Jenness could hardly bear to tear herself away, but she finally went off with one of the reporters, named Peter MacDonald, who had to rush back to his office and get out a story for an extra. He took her in there with him, and she telephoned right from the building where the newspaper is printed."

"It seems to me Peter MacDonald is always turning up where Jenness is and taking her some place she wouldn't see if it weren't for him." Judith remarked.

"Yes, and she's going to get to go to the House of

Representatives tomorrow to hear the Declaration of War, because she's a congressman's secretary. She said she never was so thrilled in all her life, but she couldn't hardly believe yet that it was true. You know Mr. Vaughn's made all those speeches to prove that the United States would never get drawn in, and she's typed them out and listened to the talk in his office, and all. I asked her if he was embarrassed, having said so much in public and then finding out he was wrong all the time, and she said no, why should he be? She'd have been put out with me if she hadn't been so excited. She certainly thinks the sun rises and sets on his head."

"I guess he's an able man," Dexter said generously. "Not that I've ever agreed with him. But we've all got a right to our opinions."

"Yes, that's what Jenness has always said. She's always said it made her blood boil to hear people talking as if the isolationists weren't sincere. She and Jerome quarrelled so, the last time they were home together, I thought they'd raise the roof. Jerome must be pretty excited too, right now. Likely he'll call up himself before the evening's over, if he gets the chance. He'll want to speak to you, if he does, Dexter."

"I guess maybe he will." Dexter's words came slowly again now, and he hardly looked at Judith as he gave her his hand to steady her when she jumped out of the sleigh. Jenness was excited because she was having a better time than she had ever had in her life, but Jerome would be excited because now he would feel sure that he was going overseas, and Dexter, who was Jerome's best friend, would be left behind. "I'll put the team up and then I'll come on into the house," he continued, pulling himself together. "That is, unless I can help Mr. Farman with the chores."

"He started them early. He's most through. He wanted to be through when you got home. He figured, like I did, that you'd stay to supper with us." Serena put her hand on the living room door and opened it wide. "He said he thought, by and by, we'd all be glad we'd spent this evening together."

CHAPTER 2

As DEXTER went limping home, after leaving the Farmans' house, he knew his thankfulness that they had spent this evening, at least, together, would date from that very night.

His own home was not far away, and he was accustomed to covering the intervening distance on foot. Walking was a slow process for him, but it was not a painful one, from the standpoint of physical effort, and he always found that after the stimulus of Judith's presence, he welcomed the sense of returning composure which he achieved through solitary exercise. From Farman Hill he struck westward, instead of going due north as he and Judith had done at the end of their drive; it was a less lonely stretch of road than the other, and there were still lights in some of the houses he passed. As he left the first hollow and walked up the second slope, he noticed one especially, in which all the upper windows were illuminated. It was a house which had been abandoned for a long time, and only a year and a half before, its condition had been almost as dilapidated as that of the ones which he and Judith had passed that afternoon. But some newcomers had bought it and restored it; everything about it looked tidy and prosperous now.

"The Hellmans are keeping pretty late hours," he said to himself. "I hope it isn't on account of sickness." He paused for a moment, undecided whether to go to the back door and inquire, in neighborly fashion, if there were anything he could do to help. But there was no light downstairs, even in the kitchen, and he knew that there would have been, if the doctor had been expected, or if some emergency had required the use of hot water during the night. Then, while he hesitated, the lights upstairs went off too, not one by one, but with a suddenness that was

14

almost startling. Dexter found himself blinking in astonishment at the blank facade, and again the sensation that
beyond it everything was not well, perturbed him momentarily. But he shook the feeling off, and walked on over the
second slope.

How pleasant the living room at the Farmans' had been
that night when he first went into it, how permeated with
peace that seemed impregnable! It was essentially Serena's
room, and even Judith's presence, insistent though this was,
did not disquiet him here. He had always loved it, and had
always been aware of its atmosphere, ever since he was a
child; but previously, if anyone had asked him to describe
its physical attributes in detail, he would have been hard
put to do so. There was an old water box at the west side
of the room, beyond the window shelf where Serena's
geraniums and begonias bloomed, and no matter how still
the room was, there was always the sound of flowing
water tinkling through it. Dexter could have told anyone
that he liked this, that it was soothing and pleasant, and
that he associated it with the small ancient picture of a
watering trough, inclosed in the same frame with the
mirror which it surmounted, that hung over a gate-legged
table standing between the big fireplace and the door into
the elder Farmans' bedroom. But probably neither the old
water box nor the old picture would have seemed very
important to anyone but him. Probably it was the tall secretary which stood on the other side of the window shelf,
or the tall china cabinet which matched it, and which stood
at the opposite end of the room, between the east door
and the grandfather's clock, which were really important.
Or perhaps the handhewn beams overhead, or the wide
boards of the floor, or the wainscotting on the walls, all of
which he was now really observing for the first time. Dexter
did not know and he did not care. He did not know either,
that often in moments of great portentousness, inanimate
objects take on the same vital aspects as the human beings
they surround and to whom they belong. But he did know
that the firelight had never seemed so glowing or the lamplight so soft, as they did at their source that night, and
that they had never seemed to melt away so mysteriously,

until they merged with the dark shadows on the still walls, and became a part of these.

Dexter had been alone in the living room for a time that night, before Daniel Farman came in from the barn, and while Judith was helping Serena with the supper. It was then that he first noticed the uncanny brightness of the fire and the softness of the lamplight, and the strange way in which these were engulfed by the beams and the wainscotting. He did not turn on the radio, and the old-fashioned telephone, attached to the wall, emitted nothing but the occasional rumbling which indicated that someone else was using the party line. The water trickling through the old water box still made the only steady sound in the room, though beyond in the winter kitchen, Judith's fresh voice and Serena's gentle one rose clearly, and Dexter heard them with enjoyment. He did not feel like smoking; he preferred to wait until after supper, when he and Daniel would light their pipes together. He sat down in the old rocker which was always drawn up near the hearth, and Pinkham, the family cat, who had been dozing on the hearthstone with his paws tucked underneath him, jumped into Dexter's lap and curled up there, purring like a tea kettle. Dexter was fond of Pinkham. He sat stroking the cat with affection and gazing contentedly, first into the fire and then at the doors on the south side of the room.

There was hardly any wainscotting on that side, because there were so many of these doors—one leading into each of the closed, cold parlors, one leading into the closed, cold hallway, and one leading into the warm dark cellar. The doors were panelled to match the walls, and they all had old latches, and grooves under the latches worn by many hands. At one time or another these doors had been used a great deal, through the course of years. But Dexter did not associate them with use. He was accustomed to seeing them with that shut, secret look which they had now. It was the two doors on the north side, at either end of the fireplace, that suggested service, that brought the winter kitchen and the family chamber to which they led into a harmonious whole with the living room.

Dexter was still staring at the north doors, when Judith

came in from the winter kitchen to pull the gate-legged table out from under the old mirror, and place it in the middle of the room before setting it. In spite of the spaciousness of the Farman house, there was no regularly appointed dining room in it. The family, and their friends, usually ate in the living room, though sometimes, in very mild weather, they used the summer kitchen beyond the winter kitchen for this purpose, and sometimes, on very grand occasions, one of the frescoed parlors. Jerome, while he was still coming home from college for summer vacations, had always encouraged the former custom, and Jenness, when she returned briefly from Washington, still encouraged the latter. But Judith, like her mother, clung tenaciously to the living room. She drew out the gate-legged table in a purposeful way and started to put food on it, ignoring the arms which Dexter stretched forth as she went by.

"There isn't any hurry about supper, is there?" he asked. "Come here for a minute."

"It must be six o'clock," Judith said, and as she spoke, the tall clock struck, slowly and sharply, each note vibrating into gradual stillness before another began. "There! I told you so! . . . The chowder's almost done," she went on practically, beginning to take china and silver from the tall cabinet, "and Dad'll be hungry when he comes in from the barn. Besides, Mom wants to get things cleared away so she can sit and listen to the radio without having the dishes on her mind."

"Did she say so?"

"No, but I know it just the same. And you heard what she did say, that she thinks Jerome will call before the evening's over . . . Are you sure you didn't have enough lovemaking while we were out in the sleigh to last you for a while? Until we say good night, anyway?"

"I never have enough to last anytime at all. I always want more. And now that we're definitely engaged——"

He rose, with his usual awkward slowness, and the next time she went swinging past him he managed to put his arm around her waist and draw her down to his knees as he reseated himself. She humored him to the extent of leaning back against his shoulder and putting her own arm around his neck. Then, finding the position unexpectedly pleasant, she relaxed and curled up in his lap, laying her cheek against his again, as she had that afternoon. The coolness that came from the frosty air was all gone now; instead her warm face reflected the glow of the fire and the softness of the lamplight; in a minute or two she might easily have been drowsy. But a question which Dexter asked her roused her more than his kisses.

"Does this room seem queer to you tonight, Judy?"

"Queer? Of course not! What makes you ask such a question?"

"Because it does to me. While I was sitting here alone, everything in it seemed to come alive—the secretary and the cabinet and all. The clock spoke up pretty sharply for itself just now, didn't you think so? And the water's always telling some kind of a story. But those closed doors on the north side there, they're keeping a secret instead. Talk about a house divided against itself——"

"Dexter, dear, you haven't started a temperature or anything, have you? Or are you just upset because Mom admitted that Jenny and Jerome fought so the last time they were here together? Maybe that's what gave you the idea of a divided house. But you must have always known how they squabble over nothing. Perhaps I better feel your pulse and stick a thermometer in your mouth, just to make sure you're all right."

He smiled as she put her fingers, with mock anxiety, on his wrist, but at the same time he shook his head.

"Don't bother. I do know Jerome's habits, and Jenny's, as well as I do yours. And I haven't a feverish feeling. But it's a weird one all right. Sure you haven't got it too?"

"Yes, I'm sure. Dexter, I must go. Mom'll be wondering what's become of me."

"I wouldn't worry about that if I were you. I think maybe she'll guess how you happened to be detained."

He tried to draw her closer again, but as he did so the latch on the east door was lifted, and Judith slipped away from him before her father actually entered the room. Daniel Farman was a stocky, rugged man, whose native intelligence was more obvious than his excellent education. Strangers in the vicinity—the Hellmans for instance—considered him uncouth, and wondered how a woman of Serena's gentleness and refinement could ever have married him. But Dexter, who knew him better, regarded him with extreme respect. The younger man rose now and spoke deferentially to his elder, though such careful courtesies were not customary in the village.

"Good evening, Sir. You see I'm still hanging around. Mrs. Farman asked me to stay to supper. I hope I'm not intruding, at a time like this."

"No, no. You're always welcome, Dexter . . . I suppose Mother told you the bad news though."

"She said there'd been some pretty alarming radio reports of an attack on Hawaii. But I guess the American people can take it, whatever it means, and that the Navy can give back as good as it gets."

"Yes, I guess so too. But Serena's almost sick at the thought of what this'll do to Jerome. It's natural for a woman to feel that way about her only son. And she frets about Jenness all the time anyhow. Jenness isn't as steady as her sister. Not that Serena's said anything. Of course that isn't her way."

Daniel unwound his long muffler and stooped to unfasten his heavy boots. He did not say anything, either, while he was doing so.

"It's getting colder," he remarked at last, straightening up. "I shouldn't be surprised but what it was ten below, by morning. The wind's shifted . . . Well, make yourself at home, Dexter. I'll be back as soon as I've washed."

His return coincided with the entry of Mrs. Farman, carefully bearing the old-fashioned tureen which contained the corn chowder. Judith had already managed, in spite of her suitor's importunities, to bring in homemade pickles, preserves, butter and bread, a deep dish of apple sauce, and a plate of pound cake. After their hearty Sunday dinner, this was considered sufficient supper. They took their places around the gate-legged table and bowed their heads.

"Lord, for what we are about to receive, make us duly

thankful," Daniel said, in his matter-of-fact voice. It was his customary way of asking grace; he used the same formula nearly everyday in the year. But this time Serena did not raise her head when he thought he had finished, and he knew she expected him to go on, as he did only on rare and great occasions. "Bless this food to our use and us to Thy service," he added. But still Serena did not raise her head, and he knew that yet more was required of him. "Keep our dear ones," he said. "Both the ones who are with us and the son and the daughter of this house who are far from home. Let none of them fail in their duty. But bring the absent back to us in Thy own good time. For Jesus' sake. Amen." Serena raised her head, and Daniel knew that now it was all right, that he could begin to dish out the chowder.

The chowder was very good. Serena had spoken the truth when she said you could not tell the corn from fresh, but neither she nor her husband did it justice. Both Judith and Dexter ate two big platefuls, however, and after supper, Daniel and Dexter drew their chairs close to the fire and smoked their pipes while Judith helped her mother do the dishes. Daniel did not suggest turning on the radio again. Instead he talked to Dexter, as one farmer to another, about matters of local interest.

"I thought I might plant the Square Field to corn this year, Dexter."

"It wouldn't be a bad idea, if the Three-cornered Piece would give you enough hay without the other."

"I'm getting hay from the Mill Lot too, these days."

"That's so. Well, we'll need to raise lots of corn, if there's going to be a war."

"What's got me guessing is how I'm going to get it in, without any help."

"You know I'll be glad to help, all I can."

"I know that, Dexter. But you need more help yourself, without trying to help anyone else into the bargain. How come you didn't have to milk this evening?"

"Hite Wendell offered to do it for me. He knew I wanted to come and see Judith. We accommodate each other that way, now and again. But just the same, I've been thinking I might sell part of my herd."

"We're going to need dairy products just as much as corn. Dexter, if we go to war."

"Yes. But like you just said, there's a limit to what one man can do. Especially if he's lame."

Daniel glanced away, without answering. Dexter seldom referred to his lameness, because he knew that when he did, Daniel felt uncomfortable and embarrassed, and he was instantly sorry he had done so now. He had broken his leg, when he was a little boy, jumping from a high beam in the Farmans' hay barn. He had been playing with Jerome and Jenness when he did so, and though Jerome had not actually dared him to take the leap, he himself had done so spontaneously and fearlessly and had betrayed his surprise at Dexter's hesitation. Then while Dexter was still standing uncertainly on the beam, Jenness had chanted " 'Fraid cat, 'fraid cat!" and Dexter had jumped. The accident had not been regarded as serious at first, so his leg had not been set as promptly or as skillfully as it should have been, and though later it had been rebroken and reset, this treatment had come too late; one leg had remained a little shorter than the other. Dexter knew that Daniel Farman had always felt a vicarious responsibility for the accident, because he had permitted the children to play, unsupervised, in the big barn, and Dexter always meant to spare his neighbor's feelings. So he had made a bad slip of the tongue, especially as Daniel's natural reticence prevented him from expressing his sincere sympathy, and since he was always troubled when he could not speak from his heart.

"Not but what I'm going to have the best kind of help I could ask for," Dexter went on, after an awkward silence. "Judith's promised to marry me in the spring, Sir. I thought maybe you'd like to know that was our plan."

"Yes, and I'm pleased to hear it. Not that it's any surprise, in a way. But I'm glad to know Judith's going to settle down at last. And right near us too. That'll make up to her mother for a lot. That and knowing you and all your folks so well. It isn't as if she was marrying some stranger."

It was at this moment that the telephone had rung, its noisy bell shattering the stillness of the room where the firelight and the shadows merged in such a strange way and the furnishings had all come alive.

Daniel Farman had risen instantly to answer it. Nevertheless, Dexter remembered, as he plodded on towards home, it was Serena, coming in from the winter kitchen without any appearance of haste, who reached it first.

"Yes," she said in her gentle voice. "Yes, this is N one five ring two three. Yes, Central. No, I'm not through yet. I haven't even begun. Please don't cut me off." It was the habit of the local operator, when she was putting through long distance calls, to ask people if they were through before they had begun, and Serena's was almost the only temper in the neighborhood which remained unruffled in the face of such treatment. It was unruffled now, but there was a note of unsuppressible yearning in her voice, just the same. This was the call for which she had been waiting all the afternoon, the call from her only son, Jerome, who was a lieutenant at Fort Bragg. And now he and all the other lieutenants at Fort Bragg and every other fort would be going to war. He would not be coming home again, though he had been saving up leave for a long time, so that when he did come, he could stay whole fortnight. But he would still be able to telephone her, for awhile yet, and when he did she would be able to hear him speaking to her, which in itself would mean a great deal. That is, she would be able to hear him if only Central . . .

There was a long wait. Daniel and Dexter and Judith, who were all listening intently too, heard a confused buzzing and crackling, but no other sound. "Can't you get me a better line, Central?" Serena was asking patiently. "I'm sorry, but I can't seem to hear anything at all. No, I'm not through. I told you a few minutes ago, that I hadn't even begun yet. Hello—hello! Yes, hello, Jerome. Why we're all right! Judy's just home from a case. She's sitting

right here beside your father. Dexter Abbott's passing the
evening with us too. It's pleasant by the fire. Yes, we're
all well. How are *you?*"

The buzzing and crackling had stopped. But still the
line did not seem to be clear. Serena was having difficulty
in hearing Jerome. She kept repeating what he had said, so
she would be sure that she understood him, that she was
not making any mistake.

"Yes, of course, over the radio," she said. "Yes, naturally, it will make a great difference to everyone, in
every way. But Dexter says the American people can take
it, whatever it means, and I guess he's right. Not only that
but give the Japs and the Germans—? There, there,
Jerome! You think we all ought to get as much happiness
out of life as we can, while we can? Why, yes, I said
the same thing to Dexter and your sister myself. You're
glad because you don't believe I'll mind? What is it you
think I won't mind, Jerome? I don't believe I heard you
right. You want to get married straight away, so that if
you're sent overseas . . . Did you say *married?* But I didn't
know you were keeping company or anything. . . . Only
a week? You want to get married to a girl you haven't
known but a *week?* Hold the line, Jerome, I want you
should talk to your father . . ."

It was the first time Dexter had ever heard a tremulous
note in Serena Farman's gentle voice, or seen a stricken
look on her calm face. But her hand was trembling now
as she handed the receiver to her husband, and her voice
was shaking.

"A girl has to have time to get ready to be married,"
she said. "Tell him that, Daniel. A boy doesn't understand
about such things. A nice girl, like Jerome would want
to marry, shouldn't be rushed into marriage like that.
Anyway, her folks wouldn't let her do it. Tell him that,
Daniel."

"You let me talk to him my own way," Daniel Farman
said. He did not speak rudely, in addressing his wife, but
he did speak firmly. His voice was still firm as he spoke to
his son. "Hello Jerome! Glad to hear from you. Yes, it
does look bad—Yes, I see, but you've given your mother

quite a surprise. How's that?—Oh, I see. How's that
again?—Yes, I'll explain to your mother . . . Jerome
says this girl hasn't got any home to go to or any folks
to consult," he announced, turning from the telephone.
"She was brought up in a convent. Jerome met her in the
jewelry store at Fayetteville where she works. She's from
Louisiana, but she had a chance to get this job in North
Carolina, so she took it. She's willing to marry him right
away, that is, if his family doesn't have any objection.
Her name is . . . What was it you said her name was,
Jerome? What's that? I guess you better spell it for me.
Well, I guess you better pronounce it too." He turned
from the telephone again. "This girl of Jerome's named
Alix St. Cyr," Daniel stated in his matter-of-fact way. "He
says she's just as pretty as a picture. He says she's an
angel straight from Heaven. What do you want I should
tell the boy, Mother?"

Of course there had been only one thing to tell him. Mrs.
Farman must have known what she would have to say in
the end, even before she surrendered the telephone to her
husband, Dexter reflected, plodding on and on through the
snow. Daniel had continued talking to Jerome for a few
minutes longer—that would be a pretty costly call, in
more ways than one, Dexter could not help thinking.
Jerome had nothing but his Lieutenant's salary, and if he
were going to get married, he would have to watch his
pennies more carefully than he had ever done before.
Jenness was careless about money, but Jerome was the
real spendthrift of the family. Whatever had he been doing in a Fayetteville jewelry store to begin with? And
then to fall head over heels in love with a strange girl
behind the counter—a girl who had no home and no
family and whose name was Alix St. Cyr! Dexter had
gazed across the panelled living room in which the being
of so many Farmans had centered, and looked at Judith,
who bore her great-grandmother's strong name so staunch-
ly, with a deeper sense of thankfulness and security than
ever before. He knew her for what she was, her faults as
well as her virtues, and they all had a meaning to him.
He would not have wanted her if she had been easy to

win, like this French girl who had consented to marry
Jerome when she had known him for only a week. Of
course it would be harder for a girl to say no to Jerome
than to him, he realized that. Jerome had always been
irresistible, like Jenness. But still . . .

"I never thought to have a Roman Catholic in the family," Serena Farman was saying. Her voice was a little
steadier now, but it was still wholly unlike her own. Dexter had looked from Judith to her mother and seen that
Serena's hands were still trembling. She noticed the glance
and slipped them under her white apron. "If she should
try to drag Jerome down into Popery——"

"Jerome spoke to me about that of his own free will,
Mother. He said she hadn't tried to influence him at all.
Except that she wants they should be married by a priest.
She wouldn't marry him unless he consented to that. But
he knew the Catholic Chaplain at the Fort already and
liked him real well. He went and had a talk with this
man, Devlin his name is——"

"Irish!"

"Well yes, I guess so. But Jerome says he was just as
kind and helpful as he could be. He'll go right ahead with
arrangements to marry Alix and Jerome, now that we've
given our consent. We ought to get off some kind of a
little present to them, don't you think so, Mother?"

"Ye-e-s. I wouldn't know what her tastes would be
though, a French girl."

"There's that set of little thin pointed teaspoons my
Great-Aunt Alma left us," Daniel suggested. "The ones
with the tablespoons to match, all marked with her name.
A person just glancing at them would be almost sure to
think they were marked Alix instead of Alma, the two
names are so near the same. You've never used those
spoons any to speak of, Mother. But I've always thought
they were real pretty. Sort of frail and delicate. I have a
notion they'd suit Jerome's girl right down to the ground."

"But they suit me right down to the ground," Judith
said feelingly. "I've always counted on having those teaspoons and tablespoons when I got married. I've been trying to tell you all the evening, but you've been so taken

up with Jerome and this girl of his I haven't had a chance
—Dexter and I are fixing to get married in the Spring."

"Dexter told me himself, while you were helping your
mother get supper," Daniel observed. "And I'm pleased
to hear it." He looked at his wife, whose expression brightened instantly in her satisfied surprise over Judith's tardy
decision. Dexter could see that she momentarily forgot the
shock Jerome had given her. "Just the same, I think it
would be fitting to give those spoons to Alix," Daniel went
on. "There's plenty more silver in the house you can have,
that's marked different or not at all."

"All right, Dad. But don't you think you could let me
pick out what I want first, before you start sending off
heirlooms to a perfect stranger?"

"She's Jerome's girl, like you said yourself," Daniel
answered. "She'll be his wife by the time the silver gets
to her. She'll have just as good a right to it as anyone in
the family. There isn't something else you could think of
to send along with the spoons, is there, Mother?"

"Well now, I don't know," Serena said doubtfully. She
appeared to ponder, and Daniel waited patiently for the
result of her deliberations. "There's a little book I found
in an old cowhide trunk when I was fall-cleaning the
attic," she said at last. "I must have seen it before, but
if I had, I'd forgotten about it. It isn't more'n six inches
long and half again as wide. But it's real pretty in its way,
just as those thin pointed spoons are. It's got a cream-
colored binding with a gold flower urn stamped on the
leather. The name of it is 'A Christian Minister's Advice
to Young Couples.' I guess some young people must have
treasured it once, because there's two little entwined hearts,
made of human hair in two different colors, pasted on the
fly-leaf. I laid the book aside, thinking I might surprise
Judith with it, if she ever did make up her mind to give
up nursing and settle down. But maybe——"

"I'm perfectly willing you should send that to Jerome's
girl. I've thought things through so long I don't need any
advice."

"Now I don't agree with you this time either," Daniel
said. His tone had not altered once throughout the eve-

ning; it was still as matter of fact as when he came in from the barn, predicting zero weather. "I think you better let your mother give you that little book. You might find something of value in it after all. I haven't said anything, but I don't know as you've managed your affairs any better than your brother has. It looks to me as if you and he had gone to opposite extremes, that's all. Anyway I don't believe we'd better start giving advice to Jerome's girl just yet. I believe the first thing we've got to do is to make her feel welcome. Maybe there's an old brooch or the like of that around somewhere, we could put in with the silver. If she's been working in a jewelry store, she ought to be able to appreciate a nice ornament."

"Perhaps you'd like her to have Grandmother Brewster's seed pearls," Judith suggested.

"No, we must save those for Jenness," Serena said. She had taken her hands out from under her apron, and they were not shaking anymore. Her voice was beginning to sound natural too—it was strange, that of the three, only the voice of Judith, his beloved, should be disturbing to Dexter. "But you're right, Daniel, like you always are. We must find something nice to send to Jerome's girl, besides the spoons. I'll look around, the first thing in the morning."

It was then the telephone had rung again.

Judith sprang up to answer it, and this was just as well, because the call was for her. It was a local one; there was no buzzing or crackling on the line, and the operator did not ask her if she were through before she had begun. Dr. Barnes was speaking from the village, and everyone in the room could hear what he was saying, almost as clearly as they could hear Judith herself.

"Hello! Oh yes, Dr. Barnes. We're all very well, thank you. Yes, terrible. Yes, both of them. Jenness is awfully excited because she's going to get to hear the Declaration of War and Jerome's gone completely off the handle. He's going to be married right away. No, we didn't know anything about it before, he's only . . . Why of course they can spare me, if you need me. The Brent twins—*both* of them? And you're sure it's scarlet fever? . . . In about fifteen minutes? If he could make it half an hour it would be easier, but I'll hurry. I know it's urgent."

"Judith—you're not starting out on another case to-night?"

The words were wrung from Dexter against his will, before he had given them conscious thought. Judith turned on him almost angrily.

"Dexter, you heard. Those poor children are terribly sick and the three others in the family have all been exposed. They'll probably come down with scarlet fever too. Dr. Barnes hasn't been able to find anyone else to go— he said he'd gone over the countryside with a fine tooth comb, looking, because he knew I'd only been home three days since I got through with old lady Grymes. You've no idea how few nurses there are to be had. I've got to be quick. Will Brent's coming by for me as soon as he can get here. Of course he'll have to stay outside and I don't want to keep him waiting."

"But, Judith, if you take a contagious case like that now, you won't be home for Christmas! You won't see Jenness! You and I can't even exchange letters! And there's so much for us to plan——"

"I'm sorry, Dexter, truly I am, but mustn't stop to argue. You heard what the Doctor said—fifteen minutes!"

She ran across the room and flung open one of the closed doors which had such a secret look. A blast of icy air came sweeping in from the front hall as she did so. Then she banged it after her, going out, and the cold current was swallowed up in the warmth of the fire. Dexter could hear her tearing up the stairs and through the upper hall to the back of the house, where she slept in a small dormer room over the winter kitchen, which a pipe running up from the stove tempered enough to make habitable. Dexter had not seen it since they were children, but he knew what it looked like and felt like, and how to get to it, even in the dark. He started across the living room himself, but he could not go as fast as Judith did, because of his lameness, and while he was still fumbling with the old iron latch, Serena laid her hand over his.

"You sit right here and wait for Judith, Dexter," she said kindly. "She'll be back in two shakes of a dead lamb's tail. It doesn't take her any time at all to get ready to go out on a case. She keeps a bag all packed . . . You and she can have the living room to yourselves while she's waiting for Will Brent to come. I was just thinking of going to bed anyway. I don't know why I should be so tuckered out, but I am. And Daniel, he's had sort of a trying day too. Judith can come into our room and say good-bye to us after we're abed. Good night, Dexter."

"Good night," Dexter said dully, letting his hand fall from the latch.

"Mother's right, Dexter. It has been rather a trying day. So long. See you tomorrow."

Daniel Farman was already opening the door into the family chamber. This was not cold and forbidding, like the front hall; it was small and snug. Dexter could see the "candleflame" four-poster, covered with a patchwork quilt, which almost filled it, the small dresser which matched the bed, the comb-backed chair standing in one corner, the Windsor chair in another. In this room he had been many times; he knew that was nearly all there was to see. But he also knew that Daniel and Serena Farman, sharing it, had never been restricted by its size or inconvenienced by its simplicity; it had sufficed. Just such a room, he thought yearningly, should suffice for Judith and himself. There was one in his own house, which his own parents had shared, but it had been closed for a long time. He had meant to speak, that very evening, to Judith about opening it again, and then he had meant to speak, the next day to Hite Wendell about papering it, with a pattern he and Judith would choose together. He had meant to get started right away, papering the whole house and painting it too, so that it would be fresh when Judith came there as a bride. But perhaps there was no hurry after all. . . .

Judith came back into the living room, followed by the same sort of icy blast she had let in when she left it. She was carrying a small, neat bag and was dressed in dark, citified clothes. She looked purposeful and efficient. She was already thinking about her new case, what its complications might be, how she could best handle these. She had forgotten all about Alix St. Cyr.

"Hello there!" she said cheerfully. "Have Mom and Dad gone to bed?"

"Yes. They started as soon as you went upstairs. So that we could have the living room to ourselves while you waited for Will Brent. It was very thoughtful of them."

"Yes, it was. I suppose they were tired anyhow though. They've had a hard day. I guess Mom's a good deal cut up about Jerome, and Dad too, as far as that goes, though he wouldn't admit it." She was beginning to remember Alix St. Cyr after all; but she was not resentful for her any longer, because she was more interested in something else. "Of course if they'd listen to Jenness, and keep at least one of the parlors open all the time, they wouldn't need to bother about things like that. You and I wouldn't need to have the living room for courting. But I guess the neighbors are right. I guess Mom and Dad have spent so much of the little they had on their children that there isn't anything to spare for extra fires and frills like that." Judith broke off with a little laugh, which did not sound particularly merry, and Dexter answered soothingly.

"It's been well spent, Judith. You're all a credit to them. You'll all make your mark in the world."

"How am I going to make any mark in the world in a place like this?"

"I don't know. But I'm sure you're going to. Surer than I am you're going to stay in a place like this, in spite of all you've said about wanting to."

Suddenly he felt very tired, and when he looked at Judith, he wondered if his face showed the lack of that gladness which had kept streaming out of his heart during the last hour. Then he was sure it must have, for she came and put her arms around him, kindly, as if he were a sick child she were caring for, instead of a strong man with whom she was in love, and he felt as if she was supporting him instead of as if he were supporting her, the way it should have been.

"Of course I am," she said, speaking cheerfully again.

"I meant what I said this afternoon about wanting to, honestly I did. I meant what I said about loving you dearly too. But I wish I could make you understand what nursing means to me, and I wish you wouldn't take things so hard. Why the way you spoke, when you said I wouldn't be home for Christmas, and that we couldn't exchange letters while I was quarantined, anyone would think the stars were going to fall!"

"I guess the stars *have* fallen over a good share of the world today, Judith. That's why I want to keep you with me as long as I can—before they fall on us too. Because they might, you know. That's what your mother meant when she said we all ought to spend this evening together, in a happy way. That's what Jerome was thinking of when he decided to get married at a moment's notice. I don't say it isn't right for you to go to the Brents', if they need you, and I guess they do. But I need you too. You don't know how much. You never have, or you'd have married me long before this."

"Dearest, if you *need* me——"

He remembered how he had winced that afternoon, when she spoke of "coddling," and he hated himself for putting his plea on that basis. But it was the only one she seemed to understand and he was desperate. After that she did not draw away from him again until Will Brent's loud knock sounded on the door.

Dexter had gone up and down another small hill and across a long level stretch, while he thought of all this. The houses he had passed, since the Hellmans', had been in darkness, but now he saw the lights of his own. It was a brick cottage, much smaller than the Farman's house, and it was also different from the Farmans' in that it seemed to promise more, instead of less, than it eventually revealed. Outside it looked cheerful and friendly. Its red bricks glowed brightly against the snow, its green shutters shone, and the little latticed stoop in front of the door gave an effect of shelter and welcome. But inside it was bare and dreary. Rhoda Abbott was an excellent housekeeper. Her neighbors said that if they ever found a speck of dust in Rhoda's kitchen they would frame it, and her chicken pies and gold-and-silver cakes were famous for miles around. But she did not put plants in her clean windows; she did not like the clutter which open fires made on her neat hearths; and she did not encourage company, because guests interfered with her careful schedule. She did not go out among her neighbors very much either, or do very much reading, because gadding about, or burying herself in books, would have interfered with the schedule too. Her solitude did not represent a hardship for her, because she had always been shy; she had loved the children she once taught, but except for them she had always preferred the company of imaginary characters. The renunciation of reading had therefore represented a real sacrifice. She ministered to her younger brother's physical needs with scrupulous care; and because she had sent him to school, helping him with his homework until he went away to college, and had herself always gone with him to church, she believed she had ministered to his mental and spiritual needs also. Dexter knew that she felt this way and he never undeceived her. Besides, he was very grateful for what she had done for him. He knew how much she had loved her school teaching and how much she had given up for his sake.

She was waiting up for him now, sitting in a straight-backed chair by the kitchen table, and knitting a long gray sock with wool which had been distributed by the local Red Cross. Before the Second World War had begun its deadly march over Europe, she had never done any form of needlework on Sundays; now she did a double stint on the Sabbath, because it seemed to have a double significance. If she had not viewed the matter like this, she would have found it hard to sit up for Dexter until he came home, for he was very late, by local standards, and five was her customary rising hour. But the knitting helped to keep her awake, and at the same time it was soothing and pleasant work. She was not sure it was right to get so much solace out of anything connected with a war, as she did out of making socks. It had come to mean almost as much to her as her abandoned reading.

Dexter came into the kitchen, closing the door carefully behind him. He had already taken off his galoshes on the porch, so that he would not track mud and snow over the clean floor. He was not supposed to sit down inside, where it was warm, to take them off, the way Daniel Farman did.

"Hello," he said agreeably. "I hope you didn't sit up for me. I mean, I hope you wanted to sit up anyway to finish that sock. It's almost done, isn't it?"

"I've only three more rows. I think I might as well do those, before I go to bed."

"It wouldn't be a bad idea, seeing that you'll have to start knitting for Americans as well as British, any time now."

She nodded. "Hite told me when he came to milk. I hadn't had the radio on before, but I did after that. Then I turned it off again, because the news was so dreadful I couldn't bear to listen. I feel like a coward to say so, but it's true."

"You might as well learn to bear it. You'll have to, pretty soon."

"Well, I'm not going to until I do have to," Rhoda said stubbornly. "Hawaii's a long way off. The war'll have to come a good deal closer to me than that before I'll feel I'm obliged to listen to bad news, whether I want to or not." She paused, tightening her thin lips and drawing in her wool. A faint color had come into her drab face and a slight gleam into her dull eyes. "And I can't help but be thankful," she said, "that you'll never be mixed up in it. I presume you think it's wicked for me to say that, you've been so crazy to get into this foreign fight. But as far as I'm concerned, I'm thankful you'll be spared."

"What makes you think I will be?" Dexter asked bitterly.

CHAPTER 3

THE FARMANS found it possible to run their place without any help because, from the first, Serena had taken charge of the milk route which had enabled them to put Jerome through college and send Jenness to secretarial school and give Judith her nursing course. Serena rose regularly at five, prepared the morning meal, and had her breakfast dishes done before she started out. She supplied four of the five stores in the village, without counting the two granaries on Depot Street, where she stopped regularly every day to pour half a pint of milk into the ample saucers which were provided for the granary cats; she also supplied fifteen families who kept no cows. It took her about an hour and a half to cover her route, using the second-hand Ford which was the only family car, and usually she hurried home as fast as she could after the milk was all delivered. This was partly because she liked to "cash up" before there was any possible chance of becoming confused as to who had given her money, and who had used a charge account, and who had torn off tickets in paying her; and partly because very often she filled up her milk cans with hot water at the creamery, and took this water home for laundry work and house-cleaning. The tank on the back of the stove in the winter kitchen was good sized, as such tanks went, and many of her neighbors who had smaller ones found these ample for all their needs. But Serena Farman, though she was not "poison neat," like Rhoda Abbott, liked to use hot water in a lavish way. The milk cans, which held forty gallons apiece, gave her just the leeway she needed.

Her habit of getting back to Farman Hill, by the shortest possible way and in the shortest possible time, was well known. Therefore Rhoda was surprised when Serena

turned in at the Abbott's back yard one morning a week
before Christmas. Morning company was especially upsetting to the famous schedule, and if the visitor had been
anyone but Serena, Rhoda would probably have retired
hastily to another part of the house when she saw the
car coming. She was good at pretending to herself that a
caller might be only someone to see Dexter, with whom
she did not need to bother, and that when persistent knocking at the kitchen door went unanswered, the intruder
would go on out to the barn. But even Rhoda had a soft
spot in her heart for Serena. She hastened to throw the
door open before Serena had a chance to knock.

"Well, this is a pleasure!" she said, speaking with unaccustomed heartiness. "Come right in, out of the snow.
Terrible cold, isn't it?"

"I must say I've seen it milder," Serena acknowledged,
smiling. "The thermometer on our side porch was just
twenty below when I started out. But I guess it will moderate a little before night. The wind's shifted. Anyway
it's warm as toast in here, besides being neat as a pin. This
early in the day, too! Rhoda, I never saw such a tidy
kitchen! I don't see how you manage it even if you do
have conveniences—" Serena's eyes wandered to the
gleaming electric refrigerator standing beside the gleaming electric range, and she realized, with a pang she could
not wholly suppress, that she could manage equally well,
if she only had such equipment as this with which to do
her work.

"I have to keep right after things," Rhoda answered
with pride. She was not prepared to make any allowance
for the conveniences. "It's a terrible struggle. And Dexter
tracks in dirt, no matter what I say. You know how men
are. Let me give you a cup of coffee, Serena. I've got
the pot setting right on the back of the stove."

"Well, I don't care if I do. I most generally take a second cup as soon as I get home, that is, after I've cashed
up. I mind the cold more as I get older. It seems to go
right through to the bone. I'd be glad to have my second
cup with you, instead of waiting."

The two women sat down on either side of the oil-cloth-covered table, and drank their coffee to the accompaniment of a running conversation about the impending chicken-pie supper at the vestry. Some of the church members had thought it ought to be given up, on account of the war; but they had been in a minority. The supper was an annual affair, widely attended, and the prompt payment of the minister's salary was largely dependent upon its success. Rhoda, whose own renowned pies were always a feature at this feast, was one of those who had been most injured at the mere suggestion that the village might do without it. Serena was in sympathy with her stand and made this clear; what was more, she was willing to go on record as having said so. It was not until the coffee was almost all consumed that she broached the subject which was uppermost in her own mind.

"We had a nice long letter from Jenness yesterday," she said. "It's wonderful how that girl finds time to write us like she does, with all her other duties."

Rhoda knew that her cue was to say something complimentary about Jenness, but she could not quite bring herself to do this. She had always thought the elder Farman girl was very flighty, and she had never believed any good would come out of her sojourn in Washington and her association with a congressman. In fact, Rhoda had always resented the unhampered ease with which all the Farman children had struck out for themselves, and the complacence with which their parents had regarded their ventures. She answered noncommittally.

"I thought you were expecting Jenness home before this."

"Well, just about now. But she's going to be later than she thought, because she used up part of the leave that was coming to her to go down to North Carolina, to Jerome's wedding."

Rhoda looked up quickly from her coffee. "Why I didn't know Jerome had him a regular wedding!" she said in surprise.

"Oh, yes! He and Alix were married in his Colonel's quarters. I guess the Colonel's always thought well of Jerome. Anyway, he and his wife offered their house.

And Jerome sent a telegram to Jenness, and said he and Alix would both like to have her be bridesmaid. So she bought herself a pink dress and caught the first train for Fort Bragg."

"You don't say!"

"I guess she had a grand time," Serena went on with pardonable pride. "Everyone was just as nice to her as could be. She stayed with a Major's family herself. This Major'd been stationed in China for awhile and his house was chuck full of beautiful things, Jenness said. And she said she never knew there were so many lieutenants in the world as there were at Fort Bragg. She said the place was just lou—she said there was an immense number of them."

Serena had caught herself just in time. She had been on the point of quoting Jenness word for word. But fortunately Rhoda had not observed this slip. In spite of her disapproval of Jenness, she was by now too interested in the story as a whole to be troubled by flaws in it.

"I guess the lieutenants gave Jenness quite a rush," continued Serena. "There was a Captain Morton, too, who was Jerome's best man. So naturally he and Jenness were thrown together a lot. But she had more to say about Alix than anyone else. She says Alix is about the prettiest girl she ever saw in her life. She sent along a picture. I was glad she did, because Jerome didn't think to. As you said awhile back, Rhoda, we know how men are."

"Yes," answered Rhoda eagerly, stretching out her hands for the picture that Serena extended. She blinked a little as she looked at it. She had always been forced to admit that Jerome Farman was a handsome youngster, even if he was as wild as a hawk; but she had always thought of him just as a youngster. Now she was forced to admit that he was a very fine figure of a man, tall and straight and keen looking. Well, more than that. There was a certain maturity about him, a kind of dignity. Not that he seemed solemn. He was smiling, for he was obviously very happy. He was looking straight ahead of him in the picture, but you knew that he was thinking about his bride, and that it was these thoughts which made him so

happy. You did not wonder, either, when you looked at
the girl whose picture had been taken with him. She
came only up to his shoulder, but that was where she
seemed to belong, when you saw them together. She had
a small oval face which was almost startling in its loveliness, and she was wearing a lace veil which fell over her
dark hair from a crown of white flowers. She was carrying a round bouquet of the same flowers too, the sort of
bouquet you saw in old-fashioned pictures, and her dress
was the same type—a white brocade made with a tight
low-cut bodice and a hooped skirt. Her sloping shoulders
looked very soft above the line of lace which finished
the bodice. There was a childlike quality about her which
moved Rhoda to tenderness as her pupils had once moved
her.

"Are those roses?" Rhoda inquired, peering at the
wreath and the bouquet more closely. "They looked to be
when I first saw them, but now that I see them a little
closer——"

"No, they're camellias—white camellias. They were
sent up from Louisiana by airmail to Alix," Serena answered, with great satisfaction, looking at the picture again
too. "And that was her great-grandmother's wedding dress.
Alix wired to some of her mother's people for it, and it
got to Fort Bragg just in time. When Jerome told us she
didn't have any folks, he meant relatives near enough to
have a say as to whether she could get married or not.
Come to find out, she's got any number of cousins and
aunts and uncles, pretty important people too, I should
judge. Before the Civil War, her family lived on a plantation named Bellefontaine, right beside the Mississippi
River. There were three acres on it covered with flower
gardens and an avenue of live oaks a quarter of a mile
long leading up to the house. And the house had fifty
rooms in it. It must have been a sight to see. But the St.
Cyrs lost it. It belongs to a rich Western family now.
When you come to think what it must have meant to
those Southerners to lose places like that, it makes you
pretty thankful to feel you've been able to hang onto a
place like Farman Hill."

"Yes, so it does," agreed Rhoda, a little absently. Her eyes were still glued to the glowing picture she was holding, and though she was impressed by Serena's outline of Bellefontaine, she was even more fascinated by what she saw than what she heard.

"Mrs. St. Cyr died when Alix was just a baby," Serena was saying. She was so happy, telling her romantic story, that she really did not care much whether Rhoda listened to her or not. "She asked her husband, with her dying breath, to promise he'd send their little daughter to the convent where she'd been educated herself. She was sure the poor little thing would have every care from the good Sisters."

"Nuns?" inquired Rhoda, recoiling.

"Well, yes. But as Daniel says, you've got to see good in all religions. He says he presumes there's lots of very respectable people, among Roman Catholics, in the South. He says we shouldn't judge them by what we've seen around here."

"The Scarlet Woman is always the Scarlet Woman. The leopard can't change his spots," Rhoda said darkly, without worrying about mixed metaphors.

"I know we've been brought up to think so. But maybe we were mistaken," Serena responded cheerfully. She was determined not to let Rome ruin romance, now that she was beginning to revel in her son's rash step, instead of grieving over it. "Anyway, of course Mr. St. Cyr was heartbroken, so he promised just like his dying wife wanted. He was young himself and in moderate circumstances. Later on he remarried and did very well that way. Jenness said Alix told her the second Mrs. St. Cyr would have been glad to give her a home anytime. She has a great big house in New Orleans. She came to the wedding and made a very nice appearance, Jenness said. And she gave Alix and Jerome a substantial check for a wedding present—a very substantial check," Serena repeated, letting the words sink in. "But Alix always wanted to be independent. Her father passed away too, some years ago. You can see how she'd feel. Of course if he'd lived it would have been different. She did spend her vacations with her stepmother, and stayed with her all last summer, and into the fall, after she graduated last June. But in October she heard, through a classmate of hers who came from North Carolina, about this job in Fayetteville and she went up and applied for it. She'd always been fond of jewelry. Her own mother had left her some beautiful pieces. She wore some of them at her wedding and Jenness said she'd never seen anything to equal them. She said from what she heard these Creoles may lose their plantations, but they cling to their jewels. Now we'd be different about that too."

"Yes," Rhoda said again. Somehow she could not feel, as she looked at the bridal picture, that a girl like Alix St. Cyr would ever need to worry very much about being independent. There would always be someone who would want to take care of her, just as Jerome Farman had wanted to do so, before she had begun to find out what it was like to earn her own living. "Well, I declare I don't know when I've seen such a sweet pretty picture, Serena. I can't thank you enough for stopping by to show it to me. And for telling me all about your new daughter-in-law too," she added as an afterthought. "It's all very interesting. I wish Dexter could have heard it. But he's gone to Thetford today, to see about some cattle. I don't know what he's thinking of, adding to his herd at a time like this."

"I'm sorry not to see Dexter," Serena said, putting the bridal picture carefully back in her well-worn pocketbook, beside her milk tickets and the letter from Jenness. "I didn't really stop in a-purpose to show you this picture or to tell you this story. I guess my tongue sort of ran away with me. What I started out to say was that now she's taken so much time off to go to Jerome's wedding, Jenness can't get home until the twenty-third, and she's coming on the Express so that she'll be sure to have a seat. It's pretty hard for me to meet the Express, or Daniel either. If it only stopped here, that'd be different. But it's a long drive to the Junction, as I don't need to tell you, and when it's time to start for there, I'm bottling my milk for next morning and Daniel's right in the middle of his chores. But Dexter said, the last time he was over, that Hite Wendell was glad to help him any time, with his. So I thought that if he'd just as lieve, maybe Dexter could meet the Express on the twenty-third. It isn't as if he and Judith could be passing the evening together."

"No, it isn't," Rhoda replied. Although she had not been able to bring herself to praise Jenness, or to conceal her horror of Romanism, she had been ready, from the beginning, to agree with almost anything Serena said, because the visitor had been so nice about the chicken-pie supper. Now that the call as a whole had been so pleasant, she felt doubly complacent, in spite of her interrupted schedule. "I presume Dexter'll be glad to meet the Express," she went on. "I'll ask him as soon as he gets home and he can telephone you this evening . . . I hope Judith's getting along all right on her case?" she ended civilly but a little stiffly. She knew that Judith did not like her, and she did not like Judith either; Jerome was the only one of the Farman children for whom she had a soft place in her heart. She dreaded the time when her brother's sweetheart would come to their home as a bride, disturbing the even tenor of their ways, upsetting all their methodical household habits. "I've heard those poor children have been awful sick."

"Yes, they have. Judy's had her hands full. There was a time when it looked as if there wasn't a particle of hope for one of the twins. But he's pulled through, thanks to the good care Judy's given him, Dr. Barnes says. She's a wonderful nurse, if I do say so myself."

"It's a pity she can't get home for Christmas."

"Yes, it is. It looks now as if it might be along the middle of January before she'll be through at the Brents'. And then you know how it is. She'll be off on another case before you can say Jack Robinson."

"I've been thinking Dexter might say something, one of these days," Rhoda ventured guardedly.

Serena laughed in her pleasant way. "Oh, he's said plenty already! And I wish she'd listen. So does her father. We've said plenty ourselves. But you know what

Judith's like, when she takes the bit in her teeth. There can't anybody stop her."

Rhoda spoke to Dexter about going to the Junction as soon as he came in that evening. All through the day she had been thinking about Serena's visit and her story, and about the picture of Jerome and his exquisite Creole bride. She kept dropping stitches as she knitted, because her thoughts were so far from her work, and she neglected her cleaning, because she could not make it seem important to dust behind pictures or scrub the cellar stairs when she was absorbed by a radiant vision. But she had a good supper ready for Dexter—tenderized ham steak from the store and vegetables she had canned herself and peach preserves and ribbon cake. He complimented her on her cake and listened attentively while she talked to him.

"Why, yes," he said at last, "I'd be glad to meet the Express. It'll seem good to have Jenness home again. It's too bad she can't be here longer. But then I'm glad she went to Jerome's wedding. I guess the Farmans will all feel better, now that they know he's married such a nice girl. I do myself."

"Will you telephone, or were you thinking of going over? You haven't been there in quite a spell."

"No, I haven't. But I don't believe I'll go over tonight at that. It's quite a trip to Thetford, in weather like this. I'm kind of tired. I guess I'll telephone."

It was true that it was quite a trip to Thetford and it was also true that he was tired. But Dexter's decision to telephone, instead of walking over the hills to the Farmans', was not based on weariness; it was based on a curious disinclination he had felt to go back there, after the turmoil which had arisen in the old living room which had hitherto always seemed such a haven of peace. Never, so far as he could remember, had he permitted more than a few days to elapse without going to see Daniel and Serena, whether Judith were at home or not. Now he had not done so since the seventh of December. He tried to tell himself that it was because he had been so busy with the Defense Program which Pearl Harbor had precipitated.

Before that, the only activity of the kind in the neighborhood had centered in an airplane observation post, manned
in a very half-hearted way. Now the dormant countryside
had been rudely awakened and its first reaction from incredulity had taken the form of righteous rage, not only
at the obvious treachery of Japan, but at the apparent
negligence of America's own logical guardians. Thus
roused, the community determined that at least in this
small section of the land, there should be no dereliction in
duty; it was arranging for blackouts, practicing test raids,
and organizing a First Aid Station, an Auto Corps and
other groups. As a bank director and a selectman, it was
natural that Dexter should take a leading part in all such
projects, and he had given more than his share of time and
endeavor to make them efficacious. But in his heart he
knew this was not the real reason for his avoidance of
Farman Hill.

Dexter did not feel at all sure that Serena had not sensed
his reluctance, and the reasons for it, and that the consciousness of his attitude had not been the underlying cause
for her own visit. It was so unlike her to sit and gossip, in
the middle of a busy morning, that he was by no means
convinced she would have considered even her surprised
satisfaction over Jerome's bride as sufficient cause for doing this. However, he felt no reluctance whatsoever about
going to meet Jenness. He had always liked her very much,
and he frankly enjoyed the vicarious contact with the
capital which she gave him, as well as her own provocative
presence. Now he saw to it that his car was shining and
spotless before he started for the Junction, and he himself
dressed with meticulous care. His sister, noticing as he
went through the kitchen, that he had on the well-tailored
suit and overcoat which he had bought in Boston and
which he did not frequently wear, commented rather drily
on his appearance.

"From the looks of you, I should think you were going
to meet Judith instead of Jenness," she remarked. "Aren't
those your courting clothes?"

"Not essentially. As a matter of fact, I usually wear my

old clothes when I go to Farman Hill. This is a special occasion."

"I don't know if Judith would like it, if she could see you taking so much pains on account of her sister," Rhoda persisted.

"She wouldn't mind at all. She probably wouldn't even notice what I had on. Judith doesn't care about clothes," Dexter answered, adjusting the silk scarf which he had substituted for his usual woolen muffler before he opened the door and went out.

His car was a new one, of excellent make. It did not take him long to drive to the Junction, and he did not have much of a wait on the windswept platform. The Express, its sides glistening with a glacial coating from which long icicles hung in an ornamental border, came steaming into the station almost as soon as Dexter reached it himself. The crowded coaches immediately began to disgorge untidy, weary-looking passengers, laden with miscellaneous Christmas packages; but Dexter knew Jenness would not be in this group. He walked down the platform to the one Pullman at the rear of the train, reaching it just as the white-coated porter lifted down a snappy-looking hatbox, two large weekend "warderobes," and a suede-covered dressing case. Then Jenness herself came down the steps.

She was smarter and more dazzling than ever, Dexter saw instantly, and she looked even younger and fresher than when he had last seen her. She was well into her twenties now, but she could have passed for eighteen anywhere. She had on a brown fur coat, snugly belted in around her tiny waist, and a ridiculous little fur-trimmed hat was cocked over one eye. The coat came barely to her knees, and her lovely legs, of which no man could help being aware, were encased in sheer flesh-colored stockings, which disappeared into high-heeled patent leather pumps. On her lapel was pinned a purple orchid, looped with silver ribbon, and she was carrying a small square box with the name of a famous florist on it. Her Christmas packages, festively but neatly tied up, were lifted carefully down by the porter after he had disposed of the bags with solicitude.

"Dexter, *darling!*" exclaimed Jenness rapturously,

throwing her arms around his neck. There was always a sweet scent about Jenness which came partly from expensive perfume and partly from natural daintiness, and little gusts of this scent were wafted in Dexter's face when she kissed him. He found it very pleasant to be kissed like this by Jenness, though he knew that neither the embrace nor the term of endearment meant anything special. She nearly always called people darling and threw her arms around them, effusively, unless she positively disliked them, and the longer she stayed in Washington, the more casual this habit seemed to become. "Is Judith still quarantined?" she inquired gaily, picking her way lightly down the platform, so that the snow would not sift into her patent leather pumps and moisten her flesh-colored stockings. "Gosh, what a break for me! Am I really going to have you all to myself this vacation?"

"I know I won't have *you* to *myself*," Dexter answered, speaking gaily too. "The entire male population will be up on Farman Hill by tomorrow." There was always something contagious about Jenny's good spirits. It was a tonic just to look at her, and talking to her and touching her certainly did something to a man. The porter had carried her bags the length of the platform so obsequiously that Dexter knew she must have dazzled this functionary also, partly with her smile and partly through over-tipping; and he was still more sure of it when the porter lingered long enough to help stow the multitudinous luggage in the back of the car, though the Express had already begun to move again. "I don't quite see how you're going to manage during a ten days' visit without more clothes than you could possibly squeeze into these four small pieces," he added, holding the door open for her. "But we're all set now, aren't we?"

"Oh, I have a trunk on the way too!" Jenness announced airily, with complete disregard of his slight sarcasm. "But that's coming on the local. I couldn't quite see anyone bothering with it tonight. By the way, I brought along my pink bridesmaid's dress. I thought if Judy did get out of quarantine before I left, I might need it again."

"Nice of you to think of it. I don't believe you will

though. But you can wear it to the church supper, if you feel you have to show it off. I'm sure it would make a real sensation in the vestry."

"You old meanie! You might at least tell me what you think of my new coat," Jenness said, flicking a few flakes of snow from her furry sleeve. "I'm very excited about it, because I just bought it, on the installment plan. Of course it's only lapin——"

"Lapin?"

"Bunny with the benefit of a French godmother. I honestly don't think anyone could tell it from that new sheared beaver everyone's so crazy about, do you?"

"I couldn't say. Young ladies around here aren't going in very heavily for the new sheared beaver, or baptized bunnies, as far as that goes. The coat's a knockout. But wouldn't it have been more practical if you'd had some leggings to match it?"

"Dexter, *honestly!*" They were now rolling along rapidly in the direction of Farman Hill, and Jenness, who was experienced in such matters, knew that when a man was driving a car, he did not like to have a girl do anything that would interfere with his steering, no matter how warmly he felt towards her. But she gave Dexter's arm a little squeeze and snuggled cozily up against him. "My feet aren't even cold," she went on, stretching them out in front of her as if to prove her point by calling attention to them. "I don't own a pair of rubbers. Whatever would I do with them in Washington?"

"You might keep them beside the word welcome on the doormat to your office, and give it a homelike touch," Dexter answered, settling back in his seat and looking steadily at the road, after one brief glance at Jenny's tantalizing pumps.

"I'll suggest it to Horace Vaughn and see what he thinks of the idea," Jenness said. She still spoke gaily, and she bent her head and buried her pretty nose in the corolla of her orchid. "Horace came to see me off," she added, as if this accounted for the orchid, and then, as an afterthought, "Peter MacDonald did too. He always seems to be underfoot nowadays."

"Do you call Mr. Vaughn 'Horace' to his face?" Dexter inquired. He had grown up in a region where the use of Christian names was almost universal, irrespective of the comparative ages or stations of persons who addressed each other in this way. He himself was almost the only one man he knew who called the elder Farmans Mr. and Mrs. Still, he was surprised and faintly uneasy at the way in which Jenness now referred to her employer. He did not think she had called him Horace when she came home the last time.

"Why, yes! That doesn't surprise you or shock you, does it? When you're thrown with a man all the time, the way I am with Horace, you can't stand on ceremony forever. And the mere fact that he's a congressman doesn't keep you in awe of him very long, when you're in Washington. There are too many congressmen running around loose."

"I knew there were a lot of them, but I didn't realize they were so loose in the way they ran around. I didn't realize you were thrown with Vaughn all the time either. I didn't suppose you ever saw him outside of the office."

"Well, he's in the office practically all of the time. He's terribly busy nowadays."

"Getting out messages to men in camps? Do you have to lick all the franked envelopes, Jenness?"

"I suppose that's meant to be a joke. Personally I don't think it's so funny to sling mud at men in public office."

"I wasn't slinging mud. I was only asking a simple question. I might even ask another. Vaughn's married, isn't he?"

"No, only engaged, and I don't like the way you ask that question either. If you must know it's only someone his mother's picked out, and he's agreed to the arrangement for the sake of peace. She doesn't live in Washington, hardly ever comes there. She's been hipped on the subject of this war from the very beginning. She thought we ought to rush right into it."

"Well, we are in it now, you know, Jenness."

"Yes, I know," she said, her gay voice slightly edged with impatience. It sounded almost like Judith's when she was annoyed. It did not give a man a lift anymore. Dexter felt disturbed by the change in Jenny's voice and disloyal because he had compared it disadvantageously to Judith's. But the involuntary reaction was stronger than his will to suppress it. "Of course the isolationists have all assured the Administration that they'll support it now," Jenness went on. "They've told the President he can count absolutely on their loyalty. And personally, I'm fully prepared for battle, murder and sudden dates, and mean to make the best of them."

"I suppose the President couldn't be blamed if he felt a little more support, a little sooner, might have helped some," Dexter remarked drily, ignoring her last remark.

"Why, Dexter! You sound exactly like Jerome!"

"I don't know anyone I'd rather sound like. When it comes to that, I don't know anyone I'd rather be."

"I'm sorry, Dexter. I know it's rough luck for you to be left behind, feeling as you do. But don't let's quarrel, just because we can't agree. Let's have a good time together. Really, I'm awfully fond of you."

She nestled closer to him again. The dashboard lights, shining up on her face, revealed it as inexpressibly beguiling. She took off the silly little hat and shook out her curls. Then she leaned back and rested her head on Dexter's shoulder.

"You and Peter MacDonald are a lot alike," she said regretfully. "You have so darn many ideals. Not that anyone would ever guess it to look at Peter. He looks almost as tough as they come. And the way he swears is a caution. But down underneath he's an old softie. So are you."

"I'm not anything of the sort," Dexter retorted. "Sit up, Jenness, and behave yourself. I'm not a softie, and what's more, I'm one man you can't vamp, either."

"That's what you think, darling," Jenness said softly.

CHAPTER 4

THE RETURN of Jenness to her native heath had always been the signal for an abnormal outbreak of local gaieties. At such times, the village was accustomed to wake from its usual state of social desuetude, ostensibly to do her honor; actually it was putting in one lick for her and two for itself. Whatever her faults might be—and the village was ready to concede her plenty—she was neither stand-offish nor secretive. She gave all her old friends the impression that she was tickled to death to see them, that she thought just as much of them as she ever had, and that she was crazy to go to their homes and have them come to hers. Once such an exchange of hospitality had been established, she was ready to rattle on indefinitely, in response to hungry questioning, about what feminine Washington was wearing and serving and what masculine Washington was thinking and doing. Indeed, it was not unusual for her to entertain a group so successfully that a party did not break up until it was time for the men to go home and start milking.

Her latest arrival was so close to Christmastime, that what with tree-trimming and present-opening, not to mention seasonal baking and brewing, she did not instantly notice that the telephone failed to ring with its usual insistence, that very few neighbors were dropping in casually to pass the time of day, and that no one invited her to a dance at the Town Hall or a card party given under the auspices of the Village Improvement Society. In addition to the gifts from her family, a number kept arriving by express and parcel post, and the box where the rural delivery carrier deposited the mail was chocked with missives on which Special Delivery stamps had been wasted. Serena, asking no questions, gathered that the contents of these letters must have been highly satisfactory, judging from the amount of time Jenness spent in reading and rereading them, and the abstraction she sometimes betrayed after doing so; while the packages, when divested of their festive wrappings, were freely opened to disclose perfumes in fanciful containers, silk stockings, diaphanous lingerie, costume jewelry, and other items perennially precious to the feminine heart.

It was natural that Jenness should be so jubilant over the quantity and calibre of the loot she was receiving from the outer world that she would not concern herself with fancied slights from the neighborhood. Besides, two of her primary preoccupations, as usual, had been to go for long invigorating walks about the place and to rearrange the mode of living on Farman Hill to suit herself. She never got enough exercise in Washington, she declared. So she regularly struck out, on snowshoes in the winter and on foot in the summer, following the Farm Road that led from the Calf Pasture through the Big Field, the Pine Lot and the Mill Lot to the Back Pasture and coming home again by the same route. Occasionally, when her unleashed energy seemed boundless, she forged much further, disregarding the Farm Road and striking out across country, going first through the Ridge Field, the Swamp Piece, the Pasture Field and the Three-Cornered Piece to the Home Pasture. From there she sometimes took a turn to the right and went back through the Square Field which brought her into the Ridge Field again. More often, she struck straight ahead from the Home Pasture through the Pine Lot to Jerome's Hill, which rose at some distance north of the farm itself, though it was an integral part of the Farman property—a valuable part, for it was covered with timber as fine as that on the Wood Lot east of the highway. The view from Jerome's Hill was superb, commanding the entire countryside, and when she had climbed to the top, Jenness could feast her eyes on the great panorama which surrounded her, while she rested from the effort of ascent. Afterwards, she could wander back through the orchard and follow the meandering course of the brook which formed the eastern boundary of the Big Field where it joined the highway.

Jenness had almost invariably taken these long walks alone, since lack of sufficient exercise was not a major problem of the locality. Nearly everyone she knew worked long hard hours, and though amenable to dancing, regarded fondness for any other form of physical exertion as a peculiarity or an affectation. Even Judith, whose energy was as illimitable as her own, pointed out that nursing required more physical effort than typing, and remained unmoved by her sister's argument that a little fresh air would do her good. In the past Jerome had occasionally been more responsive; like Jenness, he had an insatiable zest for outdoor activity; but of recent years he and Jenness had seldom been home at the same time, and when they were, they quarrelled so over the question of national defense that Jerome declined to let himself in for the endless bickering which a cross-country hike might entail. In fact, he had once turned home, when they had gone on further than the Pasture Field, saying furiously that he never wanted to talk to her again as long as he lived, and had shown he meant what he said by confronting her with hostile silence until he went back to Boston. Since then, she had not suggested that anyone should share her rambles; she seemed satisfied to undertake them alone, returning from them red-cheeked and ravenous, and still ready to reorganize everything in her parents' house.

This time she had begun, as usual, by flinging open the doors into the two closed parlors, and busying herself by keeping open fires going there and in her bedroom, with many imprecations against the old-fashioned hot-air furnace which burned only wood and heated the house inadequately and unevenly. Her father brought in extra fuel without complaint, but her mother interposed a calm word of remonstrance when Jenness became actually abusive on the subject of the furnace.

"We think we're lucky to have any at all. Lots of our neighbors don't and they seem to get on all right. Your father and I don't need to heat all this extra space when we're here alone. Not but what we're glad to have you use it if you want to. But the living room's always comfortable, and our chamber and the winter kitchen."

"Well, I think it's ridiculous to crowd into three rooms when you've got ten you could spread out in. That's one of the few nice things about living in the country—you can have space. Now in Washington I have to be cramped, though at that I'm pretty well off compared to the new-comers—girls are sleeping three and four in a room now, in any old place they can find, and paying through the nose for it too. I'm thankful I got settled in my cute little two by four, on a long lease, before this dreadful congestion began. However, that's beyond the point. . . . I don't see that it makes this house any warmer, just to say the neighbors are freezing to death. It never made me feel any better to realize that someone else was more uncomfortable than I was. I suppose this furnace was the only kind you could get when you bought it. But you could buy a darn sight better one now. I wish you would. And I wish you'd have the bathroom piped for hot water too, and another one put in upstairs. I hate this simple rural custom of having the only bathroom there is right off the kitchen, and carrying every drop of hot water you use by hand."

"The reason it is by the kitchen is because it's easier to carry hot water by hand if you don't have to lug it a long distance," Serena said, still calmly. "Your father and I make out all right with that bathroom too. After all, it's just as near our bedroom as it is the kitchen. And Judith doesn't mind going over the stairs. I guess half the time she slides down the banisters."

"Oh, Judith!" Jenness exclaimed with a deprecatory gesture.

"If Judith wanted we should have another bathroom or a new furnace, she'd contribute to it," Serena went on in the same way she had spoken before, "same as she pays board right along, whether she's here or not. Of course your father's never asked her to, but it's a considerable help to him just the same. He'll miss it after she's married. She paid for the electricity too, what we've got of it. She said she thought it was only fair, seeing we'd paid for her nursing course, and we thought she did real well to put in as much as she did. We like the living room just as it is, and we've never felt the need of electric lights in the front of the house or upstairs. But they're handy in the kitchen and our chamber and the barn. We couldn't have had the milk cooler or the washing machine without electricity either."

"I'll pay board, if you want me too, while I'm home," Jenness said hotly. "I didn't know you expected me to. I didn't know you were so close you begrudged me a little food."

"Now, now! I see you still go right off the handle, Jenness, at any little thing, same as you did before you learned city ways. You know it's not the same with you as it is with Judith. She has her things around her room here all the time, and she's always home between cases. That's not like being here just a couple of weeks out of a year. She has a different feeling about the place than you have too. She's always wanted to stay in the country. You can't drive her away from it, not for a change or a vacation or anything. She favors me and her father that way. You and Jerome must take after somebody else, though I don't know who it is. And we think the world of you the way you are. But when it comes to talking about new furnaces and extra bathrooms, which those of us who are here all the time, or a good share of it, don't feel the need of . . . Why, yes, I do think you might pay for those, if you can't get along without them for a few days."

Jenness was not at all pleased at the turn of conversation had taken. She had a good salary, but she did not save anything out of it, for living expenses in Washington were high and going up all the time. Moreover, she had not the least idea of using the money which went lavishly on her pretty back to buy modern improvements for Farman Hill. She changed the subject, rather ungraciously.

"Perhaps next year I better send you the price of my railroad ticket instead of coming home," she said. "It costs an awful lot, coming back and forth from Washington. And I don't know that anyone would miss me much, if I didn't come. What's happened to all the old crowd, anyway? I haven't seen hide nor hair of them since I got here. Even those two stupid Merrill boys, who usually pester the life out of me, haven't called up. Do you know what's become of them?"

"Why, they both enlisted in the Navy about the first of September. They've been kept together so far, and I certainly am glad, they're so devoted to each other. Their mother hears from them right along. Their letters are grand too. Just think, in the last war, the furthest away anyone got from this town was Paris, France, and only two or three boys got that far. Now the Merrills have been to Hawaii already and their mother says she wouldn't be a mite surprised if they got to Iceland next. They thought Hawaii was——"

"Mom, don't let's talk about Hawaii. I'm all fed up on it. I feel as if I'd burst if I heard anything more about it . . . The Merrills aren't much of a loss as far as I'm concerned . . . What about Chet Haskins?"

"He joined the Marines the same time the Merrills went into the Navy. He's at New River, in North Carolina."

"That dump!" exclaimed Jenness, still scornfully. "Well, what about the Wests and the Carletons?"

"They're at Camp Devens, in training."

"Good grief, Mom! Is Dexter Abbott the only male creature left, around here?"

"No. Hite Wendell's still here, and Phineas Johnson. They didn't pass their physicals either."

"You mean there isn't anyone except cripples?"

"Well, you wouldn't call Hite and Phineas cripples exactly. Hite's been bothered some with a collapsed lung, or whatever it is you call it, and Phineas has always had trouble with his eyes. Not but what they make out all right. When it comes to that, I don't ever think of Dexter as a cripple myself. He's a pretty powerfully built man."

"But he isn't much good at a dance. Aren't there going to be any dances, this year?"

"I don't know as there are, Jenness. Come to think of it, I haven't heard anyone say. Since Pearl Harbor, we've been so taken up getting the observation post started, and organizing for air practice and looking for makeshift blackout material that we haven't had time to spare for much else, what with our regular work going on just the same. Some of the State authorities came up to give us a demonstration of bomb and gas attacks at a mass meeting in the Town Hall and of course we all went to that. I never saw such a big turnout here. The Masons' minstrel show was well attended too. It was announced from the platform that all the proceeds would go to the Red Cross. And we did go on with our plans for the church supper. There were quite a few thought we ought to give those up though. I don't know but what I would have myself, if it hadn't been for hurting Rhoda's feelings. Have you gone on with parties and the like of that, same as ever, in Washington?"

"Mercy, yes! That is, two or three big balls were cancelled, but I guess that was mostly for effect. And people do some of their entertaining on the quiet now, instead of hustling to see who can get their party in the paper first. But there are more of them than there ever were. You can't get into the Blue Room at the Shoreham or the Cocktail Lounge at the Mayflower unless you have a reservation days in advance. And the private cocktail parties are just as jammed. You push and push and shriek and shriek. Everyone's trying to tell the latest war rumor and no one's listening to anyone else. It's perfect bedlam."

"I should think all that clatter would be real tiring," remarked Serena. "I should think you'd be glad to get out of it for awhile. I shouldn't think you'd mind a quiet spell while you're at home."

"Well, I don't mind it exactly. It just——"

Jenness did not want to say it was just because she had got so used to excitement that she reached the stage where she was restless without it. Still less did she want to confess that she could not get along contentedly without admiration, and the expression of it, on general principles, and that she was especially piqued because Dexter had hardly come to the house at all since she had been at home. She knew now that she had made a mistake on the night of her arrival by daring him to leave her alone. Dexter would always take a dare, even one that was only implied. She would have remembered that, since she knew as well as anyone that the whole course of his life had been changed by that desperate, deliberate leap from the high beam in the hay barn. She had goaded him into taking it, and she had never forgotten how he looked, both as he stood high above her, white and hesitating, and as he afterwards lay in a crumpled heap at her feet. She had always wished the memory of it were not so poignant and vivid. She tried to push it away from her now.

"Couldn't we at least have the regular New Year's party here?" she asked at length. "We could have some of the older crowd, in a pinch. The young married set, it would be called most places. I don't know what you call it here. And people like Rhoda Abbott. If we had her, we'd have Dexter too, of course."

She spoke with an elaborate carelessness which was completely wasted on her mother. Serena responded cordially to her suggestion.

"Why, yes, I think we could have a real nice party that way," she said. "Naturally we wouldn't think of having company any time, without Dexter. He's always seemed like one of the family, and he does more than ever now. I declare I'm thankful that everything's settled between him and Judith. It's too bad she won't be here for your New Year's party. There's no one, I don't care who it is, that can touch her when it comes to making that New Year's punch after your great-grandfather's recipe. But we'll have to get along as well as we can without her. Maybe Dexter'll make it. He might as well get his hand in, before he starts doing it in his own house. Judith'll want to keep up the custom, after she gets married."

The recipe in question was one of the most valued heirlooms in the Farman family. The first Jerome among their ancestors, who had been a famous fighter in his day, had also distilled and dispensed strong spirits, and had once won a law suit, based on defamation of character, against a customer who claimed that he had diluted the hard liquor for which she had bargained. Judging from the "kick" contained in this first Jerome's punch, his descendants did not hesitate to affirm that he must certainly have been slandered; a man who could concoct such a powerful brew as this would scorn anything milder, both for sale and for home consumption. It was made of heavy rum, laced with brandy and sprinkled with spices by way of flavoring, and disposed in two saucepans placed before the open fire, where it would warm slowly, so that the eggs which had been beaten into it would gradually thicken the mixture as they cooked. Meanwhile, heavy glasses with handles were also set around the hearth to warm, and the giant poker was thrust into the glowing heart of the embers. When the poker became red-hot, the contents of the two saucepans were poured into one and the tip was plunged into it, causing the mixture to foam and bubble all around it; then, still sizzling, it was served in the warm glasses. For generations, the Farmans and their friends had drowned their sorrows on New Year's Eve in the first Jerome's potent punch. This year, Jenness said she thought it might even make them forget the war. She also thought it would be a good idea for Dexter to prepare the punch. As her mother had remarked, it would give him a chance to get his hand in.

Neither of them foresaw the contingency which put a complete stranger in charge of their ancestral brew.

The preparations for the party were practically completed, and Jenness was upstairs changing her clothes, when someone pounded lustily on the front door with the knocker. The sound, reverberating through the quiet house, startled everybody. Although the parlors and the entry were already lighted, it had not occurred to Jenness, or to her parents, that any of their guests would seek to enter through the front hall. Only intimate friends had been asked for the evening, all of whom would automatically use the customary approach through the side porch and the living room. Serena, who was putting the finishing touches on her beautiful white hair, looked at Daniel with something closely akin to alarm.

Now who on earth do you suppose that would be, pounding on the front door, at this hour?"

"I don't know, Mother. Better let me go. Not but what it's probably all right. I'd feel easier though if you stayed here until I found out."

He shrugged his shoulders into his coat and walked

through the living room, still fumbling with buttons. Before he reached the front hall the knocker sounded again, still more loudly. Displeased by such unseemly noise and such a display of impatience, Daniel slackened his speed and opened the door halfway, in a rather gingerly manner. Through the narrow aperture he could see the unfamiliar figure of a tall lean young man, wearing a slouch hat pulled down slantwise over his forehead, and a thin overcoat, obviously designed for a mild climate, with an inadequate turned-up collar. His hands were in his pockets, and he was stamping his feet, which were encased in nothing more weatherproof than polished tan shoes. Even in the dim light, Daniel saw that he looked half-frozen; nevertheless, there was considerable self-assurance, not to say cockiness, about his general appearance.

"Good evening," he said civilly, removing the slouch hat. His face was almost blue with cold, but he was grinning, and his grin was likable. "Is this Mr. Daniel Farman's house?"

"Yes," admitted Daniel, without superfluous elaboration.

"Are you Mr. Farman?" inquired the persistent stranger, whose chattering teeth, Daniel now noticed, were a very fine feature.

"Yes," Daniel said again.

"Good evening, Sir. I'm Peter MacDonald, of the Washington *Bulletin.* Perhaps you've heard your daughter Jenness speak of me."

"I don't know," Danied repeated still warily, "I don't know but what I have." He was beginning to feel the cold himself, but he was still uncertain what to do about the intruder on his doorstep when a rustle of silk sounded overhead, and Jenness came pelting down the stairs, in a swirl of ice-blue elegance.

"For heaven's sake, Dad! You'll have us all frozen if you don't shut the door! she exclaimed. "What *is* it?" Then catching sight of the shivering form outside, she gave a slight scream. *"Peter!"* she gasped. "Where on earth did you come from? What are you doing here?"

"Strange as it may seem, I came from Washington. You

may recall that's where I hang out. Or perhaps it's slipped your mind. It's quite a while since we met, and you were pretty busy with somebody else when we parted. What's more, I wouldn't call you much of a correspondent. I guess I don't use the right kind of stationery."

Without waiting any longer for an invitation, he slipped inside the door, easily but somehow without offensiveness. Then he closed it carefully behind him, and stood grinning down at her with an expression which indicated that he was extracting considerable enjoyment out of the situation. Daniel, wisely awaiting developments, reminded himself that it was always imprudent to form snap judgments, and at the same time secretly admitted that against his will he was rapidly taking a liking to this young man.

"This isn't a social call," Peter MacDonald was saying to Jenness, looking around for a chair on which he could lay his slouch hat, "it's an assignment. I'm going to do a feature article on *'The Super Secretary'* for our Sunday supplement. Describe you in your own ancestral home, surrounded by your affectionate family and celebrating ye Yuletide in ye good old-fashioned way. Didn't you know that secretaries are hogging all the limelight nowadays? Debutantes are back numbers compared with them, and even Hollywood stars are getting to be old stuff. My piece is going to have a full-page spread, with pictures. I've got my camera with me. . . . And my grip," he added, grinning more broadly than ever. "They're both in the *Drive U-R-Self* jalopy I hired at the Junction. There doesn't seem to be any real hotel nearer than that, or even a modest tourist camp displaying a tempting Bide-a-Wee sign within several miles. So I thought perhaps you wouldn't turn me out in the cold on New Year's Eve. Especially as this particular cold happens to be something like fifty below."

"Pete, you're the absolute limit. You can't fool me. Of course that feature story line is the bunk and——"

"It's the gospel truth. I've got the orders down in black and white. Special rates on the story too, if I can get it off by tomorrow. You're news in Washington now, Jenness. Not just on general principles, because you're in the afore-mentioned popular category either. Ever since Vaughn said, at that damn committee meeting, that he needed a special allowance to cover a raise for you, because you were invaluable in so many ways——"

"Oh, shut up!" she said quickly. "If you have pulled off an assignment, either there's something phony about it or else it's your biggest mixture of graft and brass yet. I don't wonder my father couldn't remember hearing me speak about you. I've hardly ever done it. Why should I?"

"Because you were too busy talking about Vaughn, I suppose. I can't imagine any other reason."

"Shut up, I said! Look, we're right on the point of having a party——"

"I'm sure Mr. MacDonald's more than welcome to our New Year's party," Daniel said slowly. As he spoke, he indicated the door of the West Parlor, and took Peter's arm. "Here, let me have your hat," he went on. "I'll hang it up on the rack with the others. Maybe you'd like to keep your coat on until you get thawed out a little. But come and sit down, while I tell my wife we've got unexpected company. She'll get you something that'll warm you up, while you're waiting till we make our punch. And don't let Jenness give you a wrong impression. There's plenty of room in this house, and if you're a newspaperman, I guess you've slept in worse shakedowns than you'll get here, many's the time. And there's always plenty to eat in the house, such as it is. I hope now you've found your way to Farman Hill, you'll stay with us awhile."

CHAPTER 5

PETER MACDONALD accepted with alacrity Daniel's invitation to step into the West Parlor. The suggestion that he should keep on his overcoat for a few minutes also seemed to him a good one, and before he had "thawed out" enough to remove it, his practiced eye had taken in the details of his surroundings and his alert mind had grasped their significance.

Some reportorial instinct had told him that Farman Hill would make good copy, though he had never known how much, or how little, of what Jenness had said in Washington about her background was true. He had always thought she was probably exaggerating the extreme rusticity of her family in order to make the state of sophistication she herself had achieved seem more remarkable; he also thought she might have given an imaginative touch to the attributes of her home, in order to make these seem unique. Now he already knew that she had underestimated the quality of her father, but that it would be impossible for anyone to overestimate either the excellence or the charm of her setting. Items which had escaped Dexter all his life were immediately vivid to Peter. He saw, for instance, that in the fresco on the nearest wall, the flags on the sailboats were blowing in one direction and the smoke from the steamboats in another, that the island lay on top of the water like a platter, and that the crude execution of the grass and houses was completely at variance with the graceful design of the great central tree. He saw that one of the ruby glass vases on the mantel was decorated with a golden bird and the other with a golden deer . . . Then he saw coming towards him an ample benignant figure, crowned with beautiful white hair, and carrying a little painted tray laden with a steaming cup and a heaped plate. With the approach of this figure, he knew that his search for human interest, as well as his search for local color, was over.

"Good evening, Mr. MacDonald," Serena said warmly. "There, don't get up. I'm going to set this tray right down on that table beside you, so's you can eat and drink in comfort. We had our own supper early, on account of the party we're giving tonight, but you go right ahead and eat. You must be half-starved as well as half-frozen. I'm going to stay with you so's to be handy if there's anything else you want. I declare I never was so mortified over anything in my life as I am at the way you were welcomed. I don't know what my husband was thinking of, saying he didn't

know as Jenness had ever spoken to us about you. But
fathers are queer, when it comes to young men calling on
their daughters. Maybe you've noticed that before. And
Daniel's sort of spoiled, in a way, because he's known all
the boys in the neighborhood since they were babies. But I
can remember Jenness speaking about you, whether Daniel
can or not. Why it was only the last time she telephoned,
she said you'd taken her to your office, after you and she
left the Japanese Embassy, and that she saw you write
your story! And now you've come all the way up here on
purpose to write one about Farman Hill! I can tell you I'm
pretty pleased. It'll be an honor to have a piece about it,
and pictures of it, in a paper like the *Bulletin*."

Serena had drawn up an easy chair, after depositing her
tray, and was now rocking comfortably back and forth,
watching her visitor eat and silencing as superfluous the
expressions of appreciation which he strove to voice. It
was not until the tray was completely denuded that she
rose.

"I'm going to show you to your chamber," she said.
"I've put you in the one right over the winter kitchen, because it's the warmest. My daughter Judith uses it when
she's home, but she's a professional nurse, and she's away
on a case just now. You'll find a can of hot water beside
the china pitcher on the washstand. The only bathroom
we've got is downstairs, between the winter kitchen and
my bedroom—it used to be another small bedroom, where
the children slept when they were little. Jenness has been
after us to put in another bathroom upstairs, and I'm
beginning to think she's in the right. I don't want that any
guest of ours should be put to inconvenience, and I'm
afraid you're going to be. Because the living room is filling
up fast, and naturally you don't want to barge right into
strangers, the first thing, on your way to wash. Well, here,
you come with me. And when you're ready, you come
right on downstairs again. Everyone will be awfully
pleased to meet you."

There could, indeed, be no question about the kindliness
of the group into whose midst Peter was ushered fifteen
minutes later. He was presented first to Mr. Litchfield, the

Congregational minister, and Mrs. Litchfield; then to Mr.
Haywood, the principal of the High School, and Mrs. Haywood, and to Mr. Childs, the President of the Bank, and
Mrs. Childs. In the course of the next minute or two, another guest was identified as the local Representative to
the State Legislature, and another as the leading local
industrialist. But the interest of the gathering, when Peter
entered the living room, seemed to be centered on a spare
middle-aged woman whose joyous expression transfigured
her otherwise drab appearance; and having first presented
the outsider to the town's foremost citizens and their wives,
with a regard for precedence which would have done
credit to the Capital, Mrs. Farman hastened to shift her
introductions to this quarter.

"Let me make you acquainted with Miss Rhoda Abbott,
Mr. MacDonald," she said. "She's been telling us about a
piece of good news she's just had, and we've all been con-
gratulating her. I'm sure you'll be interested in hearing it
too."

"You bet I would," Peter said with complete sincerity.

"Why it's like this, Mr. MacDonald," Rhoda explained.
She spoke shyly at first, but as she went on, she seemed to
forget that she was addressing a stranger, and her voice
became increasingly glad and eager. "I used to teach school
when I was young, and then after awhile I stopped, because—well, for family reasons. I never dreamed I'd have
a chance to begin again. I thought teaching was all over
and done with, as far as I was concerned. And yesterday,
in the morning mail, I had a letter offering me my old
school back again! A nice little school right near St. Johnsbury! The flighty young teacher they've had for the last
few years has left them flat to go into a factory where she
can earn three times as much money. And in the middle
of the year like this, of course it's hard for them to get
anybody, especially now that so many desirable teachers . . ." She broke off, but not with embarrassment; in her
happiness, she felt no shame at the knowledge that the long
lost opportunity to teach had come to her only because no
one else was available. "If my brother weren't going to be
married," she continued, "I wouldn't think of leaving him.

I've kept house for him ever since our parents died, when he was a little youngster. But it'll be such a short time now, he says he's sure he can manage alone. And he's handy in a house. I'll say that for him. He's urged me to accept and I'm going to. I was telling the others about it when you came in. I'd appreciate your views too, Mr. MacDonald."

"Why, yes, I'm sure you should accept," Peter answered without hesitation. "Any man would want his sister to take advantage of a swell change like that. At least I know I would." He looked from Rhoda Abbott to the tall personable figure beside her and held out his hand. "This is your brother, isn't it? I'd like to congratulate you too, Mr. Abbott. I understand you're a very lucky man.

"Thank you. It's beginning to look as if I were. But I'm sorry Judith isn't here tonight, to answer for herself."

"Well, I'll answer for her," Serena said heartily. "While we're telling good news, I want you all should know that the next time you come here, it'll be to wish her and Dexter well, at their wedding. I'm inviting you all now . . . that means you too, Mr. MacDonald."

"I'll be right here," promised Peter. "That is, if we can find a way to feature it in the *Bulletin,* and I don't see why we shouldn't."

" 'Romance Run Riot on Farman Hill,' or something restrained and refined like that, perhaps, darling," Jenness suggested laughingly. She had been standing slightly apart from the others while the introductions, which she herself had made no move to facilitate, were taking place. Now she came forward, her silken skirts rustling about her as she walked. None of the others was in evening clothes. The women had on serviceable short-skirted dresses, some severely plain, others finished with neat little lace collars at the neck; the men were wearing their Sunday suits, for the most part locally tailored. Jenny's ice-blue elegance, her bare neck and arms, the sweet scent that enveloped her, were all alien to these. But she had never looked lovelier, and nothing in her bearing or manner indicated that a stormy interlude had preceded the present festive gathering. She looked archly at Peter, her expression of playful

pride tinged with possessiveness. Her anger against him
had spent itself almost as quickly as it had flared up, for
very brief reflection had sufficed her to decide that her de-
fiant attitude had been both unjustified and unwise. Now
she was almost purring with pleasure at this opportunity to
impress her neighbors, Dexter especially, with the importance of her visitor and the flattering purpose of his journey. "I suppose I ought to warn you that Mr. MacDonald
will probably write you all up," she went on. "He was
careful to explain, as soon as he got here, that he wasn't
making a social visit, so that I wouldn't be too much set
up. I believe his first bright idea centered in the parlor.
Just the same, perhaps we ought to let him have some
punch. He might think that was even better copy than the
frescoes or the natives. How about it, Dexter? Shall we
get started with our brew?"

"You better keep away from the fire, with those damn
hoops," Peter said tersely. "Why shouldn't I get busy on
this famous punch myself? I'm a pretty good bartender, if
I do say so. Couldn't I help?"

He could and he did. He must be handy in a house too,
Rhoda Abbott told him approvingly, a few minutes later.
Dexter had welcomed his cooperation, and the two had
gone out to the winter kitchen together; the sound of their
voices, engaged in hearty masculine discussion, was audible
above the noise of egg-beating, and presently they came
back, each carefully bearing one of the precious saucepans
and a large wooden spoon. It was Daniel's proud pre-
rogative, which he never surrendered to anyone, to plunge
the poker into the fire, and Serena had already set the hobnail glasses down on the hearth to warm. But the two
young men knelt down before the chimney piece side by
side, bending over their respective saucepans, with every
sign of great congeniality.

"Say, that's some smell isn't it? I'm drooling at the jaws
already."

"It'll be better still in a few minutes. Just you wait."

"Them's harsh words, partner. Could it stand another
dash of nutmeg, do you think?"

"Clove would be better. I'll get it."

"No, let me. There now! How about stirring mine a little next? Isn't it about time?"

"Well you can move your spoon around some if you want to, but I wouldn't stir too hard. Just let the mixture thicken naturally. Pouring it back and forth from one saucepan to the other blends the liquors enough."

"I see. Give me a high sign when you want me to start pouring."

"I think maybe you better let me do the pouring the first time, if you don't mind. There's a kind of trick to it. Then after you've seen how I do it———"

"I get you."

The guests were all clustered around, watching the process intently. Most of them had witnessed this annual rite many times before, but that did not rob it of its zest. Temporarily the success of the church supper, the good news about Rhoda's school, even the careful new plans for moving the air raid observation post, were all forgotten. With complete absorption, the assembled company awaited the crucial moment when Daniel would make his portentous announcement that the poker was ready for use.

"Move apart a mite, boys. I've got to have a look. Well, I guess you might as well get your mixture all into one saucepan. Now stand back. Here she comes, folks. Steady there, steady!"

Grasping the giant poker with both hands, Daniel lifted it from the flames. The tip had turned to fiery rose which faded softly into more temperate color six inches from the end. With a swift, spearing motion, Daniel plunged the point of the poker into the brimming saucepan; as it pierced the thickened rum, the liquor began to hiss like a snake. Foam covered it in a creamy froth, and overspread the sides of the saucepan; a rich scent rose from it, permeating the air with heady sweetness. Still watching it tensely, Daniel shook his head from time to time, as if to ward off possible premature interference. At last, taking a deep breath, he drew the poker slowly out of the saucepan, and turned to his wife.

"All right, Mother. Let's get this punch into the glasses before it begins to cool off. Dexter, you can take the extra saucepan back to the kitchen now. We won't need that any more. We'll keep the other here to take care of refills though. You can look after that, if you've a mind to, Peter. How about those little oatmeal cookies I saw you putting in a silver dish, Jenness? I guess you can pass those around now without any danger of having your skirts catch on fire. It's a good thing Peter called you off just when he did though. We all know how easy it is for you to flare up."

The preparations had been perfectly planned. By the time the guests were all holding their warm glasses, filled with spiced and foaming punch, the hands of the grand-father's clock in the corner were pointing towards twelve. Jenness had just finished passing the cookies when the clock began to strike. As the last note died away, with lingering vibrancy, Daniel raised his glass.

"Happy New Year everybody! I wish you all a Happy New Year!"

Customarily he said no more. It was not his habit to make speeches, either in public or in private, any more than it was his habit to ask long blessings; when he had proposed one toast, his guests, who were aware of this, began, in their turn, to toast him. But now he raised his hand, showing that he had something more to say.

"Friends, since we last met together here, there's been a wedding in my family. I'd take it very kindly if you'd all join me in drinking a toast to my son, Jerome, and his wife. We don't know just what the future's going to bring to them, but it never does any harm to wish any young couple happiness, especially on New Year's . . . Then like my wife says, the next time you're all here, it'll be for my daughter, Judith's, marriage to our good neighbor, Dexter Abbott. Judith isn't here tonight, you all know why. But Dexter is, and I know there's not a person present who doesn't wish him all the happiness in the world, war or no war . . . Rhoda too, who's had such a fine piece of luck in getting her school back. We wish you well in your teaching, Rhoda. We hope you'll be very happy in St. Johns-bury . . . Then we're favored by having a stranger in our midst too. I never would have thought, myself, that a man could find anything to write about, on a quiet place like Farman Hill. Looks to me like the world had kind of gone by us here, and I've always been glad of it myself. But the different parts of the world are closer together than they used to be, I don't need to tell you that. So maybe Farman Hill's part of a world story after all. Anyway Peter Mac-Donald thinks it is, and I guess he knows where he can find a story, same as I know where to plant a crop. So I want you all should join me in wishing him luck. I wish you Happy New Year, Peter, the same as I wish it for my son and my son-in-law."

"Thank you, Sir," Peter MacDonald said. He had already taken several quick gulps of his punch in responding to the other toasts, and it had been very hot as it went down. Probably that was why he chocked a little now, in taking another gulp that was quicker still. And he had been half-frozen as well as half-starved before he reached this haven. He must have caught cold, driving down from the Junction or standing out on the doorstep. Otherwise there was no reason, of course, why his voice should have been so husky.

It cleared sufficiently for him to join, very lustily, in the singing which took place around the old rosewood melodeon in the West Parlor, after all the toasts had been proposed, and all the healths drunk, and the glasses had been stacked in the winter kitchen sink, to await washing the next morning. Jenness, who persisted in reminding Peter that he had not come to make a social visit, managed to sidle up to him and whisper she was sure he would want to jot down the unique history of this melodeon for his feature story: it had been bought by a Farman grandfather to accommodate the village as a whole, at a time when the community had been saddled with a very unpopular pastor. During this period, it was the second Jerome—grandson of the man who distilled and dispensed strong spirits—who had been called on to preach funeral sermons far and wide, in place of the unpopular pastor, whom no one would admit to a house of sorrow; and of course it was essential that there should be musical accompaniment to these mournful orations. So a melodeon with folding legs had been found in Boston and sent North at great expense and effort; and whenever Jerome the second fared forth to a funeral, his womenfolk meekly went with him, balancing the folded melodeon on their well-covered knees while he drove a progenitor of Nell and Gypsy. Afterwards, one of these ladies played the doleful tunes with which the sermon was interspersed, and another led the singing. Altogether, the Farman family made a valuable contribution to community life through the medium of their melodeon.

"I'd say the Farman family was still doing it . . . Do we sing with the rest of the gang or do we stay over here in a corner discussing ancient history and giving the false impression that we want to neck?"

"I strive to please, darling. We can do whichever you like."

"Well, I don't know that I'd add anything to the chorus, but I'd like to try. We can talk about ancient history—and some other things—later on. I won't hold out any false promises about making love to you."

Serena was already seated at the melodeon. There was no discussion as to what she should play. Everyone seemed prepared for her selection. As she struck the first notes, the group began to hum softly in unison. She repeated the first measure, with a slight inclination of her head, and everyone began to sing:

> Blest be the tie that binds
>   Our hearts in Jesus' love:
> The fellowship of Christian minds
>   Is like to that above.

> Before our Father's throne
>   We pour united prayer;
> Our fears, our hopes, our aims are one;
>   Our comforts and our cares.

*   *   *

When we at death must part,
    Not like the world's, our pain;
But one in Christ, and one in heart,
    We part to meet again.

*   *   *

The end of the hymn marked the signal for general departure. It seemed natural for Peter to stand at the side door with the Farmans as they said good night to their guests, and Jenness slipped one bare arm lightly through his, thus bringing him still more intimately into the family circle. Everyone shook hands with him again, as well as with the Farmans; everyone told him again that it was a pleasure to have met him, adding that he must not think of hurrying away. Several of the men suggested that he might like a day's hunting, and several of the women spoke about Saturday night supper and Sunday dinner. He answered gratefully but noncommittally.

"I'll talk with my office in the morning after I've written my story. I'll let them know it's on its way and that I've got some swell pictures lined up. Then I'll find out whether I could stay up here long enough to do another piece and take some extra photographs. If I can do that, I can wedge in the hunting and the parties too. I don't know anything I'd rather do. But the managing editor may tell me to hop aboard the first train. Somebody has to do the dirty work on a newspaper, and on the *Bulletin,* that's usually me. Good night, Mr. Litchfield. Yes, I'd be glad to bring my camera down to the church if I'm here over the weekend . . . Good night, Mrs. Childs. If you really think the High School kids would get anything out of a talk from me, I'll try and make it . . . So long, Dexter. You and I'll be seeing each other again anyway."

The last guest went down the steps, carefully, to avoid slipping on the snow. The cars which had been parked in the yard, with well-wrapped engines, started up again, most of them sputtering and back-firing before they got under way. Then they went chugging slowly off down the hill, one after another, for the snow plough had not cleared a place sufficiently wide for them to go two abreast. Their cheery lights disappeared, and the cheery noise they made died away in the distance. Daniel bolted the door carefully and turned away from it with a look of satisfaction.

"I shouldn't be surprised but what the weather moderated tomorrow," he said. "The wind's shifted . . . Well, I think that was a real nice party. Everyone seemed to have a good time. But you've had a hard day, Mother. You must be all tuckered out. I guess maybe——"

Jenness laughed . "You must interpret for Peter, Dad," she said. "If you don't, he won't understand that when you say the wind's shifted it's just an expression of general optimism, and that when you say Mom's had a hard day, you're reminding her that a courting couple wants the living room to themselves. I'd be terribly disappointed if Peter didn't get the idea."

"Say, what do you take me for anyway? I get the idea all right. What's more, 'Every prospect pleases and only man is vile.' But I haven't time for a petting party now. I've got to sail right in on my piece . . . My typewriter won't disturb you, will it, Mrs. Farman, if I take it into the parlor and shut the door?"

"Why, no. We'd never hear it, with the living room between and all, even if we didn't sleep sound, and we always do. But you must be tuckered out yourself. Couldn't you have a good night's rest and then the first thing tomorrow——"

"I wish I could, Mrs. Farman. But my piece has got to go out on the milk train. After that I'll snatch a little sleep, because it still won't be light enough to take pictures. But I'll count on Jenness to wake me up about nine. That's her regular hour for reporting on duty. She can report to me for once, instead of to Horace Vaughn."

"Oh, I'm going to sit up with you while you write your piece, darling," Jenness said airily. "I wouldn't dream of deserting you when you have to toil through the dark watches of the night. Besides, I'd like to see what you've said about me before anyone else does. I might anticipate some of the editing your boss would do."

"You might, if I thought you were any kind of an edi-

tor," retorted Peter. "Or if I hadn't found out what a
damn nuisance you make of yourself when I'm trying to
write." He wheeled her around, and pointed to a colored
print, visible through the open door of the West Parlor; it
represented a simpering, ringleted girl in a flounced blue
dress, coyly sporting with some fluttering white doves, and
captioned *"The Siren"* in fanciful letters. "An ancestress, I
presume," he observed, "whose amiable traits you've inherited. Only you don't bother with doves. You get right to
work on men. However, we'll let that pass for the moment.
And you don't need to worry for fear I'll say anything,
in this piece, about your style of living in Washington,
even if it is beginning to look suspiciously high, wide and
fancy for a girl who earns what you do. This time I'm
going to present you merely as the simple village maiden,
the local girl who's been good while she's made good. I may
want to tell all later on, when I know all, which unfortunately I don't as yet. So fear not, as far as that is concerned.
But I won't have you around while I'm working, not if I
have to carry you upstairs and put you to bed and lock the
door on the outside myself. If you really want to show your
affection for me, you can get up at four instead of nine
and ride down to the station with me. Being unfamiliar
with these parts, I might miss the milk train, without some
help. I think I can still handle you in the open. But I'm
taking no chances with you in those dark watches of the
night that you speak of with such feeling."

"Honestly, Peter! . . . You talk just like Dexter, only he
doesn't do it in front of my parents! What will Mom and
Dad think if you keep maligning their dear little daughter?"

"I guess they're onto their dear little daughter themselves, just as Dexter is," Peter said cheerfully. "If they're
not, it's time somebody put them wise. It might as well be
me as anybody. Run along now like a good girl, or at
least a good imitation of one. Oh, very well then" . . . He
picked her up, with surprising swiftness and ease, and disappeared through the doorway with her struggling form in
his arms. For a few moments, Serena and Daniel could
hear shrieks and protests coming from their daughter, and

one or two terse, imperative remarks from her captor. Then there was complete silence. Serena looked questioningly at her husband.

"Don't worry, Mother," he said. "Looks to me as if Jenness might have met her match at last. And it wouldn't be a bad match either." Daniel paused, enjoying his own little joke, "Peter'll be down again in a minute," he concluded. "I wouldn't say anything to him about Jenness though, if I was you, unless he says something first."

They waited, without speaking to each other again, for the sound of Peter's step on the stairs. It did not come instantly, and when they did hear it, they heard him whistling too. He did not sound either guilty or depressed. He came into the living room and grinned agreeably at them both.

"The press, like Marines, has the situation well in hand," he said. "Jenness and I won't disturb you, will we when we start for the station? She is going with me to the milk train. Meanwhile I'll have to do some tall hustling to get my piece written. But before I start in and before I forget it . . . I want to ask you how it happens that some people named Hellman, neighbors of yours, I believe, weren't present at your friendly little gathering this evening. They've got a very distinguished guest staying with them too, if I'm not mistaken . . . a cousin of theirs named Lentz. He's quite a pal of your daughter's—in and out of Vaughn's office every hour of the day. In fact he's supposed to use it as his headquarters. I had an idea he'd be the first person I'd run into when I came here—my office had the same idea, or I mightn't have come. There's nothing phony about the piece on the perfect secretary, but I thought I might get another piece too. I'll walk down the hill in the morning, after my pictures are taken. Dexter says the Hellmans' house is just about halfway between this one and his, so I'll drop in there on my way to the Abbotts'. I've definitely decided to stay over, if you're sure you don't mind, and if I find when I telephone my office still sees things the same way I do. I'm sure the hunting's too good to miss, around here."

CHAPTER 6

As Serena had told Peter, she and Daniel usually slept so soundly that it would take far more than the muffled sound of a distant typewriter to disturb their well-earned rest. Yet long after Serena was slumbering with tranquility which matched her name, Daniel lay awake in the dark early hours of New Year's Day, a prey to troubled thoughts for which Peter was responsible.

These had nothing to do with Peter personally. The liking which the elderly farmer had almost immediately taken to the young newspaperman had increased as the evening advanced. Neither did it have anything to do with Peter's behavior towards Jenness, or his intentions regarding her; as Daniel had told Serena, he thought the girl had at last met her match, and he was thankful because the match was such a good one. But some of the remarks Peter had dropped troubled him greatly, and so did the disclosure that there had been an ulterior motive for the visit.

Just what had Peter meant by his reference to Jenny's mode of life as high, wide and fancy? Was the girl, in whom frugality should have been an integral trait, plunging into debt? Her father knew how much she loved pleasure and finery, and he had never seen her as restless, or as extravagantly dressed as she was now. He had an idea that it took a good deal of money to gratify tastes like hers; could she be borrowing to do it? Or, if she were solvent, was she supplementing her secretarial salary in some way? Obviously Peter suspected that she might be, and it was equally obvious that in spite of his jocular manner, he did not approve of what she was doing, or at least of what he thought she was doing; if her parents knew the whole truth about it, they would probably approve still less. . . . Then what about this man—Lentz, was that his name?—who was visiting the Hellmans? The Farmans had not thought of inviting their prosperous neighbors to the party because the Hellmans were new-comers in the vicinity, and as such not spontaneously in-cluded in small groups of old and intimate friends, with-out some special reason. But if their guest was a "pal" of Jenny's, of course this constituted a special reason. She needed only to say that she would like to have the Hell-mans and Mr. Lentz come to Farman Hill and they would immediately have been made welcome there. And she had not said so; she had not mentioned Mr. Lentz at all. She had not revealed the fact that there was an outsider in the neighborhood who was also a friend of hers. This was especially strange, since she had been so eager for company, and since a visitor from Washington should have been able to supply her with exactly the sort of excitement she craved. It was all very puzzling and very disturbing. Her father decided to get to the bottom of the matter that very day.

He had just begun to doze, when he heard Peter and Jenness come quietly into the living room together. They were walking on tiptoe and speaking in whispers; Serena did not rouse at all as they went by, and almost imme-diately they cautiously drew back the latch of the east door, and with equal caution closed it after them in going out on the porch. The *Drive-U-R-Self* car started protest-ingly on its way, as the other cars had done three hours earlier, and then there was silence again, that silence of the countryside which is so deep that often an anxious listener involuntarily waits for something to shatter it, feeling it too profound to be borne. It was thus that Daniel waited, every moment adding to his sense of strain.

He had not even drowsed when he heard Peter and Jenness returning, in the same quiet, careful way that they had left. There was no smothered laughter as they crossed the living room, no interruption in their progress suggesting a stolen or spontaneous embrace. They went forward steadily, but so warily that no sound came from their footsteps after they entered the hall and while they were mounting the stairs; the previous profundity of silence again engulfed the house. Reluctantly, Daniel wakened Serena so that she would not be late in starting on her milk route, and rising, dressed and went out to the barn. The snow glistened in the starlight, and the black sky and white ground seemed united in this luminosity. Ordinarily such an aspect of union between earth and heaven would have uplifted and comforted him. But it was the ominous silence rather than the unbroken radiance which obsessed him now.

He said nothing to Serena about his worries while they were eating their breakfast, though they were alone, as neither their daughter nor their guest had put in an appearance, and it was hard for him to break the confidential habit of half a lifetime. When he came in for his second cup of coffee, after he had finished the chores and Serena had returned from the milk route, there was still nothing to be seen of Jenness, but Peter was busily taking pictures. He had come downstairs while both his hosts were out, he said, and had helped himself from the coffee-pot on the back of the stove; he had also fried himself some eggs and toasted himself some bread. There was no question about it, this mountain air certainly gave a man a hell of an appetite. Now he was obviously enjoying his photography, and Daniel and Serena gladly facilitated his efforts. Daniel helped him move the furniture away from the walls, so that the frescoes would be unobscured; Serena admitted him to her bedroom, so that he could "take" the candleflame bed, which she had spread with her best quilt, and from one of the cupboards she drew the quaint doll which had belonged to Alma Farman, and which Alma had left to Jenness at the same time that she had left Serena the spoons marked with her own name. Propped up in a comb-backed chair, the doll made a picture about which Serena and Peter were equally enthusiastic. Then spontaneously Serena offered other suggestions.

"I don't know as you'd care about going out into our summer kitchen," she said. "Of course it's colder than charity there now—we never use it in wintertime. But you could bundle up. It's the oldest part of the house and it might interest you. Come to think of it, I guess it was all there was to the house at first! The winter kitchen and the two little bedrooms and the living room were built next. Then the front part of the house was added last. We generally call the summer kitchen the back room, though I don't know why we should—the grain room's out beyond it, and so is the old wash room— we used that for washing ourselves as well as our clothes, until we made one of the bedrooms into a bathroom, like I told you. The stone hearth in the summer kitchen is the biggest one anywhere around here, and the hand-hewn beams are just huge—square and thick and black with smoke. The door that leads into the back yard's peculiar too. I guess it was hewn from a virgin tree, because it's all in one piece; it still has a great cumbersome wooden latch and latchstring, and the cupboards fasten with wooden buttons too. There are four cupboards in the summer kitchen, and they've all got names; there's the north cupboard and the south cupboard and the red cupboard and the cheese cupboard. We still use 'em all. And some of the old utensils too. Do you want I should show them to you?"

"You bet," Peter answered. While she talked, he had been making hurried notes with a soft pencil on a wad of folded spongy-looking paper. Now he picked up his camera again. "Is this the way we go?"

"Yes, but good land! You've got to put on your overcoat before we go out there. Better let me get you a muffler too—here, take this one!" She snatched up a length of worsted lying on a near-by chair, and wound it around his neck and shoulders herself, giving it a little pat as she tied it securely. "There now!" she said. "I'll put everything I wore on the milk route back on, hood and mittens and all. Then we can start, and we'll be as snug as bugs in rugs, both of us."

Peter's heart warmed to her friendliness, but he still thought, rather grimly, that there was nothing very snug about the summer kitchen in midwinter. He could see his own breath as well as Serena's while they talked together, and his hands were so numb that he could hardly manipulate his camera. But in spite of her thick red mittens, Serena handled without clumsiness the utensils she showed him.

"This wooden piggin was always used to hold salt," she told him. "Sugar was kept in a wooden bucket too. And those big iron pots are soap kettles. You can see how easy it is to take this cheese press apart—it's just put together with wooden pins. And speaking of cheese, you'll notice the cheese cupboard's the only one that doesn't have solid wooden panels. In the old days, when cheeses were put on the shelf to ripen, there was cheesecloth stretched across those open spaces. But cheese-making on Farman Hill went out about the same time as horse-breeding. I guess we haven't as much gumption, or something, as our forefathers had. They could turn their hand to anything and they seemed to find the time and the strength to do everything too. When I came here as a bride, I found a big box of hand-dipped candles, shoved away in a corner of the red cupboard, that must have been made in this very room; the mold's right there beside them. And part of the summer kitchen was partitioned off as a cobbler's shop, once. Another thing I found when I first came here was a little chest with some pieces of leather in it, and a baby's shoe, half made. I've always wondered who that little shoe was made for, and why it wasn't finished. I hope the baby didn't die."

"We'll have to write a story about that too someday," Peter said. He had taken the spongy-looking piece of paper out of his pocket again, and was making more notes. "And we won't have the baby die in the story. We'll have him grow so fast that the shoes weren't done in time for him to wear them, so the cobbler put them away thinking they would do for his little brother, and then he never had any little brother. But he grew up to be a very solid citizen himself. What's that queer-looking thing you've got in your hand now?"

"Why that's a hackel! Hackels were used to clean wool with. And those old wooden tweezers were for squeezing out lard . . . I don't know as you want I should tell you all this or if any of these things will make good pictures."

"They'll all make good pictures. So would that hooded cradle and that big spinning wheel. But couldn't we move those into the living room by the fireplace? There'd be more human interest to the photographs if I could get some figures into them. I'd like to have a picture of you rocking the cradle and Jenness sitting at the spinning wheel. We could put that old doll in the cradle, and you must have some old clothes you could dress up in. We could scatter some of these other things around too, for accessories— the mortar and pestle and the candle tray with the snuffers, for instance."

"Why I think that's a real nice idea! Let's take the cradle and the spinning wheel in together, right now. I presume you don't mind a little dust. I'll bring in the smaller things myself later on, and give them all a good cleaning after I get them into the living room."

Peter did not mind a little dust, and though he appreciated all the merits of the summer kitchen, he was not sorry for a pretext to leave it, now that his main purpose in visiting it had been met. He and Serena placed the cradle and the spinning wheel at effective angles from in fireplace, and put the mortar and pestle and the candle tray with the snuffers on the gate-legged table under the mirror that Dexter loved. But as there was still no sign of Jenness, photography was temporarily abandoned, and Peter gratefully accepted some doughnuts and another cup of coffee, which Serena said she hoped would "stay" him until dinner was ready. Her plans for this were apparently extensive, for she excused herself, after a glance at the tall clock, saying she didn't know where the morning had gone to, and hurrying out to the winter kitchen. Daniel, who had remained in the living room, biding his time, during his wife's excursion with Peter, now seized on the chance for which he had been waiting.

"I'm glad to see you kind of settling down," he said, declining a proffered cigarette, but lighting his own pipe. "I judge you talked with your office, and that they've told you that you needn't hurry back."

"Yes. I phoned while you were still out in the barn. Sheppard agrees with me that it might be worth while to hang around here for a few days. Sheppard's the managing editor. So I'm going to. That is, if you're sure I won't be in your way."

"You needn't to worry about that. I told you, last night, I hoped you'd stay awhile on Farman Hill, now you've found your way here, and nothing's happened to make me feel any different. Just the same, I'd like real well to know what you meant when you said the Hellmans had a very distinguished guest staying with them who was a friend of my daughter Jenny's."

"I meant what I said. They have got a guest, unless I'm all wrong. Perhaps I should have called him notorious instead of distinguished. But he and Jenness are great pals. Or if they're not they give a damn good imitation of it. And I suspect that they've been meeting here——"

"Jenness hasn't been off the place. And she hasn't ever said anything to me about being on friendly terms with a man named Lentz. She's never said anything at all about any such man."

"You're sure about that, are you, Sir? You know you weren't certain, when I first turned up here, whether she'd ever said anything about me. Then when Mrs. Farman was good enough to jog your memory, you recalled that she had."

Peter grinned, but his manner was more respectful than his words. Daniel took no offense at them.

"This time I don't need anyone to jog my memory," he said. "I know damn well, as you'd put it, that I never heard anything about a man named Lentz. And I'd like to."

"You don't remember reading anything about him in the papers?"

"In the papers? About a cousin of the Hellmans'? About a friend of Jenny's?"

"Well, he wasn't described in the papers as a cousin of the Hellmans' or a friend of Jenny's. He was described as an undeclared foreign agent and the author of a considerable quantity of subversive literature which had apparently been distributed under the franking privilege of certain congressmen."

"I guess I do need my memory jogged after all," Daniel said. A note that was partly surprise and partly pain had crept, almost imperceptibly, into his matter-of-fact voice. "I do remember now that I read something about a Max Lentz—Max is the name, isn't it?—who was suspected of being and doing what you say. I didn't read much. We get the Sunday papers from the store, when we go to church. But we don't subscribe to anything but our local one, and there were just a few lines . . . I hardly noticed them. And somehow I didn't connect them with Jenness. I suppose I should have."

He looked up, and Peter saw there was something akin to appeal in his troubled eyes. Peter cursed inwardly because he suddenly felt troubled himself when he saw Daniel's expression.

"Oh, hell!" he said uncomfortably. "I didn't mean to spring anything on you like this, I swear I didn't. And then I didn't know you'd be so darn nice to me and everything, welcoming me into your family, and introducing me to your friends, and all that. I thought it was just another assignment, and that maybe I'd get a scoop out of it on the side. There's been plenty written about what Lentz is doing, or alleged to be doing, in Washington, but as far as I know his rural activities have been kept pretty quiet. I'd never have stumbled on the trail of them myself, if it hadn't been for a tip Jenness gave me without knowing it. Of course I wanted to see Jenness too. I'm crazy about her. But that feature story was my own bright idea. I hounded Sheppard into sending me here, and at that he wouldn't have let me off my regular beat if it hadn't been for the chance of getting the other too. I was a bloody fool not to stay on the Hill, where I belong. I guess I better go back there, before I do any more damage."

"You haven't done any damage yet, as I know of," Daniel said. He was speaking more calmly again now, but there was determination in his voice too. "I do want you should tell me the whole story though, now you've told me a part of it. You say this man Lentz is using

Vaughn's office and those of other senators and representatives as headquarters?"

"I said he was *alleged* to be using them as headquarters. Nobody's proved yet that he's done it."

"Is anyone going to *try* to prove it?"

"Well, somebody might. You never can tell how those things are going to end. The trouble started in a small way more than a month ago. A bitchy columnist carried a tidbit about the wad of greenbacks revealed by the beautiful secretary of a congressman well known for his persuasive powers, when she opened her handbag to take out her vanity case, while lunching at the Senate Restaurant. Of course the inference was clear enough, and another congressional secretary, with the best will in the world, wrote an indignant letter to the editor which was published in 'Comments from Our Readers.' This girl scout was bent on doing her good deed. She divulged that she knew the secretary in question had been to see the Congressional Record Clerk on business for her boss. You see, this clerk handles the Government Printing Office orders for franked material. So it was natural the secretary who so indiscreetly repaired her complexion should have had money with her to pay him. And so on and so on. It was one of those good intentions hell is proverbially paved with. The eagle eye of one of my own best buddies fell on this item, and he hotfooted it off to the Government Printing Office himself. Any newspaperman can get access to its records. So he found out it was Vaughn's secretary who had been there, and that the twenty grand she spent there had been for reprints of isolationist speeches. And then he wrote a piece about that."

"Just a minute, Peter. When you say 'Vaughn's secretary' you mean Jenness, don't you?"

"I told you nothing had been proved . . . Well, yes, Sir, I do."

"Then don't you think it would make things plainer if you said so, while you're telling me the rest of this story?"

"All right. There's a rumor going around Washington that Jenness bought up several hundred thousand reprints of isolationist speeches and sent them out under a frank."

"But I thought you said Lentz wrote the speeches. How could they go out under a frank unless they were congressional speeches?"

"Oh, congressmen *delivered* the speeches all right! Representatives and two or three senators! But there was a striking similarity to these speeches, content and phraseology and all. It was easy enough to tell they were all written by the same ghost. You really didn't believe that those so-and-so's on the Hill *write* all their own speeches, did you?"

"I don't know as I ever gave it much thought. I just took it for granted they did. I took it for granted that when our congressmen, that we've elected ourselves to represent us, made speeches they were voicing their own honest views and our will. I never thought they'd hire foreign traitors to write speeches for them."

"Not many of them do, Sir. Congressmen are a pretty decent lot, taking them by and large. Of course quite a few of them let 'public relations experts' help them polish off their English and give them a few hints of what it's all about. But there's nothing dishonest about that in itself though it can become dishonest in the hands of a man like Chester Slade, the secretary of the far-famed 'Better Bill Britain Commission.' And Jenness is as smart as they come, but she's superficial and she's scatterbrained. She won't take the trouble to think things through. Besides she believes everything that goes on in Vaughn's office is O.K. He has her absolutely mesmerized. Generally it's the other way. She winds most men around her little finger, as I don't need to tell you. But she thinks he's a little tin god on wheels, damn him! Not that he hasn't stood up for her—so far. He says that these insinuations are all 'absolutely nonsensical and fantastic.' "

"What do you think yourself, Peter?"

"I think it's all a damn mess. And of course it's likely to be a darn sight worse now than it was before Pearl Harbor, when the rumors first began. Everyone's edgy, everyone's suspicious and excited. That's why I say you never can tell what the outcome of anything will be. Once it gets started, it can go like a house afire. But I still think

if Jenness will only tell the truth and shame the devil she'll
come through all right. If only she doesn't lie——"

The door leading from the front hall opened and Jenness, wearing a jade green dress, entered the room. Her
long sleep had refreshed her. The late hours of the night
before, and the interruption to her slumbers caused by
her ride to the station, had left no mark on her. The dazzling quality of which Dexter had always been so poignantly conscious and which had overwhelmed countless other
men, emanated from her like a radiance. Her bright hair,
her sparkling eyes, her provocative figure were all component parts of her magic. She crossed the room with
lithe grace, and perching on the arm of her father's chair,
leaned over to stroke his thinning hair and kiss his seamed
forehead.

"Hello, Daddy, dear!" she said fondly. "How are you
this morning, after all that unwonted dissipation you in-
dulged in last night? You haven't got a head or anything,
have you?" She continued to stroke his hair and to nuzzle
his brow for a minute, before glancing over at Peter in
the same playfully possessive way in which she had regarded him at the party. "Hello to you too, darling!" she
said at last, blowing him a kiss in his turn. "I hope you
have those silly pictures of valuable antiques all made.
Because I feel like having fun today. I feel like having
fun with *you*."

"Jenness," her father said sternly. "Jenness, I want you
should sit up and answer me some questions. I don't want
you should hold anything back. There's nothing to be
afraid of, not if you'll just tell me the truth."

"Mercy, Daddy, you sound just like a judge! Why
shouldn't I tell you the truth? Do you want me to tell
you the truth about Peter? He's a big bad wolf, but——"

"I know the truth about Peter already," her father said,
still more sternly. "There's nothing you need to tell me
about him. I want you should tell me the truth about
Horace Vaughn and the men you've met in his office."

"I don't know so much about the others but he's a very
eminent congressman. He went to Yale, he belonged to
Skull and Bones. Now he lives on Massachusetts Ave-

nue, he belongs to the Metropolitan Club, he plays golf at Burning Tree. He's very polished and pleasant and still he looks something like a Viking god."

"I don't mean all that stuff and you know it. I want you should tell me what he's doing, in days like this, mixed up with a traitor like Max Lentz, and what you're doing, mixed up with either one of them."

Jenness stopped stroking his hair. She had disregarded his first suggestion that she should sit up, but now she rose. Then she strolled over to the old waterbox, lifted the lid, and dipped the china cup that hung beside it into the clear water.

"I haven't any idea what you're talking about," she said. She looked across at Peter and began to sip, slowly, from the china cup, as if the water had a delightful taste and she were savoring it. She did not speak again until she had drained the cup. "I never heard of a man named Max Lentz, not in my whole life."

CHAPTER 7

PETER HAD not taken his eyes off the girl from the moment she sauntered into the room; all the time she had been fondling her father and sipping her water he had continued to look at her fixedly. But he had neither moved nor spoken. Now he stepped forward abruptly and grasped her arm.

"All right, prove it," he said tersely. He did not shout at her, and he did not storm or swear; but Daniel saw Jenness shrink away from him, and knew that something about Peter's voice and manner, perhaps their very control, had made her cringe. "Climb into my car and come over to the Hellmans' house with me," Peter went on, still tersely. "If Lentz isn't there, I'll admit my hunch about his meeting you here and cooking up more mischief must have been all wet. I'll grovel on the ground. Even if he's there, and is surprised to see you, I'll give you the benefit of the doubt. I'll know all right whether he's bluffing or not. But if he gives himself away, I'll tell the world you're the damnedest liar I ever knew in my life, and nothing you can do or say will make me keep my mouth shut."

"What do you mean, you'll tell the world?"

"I mean just that. The pretty little story I wrote in the night will go straight into the ash can. It's not too late now to keep it from being set up. Another telephone call would do that. And the substitute would be pretty hot stuff. I'll stand by you, no matter what else you've done, if you haven't lied—that's what I've been trying my level damnedest to do right along. All the build-up I've given you so far has been meant to prove, when it came to a showdown, that you couldn't possibly have been anything except a victim of circumstances. But if you have lied, I'm through with you. I can stand anything but a liar. It wouldn't make any difference if she were Helen of Troy and Cleopatra and Mary Queen of Scots and the Duchess of Windsor all rolled into one, I'd still hate and despise her. And you're a long ways from being that. Come on, let's get going."

"Daddy, are you just going to stand there and let this— this cheapskate go on insulting me and browbeating me?"

"He isn't a cheapskate, Jenness, and it doesn't look to me as if he'd wanted to insult you and browbeat you in the first place. It looks to me as if he'd wanted to help you all he could. But I'm afraid you've made it real hard for him. I'm afraid you've driven him to feeling the way he does now. And I guess you'd better go along with him, like he says. I guess it's your last chance to prove you're right and he's wrong."

Daniel spoke in the same pained, troubled way that he had spoken to Peter, before Jenness came into the room. But he showed no sign of weakening under his daughter's appeal, and Jenness, watching him closely and covertly, saw that his face was set in grim unnatural lines. She did not attempt another plea; instead she answered defiantly.

"All right. If he'll stop clutching me until I'm black

and blue, I'll go and get some coffee. Neither of you seems to remember that I haven't had any breakfast, or realize that I might like some. Then I'd like to go and get a coat too. After all, it is below zero out, and I haven't anything on except a dress and a slip."

"I'll bring a cup of coffee to you here and I'll get your coat for you. But I'm not risking another kind of a slip, not now. Mr. Farman, I'm counting on you not to let Jenness leave the room while I'm out of it."

Peter strode over to the kitchen door, jerked it open, and closed it carefully after him. Jenness sidled up to her father again.

"Daddy, aren't you going to do anything at all? Are you going to let him bully you too?"

"There isn't anything I can do, Jenness, not now. And he isn't bullying me. He's showing me that he's got faith in me."

The kitchen door opened again, and Serena came in, carrying the same little painted tray that she had taken to Peter the night before. Peter followed her, but he did not stop. He walked straight through the living room as if it had been empty, and Jenness knew that he had gone to get her coat. She also knew that when he came back with it, he would expect her to put it on and go out with him at once, and that her father would do nothing to prevent this plan. She turned to her mother.

"Mom, darling," she began. But Serena stopped her.

"I haven't heard everything that's been going on in here, by any manner of means," Serena said evenly. "Not more than one word in three, I presume. Of course the door's been shut all the time. But I got the gist of the talk just the same. I don't know yet just what you've done, Jenness, but I do know this much: whatever it is, it's no credit to yourself, or your family, or this nice young man who's come all the way up here to visit you. I never expected to live to see the day when one of my daughters would disgrace me. But a person can't tell what's going to happen in this world. I guess I have lived that long, after all."

She turned away, and began to break little leaves from

the begonias and geraniums that stood in the sunny window. The leaves were not really withered, Jenness noticed. It was just that her mother wanted to do something with her hands, so that she would have an excuse for not talking any more until Peter came back. Then there was no help in that quarter either, Jenness said to herself, listening against her will to the flowing water and the ticking clock, which made the only sounds in the quiet room. She was caught, as Dexter had been caught before he jumped from the high beam, and she wondered, wildly, if she would be mutilated too, all the rest of her life, because of a dare she could not escape, or whether she could land safely, just this once more, as she had so many times before, when she had taken a mad chance. Horace Vaughn had told her that there was nothing to be afraid of, and because she wanted to believe him she had told herself that she did. But now she knew she had been frightened from the beginning, and Horace Vaughn was not there to shield her. Even Dexter, who might have shielded her for old times' sake, or Judith's sake, or out of sheer kindliness and goodness was not there. Only Peter, who did not believe in her any more, and who was hard and bitter in his disillusionment . . .

Her panic mounted while she waited and waited for Peter, finding the tension increasingly unbearable, and yet dreading increasingly the moment of his return. When at last he came back, he had his own coat as well as hers slung over his arm, and he was carrying his camera and his grip.

"I think I'll take some pictures of the Hellmans' house while I'm about it," he said. "Here you are, Jenness. Let's get going."

Serena pushed the leaves she had been plucking into a neat little pile and looked steadily at Peter. "You're coming back though, aren't you?" she asked.

"It's awfully good of you to invite me. And I did want to stay, you know that. But now I'm not so sure I should."

"I'd be real sorry if you didn't. I was sort of counting on having you. I've got a nice dinner almost ready."

"If I can't eat it today, won't you give me a rain check and let me have it some other time?"

"You'll always be welcome here, as far as I'm concerned. And my husband feels the same way. That's so, isn't it, Daniel?"

"Yes, that's so."

They both shook hands with him. Then Serena put her little crocheted shawl around her shoulders and went out on the porch with Peter and Jenness. After Peter had started down the steps, he turned back, taking off his slouch hat.

"Don't worry," he said. "I may be all wrong after all, you know. If I am, you'll want to kick me out. I'd have to go then anyway. And I promise not to spank this bad girl of yours. I'll let you do that, if she needs it, after I bring her back to you. We won't be long."

He put his arm around Serena and kissed her. Then he went out into the snowy yard and stowed his camera and his grip in the *Drive-U-R-Self* car. He did not say anything to Jenness when she got in beside him, beyond asking her, as he might have asked a complete stranger, if he should turn to the left or the right to go to the Hellmans'. Jenness tried to answer with equal brevity. But she found she could not stand the silence any longer. It was doing something dreadful to her and this was growing worse every minute. She felt as if she had nails in her stomach and a large jagged bone in her throat. But she tried to mask her terror with mild mockery.

"My mother seems to have made quite an impression on your hard heart."

"She has. So has your father."

"It's a pity it doesn't extend to the rest of the family."

"Well, I haven't met your brother and sister yet. I don't see any reason why it shouldn't extend to them."

"I wasn't talking about my brother and sister. I was talking about myself. I don't see how you can be so fearfully cruel to me, Peter, all of a sudden, when you've pretended and pretended——"

"*Pretended!* You're a great one to talk about pretending! I've never pretended anything. I've been crazy about you from the moment I laid eyes on you, and you know it. But I've never trusted you. If I had, I wouldn't have given you a moment's peace until you married me, after I first proposed to you."

"I think another proposal from you would be awfully pleasant, darling."

"Oh, you do, do you? How long since? You were ready to claw my eyes out a few minutes ago. I'll say this for you: you can change your front faster than any female I ever saw. Last night you'd have left me to freeze on the doorstep, if you'd had your way; but inside of an hour you were cuddling up to me like a kitten. Now this morning you started out by baiting me, then you lied to me, then you railed at me, and now you're trying to wheedle a proposal out of me. You're wasting your time, Jenness, whatever way you look at it. You ought to have sense enough to see that."

"You'll be sorry, pretty soon, that you've treated me like this. You'll ask me to forgive you and I won't do it. You've talked to me about giving me a last chance. You don't seem to think things might be the other way around."

"No, I don't. If I'm wrong, that'll be my tough luck. But we can go into that later on. I'm not out on a petting party now anyhow. I'm out after a story, and I never mix the two. So you might tell me if I'm on the right road to the Hellmans' house. Of course I know you're quite capable of lying about that too. But you'd only delay the showdown. And if I were you I'd have it and get it over."

"I haven't the slightest desire to delay it. After all there isn't anything for me to be afraid of."

"Then why in hell are you in such a blue funk? You've been scared stiff, Jenness, for the last hour, and you've pretty nearly reached the final stages of fright now. All of which seems to support my own theories pretty well. If you had a clear conscience, you wouldn't be so jittery."

"I'm not jittery . . . That's the Hellmans' house straight ahead of us, in case you're still interested—the pretty one with all the fresh paint on it."

"Fine. I see they've been making good use of their ill-gotten gains. Climb out of the car, will you, while I take some shots of it from here? We'll get some close-ups of it afterwards."

"So you won't even trust me in the car alone?"

"I don't trust you anywhere, under any circumstances. I've told you that about ten times already."

"You could take the keys, you know, and I couldn't do a thing. Not that I could anyway, or that I'd want to. But I'm terribly flattered because you think I'm so dangerous."

"If you enjoy feeling flattered, that's quite all right by me. It may help to calm your nerves. But I didn't give you the feeling. Come on, I said, climb out."

Jenness voiced no further objections. Since her declarations of indifference were so unconvincing, she decided, rather tardily, that she must make her manner, rather than her words, give the desired but difficult effect of jauntiness. She stood hugging her lapin coat around her and stamping her slippered feet, a half-martyred, half-impudent look on her lovely face, while Peter took one shot after another. Then, at his next signal, she got meekly and silently back into the car. This process had been twice repeated, each stop bringing them nearer to the Hellmans' house and permitting views from closer and more varied angles, when another car went slowly by them, as if its occupants were slightly uncertain of their direction, and finally turned in at the Hellmans' driveway. Peter, who was changing a film when it passed, looked up, at first carelessly, and then with increasing alertness. As the first passenger got out, he gave a smothered exclamation, snapped the sides of his camera together, and jumped back into the *Drive-U-R-Self* car, pulling Jenness unceremoniously in after him.

"What's the matter *now?*" she said petulantly. She had begun to realize that Peter had not even noticed her martyred look, much less been stirred to sympathy by it, and the situation was becoming more and more obnoxious and alarming to her every minute. "Have you gone completely crazy, Peter?"

"I never was saner. The first man who got out of that car was Thirkell. I'm not sure who got out next—Bates,

I think. But I'd know Thirkell in the middle of the Libyan Desert."

"Thirkell? Who's Thirkell?"

"One of Hoover's hand-picked, hand-tailored, soft-spoken Rhodes scholars. About the slickest, surest, fastest worker in the whole F. B. I. And Bates always teams up with him. The third man must be a driver they've picked up locally. You don't happen to know *him*, do you?"

"Yes. He operates *the* village taxi."

"I thought so. Then Thirkell came on the train and hired him at the station. It all fits in."

"What's Thirkell doing here?"

"I should think a bright girl like you might guess. But if you don't know now, you will in a minute. The game's up, Jenness. The F. B. I. never makes an arrest until the evidence is all in. And there aren't any third degree methods. It's all as affable as a tea party at the British Embassy. 'Mr. Lentz, I presume? Such a pleasure to find you in your rural retreat. But I hope I can persuade you to leave it. Because Mr. Hoover is counting on your early return to Washington. He's very eager to have a little chat with you. It seems there's been a slight misunderstanding on your part about the proper use of congressional franking privileges. Probably very simple to clear up. But just for the moment——' "

"Do you mean that Thirkell's followed Lentz all the way from Washington? That he's going to arrest him *here?*"

"I mean that he'll already have arrested him before I can get there to see it, if I'm not damn quick about it."

He had gone on driving fast, intently observing the lay of the land, while he was talking. Now instead of following up the other car, he drove the one he had hired through the open gate of a large barnyard, and brought it to a swift stop at the further end of the barn, out of sight from the house. Then he switched off the engine, locked the car, and dove for his camera.

"This time I am going to take the keys," he said. "I've got to leave you in the car. I haven't any choice. And it's your only chance as well as mine. If you don't keep out

of sight now, you're a goner. Of course you may be anyway . . . No, I can't stop to explain. I'll do that later. But
you better believe me when I say you've had a lucky
break."

He plunged away into the snow, pulling the collar of
his thin overcoat up around his ears and pulling down his
slouch hat. After he turned the corner of the barn, Jenness
could not see him, and presently she could no longer even
hear his crunching footsteps. The barnyard was empty, as
the cattle throughout the region were now kept inside because of the cold, and the only sounds that came from
the barn were those of muffled munching and the occasional creak of a stanchion. She unfastened the nearest
door from the inside, but before she had stepped out into
the snow herself, she had realized the futility of attempted
flight. If she started down the road, Peter would overtake
her. If she hid in the barn, he would find her and drag
her out of it. If she tried to get into the house by a round-
about way, she might be intercepted and questioned. She
was still not so far lost to logic that she did not sense the
danger which the appearance of Thirkell and his associates
might mean to her personally, if they actually saw her on
the Hellmans' property; their probable knowledge that
she was staying in the vicinity, their possible suspicion that
she might have an ulterior motive for doing so, were
menacing enough. Furiously she admitted to herself that
Peter was right, that her best, perhaps her only chance
of skinning through to safety lay in non-discovery. She
slid back onto the seat, shaking now with cold as well as
fear, and closed the door again, her frenzy increasing, as
it had in the house, with every moment of Peter's absence.
She had begun to cry, so hysterically that she had not even
seen him coming, when he unlocked the door and got in
beside her.

"Now, now," he said quickly. Jenness instantly caught
the bantering note in his voice, much lighter and gentler
than the satirical sternness with which he had previously
spoken, and knew at once that he must have accomplished
his purpose, and that momentarily his relief and elation
had submerged every other sensation. But he did not put

his arm around her, as she hoped against hope he would
do next, and he did not stop to soothe her; he immediately switched the engine on and began to turn the car
around. "Instead of crying, you better say a little prayer
of thanksgiving," he went on. "You've had a damn narrow
escape. It may be only a reprieve at that. I can tell better
when I see where that other car's going next."

"What's—what happened?"

"I'll tell you that in a few minutes too. Don't bother
me, talking to me now. Blow your nose and put some powder on it."

He steered the *Drive-U-R-Self* car expertly through the
bumpy barnyard, betraying none of the haste with which
he had forged through it before; then he swung it up into
the road again. But he made no attempt to catch up with
the other automobile, which now contained a fourth oc-
cupant; in fact Jenness thought that he was deliberately
delaying, in spite of the intentness with which he was
watching. When it took the left-hand turn south, towards
the long stretch of lonely road where the deserted houses
stood, instead of going straight ahead towards Farman
Hill, he gave a brief, profane exclamation of satisfaction,
pushed harder on the accelerator, and began to talk rapidly and eagerly.

"Look, they must be going straight back to the station.
That means they're taking Lentz somewhere for detention
before they take him to Washington. They're taking him
by train, wherever he's going, and they're not interested in
you at the moment. If they had been they'd have gone on
to your house . . . Where's the nearest airport?"

"I—I can't think. They're talking about having one
here."

"Well we can't use that now. You better think where
there actually is one, and damn quick, too."

"Honestly, Peter, I'm not sure. Perhaps it's Concord—
no, I guess it must be Montpelier."

"Yes, I guess it must be. All right, you're driving me to
Montpelier with me, so I can catch the next plane."

"Oh, Peter, please drop me off! I won't take you out

of your way at all to leave me at home! The road to Montpelier goes right by our house and——"

"And then you can go straight to the telephone and talk to Vaughn before I've read the riot act to you. Look here, you ought to be thanking your lucky stars for the way things have turned out, not trying to pull any more fast ones and getting right back into hot water again. Do you mean to say you wouldn't enjoy a nice long drive with me, this beautiful winter day? Why I should think you'd welcome the chance to go on with your efforts to wheedle that proposal out of me!"

Again she was conscious of a mood softened partly by relief and partly by elation. But her own fear was still unassuaged, and her own rage was still enmeshed with it. She retorted furiously.

"I think you're the biggest bully and the most unspeakable cad I ever knew in my life! You seem bent on making me miserable in every way you can. You might at least tell me what's happened."

"I'm going to tell you what's happened, or as much as it's healthy for you to know, now that I haven't got to watch Thirkell like a hawk and at the same time take care he doesn't see hide or hair of me."

"Well, what *did* happen?"

"I was nonchalant, after the manner recommended by the famous cigarette ads. I walked through the barnyard gate into the back yard and nodded in a very friendly way to your local taxi driver. Then I said, 'Mr. Thirkell's just gone into the house, hasn't he?' I gather that the taxi driver is what's sometimes disparagingly called a dumb yokel. He nodded back at me. I didn't have to do any lying myself. He simply took it for granted that if I talked about Mr. Thirkell in that casual way, the two of us must be in cahoots."

"So you wouldn't be too holy to resort to the heinous crime of lying yourself?"

"There are lies and lies. You know that as well as I do. But I didn't tell any . . . Incidentally wouldn't this be the place where we cross the Connecticut River into Vermont?"

"It would."

"Helpful if you would have mentioned the matter without prodding. Remember I'm a stranger in these parts. What's the name of the next village?"

"White Falls. You'll see the Montpelier sign when you get halfway down the main street."

"You bet I'll see it if it's anywhere in sight . . . Well, as I started to say, when you so rudely interrupted me, I took a few more pictures of the Hellman house, and then I told the yokel I thought it would be a good plan for me to watch the windows while he watched the door. That took *him* into partnership. He was very much flattered. I could tell by the way he nodded the second time. I wouldn't call him garrulous exactly. Probably one of those strong silent men you read about."

"For heaven's sake, skip it! Do you mean to tell me you walked right up to a window and looked in, just like that?"

"Oh, I did it very warily! I stood at the side, half hidden by a neat shutter that I pried just the least bit loose. I didn't want to take any chances of having Thirkell see me, if he should happen to look *out,* just about then. I wanted to see—and hear—everything I could first. And he didn't look out. He was too busy arresting our friend Mr. Lentz with great neatness and dispatch. Very politely, however, exactly as I told you he would. He even passed around cigarettes. The Hellmans were completely bowled over. I think they're probably still in a daze. Thirkell called Mrs. Hellman *Gnädige Frau.* His German is unimpeachable. Also his French, Spanish, Italian, Portuguese, Russian, Arabic and——"

"You mean everything is all *over?*"

"No, only the first act. Lentz has been indicted on several charges; his activities as an undeclared foreign agent, including the misuse of congressional franking privileges, which I mentioned to you before, in passing, is only one of them. But he's still got to be tried. It'll probably be several weeks before the trial takes place."

"And what's going to happen in the meantime?"

"Well, in the meantime I think you'll probably get a

nice little notice suggesting that you better be one of the witnesses. I don't imagine you'll like that particularly. But at least it's a lesser evil than being under arrest yourself. I told you that you'd had a close shave. As a matter of fact you've had a couple of 'em. Thirkell didn't see you on Hellman's property and I couldn't take you into the house with me and bring you face to face with Lentz. I had to keep you out of sight to save my story."

"Save your *story!* Didn't you give any thought at all to saving *me,* you louse?"

"Not very much," Peter responded cheerfully. "I kept telling you I was through making any special effort to do that. But the story's another matter. And I've got a honey —God, what a scoop! I'll go places on the strength of this, faster and further than I've ever managed to go before."

"What do you mean, you'll go places?"

"I mean it literally, just as I meant it literally when I said I'd tell the world if I found out you'd lied to me. Well, I'll have to wait awhile to do that, because, as I also said before, I'm willing to give you the benefit of the doubt as long as possible, and I probably can't prove anything until I get you and Lentz together—or until I hear you on the witness stand. But I may start going places before you reach there. I certainly wouldn't let a picayune trial keep me from starting for the other side of the world as a war correspondent."

"Oh, Peter—please—please don't go off to the other side of the world! Don't leave me to face a trial without anyone to help me! I'd die if you did! I couldn't bear it if I were called as a witness! I'd—I'd——"

She was crying again, hysterically, as she had cried before, and she had seized his arm, not in a conscious attempt to stop him from steering, but in a desperate groping for support. Far from being soothed by Peter's recital, she was more frightened than ever, so frightened that her fury was now engulfed by her fear, instead of being merely interwoven with it, and Peter, instead of seeming like the villain in the piece, seemed like a possible savior. But her appeal was ineffective. He did not speak to her reassuringly again. Instead he swung quickly away from her, keeping a firm grip on the wheel, and pressing harder than ever on the accelerator.

"I wonder why women always cry and clutch a man at the wrong time," he said dispassionately. "Now if you'd only done that this morning, instead of looking me up and down as if you'd never seen me before, and lying to me, I might have weakened. I hope I wouldn't have been such a bloody fool, but still I might have. After all, I have been crazy about you for a long time. However, I've got something else on my mind now and I never felt less vulnerable. Besides, I'm sitting pretty. If I can get a story like this one on the Lentz arrest in a place like Farman Hill, I can get a darn sight bigger one in a place like Manila or Moscow. Sheppard'll see that. Like most managing editors, he doesn't see more than half of what goes on right under his eyes, but he'll see that much."

"You said you'd give me the benefit of the doubt. You don't know yet that I have lied to you."

"Yes, I do. It hasn't been proved, because you've had a couple of lucky breaks, as I said before. I wish you wouldn't make me keep repeating myself. I'll stand by you publicly. I won't kill the pretty little story I wrote in the night, if that's any consolation to you. No one will pay much attention to it now anyway. Everyone will be too busy talking about the other, the one about the arrest. So what I've written about you and your charming ancestral home and the idyllic existence you lead there won't amount to Hannah Cook. But the Lentz story——"

Peter leaned forward, as if to impel the *Drive-U-R-Self* car to greater and greater speed. From the beginning of the mad ride, he had apparently been oblivious of such impediments to progress as drifts and ruts. Now the racing car lurched so violently that Jenness was thrown against him. She gave a sharp cry.

"Oh, Peter, you must stop! I'm hurt! I've got a terrible pain in my shoulder! I can't stand this. I can't stand any of it."

"There must be a hospital in Montpelier," Peter remarked, still dispassionately. "If you're hurt, the quicker you get there, the better. We can find someone at the airport to drive you over. Not that I think you are. You're shaken up, that's all. A little shaking up will do you good. We haven't much further to go. That is, I don't suppose we have. Where are we now?"

"We're almost to Barre, and that's about six miles this side of Montpelier. That is, I think we're almost to Barre. We've gone so fast, I've hardly been able to see."

"Well, you're not out to view the scenery today. It's worth it though."

For the first time he ceased to watch the road intently and glanced swiftly around him. They had just come up from a hollow where the shadows cast by twin groves of evergreens had obscured the road and the small stream which bordered it was icebound. Now that they were on the open heights again, the sun streamed all around them, and the brave little brook gushed riotously out of the crevices it had forced through the ice. The snug buildings of two or three scattered farms dotted the landscape with cheerful color, and near one of these some children, enveloped in bright woolens, were sliding down a hillock, shouting as they went, and scrambling up it again, tugging their sleds after them. Beyond, in the next valley, half a dozen small green-shuttered houses were clustered around a little white church with a plain steeple, at one and the same time protecting it and protected by it.

" 'Vermont Is Where You Find it,' " he observed. "I don't wonder so many people wish finding could be keeping, when they come here. But that's beyond the point, at the moment. Now listen. I know you mean to telephone Vaughn, and of course I can't stop you. I suppose he isn't in Washington, on account of the holiday recess. But I also suppose you know where he is, and that you can reach him. He always leaves you a record of his itinerary, doesn't he, when he goes rushing hither and yon making speeches to prove how invulnerable we are on this hemisphere? But perhaps his latest tour has been cancelled since Pearl Harbor. Anyway, I can't stop you from telephoning him. But I can advise you not to. And I do. Because it may be a truism that anything you say will be used against you, but it's also the truth. You don't know who'll be listening on the wire or what they'll do after they've heard. I wouldn't risk phoning my own story, not for a million. Go home and keep quiet. Don't telephone, don't write, don't talk, don't run around. Just sit tight in that ancestral home of yours aforementioned for the next two days. Then start back to Washington exactly when you'd planned and exactly as if nothing had happened. When you and Vaughn get together for one of your cozy little chats, after office hours, you can hash everything out then, in whispers. But don't try to do it any sooner or any differently. If you do, you'll lose everything you've gained so far."

"I—all right, Peter. I'll do just as you've told me. I want to follow your advice. Really I do. But suppose Horace telephones me?"

"He won't. He'll be too cagey. Or too scared himself. Or something. Anyway he won't do it . . . Now when I said don't talk, I didn't mean, don't talk to your parents. Because I think that might be a good plan. What's happened so far has been an awful shock to them. If you're called as a witness in a trial, it'll be a worse one. Probably your father would try to come to Washington, if that happened. And I don't suppose it would be so easy for him to arrange. He'd need some notice."

"I don't see how he could arrange it. He hasn't got anyone to help him with the work on the farm. And he hasn't any spare money, Peter. He's never been to see me, or Mom either, because they couldn't afford the trip. You haven't any idea how little they live on."

"Oh, yes, I have. But your father's credit's probably all right. He could probably borrow all the money he needed, in reason. He could mortgage the farm, if it came to that."

"*Mortgage the farm!* Why Peter, you don't understand what that would mean to a Farman! It might kill him.

"No, it wouldn't. He'd hate it like hell, but it wouldn't kill him. He's a good deal tougher than that. If you're so worried about him though, you might have thought, a little sooner, what all this might mean to him. You might even lend him some money yourself."

"I haven't got any money saved up either. It takes an awful lot, Peter, to get along at all in Washington. You know that."

"Yes, I know that. Especially when 'getting along' includes fur coats and blue satin dresses and trick apartments and little items like that. But I suppose ladies must live, no matter what happens to the old homestead. What about Dexter Abbott? Wouldn't he help? He seems like an awfully good egg to me. Or is he strapped too?"

"Oh, no! Dexter has got plenty of money. Not that you'd ever guess it. He never seems to spend much."

"Well that's one pretty good way of having it. I'd have put him down as thrifty myself. But not stingy. He doesn't look stingy to me, or mean. But when a fellow's as handsome as he is, you can't always tell what's behind their good looks, at first sight."

"Dexter—*handsome!*"

"Don't tell me you never noticed it. A girl as keen about good-looking men as you are."

"But he's lame!"

"Byron was lame, as I recall it, but he was the greatest lady-killer of all time except maybe—what was that Italian chap's name? Except maybe Cassanova. Not that Dexter is their type. But I should think he might make quite a dent in a feminine heart at that. Your sister's certainly got something there. Sure you haven't ever tried to get it away from her?"

"Of course I'm sure. I wish you wouldn't keep on talking as if I were a complete fiend."

"But you are," Peter said agreeably. 'Well then, about Dexter Abbott? I think he might help, if it came to a showdown. And I think you might talk to him too. You might even do it today. Because, after you've taken this jalopy back to the place where I hired it—always supposing you're not in the Montpelier Hospital—you still have to get home, don't you? I think you could telephone Dexter and tell him I had to leave unexpectedly from Montpelier, so I entrusted the *Drive-U-R-Self* car to you, and now you're at the Junction and would he please come to get you? Then on the way back to Farman Hill you could tell him——"

"What shall I tell him, Peter?"

Peter leaned forward again, bearing down with renewed force on the wheel. A bleak look had come into his thin face. He did not speak cheerfully any more.

'You might tell *him* the truth," he said bitterly. "Not that it'll matter to him whether you do or not, as much as it did to me. He isn't in love with you. He hasn't kept hoping against hope that he wouldn't find you out. Shut up, Jenness. There's nothing more for you and me to say to each other. I want to get my mind on my story."

CHAPTER 8

PETER'S PLANE connections were as nearly perfect as anything could be in a chaotic world. He reached Washington before midnight, and the following afternoon his scoop, headed with banner lines and illustrated with his own photographs, was spread as a copyrighted story in bold-faced type across the front page of the *Bulletin*. The news commentators gave it first place in their radio reports that evening, stressing its tremendous significance; and the following morning the A. P. and the U. P. began their dispatches with the heading "Peter MacDonald of the Washington *Bulletin* says—" Before it was time for Jenness to take her train back to the capital, Farman Hill, not to mention the whole township, was seething with excitement, half-horrified and half-exultant over the national notoriety into which it had abruptly been plunged after nearly two hundred years of unobserved quietude.

There had been nothing in Peter's story linking the names of Jenness and Lentz. But the fact that Lentz, who had been indicted as an unregistered foreign agent, had been misusing the congressional franking privilege and that Jenness was a congressman's secretary was enough to turn the eyes and ears of the agitated countryside in her direc-

tion, and set all tongues wagging. Moreover, the alerter
followers of current events began to recall news items to
which they had previously attached little importance, to
hunt up old periodicals and reread them in the light of the
startling headlines which suddenly stared them in the face.
Jenness, who had chafed under the indifference of the village when she first went home, now shrank in alarm from
its importunities. She did not need Daniel's quiet suggestion that perhaps it would be just as well if she stopped
answering the telephone and the knocker. She spent most
of her time in her own room, feverishly assembling her
scattered belongings so that they would be in readiness to
take away with her, or cowering under the bed covers,
hoping that drowsiness would numb the shooting pains in
her head, hating the stillness, dreading the sounds that
might shatter this. At mealtimes, she called down to her
mother that she was not hungry, and eventually Serena
came upstairs, carrying the little painted tray. But Jenness
hardly tasted the appetizing dishes with which it was set.
She pushed them aside and asked feverish questions.

"Who was it that came here about an hour ago, Mom?
I heard someone knocking and knocking and then I
thought they walked right into the living room."

"You're fancying things, Jenness. No one walked into
the living room. I've got the door locked. It's the first time
I ever did have it locked, in the daytime, since I've lived
here. But it's locked now. You don't need to see anyone
you don't want to see."

A few persons did penetrate to the barn, for Daniel
could not abandon his livestock even to shield his daughter; he was obliged to go about his chores as usual. He
was proverbially tight-lipped, however; his neighbors, discussing their reception among themselves later on, admitted that he had acted much as usual. Serena could not
forsake the customers on her milk route either, and these
waylaid her as she went from house to house and store to
store and stopped at the granaries to fill the cats' saucers.
But Serena, usually so soft-spoken, could be tight-lipped
too, and her well-known habit of making her rounds with
dispatch saved her from seeming brusque now. When she

said she must get back home, that she did not have time to stop and talk, she was only saying what she had always said.

In spite of her alleged haste, however, she did turn in at the Abbott Homestead, on the pretext of saying goodbye to Rhoda, who was about to leave for her school. Rhoda, like Jenness, was preoccupied with her packing, though unlike Jenness, she was not doing it fearfully and feverishly, but proudly and methodically. She took Serena into her bedroom and showed her the neatly folded garments in the battered, old-fashioned steamer trunk which stood at the foot of her spool bed, and explained their scarcity without apologizing for it.

"You can see that trunk isn't more than half full, but I'm almost ready just the same. It's quite some time since I've had many new clothes," she said simply. "You know how it is, Serena: We seldom ever need to wear anything fancy here, and when you get into a rut like I have, going hardly anywhere except to church, you put on the same dresses year in and year out. If the materials are good in the first place, they stand a lot of wear, and I never set much store by style myself. But children take lots on notice about a teacher's appearance. I'm planning to buy me a whole new outfit in St. Johnsbury Monday. School doesn't open till Tuesday, so I'll have plenty of time. And Dexter has been real generous. He's given me a hundred dollars to do just what I have a mind with. Dexter is an awfully good brother, Serena. I feel bad, now that the time's actually come to leave him, even if I am pleased as punch about getting my old school back. If I didn't know that Judith——"

"Where is Dexter? I'd like to see him for a minute too, as long as I'm here."

"Why he must be around somewheres. He's been saying he might start logging, but then he decided to put it off till next week. I presume he's in the barn. I'll call him."

"Don't you bother, Rhoda. I'll go right out to the barn myself. I haven't been there, since Dexter put in those steel stanchions everyone's talking about, and the new drinking troughs. I'd admire looking at them. Well, goodbye, if I don't see you again. You'll be back for spring vacation, won't you?"

"Yes, in April. It'll be here before we know it too. Goodbye, Serena."

The two women kissed each other, affectionately though without effusion. But when Serena's hand was already on the latch, Rhoda detained her.

"I didn't think to ask you before, Serena, what the latest news is from Fort Bragg."

Serena paused, her grave face brightening. "Why it's good," she said. "It's very good. Jerome and Alix spent the first week after they were married at the Officers' Club on the Post. It must be a real pleasant place, the way they describe it, with game rooms and a cocktail lounge and the like of that inside, and tennis courts and a golf course right on the grounds. But of course they wanted something more homelike and private than that, and finally they found a little apartment in a big house that's been remodeled a-purpose to accommodate young married officers and their wives. It's in a small town called Raeford. I gather from what they write that they're very nicely situated. The house is the real old Southern type, furnished with antiques, like what they've both been accustomed to, and the rooms are huge, so they've got all the space they need, though they've only three. And their landlady's awfully kind to them. She's teaching Alix to cook. I was sort of surprised to find out Alix didn't know how before, but come to think of it, I suppose she didn't have any occasion to, at the convent, and then her stepmother, being so wealthy, probably kept hired help all the time."

"Yes, that's so," Rhoda agreed. "It does seem strange to think of a grown girl not knowing how to cook, but then the circumstances were peculiar."

"And she likes it," Serena hastened to add. "She likes cooking and everything about housekeeping. She writes me long letters, telling me all about it. She buys chickens from her landlady, and fries them. She hasn't said anything about making a fricassee, so I'm going to send her a recipe. But she's made a pecan pie, out of nuts that grew right there in their own yard, same as butternuts grow here. Out

beyond there are fields with cotton and tobacco growing
in them."

"You don't say!" Rhoda exclaimed, with sustained interest.

"Yes. She's had some trouble with her marketing and
that frets her a little. It seems the merchants have two sets
of prices, one for anyone connected with the Army and one
for the natives. We wouldn't think well of it, if anything
of the kind happened here. But in Raeford it's the regular
practice, right down to toothpaste. And Alix is enjoying
the social life. Her landlady is President of the Women's
Club, and she invites Alix to all the meetings. It helps pass
the time for her while Jerome's away at Fort Bragg. And
of course they've made friends with lots of other young
officers and their wives. There's another bride there who's
a Russian. Alix says this Russian is 'very charming and
well educated.' She used those very words."

"You don't say!" exclaimed Rhoda again, her interest
growing keener and keener.

"Yes. She and Alix are great friends. I don't doubt but
what this Russian is really a very nice girl. But I'm glad
my son didn't marry one."

"Well, that's natural, Serena. And I believe you're going
to find Jerome made a wise choice. I believe you're going
to like Alix better and better, when you get to know her.
I'll never forget that picture of her you showed me, when
you stopped in here before. She's a sweet pretty girl, if I
ever saw one. So ladylike too. Not like—" Rhoda bit back
her words hurriedly. She had almost said "not like Jenness," and though she could not help being secretly gratified because her dismal predictions in regard to Jenness
had been more than justified, she was too kindly to enjoy
rubbing salt in her friend's wounds. "Not like some of
these modern girls," she ended lamely, with a guilty blush.
"Well, I mustn't keep you any longer, but I felt I just had
to ask. I took such a liking to Alix, from her picture.
Goodbye again!"

"Goodbye," Serena said, lifting the latch to go out.

She did not have to search far to find Dexter. She discovered him in the small room at the front of the barn

which he used for an office, keeping his herd books and doing his town accounts there. He had installed a large old-fashioned roll-top desk in it which was dominated by a photograph of Judith in her ruffled graduation dress, holding her rolled, beribboned diploma, and he had hung his own college degree and some ancient prints and engravings above the plain bookcases which he had built around the walls. There was a round rug that Serena herself had braided for him on the painted floor, and a Franklin stove, that gave forth a cheerful glow, stood in one corner. As Serena sat down, gratefully, in the chair Dexter pulled towards the fire for her, she looked around her with appreciation.

"I declare, Dexter, you've made this little office real homelike! Nobody'd ever think it was in a barn."

"The barn's my natural province. Rhoda doesn't like to have me clutter up the house," he said smiling. "I suppose I can, pretty soon. But I probably won't want to then, I'll miss her so. I'll want to keep it just as she left it. I can't realize yet I'll be all alone here, after tomorrow."

"But just for a short while, Dexter. Because pretty soon, you and Judith——"

"Yes, of course, Judith'll be here in no time at all. But I have an idea Judith won't want me to clutter up things either. I have an idea she likes a tidy house too."

"Yes, she does. It was about Judith, Dexter, I wanted to see you."

"I'm very glad. I was afraid it might be about Jenness. Of course you know if there's anything on earth I can do——"

"Yes, of course I know that. Daniel knows it too. It's—it's considerable comfort to us, Dexter. Because we don't know what's going to happen next, as far as Jenness is concerned."

"I blame myself because I didn't say anything to you, of my own accord, before you got this awful shock. I read more papers than you and Mr. Farman. I was afraid something like this might happen. In fact I hinted as much to Jenness when I met her at the Junction. But she wouldn't take me up on it. She won't talk to me freely any more, the way she used to. I tried again to make her, when I was driving home after she'd left MacDonald at the airport. But it wasn't any use."

Serena nodded. "I know. She won't talk to her father or to me either, except to say that she knows Horace Vaughn will look out for her and that this is all a lot of nonsense anyway. But she's terribly frightened, we can see that. And tomorrow she's going back to Washington. I'm frightened myself, Dexter, to have her go."

"I suppose it's the best thing she can do. If she stayed here, people would say she was trying to hide; they'd be sure then she did have something to conceal. And we're not certain there is yet. She's got into bad company, I'm afraid there's no doubt of that. Not only in Washington. Here too."

"*Here!* Why she hasn't seen anyone here, hardly. She complained that no one dropped in like they used to. When we were planning the New Year's party, she said——"

It was Serena's turn to bite back her words. Jenness had said there seemed to be no male creatures left, anywhere around, except cripples. But that was the last thing Serena wanted to say to Dexter. He finished her sentence for her, without awkwardness.

"I know she missed the excitement of having the old crowd around her, the Carletons and the Merrills and all the others who have either gone to camp or enlisted. But I think she may have found at least one other companion that she didn't tell us about. I think when she went off on those long walks of hers, she didn't always go alone."

"Why I saw her, everytime she started out!"

"I'm sure you did. And everytime she came home. I know your nice custom of coming out on the porch." He leaned forward, smiling at her affectionately and taking her hand in his. "But I think once in a while she met someone, while she was out walking. In fact I know she did. I saw her myself, with a man I didn't recognize, one afternoon when I was coming home from the Junction. She was strolling along beside the brook, in the Big Field."

Serena looked at Dexter with dumb misery in her mild eyes. He pressed the work-worn hand he was holding.

"That doesn't mean anything in itself, you know," he said gently. "I wouldn't have given it a thought, if she hadn't stepped behind some bushes, as soon as she heard a car coming, and beckoned to this man who was with her to hide too. Normally Jenness would watch to see who was in the car, and if it was anyone she knew, she'd have waved and shouted. In fact, she'd probably have waved and shouted whether it was anyone she was sure she knew or not—she'd have taken it for granted it must be a new neighbor she hadn't met, or an old codger she'd half forgotten. Jenness has always been so friendly that it's like her to be hail-fellow-well-met."

"Yes," Serena said wretchedly, "she always has been friendly. So if she hid when she saw you coming—if she's been meeting someone on the sly—why, that would explain what Peter meant when he talked to Daniel about her seeing Lentz here, and about that wicked man's 'quiet rural activities'!"

"It *might*. Nothing's certain yet, Mrs. Farman. We don't *know* that she's done anything wrong herself. We can still go on hoping she hasn't."

"Yes, we can still go on hoping. But from what you've just told me, things look pretty bad, even worse than they did before. And Daniel thought anyhow that maybe he ought to start making plans to go to Washington. He thought maybe I ought to go with him and I agreed. Just in case anything should happen, you know. Because it wouldn't be so easy to get away, all of a sudden, unless we did plan beforehand, what with no help on the farm and—and all."

Serena could not bring herself to say "and no money," not even to Dexter. But he knew what she meant. He answered her with increasing gentleness.

"I'm sure Hite and I can manage to look after the cattle and the milk route too if you and Mr. Farman find you do have to go. I don't know just how we'd work it out, but we'll find a way."

"Well, Daniel and I were talking it over last night, after we went to bed. And we thought maybe Hite could look out for your stock right along instead of once in a while,

seeing he's so near anyway, and boards with his family
and all. It wouldn't put him out much of any, except that
he'd have to give up some of his paper hanging for a few
weeks, but we thought he'd be willing to do that, in a
pinch, and that everyone he'd promised would understand
too. And then we thought maybe you could move up to
our house."

"Well, I could, of course, if that would make your minds
any easier. I could come down here every day, just to give
things the once over—not that Hite isn't trustworthy, but
a man does like to keep his eye on his own stock if he can,
you know that. I can look after *myself* just as well in your
house as I could in my own. And with Rhoda gone——"

"Yes, that's what we thought. And we thought maybe,
if you were right there, and she saw how it was and all,
Judith would marry you straight off as soon as she got out
of quarantine. She'll be out in just a short time now. Maybe before Daniel and I would have to go to Washington.
That is, if we do have to go. And it *would* ease our minds.
Things would look a lot different to us, Dexter, if you
really were our son-in-law, if we had a right——"

"You've got every right. You know I've always felt as
if you were my mother. Well, now you're going to be.
Straight off, just as you said. Don't worry anymore, please
don't—Mother Farman. Judith will see how it is. I can
talk to *her*. She's not like Jenness. She's steady and sensible
and straightforward. You don't know how thankful I am
that she is. I'll go and get her, the minute Dr. Barnes will
let me, and on the way home I'll tell her—please, Mother
Farman—please don't cry."

She did not, very long. She went on talking to Dexter
for a few minutes more, and before she had said everything she had come to tell him, she dried her eyes, and
looked up at him with an attempt at a smile.

"There, I'm real ashamed at giving away so," she said.
"I'm sure I don't know what made me. I don't usually cry,
not in a month of Sundays. I won't deny but what I worry.
I feel different though, now I've had this talk with you,

Dexter. I feel as if everything might come out all right after all."

"That's the way I want you to feel. I can start moving tomorrow, if you'd like to have me, as soon as I've taken Rhoda to the station. I guess perhaps I won't say anything to her about it beforehand. It might upset her, just as she's leaving."

"Yes, that's right. I wouldn't say anything to Rhoda."

"And perhaps it would be just as well not to say anything to Jenness either. You'd like me to take her to the station too, wouldn't you?"

"If you're sure it wouldn't put you out any. We're asking a lot of you, Dexter, we know that."

"You go right on asking. That's what I'm here for."

He went out of the barn with her, helped her into the secondhand Ford, and stood looking after her until it swung out of sight over the crest of the hill. Then he went back to the books on which he had been working when she came in. As a selectman of the town, it was one of his duties to appraise property and report on his findings; though Town Meeting Day was still comfortably far off, he liked to have everything ship-shape well in advance. He had found more than usual to do this last year; a number of places had changed hands, and most of those which had been bought and sold indicated revaluation. Modern improvements had been installed in a number of houses, and in several cases, sizable additions had been put on them as well. Barns and other outbuildings had not been overlooked in these projects of renovation, for larger herds had required larger quarters; the dairy business had never been better. Besides, a new store and a new gas station had been opened in the village, and a new tourist camp built near it. The bank of which Dexter was a director had approved a number of loans, but most of these had already been paid off. The newcomers were nearly all prosperous; there would be no trouble about collecting their taxes. And these taxes, as Dexter reckoned them, would come to a substantial sum. When Serena had come to the office, he had been making a rough estimate of the extra amounts on which he thought the town could safely count. Now he picked up his pad of scratch paper and looked at it again. Adelbert Hellman's name headed the list with taxable farm property valued at twenty thousand dollars; but Karl Wagner, the new merchant, ran him a close second. August Lippman, Berthold Becker and Hilda Krauss would all find their local responsibilities heavy also . . .

An eerie feeling of uneasiness crept over him as he glanced at the list, his eyes straying from the figures in the right-hand column to the names on the left. It was the first time he had grouped them in this way, and together, they seemed to take on a meaning which separately they had not possessed. He read them over once more, half aloud— Hellman, Wagner, Lippman, Becker, Krauss—why those were all German names! It seemed incredible that he had never thought of it before, but it was true. Among the new taxpayers, who were bringing so much welcome revenue into the community, only the Whites and the Jenkins were outside the alien category.

He laid the pad down on his desk and walked over to the window, intent on a new train of thought. But glancing out, almost subconsciously, he saw that he had another caller. A tall, solidly built man was approaching the barn, without haste but with every indication of self-assurance. As he came closer, Dexter could see that his face was florid, but there was nothing about this ruddiness which suggested that he was cold; like the frosty blue of his eyes, it seemed a natural part of his fair coloring. He was wearing a handsome coat, rather formal in style, its wide fur collar buttoned up closely around his throat, and his hands were encased in heavy leather gloves. Dexter guessed that the coat and the gloves were both fur lined before his caller, courteously accepting his inviation to enter, removed them and revealed that this was indeed the case. He took the seat beside the fire, recently occupied by Serena, introducing himself and broaching the object of his errand almost simultaneously.

"I hope I do not intrude, Mr. Abbott? No? This is a good time for you to receive a caller? The lady of the house—your sister, is it not so?—told me that I should find you here, and that she did not think you would be so occupied that it would be inconvenient for you to receive me. Well! I shall nevertheless be brief. My name is Meyer, Gustav Meyer. I am associated with the real estate company of Archer, Lamb & Archer in Chicago. Doubtless you know it by reputation; it is one of the first firms in the city. But let me give you my card."

He produced it, with something of a flourish. Dexter took it, studied it for a minute, and then laid it down on his desk beside the pad of scratch paper on which he had scribbled the names of Hellman, Wagner, Lippman, Becker and Krauss.

"I don't happen to, but then I almost never get to Chicago," he said civilly. "Most of us around here think of Boston as our big center. Is your firm interested in New England real estate, Mr. Meyer?"

"Yes. That is it exactly, Mr. Abbott. You have grasped my purpose immediately. Mr. Willis Archer, the senior member of the firm I represent, is very much interested in New England real estate, especially in the rural regions along the Connecticut River. He feels that an excellent market has been inexplicably overlooked. Such splendid scenery! Such fertile soil! Such wonderful dairy country! Such fine timberland!"

"You couldn't describe them better if you came from one of our own state publicity bureaus, Mr. Meyer."

"Ah! I see you like your little joke, Mr. Abbott. I also. But on this occasion I am most serious. Not to take up too much of your so valuable time, I should venture to inquire if by chance you know of some desirable properties in your own beautiful town which might be for sale."

"I'm afraid I don't. As it happens there's already been quite a boom in real estate here. All the places that were on the market have been sold already."

"All? You're positive of that, Mr. Abbott? Because I have here the name of a property which Mr. Willis Archer feels certain would be very interesting to one of his best clients."

"The *name* of a property? We don't often name our places around here, Mr. Meyer, the way people do in the South. I'm afraid I don't know what property you mean."

"Excuse me. I did not speak correctly. I know you are right, Mr. Abbott. I know that New England properties are not invariably named in the same manner, shall we say, as southern plantations. But often they go by the names of the family who own them, is it not so? For instance, I believe this property of yours is locally always called the Abbott Homestead. The one to which I refer also goes, I think, by the name of a family. It is called—" Mr. Meyer paused to consult a piece of paper which, up to that moment, he had held neatly folded in his well-kept hands— "it is called Farman Hill."

"Then I can tell you very positively, Mr. Meyer, that the property in which you are interested is not for sale."

"You are sure, Mr. Abbott? Excuse me. Of course I should not dispute you. But sometimes outsiders are informed of matters which are not discussed in a neighborhood. Is it not so? Now Mr. Willis Archer has been informed most reliably that the Farman family might be persuaded to sell this property if the figure were sufficiently high. And it would be substantial. It happens that this distinguished client of Mr. Archer desires a country estate of a certain elevation. It appears that Farman Hill meets this particular requirement. The distinguished client also desires a certain amount of woodland. In this respect it appears that Farman Hill more than meets the requirement. If I am not mistaken it has on it—" Mr. Meyer again consulted his neat paper—"a large lot covered with pine, and somewhat apart, another large timber lot. This is not to mention a second elevation, even higher than Farman Hill itself, which is, I believe, called Jerome's Hill, and which is well covered with healthy spruce and balsam fir."

"You couldn't have described it better if you'd done it from a surveyor's map. Or did you?"

"Excuse me, Mr. Abbott. I do not think I quite follow you."

"It doesn't matter. I'll have to repeat, I'm quite sure Farman Hill isn't for sale."

"But the house," persisted Mr. Meyer. "The house, as it happens, also meets our very distinguished client's requirements exactly. This gentleman has a very keen appreciation of quaint indigenous characteristics in early American architecture and cabinet making and decoration. So he is intensely interested——"

"In the frescoes? Or the hand-wrought beams? Or the candleflame bedroom set? Or the piggins and the hackels?"

"Ah, I can see that you are yourself a connoisseur, Mr. Abbott! Then surely you can understand the eagerness of our client!"

"No, I'm not a connoisseur. I never even noticed those things much until lately. But I've seen them around ever since I was a little boy, and I happen to know that none of them is for sale. Of course if you don't believe me you can go and ask Mr. Farman. In fact, I don't see why you didn't do that in the first place. After all, Farman Hill doesn't belong to me. It belongs to him."

"Excuse me. It is because the word of a valued friend has so much weight, is it not so, Mr. Abbott? You might advise Mr. Farman to sell if you thought it would be a real advantage to him, might you not? Mr. Archer felt sure that you might. And then, Mr. Archer also reasoned, that if I came to you first, you might be able to tell me what figure, in your opinion, would be attractive to Mr. Farman. You know the value of the property and you need not hesitate to mention a large sum. Thirty thousand, perhaps?"

"I don't think Farman Hill could be bought for thirty thousand."

"Thirty-five thousand, perhaps? Forty thousand?"

"I don't think those figures would be attractive either."

"Would you care to mention a figure yourself, Mr. Abbott?"

"Well, had your very distinguished client thought of a hundred thousand?"

Mr. Meyer gave a short, formal little laugh. "Again I see you enjoy your little joke, Mr. Abbott," he said agreeably. He refolded the neat little piece of paper he had been holding, and extracting a handsome pigskin billfold from his pocket, inserted the memorandum between the crisp greenbacks with which it was distended. Then he rose and picked up the fur-lined broadcloth coat.

"All that pine," Dexter said pensively. "All that spruce and balsam. And the elevation—I mean the two elevations. With authentic antiques like piggins and hackels thrown in too."

"I believe our distinguished client might go as high as fifty thousand, Mr. Abbott."

"Now you mention it, I believe he might," Dexter said, still pensively. "Why don't you get in touch with him and find out? You might mention the figure I quoted too, while you're about it. Let him think it over for a few days. And then come back and talk to Mr. Farman. I'll be very glad to tell him about your little proposition in the meantime, now that you've put it to me in such an urgent way. But he'll need a few days himself, to think it over, I'm sure of that. Why don't you come back next week, Mr. Meyer? Or the week after? By the week after I believe I'd be in a position to give you a very positive answer."

CHAPTER 9

DEXTER HAD very little opportunity for uninterrupted deliberation during the next few days. As the moment for her departure approached, Rhoda felt her heart failing. She sensed the fact that her brother was perturbed, and assumed that it was the thought of his impending separation from her which was troubling him; so she found a dozen pretexts for detaining him every time he came near her. Over and over again she cautioned him about not letting the pipes freeze or leaving the fires untended, about the system of airing the house which she had found most satisfactory, and about the relative proportions of the different ground feeds in the mash she gave the poultry. Mrs. Wendell, Hite's mother, had agreed to come in twice a week to clean, and to take the laundry home to do with her own. This was an act of sheer neighborliness, for the

Wendells were in comfortable circumstances, and she had never before gone out to work or taken in washing. Rhoda went on to caution Dexter that he must be careful how he spoke of this accommodation; it would never do to give a wrong impression about the Wendells' means.

He promised readily, if with some abstraction. It was hard to listen respectfully and attentively to all Rhoda's trivial advice, when his mind was on matters of so much graver import, and he disliked the mild deception of faithfully promising to follow it, when he knew that her back would hardly be turned before he would be on his way to Farman Hill. Besides, Rhoda was flustered as well as worried, because she insisted on doing too much, and the atmosphere she created was one of disquietude. She had scrubbed the already spotless house from attic to cellar, the previous week, washing all the curtains, blankets and bedspreads into the bargain, and when Sunday morning came she was exhausted; but she insisted on going to church and taking her usual place in the choir, though this meant a last minute rush to prepare and clear away dinner before going to the station. Distress had already unnerved her; and by the time Dexter finally watched her train pull out, after reassuring her as to the safety of the steamer trunk in the baggage car and placing her worn Boston bag beside her on the faded plush seat of the day coach, fatigue had further undermined her self-control. Tears were rolling down her pale cheeks as she waved to him from the unwashed window. He turned away, doubly distressed himself because this sister to whom he owed so much had not been able to sustain the high note of happiness on which she had begun to reshape her life.

There was no spare time for him to spend at home before taking Jenness to the Junction to catch the express, so he went straight from the local station to Farman Hill. Usually the quiet old house was completely upset by the flurry which characterized her departure. She seldom started to pack until it was almost train time, and then she called on everyone within hearing to help her assemble her scattered belongings and fling them into her baggage. Now all her suitcases were already lined up in a neat row by the living room door when Dexter entered, and Jenness, dressed for traveling, was standing near the window with the air of impatiently watching for him to come. Like most men, Dexter was not especially clothes-conscious; but he noticed, with some surprise at his own observance, that she had on another new outfit, different from the one in which she had arrived. Instead of the little fur hat, she was wearing one trimmed with tip-tilted scarlet wings, and a spotted veil was swathed around her face and fastened at the nape of the neck. Her tailored suit was scarlet too, and a short full jacket of black fur, with a matching muff, lay on a chair beside her. He could not help feeling that as a final gesture of defiance, in leaving home, she had put on the most conspicuous and the most costly clothes she owned.

"Why, Jenness, you look just like a redbird!" he said pleasantly. "And poised for flight already! We'll miss your bright plumage on our quiet countryside."

She turned away from the window, and he could see, even under the veil, that she was wearing much more makeup than usual. Her naturally exquisite complexion required no artifice to improve it, and Dexter, who had conservative ideas on the subject, had always been thankful that Jenness recognized this fact. It was a shock for him to see the smudgy blue shadows under her eyes and the crude overlay of vermilion on her lips. But at least it was a relief to find that she had mastered her hysteria, even if her bravado had such a hard quality.

"Don't be so silly, Dexter," she said sharply. "It isn't in character for you to talk poetically. Besides, you know perfectly well you'll be glad to get rid of me."

"You're mistaken. I never was sorrier to see you go," he answered.

"You don't need to be so nasty-nice about it. I know what you really mean. You don't mean you'll miss me. You mean you think I'm going to get into some kind of trouble. Well, as it happens, I know I'm not. I've had a wonderful letter from Horace Vaughn this morning. I've told him a hundred times not to waste money sending me letters by airmail special, because they're not delivered any quicker, in this godforsaken neck of the woods than if they're sent by ordinary mail. But this morning Phineas Johnson did telephone that a letter had come in for me, and Dad picked it up at the Johnsons' house when he and Mom went to church. I don't think for a moment Phineas telephoned out of kindness—he's never done such a thing before. It's just that he's snooping, and scenting some kind of a scandal, like everyone else. Well, I hope that sometime you'll find an excuse to tell him what was in the letter. Horace said he didn't think there was the slightest chance I'd be called as a witness, if this man Lentz you're all raving about actually was brought to trial, and he thought that was most unlikely too. He called the whole thing a tempest in a teapot, stirred up partly by dirty politics and partly by the yellow press. But he said that if anything *did* happen, he'd tell the world I had nothing to do with the silly muddle. You can read the letter yourself if you like. Horace says 'You're a hundred percent O. K., Jenness. I'll back you to the limit in everything.'"

"I'm very glad," Dexter said quietly.

"Well, you know he said in the first place that all the charges against me were 'absolutely nonsensical and fantastic.' This is only more along the same lines . . . Don't you want to read the letter?"

"Not especially. I get the idea from what you've told me. Thanks just the same."

"Well, if you're not going to sit down, we might as well start for the station."

"There's no hurry. But we can if you like. That is, if you've said goodbye to your father and mother. They didn't know you were going quite so soon, did they?"

"I don't suppose so. Dad brought down the bags and then he went out to the barn. I think he invents things to do there so that he can escape me. I don't see how he could spend so much time on a hundred cows, let alone fifteen. And Mom's upstairs somewhere putting things to rights, as she calls it. I told her everything would be all right anyway as soon as I'd gone."

"Jenness, I wish you wouldn't talk so. Your father and mother do feel terribly, and you make it harder and harder for them all the time. You haven't said a word to relieve their minds. If you only would, before you go——"

"Why I offered to show them Horace's letter too! And they wouldn't bother to read it, any more than you would!"

"They don't care what Horace Vaughn says, Jenness. They care about what you might say."

"Oh, stop picking on me, Dexter! You're as bad as Peter MacDonald! There isn't anything I *can* say. There isn't anything *to* say."

"All right. I don't want to pick on you, Jenness. Perhaps it would be just as well if we did get started."

It had been even worse seeing Jenness off than seeing Rhoda off, Dexter reflected, in the course of the bleak and dreary drive back to Farman Hill. To the very end, he had kept on trying to break down her resistance and reserve, not with threatening abruptness, as Peter had done, but with gentleness and patience, and as far as lay in his power, with adroitness. He knew that he lacked subtlety, but he hoped that sympathy might serve as a substitute. However, he was no nearer success when he stopped than when he began. He left her, not as he had left Rhoda, with tears she could not suppress streaming down her cheeks, but with her head tossed back under the scarlet wings that surmounted it, and her painted face impudent under its spotted veil.

He stopped in at Farman Hill a second time, on his return, but only long enough to say he would not spend that night there after all, if Mother and Father Farman did not mind. So far, he had not had a minute to himself, and there were a number of things he must see to at home. There was the water to shut off from the house, for instance; he thought he could do it all right alone, but he might have to get in a plumber, and in any case it would take several hours. He did not think he would move his herd books and his town accounts; after all, he would have to go down to see his stock every day, and he could continue to use his office in the barn. But the house would have to be completely closed. There were no plants and no pets to provide for, because Rhoda had never wanted to bother with any; on the other hand, there were all her pickles and preserves in the cellar which he would have to move. And he must tell Mrs. Wendell that she would not need to come in to clean or take home laundry after all; even more tact and time would be required for this than there would have been in explaining her disinterested efforts in his behalf. When it came to that, he would have to take time to write Rhoda, before someone else beat him to it, giving the wrong impression; he would not put it past her to come home, if she thought he had moved because he was lonely or because he could not manage for himself after all. His personal packing would not take any time to speak of. But there were all these other things . . .

Yes, that was so, the Farmans agreed. They were entirely reasonable, they did not press him in any way. Yet he saw how pitifully eager they were to have him with them; and all the next day, and the day after, he went from one necessary task to another with a sense of haste, reluctantly pausing to eat a cold hurried bite standing, in Rhoda's deserted kitchen, and sitting up far into the night to write her the difficult letter. Before it was posted, he received one from her, revealing that she had made a quick recovery both from her weariness and her qualms of conscience. The day's shopping in St. Johnsbury had been an unqualified success: she had found exactly what she wanted to wear, very reasonably—everything was marked down because it was after Christmas, and the hundred dollars he had given her had been more than enough. She had gone on to her destination that same evening, and everyone had been so glad to see her that she was very much touched. She had her old room back, with the Goodwins, in whose house she had boarded before—a nice, warm, pleasant room, facing south. There had been everything she liked best for supper too. Mrs. Goodwin had remembered her tastes, all these years. And the school building was improved some, but not so much but what she felt right at home there . . .

The tone of Rhoda's letter gave a modicum of relief to Dexter's overburdened mind, but this was offset by the effect of one from Peter MacDonald which arrived by the

same mail. He felt like a dirty dog. Peter wrote, because
he had gone off without a word, when Dexter must have
waited dinner and delayed a hunting trip on his account.
He hoped Dexter understood how it was, even if like the
late lamented Will Rogers, all he knew was what he saw
in the papers. Aside from his own regret at seeming so
damned ungrateful, and his uneasiness over the hell of a
hole into which Jenness had undoubtedly slipped, Peter
was feeling pretty good; he had got both a raise and a
bonus on the strength of his scoop, and he had hopes that
he might also get a foreign assignment. Of course he had
been told he was to cover the Lentz trial, but he was holding out for the other, and he thought he might pull it off.
He didn't want to touch the Lentz trial with a nine-foot
pole; from what he could pick up, Jenness was sure to be
called as a witness, and he would rather be on the other
side of the water when that happened. After he got back
from the Halls of Montezuma and the Shores of Tripoli,
he'd like to see Dexter again, if not on Farman Hill, where
he'd probably be about as welcome as a polecat, then in
Washington, where his stock was rapidly rising. They ought
to be able to get some good hunting near-by in Virginia.
Some friends of his had a private little place not far from
Aguia, where they shot wild turkeys and wild geese. He
went there himself every weekend that he could get away,
during the season, and liked it a lot. He thought Dexter
would like it too. He sent his best . . .

Driven by the urgency of settling in on Farman Hill before definite word of the threatened disaster to Jenness
could reach there, Dexter redoubled his efforts to reorganize conditions at the Abbott Homestead, and finally succeeded in making all necessary adjustments and leaving
there three days after the departure of Rhoda and Jenness.
He was late for supper and he was too tired to eat; but
he noticed that Mrs. Farman had regarded his special tastes
with the same touching care that Mrs. Goodwin had bestowed on his sister's, and he tried hard to do justice to
the good things she set before him. After supper, Daniel
brought out some small glasses and filled them with apple
brandy—a rare gesture on his part, for he entertained as

abstemiously as he lived, and it was only on such great occasions as New Year's parties and wedding feasts that he offered liquor to his guests. But tonight Dexter was thankful for the unexpected cheer of the spirits. He emptied his glass quickly, and Daniel, without speaking, took it away and refilled it, together with his own. Then, as they settled down beside the fire with their pipes, sipping more slowly and relaxing after the prolonged strain they had both been under, Dexter broached the subject which he had succeeded neither in dismissing from his mind nor in solving.

"I've been waiting to tell you about a rather strange visitor I had the other day," he said. "Everything's been so upset I haven't had a good chance before. But I don't want to let it go too long. Maybe this is as good a time as any."

"Maybe it is," Daniel agreed. "Unless you should want to wait until Serena has finished the dishes."

"No, I'd rather tell you first. Then we can talk it over with her afterwards . . . A man came to me representing a Chicago real estate firm—Archer, Lamb & Archer, the firm's name is. But the name of this man was Gustav Meyer."

Daniel, puffing away at his pipe, did not answer.

"It was a funny thing, but when this man came in, I'd just been making up a rough list of the new taxpayers in town. I didn't realize, until I saw them grouped together that way, that all but two of them had German names. Did you ever think of it yourself?"

"No, I don't know as I have. To tell you the truth, I don't know as I'd always recognize a name as German when I did see it. Of course I know now that Hellman's a German name, but I never gave it any thought until this matter of Lentz came up. What are the others you had in mind?"

"Well, Wagner for one. And Lippman and Becker and Krauss. Of course Becker's been Americanized. But the others are unmistakable, and Becker looks and acts more like a German than any of them—or what we think of when we say anyone looks and acts like a German. Not that I know much more about it than you do, Sir. But from what I do know, I'd say Becker was what's called typical. And so was this man Meyer who came to see me on Saturday."

"I presume he told you what he wanted."

"Yes. He said his firm felt that rural New England had been 'inexplicably overlooked' as a market. He went into raptures over the scenery and the soil. Not to mention the timberland and several other aspects of the countryside."

"He was thinking of investing around here?"

"Yes. He asked me if I couldn't give him the names of some attractive properties. I said no, that they'd all been sold already. And while I was saying it, I kept thinking about those other Germans who'd bought them. But then he suggested one himself."

Again Daniel went on puffing at his pipe, silently waiting for Dexter to continue.

"I suppose there's no use in beating around the bush. I may as well tell you first as last that the place he suggested was Farman Hill. He described it to me in great detail. And then he went on to say it suited a very distinguished client of his in every respect. I gathered that the elevation and the wood lots were the features this client particularly coveted, though the architecture and the antiques were mentioned too, in passing. He knew all about Jerome's Hill and the frescoes and the summer kitchen. You'd have thought, to hear him talk, he'd spent as much time on the place as I have."

Daniel leaned forward, and began to knock the ashes out of his pipe. Then he took another slow sip of the apple brandy before he answered.

"I presume you were afraid this would be a sort of shock to me, Dexter," he said at last. "Maybe I ought to have spoken first, but as you say, there hasn't been any good chance. I knew what you were going to tell me, before you began to talk. I had a letter from this man Meyer myself, this morning. He said you'd advised him to wait awhile before writing, but that his client was in a hurry, and that he'd rather got the idea you were personally averse to the sale and that you'd probably take your own time about consulting me."

"Of course I'm personally averse to the sale. But that isn't what prevented me from speaking to you about it. The only thing that prevented me has been lack of time. There's certainly no reason why I should dread talking about it, when I knew you'd be ten times as averse to the idea as I would."

"Yes, that's right. I am averse to the idea. And I haven't dared speak to Serena about it. I figure she's had about as much to stand, lately, as she ought to. But I've been thinking about it all day, just the same. I've been thinking that fifty thousand dollars is an awful lot of money. More than I ever saw in my life. More than I ever expected to see."

"You don't mean to tell me you thought you would sell?"

"Easy there, Dexter. I hadn't got that far. But let's say, just for the sake of having something to go by, that I got far enough to think I might sell, if I found it wouldn't be too big a blow to Serena. I'd been looking at it differently from you. I hadn't thought about having Farman Hill pass into the hands of Germans, along with half a dozen places right in this same village. I hadn't thought what that might mean, and I still don't understand rightly. But I can see you think it might mean something that wouldn't do the village any good."

"The village! It isn't just the village! It isn't just the township or the country or the state. It's our country!"

"Yes, I see that now. I told you we'd been looking at it differently."

"But even if it weren't for that I don't see how you could bear to part with it. Why, there have always been Farmans on the Hill, ever since the Upper Connecticut Valley was settled."

"Yes, that's so. I won't deny but what it would be a wrench to leave it. I won't deny but what there isn't any other place I could live that would seem like home to me, not even yours, Dexter. But fifty thousand dollars go a long way towards taking care of Jenness if she was in trouble."

It was the younger man's turn to look speechlessly at his companion.

"I told you that you and I had been looking at this matter differently," Daniel said. "When you have a daughter yourself, Dexter, you'll find out you'd want to do anything you could to keep her out of harm's way. Even more than you would a son. A man's proud of his sons, he's in a hurry to have them become men and get sons of their own; he wants to see his name go on. In a way, a son's a symbol of immortality to a man, if you understand what I'm trying to say. But at the same time he expects a son to stand on his own feet and look out for himself. He doesn't have much respect for a boy who can't. Now a daughter—well, a man likes to baby his daughter. He likes to have her sit on his lap and cuddle up to him. He likes to feel he's taking care of *her*. She's his little girl, even after she's grown up. When she's going to have a child, he remembers the times his own children were born, how their mother suffered, and it seems as if he couldn't bear it to have his little girl suffer like that. It isn't the same when he can't see travail as a part of shared rapture, when another man's caused the suffering. He doesn't think of the name going on then—of course it isn't, for his daughter's got a new name. But even if it weren't for that, he wouldn't feel the same about his daughter's child as his son's child. Now if I heard tomorrow that Alix was in the family way, I'd be so pleased I wouldn't know what to do. In fact I keep hoping, every letter that comes . . . It's too soon to tell of course, and still I've got it on my mind and keep waiting to hear. I'd be sorry if she had a hard time, in childbirth, but I wouldn't grieve over it; I'd say it ought to be worth it to her, to bear Jerome's son. And somehow I've always thought Judith would get along all right. She's stronger than the average and takes things in her stride more. Besides, I've known for a long time that you'd be her husband, and somehow I feel a girl would be safe with you, whatever happened. But Jenness—why if it was Jenness who was going to get married this month, I'd worry, the best I could do. I can't think of her except as my lovely

little girl—my little girl with big blue eyes and rosy cheeks
and curly hair, who still sits on my lap and kisses the tips
of my ears and plays with my forelock."

Daniel paused and blew his nose. Then he took another
slow sip of brandy.

"I seem to have sort of got off the subject," he said at
last. "We were talking about selling this place, and here
I am rambling on about girls having a hard time with their
babies, just like an old woman who loves to gloat and
gossip. But maybe I'm not so far from where I started
after all. Because Jenness may be facing something a lot
worse than childbirth. So I feel just that much worse about
her. I feel it's just that much more necessary to do everything I can to protect her. And if fifty thousand dollars
would do it . . . I know these high class lawyers cost
money. I don't know just how much, but it's a-plenty,
when they take a client whose case they practically guarantee to win against heavy odds. And then, afterwards, Jenness might like to go away somewheres till everything blew
over. People forget pretty fast if there's nothing around
to remind them of a scandal and Jenness has always
hankered to take a European trip. Well, of course that's
out of the question now. But maybe Mexico—I thought of
Mexico."

"But you wouldn't be satisfied to have her acquitted,
if she had to face a trial, just because she'd had a clever
lawyer! You'd have to be convinced yourself that she was
innocent! You'd never feel her name was really cleared if
you'd bought off justice! You've been like a father to me all
my life, sir, and I know——"

"Yes. Yes. You know a good deal Dexter, I'll admit
that. But you don't know yet what it's like to have a daughter. Maybe, next year at this time, you'll understand better
how I feel—that is, how I have been feeling all day. But
now—now it isn't a case any longer, of looking at things
differently from you, when it comes to a question of selling
Farman Hill, or keeping it, out of sentiment, either way.
After what you've told me, I've got to think of something
else too. I've got to think what it might mean, not just to
sell Farman Hill, but to sell it to Germans, which I didn't

think of before, like I told you . . . Did you have something in mind that it might mean, Dexter?"

"Well—not exactly. But last night, before I went to bed, I happened to pick up a magazine, and it opened up on a page that startled me, seeing it right after seeing Meyer. The name of the piece was *'Nazis In The Wood Pile,'* and after I'd glanced at the first paragraph, I read it straight through. I was darned tired, but I couldn't stop until I'd finished it. This piece described the way Germans had bought up places with timber land on them, every time they'd started out to occupy a country or part of a country. I brought the magazine along with me, in my suitcase, I thought if you weren't too tired, maybe you'd read it yourself."

"I will, Dexter. I'll read it tonight. I am tired but I'm not too tired to do that. I guess it's important I should do it. But was it just this article in a magazine——?"

"No, it wasn't just an article in a magazine. I couldn't go to sleep after I did go to bed, and I went on thinking— wasn't this road up the Valley the main thoroughfare to Canada during the Revolution? Didn't the British Army and the Continentals both use it?"

"Yes, but——"

"Well, couldn't it be a thoroughfare again? A main military route? I don't see why not. And even if the thoroughfare's ancient history, the Great Circle isn't."

"The Great Circle?"

"The beam that the transatlantic planes follow. We're right under it. I may be all wet, as Peter MacDonald would say, but I can't see anything wrong with Jerome's Hill, or Farman's Hill either, for a signal station. And then there's the question of our proposed airport. That isn't without its potentialities."

Daniel Farman picked up his brandy glass again. There was nothing in it. Sip by sip, while he and Dexter had been talking, he had emptied it. He made no motion to refill it a second time, but he held it in his hand, staring at it for a long time. Then he set it down on the gate-legged table and looked steadily at Dexter.

"I see," he said. "I see what you're thinking. You're

thinking that if I sell this place, it may be used to help sell
out this country. You're thinking I'd be a traitor if I did
that, even to save my own daughter. And you believe my
daughter's been a traitor already. You're right, Dexter.
It's hard for me to say it. But I know you're right."

CHAPTER 10

THE DREADED letter from Jenness was in the mail left
by the rural delivery carrier the next day. It was addressed to both Daniel and Serena, and Serena called to
her husband to come into the house before she broke the
seal.

"Dear Dad and Mom—" she read aloud. Daniel stood
over her, with his arm around her shoulder, while she
sat in the old rocker by the fire. But he could not see to
read without his glasses, and he had not stopped to get
these when Serena called him.

> *"I have been summoned to appear before the Grand
> Jury in connection with the Lentz case. Everyone
> seems possessed with the idea that I know something
> about it. Also, though I can't imagine why, I am be-
> ing accused of fooling with some mysterious mailbags.
> It's all an awful headache. The summons was served
> on me as I was coming back to my apartment this
> evening, when I happened to be all alone. I tried to
> get Horace Vaughn on the telephone, but he had gone
> to dinner at the Argentine Embassy and I could not
> reach him. Then I tried to get hold of several other
> friends, but they were out too. It is always that way
> in Washington; you never can reach anyone in a hurry
> because everyone is going around in circles. I even
> tried to get Peter MacDonald, as a last resort, but
> there wasn't any answer at his apartment, and the*

operator at the Bulletin *Building said she didn't have any idea where to reach him. It sounded to me as if she were making a great mystery out of nothing.*

"Of course I'll talk to Horace in the morning and I'm sure he'll fix up everything for me. But if you really want to come to Washington, as you said you did before I left home, I suppose this as good a time as any. I'm sure I don't know where you'll stay, because there isn't a hotel I know of in town where you could get in with a shoehorn, and prices are so high they'd knock you over, just to hear about them. But I'll try to find something if you decide you do want to come. I'm sure Dexter will lend you the money, if you ask him, because I know he has plenty, and I could tell from the way he talked, when he took me to the station, that he would like to do anything he could for you. Of course everything is practically the same as if he were married to Judith already, so I don't see why you need to hesitate.

Love,
Jenness.

P. S. Don't pay any attention to what the newspapers say about the trial. They're always full of wild rumors and dirty lies.

Serena stopped and handed the letter to her husband. While he was rereading it to himself, having meanwhile gone for his glasses, she removed her own, which she had taken time to put on in the first place, and wiped her eyes. Then she sat very still, not rocking at all, waiting for Daniel to speak.

"She doesn't sound frightened. She's got hold of herself," Daniel said at last, putting the letter back in the envelope and handing it to his wife.

"She'd begun to get hold of herself before she left here. But she's still frightened inside. I can tell."

"Yes, I guess maybe she is. What do you want we should do, Mother?"

"I want we should start as soon as we can . . . I'm

some surprised Jenness doesn't suggest we should stay with her. I should think she could make room for us if she tried. She's got a studio couch in her living room. She could give us her bedroom and sleep on that couch herself. It kind of hurts my feelings that she doesn't offer to. It makes me feel she doesn't want us around, not too close anyway. Just handy in case she needs us."

"This isn't anytime to think of hurt feelings, Mother. I guess all children hurt the old folks' feelings now and again, half the time without meaning to or knowing they've done it . . . Is Dexter here?"

"No. He went down to the Abbott Homestead right after dinner. He said he wouldn't be back till suppertime. He wanted to work on his town accounts. And he said, if he got to a good stopping place on those, he was going out to try to find some one to help him with the logging."

"It wouldn't be fair to Dexter to start off tonight. He's carrying a heavy load as it is, Serena."

"Yes. I don't know how he'll manage. Do you suppose it would do any good if I should call up Judith and see if she couldn't get off her case a little sooner than she'd figured? None of the other Brent children have been taken sick, thank heavens, and the twins must be almost well by now."

"It wouldn't do any harm to try. But I'd be careful what I said over the phone. It might be better to write."

"She wouldn't get the letter until tomorrow afternoon. And it seems so silly to write your own daughter, when she's in the same village with you."

Serena went to the old-fashioned telephone, and tried to ring the Brents' number. Someone else was talking on the line, giving a new recipe for a cake to a neighbor, and it was some time before she could get in. When at last the line was cleared, she heeded Daniel's injunction to speak cautiously.

"Is this Brents'? Ruby, this is Serena Farman. Why I'm well, thank you. Yes, he's well too. Yes, you've heard right. With Rhoda gone and all, we thought it would be a convenience on both sides. Yes, we had a letter on the afternoon delivery. She's always been wonderful about writing. Why no, nothing special. I do hope the twins are better. That's fine, Ruby, that's just fine. Well naturally it makes me feel good, to think you have such a high opinion of her. Would it be so's I could speak to Judith, Ruby, without putting you out any? . . . Hello, Judith. Why we're all right. Yes, he has . . . Judith, I don't suppose you have any idea yet, have you, when you'll be getting home? No, nothing's wrong, but it's a long, long time since we've seen you and we were sort of hoping . . . Sunday—and this isn't but Thursday. Well, of course you ought to stay as long as you are needed. All right, Sunday in time for supper. Well, good-bye, Judith. No, there wasn't anything else . . . You heard, Daniel," she said, turning from the telephone. "Judith says she can't possibly leave the Brents' before Sunday. And then of course we'd have to wait and find out if she'd be willing to marry Dexter straight off. We couldn't leave them here together unless they were married. Not but what you and I would know everything was all right. But it would cause talk. I couldn't stand it if a fine girl like our Judith was to cause talk, especially so soon after . . . But if we wait too long, then maybe Jenness——"

"There, there, Mother. There'll be some way. You mustn't let this get you down. We'll see what Dexter has to say when he gets back here at suppertime."

Dexter was very definite and direct in what he had to say. They should start for Washington at once, in his opinion—Well, they couldn't get off until the next day, that was true enough, but he thought they should certainly go then. As far as Judith was concerned, he would try to persuade her to go right to the parsonage with him, and let Mr. Litchfield marry them Sunday afternoon. He'd see about a license and a ring the next day, so that he'd be ready, in case. . . .Yes, he knew it would be a disappointment to Father and Mother Farman not to have the wedding on Farman Hill, the way they'd always planned; but they could have a wedding party for all their friends later on, and that would be almost the same. He hadn't been at all sure, for a long time, that cave man methods might not have been best with Judith from the beginning;

now he'd have a chance to find out. But if worse came
to worst, he could always move back to his own place.
Yes, of course, the water was turned off, but he could
turn it on again. Why, no, it wasn't any trouble to speak
of. They were not to worry about anything. He could manage. And they mustn't think they couldn't manage either.
There was sure to be some place they could stay in Washington. If Jenness couldn't find them one, Peter MacDonald could. And he himself had stopped in at the bank
while he was out that afternoon and got a check cashed.
He'd thought they might need some ready money. Now
listen, there was no use going into all that for the time
being. They could talk it over later . . .

After prolonged persuasion, Daniel accepted the thick
envelope that Dexter held out to him, turning it over several times without opening it. Finally he cleared his throat
and spoke.

"I'd feel better, Dexter, if we did this in a businesslike
way. Not but what I'm grateful. But I don't like to be
too much beholden to any man. If you'd take a small
mortgage——"

"All right, I will, if it would really make you feel better.
But there isn't time to arrange for it now. We'll have to
do that after you get back. It can wait."

"Then I'll give you my note. I'll make it out now."

He rose and walked over to the old secretary. None of
them spoke while he sat down again, pulling out the folding writing shelf, searching in one of the pigeon holes for
stationery, and taking the brass top off the inkstand. He
had begun to write painstakingly, with a scratchy Spencer-
ian pen, before he remembered that he would have to
open the envelope, after all, in order to fill in the sum that
he owed Dexter. He counted the bills slowly, and after
putting them back in the envelope, sat very still, with his
head bent and his hand shielding his eyes. There was something about his attitude which suggested prayer. Then he
took down his hand and picked up the pen again. It
scratched on and on through the silence, recording his
obligation.

"There," he said, at last. "There." He folded the paper

and handed it to Dexter, clearing his throat again. "I think you'll find that's in order. I want you should know I appreciate what you have done, Dexter. If you'd been my own son—well, there. I want you should know too that Serena and I had another talk last night. We both read that piece in the magazine you brought, and we talked that over, and what you'd said to me and all. I told Serena about Mr. Meyer's letter. I told her what I thought first, and then what I thought afterwards, when I seemed to see things plainer. But I said this was something we ought to look at from every side. If we had fifty thousand dollars, even if we spent a good share of it on Jenness, we'd probably have enough left so we could take things a lot easier ourselves. Serena could give up her milk route. She's getting to an age when it isn't so easy, getting up at five in the morning and going out into the cold. I reminded her of that. And I reminded her that we didn't know, for sure, that there was anything the matter with Meyer. He seems to represent a reliable firm. We could string him along for a little, looking it up. Besides, I reminded her that if there were four or five other places in this neighborhood already sold to Germans, one more or less probably wouldn't make much difference in the outcome, if they should cause trouble. I thought of something else too. I thought if the F. B. I. knew enough about the neighborhood to track down Lentz here, it wouldn't be surprising if they knew a lot of other things about it. I said maybe we could sell the place, and then tell the F. B. I. all the circumstances, so that they could keep an eye on it, if they weren't doing it already. And Serena put me to shame. She asked me if that wasn't a good deal like what Judas did, after he'd taken the thirty pieces of silver. He told, when it was too late, to the F. B. I. in Jerusalem."

"Now, Daniel, you mustn't give me all that credit. You know you said yourself——"

"I'm going to give you all the credit that's coming to you, Mother. I said we ought to look at this offer from every side. And you said there wasn't but one side to it, that you could see. You said the minute anybody started to wonder whether a thing was right or not, they might just as well make up their minds that it wasn't, first as last. Because if it was right, you didn't wonder. You knew."

"Yes, Daniel, but you said something too. You said people had to do different things in a war. You said they couldn't all go out and fight, but they could all make sacrifices. You said maybe the Lord meant this should be our sacrifice. You said maybe He gave us this chance, so that our son who's going out to fight and maybe die for his country would know we were trying to do our share. We wouldn't want Jerome to think we hadn't. We wouldn't want him to hear, while he was off on foreign soil, that we'd sold his own home to the same enemy that he was fighting. We've got Jerome to think of as well as Jenness, Dexter, Daniel sees that as clear as we do. Just because we're sorry for Jenness, we can't shame Jerome."

"You never will, Mother Farman," Dexter told her, and put his arm around her, holding her fast.

He felt extraordinarily lighthearted as he started off to get Judith, three days later. In the meantime a letter had been sent to Mr. Meyer, telling him that Farman Hill was not for sale at any price; and a wire had come in from Serena and Daniel, saying that they had reached Washington safely, that they had found Jenness well, and that they were installed at a pleasant boarding-house in Alexandria. With his mind relieved on both these scores, Dexter had gone cheerfully about his double duty of caring for two farms, besides running a milk route and cooking his own meals. There was no denying that this represented long hours and hard work; but there was an exhilaration in finding that despite its manifold complications, he could still swing it. And presently it would not be so hard; when Judith got home, she could do the housework with one hand tied behind her, as she had often said herself. She could take over the milk route too, and the care of the poultry; he would not even put it past her to help in the barn, if she had a notion; Judith had milked a cow as well as any boy in the neighborhood, when she was a sturdy little girl. She was still sturdy—and staunch, and steadfast. What a helpmeet she would make, Dexter thought with thankfulness, as he had thought so many times before; how prosperously and purposefully they would go on through the years as partners, working together side by side. And she would be none the less his helpmeet because she would be so wholly his beloved, as his relentless longing for her now increasingly revealed her. Like many another man who has lived continently, not because he lacked passion but because he curbed it, Dexter discovered that a time had come when it threatened to break all bounds with an insistence which could no longer be denied. He found assuagement in the certainty that Judith would understand and minister to this urgency, and again he rejoiced in the thought of all she was and all she would become. The healthy childhood she had spent on the farm had enabled her to absorb natural laws easily and decently as fast as she observed them. Her preparation for nursing and the practice of her profession had disciplined and developed this early aptitude; her entire outlook on life was wholesome and hardy. She knew that physical fulfillment was as normal and beautiful as spiritual fulfillment, she understood both the power and the dignity of sex, its vital place in the harmonies of creation and in the eternal struggle for survival. There would be no false modesty in her reception of her bridegroom. Far from demanding solicitude and delay at such a time, she would regard him as a weakling if he did not exact the immediate consummation of their marriage, and she would despise herself as a coward if an instant's recoil betrayed her into unwarranted resistance. Afterwards, she would yearn for caresses, and respond to them with her whole heart. But the elemental act must come first. Dexter knew that the time for it was ripe, that it could not come soon enough . . .

Before leaving, Serena had asked Dexter whether he felt, as she did, that the small room she and Daniel had occupied so long would make the best bridal chamber; it was so snug, she said, looking about it with loving eyes. Of course he was welcome to any of the rooms upstairs that he wanted; but they were cold at this time of year, and the little downstairs bedroom was always warm. Besides, the others were so far from the bathroom. It was

convenient, no matter what anyone said, to have a bathroom between a bedroom and a kitchen. Dexter agreed
with her, unreservedly. Later on, when she and Father
Farman came back from Washington, of course he and
Judith would move upstairs, if it still seemed best for them
to remain on Farman Hill, instead of going back to the
Abbott Homestead. But for the present they would sleep
downstairs. He was sure Judith would agree this was the
best plan too. He was grateful to Mother Farman for
offering him the snug little bedroom.

Daniel and Serena had not heralded their departure,
but they had not made a secret of it either. Everyone in
the village knew by this time, that they had gone to Washington to be with Jenness. Nothing had been published
about her impending appearance as a witness, but the
neighborhood guessed that this was probable from the
announcements about the trial which had appeared, and
in its preoccupation with Jenness had failed to concern
itself with Judith's probable plans. No one except Dr.
Barnes knew that she was so soon to leave the Brent's, because no one had remembered to ask exactly when she
would be released. There was a complete and merciful
absence of curiosity about her and Dexter. But Serena
had written her a line, and had told Dexter she was doing
it, asking Judith to let him know if for any reason she had
changed her plans, and did not want to come home on
Sunday after all. In the absence of any such message, his
spirits soared higher than ever. Her silence, as he interpreted this, could mean only one thing.

As he closed the door of the house after him and went
out into the yard, the thought suddenly came to him that
it would be fun to get out the old yellow sleigh again, and
go for Judith in that. They had had such a good time,
that other Sunday when they had ridden around in it, all
the afternoon! And this was much the same sort of a day,
with undisturbed snow still lying deep on the ground and
the sky curving over the molded mountains in a dome of
turquoise. He backed his car, which he had already taken
out, into the shed again, and went on into the stable where
Nell and Gypsy were still kept. He would have a struggle

to get Gypsy out of the barn, he knew. From the time the old horse was a colt, Gypsy had always halted on the threshold, no matter how often he was taken from his stall, and stopped there, turning his long white head first in one direction and then in another, as if he were surveying the scene before him with infinite satisfaction. His keepers might be hard-pressed for time, they might do their best to hurry him; but neither pushing nor pulling had any effect: he would not move until he had looked both up and down the valley and finally turned to gaze at "Old Moosey," as the elder inhabitants designated the highest of the molded mountains. The effect he produced was one of uncanny human intelligence, for he seemed to drink in the encircling beauty, entirely aware of its charms; but the trait was irritating, like another one he possessed: he had an unnatural fondness for eggs, and kept careful watch of a nest built in a box handy to his stall. The disappearance of these eggs had been a mystery until he was caught in the act of devouring them. After that the box was carefully watched by others besides old Gypsy, and eventually it was moved. Serena often said, with her pleasant smile, that poor Gypsy's strength had waned from that time; absence of eggshells had apparently impaired his digestion!

Dexter had smiled with her over Gypsy's idiosyncrasies, many a time, and himself shared the fondness of the Farman family for the old horse. But today he grew impatient, waiting for Gypsy to finish his leisurely appraisal of the scenery and suffer himself to be led into the yard. Dexter had almost decided the idea of the sleigh had been a mistake, when Gypsy started down the incline of the great door of his own accord, and patiently permitted Dexter to hitch him to the sleigh. Once on the road, he gathered speed, as if he knew there were reason for haste. The sleigh bells tinkled merrily as he sped along, and the runners slid over the smooth snow with increasing velocity. Long before he had reached the Brents' house, Dexter was glad he had taken the sleigh after all.

He drew up at the door with something of a flourish. It flew open instantly, and Judith, wearing the same dark citified clothes in which she had left Farman Hill, and carrying the same small neat bag, came out to meet him. He had never seen her looking lovelier. In spite of her long confinement and the gruelling work that had gone with it, her color was fresh and rosy, her eyes clear and bright, her carriage erect and buoyant. Again the realization of her inexhaustible vitality, and of the soundness and strength which gave meaning to her beauty, struck him with full force. No man on earth could require more of his mate than Judith could give to him.

She did not try to prevent him when he put his arms around her. Instead she put hers around him too, and kissed him, still standing on the little porch, with an intensity that startled him. She had never embraced him like this before, not even in the course of that last ride, when they had let the reins hang over the dashboard, and gone blindly on and on. The joyousness in Dexter's heart, which had grown by leaps and bounds during the last days, now seemed to swell it to the bursting point; the passion which had so long been suppressed seized him in an overpowering grip. His voice shook when he spoke to her.

"Judith—Judith—it's been so long—I couldn't have stood it if it had been any longer!"

She made a slight movement, as if trying to free herself, but he shook his head, with his lips still against her, and she did not force the issue. It was not until he released her of his own accord that she moved towards the steps and held out her hand so that he could help her into the sleigh.

"I'm so glad you brought Gypsy," she said as he tucked the fur robe around her. "Did you do it because we had such a nice ride the last time we went out together?"

"Yes—you remembered then too?"

"Of course I remembered. I won't forget that ride, Dexter, as long as I live—or this one either. Did you have a hard time, getting Gypsy out of the barn?"

"You bet I did. He seemed to enjoy the view more than usual. I began to think I'd have to build a fire under him, before I could budge him."

Judith smiled. Dexter had never seen her smile when it

was so sweet. He gathered the reins into one hand and felt with the other for hers, under the fur robe. When he found it and gripped it hard, she returned the pressure.

"So Mom and Dad thought they had to go to Washington?" she asked conversationally. "Dad sent me just a line. Of course I was terribly surprised and I'm still terribly mystified. But he said you'd explain everything."

"Yes. I will pretty soon. Of course you guessed they felt Jenness needed them right away, or they wouldn't have started off without seeing you. I'm afraid they had a hard trip. But I've had a wire telling me they finally got to Washington all right and giving me their address. I'll show it to you when we get home. But there's no hurry, is there? I thought we'd go somewhere else first, if you didn't mind."

"No. I don't mind. It's a nice day for a ride, just like that other. And I want to talk to you."

"I want to talk to you too. I'm going to tell you what's in my heart without any beating around the bush. I want you to come to the parsonage with me. I want you to marry me this afternoon."

"Oh, Dexter! I—I couldn't do that!"

"Yes, you could. I know what you're going to say—that it wouldn't be fair to your father and mother. But they want you to. They think it's best too. I talked it over with them before they went away. And I have the license and the ring and everything."

"You haven't!"

"Yes, I have. We'll just swing around by the parsonage, Judith, and hitch Gypsy outside and in fifteen minutes we'll be man and wife. It's as simple as that."

"I wish it were, Dexter. But it isn't."

"Why isn't it? Don't you believe I'm telling you the truth about your father and mother?"

"Of course I believe you. But——"

"You can't tell me it's because you don't love me enough. No girl who didn't love a man with all her heart and soul would kiss him the way you just kissed me. She couldn't."

"No, she couldn't. I do love you, Dexter, with all my heart and soul, but——"

"There aren't any buts. You're going to marry me this afternoon if I have to hog-tie you and carry you into the parsonage over my shoulder like a bag of meal. You're going to marry me if I have to hold a gun to your head all the time. Mr. Litchfield's reading the service. But you'll be married to me before night, no matter what I have to do."

"Don't—don't joke, Dexter. I'll cry if you do. And I mustn't cry. You mustn't make me. You must help me explain."

"I've told you there isn't anything to explain."

"Yes, there is. Dexter, you've got to listen. I'm going away."

"Going away! You must be crazy to think I'd let you go away at this stage."

"You can't help it, Dexter. I'm going."

"Where?"

"I don't know yet. Wherever I'm sent. I'm going to be an Army nurse."

"Judith, I'll say the same thing you said to me. Don't joke. This isn't any time for joking."

"I'm not joking. I'm telling you the truth."

"You've always told me you wouldn't go away from here for anything in the world."

"I believed it too, when I told you so. I've never wanted to go away from here. I don't want to now. But there's something inside of me that makes me, just as there was when I decided to be a nurse in the first place."

"When did you find that out? *How* did you find it out?"

"A few days ago. No, it must be a week now. I got a questionnaire from the Red Cross. It's just a form. If I understand it correctly, it's been mailed out, in bulk, to registered nurses all over the country. It doesn't require anything of a girl, the way the draft requires men to register. But the Red Cross acts as a Procurement Bureau, asking for volunteers. There aren't anywhere near enough nurses for the Army or the Navy either. There's terrible need for them."

"There aren't anywhere nearly enough nurses for this

town. You've told me so yourself, dozens of times. You said so when Dr. Barnes sent for you to go to the Brents'. You said he'd been through the countryside with a fine tooth comb before he called you, because he knew you ought to have a rest. There's a terrible need for nurses right here."

"Yes, that's true. But older women can do the nursing around here, if they have to. As the war goes on, they'll be pressed back into service, just as older teachers, like Rhoda have been. They'll be happy getting back to their work too, lots of them, just as she was. But to go overseas, to live in a tent, to manage with all kinds of makeshifts and stand up under all kinds of hardships—you have to be young to do that and strong and brave and willing. Older women can't take it, no matter how hard they try."

"Judith, if you'll give up this wild idea about going away, I'll never say another word to prevent you from nursing around here after we're married. I swear I won't. You can take one case after another, if you'll only stay."

"You're saying that, Dexter, because this decision of mine is a terrible blow to you. But you never felt that way before. And you wouldn't again after we were actually married. You'd want me with you all the time. I wouldn't put it past you to make me stay with you all the time. I've said that before when I was only half in earnest. But I'm in deadly earnest now. Tell me the truth: If I married you this afternoon, would you let me start out on a case again tomorrow morning, if someone needed me?"

"Of course I would if I promised. I do promise."

He tried, as he had never tried before, to make his voice carry conviction. But even while he was speaking, he knew he had failed because he did not speak single-heartedly. He could not suppress the vision which now obsessed him: of Judith coming home with him to Farman Hill in the yellow sleigh after the simple ceremony at the village parsonage. Of their supper, prepared in the winter kitchen and eaten in front of the living room fire on the gate-legged table—a hot, hearty supper, with some of Daniel's old apple brandy taken with it and putting extra warmth into the veins which were already riotous with hot young blood. Of Judith expectant and ready when he joined her in the small snug chamber. Of their swift, primitive mating, forceful on his part, controlled on hers, not for lack of love on either side, but because that was the way of a man with a maid and a maid with a man, as they understood it must be at the first. Of their joy in each other when he was doubly a man and she was no longer a maid, and they were freed by their new knowledge and their new interdependence. Of daylight coming quietly into the dark room, revealing a new Judith, softened yet quickened, conquered yet triumphant. Of seeing her while she rose and dressed and prepared breakfast and went about the small intimate tasks in the house which was now their home. Of constraining her from overtaxing her strength while exulting because she was so strong. Of leaving her reluctantly to perform the inevitable duties of the day, and hurrying back to find her watching for his return. Of talking with her about the problems they must face together and the joys and sorrows they must share. Of waiting with impatience for another night to come and hearing her confess that she had found the gloaming long too. Of reunion, spontaneously sought and voluptuously prolonged, because now it came through mutual desire and meant mutual delight. . . .

If the vision had ended there, he might have promised. But he knew that the first revelation of his beloved would be only a prelude to all that permanent possession of her and permanent partnership with her should mean. His need of Judith went far deeper than any ephermeral desire which could be satiated over night; it was enduring. He had sought her in marriage because he wanted her for his wife, in every sense of the word; if he had wanted less, he could have been appeased with less. But he knew that once she was his he would never let her go, no matter how hard he had to fight to keep her, and he could not make a lie sound like the truth or take her under false pretenses.

"No," he said. "I can't promise after all. It isn't just being together tonight that counts. It's being together always. That's what marriage means. I'll have to take back what I said. But don't punish me, Judith, for telling the truth when I could have lied to you. Don't do this dreadful thing. You don't know what it would mean if you did. Not just to me. To your father and mother too. I suppose you've read the papers, a little anyway. I suppose you've guessed that Jenness is involved in some kind of a terrible scandal, that she's almost broken your parents' hearts. They've gone to her, fearing the worst. You've got to stand by till they come home. They've faced a great temptation too, and put it behind them as unworthy of them. I can't take time now to tell you about that, but you'll have to believe me when I say they've been through a fearful struggle and that it's left its mark on them. They've aged this last week, both of them; it's pitiful to see. They need your strength to lean on. That isn't all either. I know they both believe they'll never see Jerome again. They haven't said much—they couldn't. But they've betrayed their fear in countless little ways. They've lost Jenness in one sense and they're going to lose Jerome in another. They haven't anyone left but you. You mustn't fail them."

"I shan't fail them by leaving them. I'll never do anything to disgrace them, and I'll come home safe and sound. But I have to go. I can't explain to you, Dexter, because you've never understood about my nursing. You didn't even ask, when you came for me this afternoon, how the little children were that I've cared for through a long hideous illness. You didn't think of them at all. If you understood you would have. Perhaps the reason I can't make you understand is because I don't fully understand myself. But I suppose it's something the way a nun feels, or a missionary. Not that personal happiness and human love don't matter, but that there's something else which matters more."

Dexter had only half listened to her. All the time she had been talking he had been gathering his forces for one last appeal. He knew that if he failed again, he would have failed for all time. He let the reins slide away from him, as he had done before, and put one arm around her shoulder, while he still gripped her other hand.

"I'm terribly sorry I didn't ask about the children," he said. "Of course I should have. It must have seemed awfully unfeeling or awfully forgetful or both. But you see, dearest, I didn't have room in my heart or my mind then for anyone but you. You're not just my sweeheart, Judith. You're my world. Your father and mother would have each other even if they lost everything else. I wouldn't have anyone to live for if I didn't have you. I can't even be anyone myself without you. I can't do brave deeds. I can't fight big battles. I'm a failure, I'm a cripple, I'm only half a man. But your love would make me whole, your strength would save me. Don't desert me, Judith. Don't leave me to perish."

She tried to look up at him, meeting his eyes in the same way that she had always done. She could not do it this time because her own were full of tears. But somehow she kept her voice steady while she answered him.

"Please," she said. "Please." She stopped and waited a minute before she went on. "I shouldn't have come out with you," she said at last. "I shouldn't have brought my bag. I knew all the time I wouldn't use it. I knew I wasn't going home with you, just out for a ride and then back to the Brents' for the night. But I thought if I didn't bring it you'd suspect right away, and then we couldn't be happy together, not even for a few minutes. I would have to start right in, explaining. As it was, we did kiss each other, you did find out how much I love you. But it's no use, Dexter. I've promised. I filled in the questionnaire and sent it back to the Red Cross in Washington the day I got it. I said I'd go anywhere, any time. I've had another paper, a personal one this time, telling me to report at the Army Base in Boston for a physical examination before I'm sent off somewhere else. I'm leaving in the morning."

PART II

Washington, D.C.

January–February 1942

wouldn't get anything — — — Come on, Dad. We go

CHAPTER 11

THE COLONIAL EXPRESS from Boston to Washington was nearly three hours late, and Serena Farman, who had been crowded into a coach seat since early morning, was so tired that she was secretly sure she would never feel really rested again. But she managed to put cheeriness as well as sympathy into the smile with which she looked up at Deniel. He had made the great mistake of trying to secure some sandwiches when the train stopped at New Haven, and his side of the seat had been instantly snatched, over Serena's appealing protest, by a bulgy, belligerent woman. This woman snorted and panted and ate a succession of sausage-stuffed buns and overriped bananas, that she extracted, one after the other, from a covered basket which she kept pressed to her ample bosom, and which, apparently, constituted her only baggage. She effectually separated Serena from Daniel, having declined, with a vehemence Serena found terrifying, to take the place next to the window, because "it sent creeping chills all through her to feel the cold air right through the dirty panes." But every now and then Serena leaned forward and tried to say something encouraging.

"It isn't much further, is it, Daniel? That was Wilmington we just passed, wasn't it?"

"Yes. Baltimore must be the next stop. And that's less than an hour from Washington."

"Why we'll be there before we know it! And after we've had a good night's rest——"

She paused, remembering that they still did not know where they were going to stay. No message from Jenness, reassuring them on this point, had reached them before they left Farman Hill. But they continued to be confident that she would meet them at the station, and that then everything would be explained and arranged.

Serena could not help wishing they had taken a Pullman. She had ventured to suggest that they should do so, when they went to buy their tickets, but Daniel had firmly refused. It was Dexter's money they were using, he reminded his wife; they had no right to spend it as they might have their own, if they had been provident enough to have had any laid by for a rainy day; they must never forget how beholden they were to Dexter, they must scrimp and save in every way they could. Not only for Dexter's sake either, for their own as well; the less they spent, the less they would have to pay back. Serena had instantly agreed that Daniel's viewpoint was proper. But now, as she watched him standing in the crowded aisle, clutching the seat ahead with his horny hand to steady himself, and saw the deep lines of weariness in his steadfast face and the telltale sagging of his staunch shoulders, she regretted the comfort that had been sacrificed to principle, even while she reproached herself for doing so.

She had kept hoping that the repulsive creature beside her would get off at Baltimore, or that at least someone else might, so that Daniel could get a seat somewhere, even though it was not with her. But the belligerent woman, having exhausted the unshared contents of her covered basket, settled back to take a noisy nap, undisturbed by the turmoil which seethed around her, and the passengers already blocking the aisle were jammed still more closely against each other by the newcomers who in turn pressed against them. Daniel was shoved forward by these newcomers, and Serena lost sight of him completely. She tried not to worry, but she could not help wondering whether he would be able to get back to her again, and how she would manage if he did not. They had only two bags apiece, but one of these was so ill-shaped that it was clumsy to handle and another had a defective catch; they would be hard for her to carry alone. Besides, if the crowd in the station were comparable to the crowd in the train she might have difficulty in rejoining him.

She was not wearing a watch, so she could not keep

track of the time, but she was sure it must be much more than an hour since they had left Baltimore and still the train went rocking and clattering along. Then its motion gradually became slower and jerkier, and she thought that at last they must be coming into the Washington station. But when she looked out of the window, she saw that there were no lights anywhere; the train was shuddering to a stop in the middle of a dark dismal field. The unnatural hush which falls upon a train when its normal progress is suspended and its normal noises cease, descended on the crowded car, engulfing it gloomily, though occasionally a voice, jocular or enraged, desperate or inebriated, pierced the strained silence with its futile questioning; then it sank into stillness again. Serena, feeling desperate herself, leaned forward and spoke to the woman in the seat ahead of her, who had been quietly crying for a long time.

"Have you any idea what's happened?"

"No, I haven't. We may have been sidetracked to let a troop train pass. Or maybe just a freight. They're sending freights ahead of passenger trains a lot nowadays. And we're so late we lost the right of way ages ago."

"We wouldn't be held here so long, just to let another train by." The paunchy man sitting beside the woman Serena had approached turned around and spoke importantly, as if he were an authority on the delays of wartime travel. "We must have had a hotbox. Probably we'll be here another hour or so."

"Hell, if we are I've missed my connection for Texas. It's taken me two weeks to get my reservations and I had them straight through——"

"I haven't a train connection to make, but I'm on my way to see my sick daughter, down on the Northern Neck. She's got pneumonia, and my son-in-law didn't have anyone to leave her with but a no-count nigger, while he drove up here to meet me. If she should die before I got there——"

"Well, boys, it's the hoosegow for us tomorrow all right! We'll get to Quantico just about in time for reveille. I told you we were running too close to the wind when I first began trying to pry you loose from those dizzy dames. You'll have plenty of time this next week to think about their winning little ways——"

'Whatcha say we have another swig at the bottle, fellahs? There's a little left in the bottom of this one, and I got another I can open——"

" 'Sal right by me. If you can't drown your troubles any other way you can always drown 'em in drink."

"Wouldn't you think the conductor would come and *tell* us something?"

"Jeepers creepers, how would the conductor get into the car in the first place? If he should try to open that damn door, every poor bastard anywhere near it would be mashed to a bloody pulp."

The silent car had suddenly become clamorous. Some of the passengers were truculent, some tearful, some roistering; but none of them was silent. Serena leaned her aching head against the window-frame and closed her tired eyes to the sight of the dark and dismal field, though she could not close her ears to the oaths and imprecations and sobs echoing around her. These went on and on. But the train continued to stand still. It was not until she had become convinced it never would move again, that it shuddered once more into reluctant motion, and began to creep slowly along, as if proceeding over a high and dangerous trestle. After another long interval, an occasional faint light penetrated the gloom through which they were traveling, and as these gleamed more closely together, some of the passengers who were seated tried to reach for their wraps and their bags. Serena was so tightly squeezed in beside the bulgy, belligerent woman that she could not do this, and the woman was still sleeping soundly and snoring loudly. She did not wake until the train came to a standstill as sudden as its previous one had been slow. Then, with one last resounding snort, she heaved herself to her feet and wedged herself into the emptying aisle.

Serena struggled up, aching from head to foot, but thankful she could stretch her cramped limbs at last. Wisely, she stood still, realizing, now that her tired head was beginning to clear, that Daniel would seek her where he had left her; and presently she saw him coming towards her, answering her resolute smile with one of his own. He slid into the seat beside her and took her hand.

"No use trying to get out of this in a hurry, Mother. We might as well wait till the worst of the crowding's over."

"I presume you're right. But we wouldn't want to be so long, getting to the gate, that Jenness would think we hadn't come, after all, and go away herself."

"If she's waited a few hours for the train already, she'll wait a few minutes longer. Anyhow, we wouldn't get to the gate any quicker, Mother, if we did try to buck this mob."

He lifted down the bags, handing her those which were easiest to carry, and himself holding on to the clumsy one and the one with the defective catch. Then he started along the aisle ahead of her, walking without haste, and taking the steep steps without haste too, before he deposited his burdens beside the track and turned to help his wife with hers. They were still so far out in the yard that they had to walk a long way to reach the platform, and there was almost no light, so that they could barely see to pick their hard and unfamiliar way along. Besides, the congestion and confusion which had prevailed in the train were infinitely worse here: Pullman passengers, surrounded by their multitudinous suitcases, stood at the doors of the cars they had quitted, calling, in loud and aggrieved voices, for redcaps who failed to appear, while they themselves gave no gangway. Baggage trucks came clanging and charging out of unseen regions, bearing down on startled pedestrians whom they scattered without warning. Baggage cars disgorged trunks, boxes, crates, coffins and pet animals. Some of the weary travelers, straining ahead with bewilderment, stopped to comfort crying babies, to recapture lost companions, or to shift heavy loads from one arm to another; still others, frantic from haste, tried to batter their way forward with appalling roughness. Beside the gate which had opened to disgorge the incomers from the Colonial, another had opened to receive the outgoers on the Statesman. Before one crowd had left the

concourse and the other had reached it, the two met in
head-on collision.

But the platform had been the embodiment of peace
compared to the concourse. As Daniel and Serena finally
struggled through the gate, looking hopefully for Jenness
in the throng that encircled it, they were confronted by a
moving mass of humanity so dense that at first it seemed
to have no marks by which one atom in it could be distinguished from any other atom. It was only gradually,
as they gazed at it in fascinated horror, that they could
see this mob was made up of soldiers and sailors and the
officers who had them in charge, civilians, both male and
female, of every sort and description, pitiful old men and
self-assertive girls, porters and policemen. Eventually a
difference in headgear also began to make itself manifest:
There were soft fedoras with faded hatbands and stiff caps
adorned above the visors with naval and military insignia;
there were silly little flower turbans pulled down over some
women's eyes, and limp-brimmed felts, trimmed with bed-
raggled feathers, perched high on the straggling locks of
others. The red caps of the porters, the white caps of
the sailors and the khaki overseas caps stood out especially. After the headgear, the faces beneath these became
visible: faces strained and sad, faces eager and hopeful,
faces rubicund and fleshy, faces white and unwholesome,
faces black and beaming. Eyeglasses, beards, surgical
dressings and veils stood out on some of these faces; little
by little they became less uniform and nondescript. But
they were all strange and all preoccupied and some of
them seemed hostile. A muffled roar, not unlike the sound
of the sea, rose from this heterogeneous mob, to which
the headgear and the faces belonged; and, like the sea,
it seemed to ebb and flow without progress or direction
and without rifts. Only one small cleared space was roped
off from it. This was encircled by a ring of photographers,
who were holding their instruments high over their heads,
and flashing their blinding bulbs in swift succession. The
object of their attention was invisible beyond the fringe
of immediate onlookers. But their hoarse voices rose impellingly above the muffled roar of the mob.

"Now just one more shot! With a Marine this time! Aw, come on! You can't pass up the Marines! Not after you've done your bit for the Army and Navy both!"

Involuntarily, Daniel and Serena were propelled towards the enclosed circle. Just as they reached it, one of the photographers lowered his instrument and started through the crowd, using his standard as a battering ram. Daniel and Serena were swept into his place, to see a girl standing with her back to the iron railing between the gates, and her hands clasped around the arm of a sheepish-looking young officer, who was laughing in an embarrassed fashion, and turning his eyes away from the glare of the flashlights. The girl was a platinum blonde, wearing showy clothes and gaudy make-up; orchids cascaded from her shoulder and her wrists were banded with tinkling bracelets. But in her cheap, bold way she was beautiful. Her painted lips, parted in a bewitching smile; her abbreviated dress, cut with a plunging neckline, revealed long, lovely legs and the outline of pointed, provocative breasts. Serena, catching sight of her, drew in her breath sharply.

"Why, Daniel, that girl looks like Jenness!" she said. "I declare I'm half blinded by all these lights, and I'm so tired, I can't see straight, any more than I can think straight. But—it *isn't* Jenness, is it? Jenness with something done to her hair?"

"No, no, Mother. Of course it isn't Jenness. I don't see how you could ever come to think of such a thing. You must be even more tuckered out than I thought. You don't suppose Jenness would stand up in a public place like this, and have her picture taken with a parcel of strangers, do you? We'll find Jenness any minute now, and then you'll see the difference. You stay right here so's I can locate you. I'm going back to the gate to look for Jenness again."

"That's Melisande Darcy, the new movie star," the photographer standing next to the Farmans said good-humoredly. "I guess you've just come to Washington, or you'd have seen her sweet face staring out at you every time you picked up a paper. She's spent the last week here, mostly sitting on senators' laps, as a dual contribution

to photographic art and the war effort. Now she's decided
to give the armed forces a break as her last generous
gesture before she takes the train back to California. It
was put right up to her that they needed her to boost their
morale . . . Look here, I'm not trying to butt in, but I just
heard you say something about a girl named Jenness. It's a
rather unusual name. You're not Jenness Farman's father
and mother by any chance, are you?"

"Why, yes, that's just who we are," Serena and Daniel
answered in thankful unison. "Do you know Jenness?
Have you seen her anywheres around this station? We
looked for her to meet us, but we're afraid we missed her
in the crowd at the gate, and we——"

The photographer folded up his machine and backed
away slightly from the circle. "Yes, I know Jenness,"
he said briefly. "Of course all the photographers in Washington know her by now, almost as well as they know
Melisande Darcy. There's something about this dame that
makes you think of her too, isn't there? You noticed it
yourself, Mrs. Farman. I couldn't help overhearing what
you said. Only of course Jenness has got a lot more class.
Look, I don't believe she's at the station tonight. I know
she had a heavy date on. But Joe is—Joe Racina, you
know, of the *Bulletin*. I'm on the *Bulletin* too—Marcy
Heath my name is. Joe went to the gate himself but *he*
must have missed you. You both stay here and let me
go back there. I'll find him for you."

"But why should Mr. Racina—that is, you see we
don't know Mr. Racina," Serena began in bewilderment.
Marcy Heath interrupted her.

"No, but Jenness described you to him. She called up
the *Bulletin* and tried to get Peter MacDonald to come
and meet you. She can't seem to get it through her head
that Pete isn't to be reached at the home office any more.
So she was switched on to Joe instead, which must have
burnt her up, because she hates Joe like poison. But just
the same he's a good fellow and he was always a great
pal of Pete's, see? So he said he'd be glad to come to the
station, and you'll like him. Well, speak of the devil and
you hear his hoofs—if this isn't Joe right now!"

Another self-assertive man had come charging through
the crowd, who—Serena thought quickly—bore a general
resemblance to Peter MacDonald which was as confusing
as the general resemblance which Melisande Darcy bore to
Jenness, though it was as reassuring as the other was disturbing. Like Peter, he wore a thin overcoat with an up-
turned collar and a slouch hat pulled down over his eyes;
like Peter he had a nice grin; and like Peter he was built
on long lean lines and had a brisk and purposeful manner.
But he was obviously older than Peter, and he lacked
Peter's fresh color and merry twinkle. His lean face was
sallow, and there were dark pockets under his black,
bloodshot eyes. He reached out and with friendly abruptness took the bag Serena was carrying.

"If I can't do a simple little thing like meeting a train,
I guess I better go back to the sticks where I came from,"
he said apologetically. "I'm terribly sorry, Mrs. Farman.
I'll explain later. But if you and Mr. Farman will just
come along with me now, I'll get you out of this madhouse
by the shortest possible route. If it's any comfort to you to
know it, you've seen Washington's worst wartime feature
first. You've probably heard the story about the poor
fellow who dropped dead at the ticket window before he
could get his reservation. Fact. The lobby of any hotel
runs the Union Station a close second when it comes to
bedlam. You've probably heard about the other man who
wired for a suite and was given a seat. The manager
thought he'd made a typographical error. Fact. Well you
haven't got to cope with a hotel tonight. I've spared you
that much anyway. This way, please. So long, Marcy. See
you in the morning. Thanks for holding the fort for me."

Without apparent difficulty, Joe Racina drove through
the crowd which a quarter of an hour earlier had seemed
so impenetrable. Daniel and Serena followed gratefully
in his wake. Their escort skirted the doors through which
a large proportion of the mob was endeavoring to squeeze,
and plunged through one that was comparatively unobstructed, at the extreme end of the concourse. They were
doubly thankful for this detour when they got outside,
and witnessed the mad struggle to secure transportation

from which their benefactor had saved them. The crowds, shouting and gesticulating, were now gathered around a series of metal standards, variously labelled. The first to catch the eye bore the inscription "NAVY—ARMY—MUNITIONS—ARLINGTON," the one next to it "SOCIAL SECURITY —RAILROAD RETIREMENT—WAR COLLEGE—TEMPORARY BUILDINGS A—B—C—D—E—R—S"; but these were only two out of many. Overall, three large signs were boldly lettered alike in heavy black with an urgent appeal: "YOUR COOPERATION IS SOLICITED TO IMPROVE TAXI SERVICE BY CLUBBING TOGETHER IN THE USE OF TAXICABS." The cabs in question, as they slowed down beside the standards, were besieged, before they came to a standstill, by desperate groups, evidently prompted less by a desire to cooperate than by a determination to beat another desperate group to the draw. Pell-mell they leapt in, snatching their suitcases from their porters, and yelling to their drivers to be on their way. The starters, swallowed up in this strife, did not even attempt to stop the hordes hurtling past them.

" 'Clubbing together' is good," Joe Racina remarked genially, as he guided his protégés further and further to the right. "Hell, you couldn't club them *apart* no matter what kind of a deadly weapon you used. Anything can happen in a taxicab nowadays. Only last week a big butter-and egg man was shoved in beside a dizzy blonde, and before they'd got as far as the Occidental he invited her to dinner. Now they've made a match of it. On the other hand there were four timed souls from Dubuque who got to talking things over on their way to a Government bureau and decided there wasn't any use in bearding the alphabet official they'd come to see, so they turned around and took the first train west they could get aboard with a running jump. Fact."

While he talked, Joe Racina went on leading the Farmans past a long line of parked cars and finally reached a battered Buick standing near the end. This he unlocked with an air of triumph.

"Well, here we are, on our way to Dublin Bay," he announced. "That wasn't so bad, was it, once we got started? The trip down must have been pretty grim though. Look, wouldn't you like something to eat before we start out to Alexandria? I'm afraid you didn't get much of a supper, with diners the way they are now. We could stop in at O'Donnell's or one of the places down by the water-front."

"Well, we haven't had anything to eat since we left Boston," confessed Serena. "You see we came by coach, to economize. But we don't want to put you out, Mr. Racina, any more than we have already. If you'd just take us to our daughter's apartment, I'm sure we could have a hot drink there, and something out of her icebox. Then we could sort of talk plans over with her. I understood Mr. Heath to say she'd had to go to a party this evening, but it's so late now I guess she'll be home by this time."

"She won't be home for ages," Joe Racina said rather curtly. "I've taken her out of the town myself, I know the hours she likes to keep. You just let me take over for tonight. We'll have a good stiff Scotch and soda and a nice hot oyster stew at O'Donnell's and then we'll strike right out over the Memorial Highway. I've got a fine room for you in the house where I live myself. A great piece of luck too. The couple who had the room moved to the White House yesterday for an indefinite stay. Fact."

Neither of his passengers felt equal to protesting. They suffered themselves to be taken to the strange restaurant, where they were confronted by a fantastic façade adorned with ornamental anchors, life preservers, hawsers and so on, and a window display of live lobsters, crabs, and fish of various sorts and descriptions, reposing on ice. Inside, the panelled walls were flanked by a series of stalls, and a glittering bar, manned by colored bartenders, ran across the rear of the room. It was filled with smoke, and it was almost as noisy and crowded as the Union Station. While Joe Racina was looking about for a free table, he was hailed by a number of kindred spirits, and after he and the Farmans were settled, he explained to them the identity of several.

"That pudgy geezer who spoke to me first is Herb Parrish of the *Enterprise*. One of the smartest reporters in

Washington too. He's covering the Lentz case, for his paper, so you might like to meet him later on. It never does any harm to be on speaking terms with the press. I've got to do that job for the *Bulletin,* worse luck, now that Pete's walked out on us, and I'll give you all the tips I can. The gaunt specimen with Herb is Newt Evans, who pretends to do publicity for FWA, but does it mostly for good old Newt himself. Back on them are two congressmen from Missouri, both so new they're still wet behind the ears. I feel sort of sorry for them. The oldtimers will make pretty short work on their great ideals about public life. Why they actually still believe that statesmen write their own speeches!" Joe Racina paused, noticing a pained expression which puzzled him on his protégés' faces. Then, gathering that it was his last remark which had caused this, he added lamely, "Of course a few of them do."

"Is Mr. Horace Vaughn here by any chance?" Daniel inquired, looking around him attentively.

"Gosh, no! You'd never find him at O'Donnell's. He'd be at Pierre's or the Salle du Bois if he went to a restaurant at all. But Embassy Row is more in his line. Socially he's very keen for America last, in spite of his political proclivities. Well—here's mud in your eye!"

His guests did not toss off their tall drinks with the same speed that Joe did, or call for rapid refills, but they gradually emptied their glasses, and took fresh heart when the stimulating warmth of the whisky began to creep through their veins. The stew also slipped down easily. It was the best stew she had ever tasted, Serena told Joe, with gratitude; it gave her the notion that she ought to make oyster stew oftener herself. You could get real good oysters at the Junction, if you went for them; but she wasn't apt to think of it, because most generally she made chowders out of corn she had canned herself. Joe nodded understandingly, and said Pete had told him about the wonderful things she had given him to eat on Farman Hill, and about the New Year's punch. Didn't Mrs. Farman think they could make some punch at Mrs. Porterfield's in Alexandria, where he was taking them? There were big fireplaces in every room, and the one in the present dining room, which had originally been the kitchen, was simply tremendous. He had already bought some heavy rum and spoken to Mrs. Porterfield; she was perfectly willing they should make an experiment. Probably Sunday would be the best time. He didn't mean the next day, he knew they'd be too tired for that, after their trip. But possibly the following Sunday——

"Why, yes we'd be glad to accommodate, if we could," Daniel said willingly. "Of course we wouldn't want to put your landlady out any . . . Speaking of Peter, it's a considerable disappointment to hear he's not around Washington any more. That is, I understood Mr. Heath to say he wasn't. Is that correct?"

"Yes, that's correct. He's on his way to the Philippines. Naturally we didn't want to go yelling around about his itinerary until he got to Hawaii. But his first piece came in today and it's a lulu."

"I'm sorry he's gone. We liked him ourselves, and besides, we felt he might be considerable help to Jenness, if he had a mind to."

"Well—" Joe Racina began to draw patterns on the tablecloth with an unused fork. "Peter did like Jenness a lot. I guess you gathered that. But evidently there was something that didn't jell. Anyway, he was dead set on a foreign assignment. Now he's got it, the lucky bum. He'll probably write a book too, like all the other foreign correspondents, and make a mint of money before he gets through. It's too bad he couldn't have made it a little sooner—of course that would have helped with Jenness. But when it comes to helping *her*—why I'll be glad to do what I can for her, pinch-hitting for Pete, and so will the rest of the gang. I've got her a good deal on my mind, when it comes to that. I was the sleuth who went nosing around the Government Printing Office and found out that Jenness had spent twenty grand there for reprints of isolationist speeches. Of course when I found that out, I had to write a piece about it. I wouldn't have been fair to the *Bulletin* if I hadn't. Then on top of that Marcy Heath got some shots of the mail bags while they were being moved, as a result of another tip I had and I wrote a piece to go with his pictures. So altogther I know I'm responsible for part of the mess Jenness is in, and I'd be only too glad myself to see that she got out of it, quite aside from the way Pete may feel. I hope you can persuade her to have a good lawyer. A hell of a lot is going to depend on that."

"Naturally she'd want a good lawyer if she had one at all. But why does she need one just to advise her to get up and tell the truth?"

"Well, you've found for yourself, just as poor Pete did, that Jenness isn't so keen on telling the truth. So I think she'd better have legal advice on that point, and I'm scared stiff that her judgment as to what constitutes a good lawyer mayn't be much better than it has been a good many other things. Now I think I know just the man for her. Waldo his name is, Ned Waldo. He lived in Marcy's home town when Marcy was a kid. He was State District Attorney then, and the district's a country one, where attorneys practice both civil and criminal law. Well, the erring daughter of one of our leading citizens bumped off her gentleman friend here in Washington—she'd come here to take a Civil Service job but she managed to have a love affair on the side—and her father got Ned to come on and defend her. He did a brilliant job. It was so good that he was offered another case similiar to it right away —one involving a strange death in a disorderly house. He won that too and it didn't take him long to decide his talents had been wasted out in the sticks. He's practiced here ever since. He could get Jenness off if anyone could."

"We're not asking that justice shan't be done," Daniel said quietly. "All we want is that Jenness should have a fair hearing. Of course her case isn't anything like those you've mentioned."

Joe Racina brought the fork he was holding to a slow stop and lifted it a little, gazing at it in a meditative way for a minute. Then, still slowly, he resumed work on the interrupted pattern with which he was adorning the tablecloth.

"Of course not," he said. "But Waldo *is* able, and he knows Jenness and likes her. As a matter of fact she's been out on his boat with me two or three times. He's very chummy with the press, and he's got quite a nice little cruiser—it's anchored near here, right now, by the Twelfth Street wharf; you can take a look at it if you like, after we leave the restaurant. So I just thought . . . but maybe at that you'd prefer the lawyer Vaughn's picked. Vaughn doesn't know any criminal lawyers. He wouldn't. You'll realize yourself, after you've taken one good look at him, that all his cronies would have fat corporation practices. But he asked a friend who asked a friend and this friend suggested Tom Loper. I knew him when, too. He's got a very reputable criminal practice—now. And he deserves all the credit that's coming to him for sticking to night school at George Washington University until he passed his bar examinations. He had to do his law work after he'd slaved in a fish market all day. And that takes guts, whatever you say. He's smart, but he isn't very subtle. I'm afraid he wouldn't always give Jenness the best advice. For instance, I'm sure he'd take her before the jury dressed to imitate Mae West in that siren's most flamboyant moments—she'd look something like that dame you just saw at the station. And she ought to look like the girl Pete did such a swell job of describing in that Sunday feature of his—very, very neat, but not at all gaudy. That's just one point—there are lots of others. But maybe you get the general idea."

"Yes, Mr. Racina, we do, and it's a good one. But there's another point we've got to consider too, and that's expense."

"Well, lawyers are a good deal like doctors in one way—there's nothing so expensive in the long run as a cheap one and nothing that's such a good investment in the end as an expensive one. Waldo might cost you a little more in cold cash than Loper and then again he mightn't but it would be a darn sight better to pay him whatever he asks than to have Jenness paying the piper."

"I see what you mean about that too. But we may not be able to raise as much as he wants."

"Oh, I think you can. I'll see what I can do to give Waldo the idea there's no gold mine involved, if you decide to take it. In any case there's plenty of time to worry about that later on. It's getting late and I know you want to be pushing along. Not that it's as far to Alexandria as Jenness and her crowd like to make out. It was a pretty drive too, until all the lights got dimmed. But now that we have to creep along the river, it does take longer."

The heartening effects of the Scotch and soda had begun to wear off. Daniel and Serena were both very silent on the ride across the river and along the Memorial Highway. Joe Racina continued to talk to them cheerfully, calling their attention to the anti-aircraft guns perched high on wooden platforms along the way, and to the sample air raid shelter which had just been erected on the northern outskirts of the pleasant little Virginia city. He told one or two more ludicrous, improbable stories murmuring "fact" at the end, and when he did this a wry, fleeting grin momentarily illumined his somber face. Finally he turned the Buick into a side street, proceeding at a snail's pace through the darkness.

"No one needed to start dimouts in Alexandria," he remarked drily. "All its most distinguished citizens still carry their own lights when they go out to dinner. Fact. Besides, you'd break your neck or at the very least your leg if you tried to hurry, even in broad daylight. The cobblestones were all laid down by the Hessian prisoners during the Revolution and of course it would be a desecration to replace them with concrete. I don't know who laid down the bricks for the pavements, but any number of innocent victims have laid down their lives on them since. Be careful getting out of the car, Mrs. Farman. I don't want to present you to Mrs. Porterfield in a crippled condition, if I can help it."

The car rocked uneasily into a deep gulley separating the street from the sidewalk, and came to a violent standstill. As she climbed stiffly out, Serena felt that Joe Racina had not exaggerated in describing the paving and lighting conditions of George Washington's home town. Many of the bricks were missing in the sidewalk over which she cautiously stepped, and others rose in irregular hillocks, as if they had been forced upwards by some kind of a subterranean disturbance. At first she felt this rather than saw it, for there was no illumination nearer than the next cross-street. As her eyes became accustomed to the darkness, however, she was able to discern not only the peculiar pavement beneath her feet, but rising before her, the gray bulk of a long narrow house, flanked by a wide yard railed in by black iron and dominated by a huge magnolia tree. The glossy foliage of the magnolia was a great surprise to her; she had never seen green leaves in wintertime before and the sight was somehow encouraging. To be sure, the drabness of the house and the heaviness of the iron railing tempered the verdure of the tree; nevertheless, the whole gave an effect of dignity and stability. She was prepared to like the place even before Joe Racina opened the panelled door with a latch key and, followed by Daniel, she entered a spacious hallway. The illumination in this hallway, emanating from two gas jets shielded by red globes, was not much brighter than the street lamp, but as the strangers' eyes became accustomed to this, they saw that the entrance was adorned with two arches, one of them framing the straight stairway ahead of them, and the other opening, on their left, into a Victorian drawing room papered in pale blue and furnished in rosewood. Joe had whistled as he closed the door after him, and fastened a dangling chain across it. At the same moment, an elderly lady had appeared from some region at the rear of the hall and now she was coming unhurriedly forward. She was very tall and very thin, and she was wearing a nondescript black dress made with a high collar and revealing only a few inches of black stocking between her plain shoes and her plain dress. Her iron gray hair was primly arranged, and large spectacles partially concealed the fine network of wrinkles on her pale face. As she drew closer, Serena saw that she was wearing a large cameo brooch with matching earrings, and a number of old-fashioned rings with fanciful gold settings. But she did not require the jewelry to give her an air of elegance. Serena knew that she must have had that even as a small child, and that she always would have it, no matter how old and faded she became or how grotesquely she was dressed.

"Here comes my best girl," Joe Racina announced proudly. "I propose to her regularly every week, but she keeps putting me off. I think she favors a Culpepper beau she has, one of that sporting horsey crowd. Fact. Mrs. Porterfield, may I present Mr. and Mrs. Farman to you? They've had a hell of a trip. No, I won't apologize. You know I can't get along without one or two little hells while I'm talking any more than you could get along without your earrings. It wouldn't be in character."

"I reckon Mr. and Mrs. Farman are right good judges of character already, Joe, without any help from you," Mrs. Porterfield observed. Her tone might have seemed dry if she had not spoken with such a pleasant drawl and such a sweet smile, and if a glint of merriment, obscured but unhidden by the large glasses, had not brightened her faded eyes. It was easy to see that she regarded Joe Racina indulgently, that he was, indeed, a great favorite of hers. "You-all must be mighty tired," she went on, giving a beringed hand, which proved startlingly soft, to both of the Farmans in turn. "I reckon you'll want to retire right away. If you'll come with me, I will show you to your apartment. It is the one formerly occupied by my dear parents, so I especially hope that it will please you. Joe will bring up your belongings. Rosetta and Justin have gone home—you probably know that in the South our servants do not live with us. These faithful persons have been in my employ for more than twenty years, but if I suggested that they should stay twenty minutes after dinner was cleared away, they would at once apply for government jobs, as all my friends' former household staffs have done.

Again she smiled indulgently, as if she rather sympathised with her faithful servitors' insistence on nocturnal independence. Then she turned and led the way up the long straight stairs. Near the top of these there was a landing from which three steps led straight ahead and six to one side, indicating that the second story was on two levels. Mrs. Porterfield turned again and went up the longer of these flights of small hallway flanked with panelled cupboards, and finally she opened the door into an immense high-ceilinged room, furnished in black walnut and equipped with a stationary marble washstand. The monumental bed had clusters of carved fruit on the headboard and was covered with a burnt-orange spread which matched the upholstery. The gilt clock and the gilt vases on the black marble mantel also matched and were embellished with classical figures. Steel engravings representing the funeral of General Latané and the home life of General Washington hung on either side of a wardrobe even more massive than the bed. But the room, though gloomy and overpowering, somehow had distinction. Serena had never seen one like it before, but she instantly understood that it was in character, like Mrs. Porterfield's cameo earrings and Joe Racina's casual profanity. She addressed herself to her hostess with appreciation.

"I'm real touched that you should have put us in your parents' room," she said. "We'll be careful not to disturb anything. And I do hope we haven't put you out too much, coming late like this. You must have had to sit up for us a long spell."

"I had not even thought of retiring," Mrs. Porterfield assured her. "I hope I have everything arranged for your comfort. The bathroom is on the other side of the stair landing. You go down the first six steps of the stairs and then turn and go up the three others. I hope that will not seem an inconvenience. My guests usually keep their towels on their own washstands. There is some port wine in this decanter, and here are some beaten biscuits, spread with Smithfield ham, folded in the napkin beside it. I understood that you were to have dinner with Joe, but I feared you might be hungry in the night. I hope you will have a refreshing sleep and that I shall have the pleasure of seeing you in the morning. On Sundays my guests generally breakfast with me at half past nine and afterwards most of us attend services at Christ Church together. But if some other plan would be more agreeable to you——"

She paused, awaiting the expression of their preference. Serena and Daniel exchanged glances.

"If you'll excuse us, Mrs. Porterfield, I think maybe we ought to get started to town in good season, without bothering you or your hired help about breakfast," Daniel suggested. "It's important that we should talk with our daughter as soon as we can, and I think we ought to get to her apartment before church time, seeing that she was prevented from meeting us tonight. Then we can go over plans with her and——"

"I don't like to butt in every time you say you want to talk over plans with Jenness." Joe Racina did not interrupt quite as curtly as he had before, but again there was insistence in his voice and again Daniel and Serena both reluctantly realized that he was forestalling an inopportune call at their daughter's apartment. "This was a pretty late party she was going on tonight," he went on. "She was all tied up with it before she knew just when you were coming, so she felt sure you'd understand. But *she* wouldn't understand if you went and pounded on her door the first thing Sunday morning. It would burn her up. Look, you've had a hard trip—a hell of a trip," he amended, stopping to grin at Mrs. Porterfield. "Why don't you take it easy tomorrow? You don't know what you'll be missing if you don't try one of Mrs. Porterfiield's Sunday breakfasts. She has scrambled eggs and sausage and waffles and hot rolls, like everyone else, but then she also has kidney stew, a kind that's absolutely unique and makes you feel better about this wicked world. After breakfast you can take your time getting unpacked and read the paper, while you're waiting for Jenness to call up—you'll want to see that piece of Peter's on Hawaii—we're giving it a big spread. As a matter of fact, I think you'd have plenty of time to go to church before you hear from Jenness, if you care to. She likes to have her sleep out. But if you just leave her alone, I think eventually she'll suggest that you have supper with her at her apartment. *Then* you can start planning. It can't possibly do any harm to put it off that long, because you can't get going till Monday anyway. If the day drags, after you've heard from her but before you can go to see her, you could do a little sightseeing. There are lots of things to see right here in Alexandria—George Washington's fire engine, for instance, and the house where his girl friend lived. Don't tell me you didn't know George Washington had a fire engine and a girl friend? Fact."

Again Daniel and Serena exchanged glances. It did not seem right or natural to either of them to wait for twenty-four hours before seeing Jenness, when they had come to Washington on purpose to do so; neither did they feel they ought to squander Dexter's money by wasting a whole day, even though this day was the Lord's, and they knew their burdened minds would not be relieved until they had entrusted their daughter's case to a good lawyer. But something told them they would only lose in the end if they sought to force an issue now.

"Well, thank you kindly, Mrs. Porterfield," Daniel said, speaking for both. "We'd be very pleased to have breakfast with you at half past nine, seeing as how you're good enough to ask us. We wouldn't want you should think we didn't appreciate your hospitality. Because we do. More than we can say. We'll never forget what it's meant to us, having Mr. Racina bring us to your home tonight, never, as long as we live."

Daniel Farman had spoken solemnly, for the occasion was a solemn one for him, as he knew it was for his wife. But after they had undressed, in the great formal room, and had knelt side by side in prayer, according to their nightly habit, they were able to compose themselves in the huge bed and await the coming of slumber with comparative tranquility. The peace of mind they had achieved with such effort was undisturbed by the image of Jenness as she was at this same time. Mercifully they could not see her face as she tried to wrench herself free from the man who bent over her or hear her voice as she cried out.

"But you told me you only wanted to come in for a nightcap. . . . Not three either. Just one. . . . You've said over and over again . . . No, I haven't led you on, not purposely. . . . You haven't any right to bargain with me anyway . . . Don't, darling, don't!"

CHAPTER 12

JOE RACINA had not exaggerated the attraction of Sunday morning breakfast at Mrs. Porterfiield's. When Daniel and Serena went downstairs the next morning, they made their way, without difficulty, through the long blue drawing room and a small rectangular sitting room behind it to a large sunny dining room. There they found their hostess already seated behind a silver coffee service, set forth at one end of a long table covered with a well-worn cloth, and already partially surrounded by other guests. She effected presentations to these persons so easily and graciously that almost immediately the New England couple ceased to feel that they were among strangers.

"Good morning, Mrs. Farman. Good morning, Mr. Farman. I do trust you-all rested well. Permit me to present you to some of your fellow guests. This is my sweet friend, Miss Lily Twitchell. Miss Lily has honored me by making her home with me for twenty years, ever since she lost her dear mother. And here at my left are Captain and Mrs. Webb. Captain Webb is in the Chemical Division of the Navy Department, mighty interesting work. And Captain Buchanan, just opposite you, is in charge of camouflage. I never did get used to this idea of changing the looks of one thing so it would look like something else until Captain Buchanan explained its importance to me. Miss Sybil Blodgett and Miss Maude Waggaman are both connected with our fine local Red Cross. Mr. Racina, whom you know already, and Mr. Weatherby, our other journalist, have not come down yet. But I am sure they will be joining us at any minute now."

Having created a genial atmosphere, Mrs. Porterfield gave it a spiritual touch by asking a brief blessing before beginning to pour the coffee. Filling the porcelain cups, which were none the less elegant because they were so ample, with a rich mixture of mocha, cream and sugar, she passed these herself. Meanwhile, a beaming negro, whose teeth were whiter than his somewhat sabby jacket, encircled the table in an efficient but unhurried manner, offering one heaped dish after another and murmuring exhortations designed to tempt his beneficiaries to unstinted indulgence in the specialties of the house. Before any of the supplies showed the slightest sign of being exhausted, he disappeared into the kitchen to return with reinforcements in the shape of fresh delicacies. Daniel and Serena had never before seen food supplied in such a lavish and leisurely way, and they had never eaten so richly flavored or so attractively presented. Even more than the seafood at O'Donnell's Restaurant, it put new life and new courage into them, and they were glad to concentrate on it, answering direct questions politely, but making no effort to take an active part in the general conversation.

"If this is your first visit to Washington, Mrs. Farman, I hope you won't judge it by conditions as they are now. Of co'se it's never been the same since the New Deal came in. But the alphabet agencies only started the overcrowding. It's all the new war workers——"

"But, Miss Lily, we poor war workers aren't responsible for the terrible climate. I've had one cold after another ever since I came. I never used to have colds in Philadelphia——"

"The climate is dreadful but I don't mind that as much as I do the awful row houses. I never could abide a city with row houses. Now Minneapolis is such a pleasant open city——"

"What do you think of General Emmons' report on the strengthening of Hawaiian defenses and the smashing of Japanese espionage? Personally, I'd like to see a little more action and hear a little less soft-soaping——"

"If you want to know what's really going on, you better read Pete MacDonald's follow story to yesterday's release. It's hotter than any hula that ever came out of Hawaii."

This last remark was made by Joe Racina, who had come in tardily, and who more or less set the tempo for the talk from that point on. His fellow journalist, Bruce Weatherby, did not appear, and Joe, in response to rather pointed questioning, murmured something vague about a tall Saturday evening and adroitly changed the subject. Breakfast went on and on, but when they finally rose from the table, Joe suggested that he should show the Farmans the way to the Presbyterian Meeting House which he thought they might enjoy more than Christ Church, and which was only a few blocks away; in broad daylight, they actually might be able to walk there without breaking their legs. They accepted his invitation gratefully, and were agreeably surprised at finding the day so mild when they went out into the sunshine; they had not realized they would find such a change in temperature, and like the strange abundant food, the strange warmth was welcome. So was the sight of more magnolia trees, green and glossy like the one in Mrs. Porterfield's yard, and the glimpses of box, also strange and green and glossy, beyond the latticed doorways leading into walled gardens beside houses made of mellowed brick. Joe Racina sauntered along beside them in the same leisurely way that characterized the movements of Mrs. Porterfield and the rest of her household. Sunday was his day off, he said; all the rest of the week he was on the run, breaking Commandments right and left; he rather enjoyed keeping the Fourth by way of a change and a contrast. He spoke soberly, but there was a telltale twist to his lips, and the dark circles around his eyes disappeared into the wrinkles.

"I presume that's the Meeting House where we're headed?" Daniel asked, indicating a gray stone structure which came into view as they turned a corner.

"No. That's St. Mary's, the Catholic Church. The Presbyterian Meeting House is right back of it."

"We never were in a Catholic Church," Serena confessed, looking at the gray structure with timorous interest. "There's one at the Junction, but the Canucks and Poles who work on the railroad are the only people around home who go there. Is—is it much different? I've wondered quite a lot lately. You see our son Jerome, who's a Lieutenant at Fort Bragg—well, he married a girl from Louisiana named Alix St. Cyr and she's a Catholic. They were married by a priest, and I sort of suspect that sometimes Jerome goes to church with her now. Not that he's told us that, in so many words. He wouldn't want to worry us. But he said he likes this priest, Devlin the man's name is, real well—"

"You wouldn't like to go to St. Mary's this morning, would you, instead of to the Meeting House? I'll go with you, if you like. I've strayed a long way from the fold, but I used to be an acolyte myself when I was a kid, so I know all the ropes. We could sit in one of the back pews and you could leave at any time if you found you weren't at ease there. But I think you would be. You don't feel ill at ease at Mrs. Porterfield's, do you, just because her house is different from yours? Come on, let's find out."

Serena did not know just what she had expected, but certainly it had never occurred to her before that ease might be a primary sensation in church. She marveled at the lack of restraint with which Joe Racina flung open the door and entered a pew at the rear, nonchalantly ushering Daniel and Serena into it before him. He even seemed quite unembarrassed by the presence of a long row of women clothed alike in black dresses and black veils, with white fluting around their calm faces, who Serena judged must actually be nuns in the flesh. Joe Racina turned around and nodded to several of these black-robed women, saying "Hello, Sister!" very heartily, and in return they smiled and saluted him. Then presently a little boy, also wearing unfamiliar black and white garments, emerged from a side door near the front of the church and began to light a series of high white candles that rose among flowers. Joe Racina nudged Serena gently.

"That kid looks just the way I used to look," he observed. "Fact. Listen, you don't have to keep kneeling down and getting up all the time if you don't want to. You can just sit still and watch. Or go out whenever you feel like it. Except after they get started ringing some little bells. When they do that you must sit still until you see other people begin to move . . ."

"It was beautiful, Mr. Racina," Serena said as they went out into the sunlight again an hour later. "I don't know how else to put it. But that's the word that comes natural to me. It was just beautiful. Wasn't it, Daniel?"

"Yes," said Daniel, looking across the street at nothing in particular. "It was. I think you got the right word for it straight off, Mother. I don't think you're called on to say anything else about it."

"It means a lot to us to find it was like that," Serena said. Increasingly, it was "coming natural" for her to talk to Joe Racina and she went on eagerly. "On account of Jerome, you know. I feel different about his marrying a Catholic, now that I've been inside such a beautiful church. I can tell every thing about it can't be evil, like we've always heard. Not but what I thought Alix was a good girl herself. Only I was afraid she'd had bad influences to combat, brought up by nuns. And when I saw those women behind us—sweet-faced, that's what they were. Alix is sweet-faced herself, from her picture. I wish I could see her."

"Why don't you go down to Fort Bragg and make your son and your new daughter-in-law a little visit? It isn't far from here, and I should think you'd enjoy it. You have several days to spare before the hearing."

"Ye-es. But of course we haven't got the matter of a lawyer settled yet. And then we have to think of expense, Mr. Racina, like we told you before. We're—we're in sort of straitened circumstances and it would cost money to travel to North Carolina. We had to borrow from a neighbor to come to Washington in the first place. We don't want to be any more beholden to him than we have to. Not that he'd begrudge it to us. He's real free-handed. And he's going to be our son-in-law pretty soon. But that doesn't give us any right to sponge on him."

"I see," Joe Racina said gravely. "Well, it was just a suggestion . . . Did you say your son married a St. Cyr? I'm from New Orleans myself—I was born Giuseppe Mangiaracina, but I had to edit that before it was practical for newspaper work. I've known lots of St. Cyrs. That is, I've known about them. Not that our orbits touched. My grandfather was an Italian immigrant, who had a little bakery on Erato St., and my father and uncles worked with him. But of course we heard of the St. Cyrs as a glorious legend —everyone did. This young lady's father wasn't Adelard St. Cyr by any chance, was he? Adelard St. Cyr married a second time, and his widow is one of those fabulous de Greves who——"

"Why Jerome never happened to say," Serena answered, still speaking so eagerly that she did not give Joe a chance to finish his sentence. "Her father did marry a second time though, I know that much, and his widow's real well-to-do. She's been awfully good to Alix. But I guess Alix is like us in one way, even if she is from Louisiana. She doesn't like to feel beholden to anyone. So she took a job in a jewelry store in Fayetteville, and Jerome met her when he went in there to buy me my service pin. I'm real pleased, Mr. Racina, to think Jerome's married a girl who wouldn't want to sponge on anyone, even her own stepmother."

"I see," said Joe Racina again, still more gravely. "Well I guess you've got all kinds of good reasons to be pleased with your daughter-in-law. I hope you'll change your mind about going to see her. But of course you want to see Jenness first. Let's mosey along the house and find out if a call's come in from her. Not that I think it will have yet. It's only a quarter of one now. She won't be waking up for another hour or so. By the way, I must get you a latchkey. The doorbell doesn't work, and Rosetta and Justin always use that as an alibi for not coming to the door. Of course you can make enough noise with the knocker to raise the dead, but that's beyond the point. One of the reasons I feel so at home with Mrs. Porterfiield is that the doorbell to our house in New Orleans never worked either. It's a good old Southern custom to let them stay out of order once they get that way. We're all doless below the Mason and Dixon line. Well, here we are."

The telephone call had not come in, and Joe had been

fairly accurate in predicting the time that it would. Jenness still sounded sleepy when she made it. She was sorry about the night before, she said, but she really hadn't expected them until the first of the week, and it was just one of those things she couldn't get out of. Important from the viewpoint of the tiresome old hearing too. She was sure Joe had looked after them all right. She wasn't feeling especially friendly to him, because if he hadn't been such a nosey old Paul Pry, it would have saved her a lot of trouble. But after all there was nothing to worry about, really, and she had to hand it to Joe: he certainly could find a needle in a haystack and for that very reason she knew he'd done a much better job, meeting them, than she could have herself. And probably they'd like that mouldy old boarding house where he lived better than any place she could have found them in town. He'd tried to persuade her to go there before she got her apartment, but one swift glance at Mrs. Porterfiield's cameo earrings and black cotton stockings had been enough for her, even before she saw the blue wallpaper and the groaning board, not to mention the groaning boarders. Well, anyway . . . Would they like to come in after dinner? She was not going to have any dinner herself, just brunch, and she didn't have much on hand for supper, when it came to that. But she didn't suppose they'd need much, after gorging themselves at Mrs. Porterfield's. Well, around five. No, wait a minute—she'd forgotten about that damn cocktail party. They better make it seven-thirty.

"Seven-thirty!" Serena protested, as Daniel, who had done the talking this time, turned from the telephone. "Why that's not right after dinner, Daniel, that's way past suppertime!"

"We eat supper later down here than you do up North," Joe Racina said soothingly. "Seven-thirty's a good time. You won't be able to do anything but sleep for a couple of hours after dinner, you'll be in such a state of repletion from fried chicken and candied yams and spoon bread and fruit cake. Then we'll get in a little of that sightseeing I told you about, and afterwards I'll drive you in town. I'm going to that damn cocktail party myself, but it'll be all right if I don't get in till the tail end. I can drop you at the Potomac Plaza—that's the chromium plated palace where Jenness lives—before I go there. If she isn't back herself you can sit in the lobby and gaze at the "Modern-Age" furniture. It's the most completely streamlined place in Washington. You ought not to overlook it, while you're taking in the other sights."

Joe Racina certainly had the happy faculty of contributing to their comfort, not only physically but mentally and spiritually as well. With the same ease with which he had rescued them from the bedlam of the Union Station and introduced them to the beauties of the Roman ritual, he now made it seem logical for them to wait another whole afternoon before seeing Jenness. The day did not drag for them after all. They read Peter's Hawaiian piece with excitement; they relished their dinner and relaxed for their nap; they enjoyed their sightseeing. When Joe finally deposited them at the wide plate-glass door, framed with slabs of polished marble, which led in to Jenness' "chromium plated palace," they found themselves so loath to part from him that Serena managed to put their reluctance into words.

"You couldn't come with us to see Jenness, could you, Mr. Racina?" she asked. "Maybe if you did, we could all talk about that lawyer you think she ought to have, and get somewhere. Daniel and I've thought it over, and we believe, if you're convinced Mr. Waldo's the best one for her, she ought to have him. But I don't know as we can convince *her*. I don't know if she'd listen to us."

"She won't listen to me either," Joe Racina said briefly. "Not about anything. No, I won't go in with you. It's better for you to see her without me, for all kinds of reasons. If I don't get held up at the cocktail party by some politician with a pet project, I'm going down to the office to do a little work later on. You might give me a ring when you're ready to go back to Alexandria. Here's my number. Or if I find I do get sidetracked, I'll give you a ring, tenish. Yes, I know that number. Right? So long."

His departure left them inexplicably bereft. It was hard for them to understand how the presence of a man whom

they had never seen, twenty-four hours earlier, should seem
so supporting; but the fears they had half forgotten, while
he was with them, assailed them again now as they sat forlornly in the streamlined lobby of the Potomac Plaza,
waiting for Jenness. It was sparsely furnished in tubular
metal furniture, upholstered in pale leather, with a slippery
semi-circular seat curving close to a cubby-hole enclosed
in bleached wood, where a receptionist, as streamlined as
her surroundings, was modishly enthroned. She looked at
them with a cold stare and spoke to them haughtily before
they had attempted to approach her.

"We have no vacancies whatsoever. We haven't had
one in months."

"We didn't expect to find a vacancy. We only——"

"We don't have a waiting list either. We've found it's
too much trouble to keep track of one."

"But we only wanted you to ring Miss Jenness Farman's
apartment to see if she's come in yet."

The receptionist finally condescended to perform this
service, but she appeared to take a malign satisfaction in
announcing that Miss Farman's apartment did not answer.
After that she paid no more attention to them and they
lost hope completely. They did not so much as see Jenness
when at last she came breezing in through the marble-
framed plate glass door, because they had long since
ceased to look hopefully towards it every time it opened
and shut, and to tell each other she would be along any
minute now. They had slumped down on the slippery
circular seat and were gazing mutely in the opposite direction, at a skeletal spray of artificial flowers which rose
from a small bare table. Even while she was rustling rapidly down the lobby they paid no attention to her. It was
not until she was almost upon them that they recognized
their own daughter in the striking girl wearing a slinky
black dress, with a large jewelled pin on her left shoulder
and a black parasol hat tilted back from an exaggerated
pompadour. She bent over and kissed them both with
startling swiftness, leaving little arcs of lipstick on their
cheeks as she did so.

"I'm *so* sorry!" she said breathlessly. "But I just had

to go to this particular party—there were all kinds of reasons why it was important. I didn't mean to stay more than a few minutes though—I thought I'd just make a dashing entrance, and mill around for a few minutes, and then leave. But every time I tried to break away someone detained me. I knew practically everyone there. Usually you don't, at a cocktail party. You have to keep telling people who you are. Not that they really care, and half the time they can't hear you, no matter how loud you shriek, there's such a racket going on. But you bellow at them just the same. Sometimes even your hostess doesn't recognize you, she's in such a dither by the time the party gets under way because she's taken so many drinks to fortify herself against fatigue. Or maybe she didn't know you in the first place—your name may have just been put on a list by her social secretary, or a friend of yours who is a friend of hers may have dragged you along. Well, anyway, I finally escaped, and I've brought the most marvelous person with me to make up for being late. This is Mr. Thomas Loper, Mom. Dad, Mr. Thomas Loper. Mr. Loper's going to stay and have supper with us. You'll realize what an honor that is when I tell you he's practically the most important lawyer in the District of Columbia. And he's going to explain to you that there isn't a thing to worry about. Why my appearance in court isn't going to be anything but a formality! I'll only be there a few minutes! And then everything will be all over and you can go home. It's so simple, the way Mr. Loper explains it, that I don't see why I ever got panicky. I'm almost sorry I bothered you about coming down."

The lank, swarthy, blue-chinned man, extolled in such glowing terms, had remained so far in the background until she began her presentations, that her parents had not realized he was her escort. Now he came blandly forward, extending a short square hand covered with fine dark hairs. There were tufts of similar hair above his glittering eyes and protuberant ears, but the top of his head was only scantily covered with it, and his partial baldness made the peculiar shape of his crown more noticeable. It was long and flat, and he moved it with a swiftness which was at variance with the slowness with which he moved his body. He was immaculately and rather formally dressed. His collar and cuffs were so white and stiff that they had a glaring quality, and there was a scoured look about his long neck and lean hands, as if he had been so afraid they would not look clean that he had scrubbed them too hard. He wore a pearl stickpin, a heavy watch chain, and a massive ring set with a carbuncle.

"Now then, everyone ought to have a glimpse of Washington in wartime," he said genially. "I'm sure Mr. and Mrs. Farman are grateful to you for giving them such a plausible pretext, Jenness. But your daughter's right, Mrs. Farman—there isn't a thing on earth to worry about. We'll talk it all over. Not here, of course, in this public place. We'll just wait until we get to the cute little hideout Jenness has upstairs. You'll see that it's a perfect place for confidences."

Jenness had linked her arm through her father's, and was already guiding him towards the elevator. Mr. Loper, now put one of his lean hands under Serena's elbow, propelling her in the same direction. The operator nodded with a friendly smile as they got into the elevator, and spoke enthusiastically to Jenness. "That was a swell piece your boy friend had in the *Bulletin* this morning," she said in a voice as warm as the receptionist's had been cold. "I declare it's the first thing I've read that's made this war seem real to me. I felt as if I was right there in Hawaii with him . . . I'd like to be too," she added, bringing the elevator to a smooth stop. "I don't mean on account of him personally. I'm not that kind of a chiseler. I mean so I could get in the fight myself. Maybe I can at that, later on. I hear there's talk on the Hill about a bill to let women into the Army. Was that your other boy friend's idea, Miss Farman?"

"I haven't any idea what you're talking about," Jenness said freezingly. "I haven't had time to read the paper today, and if I listened to all the gossip there is on the Hill about fool bills that never get introduced after all, I wouldn't get anything else done. Come on, Dad. We go this way, around to the left. You're still looking after Mom, aren't you, Mr. Loper?"

Mr. Loper, still speaking smoothly and still keeping his hand under Serena's elbow, assured her that he was. Serena, feeling increasingly uncomfortable, walked along beside him in silence. She felt sorry for the friendly little operator who had been so curtly snubbed, and she could not avoid the impression that Jenness' irritation had been caused by the elevator girl's artless references to "boy friends," rather than to the praise of Peter's piece or to the question about pending legislation. Serena somehow felt that Jenness did not want anyone to talk about Peter at all, and that such references as were made to Horace Vaughn should be guarded and respectful, unless Jenness herself introduced the subject first. Serena had seen Mr. Loper watching Jenness very closely, all the time the elevator girl had been talking, and the expression on her daughter's face, under his scrutiny, had taken on the same tinge of fear mingled with anger which had intermittently disfigured it during the Christmas holidays. It was all very well for Jenness to keep on saying there was nothing to worry about. Serena knew that the girl was terribly worried, and she was more and more afraid herself that part of this fear was based on the dread that someone might disclose facts she wanted kept secret . . .

"Well, here we are!" Jenness was saying, taking a key out of her smart initialed handbag and turning it in the lock. Her voice had regained its quality of bravado; she threw open the door with an air of triumph, ushering her visitors into her apartment with pride. The room was furnished in the same modernistic manner as the lobby downstairs; with pale, highly-polished woods and pastel-colored upholstery; the only ornaments in it were some crystal figurines on the low tables, and the only pictures on the walls were a couple of stylized prints. It looked bare and stiff to Serena. Everything in it seemed to her too new and too studied. She instinctively felt that it had never really been lived in, like the rooms on Farman Hill, just as she instinctively missed not only the homely warmth of an open fire but also the companionable grouping of chairs which the absence of a fireplace made impossible. However, she tried to put heartiness into the expression of admiration which she knew Jenness was awaiting.

"Why, this must be nice and light in the daytime with all those windows!" she said, glancing towards the front of the room. "Picture windows, did you say you called them? I always thought of city rooms as dark. You're up real high too, aren't you, Jenness? I realized that coming up in the elevator. You must get plenty of fresh air this way."

"Yes, I do. I'm on the top floor. And it is nice and light. I've got a cute little balcony too and a grand view. Come and see."

She opened a French door, lightly veiled with cream-colored glass curtains, and stepped outside. The "balcony" was hardly more than a wide ledge, enclosed by the rooms which jutted out slightly on either side of it, and safeguarded by a fanciful metallic railing which formed part of the architectural embellishment of the façade. Measuring mentally, Serena saw that two chairs could not have been placed there side by side, because it was too narrow; but it was long enough to permit them to be placed opposite each other, if two persons should care to sit that way and look at the view. It was already so dark that she could not see this; but she could well imagine that, as Jenness said, it might be extremely pleasing, though she could not herself escape a slight sensation of pitching forward.

"You don't ever get dizzy when you come out here, do you,' Jenness?" she inquired, trying not to sound anxious.

"No, of course not. You wouldn't either, after the first minute or two. It's only because you're up so high and the balcony's so shallow that you get the feeling. But I love the height, and there's all the room I need. It's lovely in the spring. But it's too cold to stay here now. Let's go and fix some drinks," Jenness said, stepping inside again and closing the French doors with care. "I want you to see the kitchenette too. You'd never believe so many things could fit into such a small space or that you could

save so many steps by having everything right together. It
would spoil you for housekeeping on Farman Hill after
you'd kept house here for a while, just as it has me. When
we get the men started on their highballs, we'll go into
my bedroom. Then you'll really see something. I went
to town when I fixed that up. Dad can hobnob with Mr.
Loper while we're powdering our noses. Well, I just meant
that figuratively. Of course I know you don't use any
makeup. But we can have a nice cozy time together just
the same, can't we?"

She was her most beguiling self again. Serena followed
her willingly into the kitchenette, and here the older woman's expressions of admiration were unforced; she had
never imagined that anything could be so compact and
convenient. She could understand now how easy it was
for Jenness to do her own housework, holding down her
office job too, and still have plenty of time to give parties
and go to them. It was all wonderful—the tiny refrigerator,
the tinier range, the gleaming sink that was tiniest of all.
And that cupboard space! Why there wasn't an inch that
hadn't been utilized! She paused long enough in the living
room to tell her husband that he must go and see the
kitchenette too. But Daniel, who was already deep in conversation with Mr. Loper, answered her rather abstractedly, and accepted his highball from Jenness with only a
nod of acknowledgment. Serena did not mind this. She
was glad to feel that the two were making progress, and
she herself was now eager to inspect the remainder of
Jenness' quarters. But the feeling of uneasiness which, in
the kitchenette, she had almost shaken off, oppressed her
again in the bedroom. This was not bare, like the living
room, but filled, in a fluffy sort of way, with ultrafeminine
furnishings. The wide low bed was covered with a lacy
counterpane which swept down from a headboard of tufted
satin; the dressing table was also draped with lace, and
two silly little lamps with lace shades reflected the glitter
of the plate glass on which the fanciful toilet articles were
arranged. There were white fur rags on the floor, but aside
from these, the prevailing color in the roow was pink,
and the tiles in the adjoining bathroom were pink too. A

faint powdery smell, suggestive of expensive cosmetics rather than of good fresh air, permeated the atmosphere. Serena was relieved, after all, that Jenness had not suggested her parents should stay with her; she knew she never could have rested easily in that strange looking bed, with no footboard at all and no legs to speak of, and the corners of her mouth twitched, momentarily, at the thought of how Daniel would have looked in it. She had not seen anything that resembled a studio couch in the living room either, only that queer cubic sofa. Perhaps Jenness had recently redecorated the apartment and done away with the studio couch at the same time, thugh she had not said anything about doing so. But certainly everything looked brand new. Too new, she thought again, to be homelike. But the bedroom, despite its powdery smell and its lacy frills, did have something the living room lacked. It seemed more inhabited.

"I presume we ought to be getting back to the men folks, oughtna's we, Jenness? Or else starting supper?" she inquired. She hoped she had said enough so that her daughter would not feel she had slighted the lace spread and the fur rugs; but she was secretely longing to get out of this bedroom, which she did not like at all, and return to the intriguing kitchenette. "I've got a piece of news for you though that maybe I better tell you first, so you won't be surprised if we should get a call later in the evening. I'm expecting to hear, any minute, that Dexter and Judith were married today. Dexter went all over it with your father and me, and we decided it would be the best thing all around. Not but what we would have liked to give them a real nice wedding. But you see Dexter has moved over to our house to stay, and of course none of us wanted to cause talk—so——"

"*None* of you! Did you consult Judith while you were making this cute little plan?"

"Why no, how could we? She was still down to Brents'. But she was aiming to get out of quarantine today, and Dexter was going to explain everything to her when he went to fetch her. How you needed us most right now and all."

"I think you and Dad and Dexter must all be crazy. Or I'll think Judith is, if she lets herself be bulldozed into getting married like that."

"Why, Jenness! You don't think your sister would stay alone in the house with a man unless she *was* married to him, do you?"

"I don't see any reason why she shouldn't, if the man was Dexter. I think she'd be perfectly safe."

"Yes, of course she would. But I don't like the way you say that, Jenness. If you said it so's to show that Dexter is an honorable man and wouldn't give way to temptation, that would be all right. But you didn't. You said it as if you were slurring Dexter, as if you thought he wouldn't hanker for Judith according to nature. He's wanted her for his wife a long time. He's never even looked at another woman."

"If he had, perhaps he'd have more idea how to manage Judith."

"Jenness, it isn't becoming in a good girl to talk like you are. I don't know what's come over you. I'm not going to sit here and listen to you another minute."

"Well, you don't have to. But you needn't get so excited either. You didn't let me finish what I started to say. I didn't mean that Judith would go and live in sin, as you'd call it, with Dexter on Farman Hill. I meant she wouldn't go there at all. She'll find some pretext not to. You wait and see."

"She couldn't find any pretext. There isn't anything against Dexter, not a thing in the world."

"Maybe there isn't. But there isn't much *for* him either, that I've ever been able to see. Judith can do a lot better for herself than that. If she's got half the sense I think she has, she will, too . . . Well, don't let's keep on arguing about it and getting nowhere. When the telephone call comes through we'll find out, fast enough, which of us was right. Meanwhile, I think it would be a good plan to start supper."

In spite of the disparaging remarks she had made about the state of her larder, the supper was very good, and Jenness had it ready to serve in two shakes of a dead

lamb's tail, as Serena willingly admitted. There was an
aspic salad, with shrimps and celery in a tomato jelly,
which Jenness had prepared beforehand, and which she
now set out in an attractive mold, on a pretty glass platter.
She also had a "Swedish platter" of sandwiches, astonish-
ing in its tempting variety, and while coffee was perco-
lating in an electric pot, she reheated some creamed mushrooms which had previously been put in a double boiler.
All her dishes were made of glass instead of china, and
when she had set the table, which was already adorned
with the crystal figurines, adding a glass bowl filled with
paper-white narcissi and tall white candless in glass candlesticks, the total effect was entrancing. After the salad and
sandwiches and mushrooms had all been devoured, she
removed the plates, but not the cups; she had another
pot of coffee "perking," she said, and she would bring
that in with the dessert, which was strawberry shortcake.
No, she wasn't extravagant, really. It didn't take many
strawberries for such a small party, and she thought Mom
and Dad deserved that much of a treat after all the trouble they had gone to by coming to see her. As for Mr.
Loper, of course he deserved a treat too, because he was
going to fix everything so that none of them would have
a care in the world, as soon as he'd finished his cigar.

"I declare, I never knew you'd make such a nice little
housekeeper, Jenness," Serena said, as she helped her
daughter stack the dishes neatly in the sink. "That supper
would have been a credit to anyone. And your apartment's as neat as a new pin—seems to me the bedroom
needs airing some, but maybe that's just my imagination.
I can't help wishing that as soon as this trouble's blown
over, you could marry and settle down, same as Judith's
planning to. It's fine to see a girl able to hold down a
big job the way you have, but after all there's nothing that
means so much to her in the long run as a good home
and a good husband. And you'd make a man a good wife.
You've sort of got your restlessness out of your bones
now, haven't you, Jenness? You wouldn't mind settling
down if the right man should ask you?"

"Oh, Mom, don't keep talking about settling down! I think it's a horrid phrase! It makes me think of a hen."

"Yes, but once you were married, Jenness, you wouldn't think so. You'd want to give all your time and strength to your husband and your children."

"Mercy, Mom, I wish you'd get some more modern ideas! If I did get married, I wouldn't think of having a child for five years at least, and if it was as bad as some people make out, I'd never have but one. And I'd want my husband to do things for *me*. I'd expect him to give me a swell house and a snappy car and oodles of jewelry."

"Those aren't the things that matter most, Jenness."

"They're the things that matter most with me. They're the things I'm going to have. You wait and see. Of course I know I'd have to do something to get them. Men are terrible traders. But if they can get what they want most——"

"Maybe you don't know yet, Jenness, what they want most."

"Yes, I do. Where do you think I've been all this time? Of course I know what they want most. I don't mean sissies like Dexter. I mean real he-men. If a girl can give them what they want, she can do a little trading herself."

"Jenness!"

"Well, she can. I know what I'm talking about. I'm glad of it too. And I'm glad I've got what it takes. Now, here we are arguing again over nothing at all. Let's go back to the living room."

They found, on their return, that Mr. Loper was already comfortably settled with his cigar, which he seemed to be greatly enjoying. He paused every now and then to contemplate its fine ash and savor its excellent aroma, while talking to Daniel in an agreeable if slightly supercilious way. He looked across at Jenness, as she sat down herself, with an expression which indicated he was counting on her to help him convince these unsophicated parents of hers that they must not meddle with his adroit management of her affairs.

"I've been following your suggestion that I should start

explaining the situation to your father, Jenness," he said easily. "I'm sure he understands now, just as you do, that there's no reason for anxiety, none whatsoever, if you follow the course I've mapped out for you."

"No, I'm not sure that I have followed you," Daniel said painfully. "From what you've just told me, it sounds as if the story was to be she never heard of Max Lentz. But she's not only heard of him, she knows him. She met him, time and time again, on our place at Farman Hill. She went out walking with him there almost every day."

Mr. Loper laughed, his manner easy again. "I didn't dream you belonged to that school of thought, Mr. Farman," he said. "Of course the method's effective sometimes. But I still think the other way is better, in this case."

"I don't know what you're talking about."

"I'm merely trying to say that under certain circumstances, one very effective way of undermining fantastic charges is by giving still more fantastic evidence. Of course you know your statement that Jenness went for daily walks with Max Lentz is fantastic."

"She was seen," Daniel said stubbornly.

"Why of course she wasn't, Mr. Farman."

"She went walking everyday from the Home Pasture through the Pine Lot to Jerome's Hill and back by the brook in the Big Field where it joins the Highway. She always started out alone, but she didn't always go on alone."

"I'm sure she didn't. A pretty girl like Jenness would be almost sure to find a willing escort wherever she went walking, even on a lonely country road. We all know what a pleasant way such things have of happening. Almost as if a kindly fate took a hand. But it's absurd to say her escort on these occasions was Lentz."

"Maybe you wouldn't call him an escort. But he met her. Didn't he, Jenness?"

"No," said Jenness coldly. She did not look at Mr. Loper, as if seeking for guidance, when she spoke. She looked straight at her father, answering without hesitancy.

"Why, Jenness, however can you say that? However can you lie like that to your father?"

Serena's voice was stricken. Daniel put his hand firmly on her arm.

"Mother, I want you should let me talk to Mr. Loper right now. You can talk to Jenness afterwards, if you're a mind to. It doesn't make any difference what you say, Mr. Loper, or what Jenness says. My wife and I know she met Max Lentz on those walks of hers. What's more, we know she gave him the plans to our place. She helped him work out a scheme to sell it to a German named Gustav Meyer. It was a pretty shrewd scheme too. It pretty nearly worked. If it had, we'd have had another German family in Farman, all set to make trouble there, same as the Hellmans and the Wagners and the Lippmans and the Beckers are set to make trouble there already."

"I'm very sorry to hear that you've had such an over-powering Germanic invasion in your peaceful village, Mr. Farman. However, you're still showing a very fanciful spirit in attributing any part of this influx to your charming daughter. She made a great effort to go home at Christmastime, because she hoped her visit would give you and Mrs. Farman pleasure. But she had no motive beyond enjoying a healthful respite from her regular work. She holds a very responsible position and she fills it very capably and conscientiously. She's considered one of the most outstanding secretaries on the Hill. Her employer places entire dependence on her. She's been unremitting in her devotions to his interests."

"Perhaps he placed too much dependence on her. It wasn't to his interest, or hers either, for her to mail out subversive speeches under a congressional frank."

"I'm afraid I must remind you that it is very dangerous to jump at conclusions, Mr. Farman. Now you do not impress me as a man of rash judgment. But you are being very harsh, very harsh and unjust, to your daughter. I am beginning to fear your visit will not be a source of much comfort or help to her after all. She is nervously very much unstrung, and she is completely exhausted. She was desperately in need of the rest she counted on getting during her hard-won holiday. Personally I feel extremely sorry that she did not get it. It seems too bad that this pleasant vacation to which she had looked forward so much, and which might have done so much to restore her, should have been spoiled for her. By the intrusion of such a low type of news-sleuth as Peter MacDonald. By the suspicion of her parents. By the spying of neighbors whom she thought were devoted friends. No wonder she is unstrung now."

"She's unstrung because she knows she's done wrong and she's afraid of what's going to happen to her when everybody's found her out."

"Mr. Farman, I must repeat that if you're going to take such a threatening attitude towards your daughter, it would be better if you should leave. It would be most prejudicial to her if she should become hysterical before the Grand Jury, and she may be, if she becomes impregnated with false fears."

"I'm not impregnating her with false fears. I'm trying to make her understand that perjury's a criminal offense, and that if she's caught lying on the witness stand the way she's lied to us, after she's sworn to tell the truth, the whole truth and nothing but the truth, she'll get a prison sentence."

He rose, glowering in his righteous wrath, "Come, Mother," he said sternly. "There isn't any use our staying here now, not a particle. We better telephone Joe Racina at the *Bulletin,* like he suggested, and let him know we're ready to go back to Alexandria." He turned from his wife to Jenness, and spoke still more sternly. "We'll stand by, until the hearing and whatever comes out of it are over. You're our daughter, whatever you've done and whatever you're figuring on doing, and we shan't forget it, even if you've forgotten yourself what kind of stock you come from. But I never thought I'd live to see the day when I'd be ashamed because a child of mine was taking part in a war. You're in this one, Jenness, just as much as Jerome is. Only you and he aren't fighting on the same side."

CHAPTER 13

THE DRIVE to Alexandria was sad and silent. Joe Racina's pleasantries, which had been so cheering before, were ineffectual now. He made a few unrewarded efforts to lighten the gloomy atmosphere by telling them a little more about himself, in an off-hand manner designed to prepare the way for finding out what had happened between Jenness and her parents, without making his questions too crude. His grand job on the *Bulletin* was a comparatively new one, he said, and his discoveries in regard to the orders from the government printing office and the disposition of the Congressional mail bags had constituted his first real "break." Before coming to Washington, he had worked on the *New Orleans Item,* first as a campus correspondent while he was at Tulane, and later as a regular staff reporter. There had also been a brief interlude of teaching, between the time he got his B.A. and the time he got his M.A.; but he had hated that; it was newspaper work that was really down his alley. Peter MacDonald was his best buddy. He hoped he could do as good a job on Jenness as Peter would have done . . .

None of this called forth any encouraging or enlightening response, and gradually he himself subsided, and permitted his thoughts to wander from the perturbed couple, who had so unexpectedly been catapulated into his keeping, to his pal Pete, who was off to the Orient, the lucky bum, leaving him behind to hold the bag. War or no war, he was sure Pete would find some way of basking now and then on the sands of Waikiki, and of savoring the delights of *luaus* as the end of a hard day's work. He was recalled from his visualization of these imaginary scenes to the actualities of the moment by a cry from Serena, so sharp and sudden, that instinctively he jammed on the brakes and turned to her in alarm.

"Good God, what's the matter?" he asked, speaking sharply himself. "Are you hurt or something?"

"No—no, I'm not hurt," Serena answered, with an obvious effort at self-control. "But I've just thought of something that—that sort of upset me. You see, Mr. Racina, we were expecting our other daughter, Judith that is, to call us this evening. About a very important matter. And she didn't. I got so excited—well, about other things, at Jenness', that I forgot all about this matter. Didn't you, Daniel?"

"Yes, I did, and that's a fact," Daniel confessed ruefully. "I don't see how I ever came to, any more than I see how you could have, but I did. We ought to have heard from Judith hours ago. It's strange that we haven't."

"Don't you think we might call *her* up when we get back to Mrs. Porterfield's?"

"Well, no, Mother, I don't believe we better do that. It must be getting on towards eleven o'clock. I don't think it would be just the thing to call Judith up as late as that, not tonight anyway."

There was a short silence. Joe, without being informed of the circumstances, realized there was some special reason why a late call should be considered especially inopportune on this particular night.

"Of course it wouldn't." Serena's voice sounded apologetic and a little embarrassed. "I don't know what I was thinking of, Daniel, to suggest such a thing, I declare I don't. I can't help but worry though, just the same. Don't you think, if we haven't heard from Judith by noon tomorrow, we might call her then?"

"Well, suppose we don't cross that bridge till we get to it," Daniel said temperately. "I haven't a doubt but what we will hear from her before noon tomorrow. Likely as not she clean forgot it tonight. It wouldn't be so strange if she had, would it?"

"Yes, it would. Jenness might forget what she'd promised to do, but Judith never would," Serena persisted.

"Judith or Dexter either. They're dependable. They wouldn't want us to worry, just because they were happy."

"Not if they remembered us. But I can't say I gave my parents a thought, under the same circumstances. I don't believe you did yours either, Mother."

Serena murmured something indistinct, which admitted nothing, as to either the past or the present.

"We've got to think of the expense too," Daniel reminded his wife gently, as if he realized that she was still unconvinced.

"It doesn't cost any more to telephone from Washington to Farman than from Farman to Washington, does it?" she inquired, with a touch of returning spirit. "If we call them first, they won't be put to the expense of calling us. I don't see what difference it makes."

"All right, Mother. If we haven't heard from Judith and Dexter by noon tomorrow we'll call them," conceded Daniel.

"I hope you'll call me too," Joe Racina suggested. "I have to get to work early, weekdays. I leave the house around six. It seems too bad you should have to keep on hanging around, waiting first for one daughter and then the other to telephone. But I suppose it can't be helped, if this is important too. After you do hear though, you might like to come in town again and meet me somewhere. I've got a pretty heavy day tomorrow, but I can always squeeze in one thing more, if it's important."

"After I've heard from my daughter, Judith, I aim to go to the House Office Building and have a talk with Horace Vaughn," Daniel stated, in his matter-of-fact voice.

"Well, that might be a good idea—or it mightn't. Of course after twelve the House is in session anyway. You probably wouldn't be able to get hold of him, in his office. He'll be on and off the Floor and pretty busy. It might be better to wait until the next day. But of course early in the morning he's generally at a committee meeting."

"He must be in his office sometime in the course of the twenty-four hours," Daniel said, speaking more grimly. "I aim to see him. If he isn't in when I get to his office, I'll sit there and wait for him. There isn't any rule that makes it unlawful to sit around and wait for a congressman to turn up, is there?"

"If there were, the jails would be even fuller than they are now," Joe replied, with a grin. "Well, you know how to reach me now. Let me hear from you."

The next day was even more hectic than he had foreseen; the creation of the War Labor Board and the appointment of Nelson as War Production Chief complicated a schedule already crowded by the necessity of covering other major events. His own harassment and preoccupation effectually banished the problems of his protégés temporarily from his mind. But when he returned to Alexandria that evening, and found them both stationed in the small sitting room back of the blue parlor, their kindly faces clouded with anxiety, his heart smote him.

"Why, hello there!" he said, trying to speak with special cheerfulness. "Don't tell me you still haven't heard anything?"

"Not a thing," Serena said in a troubled voice. "We called up our home at noon today, like we agreed we would, if we hadn't got any word by then. But the operator said N—one five two three didn't answer. She offered to report to us again in twenty minutes. She's called us every twenty minutes all the afternoon. But she keeps right on saying the same thing. We asked her to call the Abbott Homestead too—we thought Judith and Dexter might have gone there for some reason. But that phone's been disconnected. I guess Dexter must have given the order before he moved up to our house. It would have been natural he should, so as to save expense. We just can't make out what could have happened on Farman Hill and we can't help but be worried. Of course Daniel hasn't gone in to see Mr. Vaughn. He's stayed right here with me."

"Of course," Joe agreed. "Well, as I said before, there's plenty of time for that visit anyway. It's better to do things one by one. Isn't there anyone else in your home town you could telephone to?"

"Yes, but we don't want to cause talk. You see, Mr. Racina, we expected Dexter and Judith were going to be married yesterday afternoon. Just a quiet ceremony at the parsonage. We were disappointed not to give them a nice wedding in our own home, but it seemed best they should get married right away, as long as we had to come to Jenness. Dexter had the license and the ring, and he was aiming to tell Judith how it was when he went to fetch her at Brents', where she'd been nursing—a scarlet fever case. We hadn't wanted to say much to her about Jenness over the telephone, because of course there's nothing but party lines where we live, and when time hangs kind of heavy on people's hands they're apt to listen in. There wasn't time to write much of a letter either. But Dexter and Judith had been keeping company ever since they were children and there wasn't a reason in the world why they shouldn't become man and wife. I don't see——"

In spite of herself, Serena's lip was trembling. Joe redoubled his efforts at cheerfulness.

"Why of course there isn't anything the matter! They just forgot, that's all. What do you expect in a b. and g.?"

"They wouldn't forget, not Dexter and Judith. You don't know them as well as I do. Daniel's kept saying too they might have forgotten, but I know different."

"Well, I'm sure we'll be finding out who's right any moment now, and then Mr. Farman and I'll be saying 'I told you so' . . . Hasn't Jenness got in touch with you either?"

"No. I guess we may as well tell you straight out. We parted from Jenness in anger last night. We haven't any use for that lawyer she's called in, and when Daniel showed it, pretty plain, arguing with him, she and her father had words. She was real stubborn, and saucy too. I don't wonder Daniel's put out with her. I'm afraid it isn't going to be easy making the next move though."

"But I understood you to say you were going to retain the lawyer for Jenness. If you are, you'll certainly have the right to choose him too. I knew you wouldn't like Loper. You better get rid of him right away. I don't think you'd have much trouble, if you told him you wouldn't pay him."

"Well now, that's an idea." Daniel replied, brightening. "And maybe I could see this man you recommended— Waldo, was that his name?—and lay the matter before him too. Not as if it was settled we'd hire him, you understand, but just to talk things over."

"I'll fix it up the first thing in the morning. But now I'm going to fix you a drink. You need a good stiff one before supper."

Daniel disposed of his drink, but Serena choked over hers and neither of them did justice to the excellent and abundant supper that followed. It made them feel conspicuous to rise and hasten to the telephone twice in the course of the leisurely meal, especially since both times they were obliged to return to their places without results. Mrs. Porterfield remained graciously unperturbed in the face of these excursions; but they thought they detected mingled condescension and curiosity on the part of their fellow guests. The first call interrupted a story Miss Lily was telling about the notable heroism her grandfather had displayed at the Battle of Bull Run; the second interrupted a story that Captain Buchanan was telling about the exigencies of his China duty. When they went back to the small sitting room after supper, they found that Miss Blodgett and Miss Waggaman were planning to use it for a backgammon game, and that they would be very much in the way if they stayed there. Torn between their reluctance to seem intrusive and their determination to solve the mystery which baffled them, they were trying to confer with each other in muffled tones as to their best course, when the telephone rang again, without a lapse of twenty minutes, and they sprang simultaneously to answer it.

"This isn't our house answering, it's Boston calling us," Serena, who as usual had succeeded in reaching the telephone first, turned to say. "Now, Daniel, what do you suppose . . . Miss Judith Farman calling Mr. or Mrs. Daniel Farman? Yes, this is Mrs. Farman. Why, Judith, whatever . . . You didn't go home at all? You went out for a sleigh ride with Dexter and then went back to Brents' and stayed all night and started for Boston this morning? But, Judith, I don't understand! Where's Dexter? What's happened to him? We've tried and tried to get you on Farman Hill, we've worried and worried . . ."

"You let me talk to her," Daniel said, taking the re-

ceiver from her. He spoke firmly and acted decisively, as
he had on the evening when Jerome telephoned from Fort
Bragg. This he knew was another crisis, even graver than
that one. He must spare his wife all that he could, but first
he must find out the exact nature of the new calamity that
was threatening them. His glance, usually so kindly, fell
rebukingly on Miss Blodgett and Miss Waggaman, who
were still lingering stubbornly in the small sitting room,
loath to relinquish their hold on it; he made it evident that
this was a private message, that it must be respected as
such. "Hello, Judith, this is Dad," he went on, when Miss
Blodgett and Miss Waggaman had reluctantly withdrawn.
"I want you should tell me exactly what's happened.
What's that? Yes, I can hear you all right, but just the
same I don't follow you . . . I think that's pretty hard on
Dexter, Judith, I think you owe something to him too. Yes,
I'll *tell* your mother, but that's not saying I can *explain* to
her. You haven't explained to me yet, not so as I can follow you. Of course we'll be glad to see you, that is, if
we're still here. I don't know but one of us ought to strike
right out for home, so's to be with Dexter. You don't seem
to think anything of his being on Farman Hill, all by himself, in the dead of winter, with two farms to look after.
Your mother and I'll have to study some, what's best to
do. Yes, we'll look for your letter and Dexter's too in the
morning. Good-bye, Judith. I hope you're not ever going to
regret this course you've taken."

He replaced the receiver slowly, and for a moment sat
bowed and motionless, as if all his strength was spent and
he did not know how to gather his forces together again.
Then, still slowly, he dragged himself to his feet and put
his arm around his wife. "You come upstairs with me,
Mother," he said gently. "I'll tell you what Judith said to
me when we get to our own room, and we'll study on what
we ought to do, like I told her. We'll study and we'll take
it to the Lord in prayer. I've got faith to believe everything's going to be all right yet. You've got to have faith
too." He turned to Miss Blodgett and Miss Waggaman,
who had withdrawn no further than the blue parlor, and
addressed himself to them with dignity. "You can have

the sitting room to yourself now, for your backgammon game," he said, and his voice was calm and courteous as he spoke. "My wife and I won't be needing the telephone any more this evening."

He managed to go on speaking calmly, and his voice deepened into tenderness while he talked to his wife. He had led her quietly up the long stairs, and closing the door of their bedroom after them, had drawn up one of the big rockers for her, and seated himself in another, opposite her. He held her hands in one of his, stroking them with the other.

"Listen, Mother," he said, "I know how bad you feel, but you must try to bear up. We can't change Judith's mind for her, you know that. We never could, even when she was a little girl. She's made up her mind her country needs her more than Dexter does, and she's left him to be an army nurse. It's done and it can't be undone. She's going to take her physical examination tomorrow morning, and then she's going to wait and find out where she'll be sent. She hasn't the least idea, but she said maybe she'd be passing through Washington herself before long, and if she did, that would give her a chance to talk to us better than she could over the telephone. She's written us, airmail special, and she says she was sure Dexter had too. We ought to have both letters in the morning. She's gone to stay with that sister of Dr. Barnes who lives in Winchester, Mrs. George Hurlburt. Mrs. Hurlburt's daughter Laura has just signed up with the Red Cross too, and the two girls are going in to Boston together to be examined. She's with friends, Mother, in a good Christian home. That's something to be thankful for."

"It doesn't help Dexter any, just because Judith's with friends in a good Christian home. He's all alone on Farman Hill, like you said yourself."

"I'm not forgetting Dexter, any more than you are. This'll be a hard blow to him—well, I guess it's what you'd have to call a body blow. But he'll get to his feet again, even if we find he hasn't been able to take it standing.

Dexter has got good stuff in him. It's more than good stuff, it's strong stuff. He'll come through all right in the end."

"Yes, Daniel, I know he will. But the end's a long way off. What's he going to do in the meanwhile?"

"He'll have to decide that for himself, same as Judith's decided for herself. We can't plan his life for him, any more than we can plan hers. But maybe we can ease the way for him, so it won't be quite so hard. It'll be hard enough though. I know that just as well as you do, Mother."

He rose, giving her hand a final pat, and began to pace slowly up and down the room. Serena, crying more quietly now, did not speak to him. She knew that he was deep in thought, "studying" as he himself had cogently put it, what was best to do.

"I think if you don't mind, I'll slip up to Joe Racina's room for a few minutes and tell him what's happened in a general way," he said at last. "Joe didn't hang around like those nosey women—he doesn't even know yet we've had our call. I'd kind of like to tell him. Then in the morning, after we get our letters, you and I can have another talk."

Daniel was guided to Joe's quarters by the sound of the typewriter. He found the newspaperman smoking furiously, sitting at a huge littered desk in a room so fantastically untidy that it gave the effect of never having been put to rights. Since the rest of Mrs. Porterfield's house was kept in a condition of decorous order, Daniel gathered that Joe, rather than his hostess, was responsible for the state of this apartment. Even in his overburdened state, the thought crossed Daniel's mind that it was just as well Serena had not come with him. She never would have rested again until she had given this room a good thorough cleaning, not to mention pressing Joe's clothes and admonishing him not to drop ashes around at random. He also knew that such action on her part would have brought the fledgling friendship with Joe to an abrupt end.

Joe had shouted "Come in!" almost angrily when Daniel knocked on the door, but as this opened, and he discovered the identity of his caller, his scowl softened to a smile, and he jumped up and came quickly forward, scattering ashes as he came.

"Why, come in, Mr. Farman," he said cordially. "I'm sorry I yelled at you like that. I wouldn't have, if I'd known who it was. I've had to put up some defenses though. If I hadn't, some of my fellow guests here would be running in for cozy little chats every evening. And evening's the time I have to keep to work for Joe Racina. I'm still hoping that some day I'll knock off a piece, after hours, that the *Post* will jump at. Not that it's ever given me any encouragement . . . Won't you sit down? That is, if you can find a chair that hasn't anything on it. Here, take this one. I hope you've come to tell me you've heard from the bride and groom."

"I don't want to disturb you while you're working. I realize it's imposing on you, coming in like this. Well, I have heard from my daughter Judith. But she didn't marry my neighbor Dexter Abbott after all. She decided to be an Army nurse instead. She'd decided before we left home, only we didn't know it. She's got as far as Boston already. She didn't telephone until she got there, because she didn't want everyone in the village minding her business for her. We haven't heard from Dexter yet. Judith said we'd probably hear from him as well as her, in the morning. But no matter what he's written I think either my wife or I ought to go back to the country. I don't know which of us he needs most, or which Jenness needs most. We've got to decide what to do."

"I should think it might. It's a darned shame, Mr. Farman, that you've had this additional bad news."

"Well, it does seem as if we'd had our share lately, but I guess everyone feels that way sometimes. There's another thing, though. There's never been a mortgage on my farm any more'n there's ever been a scandal in my family. And now to have both of 'em to come together like this———"

"Do you mean to tell me you mortgaged your farm to Dexter Abbott so that you could help out Jenness?"

"There wasn't time to execute a formal mortgage. But it amounts to the same thing. My neighbor Dexter Abbott gave me all the money he had to spare and I gave him my note for it. He as good as owns Farman Hill, the way things stand now. And Farmans have owned the same house, and cultivated the same land, for nearly two hundred years. We've had to work hard and we've had to scrimp considerable, but we've always managed to hang on."

"Well, that's the way it was with my people—scrimping but still managing to hang on, I mean. Not that we've owned the same land for two hundred years, or any land to speak of, anytime, as far back as I know anything about the family. My grandmother was a Mexican refugee who escaped over the border in charge of an aged aunt, with all their worldly possessions in one huge unwieldy trunk— how they ever dragged it around with them is a mystery, but they did, and for years afterwards, they kept on diving into it for practically everything they needed. My grandfather had been trained for a bookkeeper, in Italy, and came over to visit some relatives while he was waiting to go into the army. Then he found out he'd been turned down, on account of the same damn asthma that's kept me out of the scrap now. So he decided to stay on where he was. But he didn't know enough English to do bookkeeping here, and he became a baker instead. He and my grandmother married on twelve-fifty a week and brought up five children on it. Brought 'em up damn well, too."

"You don't say," Daniel observed with unfeigned interest, regarding Joe with fresh respect. The details of Joe's journalistic career had not made much impression on him, but this was different. Momentarily he almost forgot the troubles and problems which had impelled him to seek Joe out while he "studied" on them. "And they didn't so much as own their home?"

"Lord, no! They rented half a double-barreled shot-gun house on Erato Street for ten dollars a month. Later on the landlord raised the rent to twelve dollars and that was a blow. But they managed. There was one bad interlude, though. The traditional rich relative, who had hotel interests in Texas City, persuaded my grandfather to take his savings and——"

"Take his *savings!*"

"Yeah. He'd saved about five hundred dollars at this point, and the rich relative persuaded him it would be a wise move if he invested it in hotel stock, taking over the bakery end of the business. So we all went, bag and baggage, to Texas City. But it was a mighty poor move. Presently my grandfather's five hundred bucks were blown in with everything else that had been wasted before we got there. So my brothers and sister and I were sent out to peddle cakes and pies at the army camp near there. The officers were darn nice about letting us come. Just said it would have to be the same time every day, so the men would be sure to have enough clothes on when my little sister showed up. We made enough money peddling pies to take us back to New Orleans and it was years and years before any of us ever left it again. We wore copper-toed shoes and had our hair cut wholesale, at a reduction. But we contributed twenty-five cents a month towards our tuition at the parochial school where we went, and there was always enough money for us to go to a show once a week—the shows cost five cents in those days. And we always had old-fashioneds to drink every Sunday. My grandfather used to go to the bar that was catty-cornered from our house and bring the mixed liquors back with him in a pitcher. He and my grandmother each had a glassful, and the rest of us smaller drinks in proportion, according to age—the current two-year-old would get about a teaspoonful, and the current baby about a drop, for example, but no one was left out. They were damn good drinks, too. You better let me mix you one of the same brand right now."

Joe shoved back his papers, and shambling over to his makeshift bar, began expert preparations. Daniel continued to watch him with respect and attention.

"Here you are," Joe said, handing him a glass. "Let's have a toast to those old boys and girls, in your family and mine too, who managed to hang on even when they did scrimp considerable. You can't make me believe you won't do it too, just because your daughters have gone back on you. Especially as you've still got your son."

"Yes, we've still got our son. But you know Jerome's

in active service, attached to the Air Corps. He's liable to go overseas anytime. Not but what we want he should go. It's his duty and we want he should do it. Just the same we can't help but think if something did happen there wouldn't be any Farmans on the Hill any more. Not unless our new daughter-in-law should be in the family way before Jerome's sent off. And we haven't heard anything yet. Of course there hasn't hardly been time."

"Then don't give up hope about that either. Probably you'll have half a dozen little Farmans to help you carry on before you get through. I never knew a St. Cyr yet that didn't have a lot of children. There was one who had five in three years. Fact. So I think your daughter-in-law will too. The women in that family are all small and fragile looking—you'd think a breath of air would blow them away. But they've had big bouncing babies, one right after another, and run their own plantation at the same time, when their husbands weren't there to do it —as they haven't been, more than half the time. The South's been through a good many wars before this one."

Joe lighted another cigarette and his eyes strayed, involuntarily, from his visitor to the typescript on his machine. The story he was writing was about one of those wars, and he had seemed to be there, in the midst of it, when the knock came on his door. Now the vision was shattered; it would take him a long time to pick up fragments and piece them together again. He could not help wondering, with desperation, whether the time would ever come when he could write in peace. If he could, he might still do a good job, one the *Post* would applaud and print and pay for and that some big publisher like Harpers would later promote in book form. But when he saw that Daniel had noticed his errant glance he was instantly sorry he had betrayed himself, and impatiently brushed a few ashes from his unpressed suit as a sign of contrition. The man was so lost and friendless, and yet so self-controlled and estimable that he evoked respect as well as sympathy, and Joe disclaimed any desire to get back to work when his visitor rose. Daniel shook his head.

"I know better," he said trying to summon a smile. "I

ought not to have come in the first place. I ought to have
realized that writers are kind of like farmers in one respect;
their work isn't ever done. But it's done me good to talk
to you even if we haven't got very far. I don't know as
we could have tonight anyway. We've got to wait and see
what the morning brings forth. And I'm real pleased about
what you've told me about the St. Cyrs. I shouldn't be
surprised but what you're right and that we might have
some good news pretty soon.

"If you shouldn't, don't be in too much of a hurry to
blame it on your daughter-in-law. The mails are pretty
irregular, and some letters never reach their destination.
Why during the Christmas rush, one of the carriers got so
discouraged that he dumped a whole sack full in a sewer!
Fact. Made a darned good story. We carried it in a box."

Daniel failed to appreciate the news value of such conduct. The peculiar methods of the Alexandria carriers, as
these might affect him personally, added to his worries
during the night. But apparently the functionaries in question had recovered from the strain of the Christmas rush,
for the next delivery took place according to schedule and
the good news for which he had been hoping came through
the next morning in the same mail with the bad. Serena,
looking at the three postmarks, decided to open the letter
from Fort Bragg first, less because she anticipated the
tidings it might contain than because she dreaded the tidings in the others. As she slit the envelope, and drew out
the monogrammed sheets from inside, she wondered momentarily how Alix could afford such expensive stationery;
note paper like this, heavy and creamy and gold-engraved
must, she was sure, cost money. But almost instantly she
forgot the medium Alix had used in the contents of the
letter.

> *"Dear Mother Farman"*—she read——
>
> *Jerome thinks you and Father Farman would like
> to know that I believe I am going to have a baby.
> If I have not counted wrong or anything, it will be
> born around the first of September. We are both very*

pleased about it. Jerome is sure it will be a boy. He says, up to now, the first Farman baby has always been a boy, and I should be very sorry to break the record, so I hope I shall not disappoint him.

Sometime soon perhaps you will let me know if you have any baby clothes put away. If you have, and will let me, I should like to use them. Mine have all been saved for me by my Aunt Odilisse and of course I shall use those too. I am writing to her asking her to send them to me as I have not seen them in a long time, and have forgotten just what there is. When I know what you can lend me and look over what I I have myself, I will know what to make new. I want to make the baby's clothes myself, that is, whatever is still needed. Probably Jerome has told you that I am very fond of sewing, and by and by, when I cannot go out so much, the needlework will pass the time while I'm waiting for the baby.

I am very well, so there is nothing at all for you to worry about and of course I am very happy, not only about the baby but about everything. We are very comfortable in our apartment, which is beginning to seem very homelike, and Jerome says I am getting to be a very good cook, but I think that is partly because he is having things to eat that are new to him, collards and grits, for instance, and he enjoys them on account of the novelty. Last night I made him a fried apple pie and that was new to him too.

Jerome is now Assistant Supply Officer and I am very proud that he is doing so well in his work and getting recognition for it which he deserves. He has been coaching the Air Corps football team in his spare time, and thinks it is the snappiest one on the Post. He says it takes at least three men to stop his quarterback. His team has played with others at Fort Bragg and once with the Marines. He has enjoyed these games very much, but the parachute attack at Pope Field which took place during the Carolina maneuvers was even more exciting. Two of Jerome's classmates from Norwich University came down for these maneuvers and we had great fun entertaining them at dinner and showing them around. They acted as line men at one of the football games. But something very sad happened at maneuvers too: one of the jumpers was killed. He broke his neck when he landed. He was swinging as he came down and landed when he was at the top of his arc so he couldn't land on his feet. It sobered us all very much to think of the death of this young man, and made us doubly thankful that we were so well and so happy.

Of course Jerome does not have liberty as often now as he did before Pearl Harbor. Sometimes he does not get home more than twice a week, but I always know he is coming, so I do not mind waiting for him. He says if I had only married him sooner, he could have driven back and forth every day except when he was O. D., and that we could have gone to polo matches in Pinehurst and done all sorts of things like that. This is absurd because I married him ten days after I met him so how could I have done it any sooner? I do not miss going to polo matches, because I have seen hundreds of those already, and I do many things with him that I never did before. This includes having dinner with him at the Officers' Club the evenings he cannot come home and going with him to dances and cocktail parties on the Post. (Of course I shall be careful after this not to dance long enough to get overtired.) But we also have good times by ourselves in Raeford. On Saturday evenings we nearly always go to the movies, and later stroll along the main street watching the Negroes, who are still more or less of a curiosity to Jerome, and whom I enjoy too because they have always been part of my life. They practically take over the shopping district on Saturday nights and play and dance and sing in the streets. It is all very carefree and gay and sometimes rather uproarious, but harmlessly so.

One Saturday evening when we were coming home, just after we turned from the paved street to the sandy road where we live, we heard a pitiful little whine,

*and there lying beside some bushes was a poor little
sick hound. We could not be so heartless as to leave
him out there in the cold, so we carried him home and
fed him and bathed him. He curled up at the foot of
our bed and went to sleep and the next morning he
was better. I reckon he was mostly hungry and lone-
some. Pretty soon he began following me around with
large grateful eyes while I did my housework and
licked my hand whenever I took him more milk, and
presently I realized I had become attached to him too
and that we belonged to each other. This is the first
time I have ever had a dog of my very own. He loves
the fireplaces and would burn himself by lying too
close to them if I didn't watch him carefully, but
otherwise he is very intelligent and learns quickly.
Jerome has named him* Lucky *and I think that is a
good name for him. It was lucky for him that we
found him, but it was lucky for us too. He is great
company to me while Jerome is away.*

*There are about thirty Army families in Raeford,
so we have formed an Officers' Wives' Club, and
usually we meet for luncheon and bridge once a week.
(That is our 'day off' for the rest of the time we sew
and knit for the Red Cross.) We have a calling committee in this Club, and when a new Army family arrives, we call and also make immediate arrangements
to extend hospitality. So there are no lonely periods
for newcomers. Of course I have never had one anyway, for I have always had the thought of Jerome
even when he was not with me, and now I have Lucky
too and presently I shall have the baby. I don't see
how any girl could ask for more than that, and I thank
the Holy Mother every night for the great bounties
with which I have been blessed.*

*There may be a move at any time now, for the
men are all getting winter flying equipment and it is
too hot here for furlined clothing. Jerome says it is
quite likely that he will get ordered off on short notice,
and like everyone else is always waiting for something
to break. But no one knows what is going to happen*

*or when so I do not think about the future very much,
except as it concerns the baby. Instead I think about
the perfect present and that is enough.*

    Respectfully and affectionately, your daughter,
                Alix St. Cyr de Farman

"Well!" Serena said, looking up from the letter. "Well!
Listen to this, Daniel." She read it over again, aloud this
time, and when she had finished, she handed it to him,
so that he could read it himself. But she could not wait
for him to do so, with characteristic deliberation, before
she began to comment. "In September. I've always thought
September was the best month to have a baby, unless it
was May. It's neither too hot nor too cold then. I'm real
pleased to think she'll have comfortable weather for her
confinement. I must go through the baby clothes we have
up in the attic the first thing after we get home. Then
she'll know just what she can count on. I could help her
with her sewing some too. I'm glad she wants to use
Jerome's baby clothes and make some herself. Aren't you,
Daniel?"

"Yes," he said, with his eyes still on the letter. "Yes,
I am glad. And I'm pleased with this news too—with the
news itself and with the way it's written. This is a fine letter
from Alix, Mother."

"It's sort of taken the edge off Judith's, getting this other
first, hasn't it? Well, I suppose I ought to open her letter
next."

"I suppose you ought to. It never makes hard things
any easier to put 'em off, Mother."

"This is for both of us. I'll read it aloud right away."

Dear Mom and Dad——
    *I could tell from your voices when I talked to you
just now that you thought I'd done wrong to leave
Dexter. It was hard for me to do it, honestly it was.
I've always loved him and I know I'll never love another man. I still hope we can get married, after the
War's over. I tried to tell him so, but he wouldn't
listen. He kept saying if I didn't marry him right then*

and there, I never would. He didn't act like himself at all. He acted half crazy. So there was nothing to do but stop arguing with him, after awhile. We had a dreadful drive. He wouldn't even kiss me good-bye. He said we weren't engaged any more. Of course I consider that we are and when he calms down a little he will too. I intend to write him regularly just as if nothing had happened.

As soon as I know anything definite about my plans I'll let you know. I'm not a bit worried over the result of my physical. I'm a little tired after the strain of the Brent case and a little upset about Dexter, thought I keep telling myself I ought not to be. But otherwise I never felt better. I hope I get a hard post somewhere overseas. But probably it'll be just my luck not to, just because I want it so much.

I think Jenness is a disgrace to the family. I've absolutely no patience left with her. I wish you wouldn't bother with her any more. She's made her own bed and she ought to lie in it without having anyone smooth things out for her. Do go home, where you'll be happier yourselves and where you can look after Dexter until I get back.

> *Your loving daughter*
> *Judith*

"Well," said Serena again. "Well." But her tone was very different from the one in which she had spoken after reading the letter from Alix. "Do you think that's fine letter too, Daniel?"

"No," he said drily. "I don't think it's fine at all. Judith told me—and she said she told Dexter—that she was throwing him over because she was consecrated to her work, like a nun or a missionary. I don't doubt but what she thought she was sincere when she said it. Judith isn't a liar like Jenness, I'll say that for her. But just the same that letter doesn't sound to me like one a consecrated woman would write. It sounds to me like a letter from a girl who wants to have her cake and eat it too. I've known for a long time, whether she realized it or not, that Judith was fed up with Farman, that she was itching to get away from there, just like her brother and sister. She was fed up with Dexter too—he'd become just another habit to her. But she'd said so often she didn't want to get away and that of course she was going to marry Dexter, that she had to find some kind of an excuse to save her face. The War's given it to her. She isn't joining up with the army because she's got a sense of consecration —mind you, I'm not saying there's not lots of girls who do. But Judith's joining up so's she can put on a fancier uniform, and travel around this country anyways, and maybe around the world, and meet up with a parcel of soldiers, good, bad and indifferent, who'll give her more of a thrill, in one way or another, than one steady, lame farmer. Not but what she'll be glad to come back to the farmer after she's had her fling, if nothing better breaks for her in the meantime."

"Daniel, that's an awful way to talk about your own daughter."

"I'm just facing facts again, Mother. And I said Judith didn't realize all this herself. I said I knew she was convinced she was making a great sacrifice."

Daniel picked up the letter, and studied it himself for a few minutes. "There's just one part of this that makes sense to me," he said. "That's the part where it says we better stop thinking so much about Jenness and think a little more about Dexter. I told Joe Racina as much, half an hour ago. One of us ought to go back to the country, Mother. Only I can't decide which one it ought to be."

"Maybe Dexter's letter will give us an idea."

"That's right. We haven't read Dexter's letter yet. And I dread to, Mother, just as much as you do. But we better get it over."

"Dear Mr. and Mrs. Farman"—they read, holding the letter between them——

By the time you get this, you'll have heard from Judith. That is, I hope you will have. She promised me she'd telephone you from Boston. But after all, her promises don't amount to much.

Perhaps somebody else could have persuaded her to change her mind. I couldn't. I tried every appeal and argument I could think of, and none of them did any good. Now that I look back on it, I think I would have known long ago that she didn't intend to marry me, if I'd only faced the issue. And I couldn't. Or at any rate I didn't. So probably I deserved what was coming to me. A man doesn't get anywhere if he won't face facts.

But I'm facing them now, and I've told Judith she'll have to face them too, at least as far as I'm concerned. I've told her that I don't look on her, any longer, as my future wife. If she didn't love me enough to marry me today, she doesn't love me enough to marry me later on, from my point of view. I know now that her love isn't good enough for me. I don't want a half-hearted kind of love. I want everything or nothing.

Of course I don't know how this decision of mine will affect your own feelings for me. I shan't blame you if it turns you against me, for after all, Judith is your daughter, and it would be natural if you could see her side better than mine. But no matter how you feel, I want you to know that you can count on me to stand by, if you want me to, as long as Jenness needs you. I'm not going to stay on in this house alone. I'm going back to my own. But of course I'll have to get the water turned on again, and the fires started up, and that'll take me two or three days. I guess everyone in the village will think I've gone crazy, opening it up, when I've just closed it, but I can't stay here. I'll sleep in my office in the barn until I can move back into the house. But of course I'll come here every day to look after the stock, and I'll keep the fires going in the house too, and see that the pipes don't freeze. I'll do everything I can to safeguard the place, just as I would have if I'd been your son-in-law by this time. I hope you'll still want me for your friend, because I've always been fonder of you, next to Judith, than anyone in the world. But even

if it meant forfeiting your friendship, I'd still have to
say I'll never marry Judith now.

Your neighbor,
Dexter Abbott.

They looked at each other above the scribbled sheets.
Then Serena, the mild, the quiet, the peace-loving, rose
resolutely.

"I'm going home," she said. "I'm going right away. You
can stay and look after Jenness if you're a mind to, but
I guess I still know where I'm needed most, even if my
daughter Judith doesn't. While I'm packing, you telephone
and find out what's the first train I can catch. And go ask
Mr. Racina if he will drive me into the depot and help
me fight my way through it again. While you're about
it, you better send a telegram to Dexter. Tell him to stay
right where he is till I get home. Tell him he isn't going
to stay in that house, or his own either, alone, with no
one to do for him, not while I've got breath left in my
body. Tell him I said so."

CHAPTER 14

THE DISTRICT Court House was a majestic gray building
with wide-spreading wings and classic columns, but it was
located in a forlorn neighborhood and flanked by a scrubby
little park. Most of the battered benches scattered about
this park were occupied by dispirited-looking loafers, or
by slatternly Negro women airing their charges in dilapidated baby carriages. Daniel Farman looked about for
some moments before he discovered an empty place.
When he finally succeeded in doing so, he took it wearily
and sat staring disconsolately into space, finding, in the
unseasonable warmth of the day, his only element of
comfort.

He was waiting, it seemed to him endlessly, for Jenness to emerge from the Grand Jury Hearing Room. The Grand Jury did not meet in the stately old District Court House, but in the modernistic Municipal Court Building, diagonally across the green from this. He had gone there with her and had stayed there with her, until she was called out, in the Witnesses' Waiting Room, which was stuffy and smoky and crowded with dirty and disreputable-looking characters, whose appearance was strangely at variance with the polished marble and shining metal which characterized the Municipal Court Building, and which reminded Daniel in a vague general way of the décor in the apartment house where Jenness had chosen to live. Afterwards he had gone with her as far as the entrance of the Jury Room. But there he had been told by the bailiff in attendance—a gaunt, dyspeptic-looking man with a disfiguring birthmark—that he could not go any further. No one had suggested that he might like to watch for her close by, and indeed he had no desire, either to return to the stuffy Waiting Room, or to linger in the corridor among loungers who looked at him even dirtier and more disreputable than the characters he had seen crowding the Witnesses' Room. He had kissed her good-bye with some embarrassment, partly because he had never embraced any member of his family in public before, and partly because Jenness herself accepted the caress impatiently rather than clingingly. She actually seemed eager to be rid of him. So he had said, rather lamely, that he would wait for her in the little park he had noticed on the further side of the Court House, and had turned sadly away. A moment later he had turned back again, impelled to urge her once more to tell the truth and shame the devil. But she had already disappeared, and with a fresh pang of anxiety because there was no chance for that last word which might have saved her before she had been swallowed from sight, he went out into the street.

He had reached Jenness' apartment early that morning—considerably earlier than she had told him to come, as a matter of fact—but Loper was already there when he arrived. The lawyer was in his blandest mood. Nothing

in his manner indicted that he bore Daniel the slightest
ill will because of the anger with which the New Englander had denounced him on the occasion of their first en-
counter or the strain which had marked their subsequent
meetings. He made no reference to Daniel's efforts to dis-
suade his daughter from retaining him as her counsel, and
to entrust her case to another lawyer. But there was an
adamant quality in his amiability. He seemed bent on
preventing Daniel from talking to his daughter privately.
His very presence in Jenness' apartment so early in the
morning indicated that he had made it a point to get
there first; and when Jenness went into the kitchenette
with the coffee tray, and into the bedroom to put on her
wraps, he rose, in each instance, and walked over to the
open door, chatting with her while she performed her
small household tasks and put the last touches on her
make-up. When Daniel suggested getting a taxi, Mr. Loper
was voluble in his protests. Of course they were all going
downtown together in his car, he said. He had it right
outside. Surely a man who was careful about expenditures,
like Mr. Farman, would not waste money on taxi fare!
He did not stress the satirical note in his smooth speech,
but it was there, and it silenced Daniel. Then he did not
let them out at the entrance of the Municipal Court Building and go to park his car without them, but drove straight
to the parking lot on the further side of the scrubby little
green. Afterwards he walked back to the Municipal Court
Building with them and stayed with them until he had
ushered them into the Witnesses' Waiting Room, where,
of course, they could not talk privately. And all the time
he had conversed with them unctuously on a variety of
irrelevant topics, so that without brusquely interrupting
him, it would not have been possible for Daniel to get in
a word edgewise.

The lawyer had left them at last, saying he had some
business with the Clerk of the Criminal Court but that
he would be back later on; and now that he was actually
gone, Daniel was almost sorry he had not broken in on
him anyway. As Daniel sat on the park bench, thinking
things over, he realized there had been several points at

which he might have done so, trying at least to create a last-minute diversion. But it was too late now. He had not made a single dent in the lawyer's armor and he had been equally unsuccessful in his efforts to deal with Vaughn. The day after Serena's departure, the Congressman had personally telephoned him, and courteously invited him to dinner at eight that evening, "so that he might have the pleasure of meeting his invaluable young secretary's father and talking with him on matter of mutual interest." The invitation had put new heart into Daniel. But he had hardly set foot inside the Vaughn establishment when he realized that this courtesy had been a mockery. He knew, in a vague way, that Vaughn was wealthy; but he had been totally unprepared for the ostentatious scale on which his daughter's employer lived. The grilled door of the English basement house was opened for him by a servant in livery, and another such servant asked his name, in a supercilious tone of voice, before announcing him at the entrance of the formidable drawing room. He noticed that both of these men looked at him covertly but condescendingly, and he gathered, even before he saw the elegance of Mr. Vaughn's superbly tailored dinner jacket and resplendent white linen that the neat black suit, which he had long kept so carefully to wear only on the most momentous occasions, was the cause of these glances. He was regretful, on account of Jenness, that his appearance did not do him—and her—more credit; and his discomfiture was further increased when he discovered that he and his daughter were not the only guests, as he had assumed that they would be. Mr. Loper was also there, wearing dinner clothes as immaculate as Horace Vaughn's, though producing a less sophisticated effect, partly because he had departed from conservative custom to the extent of wearing a maroon tie and maroon studs. He was accompanied by Mrs. Loper, a wren-like little woman, surprisingly clothed in a gaudy dress covered with sequins; and the sixth member of the party was an exotic personage addressed as Marquesa, whose identity was not at all clear to Daniel, and whose command of the English language seemed to be extremely limited, though she had

certain arts and graces generally conceded to be international in character. Mr. Vaughn greeted Daniel very cordially, and presented him to the ladies with a graceful
compliment to each, adding that no introductions were
necessary as far as Mr. Loper and Mr. Farman were concerned, since they were friends already—a statement which
Daniel accepted rather grimly. At this point the two men
in livery began to circulate with cocktails and hors
d'oeuvres, and soon thereafter dinner was announced.

This consisted of six courses, most of them unfamiliar
to Daniel, and the menu, rising in a silver standard before
him, did not help him, as it was written, with many dashes
and flourishes, in French. But he could not help wondering, as he progressed from caviar to green turtle soup and
from lobster thermidor to guinea hen, what sort of a meal
Horace Vaughn would call formal, if this was a casual
one. The table was overlaid with delicate lace and decorated with crystal and camellias. In addition to the flat
silver, it was further adroned with various objects which
elicited exclamations of admiration from the Marquesa,
who condescended to address Daniel long enough to ask
him if he had ever seen more bea-u-ti-ful maté cups, and
whether he could de-ter-mine the age of the muffineers
by the hallmarks. A different wine accompanied each
course, and the goblets in which these beverages were
served were encrusted with gold. There was considerable
discussion as to the relative merits of the different vintages,
and strange words like *clos* and *château* were sagely
bandied back and forth. Daniel, seated between Mrs.
Loper and the Marquesa, soon abandoned his first feeble
efforts at conversation, though he eventually made the
startling discovery, from a remark Mrs. Loper inadvertently let fall, that the Marquesa was a native of Kansas City,
and that the English language was therefore not an altogether alien tongue to her, in spite of the coy hesitation
and pronounced accent with which she spoke.

Daniel had expected, after he discovered the presence
of other guests, that the war would be the main topic;
but it was not even mentioned, and neither were any national affairs of world-shaking significance. Instead, there

was a discussion of social events, many of them trivial or
tawdry, to his way of thinking, and a dissection of prominent persons, all of whom seemed to have emerged from
disreputable backgrounds which they strove, more or less
successfully, to keep secret, or to be engaged in illicit or
abnormal love affairs, which were allegedly the talk of
everyone about town "in the know." The Marquesa's
English improved with the description of each victim
whom she tore to pieces, and her accounts of their misdemeanors were as graphic as they were lively. The others
followed the pace she set, and if he had been mute for no
other reason, Daniel would have been silenced by shame
long before they reached the *baba au rhum*. It was horrible
for him to hear his daughter casually using words which
he would not have supposed she even knew, in sly and
sordid reference to persons with whom she apparently associated as a matter of course.

When the dreadful dinner was at last over, Daniel had
a brief moment of hopefulness, for Horace Vaughn said
that the ladies would leave them "in the good old English
custom," and that the men would linger over their cigars
in the dining room. But there was no privacy either. The
two liveried men-servants still continued to hover around,
replacing filled ash trays and replenishing enmpty glasses;
Daniel was conscious every minute of their intrusive presence, and he did not feel at all sure they were not deliberately eavesdropping. Meantime Horace Vaughn emanated
the goodwill which a man of means and importance, well-
lodged, well-dressed and well-nourished, is pleased to
show, in his more expansive moments, to those who are
indisputably his inferiors. The expression of his handsome
face, now slightly flushed with wine, was agreeable; his
manner was gracious and relaxed; he leaned back in his
high leather chair and easily introduced the subject which
Daniel had been trying so long and so futilely to broach.

"I'm very sorry to hear from Jenness, Mr. Farman, that
you've been anxious on her account. I want to take this
occasion to tell you there's not the slightest reason why
you should be. I'm sure you'll agree with me when you

really understand the circumstances. Would you allow me
to explain them to you?"

"I'll listen, while you talk," Daniel replied.

"Thank you, Mr. Farman. Now here is the situation in
a nut-shell: "There are, unfortunately, a large number of
men in this country—and quite a few women also—who
have long been determined to involve this country in
foreign wars. They have now succeeded. Some of these
persons are members of the press; others are members
of the House and Senate; others are still more prominently
placed. No matter how differently they may be situated,
however, they have been united in their efforts to discredit
all those who have not agreed with them. Does this seem
fair to you?"

"No. Not where that's really the way of it. Everyone's
got a right to his own opinion. This as a free country. And
of course there are plenty of sincere isolationists. Most of
the voters in my own town wanted to keep America out
of the War and they're a pretty honest lot of men. No
one in his senses would say any different."

"Exactly, Mr. Farman, exactly. But unfortunately, in
these frenzied times, a great many persons seem to have
lost their senses. An effort of the sort I have attempted
to describe has been made to discredit me, personally. It
does not trouble me because I am above such baseless
slander and eventually it will die down and come to nothing. But in the meantime, your chaming and capable and
of course wholly blameless daughter has been temporarily
involved in it and this I regret. So I have taken steps to
prevent the annoyance to you and to her from continuing.
I have retained Mr. Loper here to safeguard her interests.
I must ask you to accept my word there is no one here
in Washington better suited to do this than he is."

"I don't doubt but what Mr. Loper's an able man. But
he and I don't see eye to eye in this matter. We've found
that out already."

"Then if you'll forgive me for saying so, I really think
you should be guided by Mr. Loper's judgment. I know
that you are an able man yourself, Mr. Farman, able and

upright. But Mr. Loper's in a better position to know the facts and——"

"He may be in a better position to know what's taken place in your office. I'm not acquainted with this mystery of the mail bags I've heard some muttering about. But he's not in a better position than I am to know what's happened on Farman Hill. He tries to tell me my daughter Jenness never saw Max Lentz, never in her whole life, and I know different."

"Now, now, Mr. Farman," interposed Mr. Loper, raising a deprecatory hand.

"Mr. Loper, you will excuse me, but I think I have the floor at this moment, as we say in the House. Mr. Farman, I'm sure none of us wants to spoil this pleasant evening by an altercation. Mr. Loper and Jenness have both told me already that some heated words were exchanged in her apartment last Sunday. Now I hoped that by asking you here to dinner together tonight I might act as a peacemaker. I rather pride myself on my menage, even though this is more like a bachelor's establishment, since my mother has so far been prevented from joining me in Washington this winter. I am hoping that she will be coming down a little later, but in the meantime, I am doing my best to run my household without her guiding hand, and on the whole the results are fairly satisfactory, I think. You'd say that was a creditable dinner we had tonight, wouldn't you? And this Courvoisier's really almost a collector's item. Unfortunately I haven't much of it left, and I can't get any more with this unfortunate war going on. But I felt that on this occasion—the influence of good food and good wine do so much to temper a man's moods, don't you think so, Mr. Farman? And now that you and Mr. Loper have met as fellow guests at my table——"

"I didn't know we were to meet as fellow guests at your table. I understand you and I were to talk together in private, as man to man. I'll be plain with you and tell you I wouldn't have come, if that hadn't been my understanding. And I'll be still plainer and tell you that's the way I want to talk to you and propose to talk to you."

Daniel had risen from his chair. Despite his best efforts,

his anger was mounting again. It had never wholly cooled, as far as Loper was concerned, and now Vaughn was kindling it anew. Besides, something else had disturbed him. While Vaughn was talking, he had seen Jenness move from the chair in which she was sitting, at the further end of the drawing room, to one close to the French door leading into the dining room, which stood ajar. The move had taken place when Vaughn had begun to talk about his mother, and Daniel felt sure Vaughn had observed it too. He had noticed a flicker of annoyance on the Congressman's urbane face. It disappeared almost as quickly as it had come. But it had been there. Daniel could have sworn that he had seen it.

"I'm sorry you haven't enjoyed the evening, Mr. Farman," Horace Vaughn was saying. He still spoke evenly, but a slight chill had crept into his voice, and his easy manner had stiffened slightly too. "I went to considerable trouble to put myself at your disposal and to extend hospitality to you. In fact, I cancelled another engagement, one of considerable importance, in order to clear my calendar. I'm afraid I can't suggest a time for another meeting before the Grand Jury considers the case we're interested in. I'm dining out every other night this week. And in the daytime I have to rush right from one committee meeting to another. I have to visit the government departments. I have to receive a countless stream of importunate constituents, not to mention a large number of official callers. And after all, I do have to spend some time on the floor of the House. That duty may seem incidental to you but I assure you I take it very seriously. If you will think that over, Mr. Farman, and consider how integral a part of my life such service is, I am sure you will hesitate to impugn my loyalty to the United States Government."

"I have hesitated to impugn it. But I've got my own opinion just the same. And I do say my daughter knows Max Lentz and that I won't retain a lawyer for her who says different."

"I have already retained Mr. Loper for Jenness, Mr. Farman. That is my contribution to the cause of justice.

One that I am delighted to make. One that I sincerely hope you will not complicate with her appearance before the Grand Jury so close at hand."

"You mean you've gone to work and hired him, right over my head, without giving me a chance to have my say?"

"It's not customary to speak of 'hiring' a lawyer, Mr. Farman, any more than it is customary to speak of hiring a doctor or a clergyman. At least it is not customary among persons of my acquaintance. But if you are asking whether I have assumed the financial responsibility for Mr. Loper's services, I am happy to answer in the affirmative. Jenness has told me that the consideration of cost is a serious one with you. Please dismiss it from your mind. Surely it is a very slight return for her faithful service to me if I perform this slight service for her. After all, she would never have become implicated in this unpleasantness my enemies have stirred up if she had not been in my employ. I feel responsible for her. I never shirk my responsibilities, Mr. Farman, especially when they are so unmistakably indicated. I really do not think there is anything more to be said on the subject. Shall we join the ladies?"

There *was* nothing more to be said on the subject, nothing, at least, that Daniel could say. He had been outwitted at every turn. Jenness herself had accepted Loper. Vaughn was paying him. Joe Racina's shrewd observation that money would make a difference had become valueless under the arrangement which he was powerless to prevent. The hearing before the Grand Jury was imminent. There was no time and there were no means for Daniel Farman to do anything.

His sombre thoughts reverted to all this while he sat on the park bench waiting for Jenness to rejoin him and wishing there were something he could do to while away the weary moments. Then he saw that a flock of dusty pigeons was hovering expectantly around him, and after he had observed that neither the unshaven loafers on the bench at his left nor the shapeless slattern on the bench at his right had paid any attention to them, he walked across to the uninviting cafeteria which he had noticed in passing and asked the blonde behind the counter if he could buy half a loaf of bread. She gave him the same look of curiosity mingled with condescension which he had noticed on the faces of so many of the persons to whom he spoke in Washington.

"We don't sell bread by the loaf or the half loaf. We sell it by the slice or the sandwich at lunchtime and suppertime. But for breakfast we got buns and biscuits and toast and——"

"I didn't want it for myself. I wanted it for some pigeons in the park. I thought if I could buy me loaf bread it would crumb easier."

"Well, I'll ask the manager. No one ever come in here before, asking for half a loaf of bread to feed pigeons."

The blonde disappeared into concealed regions of the dingy establishment, and Daniel, sniffing the steam from a big metal container, was tempted to buy himself some coffee and a bun to go with it, and sit in the cafeteria for a while before he went back to the park bench. But he did now know just how long Jenness would be detained before the Grand Jury; after all, it might be a very short time. So when the blonde came back, and said he could have the bread, but he would have to take a whole loaf, and pay fifteen cents for it, he bought it and returned to the park. The pigeons were still clustered about the place where he had left them, as if confident of his largesse. He turned back the wrapper from the loaf, crumbled part of the bread and began to feed them. . . .

If Serena could only have remained with him, his stay in Washington would not have been such an ordeal, he reflected, scattering the crumbs. Not but what he had thought all along she had done right to go back to the country, and now that he had heard from her, he was more firmly than ever convinced of this. She had succeeded in forestalling Dexter's actual departure from Farman Hill, she wrote, and he had not been rude to her or unkind. He was faithful about all the chores too; he never went down to his own place till they were done. But he had shut up like a clam. He did not talk about Judith, or about anything, as far as that went. Sometimes he did not say a single word, straight through a meal; and when he did speak, it was only about the weather, or the like of that. And he was out a lot nights. He had asked her, when she first got there, if she was afraid to stay alone, and when she said no, he had taken her at her word, and gone off. He hadn't said where he was going or what he was doing and she hadn't liked to ask. But she was bothered some, because of course Dexter had never been one to run around nights. And she wasn't sure, but she thought, once or twice, she had smelled liquor on his breath, and that wasn't like Dexter either. She wasn't saying he might not have taken it medicinally. It was still terribly cold, way below zero, and she didn't know how much of a fire he could keep up in the little office he had in his barn, when he wasn't there to watch over it. That was another thing she didn't like to ask, because she didn't know how much he was in his office. She sort of suspected it wasn't much. . . .

Daniel was not surprised at this information. He had already written Serena, reminding her he had predicted, before she left Alexandria, that something of this sort might happen, and now that it had, he hoped she wouldn't take it too hard. There wasn't hardly a man who didn't stray from the straight and narrow path sooner or later, and sometimes the closer and longer he kept to it the further off he got when he did go. Daniel thought she was doing just right not to say anything to Dexter. After all what was there she could say? And Dexter would snap out of it after a while. Meantime he was glad she was there to stand by . . .

He had been sincere when he wrote this; but it did not alter the fact that he and Serena had never before been separated, in all the years of their marriage, and that was acutely and endlessly conscious of her absence. The feeling went deeper than merely missing her; he felt crippled as well as forsaken. They had always leaned on each other, and he felt no shame in his share of this interdependence. It was an attribute of essential unity such

as a man ought to have with his wife. That was the sort
of unity Dexter had craved with Judith and of which she
had robbed him at the eleventh hour. Daniel could understand that the bereavement which in an older man would
cause desolation would in a younger man bring about
mutiny.

Judith herself had written again, in a cocksure manner.
Her physical examination, and the red tape surrounding
it, had consumed a whole day. But she had not minded
that. She had been so intrigued with everything about the
Boston Army Base that she was glad of a chance to spend
considerable time there. She had been advised, almost immediately afterwards, that she had passed all right—of
course she had been certain all along that she would—
and now she had been told to report at the Morris Field
Air Base Hospital in ten days. Of course that would have
given her plenty of time to go home, and she would have,
if things had only been different there. In fact it would
have given her time for a honeymoon. She had written
Dexter again, renewing the proposition she had made
him before, that is, offering to marry him if he would
not put any impediments in the way of her departure.
But he had not even answered, though as it was they would
have had more time together than she had supposed when
she made her initial suggestion. Well, that was that. She
had now taken the Army Oath, and she had had a sort
of trembly feeling while she was being sworn in. She had
thought for a moment she was going to cry, but she had
managed to keep her voice steady, and afterwards she
had felt fine, probably much better than she would have
right after promising to love, honor and obey a stubborn,
unreasonable man like Dexter. She was glad she was going
to North Carolina. Of course she would have preferred
an overseas assignment but this might come later. Laura
Hurlburt was assigned to Morris Field too, which was
grand. Laura wanted to take her car South and had been
given permission to do this and provided with an allowance for traveling expenses. They were taking three other
girls with them and it would be a real lark. They would
be passing right through Washington and were planning

to spend at least twenty-four hours there, so she would be seeing him pretty soon. She had told Laura about Mr. Porterfield's and Laura agreed with her that would be a fine place to stay if Mrs. Porterfield could wedge them in. How about it?

Mrs. Porterfield had been helpful: there was the old attic playroom, she said, where the toys she and her sisters had cherished as children were still enshrined. She had never put it at the disposal of guests, partly because the memories it held were so sacred to her, and partly because there was no running water on that floor; but she would be glad to accommodate Mr. Farman's daughter and her friends by turning it into a makeshift dormitory for a night or two. She could always locate a few extra cots; and doubtless the young ladies would not always find running water in the field hospitals where they might soon be serving. She added that she was sure she could count on them not to disturb her childhood treasures; she had safeguarded them for a long while, and she was still hoping that sometime another little girl would enjoy them. Daniel gravely gave her the assurance she sought; he knew just how Mrs. Porterfield felt, he said. There was an old doll at Farman Hill that his wife set great store by; he remembered hearing her caution Jenness and Judith, over and over again, when they were children, not to tamper with it. Judith had always been careful about such things anyway, though Jenness had been more destructive; and now that she was grown up, she wasn't much better than she had been when she was a little girl; she was always throwing things around and breaking things. If it were Jenness, he'd feel different about telling Mrs. Porterfield everything would be all right; but of course there was no question of having Jenness stay with Mrs. Porterfield . . .

He wished, overwhelmingly, that there were. If he had only had her with him, under that time-honored and substantial rooftree, he might have had more influence with her. He was so ill at ease in her incongruous modernistic apartment that he could never settle down there for a good talk; and of course the atmosphere of Horace Vaughn's house had been still more alien to him. He could not

understand how any man, even a pompous specimen like
the Congressman, could be at ease in such stiff surroundings; and the vagrant speculation crossed his mind that
perhaps the house actually belonged to Vaughn's mother,
whom he had heard from Joe was a great heiress, and
that it might represent her tastes and standards rather
than his. Daniel assumed that the portrait which hung over
the drawing room mantel must be Mrs. Vaughn, and now
that he thought of it, he could understand how a woman
who looked like that would have a house of this type. She
was represented in full but prudish evening dress, with a
tiara resting on her neatly frizzed hair and a dog collar
encircling her thin throat. No suggestion of spontaneous
merriment enlivened the set smile on her thin lips, and her
pose was stilted, the rigidity of the figure suggesting the
careful corseting of another era. Yes, Daniel could see now
that such a woman would possess, by preference, an English basement house with iron gratings and keep men-
servants dressed in livery to wait on her and ornament
her table with strange silver objects. Vaughn's scale and
manner of living were actually his mother's, and the fact
that he had kept them unchanged when she was not with
him indicated how completely he was under her domina-
tion.

He was still thinking about Horace Vaughn in connection with Jenness when Jenness herself came across the
scrubby little park. A pang of relief shot through him as he
saw her advancing towards him with her customary swiftness and assurance, moving with grace and holding her
shining head high. Of course there had not been the slightest reason for supposing that her lovely free motion would
be in any way impeded, and yet Daniel had been obsessed
by an irrational dread that it might be. She lifted one
smartly gloved hand a little and waved it in sprightly
salute. Then she began talking to him, vivaciously, before
she had finished crossing the strip of concrete which still
separated them.

"Well, that's over!" she said gaily. "It wasn't bad at all.
I told you all along there was nothing to get hot and
bothered about. A lot of old sobersides sat around a big

rectangular table with a polished black top and asked me a few silly questions in a very mournful way. When I'd answered them, they said I could go. That was all there was to it."

"You didn't have to take an oath?"

"Oh, yes, I had to take an oath."

"And then you lied under oath?"

Jenness sat down on the bench and slid her arm through his. She still seemed gay and carefree, and the gesture was spontaneous and affectionate. But there was a warning note in her voice when she answered.

"If you don't stop talking on me like that, Daddy, I'm going to lose my temper one of these days. I'm getting pretty tired of being called a liar. And I don't like your attitude towards my friends at all. Here Horace gave up a whole evening entertaining you in his beautiful house, and you acted like a perfect bear all the time. You hardly said a civil word to anyone, not even to the Marquesa, who's such an out and out charmer—why any party she goes to is just *made!* And you seem to have a permanent chip on your shoulder as far as poor Mr. Loper's concerned. I don't see how he can keep on being so pleasant to you, when you go out of your way to insult him all the time."

"I'm not going out of my way to insult him. But I don't like him and I don't trust him. The same goes for the Marquesa. I don't know much about such women, but if she isn't what used to be called an adventuress then my name isn't Daniel Farman. I don't believe Horace Vaughn would have had her to dinner, if his mother had been at home, or the Lopers, or you either, Jenness. Free and easy ways like you all have, and loose talk like I heard don't fit in with that kind of a house."

"Well, his mother isn't at home. And she's a silly old snob. No one who has what it takes ever wanted to go to her stupid parties. They were just a list of names."

"Maybe. But I guess they were respectable names. And I guess from what little I know Mrs. Vaughn's a truth-telling woman, whatever else she is. I can't say as much for her son. I don't think Horace Vaughn's got the truth in

him. Nor you either, Jenness, anymore. I wouldn't call you
a liar if you weren't one. It isn't a name any man would
choose to call his own daughter."

"You're not sitting there trying to think up some still
worse ones you can call me, are you, Daddy?"

"No," Daniel said painfully. "Of course I'm not." A dull
red flush spread slowly over his face and neck, adding to
his discomfiture; but he persisted. "Just the same, Jenness,
I don't quite like the way the men I've met since I came to
Washington speak about you. I don't mean they've said
anything against you—naturally they wouldn't do that, to
a girl's father. But the photographer at the depot—Marcy
Heath, was that his name?—said something about all the
photographers in town knowing you as well as they knew
that cheap movie actress; and then Joe Racina said you'd
been out with him several times on Mr. Waldo's boat, and
he didn't say a word about any other womenfolk being
along. Of course, maybe they were, the Marquesa and such
like, but I haven't heard a word about your having any
nice female friends or seen you with a single settled-look-
ing woman. And even Peter MacDonald, when he was at
the farm, threw out some hints about your living high, wide
and fancy, as if there was more to it than met the eye."

"Peter!" Jenness exclaimed angrily. "Well, of course, if
you're going to listen to a sorehead like that, or cheap-
skates and Dagoes like Marcy Heath and Joe Racina——"

"They're all respectable men, no matter what kind of
names you call 'em," Daniel retorted. "A sight more respectable, to my way of thinking, than Horace Vaughn. I
won't deny but what it's worried me, Jenness, having you
so friendly with him, especially since you told Dexter he
was keeping company with a girl in his home town, too.
It's one thing for you to work in his office, and it's another
for you to be out nights with him all the time and going
to his house when his mother's away from home. It would
cause talk if a single girl did a thing like that in Farman."

"But Washington isn't Farman, Daddy, thank goodness!
Everyone knows that Horace isn't in love with Marion
Pierce, that she's just what's called a 'suitable match,'
whose family's been friendly with the Vaughns for years.

Her mother and Horace's hatched this thing up when Marion and Horace were both in their cradles, or he was, anyway. I think she's actually older than he is. He doesn't want to break with her altogether when his mother's heart's giving her so much trouble. He's just waiting for a good chance to do it, though. In the meantime, everyone expects him to step out a little, in a harmless way."

"I hope it is harmless, Jenness, and I hope no one thinks any different about it." Daniel paused for a moment, waiting for Jenness to protest that of course no one did. But she said nothing, and he went on, "It seems to me there's something fishy about all this somewhere. I can't help feeling if you lie to me about one thing, you might about another. And I can't help feeling either that there's something back of these lies you're telling about Lentz. You can't have any reason to shield him. But I wouldn't be surprised but what you were shielding someone else. Did you tell the Grand Jury you didn't know Lentz, Jenness?"

"I'm not suppose to talk about what happened before the Grand Jury. It's always a secret session. I thought you knew that much about legal procedure."

"Well, I do. I'm not trying to make you talk out of turn and of course I don't want you should betray any confidences. But I am uneasy, Jenness. If you can't tell me what happened before the Grand Jury, you might just——"

"I can't talk to you about anything now. Here comes Mr. Loper. He must have finished his business with the Clerk of the Criminal Court. He said if he did he'd join us here. You wouldn't want me to discuss anything private before him, would you, feeling about him the way you do?"

Daniel had been so absorbed with Jenness that he had not noticed the approach of the lawyer. Mr. Loper was now advancing across the same strip of concrete which she had so recently traversed, and like hers, his manner was nonchalant and sprightly.

"Well now!" he said buoyantly. "Well now! Everything's going very nicely and I hope you and Jenness will be my guests at luncheon today, Mr. Farman. There's a little coffee house just across the street that's not bad, not bad at all. It isn't much to look at, but the food's very good. If you're as hungry as I am, perhaps we better eat right there, instead of taking time to go uptown. But if there's any place you'd prefer—The Occidental, perhaps? Or the Pall Mall Room at the Raleigh? Or Olmstead's? The only trouble is that these popular restaurants are so crowded nowadays it's almost impossible to get service. But it's just as you say. I want you to have an enjoyable lunch."

"I think it would be fun to have lunch down here, don't you, Daddy? And then I could get back to the office more quickly, too, than if we went downtown. I've been away from it all the morning and really—of course, Horace wouldn't say a word, not if I stayed away all day, he's so considerate. But——"

"I beg pardon, Sir. Could I speak to you a minute?"

Another man had come up behind Mr. Loper while Jenness was talking. As the lawyer turned, swinging slightly to one side, Daniel saw it was the same bailiff who had stopped him at the entrance to the Grand Jury Hearing Room. He recognized the man readily by the purple birthmark which ran half-way across his gaunt face. Daniel had felt from the beginning that there was something sinister about his manner as well as his disfigurement; now the bailiff's reappearance stirred his dormant but persistent sense of foreboding. Loper, however, answered with no evident apprehension.

"Certainly, Sims. What is it?"

The bailiff lowered his voice discreetly before he answered. But Daniel caught the words just the same.

"The District Attorney would like to speak to you for a minute, Sir. He asked me to see if I could find you. He was under the impression you hadn't left the Court House yet. But I remembered hearing the young lady's father say, when he left her at the Grand Jury Room, that he'd wait for her in the park. So I thought you might have joined them."

"Well, I'm glad to find you're so observant, Sims, and that you have such good sense. Tell the D. A. I'll be right along." Loper turned back to Daniel and Jenness, still smiling. "I'm afraid we'll have to suppress the pangs of hunger a little longer," he said. "Something's evidently come up. But why don't you walk over to the coffee shop and wait for me there? I don't imagine I'll be more than a minute. Anyway, I'll join you as soon as I can."

He lifted his hat jauntily and followed the bailiff, his step quickening a little as he walked. Daniel looked at his daughter.

"Did you hear what that man said, Jenness?"

"No, I couldn't, he muttered so. Did you?"

"Yes. He said the District Attorney wanted to see Mr. Loper."

"Did he say what about?"

"No. Leastwise, I don't think he did."

"Well—you're not going to start worrying about *that* now?"

"I'm worrying about the whole setup, Jenness. I can't help it."

"I'm not. I'm not worrying about a thing. But I think that bailiff's a repulsive-looking creature. I wish he'd keep out of sight—Let's push along to the coffee shop, shall we? I'm starving to death."

She opened her smart handbag, produced her lipstick and compact, and repaired her makeup in a leisurely way. Then slipping her arm through her father's she rose and sauntered towards the coffee shop. Though her progress was slower and less sprightly than when she had rejoined him, this seemed to be only because she was trying to kill time, not because her high spirits were affected in any way. She hoped they could have a cocktail while they were waiting for Mr. Loper, she said; and when she found they could not, because the coffee shop had no license, she sulked for a moment and remarked that it was too bad they had not gone downtown after all; she was in the mood for a dry Martini. But she took out her cigarette case and began to smoke, and presently she was chatting merrily and inconsequentially again. When Mr. Loper entered the shop and came up to the table where she and her father were waiting, she looked up at him with one of her archest smiles.

"Now!" she said. "Let's eat, shall we? I'm just about ready to gnaw nails."

"All right," Mr. Loper answered. "Yes, I suppose we may as well have lunch. But we'll have to make it snappy. It seems we've got to go back to the Municipal Court House. I don't know just what's caused it, Jenness, but there's been an unexpected development. The D. A.'s arranged with the Court for a hearing this afternoon in the presence of the Grand Jury."

"A hearing! What kind of a hearing? What for?"

"I'm afraid I can't soften the legal language any. You may as well have it straight, Jenness, now as later. It's 'to advise the Court of the condition that did obtain this morning and to ask the Court to direct the witness back to the Grand Jury Room for the purpose of affording an opportunity to correct her testimony and tell her story truthfully and in full.'"

CHAPTER 15

BECAUSE OF overcrowding, some of the Justices of the District Court had their courtrooms in the Municipal Court Building. Justice Emmons, before whom Jenness had been summoned, was one of these. Daniel, going heavy-hearted to the building for the second time in one day, tried to take what comfort he could in the fact that on this occasion no sinister figure could bar him from his daughter's presence in her hour of need. The scheduled hearing was not a secret session like the one which had taken place that morning; it was to be held in open court. He was free to go in and stay as long as the hearing lasted.

But so, he realized with a fresh pang, as he went into the courtroom, was anyone else who cared to. It was a handsome chamber, sheathed in panelled walnut, which, like the rest of the building, gave the impression of polish

that was too high and styling that was too modernistic. It
seemed to Daniel significant, in a malign way, that his
daughter, who had deliberately chosen to live in surroundings of this type, should now be called to answer, in
similar surroundings, for her way of living; and he was
also struck, for the second time, by the contrast between
the shabby crowd and its elegant environment. The courtroom was nearly filled already, and Daniel felt, as he
looked around him, that there was not a single person in
attendance whose presence was uplifting, or even reassuring. He was amazed to see that the men sitting next him, on
his right, were the unshaven derelicts whom he had noticed
on the nearest park bench that morning. On his left was a
decrepit old gentleman, leaning heavily on a gold-headed
cane, who mumbled incessantly to himself. In front of him,
on either side, was a miscellaneous group: two stolid middle-aged women, evidently bosom friends, holding greasy
paper bags which kept rustling and which looked as if
they might contain food; a younger woman with an avid
face, impatiently hushing a querulous child whom she had
dragged up the aisle after her and who was whooping at
intervals; an older woman whose grandmotherly appearance somehow lacked authenticity; a few soldiers and
sailors, who had apparently drifted in off the street because
time in the capital was hanging heavy on their hands,
despite the blandishments of the pert little pieces who accompanied them; some drab creatures of both sexes, suggesting retired clerks who likewise had nothing special to
do; two or three individuals of somewhat more prosperous
appearance, who were evidently lawyers waiting for their
own cases to come up. . . . Daniel remembered reading,
during his college course, that when the Queens of France
were in travail, the populace had been free to surge
through their lying-in chambers and witness the struggles
of the women whose regality had not saved them from
being brought to bed like the least and the worst of the
fishwives and prostitutes who revelled in their anguish. It
seemed to him that his daughter was now being submitted
to an indignity hardly less harrowing. He could no longer
think of her guilt. He could think only of her ordeal.

Making a desperate effort to calm himself, he glanced beyond the depressing specimens of humanity who surrounded him. On the right of the bench, the members of the Grand Jury were already assembling. There were several women among them, he noticed, and two or three Negroes. One of the women had on large horn-rimmed spectacles and wore her mouse-colored hair in a straight bang. Another was plump and purposeful; Daniel could visualize her organizing church suppers and presiding over committee meetings at women's clubs. The outstanding Negro might have been a preacher; he was very neatly dressed and his grizzled hair formed a sort of halo for his dark earnest face. But for the most part these jurors seemed to Daniel nondescript; they might all have been his fellow passengers on any Alexandria bus, unremarkable and unprovocative. Daniel speculated on the trades they might have left to do jury service, without reaching any conclusion. He would have recognized a farmer, he thought, or a small town banker. He was not sure, but he thought he would also have recognized a fond father whose daughter was in dire straits; there was a kinship about such men, rich or poor, that gave them a common look. He could not discover any such man among the members of the Grand Jury.

At the left of the bench he was amazed to see Joe Racina leaning against the railing, smoking one of his inevitable cigarettes, but for once with the air of doing it somewhat surreptitiously, as if he were prepared to extinguish it at any moment. Behind Joe were seated Herb Parrish, the "pudgy geezer" from the *Enterprise* whom Joe had pointed out to Daniel the night they dined at O'Donnell's; Luke Weatherby, the wire-service man who lived at Mrs. Porterfield's; and a number of other journalists whose identity was unknown to Daniel. When Joe saw Daniel looking at him, he nodded, and skirting the railing dividing the lawyers' table from the spectators, came and put his arm over the back of Daniel's seat.

"Well, here we are," he said with forced cheerfulness. "I was afraid we would be. I take it Jenness stuck to her story."

"How did you find out about the hearing so quickly? We only knew it ourselves an hour ago."

"Oh, a call on it came through right away to the press room. And that was relayed P. D. Q. to the city room. An hour's loads of time, as newspapers count time. Why Peter got ready to go round the world in an hour! Fact."

"I wish Peter was here," Daniel said wistfully. "I know I've said that to you before, Joe. But I've got it on my mind."

"I guess Jenness wishes so now. Too bad she didn't realize a little sooner that he might mean something to her. If she'd given him the idea in time, perhaps he'd have stayed. . . . Well, I'm glad to see this hearing was called before Loper had a chance to doll her up anyway. Remember what I said about Mae West? As it is, Jenness looks just right."

Daniel followed Joe's gaze. Jenness was sitting in one of the two straightbacked chairs by the lawyers' table beyond the railing, erectly, yet gracefully, her white-gloved hands folded in her lap, her beautiful face for once expressionless. She presented a convincing picture of good breeding, perfect grooming, and noncommittal composure. A momentary thrill of pride pierced her father's misery as he looked at her.

"So far, so good," Joe observed, rightly interpreting the look. "Well, I must be getting back to my own stall. It's almost two-thirty—the justice will be in any minute. I see the clerks are all here and the lawyers. Have you noticed Keith Bryant, the prosecuting attorney? That tall gaunt-looking man at Loper's right? The Lincoln type, but better looking and more class. I like him myself. So does most of the gang. Well, so long. I'll be seeing you after the hearing, if you're with Jenness. Or even if you're not. FAIR DE-FENDANT'S FATHER STRICKEN is a story in itself. I'm afraid you're not going to like that part of it much. God, of course you'll hate it all like hell. I'm sorry."

He was gone, the only friend on whom Daniel could count, and from now on even his support would, to a certain degree, be withdrawn. Henceforth, he would be primarily a reporter and secondarily a friend; there would

be no help for this, no matter how much Daniel needed
him, no matter how much Joe himself might wish in his
heart of hearts that it could be otherwise. Daniel tried to
stop thinking about this impending change in Joe's attitude
and to concentrate instead on the prosecuting attorney. It
was true there was something Lincolnesque about Keith
Bryant; but this was more a matter of structure and
strength than of feature and carriage. In a rugged way he
was a fine-looking man, and he moved his great body and
long limbs without awkwardness. Daniel felt that here at
last was a lawyer whom he could respect, and he wished,
desperately, that Bryant might have been his daughter's
counsel instead of being the prosecuting attorney. But
then, a man like Bryant would never have let Jenness come
to this pass. He would have forced her to tell the truth. . . .

"Everybody please rise."

The order came abruptly. Apparently the mumbling old
man beside Daniel, who sat nursing his gold-headed cane,
was either deaf or demented, for he did not move until
one of the sailors rapped him on the shoulder, while the
pert little piece hanging on the sailor's arm giggled audibly.
The querulous child also sat mulishly in her seat, quiet for
the first time, until her mother yanked her forcibly to her
feet, wringing from her a yowl of pain which ended in a
terrific whoop. One of the stolid matrons dropped her
paper bag and bent over creakingly to retrieve it. But
everyone else in the motley gathering, even the unshaven
park-benchers, had come quickly to attention. The sinister-
looking bailiff was entering the courtroom, clearing the
way as he preceded a spare little figure with a white goatee,
whose robes looked too large for him. As this unimpressive
personage passed to the bench, the bailiff stepped forward
and began to declaim, in a sing-song so rapid that the
separate words were hardly intelligible.

"All-persons-having-business-before-the-Honorable-Jus-
tice-of-the-District-Court-of-the-United-States-for-the-Dis-
trict-of-Columbia-now-holding-Criminal-Court-will-draw-
nigh-and-give-their-attention. This-Court-is-now-in-ses-
sion. God-save-the-United-States-of-America-and-this-
Honorable-Court. Be-seated-and-come-to-order."

With the exception of the mumbling old man, who did not hear this demand, and the refractory child, who would not heed it, the assembly seated itself with as much suddenness as if its component parts had been jerked down with a string. With equal suddenness, so it seemed to Daniel, Keith Bryant had risen again and began to address the Court.

"If Your Honor please, I am the Special Assistant to the Attorney General and as such I have been conducting an investigation by this Grand Jury which is present here in Court into certain alleged violations by one Max Lentz and others of the so-called Foreign Agent Registration Act, which requires that all persons who are engaged in certain activities on behalf of a foreign principal must file a statement with the Secretary of State making full disclosure of their activities, the name of their principal and the amount of money received by them. In the course of the investigation and within the past several days, the Court caused a subpoena duces tecum to be served upon Miss Jenness Farman, directing her to produce before the Grand Jury certain material referred to in the subpoena. I will read the subpoena, if I may, Sir, in part 'and bring with you the eight mail sacks of materials obtained by a House of Representatives truck from the residence of Chester Slade and delivered to the House Office Building.' "

So that was it! This matter of the "mysterious mail bags," as Jenness had called them, was the primary concern of the prosecuting attorney. Finding a grain of comfort in the thought that when he knew what they were and why they were important he could grapple better with the problem they presented, Daniel leaned forward, intent on catching every word that Keith Bryant uttered.

"Miss Farman has appeared," he was saying. "She is here now. She has been sworn and examined before the Grand Jury. I should like at this time, with the Court's permission, to summarize in just a few sentences her testimony; and then, with the Court's permission, I should like to have the Grand Jury stenographer read Miss Farman's answer to questions which were directed to her."

There was a slight stir in the courtroom. Daniel had the impression that others were straining, like himself, to catch every word, and a hot wave of resentment swept over him for the impertinence and curiosity this represented on the part of the strangers. The tapping of the old man's cane, which went on constantly, and the intermittent whooping of the refractory child ceased to be a minor irritation and became a major annoyance.

"The facts very briefly are these: Miss Farman, who is employed in the House Office Building, on November 28th of last year, gave instructions to the House mail truck to go to the residence of Chester Slade and pick up certain material there. Shortly after the truck returned, certain mail sacks were brought to the office where she is employed. She says she made no attempt to determine whether they were addressed to her or what they contained, and she says she ordered the messenger to take them away. She says that subsequently she has gone to the storeroom to which Congressman Vaughn has access and has seen there a number of mail sacks. She was directed to produce here, these sacks. She says that since being served with this subpoena she has made no effort to obey. With the Court's permission I should like to ask the stenographer to read the record of what has transpired up to now in the Grand Jury Room."

Keith Bryant paused, resting his hands without awkwardness on the table before him and looking respectfully towards the bench. The elderly little justice turned to Jenness, who had also risen, and who stood facing him with the same composure she had shown from the beginning.

"Is there any question, Miss Farman," he said in a gentle voice, "that the prosecuting attorney has correctly stated what took place? There is no necessity of reading the record if his statement is correct."

Daniel waited breathlessly for Jenness to answer. But he waited only a minute. Her reply came unhesitatingly and clearly, almost insolently.

"Well, Your Honor, I suppose I should have gone and seen the driver, but as Mr. Vaughn had already called up the Postmaster——"

Justice Emmons interrupted her. "That is not what I am asking you. I am asking you whether there is any dispute, as far as you're concerned, as to whether or not the prosecuting attorney has correctly stated what took place."

"I haven't got the mail sacks, so I couldn't produce them," Jenness said, still more insolently.

"Apparently you do not understand me. What I want to know now is whether his statement is a true statement."

This time there was an instant's hesitation before Jenness replied. But when she did so, she gave the effect of defiance, almost as if she had tossed back her head, though this had actually not happened.

"Yes, it is correct, Sir."

"Very well, that is all I want to know for the present. Now I want you to tell me next why it was that when the mail sacks came to you, you did not preserve them?"

The Justice had sounded relieved when he began, as if he hoped her acknowledgment that the prosecuting attorney had made a true statement marked a turning point in his interrogation of this bold, troublesome girl. But his relief, if it existed, was short-lived. Jenness went on with increasing assurance.

"I didn't see any reason why I should try to preserve them. I sent for one sack and there was a whole truckload of them; it was almost impossible to squeeze that many through the door. Some important constituents of Mr. Vaughn's were in the office and I was talking with them. I was very busy. I didn't have time to look through a great mound of mail sacks. Besides, I was told they weren't all for Mr. Vaughn. So I said to the driver that I just wanted him to leave the sack that had Mr. Vaughn's speeches in it. After all, that was the only one I had ordered the truck to go for."

"Your statement is what now, Counsel?"

The Justice had turned back to Bryant, asking his question with the air of suppressing a sigh. The prosecuting attorney answered with some brusqueness above the sound of the tapping cane.

"My statement, Sir, is that although these sacks were brought to the office where this girl is employed on December 10th and were thereafter taken away at her direction, and although she admits that she subsequently went to Congressman Vaughn's storeroom and saw there a number of mail sacks lying on the floor, she made no effort to obey the mandate of the Grand Jury."

"What have you to say about that?" Justice Emmons inquired of Jenness.

"I thought if the Grand Jury wanted evidence, they would send for it."

Daniel was appalled at the increasing boldness with which Jenness was speaking. He did not see how it could fail to bring forth a rebuke. But the Justice proceeded in the same gentle way as before.

"Now as I understand it, the gist of the situation at present is this: there are certain mail sacks in Mr. Vaughn's storeroom——"

"No, outside Mr. Vaughn's storeroom."

"May I explain to the Court?" Keith Bryant asked, interrupting Jenness quickly. "There is a large storeroom which is under lock and key, accessible only to members of the House, and as a matter of fact, there are vaults in that room. The mail sacks in question are within that storage room. When Miss Farman says they are not in Mr. Vaughn's storage room, she means they are not in the vault in this room. But they are within the large storage room, to which I believe some eight or ten Congressmen have access, and they are under lock and key, Sir."

"Let me ask you this, Mr. Prosecuting Attorney. Miss Farman may be in a tremendously embarrassing position. Supposing Congressman Vaughn told her not to meddle with that stuff?"

"That's it," Daniel said to himself. "Now you're hitting the nail on the head, Mr. Justice. I knew she was shielding someone. I knew she was shielding Vaughn . . ."

"Those were my orders," Jenness was saying, proudly rather than defiantly this time.

"She says that now, but she has not made any statement to the Grand Jury to that effect."

"Well, the fact is that this girl is placed in a pretty bad spot if her superior has told her not to interfere with that stuff. I don't know that she has any authority to move it with out Congressman Vaughn's authorization."

"She has the authorization of the Grand Jury subpoena which calls upon her to produce the mail sacks which were delivered to her office." Bryant turned from the Justice to Jenness and put a direct question to her.

"If you are permitted to leave here now, will you get those eight sacks?"

"I can't guarantee what I can do. I don't know. But I am sure Mr. Vaughn wants to be as helpful as he can. He has already told Mr. Loper that he did."

"Then if you were allowed to do it, you would now get those sacks and bring them down to the Grand Jury?" inquired the Justice, his quavering voice suddenly persuasive as he reframed the prosecuting attorney's question.

"Yes, I would.—I will. At least——"

"That is all I am asking," Bryant said curtly.

"When do you want them delivered, Mr. Bryant?" the Justice inquired mildly.

"We would like to have them as soon as possible. I suppose it is rather late in the afternoon to get them to-day."

"Yes. My suggestion is, that as Miss Farman now says she will do everything in her power to comply with the order contained in the subpoena, she be given until to-morrow noon to comply. If she cannot comply, she shall then report again to the Court and state her reason."

"That is all we want: either the sacks or a reasonable explanation of why they have not been produced."

"Now if everything is satisfactorily adjusted, that will end it as far as the Court is concerned. Otherwise, Miss Farman, you will appear here at two o'clock tomorrow."

"Very well, Sir."

She was smiling as she spoke. And it was over. She had emerged unscratched from the hearing which had seemed, beforehand, so formidable to her father, and which, after all, had apparently not amounted to much. Jenness had not been questioned about her acquaintance with Lentz or about anything except the mail bags, which still remained a "mystery" as far as her father was concerned. He did not

understand why it should have been so important to remove them from Chester Slade's residence, why they
should ever have been sent there in the first place, with
their subsequent disappearance should so agitate the prosecuting attorney, why this functionary should keep insisting
upon their return. And there was no chance now to find
out. The Justice, without formality, had left the room. Jenness had been swallowed up in his wake. The sailor who
had rapped the deaf old man on the shoulder to make him
rise at the bailiff's order, rapped him again now, rousing
him to reluctant movement. He was sitting in a trance,
still mumbling to himself, still tapping with his cane, content to stay where he was indefinitely. The obstreperous
child, on the other hand, was trying to tear down the aisle,
dragging her mother instead of being dragged by her. The
mother's avid face had taken on an aggrieved look. She
spoke to one of the stolid matrons, who was already opening her paper bag, preparatory to beginning a much be-
lated lunch.

"I'm all burnt up, wasting a whole afternoon listening
to a lot of stupid talk about mail bags. I thought this was
a rape case."

"Well, I can see how you'd feel let down. Me and my
friend, we feel that way ourselves. We thought it was
abortion."

Daniel, himself feeling violently ill, tried to push his way
past them. His progress was impeded by a woman who
thrust a thick sheaf of propaganda pamphlets into his hand,
and by another who took hold of his arm, imploring him to
let her tell his fortune.

"I walked all the way from New York to Washington
on purpose to tell fortunes in this courthouse," she said
in a hoarse whisper. "If I'd taken a train, the F. B. I.
would have caught me. Or a bus. Or a plane. But I've
eluded them by walking. Just put out your palm, and I'll
tell you everything the future holds for you."

"I'm telling you that mail bag hussy should be hung,"
another woman was saying fiercely, at his shoulder. He
wrenched himself free from the would-be fortune-teller and
turned furiously towards the second speaker, to find his

rage suddenly swallowed up by incredulity. It was the gentle, grandmotherly little woman whose presence in the courtroom had impressed him with its air of artificial tranquility. Directly behind him someone hissed in his ear. "Screwballs," the voice said. "Screwballs, that's what they are. Don't pay any attention to them, mister. They come to all the trials and hearings, and they always want to tell fortunes and say that all defendants ought to be hung. But they're harmless—a lot more harmless than the harpies who keep hoping to get the lowdown on the latest fashions in rape and the best methods of abortion. Now me and my pal, we specialize in Constitutional rights. We'd be pleased to talk to you about them the next time you take an airing in the park. We saw you sitting on the next bench to us this morning."

Again Daniel tried to force his way through the obnoxious creatures barring his progress. At this rate he would never get to Jenness, and he might be guilty of violence himself, through rage, before he reached her. He could see her now, but she, too, was surrounded. Joe Racina, Herb Parrish and Luke Weatherby were all crowding about her, and so were half a dozen other reporters who were unfamiliar to Daniel. Mr. Loper had taken her by the arm and was trying to cleave a passage for her to follow in his wake. The smoothness was all gone from his face; he looked angry and upset. But Jenness was still smiling blandly and managing to make pert retorts to the newspapermen.

"Look, Jenness, do you always send stuff to the storage room without knowing what it is?"

"Yes, when I don't think it's worth looking at."

"Well, what's the acid test for telling whether it's letters asking for free garden seed or heavy contributions from a new angel?"

"I can spot garden seeds a mile off—remember I was brought up on a farm. And when you speak of angels you can hear their wings."

"How about the fools who rush in where angels fear to tread?"

"Oh, I never get rid of those—in the office or anywhere

else. In fact there seem to be a number of them right here in the Court House."

"Come on, Jenness. Don't waste your time on these fellows or let them trap you into saying too much. Here's your father waiting for you."

It was evident that Loper himself intended to ignore the reporters and to get Jenness away from them as rapidly as possible. For the first time, Daniel saw eye to eye with him.

"Yes, here I am, Jenness, waiting for you. Mr. Loper's right. We must get you out of this."

He extended his hand to her, almost as if he were trying to help her bridge a wide and dangerous expanse, and managed to put encouragement as well as affection into the look with which he faced her. He could hear Herb Parrish muttering, "Well, boys, this seems to be Loper's off day. I guess there won't be any cheap whiskey from Corn Gulch handed out in the press room this afternoon." But the meaning of the remark was only half clear to him and he felt he could afford to disregard it, especially in the face of Joe Racina's even more conclusive, "What the hell? We've got our stories anyway." Then Joe detached himself from the other reporters and came up to Daniel.

"Take it easy, Mr. Farman. At any rate, take it just as easy as you can. It's all part of the picture. And speaking of pictures, you'll run into Marcy Heath as soon as you get outside—or rather he'll run into you. Marcy Heath and about a dozen other photographers. They're not allowed inside the Court House but they're lying in wait for you. They'll want to get shots of you comforting your daughter —that sort of tripe. It'll be over in a minute though."

It was not over in a minute. With her father on one side of her and Tom Loper on the other, Jenness tried to make a swift dash from the Court House to the parking lot. But Marcy Heath and his colleagues were too quick for her; and she finally faced them jauntily, explaining to Daniel in an aside that since she had not been able to make a complete getaway, she would rather be taken looking straight into the camera than holding a handbag over her face or

ducking down under the brim of her hat. Once she had
begun to pose, she did not seem averse to continuing; and
Mr. Loper's impatience was even more evident than her
father's before she finally waved her hand gaily to the
photographers and stepped into the waiting car which he
had now removed from the parking lot and brought to the
curb.

"Anywhere special you want to go now, Jenness?" he
inquired, setting the car in motion.

"Of course there is. I want to go straight to the office.
I'm not going to get trapped a second time into saying
what Horace told me to do and what he hasn't told me to
do without knowing what he wants me to say."

"Very well. I'll take you to the House Office Building."

Loper did not seem disposed to say anything further. It
was evident that he was not taking the events of the afternoon with as much sangfroid as Jenness. But Daniel had
reached the point where he was determined to question the
lawyer.

"Look here, Mr. Loper, I want you should explain this
matter of the mail bags to me. I'm still not clear about
them in my head. Why were they taken to this Chester
Slade's apartment in the first place?"

"Well, if you must know, they were taken there so that
he could mail out their contents to persons whose names
Jenness had given him."

Loper spoke with mingled rage and reluctance, glaring at
Daniel to indicate that he was a curious and importunate
old meddler. But Daniel was impervious to Loper's rebuke.
The time had come when he was grimly determined to
clear up this muddy mystery.

"Who were these persons? Why should she give their
names to him instead of getting in touch with them herself?"

"I really don't know that it's any concern of yours, Mr.
Farman. But to placate you, since you seem to need placat-
ing, I'll tell you that they were names of persons in whom
Mr. Vaughn was interested and whom he wanted to contact. Mr. Slade had some literature of his own to add to
the material Jenness had given him."

"What kind of literature?"

"Pamphlets about Better Bill Britain First—the committee Slade's secretary to—and stickers to go with them."

"I see. Well, now I understand why the mail bags went to Chester Slade's, but I still don't know why they had to be gotten away from there. You better tell me that next."

"It wasn't expedient for them to remain away indefinitely. After all they didn't belong to Chester Slade. They had to be returned to the House Office Building sometime. It ought not be hard for you to understand that."

"No, it isn't. But then why didn't Jenness take better care of them when they came back? Why didn't she look after them in the first place? And afterwards, why didn't she want to talk about 'em to the Grand Jury?"

Without replying Loper cast a withering glance at Daniel to indicate that this time he really had gone too far. Then he glanced imperatively at Jenness. She took up the challenge lightly.

"Daddy, Chester Slade had started acting like an awful fool. He's been having the jitters ever since Max Lentz was indicted, for fear he would be too, and finally he got the idea that he didn't want any more Congressional speeches that Lentz was alleged to have written around his place. Before that he'd been crazy to have Congressional speeches because he liked slipping his own stuff in under a frank. But he suddenly decided everything had got to be cleared out and cleaned up and to humor him I told one of our truck drivers to go there sometime when he was up that way. Just any time, and just to get our own stuff. Then Slade dumped this mess of mail bags on me and Horace got hot under the collar. After all he naturally didn't want anyone to get the idea he was mixed up with Lentz himself, and Slade's jitters sort of got him down. He began to think that if anything were pinned on Slade, something might be pinned on him next. Probably no one would ever have known about it in the first place, or given it a second thought even if it were found out, except that Joe Racina went snooping around, as usual, and sicked Marcy Heath into taking pictures for his pieces, then everyone began to get excited and Horace told me to watch out. He told me to leave the stuff that didn't belong to us alone. He told me to go slow with the snoopy old jury. Oh, here we are! I'll tell you more later on if you want me to!"

She leapt lightly out of the car, ran up the steps of the House Office Building and hurried down a long marble corridor with Daniel and Loper in her wake. Then she flung open the door of Vaughn's outer office, entering it with an air of possession. A sniffling clerk who was typing at a big table facing the door, suppressed a sneeze as she glanced up alertly, apparently with the intention of warding off an importunate visitor with the expertness of long practice, or of greeting a welcome one with an equal degree of cordiality. Then seeing her employer's secretary, she wiped her reddened nose and looked down again, silently continuing her typing. Jenness, paying no attention to her either, went on to the inner office, closing the door after her. The clerk, with a second sneeze which she did not try to suppress, looked up again. She was a plain elderly woman with stringy hair and a tired face, dressed in faded brown. She apparently had a very bad cold, but quite apart from this she produced the general effect of being dispirited and downtrodden. Daniel had a terrible feeling that perhaps Jenness had not always been kind to this pathetic underling of hers.

"Wouldn't you gentlemen like to sit down until Miss Farman comes out?" she inquired politely, sniffling and reaching for her handkerchief.

Daniel and Mr. Loper seated themselves. They did not try to talk to each other. There was nothing more Daniel wanted to ask at the moment, especially in front of a third person, and Mr. Loper's usual flow of plausibility had stopped completely. The clerk went on typing and sniffling, her miserable progress punctuated by more and more violent sneezes. Indistinct sounds of telephoning, interspersed by long periods of silence, came from the inner office. Then the door opened again and Jenness emerged. She did not look jaunty or arrogant any longer; she looked puzzled and angry.

"Have you seen Mr. Vaughn this afternoon, Miss Withers?" she inquired.

Miss Withers quietly inserted another sheet of paper in her typewriter, centering it and adjusting the margin.

"Did you hear me?" Jenness demanded, her voice rising.

"Yes, Mis Farman. Excuse me. I was just getting this sheet even. And I'm sorry, but I have to keep stopping to wipe my nose. It's at the dripping stage. Just like hot water you know. I can't imagine where I caught such a——"

"I asked you if you'd seen Mr. Vaughn?" Jenness demanded again, her voice higher than ever.

"Oh, yes, Miss Farman, I did. I saw Mr. Vaughn early in the afternoon. It must be about two hours since I saw him. I couldn't say exactly but——"

"Did he leave a message for me?"

"No, Miss Farman, I don't think so. He didn't leave any message at all, as far as I know."

"Well, do you happen to know where he is? I've telephoned his house and he isn't there either. All I can get out of that insolent butler is that Mr. Vaughn isn't expected in for dinner. But there isn't any dinner engagement listed on his calendar or any cocktail party either. In fact——"

In fact she expected to have dinner with him herself, Daniel said to himself. Much as he shrank from the thought, he knew it must be faced. That and whatever else was going to happen. For something else was going to happen, he was sure of that. He dreaded the moment when Miss Withers would stop wiping her nose and speak again.

"Yes, I know where he is," she was saying. Again she sneezed, and again she inserted a sheet of paper with a blue Congressional letterhead neatly into her typewriter.

"Well, where *is* he?"

"I'm doing my best to tell you, Miss Farman, as fast as I can. He didn't leave a message for you, but he did say where he was going. He told me Mrs. Vaughn had written him suggesting he should join her at their country place for a little rest and change. Of course he's been overworking for a long time, and he allowed himself to be persuaded. He didn't fix any time for his return, but I believe that when he does come back Mrs. Vaughn expects to come with him. At any rate, he left on the three o'clock train."

CHAPTER 16

"YOUR FATHER was very sorry he couldn't be here to welcome you himself. But of course you know he's pretty preoccupied with your sister these days. I'll do the best job I can of pinch-hitting for him till he can get home."

"Where *is* he?"

"I don't know exactly myself. Somewhere out in midstream."

"*What?*"

"Fact. All's quiet along the Potomac. But nowhere else these days, as far as Jenness is concerned. You must know that yourself, if you ever read the papers. She's practically preempted page one. But won't you come in? We might be able to talk this over better in the house than on the curbstone."

Without wasting any more time on discussion which seemed to him superfluous, Joe Racina reached into the car from which Judith Farman had descended in front of Mrs. Porterfield's substantial gray house, and began to lift out bags, nodding, in a friendly but offhand way, to the four young nurses who still sat inside. Judith, looking very trim and military in her new uniform, despite the exigencies of the trip which had reduced the others to various stages of dishevelment, stood for a moment regarding Joe in a rather deprecatory way, though her expression was based on a general feeling of dissatisfaction with the situation as a whole rather than on any personal hostility to him. As he imperturbably continued to take out bags, and began to wisecrack with the other girls, in spite of the fact that Judith had not presented him to them, she realized that her severe attitude was not accomplishing much, and unbent a little.

"I'm sure you're very kind. If you'll show us where we're to go, we can handle the lighter bags all right ourselves. This is my friend Miss Laura Hurlburt on the front seat, Mr. Racina. And here in the back are Miss Hazel Boyd, Miss Grace Piper, and Miss Ada Healy."

"Howaya?" inquired Joe genially, dragging out another suitcase. "I guess you must be pretty cramped after your long trip. Here, Hazel, let me give you a hand. Look out for that pavement though—that was the first thing I had to tell your mother when she got here, Judith. I didn't want to carry her inside with a broken neck. It would be still worse if I had to carry in five beautiful young ladies, all with broken necks. 'On Comet, on Cupid, on Donder and Blitzen!'"

With suppressed giggles and small shrieks the girls in the back of the car began to tumble out, accepting Joe's proffered hand and exclaiming that he hadn't said the half of it about the pavement. Though Laura continued to sit at the wheel, she also spoke to him cordially.

"Can I park here all night, or do I put the car up somewhere?"

"Oh, Laura, don't put it up! You know I want to go to a night club and——"

"Don't be so silly, Hazel," Judith said with returning severity. "You and Ada went to practically every hot spot in New York last night, and woke the rest of us up when you came in at four o'clock this morning. And now we've driven nearly three hundred miles, and we've got to get a still earlier start tomorrow if we want to see anything of Washington, with only one day to do it in——"

"You can get up early if you want to. But I don't give a damn about the Washington Monument and the Congressional Library and the Smithsonian Institute and all the rest of the dreary sightseeing you want to do. I want to hit a few more high spots before I get cooped up in a hospital ward. Can't you suggest a nice night club where Ada and

I could go, Mr. Racina? Not too—well, not too rowdy but *fun.*'"

"I want to go to a night club too," Grace Piper chimed in. "I thought you were meanies, sneaking out on me last night. You needn't think I'm going to let you get away with anything like that again."

"You didn't have anyone to take you. It's no fun dragging around an extra girl, you ought to realize that, Grace."

"You haven't *any* of you escorts for tonight," Judith said firmly. "Besides, this is Laura's car and she just as tired as she can be. She doesn't want to do any more driving and you'd have to get back into Washington to go to a night club."

"It won't be so hard fixing up the matter of escorts," Joe said drily. Even in the dimness which the street lights of Alexandria did so little to relieve, the pleasing forms and features of the Misses Boyd, Piper and Healy were by this time discernible, and it required no great exercise of will power for him to volunteer. "I haven't a thing on earth to do between now and bedtime, after I've given Judith a few pointers on the lay of the land, and, as far as I know, my pal Luke Weatherby is free too—even a wire-service man has to stop sending in dispatches eventually. Then our congenial little circle, to quote dear Mrs. Porterfield, has just been enlarged by a very lonely lieutenant. I think he's gone to bed, for lack of anything better to do, but I can wake him up. And of course you can all come in my car. But it's quite all right to leave yours here, Laura . . . Come on, let me guide you on high to your windy eerie. Then as soon as you've washed your faces, or whatever you do to them instead——"

"Oh, Mr. Racina, you're a lifesaver" . . . "Me for the lone lieutenant, girls! I want a priority on him!" . . . "Oh, go ahead and take him if you can get him! I'd rather have Luke Weatherby, if he's anything like Joe. Is he, Joe? Goodness, I know I'm going to fall for him flat——"

Chattering gaily, Hazel Gracie and Ada dashed up the steps after Joe. Laura and Judith followed him into the house and up the staircase more soberly, commenting to

each other on the gas fixtures and the steel engravings as
they went. The huge dormer room into which Joe led them,
after much climbing, stretched across the entire fourth
story, and was lighted by a single, staring bulb suspended
from a dangling wire in the center. Under the eaves, form-
ing a background for five iron cots, were dimly visible a
gray Victorian doll house, a miniature Colonial highboy
with brass knobs, a wicker baby carriage shielded by a
faded parasol, and various other objects perennially dear
to little girls. Beside each cot, towels, washcloths and
soap were neatly set forth on small tables beside water
carafes and Testaments, and at the foot of each stood a
straight-backed chair. At either end of the room, where the
wall space was highest, an old-fashioned wardrobe, lined
with comic sections and equipped with wire hangers, stood
invitingly open. Joe, setting down suitcases, made a few
random suggestions before starting off.

"Mrs. Porterfield's sitting with Miss Lily, the star
boarder, this evening, because Miss Lily's having one of
her headaches. She has them copyrighted, always uses the
personal pronoun when she speaks of them. Miss Lily's
headache prevented Mrs. Porterfield from being at the door
to receive you. But she asked me to let her know when
you got here. She wants to speak to you all for a minute.
I'll tell Luke the good news so he can join the merrymakers
and I'll go wake up the lonely lieutenant so he can be
dressing while you and I have our little tête-à-tête, Judith.
I'll wait for you in the small sitting room back of the blue
parlor. You won't have any trouble finding it."

He was pacing up and down, smoking with his customary disregard as to the fate of the ashes, when Judith rejoined him. He did not sit down or suggest that she should
do so, and his geniality seemed to be somewhat in eclipse
when he spoke to her.

"Look here," he said. "I don't know whether you've
grasped just what this mess your sister's in is doing to your
father, but if you haven't, I may as well tell you it's doing
plenty. When he went back to her apartment with her, the
day she first appeared before the Grand Jury, and found
the press and the photographers had hot-footed it up there

too, after he thought he'd finally got away from them, it was almost more than he could take. Jenness didn't help out the situation much herself either. Of course she was frothing at the mouth because Vaughn walked out on her —not that you can blame her for that, except that she ought to have had sense enough in the first place to size him up. She was calm enough in the courtroom, Lord knows; but Minnie Withers had waited a long time to give her a body-blow, and when at last Minnie got this swell chance, she knocked the stuffings out of her smug superior. Jenness held on to herself long enough to get the mail bags to the Court House on schedule, but she went all to pieces in Loper's car afterwards, and by the time she got home was hysterical. She screamed and swore at the reporters, and then she rushed out on her little tin balcony, slamming the French door behind her. Herb Parrish plunged after her and then she started shrieking that the balcony wouldn't hold them both and that he knew it; and the next thing he knew she was yelling to him not to push her off— Oh, hell, I don't know what all! Of course that balcony's plenty big enough and plenty strong enough for two persons—I've sat there dozens of times with Jenness myself; and Herb swears he didn't threaten her or lay a finger on her. I don't believe he did, for he wouldn't hurt a fly. He was only trying to get his story and he followed her because she wouldn't stay in the living room. But apparently he did make a bad break, though he still doesn't know what it was. He was raised on a farm himself, out in Iowa, and he tried to get a laugh out of her by telling her that two hicks ought to feel right at home together on a perch that was so much like a barn loft."

"I think maybe I understand. When we were children Jenness dared a—a friend of ours to jump off a high beam in a loft while we were playing in the barn at Farman Hill. He did jump and he broke his leg. He was lamed for life. I've always suspected that it preyed on Jenness' mind ever since. She's so secretive that she's never given herself away, but I've kept suspecting that sooner or later she would, if she were forcibly reminded of it when she was terribly up-set or unstrung. In fact it crossed my mind when Mom wrote me Jenness had a balcony. No matter how much she pretended to like it because it was swanky, I felt sure that deep down inside she was afraid of it. I think your friend Herb Parrish must have unconsciously hit on this queer mental twist and exposed it as last."

"Yeah, that might be it—a balcony and a beam, eh? Well, it isn't so farfetched at that." Joe stopped for a minute, as if he were scenting another story, and then went on. "Well, they pulled her in, and got a sedative inside her, and finally she quieted down more or less. But the telephone kept ringing so she didn't get any sleep. And the next morning she was a wreck, and here was another summons to appear again before the Grand Jury thrust into her hand. I didn't want her going to pieces in public, the next time she got to the Court House, especially since she'd put up such a good bluff at first; so I broke down and made a suggestion: I said I knew Ned Waldo, the lawyer she ought to have had and didn't, would be tickled to death if she and Mr. Farman would go out on his boat whenever they felt like it. I said I'd help them cover their tracks, and no one would find them there or badger them. They've been there most of the time since. That's where they are tonight."

"I must say you were resourceful, Mr. Racina. And very kind. I didn't realize newspapermen were ever so disinterested about protecting people they might have got stories from."

Momentarily a satisfied grin illumined Joe's dark face. "Oh, I'm not so disinterested as all that. I've got stories right along, slanted to suit myself. And nobody else has got any lately, because no one else has found their hideout. At the moment, my stock with the *Bulletin's* almost as high as Peter MacDonald's. But it'll be taking a tumble pretty quick now. Because I have a hunch your sister's going to be indicted tomorrow morning. And there'll be nothing exclusive for me out of that. And no satisfaction either, in seeing the pack after her again. It's damn sad when you get right down to it."

"I'm afraid I don't understand legal terms very well.

Just what do you mean when you say Jenness will be indicted?"

"I mean she'll be haled into Court and accused of a crime."

"What sort of a crime?"

"Well, everything points to perjury. After all, she has had three chances to tell the truth—once at a court hearing and twice before the Grand Jury and it seems obvious she hasn't done it. I'm afraid she's been a very useful tool to a lot of men who are part of a powerful propaganda machine. I think there's a nest of Nazi sympathizers right on the top of Capitol Hill and that this nest is pretty well feathered. And Jenness likes fine feathers."

Judith pressed her lips together hard. Then suddenly she broke into vehement speech.

"It's a sin and a shame! There's never been a scandal in the Farman family before, not once in its whole history! And here just at a time when Jerome and I are doing everything on earth we can to prove our patriotism, Jerome giving up his wonderful position and I——"

"Your brother was just wedded to that Boston bank, was he? And you could hardly tear yourself away from the peaceful countryside? I'm only asking——"

"Well, of course Jerome knew what he might be in for, eventually, when he went to Norwich instead of Dartmouth, though there wasn't the slightest prospect then that anyone would ever succeed in involving the United States again in a foreign war——"

"Do you know you sounded a lot like Jenness when you said that, Judith? You look a lot like her too—I suppose everyone tells you that you might almost pass for twins. Only of course she's a lot more physical than you are. Of which you're doubtless glad. You've been so careful not to develop the baser side of your nature. Not that you haven't got one, maybe a little less submerged than you realize. If I didn't have so much else on my mind right now, I think I'd try to find out. I have an idea that when you look at Jenness, standing up there to be arraigned, you really ought to say to yourself, 'There, but for the grace of God, goes Judith Farman.' "

"I think you're very insulting. There's not the slightest resemblance between Jenness and me except—except very superficially. And I haven't any idea of quoting the classics in court. Because I shan't be there. It wouldn't do anybody any good and——"

"And it's the only day you've got for sightseeing? Well, I guess you're right at that. I don't believe it would be any comfort to your father to have you with him. He said as much to me himself and I can see now he was right. I thought before he was just trying to save you from an experience that's shattering to him."

"Mr. Racina, I'm not going to stay here and let you——"

"I'm not going to stay here myself. I'm going out with those cute little Roxyettes you brought along for ballast. But I mustn't forget to give you the message your father left for you before I leave. He said he was going to stay on the boat with Jenness tonight because she was in such a wildly emotional state he didn't like to leave her or take her back to her apartment. He said he was sure you'd understand. I'm not so sure about that part myself, but anyway that's what he said. And he said he'd see you tomorrow afternoon. Not to give up an instructive sightseeing on his account though. He'll just come on out to Mrs. Porterfield's as early as he can, and wait for you if you're not here first. He said he wanted to have a talk with you alone, and that afterwards perhaps you and Jenness and he could all have supper together. Provided of course that Jenness is still free at suppertime. And I suppose he might have added, supposing you're willing to eat at the same table with her."

"Mr. Racina, I've told you once before that I won't let you——"

"Yeah, I know what you've told me and I know you've said it twice. But I don't give a hoot in hell what you've told me. And incidentally, you might stop telling me what you'll 'let' me do. Because I'm going to say anything I damn please. And do anything I damn please too."

He tossed his cigarette carelessly into the fireplace, and with a movement so swift that Judith could not even try to forestall it, he took hold of both her arms at the elbow and gripped them hard, bringing his dark face close to hers and looking at her intently. Then, with a slight laugh, he released her as abruptly as he had seized her.

"No," he said curtly, "I think not, after all. But only because it isn't worth the trouble. I've got too much else on my mind, as I said before. Not because I couldn't if I wanted to. And not because you wouldn't darn well like it if I did, either."

Despite the fact that she was unwontedly tired after her long ride, and that normally she went to sleep almost as soon as she got into bed, Judith lay tossing about on her hard, narrow cot for several hours. Laura, in the cot next to hers was slumbering profoundly; but Judith was still wide-eyed and wakeful when she heard the three other girls come stealthily up the attic stairs, stumbling a little in the darkness, and telling each other to hush at the same time that they went on whispering and giggling. She immediately buried her head in her pillow and pretended to be asleep, partly because she did not want to encourage a gushing account of the grand time Joe Racina and his friends had shown them, and partly because she was not in the mood for talking about anything herself. She continued to lie very still while they undressed, with occasional half-stifled outbursts of exuberance, which gradually trailed off into silence after they were in their own cots. She waited until she was sure they were asleep; then she rose and dressed noiselessly and tip-toed out of the room with her shoes in her hand. The house was still shrouded in darkness and profoundly still; but she groped her way to the little sitting room, and sat down on the sofa there. Then, suddenly overcome with exhaustion, she put up her feet and cuddled down on it, deciding that she might at least make herself comfortable while she waited. Her next conscious thought centered in the realization that she was no longer alone, and she sat up, confusedly, to see a dusky face peering into her own with undisguised curiosity.

"Oh!" she said, with embarrassment. "I—I must have

gone back to sleep! I got up early and came down here because I wanted to be sure to see Mr. Racina before he left for his office. You don't happen to know—he hasn't gone yet, has he?"

"Land sakes, Miss, Mr. Joe's ben gone bettern two hours already. The onliest time he ever has breakfas' here is Sundays. Yes, Miss. He says he has to get out of bed early so's his paper can be put to bed on time. Mr. Joe does like his little joke. Yes, Miss. And it ain't breakfus' time fo' any of the other bo'ders, not yet, Miss. But I'se mos' sure Rosetta's got some coffee perkin' on the stove already. Wouldn't you like me to bring you a cup right now? I'se Justin, Mis' Po'terfield's butler."

Judith accepted Justin's offer gratefully, but while she was waiting for the coffee to appear, she put in a call to the *Bulletin*. Mr. Racina did not seem to be anywhere around the building just then, she was informed. Would she care to leave a message? She would and did, saying the matter was urgent and charging the operator to have Mr. Racina get in touch with her the instant he returned. But though she loitered near the telephone long after everyone else had finished breakfast, he did not call her back, and her efforts to reach Jenness and her father were equally unsuccessful. Miss Farman's apartment did not answer, she was crisply informed by the operator at the Potomac Plaza; the operator believed that Miss Farman was out of town. Mr. Vaughn's office was equally uncommunicative. No, Miss Farman had not been there in several days; this was Miss Withers speaking. Miss Withers believed that Miss Farman was indisposed. Oh, this was Miss *Judith* Farman speaking, Miss Jenness Farman's sister? Well, had Miss Judith Farman tried her sister's apartment at the Potomac Plaza? Oh, indeed! No, Miss Withers was sorry, but she really had nothing else to suggest. No, Mr. Vaughn had not returned to Washington. Miss Withers understood that his absence might be prolonged. Matters of great importance had arisen to detain him at home.

Judith had intended asking for tickets to the gallery in the House, and she was disappointed because Miss Withers' uncooperative attitude deterred her from doing so. Her annoyance was visible when she rejoined Laura, who was impatiently waiting for her to begin their sightseeing, with Gracie a rather wan third. Hazel and Ada were not coming with them, Gracie said with a yawn. The newspapermen and the naval lieutenant had certainly shown them a tall time. They had been to the Troika, where they could hardly see what they were eating, the light was so murky, but of course that made it all the more romantic. They had been to Del Rio to see the slinky Spanish dancers who were simply swell; there were some old duffers there experimenting with the Conga, who were Congressmen, Joe said, but they did not have much class; according to Joe all the real swells spent their time going to stuffy dinners. After Del Rio the boys had taken them on to Bamboo Gardens and Casino Royale and the Hi-Hat Room and treated them at every one of these places. Hazel had a pretty bad hangover. Gracie did not think she would be equal to mounting monuments and tramping through cemeteries; in fact, she thought they would do pretty well if they could get Hazel patched up enough to continue their trip the next day. Ada had gone in for some pretty heavy petting. At first the lieutenant had not got anywhere with her because Ada had kept telling him she knew he was just a wolf in ship's clothing; but he had fallen hard for the gag, which he thought was original with Ada and had redoubled his efforts to please, with good results. Gracie did not think he was lonely any longer, or if he were, it must take an awfully close clinch to keep him from feeling solitary; Gracie wouldn't like to say just how close. She yawned again, and from her expression her companions gathered that she did not wholly emerge from her stupor all the time they were sightseeing, except when she willingly posed for her picture in front of the Lincoln Memorial and again in the Amphitheater at Arlington.

"Joe Racina kept telling me how snappy I looked in my uniform," Gracie roused herself long enough to inform her friends smugly. "I think he'd like some of these shots for a keepsake. Especially the one that shows me sitting in the very same chair where the President sits in that

open-air theatre. It was a swell idea of you to bring your
Kodak along, Judith."

Judith had begun to think it was not such a swell
idea after all. Originally she had intended to have the
other girls take some pictures of her so that she could
send them to Dexter; but she was tired of Gracie's yawn-
ing and posturing, and she did not believe a word of this
nonsense about silly compliments from Joe. She was sure
he was not the kind of a man who would say such things.
He would either let a girl completely alone or just grab
hold of her with a grip like a prize fighter. She didn't see
what he had meant by inferring she didn't have any sex
appeal—Dexter had always thought she had plenty. Or
letting her go like that, so quick that she almost fell over,
when she thought he was on the very point of kissing her
hard. She wondéred just what he meant when he said no
girl was going to tell him just what he could say or do,
he was going to say and do just what he damned pleased.
She recoiled from the thought of what a huge, foreign-
looking man like Joe would choose to do, as far as a girl
like herself was concerned, and then reverted to it, dwelling on it loathingly but lingeringly. She thought so much,
though so unwillingly, about Joe, that she almost forgot
about Jenness, which was just as well, because she did
not want to think about Jenness. She did not believe for
a minute that her sister's predicament was as grave as
Joe had indicated, or that her father had any reason to
be so seriously upset. Jenness had probably wound Joe
around her little finger, just as she wound everyone else,
and roused his sympathies, the way she did her father's.
No matter how naughty Jenness had been as a child, her
father had found some excuse for her; he had always
prevented her from being punished. He would find an
excuse for her now, he would still prevent her from being
punished. Nevertheless Judith wished she had succeeded
in reaching Joe Racina that morning. She had been ready
to tell him she was willing to go to the Court House after
all. But if he did not care enough about talking with her
to call her back, and if her father did not give her a
chance to locate him either, she did not know what she

could do. They were both completely absorbed in Jenness . . .

"I declare, Judith, you act almost as dazed as Gracie! I've spoken to you three times. Can't you hear me above the band? It must belong to that military funeral going up the hill. Isn't it a beautiful sight? Just look at those six white horses drawing the casket and the wagon draped with the flag and all. I think we were awfully lucky to see a military funeral, don't you?"

Judith agreed with Laura that the military funeral was a beautiful sight, though she added that probably there were a good many of these taking place nowadays, so perhaps it was not so extraordinary, after all, that they had happened to see one. As a suggestion that they had not been singled out by Providence for a special treat seemed to dampen Laura's spirits, Judith next suggested that they might as well go on to Mount Vernon, since they were back in Virginia anyway; and after they had tramped over the grounds and through the mansion they were all ready to go back to Mrs. Porterfield's to see what the other girls were doing. When they reached this haven, Judith found her father watching for her at the entrance of the blue drawing room. Her conscience suddenly smote her at the sight of his white face.

"Why hello, Dad! I'm awfully glad to see you. Have you been waiting for me long? I tried to reach you this morning, but I couldn't, so then I went out. I thought I'd get here before you did though . . . Oh, I forgot— this is my friend Laura Hurlburt, Dad, and this is Gracie Piper."

Daniel told both Laura and Gracie that he was pleased to meet them and managed to smile as he said it, but almost immediately afterwards he asked them if they would be kind enough to excuse him, because matters had come up which he thought he should discuss with his daughter privately. Then he led the way up the stairs, walking wearily, and opened the door of the Victorian bedroom, indicating with a nod that Judith was to enter it too. But when she had done this, and her father had closed the door again, trying it to make sure it was tight, he stood looking at her mutely, unable to speak. For the first time in her life, she saw that there were tears in his eyes.

"Oh, Dad, what's happened? Do tell me."

"I don't know how to, Judith, it's so bad."

"Has Jenness———"

"Yes. She's been charged with perjury."

"And what does that mean?"

"It means she'll be brought to trial."

"And then what?"

"If she's found guilty, she'll be sent to prison. And she will be found guilty, Judith. She *is* guilty. She's pleaded not guilty, but that's another lie."

"Dad, don't take it like this! Please don't! Please don't look at me like that!"

"I don't know how I'm looking at you, Judith, but I don't know, either, how you expect me to take it, as you say. I've heard your sister described by the prosecuting attorney as the key person here in Washington for the distribution of propagandist literature master-minded by German agents and sent out under a Congressional frank. I've just come from the Court House. Your sister's been photographed and fingerprinted like any common criminal. I had to stand by and see it happen. She has been admitted to bail. I was able to go bail for her, thanks to Dexter. But if I hadn't been, she'd be in jail already. I don't know how I'm going to tell your mother."

"How much bail did you have to put up for her?"

"Five thousand dollars. The prosecuting attorney asked for ten thousand at first but———"

"Ten thousand dollars!"

"Yes. The prosecuting attorney reminded the Court that Jenness, by her own admission under oath before the Grand Jury, has received $12,000 in cash within the last few months and hasn't revealed what she's done with it. He intimated that it was ridiculous for Mr. Loper to refer to her as a 'modestly paid Government employee.' Of course I don't know what she's done with $12,000 either, Judith, if she's had it, or where she got it." Daniel swallowed hard, looking away from his daughter before he went on. "She hasn't anything to come and go on now, that's sure, and I don't know where I'd have put my hands on ten thousand dollars, Judith, to save my life. But I did have five thousand, and a little better than that, from Dexter's loan. I guess I can keep going somehow through the trial. I've got to. I've got to stay with Jenness until she's put in prison. After that I can't stay with her anyway. I'll go back home to Farman Hill and stay there and hide my shame. Leastwise I will if Dexter lets me, and I guess he will. Of course Farman Hill belongs to him now, but he isn't one to bear a grudge long. He's taken this break with you real hard though. That's why your mother went home. Reading between the lines of the letter he wrote after you left, we could tell he'd sort of gone to pieces. But I guess he's pulled himself together by now. Anyway I hope so, because of course your mother'll come back for the trial. That'll mean still more expense, it'll mean putting off the day of paying Dexter back, maybe borrowing more if he's got it to lend. "I'm afraid he's pretty well cleaned out himself. I'm afraid——"

"Dad, do you have to keep talking about Dexter?"

"Yes, Judith, I guess I do. Dexter is the best friend I've got in the world. He's a friend of the whole family. You know what store he and Jerome have always set by each other. He's still fond of Jenness too, in spite of everything. I'm sort of sorry, the way things have turned out, it wasn't Jenness he was in love with. If it had been, he'd be right here now, standing by her, and things might have turned out different. If she'd been keeping steady company with a respectable young man, and he'd been seen everywhere with her, it couldn't have helped but put a stop to a lot of this gossip that's floating around about her being free with men. That gossip's done her a lot of harm. I won't say it's responsible for the decision of the Grand Jury, but certainly it didn't help any to dispose the jurors in her favor. It's the same with girls as with dogs—once they get a bad name for one thing, it's pretty hard for them to live it down when it comes to other things. Not that I believe Jenness has really been free—I believe she's kept her virtue. But she has done some things that don't look just right, and they've caused talk. Well, it can't be helped now. But as long as you don't see your way clear to marrying Dexter, after all, I can't help but be sorry he never thought of any other girl but you in that way. I'd have been proud to have him for my son-in-law. It isn't every father who can say that, Judith, and mean it, about the man he thinks is going to be his daughter's husband."

"Why, Dad, he will be my husband by and by! Don't talk as if everything were all over. I've asked him to wait again, because I felt in wartime my profession had to come first but——"

"If you felt your profession had to come first, you ought to have told him that in the first place. You ought not to have promised to marry him and then gone back on him just when he needed you most. Dexter won't ever be the same man again he was before you did that to him. But I didn't start out to reproach you. I know that's all water over the dam now and nothing I can say would make any difference. You'll do well in the Army, like Jerome, and you'll have my prayers and best wishes wherever you go. Just the same, I suppose it's human nature for parents to hope they can keep one of their children with them. And Mother and I were counting on you to stand by us and Farman Hill."

"Dad, I wish you'd stop talking as if I'd deserted you. I'm coming back to Farman Hill. I'm——"

"You'll find a considerable change when you do," Daniel said stubbornly. "Mother's found a change already, in the place and in Dexter both, and it isn't a change for the better, Judith. But we mustn't talk about this any more. For one thing, I haven't the time. I've got to go back to your sister. I left her asleep on Mr. Waldo's boat—I understand Joe's told you that's where she's spending most of her time these days. She was so plumb tuckered out I figured she'd sleep long enough so's I could get to Alexandria and have this talk with you and still get back to the boat before she woke up. Joe Racina's going to take me in his car. He's been real kind to me, Judith, all through this trouble. It's meant considerable to me to have a younger man like that I could turn to, especially when

I know things aren't going to be the same between Dexter and me."

"I shouldn't think you'd mention a quiet, refined man like Dexter and that crass, vulgar reporter in the same breath. They're not to be compared."

"Well, they're both kind and they're not either of them lazy or stupid. I won't say that the resemblance goes any further than that, but those qualities count a good deal with me in a man, even if he hasn't got any others worth mentioning. Besides, I don't know as Dexter would be so quiet, if he had anything to bring him out. Rhoda's a good woman, and she's done her best by him, according to her lights; but a boy brought up alone by an old maid sister doesn't have as good a chance as one raised by his father and mother, with a parcel of other kids whooping it up in the same house. Then if he'd ever kept company with more than one girl, or if the one had been a different kind, that would have helped some too. Well, we won't go into all that again. But speaking of Joe, he isn't what I'd call crass either. You'll see a lot worse than him, Judith, before you've been in the Army long. If you're afraid of facing male human nature the way it most generally breaks out, you'd better go back to your mother after all, and you better make up your mind to be a maiden lady."

"If you weren't so unhappy, Dad, I'd think you were trying to pick a quarrel with me. You know I'm not afraid of men and you know I haven't the least idea of being an old maid. But just the same, when I see a man like Joe Racina, who doesn't even bother to be civil and who's so lacking in every gentlemanly instinct——"

"He's put himself out considerable for me, like I've said before," Daniel remarked, rising. "I'm sorry you don't like him, Judith. Well, I guess I must be going. Joe said he'd be ready for me around five o'clock and it's after that now. I'm afraid I shan't see you again, if you're planning to leave tomorrow in good season. I hope you'll say goodbye to your friends for me, and tell them I'm sorry it was so I couldn't do more to make their stay pleasant while they were here. And goodbye to you too,

Daughter. I shall be asking God to bless you wherever you go and whatever you do; and to grant you a happier fate than your poor sister's."

He leaned over and kissed her, gravely, on the forehead. There was something about the restraint of the caress and the solemnity of the farewell which unnerved her. She put her arms around his neck and clung to him.

"Don't let's say goodbye like that, Daddy, as if we weren't really friends any more. I want to be friends. I want you to love me the way you love Jenness. Would—would you like me to go with you this evening to see her? I'd be willing to, if you'd like to have me. I don't know whether she'd be glad to see me or not, but I'd be glad to see her. Perhaps I could say something or do something that would be helpful. I've been thinking about it all day. Of course I do have to go on, early in the morning, to report in on time at Morris Field, but perhaps tonight——"

"Well now, Judith, I can't say. I don't know as Jenness would be pleased to see you this evening. It's a little late now to start thinking how you could help her. Of course she said she didn't want you should come to the Court House this morning, but just the same, I think down deep in her heart she hoped you would. And you haven't written her once since you left Farman Hill and she's been in all this trouble. I think you've hurt her feelings considerably."

"Hurt *her* feelings! What do you think she's done? Hasn't she done a good deal worse than hurt my feelings? Hasn't she——"

"There you go again, Judith, and once you get started, you don't always know when to stop. That's why I hesitate, much as I'd like to see you two sisters together again. I have a feeling it may be quite a while before there's another chance for you to meet. A long, long while." He pondered for a moment and then walked slowly over to the door and opened it. "I believe I'll ask Joe," he said. "I think Joe'd have good judgment in a matter like this. Besides, there's another thing to consider: if you went in with us, Joe'd have to bring you back here. For all I know, he may have some other plans that would prevent him. He works nights a lot at his office, and then again he tries to do magazine pieces out here in his room. He keeps hoping he'll sell something to the *Post*. I wouldn't want to interfere with his plans any more than I have already. But I'll go ask him. Then I'll come back and let you know."

Joe said it was all right by him, Daniel reported, returning five minutes later. He didn't care whether she went to see her sister or not; they'd have to thrash that out for themselves. But he didn't mind bringing her back to Alexandria after supper, provided she didn't make it too late and also provided that was all she wanted to do. He didn't see himself taking in any more night clubs for a while, partly because he was flat-broke and partly because he did want to work on a piece for the *Post* before he went to bed. Besides, he did have to get a little sleep, once in a while, and he hadn't been to bed at all the night before. But he'd have to get back to Alexandria himself anyway after he'd had supper on the boat and she was welcome to ride along with him. Judith, who had washed her face and hands at the stationary basin while her father was out of the room, and who was tidying her hair when he gave her this message, tightened her lips characteristically before voicing an equally characteristic protest.

"I don't see why he should act as if I'd invited myself to go out with him. I'm only thinking of getting to see Jenness and of having a little more time with you, Dad, you know that. I should think Joe Racina would have sense enough to realize that too. I wouldn't go to a night club with him if he asked me. I hate night clubs. Or anywhere else. I've taken an immediate dislike to him. I told you that and I don't see any reason——"

"There, there, Judith. There's nothing to get excited over. I'll admit Joe's sort of blunt in his manner of speaking, but he's waiting outside and he's expecting you to come along. We better get started."

The offhand quality of Joe's greeting did nothing to assuage Judith's wounded vanity. He was already in the car when she came down the steps with her father, and nodding carelessly, he leaned back and unfastened the rear door without excusing himself for his failure to get out. He seemed to take it for granted that she would sit on the back seat alone, and all the way into town he talked with her father about Jenness. The press would not pester her much these next few weeks, he said, while she awaited trial; he thought she could begin getting back to her apartment more. There was a limit to the amount they should sponge on Ned Waldo; he might be wanting his boat himself. Perhaps they could work out a plan so that Mr. Farman could stay in the apartment with Jenness. That would save expense, which he knew was important, and it would also provide a buffer for Jenness, which was important too. One of those folding cots now, would roll right into that big closet off the foyer, in the daytime; he thought he knew where he could get one cheap, and he'd look into the matter in the morning. Well if Mrs. Farman was likely to come back, perhaps he'd better get two folding cots; he thought it would be a good idea if she did. He wished Jenness would start getting hold of herself again and go back to the office as if nothing had happened. If you were going to begin brazening a thing out, it was better not to stop halfway. Sooner or later Vaughn would have to come back, and it would be all to the good if Jenness were lying in wait to confront him. If she could put on a good enough act, they might still get somewhere. Joe did not want Mr. Farman to give up hope. After all the damn trial hadn't begun yet and wouldn't for several weeks. Much less was it over . . .

Daniel listened to Joe with obvious attention and respect, and even seemed to derive a certain amount of comfort and support from his remarks. Neither man had addressed a single word to Judith when they turned from the lower bridge to the river front, skirting the long line of fish markets and seafood resturants, and passing the Twelfth Street wharf, where craft of various kinds were anchored, among them two or three luxurious private yachts. Just beyond these were several boats of more modest proportions, none of which showed any signs of life. But a tall weather-beaten looking man with high cheek-bones, holding a short pipe between his teeth, was strolling back and forth on the wharf in front of them, apparently aimlessly. He glanced up with a nod, as Joe brought his car to a stop.

"Hello, Sig," Joe said cordially. "Anything new? No troublesome visitors? Well, that's fine. Mr. Farman's got his younger daughter here with him. Judith, this is Mr. Waldo's skipper, the far-famed and justly celebrated Captain Sigismund Gahde. If you get on the right side of him, you many have a damn good supper, all kinds of nice, Nordic dishes. If you don't, he's quite capable of throwing you overboard. I've seen him dispose of several troublesome guests that way. Fact."

Without any answer beyond a brief guttural sound, the far-famed Captain Gahde, who was apparently a man of few words, preceded the others towards a boat which, now that they came closer, revealed one dim hatch light. They followed him over the short gangplank and down a short, steep companionway into a cabin which proved surprisingly bright and cheerful. There was a brass-bound hanging lantern overhead which gave pleasant and adequate light, and in the center, a large rectangular table already covered with a white cloth and set with white pottery ornamented with small blue sailing ships. On either side, with deep, built-in drawers underneath, were long seats covered with blue leather, which looked as if they might also serve as bunks; and above these were several gay nautical prints and a glassed-in cabinet containing silver trophies. At one end of this cabin, a door stood open into the galley, from which appetizing odors were drifting forth; at the other end was a second door, which was still closed.

"Waldo's seraglio," Joe remarked, nodding in the direction of the closed door. "Now exclusively occupied by the lovely Sultana Jenerazade. Do you think perhaps your father better prepare her for the pleasant surprise you're giving her, Judith? It might be too much of a shock if you burst in on her without any warning at all."

"I thought of that myself, Joe. I'll see if she's awake and if she is——"

Daniel went over to the closed door and knocked gently. There was no verbal answer, but after a moment there was a soft sound of stirring, and presently the door opened to reveal Jenness standing on the threshold. Her golden hair was tumbled about her face, which was still rosy from slumber. A robe of sapphire blue velvet was gathered loosely around her, and her bare feet were thrust into feather-trimmed blue mules. She rubbed her eyes and spoke drowsily.

"Hello, Daddy," she said. "I've had a grand sleep, I feel loads better. . . . Why, hello, Joe, I forgot you were coming back, or I wouldn't . . . Oh, hello, Judith—so you came along too at last, did you?"

Her voice changed entirely as she caught sight of her sister, and without moving from the doorway, she looked at her with eyes which rapidly hardened too. Judith went over to her and kissed her, finding this somewhat difficult to do in view of the fact that Jenness accepted the caress stonily, without even pretending to return it. Nevertheless Judith made an honest effort to speak gently and affectionately.

"Hello, Jenness," she said. "It is too bad we didn't get together sooner. I understood you didn't want to see me this morning, or I'd have been on hand. Apparently there must have been some mistake about that. But I'm glad I had a chance to get here this evening anyway. Can't I come to your room with you and stay there while you dress? Then we'll have a chance to talk together."

"I haven't anything special to say to you. But you can come in to see my *cabin,* if you want to. I'll be out in just a second, Daddy. You and Joe better start drinks without me."

Judith did not fail to catch the correction in the emphasis on the word cabin, or the implication that it was superfluous to consult her wishes, in the matter of serving refreshments. It was insufferable of Jenness, Judith thought indignantly, to relegate her to the rank of unsophisticated outsider, unfamiliar with nautical terms and unentitled to hospitable consideration, when Jenness herself was culpable of misdemeanors, to say the very least, which her younger sister would have scorned to contemplate. But the very impudence of Jenness' behavior made it effective; in the face of it Judith was incapable of framing a ready retort or of giving officious advice or of prying into the submerged fear of the balcony. There was a wicker chair in the "seraglio" and she sat down in this, looking around her with curiosity tinged by envy. She herself had never been on a privately owned boat before, and she was great-ly intrigued and not a little impressed. The cabin was homelike and attractive, with shaded lights, chintz hang-ings and brass beds, and a tiled bathroom was visible be-yond it. Jenness took a quick shower, and came back into the cabin completely nude, an action which seemed to add still further to her effrontery. Even when they were small children, sharing a room and a bed, their mother had spoken to them impressively on the subject of modesty, and as young girls it had never been their habit to undress entirely before each other. Judith tried to avert her eyes from her sister's svelte figure and satiny skin, as Jenness rummaged in a small chest for the fresh undies, still talk-ing insolently.

"So you decided to throw Dexter over and go in for being patriotic in a large way? Those are awfully stiff uniforms they make you wear, aren't they? I don't see how any man could get very far with a girl who had on one of those and I shouldn't think a man like Dexter would even dare to try."

"Of course Dexter has never taken any liberties with me, Jenness, no matter what I had on. And I didn't throw him over. I only decided that in view of the War we had better postpone our marriage until——"

"*You* decided! Well, what did Dexter decide? Is he just going to sit around and wait for you to get back?"

Having located a pair of black lace briefs, Jenness stepped easily into these. In the soft light, her legs below the thigh and her body above the waist looked even whiter and more alluring than before by way of contrast.

"Of course," Judith said again, uncomfortably, looking away from the filmy black triangle. "What else do you sup-pose he'd do?"

"Well, I admit there isn't much of a selection on Far-man Hill. But he might do something. I wouldn't bank on it as a fact that he couldn't, if I were you."

She had now found a bra which matched the briefs,

but which was even more scantily fashioned. It barely
covered her beautiful small breasts. But she seemed to
consider her underwear adequate, for she closed the chest,
after taking out a pair of diaphanous stockings, and began
to draw these on in a leisurely way, crossing one leg over
the other and twisting the stockings into a knot well below her kness.

"At least he didn't walk out on me," Judith said, stung
beyond endurance.

"No? Well, give him a little time, dearie. After all, it's
only a few weeks since you left him. Wait until you see
what's happened by the time you can get back to Farman
Hill. You may get a big surprise." She stepped swiftly
into some buckled slippers and drew a bright jersey dress
over her shining head. "Not that I failed to catch your
sympathetic inference, darling," she added. "But you can
take it from me that it's better to have loved and lost than
never to have loved at all—especially if the loss isn't ir-
replaceable or permanent. Well, I seem to be all set. Shall
we go out and see Joe?"

Joe, it devolved, had taken Jenness at her word and
had begun to mix the drinks as soon as Judith had left the
outer cabin. Cocktails were now invitingly set forth on
the rectangular table, together with the most enormous
platter of large, open-faced sandwiches which Judith had
even seen. Supposing that these constituted their supper,
she helped herself to them plentifully, only to find a few
minutes later, to her infinite chagrin, that they were merely appetizers. The taciturn Norwegian who, apparently,
was steward as well as skipper, began to pass back and
forth from the gallery, his weather-beaten face more im-
passive than ever, carrying one succulent dish after another; among these cauliflower with shrimp, baked tongue
with mushrooms, and a duck stuffed with prunes. Joe having taken his place at the head of the table, assumed the
role of host with surprising grace. Judith was amazed at
the ease and tact with which he presided. He did not attempt to inject forced merriment into a serious situation,
but he talked fluently and intelligently on a variety of sub-
jects, skillfully drawing the others, especially Daniel, into

the conversation. He seemed to know a great deal about different kinds of food and drink, and to regard dining as a fine art; his comments on the relative merits of the Italian and Mexican cuisine in his grandparents' menage and of the Norwegian delicacies which Sig was so plentifully providing, were enlightening and engaging. He had first become interested in such relative merits, he said, when he was a small boy entrusted with carrying his grandmother's offering of special macaroni dishes to her neighbors, who in turn regularly reciprocated with special offering of their own. There were five of these neighbors who carried on this custom—a German, an Irishwoman, a Jewess, and two Italians; and their specialties were all worthy of commemoration. He remembered especially the Irishwoman's thin flat cakes, and the Jewess's meatballs . . . Yes, there was always a lot to eat at his grandparents' house even before the family fortunes rose from twelvefifty to the dizzy heights of sixteen a week. And some bread from the bakery was systematically distributed to charity too.

Well, that was that. Joe confessed, without mock modesty, that he knew something about cookery, but when it came to farming, that was something else again. He asked eager questions concerning the rotation of crops and the suitability of different grains for different climates. He had written a story that day on the arrival of the first A. E. F. in Northern Ireland; if Judith did get overseas duty, he said, perhaps she could help him out on the local color in such pieces. He had never been abroad himself except to France and Italy when he was a kid, and he was in a terrible fog when it came to describing the foreign countryside. He had press passes for Frank Craven in "The Flowers of Virtue" the following Monday. He didn't know that those were among her favorites but Craven was always worth seeing. He hoped Jenness would have a snack with him at Hammel's that night, and go on to the show later. After dinner he suggested a game of cards, and since Daniel did not play bridge, gave the two girls a good-humored lesson in fantan. He did not even commit the error of making the first move to leave, but waited, either with real patience or an excellent imitation of it, for Judith to signal to him. Then he rose, and bade both Daniel and Jenness an unhurried goodnight.

"Perhaps before you go to bed you two will have a chance to talk over those suggestions I made on the way in, Mr. Farman. Oh, nothing much, Pauline Pry. Keep your shirt on—that is, if you have a shirt on. No, I thought not. Well anyway, I'll be seeing you. I'll wait for you outside, Judith. I'm sure you'd like a chance to say goodbye to your father and your sister without having a snoopy reporter hanging around and listening in."

She was actually sorry to see him go, the taciturn Norwegian in his wake. After Jenness herself had made it almost unbearable, his presence had mitigated the unpleasantness of this meeting; now that he was gone, the sense of strain and disharmony, tinged with scandal and sadness, was inescapable. Judith did not know what to say or do to alleviate it, and unreasonably she reproached Joe in her heart for leaving her to cope unaided with this condition.

"Well, goodbye, Jenness," she said awkwardly. "I do hope everything will turn out all right yet." Again she tried to kiss her sister, and again she found that Jenness' cheek, which looked so soft and rosy, had a stony quality. "Goodbye, Dad. I'll write you as often as I can. I may not be as good about that as Jenness. I know she's always been wonderful when it came to writing letters. But I'll try. Besides there'll be lots to tell. And don't worry about me. I'll be all right. I can take care of myself."

"Yes, Judith," her father said briefly. "Yes, I know. Goodbye, Daughter."

He kissed her undemonstratively, without the evidence of deep feeling which he had shown that afternoon, and then he stood at the bottom of the dim companionway, watching her mounting it. He did not caution her about stumbling on the steep steps, and he did not offer to go up with her and see her to the car. She missed the evidence of tenderness which this would have represented, but otherwise she was not sorry. She was glad to escape into the fresh air where she would no longer see his sad face and where Jenness would no longer treat her insolently

and act shamelessly in her presence. She was still af-
fronted by the memory of her sister's nudity and her sister's arrogance. She felt as if she never would be able to
forget how Jenness had looked with her white skin gleaming against her black laces, or how she had sounded when
she said, "Wait until you see what's happened by the
time you can get back to Farman Hill."

Joe and Sig were talking to each other beyond the short
gangplank, their voices low and earnest. Judith could not
hear what they were saying even when she got quite close
to them, and they parted at her approach, in a way which
suggested to her that they did not intend she should, nonchalant as their conversation seemed. The Norwegian gave
another low, guttural growl, which she gathered was his
way of bidding her good-night, and she walked quietly
across the walk with Joe to the place where his car was
parked. He opened the door for her with a little more
ceremony than when they had started, but he did not
speak either until they were out on the bridge again.
Then with a slight smile, hardly more than a twitching of
the lips, he turned to her.

"Well," he said. "Now that the prelude's over, do we
start the fugue?"

"I haven't any idea what you mean," she said shortly.

"Haven't you? Didn't you ever study music?"

"Of course I've studied music. I've had a very good education. I don't see why everyone is suddenly possessed to
act as if I were an illiterate or a moron."

"And I don't know just who you mean by 'everyone' unless your dear sister told you a few hideous home truths
when you retired to that virgin's bower with her. But if
you intended to include me in such a glittering generality,
you did it mistakenly. I think you're not only literate but
literal, which is infinitely worse in a woman. I was trying
to lead up to an indelicate subject delicately, which is always a mistake. It's a damn sight better to say things
straight out. My musical question was intended to clarify
my course of conduct for the rest of the evening."

"I still haven't any idea what you're talking about."

"Do all female Farmans lie? No, I guess not—your

mother's the soul of truthfulness. But you're not trying to tell me, are you that when you suggested going in to see your sister this evening, it never crossed your mind that you and I would ride home alone?"

"Of course it never crossed my mind. Not in the horrid way you're insinuating."

"I can't seem to please you whatever I do. You were furious with me because I grabbed hold of you last night and then you were bitterly disappointed because I let you go. Next you were furious because I didn't telephone you and now you're righteously indignant because I won't pretend that I don't see through you. You're just as much of a fraud as Jenness is, Judith. The only difference between you is that she lies to other people, never pretending to herself that she's not doing it, and you lie to yourself, so hard that you're convinced, or almost convinced, that you're sincere."

"I think you're the most insufferable man I ever met in my life."

"Oh no, you don't. As a matter of fact you're quite intrigued with me. You're dying to find out what it would be like to have me make love to you. You have an idea it would be entirely different from any kind of lovemaking you've had so far. Well, you're right. It would be. And I will make love to you, if you insist. I don't want to fall down completely in your eyes as an adequate escort. But I'm afraid I wouldn't put much punch into it. Because the catch there is, I'm not crazy about making love to a girl just to satisfy her curiosity. I'd want her a little less cold-blooded about it. And incidentally, a little less cold-blooded about her father and sister, when they were in trouble. I'd be afraid if she didn't show some sympathy to them, she wouldn't to me either. What's more, even if the affair were to be rather fleeting, I'd like to feel she had some dependable qualities. I wouldn't want her to keep agreeing to do one thing and then deciding to do another. Which a little bird has told me is one of your amiable habits. Of course it would be all right if she didn't agree to anything in the first place. Then I'd know where I stood. But if she told me she was coming across, she'd have to. She wouldn't have a Chinaman's chance of getting away from me."

To her own utter horror, Judith was crying. She had begun to sob almost as soon as Joe had begun to speak, and by the time he stopped she was weeping uncontrollably. Joe regarded her dispassionately.

"Look here," he said, "it won't get you anywhere at all to cry, at least as far as I'm concerned. I never saw a girl yet who was so good-looking normally that she didn't look hideous when she cried. Now listen: of course it isn't any of my business, but since you've decided it's your vocation to be a nurse, why don't you go ahead and *be* a nurse? I mean a real one, like the Lord knows we need in a war. It seems to me you've acted like an awful fool already, but I have a terrible feeling you're going to keep on acting worse and worse. I can just see you writing ghastly letters all the time to that poor fellow you walked out on, telling him about the swell dates you're having with the other poor boobs who run after you, and still reiterating that in the end you're coming back to him, just as you left him. I really think that if you cut out all that kind of nonsense, you might be quite a girl. But when a girl keeps running around and then writing home to brag about it to the only man who ought to matter, she's about on the same plane as the man who kisses and tells. That is, I think she is."

"I don't care what you think," Judith gasped, in a voice that was still muffled with sobs. "I'm going to write to Dexter if I want to and I'm going to tell him anything I like about everything I do. After all I'm still engaged to him and——"

"Well, if you're still engaged to him, I think your conduct's highly original to say the least. Here you are inviting me to make violent love to you——"

"Will you *stop!* I'm not inviting you to make violent love to me. I'm not inviting you to make love to me *at all!* I hope I never see you again as long as I live! And I won't let you have the satisfaction of thinking that I'm going to take any of your unwelcome advice either. I'm going to do whatever I feel like. You're not the only person who can do what they please and say what they please. I can too. I won't have a complete stranger like you ordering me around. I think men and women are just alike and——"

"Well, if that's the case, you ought to take a course in elementary biology," Joe remarked brutally. "I thought you were brought up on a farm and trained to be a nurse. If you haven't learned any more than that in all this time——"

"I said will you *stop!* Of course I didn't mean I thought they were alike in *that way!* I mean I thought——"

"I don't want to hear any more about what you think. It isn't worth listening to. It clutters up my mind. All I can say is, I think Dexter Abbott has had a mighty lucky escape. I would in his place. I believe he'll think so himself, as soon as his head clears. Now do you suppose you can manage to calm down before we get to Mrs. Porterfield's front door? If you go inside her house raging and sobbing like that, she'll certainly suspect the worst. And that would be too bad in view of my wholly blameless behavior. Of course if I only had seduced you, the story might have had a more dramatic ending. I could have repented and then Mrs. Porterfield could have planned a lovely home wedding in the blue parlor. And we might have lived happily ever after."

The car had come to a stop in front of Mrs. Porterfield's house. Joe switched off the engine and got out.

"None of which is to be construed into a proposal," he said. "After all, with no seduction, there doesn't have to be a sequel. Neither of us needs to repent of anything, at least as far as the other's concerned. It'll be nice if we don't have anything to regret too, won't it?"

especially, quite often took advantages in spite of Court rules. The press table was bewildering to Serena, but Daniel was familiar with most of the figures there now: the pert young cartoonist whose sketches, as effective as they were mischievous, made their deadly appearance in the *Enterprise* every day; "the bitchy columnist," described by Peter to Daniel so long ago, oozing satisfaction because of the rich returns from her first item concerning "a certain congressional secretary who had inadvertently revealed a wad of greenbacks when opening her handbag to repair her complexion"; the syndicate writer who was internationally known as the most successful of all "sob sisters," coining money from the bathos of shoddy and shameful trials which she adroitly interpreted in terms of crocodile tears. Even a well-known fashion writer had been there one day, cleverly covering not only every detail of the outfit in which Jenness appeared, but the outstanding features of the apparel worn by various other women in the courtroom. (The spectators were not all derelicts now, by any means. Numerous official matrons who carried the Vaughns on their calling lists were a prey to the same curiosity which obsessed less exalted members of society; so was the "party-crowd" with which Jenness had been in the habit of disporting herself at cocktail bars and night clubs.) The fashion writer's piece had been given almost a full-page spread on the woman's page of the *Record,* a Washington paper of which Daniel, up to then, had not been especially conscious. It was a smaller sheet than the *Bulletin* and the *Enterprise,* and it catered to a different clientele; but he was not able to ignore it after the appearance of the fashion article.

Daniel was far more afraid of these female journalists than he was of their male colleagues. Despite Joe Racina's own responsibility in revealing the use of the funds Jenness had spent at the Government Printing Office had been put —not to mention the revealing activities of Marcy Heath —and the apparently antagonistic attitude of the *Bulletin,* Daniel still felt that this paper and its representatives, who all happened to be men, were basically fair. Nor did he have any personal grudge against Herb Parrish, whose pudgy appearance did not blind the New Englander to the reporter's kind heart and alert mind. But he felt the women were out to knife Jenness. The exhibits placed in evidence might be lacking in dramatic effect; but the defendant more than made up for this lack. All the elements which aroused open scorn and secret envy in feminine breasts were embodied in the face and figure of his beloved daughter. That was why the pert cartoonist and the "bitchy columnist" and the professional sob sister were in constant attendance at the trial, whereas the men came and went. These women were gloating over the chance to write about Jenness, not merely for the sake of their eager papers and their avid readers, but for their own sakes.

On the face of things, the clothes which Jenness wore seemed quiet enough. She did not appear in a succession of elaborate costumes, each more brightly colored and fancifully trimmed than its predecessor; instead she always wore a black dress, similar in type to the one she had been wearing to a cocktail party the day Daniel and Serena had first seen her in Washington. It did not always seem to be the same dress, but it was always in very much the same style, except that sometimes it was fashioned of shiny satin and sometimes of flat crepe; that sometimes it had long tight sleeves, with a row of neat little buttons fastening it close to her slim wrists; and that at other times it had short puffed sleeves, which gave a glimpse of her rounded forearms between the lace frills with which the sleeves were finished and the black suède gloves with which her hands were covered. Sometimes, too, it had a rounded neckline which seemed to accentuate her graceful white throat, and at other times it had a neckline cut in a deep "V," which seemed to accentuate her beautiful small breasts. Sometimes it had a full skirt which spread out, accordionwise, when she sat down, and sometimes it had a tight skirt, which kept slipping up above her knees and which followed the line of her thighs. Serena had never attached any importance to what she wore and had never possessed money to spend on a wardrobe; but any clothes-conscious woman could have told Daniel, without consulting the article written by the style specialist, that the

seeming simplicity of these black dresses Jenness wore was
a delusion and a snare; that they represented the zenith of
some great dressmaker's art; and that the cost of any one
of them was greater than the total sum which most secretaries spent on a winter's wardrobe. It was probably just
as well, for Daniel's peace of mind, that he was not on
speaking terms with any such woman, and that it did not
occur to him Jenness was wearing especially costly clothes
until the article appeared in the *Record*.

With her black dresses, Jenness wore black hats and
black shoes, which also differed in detail: some of the hats
had wide floppy brims, framing her face like a parasol,
and others had no brims at all, but fitted closely to her
shiny head, outlining its exquisite shape. Some of her shoes
were made of patent leather, which shone so that Daniel
was aware of their gleam halfway across the courtroom,
and some of them were made of dull suède, cut out over
the toes and heels, which made them conspicuous too.
Daniel had heard that there was a growing shortage of silk
stockings, but Jenness had apparently not felt the pinch of
this. She wore hose that were very sheer, of a nude shade,
drawn straight and smooth and tight over her beautiful
legs. Daniel observed that whenever a man in the courtroom took his eyes off Jenness' face, it was to stare equally
fixedly at her legs. But the women eyed other things: the
black hats and the black dresses and the black shoes; the
quality of the stockings rather than the shape of the legs
they encased; the spotless gloves and smart handbags; the
fur neckpieces flung with such carelessness over the girl's
graceful shoulders; the fresh orchids which were always
pinned to these; the ornamental jewelry which gave the
final appropriate touch to each costume. With her round-
neck dresses Jenness wore an old-fashioned necklace made
of small onyx ovals set in gold and linked together with
gold, which clasped closely around her throat; with her
"V" neck dresses she wore a delicate diamond pendant
which swung at the end of a fine platinum chain. Daniel
knew all about the necklace; it was a legacy from his great-
aunt Alma, the same one from whom he had inherited the
thin pointed teaspoons. But he could not place the pendant

and Serena told him that she could not—neither that nor
the wrist watch at which Jenness kept glancing, especially
as the day wore on and she apparently grew tired. Early in
the morning she was always erect and composed, but later
in the day she became restless. She was apt to take off her
hat and toss it on the floor beside her, shaking her shining
hair free. She opened and shut her handbag, sometimes to
extract her compact and lipstick and then stow them away
again with elaborate carefulness, sometimes as if only
to listen to the clicking of the catch or watch the sides of
the bag close together. Above all, she played with her
bracelets—the wide old-fashioned ones, resembling bands
of gold braid, which she wore with the short-sleeved
dresses, and this glittering new bauble which shone in-
escapably against the long black sleeve that closed with
such neat little buttons around her slim wrist.

Sometimes the sight of Jenness hurt Daniel, though it
was always a lovely sight, and when this happened he was
apt to glance away from her towards the two alternate
jurors, sitting forlornly apart from the others. They were
essentially drab-looking men to begin with, and something
about their forlorn but hopeful aspect reminded him of
substitute players on a football team. Then his mind reverted, pleasantly for a moment, to the games of his own
college days, when he himself had played fullback at Dartmouth, and those later days when he and Jerome had
motored to Hanover together, and Jerome had been intrigued by the cadets who had come over from Norwich
University . . . After looking at the alternate jurors Daniel
usually turned to look at the regular ones. He had watched
them carefully while they were being selected and sworn,
hoping to perceive something in their faces or glean something from their statements which would give him confidence in them. There were three whose personalities were
somewhat more pronounced than those of the other nine,
but nothing about these was encouraging or inspiring. One
was a chicken fancier, who was irrepressibly fidgety and
jolly; even in the jury box his mind seemed to dwell on his
cherished coops, and he had the air of longing to fuss contentedly among them. Another was an undertaker, with a

deeply lined saturnine countenance and hands that looked clammy even at a distance; he had brought something of the funeral parlor atmosphere into the courtroom with him. Still a third was a haberdasher, who evidently considered himself a second Sulka, and whose specialty shop catered to an elite element. He never failed to appear in tailored clothes which were perfectly pressed, with a spotless handkerchief, adorned with a colored border which matched his tie and socks, peeping from his breast pocket. His attire automatically set him apart from his comparatively dishevelled companions. But he was not satisfied with this natural division; he made it clear that because of a fastidiousness and an elegance which they lacked, he desired to withdraw still further from such coarse contacts.

In his own mind, Daniel divided his courtroom sensations in two groups: those which were primarily connected with hearing and those which were primarily connected with sight. He *watched* the Judge, the jurors, the press, the defendant; he *listened* to the testimony of countless witnesses, to the endless interrogation of lawyers, to the reiterated rulings of the court. As in the case of the jurors, the witnesses who had especially impressed him were three in number. Daniel did not know exactly what he had expected to see in the person of this alleged Nazi agent, but certainly not a dapper little man, who walked as if he were accustomed to swinging a light cane, and who wore pearl gray spats and a pearl gray four-in-hand. Lentz and the haberdasher might or might not have been brothers under the skin; but they were certainly kindred spirits when it came to the skin's covering. The manner of Mr. Lentz remained breezy all the time he was on the witness stand; but back of the breeziness was an adamant quality. Being under indictment himself, Mr. Lentz was within his constitutional rights in declining to give any answers which might incriminate him later on; and it was amazing to find how much material he felt came within that category. Mr. Lentz was asked to define his occupation; Mr. Lentz refuse to do so. Mr. Lentz was asked whether his book, *Sowing Seeds of Poison,* had been used for propaganda purposes; Mr. Lentz refused to answer. Mr. Lentz was asked whether he had ever been employed by certain German publishing firms, whose names were carefully spelled out for him; Mr. Lentz refused to answer. Mr. Lentz was asked whether he had received certain substantial sums of money, whether he had written the text of certain speeches delivered by certain Representatives and Senators, whether he knew the Senators and Representatives in question. In every instance the refusal of Mr. Lentz was consistent. When the matter of his possible acquaintance with the defendant, Jenness Farman, arose, Mr. Lentz was still supported by his constitutional rights as literally as he was by the witness chair. At this juncture the prosecuting attorney pointed out, with some vehemence, that in the course of a hearing before the Grand Jury, Mr. Lentz had admitted he did, and a lengthy wrangle ensued; but in spite of Keith Bryant's every effort, Mr. Lentz left the courtroom without making any such statement there. He walked away with a triumphant smile and a jaunty step and was swallowed from sight. Daniel remembered the tale of the Cheshire cat, whose smile was visible after the noncommittal feline had vanished; it seemed to him that the same might have been said in this instance.

The next witness to make a special impression upon him was Martha Bowers, who had formerly been one of Senator Slocum's secretaries, though she no longer held this position. It was not quite clear why she had lost it, and Daniel felt there was an underlying strain of sympathy in her testimony, caused by the fact that she herself had known what is was to take the rap, thanklessly, for her employer. Nevertheless, Miss Bowers was quite definite in everything she said. She was positive that she knew Mr. Lentz—yes, the man who had preceded her on the witness stand—and that this acquaintance had been formed in Senator Slocum's office, where Mr. Lentz had been a frequent visitor. He had been there on the average of once a week over a period of several months. She was also certain that he had telephoned Representative Vaughn's office from Senator Slocum's office. He had asked for permission to do so, and when this had been granted and the connection had been made, he had said, "Hello, Jenness, is that you?" Miss Bowers had taken it for granted that he must be speaking to Mr. Vaughn's secretary, because she knew that Jenness was this young lady's first name and it was an unusual name. Mr. Loper objected that what Miss Bowers might or might not take for granted was not testimony, and these remarks were stricken from the record. But after all she had made them. She also said that Miss Farman, giving her name, had called Senator Slocum's office several times asking if Mr. Lentz had been there, indicating that she expected . . . what Miss Bowers thought was indicated was not testimony either, Mr. Loper snapped, and again her remark was stricken from the record. But it was not possible to eliminate her statement that she herself had called Representative Vaughn's office at Senator Slocum's direction to let Miss Farman know that Mr. Lentz would be late for an appointment. Or her statement that Miss Farman had made another telephone call, asking if she might use Senator Slocum's frank for mailing out this speech, and that there had been several subsequent conservations in regard to this. The mailing in Senator Slocum's office was so heavy that it was impossible for them to handle anything extra there, Miss Bowers had explained to Miss Farman, in connection with the use of the frank. But Miss Farman had said this would not matter, because she herself had engaged a large crew of girls in order to handle this material under her direction.

All of this was apparently so damaging to Jenness that Daniel could not understand why he felt sure that in her heart Miss Bowers was sorry for her fellow secretary, and that she had given her testimony reluctantly; but he had no illusions concerning the next witness, Miss Minnie Withers.

Yes, said Miss Withers, she could well remember that Mr. Lentz had paid several visits to Representative Vaughn's office; she had never taken any telephone messages from him, because Miss Farman had always insisted on handling such messages herself; but she had inevitably heard them. Daniel himself was not so sure about this element of inevitability, but Mr. Loper let it pass and Miss Withers went on to say that Mr. Lentz had always been received in the private office, whereas of course her own desk was in the outer office. She had not been a party to the conversations which took place there because after all she was only a clerk; but she had observed Mr. Lentz as he went in and as he came out—very much later. Miss Farman had also taken entire charge of the crew of extra girls who had been hired to mail out the franked speeches; Miss Withers had been kept in the outer office busy with routine correspondence. But the crew had been underfoot for several weeks, and Mr. Lentz had been coming and going all through the period of their employment. Very often, when he went out at lunchtime, Miss Farman went with him. Miss Withers did not know that they had lunch together, but they certainly came and went at the same time. Mr. Lentz had never invited Miss Withers to lunch . . .

Besides the statements of these witnessess, Daniel had heard the testimony of numerous others—the mailing platform clerks, the truck drivers who had handled the mail bags, the Grand Jury members, the F. B. I. agents. He had heard Loper argue a motion for a directed verdict. Temporarily his spirits had risen. But the Judge had promptly denied the motion and indifferently allowed Loper's claim of an exception. Daniel had next heard Loper inform the court that the defense would call no witnesses. He had heard the denunciations which Loper hurled at Bryant, increasingly violent and uncontrolled as the trial progressed, and had noticed, with a sinking heart, the impregnability with which the prosecuting attorney had weathered these assaults, the skill and strength with which he had withstood them. Now at last the end was almost in sight. Keith Bryant, towering above all his listeners, his rugged face intense, his gigantic head held high, his huge body under complete control, was making his summation to the jury.

He had begun it temperately and courteously. ("May it please the Court and Gentlemen: You have been very patient. You have listened with a great deal of attention to the evidence which has been presented here by the government in support of this indictment and I thank you personally. I think you have earned the thanks of your countrymen too.") He had next reminded the jury that the indictment contained two counts, the first charging Jenness Farman with perjuring herself in her testimony regarding the disposition of certain mail bags, the second charging her with denying acquaintance and her association with Max Lentz. Then he had gone on to define the four elements involved in the crime of perjury, and to state that the government was under the compulsion of proving each of these elements beyond a reasonable doubt. Briefly, he said, the four elements were: the falsity of the testimony Jenness Farman had given before the Grand Jury; her knowledge that the testimony was false; her belief that it was false and untrue at the time she gave it; and finally the wilfulness which had characterized her conduct.

After defining these elements, Bryant analyzed each one separately, quoting the testimony of the men who had delivered and moved and put away the mail bags, and of the secretaries working in Congressional and Senatorial offices which Lentz had also frequented and with which Jenness Farman had been in constant touch. ("And I want to remind you: these witnesses had no motive for falsity. They have no interest in the outcome of this trial. They have no reason to come here and tell you that something happened if it did not happen. Not any one of them, in any way, after being cross-examined, changed any particle of his testimony. So I say to you: they had no motive to lie, and on the other hand, the defendant Farman had every motive.") Personally, Daniel thought it possible that Minnie Withers might have had an ulterior motive; but this did not alter the fact that he believed she had been telling the truth, and he knew that everyone else in the courtroom believed it too.

The prosecuting attorney leaned forward a little, and somehow the movement, slight as it was, seemed to still further enhance the tremendous effect of earnestness and sincerity which he had already produced. He had dismissed the element of falsity and turned to the element of knowledge. ("When you come to consider whether Jenness Farman had knowledge of the fact that she did give instructions for the storage of those sacks, there can be only one excuse for it; that she had forgotten about it. Then I wish you would keep in mind that just a few weeks elapsed between the time those sacks were spirited away from Slade's apartment and the first time that Jenness Farman appeared before the Grand Jury. Is it reasonable to suppose that a young woman capable of acting as a Congressman's confidential secretary would have such a poor memory that in a few weeks she forget about an important order she had been given? Think it over, Gentlemen, and then turn your minds to the question of whether Jenness Farman had knowledge at the time she appeared before the Grand Jury that she actually knew Lentz. Well, the testimony is that she handled the mailing out of 125,000 copies of *The Man of Mars* which was the pamphlet written for Senator Slocum by Max Lentz. Would a young woman intelligent enough to hold a responsible government position be likely to forget that she had handled 125,000 copies of a certain pamphlet? a thousand, perhaps, Gentlemen—but 125,000! Could that many slip her mind? Or would she be likely to telephone a fellow secretary—as Senator Slocum's secretary has testified that she did—and say, 'I hear Lentz is coming to town today? Has he been in your office yet?' Would an efficient young woman refer in that way to a man of whom she had never heard and whom she had no interest in seeing?")

Daniel could almost hear himself answering Keith Bryant when the prosecuting attorney asked this question. He felt impelled to rise and shout, "Of course she knows him! And it wasn't only in these governmental offices that she was meeting him. She was meeting him in the country too, in the Big Field by the brook where it joins the highway. On the acreage her ancestors settled and cleared, on the property that's been handed down from one generation of Farmans to another, on the land that's part of her own home. She was ready to sell her birthright for a mess of red pottage. This is the time to tell the truth, the whole truth and nothing but the truth, so I must tell that too. She's not only doubly guilty, she's trebly guilty. I have to

tell you that about my own daughter, about my daughter
who's dearer to me than life."

It was the disturbance made by the strange woman who
was sitting on the side of him which curbed him when he
had half risen, rather than Serena's stifled exclamation of
surprise. Daniel had noticed this woman's uncanny eyes
every time she looked in his direction. The whites were
visible all around the irises, and the pupils were dilated, as
if by belladonna. This impression of dilation was further
enhanced by the effect the eyes gave of overflowing, as if
they contained some alien liquid which had no connection
with tears. The lashes encircling them were very long, very
straight and coated with mascara; they fringed these intense
swimming eyes like little sooty sticks. Even in the midst
of a hundred glances this woman's relentless stare was
inescapable. Now she had begun to mutter too, and the
mutter rapidly became a shriek.

"Hussy! Wanton! Whore! Harlot!"

She had sprung to her feet as she screamed and her
voice swelled in volume with each epithet she uttered. She
was pointing at Jenness, her shaking finger growing more
and more menacing with every move it made. Justice Bellinger was vigorously rapping for order by this time, and
the bailiff was indignantly charging down the aisle, furious
because a spectator had got out of hand before he could
reach the scene of the disturbance. He seized the woman's
shoulder and propelled her in front of him towards the
door, while she still shrieked aloud. Jenness continued to
stare straight ahead of her, a bright spot of crimson suddenly burning on each cheek, vivid through her makeup;
but everyone else had turned to stare at the fanatic. Everyone else who had not raised the question before, now
wondered whether the charges she had hurled were deserved, and Daniel cringed at the prospect of seeing it
described by the press. Beside him, Serena was quietly
crying. He could not comfort her. There was a lump in his
own throat.

Because this disturbance had caused another dreadful
diversion in Daniel's tortured mind, he found it hard to
follow Keith Bryan's definition of the third element in the

crime of perjury. Since there was no suggestion that the defendant was suffering from amnesia, the prosecuting attorney was saying, with the first touch of sarcasm which had crept into his earnest exposition, she must have believed the testimony she gave before the Grand Jury was false. Bryant treated this third element more briefly than he had the first two, passing along swiftly to the fourth, and on this he dwelt at length: Did she testify wilfully and falsely? ("Now 'wilfully' means just what it indicates. It indicates that an act has been performed of a person's own accord, under no compulsion. And here is the defendant's own testimony, which you have heard before, but which I will read again: 'I left no instruction with anyone about mail bags' . . . 'Those mail bags were never stored under my instructions.' Those answers are reiterated, Gentlemen. And then we have my question: 'You don't wish to correct any of the testimony you have given heretofore in that respect? And Miss Farman's answer: 'No, Sir.' And my next statement: 'I want to be fair to you, Miss Farman.' And her answer: 'I realize that, Mr. Bryant.' And my admonition which was coupled with still another question: 'I tell you here, in front of this Grand Jury, that there has been testimony not from one source but from numerous sources, that you were the person who gave the directions to store those sacks in Horace Vaughn's storage space in the House Office Building. Now having made that statement do you still persist in your story that you did not give the alleged directions?' And again her answer: 'I do, Sir. I didn't give any directions to place them in the storeroom or any place else.' ")

Daniel looked towards the counsel table, trying to catch Loper's eye. Could the lawyer's mind, at this point, fail to revert to Daniel's own persistent questioning on the subject of the mail bags, the day they had driven from the Municipal Court House to the House Office Building? The answer to this question must be yes, for Loper, having caught Daniel's gaze upon him, looked swiftly away again. And meanwhile Keith Bryant was proceeding with his second charge of perjury.

"I am asking you, Gentlemen, to recall this further

statement which I made to Miss Farman: 'I will give you the opportunity now to correct your testimony when you say you never met Mr. Lentz and I assure you I will never again repeat the offer. You will take advantage of it at the present time or we will be through with it. Do you want to avail yourself of this opportunity?' And Miss Farman answered: 'Mr. Bryant, to my knowledge and under oath I have never met Mr. Lentz.' This too was repeated again and again under questioning so worded as to offer additional opportunities for correcting a misstatement. But the defendant continued to declare that she did not know Max Lentz by that name or by any other that he might have assumed. That she had never talked with him either in person or on the telephone. That she would not know how to reach him even in an emergency, that she was positive of all this. And finally when I reminded her that the direct questions I was putting to her were not in the nature of a threat, but were asked solely that she might be advised how grave was the offense of giving false testimony under oath, she persistently told me she knew what she was doing. She still did so when I put it over more plainly and asked her if she realized that perjury was a felony punishable by imprisonment."

Suddenly the courtroom was very still. It seemed to Daniel that this was not only because Keith Bryant had ceased to speak. He felt—and feared—it was because everyone in it—the idlers, the vagrants, the scandal-seekers, the lounge-lizards, the lunatics no less than the jury and the Judge, the press, the clerks and the counsel for the defense were straining to hear his next words, alert to every syllable which piled his daughter's sin upon her shame.

"So much for the wilfulness of this defendant in perjuring herself," Keith Bryan had said slowly and distinctly. And then he had repeated those fateful words which formed the core of his summation: "Human beings do not perjure themselves without reason unless they are morons and morons do not become secretaries to Congressmen. The reason Jenness Farman perjured herself is perfectly plain . . . She did it because she is an important cog in the most diabolical propaganda machine this world has ever seen!"

He paused, as if waiting for his hearers to grasp the full import of what he was saying. Then he went on, still more forcefully, still more relentlessly than before.

"That is why her lips were sealed to the truth and opened only to tell lies. She was acting on the direction of the arch traitor, Max Lentz, representing the lying, murderous rogues of the Wilhelmstrasse. Thus the long arm of the Gestapo put these lies in her mouth. The long arm of the Gestapo tried to stop this trial and impede it in every way. The defendant knew that if she told the Grand Jury the truth, the Government of the United States would discover this diabolical machine, the American people would learn of this vicious propaganda. The long arm of the Gestapo has controlled her and through her has tried to control this Court. That is why she has lied and lied and lied."

The wild-eyed vituperative woman who had been ejected by the baliff had now stolen back into the courtroom again and was again seated beside Daniel. As Keith Bryant re-iterated the word "Gestapo" she looked apprehensively over her shoulder, and then looked down again, muttering under her breath. He know she felt, as he did, that this long arm had indeed reached into the very courtroom, that it was stretched over them even then, that at any moment it might descend upon them and crush them with its weight. But Keith Bryant was not overwhelmed by this vision of a menacing arm which he himself had evoked. He was pro-ceeding dauntlessly with his argument.

"Gentlemen, you have heard the testimony. You have seen many witnesses on the stand, and you have seen the master mind of this Nazi propaganda machine, Max Lentz, the false prophet of his false god in Berlin. He has been a busy missionary in our midst, sowing the seeds of poison in this country. He has employed this defendant as one of his minions in the office of one of our own legislators whose salary is paid by the American people.

"Where did the money come from that enabled his sixty-

dollar-a-week clerk to buy and to order 625,000 reprints
from the Congressional Record in less than a year?

"Where did the moey come from that enabled her to
employ hundreds of girls to address these envelopes and
send them out?

"Look at the record, Gentlemen.

"Here is the registration statement of Lentz, filed with
our own Department of State, revealing that he received
$25,000 from the Nazi Information Bureau, alone, includ-
ing reimbursements for expenses.

"That is where the money came from.

"This girl who is now on trial was not getting money
out of her own pocket. She was in a big game for profit
and she was in the employ of Lentz, the man who received a total of $70,000 from various Axis institutions in
less than a year and a half."

That is where the money had come from for Jenness to
buy fur coats, Daniel said to himself, fur coats and ice-blue
evening dresses and lace bedspreads and fragile crystal
ornaments and strawberries in January. That is where the
money had come from for a stylized apartment with a steel
balcony in a showy apartment house. A wave of involuntary relief, of which he was instantly ashamed, swept over
Daniel as he realized this; yet how could he wholly stifle
this sensation, which he saw that Serena shared? He had
told Judith, hoping against hope he was telling the truth,
that Jenness had "kept her virtue." But in his heart of
hearts, he had found this hard to believe; there was every
evidence to the contrary. Now the dreadful disclosures
Bryant had made indicated that after all this hope might
not have been unfounded; the association between Lentz
and Jenness, disgraceful as this had been, had been untinged by personal attraction. She had delivered to Lentz
the keys to the treasure-trove which he so eagerly sought
and for which he so amply rewarded her; but the girdle
of chastity was not in the loot for which he covetously
looked. It was less devastating for Daniel to believe that
his daughter had jeopardized her country's safety than that
she had sold her own honor. Traitorous as he knew the
feeling to be, ashamed as he was to harbor it, his grief was

assuaged instead of augmented for the first time during the course of the trial.

But his relief did not stultify his alertness. Bryant was still talking, no longer about tangible gains but about intangible principles.

"Now, Gentlemen, this investigation by the Grand Jury was in no way intended to stop any man from freely expressing any view, political or otherwise, which he might honestly hold. Personally I would never be a party to an investigation which sought to deprive any citizen of free speech. Neither is that the purpose of the act which requires the registration of foreign propaganda agents. Perhaps the most sacred right we Americans have is our right to speak our minds at any time and at any place, and no one of us, I am sure, would hesitate to give up his life to defend it. But in order to protect that sacred right from the foreign isms and the dictatorships of Europe, our Congress saw fit to pass a very wise law. This law did not make it a crime to spread propaganda either. But it did provide that if such propaganda were spread, those responsible for it must tell the American people for whom they were working and what they were getting paid for doing so. This provision left the American people free to decide how much credence they wished to give to the utterances of a man so paid and it is a case of this type that the Grand Jury has been investigating. It was not trying to stop anybody from saying anything, but it wanted to know the motive behind the material that was being mailed out; and I have here a sample which, to my mind, illustrates more clearly than anything I could say on my own initiative, just what was going on.

"Here is the speech *The Man of Mars* written—and, Gentlemen, there has been no denial of that fact—written by Lentz for Senator Slocum and delivered on the floor of the Senate. I quote in part: 'Propaganda, war psychosis is being artificially created. The American people are told that peace in Europe is hanging only by a thread and that war is inevitable. At the same time the American people are unequivocally told that in case of a world war, America must take an active part in order to defend the slogans of liberty and democracy in the world . . . Our defense should serve American purposes only. It should not be used as a screen for unneutral aid to the British Empire. No one, neither the Allies nor the Axis, can assail us if we are guided solely by American interests. We must take into protective custody, with the cooperation of our sister republics, every strategic point in the Western Hemisphere. We must bar from this American Hemisphere all the nations of Europe. We shall then be unassailable, even if both the Axis powers and the Allies should combine against us at the end of the present war or at any time in the future. "Europe for the Europeans"; "Asia for the Asiatics"; "America for the Americans." If we adhere to this slogan, the lamp of liberty will continue to burn brightly in the Western Hemisphere, no matter what happens in Europe or Asia. The lamp of liberty will shine on—the symbol of American civilization—a beacon of hope for all mankind.'

"Is there any significance, Gentlemen, in the fact that we have Hitler quoted as saying: 'America for the Americans and Europe for the Europeans,' that we find Hitler's registered propaganda agent writing a speech for Senator Slocum in which that identical phrase is used, and then that we find this defendant Jenness Farman mailing out not one or two or three or four, but 125,000 copies of that speech?

"How does that look to you? Does it not look as if the sender were an important cog in a propaganda ring?

"And now look at this card—*Conscription Is Coming* —'The recruiting officers are at your door. They will take your sons and put them into the Army. Then they will be shipped through the submarine zone by the hundreds of thousands to the bloody quagmire of Europe. Into that seething, heaving swamp of torn flesh and floating entrails they will be plunged, in regiments, divisions and armies, screaming as they go. Agonies of torture will rend their flesh from their sinews, will crack their bones and dissolve their lungs; every pang will be multiplied in its passage to you. Black death will be a guest at every American fireside . . . And still the recruiting officers will come; . . . And still the toll of death will grow. . . . You cannot avoid it; you are being dragged, whipped, lashed, hurled into it; your flesh and brains and entrails must be crushed out of you and poured into that mass of festering decay.'

"And that, Gentlemen, is no speech of a Congressman. That is something that was inserted in the Congressional Record. It does not appear by whom it was inserted but this was done under the extension of a Congressman's remarks. And the significant thing is that this card was taken from one of those sacks which this defendant Farman was very anxious to hide from the Grand Jury.

"I am going to stop talking now. However, before I sit down, I should remind you that you have been called here to do a duty, that it is part of your duty to protect our country and to see that our laws are enforced, and that one of the best ways of enforcing these laws is through the investigations of a Grand Jury. But no such investigations will ever bear fruit unless the witnesses called know in their hearts and minds that they must tell the truth. Your verdict in finding this girl, this defendant Jenness Farman, guilty of perjury is the only assurance the government can have that this investigation which is still continuing will disclose that enemies of our country are working behind the so-called cloak of patriotism."

Bryant's summation was over at last and he sat down, relaxed and assured, his presence still dwarfing all others about him, the force of his personality still undiminished. Loper was already on his feet. But the foreman of the jury had made a signal of distress to Justice Bellinger, and the Justice, with a hint of a smile, had ruled that the jury might have a five minutes recess. The jurors, filing out with a haste which minimized the effect of their solemnity and silence, created a diversion in the courtroom. Just before their return Joe Racina, who had gone out before they did, came back into the courtroom and beckoned to Daniel. The older man rose stiffly and joined the reporter in the corridor outside, under one of the signs admonishing its frequenters that they must not smoke, spit, throw rubbish on the floors, scratch matches on the walls, loiter in the passageways, whistle or talk in a loud, boisterous manner.

"There's still a chance that there may be a split jury," Joe whispered. "Don't give up hope."

"What makes you think there may be?"

"I've just come from the men's room. It's one of the best places to pick up tidbits during a trial. Of course the bailiff stands right outside the door and the patrons aren't supposed to talk; but there's something about the facilities that seems to loosen jurors' tongues besides relieving them in other ways, and sometimes they let something slip before they remember. I figured out they'd be having a recess to go there before long, so I went there first. I'm almost sure that chilly-looking undertaker, who's been having cramps all the morning, sympathizes with Jenness. He wasn't talking to anyone else, but he was muttering to himself, loud enough to be heard. He seems to see her as the poor little country gal whose head's been turned by her boss and Vaughn as the base betrayer who leaves her in the lurch. Of course I've slanted several of my own pieces that way. Those should have been barred from the funeral parlors for the duration, but accidents do happen."

"I know you're doing everything you can for Jenness, Joe. But one dissenting juror wouldn't accomplish anything beyond holding up the verdict for a while. It wouldn't make any difference in the long run."

"It might if he convinced enough of the others. And the man alongside of the undertaker was growling, 'That's so, that's so,' as if he were agreeing with something the old crepe hanger was muttering—That was the haberdasher. You may be sure he's appreciated the effect of those custom-made clothes Jenness is wearing. Of course I couldn't hear much anyway and presently they seemed to remember they shouldn't be saying anything and shut up. Well, we shall see what we shall see."

Joe and Daniel went back into the courtroom together. Its atmosphere had definitely changed now. Instead of being tense, this was slack. The letdown was evidently irritating to Loper for he began his closing argument by calling for quiet instead of admonishing everyone to "speak up" as he had done heretofore, and by snarling at Keith Bryant with unprecedented animosity. His own thanks to the Court and the jury for their patience were interrupted by his call for quiet and after that he did not seem to collect himself instantly. Without continuity, he reminded the jury that the government which was proceeding against Jenness Farman was not a dim and distant organization as his adversary's definitions of it would seem to indicate, but a vital body in which every American had a part, and that the jury, as such a part, had a serious obligation in a serious matter which seriously affected the defendant.

"Any conviction," Mr. Loper announced with continued lack of originality and hence with continued lack of effectiveness, "will of course mean to this lovely young lady, Miss Jenness Farman, the loss of her treasured standing in the community, the loss of the position on which she depends for her bare livelihood, disgrace and jail for herself, disgrace and deprivation for the fine family from which she comes and which is so nobly represented in this courtroom by her stricken father and mother."

As Loper pronounced his final words, he turned slowly but completely around, so that instead of facing the Judge, he ended by facing Daniel and Serena. To the unhappy New Englanders, this movement of Loper's seemed to give the signal for a similar movement on the part of everyone else in the courtroom. The deep flush which came so rarely and so intensely burned Daniel's face and neck with intolerable fire. He tried to stare stonily ahead of him. But all his will power could not keep his chin from sinking and his shoulders from sagging, any more than Serena's could keep her from sobbing.

"The Court will tell you about the presumption of innocence," Mr. Loper continued. "It is important. Of course the indictment, as the Court here will remind you, was only a charge. In itself it proves nothing. It is a complaint made against a man or a woman and until the very moment when you come to a conclusion in the Jury Room, the presumption of innocence clings to a man or a woman. It is sometimes described as a guardian angel who accompanies a defendant into a criminal court and stands at all times guard over him whispering in a still small voice, 'This person is innocent—innocent—innocent.' "

Mr. Loper's voice broke as he pronounced the word "innocent" for the third time, and he made a dramatic gesture. But the guardian angel somehow failed to materialize in the desired form. Several audible snickers resounded through the courtroom, causing Justice Bellinger, whose own expression at this moment was less serious than Daniel would have liked, to call imperatively for order. The pert young cartoonist at the press table immediately bent over the blank sheet which she kept spread out in front of her and began to sketch rapidly; Daniel was certain that the next day's *Enterprise* would contain a caricature of Jenness depicted with a grotesque angel hovering over her, and carrying a floating banner inscribed with a barbed caption. His fear that this new indignity was inevitable became a conviction, when one of the spectators near him took a scratch pad from her handbag, and begun to make a sketch of this very description, with the added embellishment of an orchid on the angel's shoulder. Her achievement, though amateurish, was sufficiently mirth-provoking to arouse fresh titters of merriment from the companions to whom she showed it, and a fresh admonition from the Judge. Daniel could remember the reverberations from the famous plea in behalf of the "angel child" during the notorious Thaw trial; he cringed at the realization that something of the same sort was about to happen now. He knew that the "bitchy columnist" would carry another juicy item beginning, "As I pointed out last October, several months before any other news writer carried the story . . ." He knew that the sob sister would somehow contrive to bring in the pearly gates and the fleecy clouds of heaven as accessories for the victim of man's oppression, assuaged by consolation from above. He knew that the fashion writer would achieve another full-page spread, showing "The latest in 'divine' styles . . ."

Mr. Loper, however, was quite unabashed. Though he had failed to sound a celestial note convincingly, he still had faith in one of a patriotic nature, and his voice began to boom as he continued.

"You are looking at a girl whose brother is an officer in the armed forces of the United States," he shouted. "A hero prepared to defend his country to his dying breath. The devotion of this noble young man to his native land was such that long before the United States was attacked, he had given proof of it. As a mere boy he had chosen to go to a military college instead of to the nearby educational institution which his father and other male members of his family had attended; before he was twenty-one he was enrolled as a reserve officer. As the first clarion call for defense was sounded, he left his profitable position in a Boston bank and hastened to an Army post. He had already been there for months when the disaster of Pearl Harbor occurred. It is likely, Gentlemen, it is reasonable to suppose, that a girl brought up under the same noble influence as this gallant young officer, a girl further inspired by his self-sacrificing example, would be guilty of the type of treachery which my opponent has so glibly laid to her door?"

For once Mr. Loper was speaking logically, Daniel thought, though the logic would have been more forceful if it had been clothed in less flowery language. But ironically this was the one instance in which logic did not hold. The precepts and example which he and Serena had given to all their children had not produced the same effect on Jenness as on Jerome and Judith; and far from yearning to emulate either her brother or her sister, she had made a mockery of everything they had done. Nor could Daniel conscientiously accept the evaluation which Mr. Loper lavished on Jerome's patriotic service. The boy's father believed, and found assuagement in believing, that he was ready and eager to serve his country; but his latest letter seemed to burn through Daniel's pocket as Mr. Loper spoke: *"I have been O. D. for the last three days, so haven't had a chance to go home, but Alix came over to the Post last Friday with some friends and we all had a very jolly dinner together at the Officers' Club. Then we went to a show afterwards. I play golf regularly at the Club. There is a very fine course and I am getting to be a pretty good player. Perhaps someday we could have a nine-*

hole golf course on Farman Hill. The Ridge Field would be a good place." Daniel was surprised that Jerome should have made such a suggestion just at this time; he himself was thinking that he would again need to expand his usual crop schedule, which normally included only corn, oats, and hay, though Dexter had always raised barley, millet, potatoes and beans as well. In the first World War the Governor of New Hampshire, "Harry" Keyes, who was himself a farmer, had come out with the slogan, "I'm planting wheat. Are you?" The slogan had been very successful; even the French newspapers published in Manchester and Nashua had blossomed out with banner lines reading: JE SEME DE L'AVOINE: ET VOUS? Daniel, like most of his friends and neighbors, had hastened to show Harry that his property was quite as capable of producing wheat as Pine Grove Farm. He should be thinking of planting wheat again now, in Harry's memory, not of making a golf course. Harry had done well as War Governor of the State . . .

"I have here a copy of the *Bulletin*," Mr. Loper was continuing, "a paper conspicuous for its venomous attitude towards the helpless and harmless girl who is the defendant in this case." Mr. Loper paused long enough to cast a glance which was itself laden with venom in the direction of Joe Racina, who looked up so very brightly and briskly that Mr. Loper hastened to glance away again and to gaze sorrowfully at Jenness, who was wearing a fresh corsage of white orchids fastened to a new silver fox scarf, and whose skirt, as usual, had slipped up above her knees, so that she did not give quite the effect of utter helplessness and harmlessness which Mr. Loper might have desired at this juncture. However, her appearance did not seem to depress him, for he continued to boom. "In spite of its pernicious policies," he announced in stentorian tones, "the *Bulletin* has published a full-page illustrated article by Peter Mac-Donald, entitled: FROM FARMAN HILL TO CAPITOL HILL: THE SUCCESS STORY OF THE SUPER SECRETARY JENNESS FARMAN. I invite—nay I urge—the careful perusal of this story, Gentlemen. If you read it you will find there is not a single line that redounds to the discredit of Jenness Far-

man. Instead we discover that she comes from that sturdy
stock which has given New England its outstanding and
enviable position in this country; that the atmosphere of
the ancestral home in which she grew to womanhood was
cultured and Christian and that her surroundings were in
every way ideal. Under these circumstances how could her
character fail to be lofty and her conduct exemplary?
There has been no failure, Gentlemen. In this respect she
is like her brother, the gallant young officer to whose
patriotic career the limitations of time have not permitted
me to do justice. And she is also like her sister, whom I
have not yet mentioned to you, but whom I am proud to
describe. For there is another girl in this notable family,
Gentlemen, a girl who with self-sacrifice comparable to
her brother's has left the home of her childhood and the
sweetheart of her youth to become an Army nurse. Already
she is prepared to minister to the wounded and dying on
the field of battle. Without exaggeration she may be called
a Florence Nightingale of our own time."

The latest letter from Judith, like the latest letter from
Jerome, was burning through Daniel's breast pocket to
his heart at that moment: *"We had a grand trip down here
to Morris Field. From Alex. we went to Fredericksburg,
then Richmond where Gracie, Hazel, and Ada left Laura
and me to go to their own post. Then on to the N. C. line,
saw lots of beautiful old estates, just like pictures, quantities of horses in the fields, got to Raleigh about 9:30
p. m. It was our hardest day of all because we wanted to
see so much, but was it worthwhile! We left R. about 10:30
next a. m. and followed Route 29 to Charlotte, it is a
wonderful place, very large, lots of stores, etc. Got here
to camp about 4 p. m. It is a new camp but nice. The
chief nurse is young and attractive, comes from Texas.
On Mon. night we celebrated her birthday, had a big dinner and dance. Tues. night, 2 sgts. invited Laura and me
to go in town with them and we might have had another
swell time if it hadn't been for the rule that nurses, as
commissioned officers, aren't allowed to have dates with
non-commissioned officers. Of course sometimes they take
a chance and do it anyway, but we thought we'd better*

not and the next morning we got a marked copy of the
Fort Banks Digest *with this poem in it:*

'NURSES? CURSES!
Sing us a song of pain and penance—
Army nurses are all lieutenants.
Whether they're blondes, brunettes or titians,
The hell of it is: They have commissions.
And privates, creatures of low degree,
Can dream but never hope to be
More to the nurses that win their hearts
Than pulses, temperatures and charts.' "

Daniel was glad Judith—was happy, just as he was
glad Jerome was happy, but he wished Mr. Loper would
not talk about Jerome as valiant while he was still free
to be out on the golf links, or of Judith as a ministering
Florence Nightingale when she was spending her free
time going to dinners and dances.

But Mr. Loper had now ceased to discuss Jerome and
Judith and had reverted to Jenness, though her father
did not feel the lawyer's description of her was wholly
accurate. "Now, Gentlemen, Mr. Bryant had read from
the indictment several significant passages which certainly
show what position this poor, defenseless young woman
was in before the Grand Jury. You have heard the suggestion of a threat, the suggestion of a felony—yes, a
felony, Gentlemen—the suggestion of jail—all the suggestions made to the defendant, as timidly and alone, she
faced a barrage of questions—and suggestions such as I
have mentioned—from the government attorneys and
members of the Grand Jury. I say 'timidly,' Gentlemen,
because naturally any young woman who undergoes such
a grilling feels upset and unstrung by the questions so
relentlessly hurled at her. Naturally, she becomes confused. What preparation can a lovely young girl such as
Miss Farman—born and brought up, as I have already
indicated to you, on a New England farm, and come to
Washington to act as a hardworking secretary—what
preparation can she have had for such an ordeal as she

must have gone through during the probing of the Grand
Jury? *She* is no lawyer; *she* has not spent years learning
and practicing how to make subtle innuendoes, how to
make glib and ready answers."

Daniel glanced at Serena. She had stopped sobbing. She
seemed to be taking heart. But he himself had no such
sense of encouragement.

"Gentlemen, you are trying this defendant for having
knowingly and falsely testified," Loper continued slowly.
"This charge then must be based on some impediment of
justice; this young woman must have put something in
the way of justice being carried out.

"But did she? I say she did not. This Grand Jury that
indicted her for perjury was supposed to have been investigating Lentz and the failure of foreign agents to register. All right then. Lentz was indicted by them prior to
Miss Farman's first appearance before the Grand Jury.
Therefore her testimony before them could not have, in
any way, impeded any investigation of Lentz. Nor has
there ever been any suggestion that this fair young defendant ever knew or had anything to do with any other
agent.

"You, Gentlemen, have listened to a great deal that
has been said concerning these mail bags that you see
heaped up there beside the table. You have heard various
witnesses testify as to the whereabouts of those mail bags
at varying times. Those mail bags went from the Better
Bill Britain First Committee to the storeroom in the House
Office Building. But Gentlemen, those same mail bags
were produced before the Grand Jury. They are in Court
this very minute, as you can see for yourselves.

"Those mail bags are intact—they have not been
touched. Nor has there ever been the slightest suggestion
that they are in any way different from the way they were
when they left Slade's place. Then what is this all about?
The mail bags went before the Grand Jury and are in
this courtroom now.

"Now, Gentlemen, in spite of this immateriality which
I am sure I have now explained to your satisfaction, Mr.
Bryant walked over toward this helpless, bewildered de-

fendant who sat here during the trial and he said: "She is a most important cog in the greatest propaganda machine the world has ever seen,' He even attempted to hook her up with the 'long arm of the Gestapo' whose sinister shadow he brought into this very courtroom. Would a young woman with her background and heritage, a young woman who has worked hard to earn her own living, would she be apt to be a tool of the Nazis? Look at this young defendant as she sits there so quietly, Gentlemen. Does she appear to you to be the kind of person a 'cog in the Nazi propaganda machine' would be?"

Again Daniel had no sense of encouragement when Mr. Loper paused. All eyes were now turned towards Jenness again, and again her father saw condemnation rather than sympathy in their glances, as he had when the vile epithets had been hurled at her. She was too assured, and far, far too beautiful to conjure up an image of a workday drudge. Indeed, something about her did actually suggest the embodiment of the classic fictional spy.

"It comes as a shock to see the United States Government—that has all the privileges and advantages—setting up its power against one lone, helpless American girl—a citizen, Gentlemen, loyal and patriotic," Mr. Loper declared righteously. "Every day when I come here I look at the statue of Lincoln out in the courtyard and I am reminded of what he said, 'Why should there not be a patient confidence in the ultimate justice of the people?' To this defendant you are now the people. You can either send her to languish in jail where the bloom of her beautiful youth will fade slowly from day to day and her belief in the essential goodness of human nature falters and fails; or you can send her home, rejoicing, on the arm of her father who patiently sits here, hoping and praying that this may happen, with the mother who has prepared for her return to the dwelling sanctified by the noble deeds of her ancestors."

Mr. Loper's final remarks were accompanied by a gesture even more impassioned than any of his previous motions, and before he sat down, he struck and held a grandiloquent attitude which was not without a momentary

effect. His reference to the Farmans, however, focussed less
attention on them than the similar one which he had made
before. The audience at this point was eagerly awaiting the
rebuttal of the prosecuting attorney, which was surprisingly brief; Keith Bryant was too wise to risk an anti-
climax. The bailiff had now gone to the door, preventing
entrance to the courtroom or departure from it. The
Judge had begun his instructions to the jury, which he
gave concisely, in spite of the clarity with which he defined
their duties. As he brought his remarks to a close, he
thanked and dismissed the alternate jurors, who to the
very end continued to look like depressed substitutes on a
football team. Then the Judge turned again to the jury
and spoke to them with great solemnity.

"You may take the case."

So this is the end, the very end, except for the verdict,
Daniel said to himself, watching the jury file out. The
testimony is ended, the arguments are over. Keith Bryant
will say nothing more, Tom Loper will say nothing more,
nor Max Lentz, nor Martha Bowers, nor Minnie Withers.
And Horace Vaughn will say nothing now either. He alone,
of all those concerned, has said nothing throughout these
six dreadful days. He has not appeared, he has sent no
message, he has made no sign. Or could Daniel be mistaken? Certainly Vaughn had not appeared. But had he
sent no message, had he given no sign? After their futile
visit to the House Office Building, Daniel had endeavored
to talk to Jenness about Vaughn. But to his amazement,
the fury she had shown in the face of Minnie Withers'
disclosure had been short-lived. Long before she had recovered from the general hysteria precipitated by her tussle
with Herb Parrish, she had rallied from that part of it
which seemed connected with Vaughn. She was sure there
was some good reason for his absence, she told her father,
in almost her first calm moment, beyond what that nitwit,
Minnie Withers, had acted so smug about. If Horace
really had gone to stay with his thin-lipped mother, there
was more to his visit than met the eye. Mrs. Vaughn
claimed to have a weak heart—Jenness could tell the

world it was weak enough in some ways—and gave her debilitated health as an excuse for her prolonged absences from Washington. Sooner or later, if she really did have heart disease, she would be seized with a fatal attack. Horace had discussed this possibility, and its potential consequences, as far as they might affect her, with Jenness more than once. Mrs. Vaughn might be in a critical condition now, or she might be putting up a good imitation of one. It was all phooey about his being overworked. But his mother might very well have put on an act, or have been seriously ill.

Daniel was appalled at the callousness with which Jenness spoke of Mrs. Vaughn, and of the happy solution which his daughter seemed to think her possible demise would be for all concerned. But moral lectures on that subject left Jenness entirely unmoved, and at that point her father was reluctant to deliver them, in any case. He dreaded to have her lose her balance again; and he felt that almost any self-argument which would convince her that Vaughn's absence was reasonable and proper did not lack its advantages at that juncture. He was increasingly amazed, however, because the more protracted this absence became, the more calmly Jenness seemed to regard it. After the indictment, while she was awaiting trial, she followed Joe Racina's advice: she went back not only to her apartment, but to Vaughn's office, and nonchalantly continued to do a certain amount of work in Minnie Withers' very teeth. Indeed, she did not leave the office until the very day that the trial began; and during this interval, on the rare occasions when Daniel had ventured to mention Vaughn's name to her, she had looked at him with a little secretive smile of satisfaction and told him not to worry, that everything would be all right.

She could hardly have been so self-assured, Daniel told himself, unless she had some sound reason for confidence. She must be hearing from Vaughn regularly, either directly or indirectly. With sudden dismay, Daniel thought of the magnificent orchids, which bloomed afresh every day on his daughter's shoulder; of the black dresses, which he now knew were so costly; then, with mounting horror, of the rich furs slung arrogantly around her, of the glittering wrist watch at which she glanced so often, of the shining pendant which dangled on a slender chain between her breasts. Were these gifts, sent with messages so adroitly worded that they could be unsigned, the poisoned hypnotics which were numbing her senses and tiding her over as long as it suited Vaughn?

In one shocked moment the dreadful doubt robbed him of the brief respite given by the assurance that Jenness had not received money from Lentz for personal reasons. But before he could either answer or dismiss the harrowing question he was conscious of a murmur and a stir. Looking up, he saw that the bailiff who had charge of the jury was again standing by the door, and that the jury members were filing back into the courtroom. They came slowly and grouped themselves in order, respectfully awaiting the attention of the Judge. This was immediately given.

"Mr. Foreman, has the jury agreed upon a verdict?"

"It has, Sir."

The stir and murmur had ceased with unbelievable suddenness. Everyone in the courtroom leaned forward instinctively, as if this change in position would make for better hearing. Then came a sense of great concentration, a deep silence.

"What say you as to the guilt or innocence of the defendant, Jenness Farman, on the first count of the indictment?"

"Guilty."

There was a sharp general intake of breath. The woman with the dilated eyes muttered, "I knew it, I knew it!" But the one who had drawn the amateurish caricature turned to her companion with an exclamation of incredulity. The syndicate writer reached for a fresh sheet of paper. The "bitchy columnist" had already begun to scribble and the pert cartoonist to sketch.

"And what say you on the guilt or innocence of Jenness Farman on the second charge of the indictment?"

"Guilty."

A buzz vibrated through the courtroom, rising in volume until it was no longer a suppressed hum but a sharp sibilant sound which the bailiff could not quell. The Judge rapped loudly and the noise of his gavel echoed above the buzzing.

"Members of the Jury, your foreman says you find the defendant guilty as indicted and that is your verdict. So say you each and all?"

"We do."

The words had the solemnity of a marriage vow. But they produced no shock. After the first two pronouncements, they had been almost inevitable. Daniel forced himself to glance at Jenness. She was standing with her gloved hands lightly clasped, her vivid face composed, her lithe body erect. She had never looked lovelier. A thrill of pride in her self control pierced her father's anguished heart. That was the way the French queen must have looked, he thought, on her way to the guillotine. Strange, that twice during this trial he should have thought of Jenness in connection with French queens.

"Your Honor, I ask that the jury be polled."

Loper was on his feet, his face flushed, his voice loud. The Judge answered with great gravity, giving the order.

"Yes. The jury shall be polled."

The clerk rose and stepped forward. He was a sandy, weedy little man with a pink nose which quivered like a rabbit's. He spoke shrilly to the jurors.

"Mr. Penniman, what do you say on the first count?"

"Guilty."

"And on the second count?"

"Guilty."

Mr. Penniman was the chicken fancier. He seemed to sigh with relief as he spoke. At last the end was in sight. In a few minutes he would be free to return to his coops.

"Mr. Moseley, what do you say to the first count?"

"Guilty."

"And to the second count?"

"Guilty."

Mr. Moseley was the undertaker. He intoned his words and wrung his moist hands. He also was preparing to officiate in his normal capacity again.

"Mr. Featherstone, what do you say on the first count?"

"Guilty."

"And on the second count?"

"Guilty."

Mr. Featherstone was the haberdasher. He removed the carefully folded handkerchief from his breast pocket and lightly patted his upper lip. The handkerchief had a discreet blue border, and blue initials enclosed in a diamond-shaped design. While patting his upper lip, he was careful to do so with one of the plain corners.

"The jury will be excused."

The men were filing out for the last time. Their manner had suddenly become less listless, their step more springing. The courtroom door closed after them and again there was a hum which rose to a buzz. Above it Loper was addressing the Court. But he was not shouting any longer. At this moment his manner had more dignity than at any time during the trial.

"If Your Honor please, I understand that to make a motion to set aside the verdict, or for a new trial, it must be done formally and in writing. But pending that I ask that the bond of this defendant may be continued and that she may be released."

The spectators, who had been busily preparing to leave the courtroom in the wake of the jury, suddenly ceased getting ready. The syndicate writer unsnapped her handbag and drew out the sheet of paper that had been folded inside. Daniel, pausing on the end of the seat which he had been on the point of leaving, saw rather than felt that his hand, which rested on the back of it, was shaking.

"I think the motion must be overruled." The Judge was speaking even more gravely than when he had ordered the jury polled and again he was weighing his words. "The constant practice of this Court is to commit upon the verdict of the jury."

"But Your Honor, this is not an ordinary case."

Loper was making a real plea. Stripped of sentimentalism and sensationalism, his manner was earnest and impelling. Daniel could see that it was not without its effect on the Judge, and looking first at Jenness and then at

Joe, he saw that they realized this too. The color which, for all her composure, had been slowly drained away, was coming back into his daughter's face. The reporter had stopped in his tracks, and was watching the Judge with intense eyes. Justice Bellinger, feeling the scrutiny, instinctively recoiled from the effect of leniency which he had produced.

"Ordinarily the defendants in this Court all look alike."

"I appreciate that. But, if it please the Court, may I point out that the defendant is not the type usually brought before this tribunal. She is not a recidivist, Your Honor. It would be impossible for her to go out of this courtroom today, and, pending sentence, again commit the felony for which this jury has now convicted her. Remember, she is not a vendor of narcotics. She is not a common thief. She is not a prostitute. She is not a murderess.

"As you well know, Your Honor, as the prosecuting attorney well knows, and as I have previously stated in the presence of the jury, there is nothing in the past life of this defendant showing that she has ever committed so much as a petty misdemeanor.

"The Farmans' reputation is beyond reproach. Their record is remarkable. The family background indicates loyalty to country and love of God. It is the antithesis of treachery. I reiterate, the defendant's brother and sister are both officers in the armed forces of the United States. At great financial sacrifice, her parents have been in Washington throughout their daughter's ordeal. I beseech Your Honor that you permit the defendant's bail to be continued, so that she may have their comfort and support until such time as a new trial may be granted or the sentence actually imposed."

Again Judge Bellinger appeared to ponder. Then he turned to the prosecuting attorney.

"I must repeat that such procedure would be contrary to the spirit of this Court. Nevertheless, I shall not decline to hear an expression of opinion from the prosecuting attorney."

Again a deep hush fell on the courtroom. Like the Judge, the prosecuting attorney seemed engulfed in thought.

His intensity was one of silence now, but his power still prevailed. At last he spoke, and from his deliberation came the miracle of reprieve.

"Your Honor, as my opponent has so eloquently pointed out, this is not an ordinary case. In this instance the government would have no objection."

"Very well. The bail may be continued. You may arrange with the clerk."

The Judge was already rising and arranging his robes. The bailiff's dismissal of the Court fell upon deaf ears. Unbelieving but undetained, Daniel and Serena walked to the defendant's chair.

CHAPTER 18

AT SEVEN in the morning, the long corridor leading to Horace Vaughn's office was still deserted. Jenness had counted on this, for by now she was well acquainted with the habits of individual Congressmen and their secretaries. The wife of a former Vice President, who was also his "chief-of-staff," had made a practice of beginning her working day around six, priding herself, with reason, on the amount of ground she could cover before the rest of the office personnel arrived. But she was a glittering exception to a prosaic rule. Nine was considered matutinal by almost every one. Jenness fitted her key into the lock of the private office and entered.

Like most congressional suites, this one was arranged with the private office and the general office side by side, each with an outside door leading into the corridor, and with an inside door connecting the two. This arrangement made it possible for a Congressman to enter his private office without the necessity of passing through his general office in order to do so, thus keeping his presence unobserved and avoiding importunate callers. His secretary seldom possessed a key of her own to the outside door of this sanctum; she was generally obliged to enter it from the inside door. It had never occurred, either to Horace Vaughn or to Minnie Withers, that Minnie should have the privilege of direct entry to his private quarters at any time. But Jenness had long been privileged in this way. She had never felt more fortunate in possessing the privilege than she did now.

Her first act, after entering the private office, was to walk over to the inside door and bolt it on that side. Of course, she said to herself, it would still be ages before that sour-puss Minnie came along and tried to get in; but it was just as well to be on the safe side. Jenness did not propose to take any chances, when it came to a question of having her conference with Horace interrupted, and if she locked the door now, that would be off her mind. When Minnie tried it from the other side, she would assume that Horace had locked it himself, for some special reason, and she would not try it again. What was more, she would not announce any callers, however important they appeared or put through any telephone calls. She would assume that the locked door signified a desire for absolute privacy, and she would defend this with fierce pride. Minnie's conscientious attitude towards her work was untinged with imagination.

Jenness had been sleeping very badly for some time now and this last night, when she had made up her mind to come to Horace's office, she had slept hardly at all. But she had not made the mistake of putting on too much makeup in a futile effort to conceal the haggardness, which, like a blight, was slowly overspreading the fresh bloom of her face. She had done it very expertly and delicately, so that no man could have told where the natural color ended and the artificial glow began; the finished effect was one of great ethereality and charm. Jenness did not look wan or faded, but she did look fragile and fine-drawn. The look was exceedingly becoming.

She had bestowed the same thoughtful care on her clothes as on her complexion. She was wearing the most conservative of all her beautiful black dresses, one of those which closed with neat little buttons around her wrists, and had no trimming except a closing, similarly adorned with buttons, at the neckline. She had on her diamond wrist watch and her diamond pendant, but the pendant hung over the flat crepe and not between folds of shiny satin which opened to disclose a white neck; and she had on her silver fox furs, but no orchids fluttered on these. As a matter of fact she had received no orchids as presents for several days, or, as far as that went, any other persents, and she had always regarded with great scorn girls who sent flowers to themselves.

Horace Vaughn liked an orderly desk and the top of this was uncluttered now: the sparsely filled mahogany trays were straight; the small stack of correspondence requiring immediate attention was neatly placed under a paper weight on one side of the immaculate blotter; the equally small stack of bills currently before Congress in which he was especially interested were similarly arranged on the other side. His calendar and his engagement pad, framed in matching leather, delicately tooled, flanked the inkstand. The engagement pad seemed unusually well filled and Jenness picked it up and attentively examined the different items on it. Then she put it down and looked even more attentively at the photographs of Mrs. Vaughn and Marion Pierce, also framed in delicately-tooled leather. She did not touch any of the papers on the desk, or look at anything else on it. When she put down the framed photographs, too, she seated herself in one of the big comfortable leather chairs drawn up beside the desk, and watched the electric clock that was fastened over the doorway, intermittently glancing away from it to look at other objects about the room. A pictorial map of his district, his diploma from Yale, and several honorary degrees which had been conferred upon him adorned the walls; the bookcases were commodious and well-filled, not only with back copies of the Congressional Record and various volumes generously bestowed by publishers upon men in public office because of some special slant, but also with biographies and autobiographies of numerous Vaughns, the town histories of the places in which they had been leading citizens, their genealogies and public papers. The room as a whole bespoke wealth, leisure and tradition and was permeated with family pride as well as comfort. Jenness had always been aware, in a general way, that it had these attributes. But she had never been so definitely conscious of them as she was now, or had she ever told herself, so defensively, that a man with a heritage like Horace Vaughn would instinctively adhere to the standards of a gentleman born and bred.

Her wait was a long one, but she did not permit it to rouse her to restlessness or impatience. Shortly before nine, she was aware of Minnie Withers, beginning to move around in the outer office. From the other side, the clerk turned the knob of the door leading to the private office and finding this locked, immediately retreated, as Jenness had felt sure she would; the little click, revealing that Minnie was trying the door, did not come a second time. At twenty minutes of ten, a key turned in the door leading from the corridor, and Jenness rose to meet Horace Vaughn.

He was looking extremely fit. He always wore his well-tailored clothes easily, after the manner of a man so thoroughly accustomed to the best money can buy that he attaches no special importance to it and gives it no special attention; but this morning his essential elegance seemed especially marked. His eyes were clear, his color fresh and his step quick. He appeared to have slept well and breakfasted well, to have come only recently from a thorough shower, and to have enjoyed a brisk walk in the open air during the interval. When he saw Jenness, he did not stop or betray displeasure or embarrassment. He continued to advance towards her, and he spoke to her agreeably if impersonally.

"Why, good morning," he said, almost as if he had expected to find her awaiting him, rather than as if she had given him an unwelcome surprise. "How charming you look, Jenness. Did you want to see me about something?"

"It isn't unnatural that I should, is it? I've tried, several times, without success, to reach you by telephone, and I've also written to you several times without receiving any answer to my letters. It's very important that I should consult you. I decided that I had better come here, without wasting any more time. As a matter of fact, there isn't any more time to waste."

"I'm sorry you've been put to so much trouble. I've been unusually busy these last few days. I'm afraid I haven't caught up with my calls and that I've let my correspondence get ahead of me. But I'm not quite sure that I follow you. Just what do you mean by saying there isn't any more time to waste?"

"Tomorrow's sentence day, Horace."

"Is it really so soon? I was under the impression that a longer period usually elapsed between a verdict and a sentence. But I haven't any control over the court calendar."

"No, of course not. But you might have some influence otherwise."

"Unfortunately I haven't, beyond the limits in which I've already exerted it indirectly. In understand that Justice Bellinger has shown exceptional leniency in your case, as a result of Mr. Loper's eloquence. If I'm not mistaken, this is almost the first instance in which he's departed from the constant practice of the Court to commit upon the verdict of the jury. But it was apparently very clear that there was to be no question of suspending sentence. The Court didn't consider this a case for probation. It merely permitted the continuance of your bail, so that you might have the comfort and support of your parents' company until sentence was actually imposed."

"Or until a new trial was granted."

"Yes, it's unfortunate that Loper's motion for a new trial was denied. Later on, however, you might possibly appeal the case——"

"But, Horace, if sentence is imposed before a new trial is granted, I'll have to go straight to prison! I'll have to go tomorrow! I'll have to stay there until there *is* a new trial."

"Yes, I'm afraid you will."

"Is that all you have to say, that you're afraid I will?"

"What else do you expect me to say? I've pointed out to you that I can't control the courts."

"Yes, that's what you're pointing out now. But for months you've kept telling me there was nothing to be afraid of. You didn't tell me that I might face a minimum term of two years in prison, that I might be kept there six years. Deprived of my liberty, separated from my family and my friends. Sleeping in a cell, eating coarse food, doing hard manual labor, wearing a uniform that's a badge of disgrace in itself . . ."

"I don't think it's really as bad as all that. I understand that prisons are model institutions nowadays. And of course there's always the chance of a commuted sentence for good behavior, or for a new trial after all."

"That's not what you told me before either. If you had, I'd have told *you* what any girl in my place would have told you: that it didn't matter how model an institution was, she wasn't going to take the risk of getting into one; that it didn't matter how good the chances were of a commuted sentence or a new trial, she wasn't going to take the risk of getting a summons in the first place. But you assured me there weren't any risks. You said that if I'd be guided by you, everything would be all right. And I *was* guided by you. I did everything you told me to."

"Yes, you were very amenable, Jenness, and very trustworthy too. I've tried to show you that I appreciated these qualities. I engaged the best lawyer I could get for you. I've paid him for his services and his services came high. I don't begrudge what I spent at all. I was glad to do this for you. But at the same time . . ."

"At the same time, paying a lawyer isn't what I thought you meant you'd do when you said you'd back me to the limit in everything. You said the charges against me were utterly fantastic and absurd."

"I still say so. But unfortunately the Attorney General didn't agree with me. Or the jury. I can't control their opinions, or their actions, any more than I can control the court's."

"The jury might have formed a different opinion or

taken a different action if you'd gone on the witness stand in my defense."

"Mr. Loper didn't think it was advisable for me to appear on the witness stand. When you retain a competent lawyer, you naturally abide by his advice."

"Did he also advise you to leave town immediately after the hearing before the Grand Jury? And to stay out of town until the trial was over? And to have your clerk and your butler say you couldn't be reached just then, every time I telephoned? And to leave my letters unanswered?"

For the first time the urbanity of Horace Vaughn's manner seemed to crack a little. He opened his lips as if to speak and then apparently thought better of it. Without making any direct answer to the questions Jenness asked him, he walked over to his desk and sat down in front of it, resting his hands on the edge of it in a way suggesting that he was eager to begin picking up the papers which lay there, and glancing at his calendar. Jenness walked over to the desk too, and stood on the opposite side of it, resting her own hands on it and leaning towards him.

"If I hadn't still happened to have my own key to your private office I'd never have been able to get in touch with you at all, no matter how much I needed you." She did not speak noisily or rudely, and she did not speak teasingly or tearfully either, but with a degree of self-control which was a source of great relief to Horace Vaughn, who had been afraid that she might betray emotionalism at any moment. Nevertheless she went on in a way which showed that she had no intention of being either sidetracked or silenced, and for some reason he flinched slightly from a recital of facts which did not sound especially creditable to him as she enumerated them, though none of them was in itself damaging. "You say you've been unusually busy since you came back to Washington, and I guess you have, from what I've read in the papers. You've been to receptions at the Polish Embassy and the Russian Embassy and the Brazilian Embassy. You've been to a dinner at the French Embassy and you and your

mother have given a big dinner yourselves. This isn't
counting a lot of cocktail parties and numerous other miscellaneous festivities. It sounds to me as if you'd been
having a pretty gala time. But you know I haven't been.
You know I've been frightened and lonely and desperate.
And still you've never come near me, still you've never
sent me any word, though you told me over and over
again that you'd stand by me, a hundred percent, whatever happened."

"I'm sorry if you've misinterpreted anything I've said
to you. I don't like to seem to stress any of my own good
offices, but I've already reminded you that I retained, at
my own expense, the best lawyer I could find for you.
It isn't my fault that he couldn't stand up against a steam
roller like Keith Bryant. And it isn't my fault either that
the members of the jury, like almost everyone else in
Washington, seemed to be victims of war hysteria. They've
probably been sitting around brooding, or working themselves up into a frenzy. That seems to be the common
practice nowadays. I doubt if any of them was in the
proper frame of mind to render a balanced verdict, which
is very unfortunate for you, of course. Personally I consider it important to fill one's time with normal pursuits,
as far as possible. That is why I have been going on with
mine. The receptions and dinners you mention were all
official functions. I don't need to tell you how closely such
affairs are interwoven with the fabric of political life. It's
practically impossible to disassociate one from the other."

"You were able to do it often enough to see a good
deal of me until I had to appear before the Grand Jury."

"Jenness, I hope very much that you are not going to
be unreasonable. By an unfortunate coicidence, my mother
had a very serious heart attack the same day that you were
called before the Grand Jury. You know this already. You
do not needed to be told that I was obliged to leave, at
a moment's notice, to go to her. But I tried to show
you, in every possible way, that you were still in my
thoughts."

His glance strayed from the papers at which he had
been gazing so yearningly to the diamond wrist watch

clasped around Jenness' impeccable black buttoned sleeve, and then, lifting a little, to the pendant and the silver fox scarf. She followed it too.

"So it was you who sent them to me? The jewelry and the furs and the orchids and the big bank notes?"

"Of course it was I. You knew that perfectly well when you accepted them."

"They all came anonymously. They'd have meant more to me, Horace, if you'd signed your name to them."

"I didn't suppose it was necessary for me to sign my name to them. I didn't suppose it was your habit to accept gifts of such value promiscuosly."

For the first time, she flushed angrily. But the retort she seemed on the point of making was bitten back. Instead of speaking sharply, she replied temperately and tellingly.

"What that really the reason? Or did you think perhaps it was more prudent, under all the circumstances, to send them unsigned?"

"I will answer your second question first. I think it is always more prudent that such gifts should be sent anonymously if they are made by a man in official life, to his very charming secretary. This is not the first time I have sent you presents of this kind, in this way, and you have never resented it before. There is no reason why you should connect my methods with the fact that you were on trial. As to your own conduct, since you have indirectly raised that point, I'm afraid I must say something which I had hoped you would never force me to say: it is beginning to look to me, Jenness, as if you had been very indiscreet."

"I'm afraid I have. But I didn't expect you to reproach me for that. I should think you'd be the last person to do such a thing."

"There is every reason why I should reproach you. I naturally assumed that you were a girl of good character when I made you, to a certain degree, my comapnion as well as my confidential secretary."

"I was a girl of good character. I'm still a girl of good character, even if it was indiscreet to become your companion, as you call it, to a certain degree."

"There's is nothing else to call it. But I was not referring to that when I spoke of indiscretion. I was referring to the fact that I have just discovered, to my pained and very great surprise, that you have been seeing a good deal of a good many other men."

"A good deal of a good many other men! Why, Horace, how could I, when I was with you practically all the time?"

"That is a slight exaggeration. You have been with me a good deal, but you have not been with me practically all the time, by any means. Please do not infer that you have. Especially since during the intervals——"

He picked up a paper cutter. It had been within easy reach all the while, and for some moments he had felt as if he would like to occupy himself in some way while he talked to Jenness, who was still standing on the other side of the desk, gripping the edge of it with her hands, but otherwise giving no sign that she was struggling to keep her self-control. She was really a very beautiful girl, very beautiful and very alluring. She did justice to custom made clothes and handsome jewels. Her bearing was really remarkable, for a girl from the country, not to mention her figure, which was remarkable for any girl, no matter where she had come from. Moreover, she had always been perfectly ladylike, never telling a smutty story, never taking one cocktail too many; and she had also been extraordinarily circumspect, never discussing their association with anyone or otherwise making it conspicuous. But there was nothing solemn or prudish about her either. She really had been a good companion—the word was more appropriate than Jenness had been willing to admit: a much merrier and better companion than Marion Pierce ever had been or ever could be. Involuntarily he compared the dullness and rigidity of Marion with the gaiety and complacence of Jenness and stifled a sigh. It was too bad that everything had to end like this. Nevertheless he steeled himself to continue.

"I understand, from reliable sources, that during the intervals of our—companionship, you at one time saw a great deal of Peter MacDonald, a representative of the *Bulletin* who is now its foreign correspondent."

"Yes, I did. But Peter wanted to marry me. He asked me to over and over again, and he wouldn't have done that if there had been anything shameful about our relationship. You can't pretend that you think there was, Horace."

"He left Washington very abruptly. At a time when it would seem to me that he might have been serviceable to you, if he were really in love with you. You are slightly inconsistent, Jenness, in blaming me for doing something which apparently you considered quite proper on the part of Peter MacDonald."

"It was quite proper, as far as he was concerned. He gave me a chance to tell him the truth. And I wouldn't. I lied to him, just as I lied to my father and mother, just as I lied to the Grand Jury—for your sake. And Peter hates a liar. He said he'd never forgive me and he won't. He took the first chance he could of getting on the other side of the world from me. But I've never blamed him. He didn't let me down. It was I who let him down. And I'm sorry I had to, because Peter's a grand person. As grand as they come. But I had to, because it was you I cared for."

Her lips were trembling a little now. She bit them and looked away. Before she looked back again, Horace Vaughn went on talking.

"Well, I suppose I shall have to accept your assurance that your association with Peter MacDonald was wholly innocent in a personal way. But I still think you were indiscreet in spending so much time with him, under the circumstances."

"Under the circumstances! Under what circumstances?"

"The circumstances of our own association," Horace Vaughn said smoothly. "I did not realize then that at a time when you were accepting a great many costly presents from me, and accompanying me here and there in public, you were also lending a receptive ear to proposals of marriage from a cheap reporter representing a sensational paper which has lost no occasion to smear me and defame me."

"I didn't lend a receptive ear! I refused him, over and

over again. But you shan't call him cheap, because he isn't!
I won't let you slander Peter by slandering me! Peter is
just as straight as they come and——"

"Jenness, you have shown admirable self-control up to
this point and I hope you will continue to do so throughout the rest of this interview. I must remind you that it
was you who sought it and also that I cannot prolong it
indefinitely. I am late for a committee meeting already.
I said I was willing to dismiss the subject of Peter Mac-
Donald. But what about the other staff members of the
same paper with whom you have constantly associated?
What about Joe Racina? What about Marcy Heath? If
it had not been for them you probably never would have
been brought to trial. It was they who made a mountain
out of a molehill with the story of the mail bags and the
pictures of them, not to mention Racina's original snooping around the Government Printing Office."

"They tried to be faithful to their paper, just as I tried
to be faithful to you. They *had* to be. It's part of a newspaperman's code. And Joe Racina's Peter's best friend. He
took over when Peter went away."

"Yes, that is what I was given to understand."

"I don't know what your dirty spies have been telling
you. When I said he took over, I didn't mean he wanted
to marry me too. I meant——"

"I was not given to understand that Joe Racina wanted
to *marry* you. After all, he is a pretty ordinary type of
Dago."

Jenness stopped gripping the desk and began to beat
on it with both small clenched fists.

"Don't you dare call him an ordinary type of Dago!"
she cried. "He isn't ordinary—he's most unusual. He's
the kindest and most cultured man I ever knew in my
life. He's got just as many degrees as you have, and
they're not honorary degrees either! He earned them all
and worked his own way along while he did it. And he
isn't a Dago either. His people are poor, but they're good
Americans. They've been Americans for two generations
already. Joe's got five brothers in the Service. The only
reason he isn't in himself is because he can't get in! There's

something the matter with his eyes and he's had asthma intermittently."

"I didn't realize I was calling forth such a heated general defense when I mentioned I understood he didn't want to marry you. You seem to hold the press in very high esteem. Next I suppose you'll be telling me Marcy Heath is a member of the Porcellian Club and a Rhodes Scholar, and that his father was second in command to Pershing during World War Number One."

"I don't think Marcy Heath ever got to college. I think he started taking pictures when he was just a kid and went on because there wasn't enough money to go around. I never asked him, because I don't know him well enough to pry into his affairs and I never happened to hear. But I do know Joe well enough to answer everything you've said about him. Joe doesn't want to marry anybody. That's not to my discredit or to his either. There are lots of newspaper friendships that don't have romance or scandal attached to them, and this is one of them. He's a friend, that's all. A darn good friend. I suppose you wouldn't believe that, but it's true. He's turned the world inside out to be kind to my parents, on top of all his work. He's arranged to have me shielded and protected——"

"On Ned Waldo's boat? Where you were already a frequent visitor?"

Horace Vaughn put down the paper cutter and rested his thumb lightly on the push button near it.

"I don't want to ring this bell, Jenness," he said agreeably. "I don't want to create anything in the nature of a scene. But I'm afraid we're getting pretty close to one and therefore I feel it is time to bring this conversation to an end. I must warn you that if by any chance you should be so misguided as to attempt to create—unpleasantness of any sort for me, I shall retaliate. And I have ample means to do so.. Besides the men I have mentioned, I find that you have also seen a good deal of a reporter on the *Enterprise* commonly nicknamed 'Herb' Parrish, not to speak of several in your home town, where apparently you have been a great belle. Not that I am at all surprised to hear this, but it does have ramifications. I must add that I am very happy that my mother is greatly improved in health, so that she is now able to resume her duties as my official hostess. Naturally, this will make some difference in my manner of living. You know that she has very conservative views, and that she has never approved of the—association between you and me. If there had been no question of the trial, with all its attendant disagreeable publicity, indirectly aimed at me, this changed mode of living would necessarily have precluded me from seeing much of you. After a little reflection, I am sure that you will realize this. I am very sorry about the sentence, Jenness, and sorrier still that I can do nothing to avert it. I shall always remember our former association pleasantly and I regret that circumstances have combined to end it. I hope you will regard the little presents I have given you as mementos of it and of course your salary as my secretary will continue until you are officially replaced. But since obviously you cannot continue to serve in that capacity I suggest that you turn over the key to my private office now."

Jenness went through the plate glass doors and across the streamlined lobby of the Potomac Plaza so blindly that she did not even see the receptionist as she passed this haughty personage. But the receptionist, whose usual manner was one of such complete detachment, waylaid Jenness as she passed.

"Oh, Miss Farman—the manager suggested that I should speak to you. He understands that you won't be needing your apartment after tomorrow and he's had an excellent opportunity to rent it. He thought it would be as much to your advantage as his to do this. He would take the lease right off your hands, and of course you would have the benefit of the difference between the furnished and the unfurnished rental price. Besides, your furniture is in such harmony with the décor of the apartment house as a whole that the prospective tenant felt this was a great attraction and was willing to pay extra for it."

"I'll let you know later. I hadn't thought about it at all. And I have my parents visiting me."

"Well, the manager said if you *would* let him know before six o'clock, because this party's going to call again then———"

Jenness did not answer a second time. She swept along towards the elevator. The friendly operator spoke to her also.

"I've been wanting to tell you for a long time, Miss Farman, how sorry I am about the way things have turned out. But there's always been someone else in the elevator before, when you were, and I thought maybe you'd rather I didn't. I'm glad I've got a chance now to say it doesn't look to me as if you'd had a square deal. I'd like you to know I feel that way."

"Thank you. It's very kind of you to say so."

"And I—I'd like to come to see you sometime, Miss Farman, if—if it's allowed. I don't know about the regulations in—in places like that. But I admire you more than anyone I've ever seen. You're just my ideal. You've got so much style and so much class."

"Thank you. It's very kind of you to say so," Jenness repeated, mechanically.

She got out of the elevator and walked down the hall to her own apartment, still blindly. As she entered the formalized living room, her father, looking out of place and ill at ease, as usual, in his incongruous surroundings, glanced up from the paper he was pretending to read.

"I declare I'm relieved to see you, Jenness," he said. "Your mother and I have been real worried. You didn't say anything, last night, about going out, and you must have slipped away early because we didn't either of us hear you. It isn't often we sleep later than you do, you know that."

"Yes, I did go out early—Where's Mom?"

"Why she's gone out too. She's gone to market. She can't seem to put her mind on sightseeing, picture galleries and Shakespearian libraries and the like of that, but she does enjoy the markets. She's never seen anything like them before, so much variety and all. She thought if she went out and looked around herself, she might find something for dinner that would be real tasty."

He did not say "for the last dinner we'll be having together" but Jenness knew what he meant. She took off her hat and coat and tossed them on one of the tubular chairs at the end of the room. Then she sat down on the sofa and stretched out her hand.

"I'm glad she's gone out. I want to talk to you, and it's always easier for me to talk to you when you and I are alone. It's not that I'm any fonder of you than I am of Mom, but I've always felt closer to you. Come and sit down beside me, Daddy?"

"Well now, Jenness!—What was it you had on your mind?"

"I went out early this morning so that I could get into Horace Vaughn's private office. I still had my key to it. He wouldn't come to the telephone when I called him and he wouldn't answer my letters. I knew he was in town because I've kept reading about him in the newspapers, the parties he was giving and going to and all. And I made up my mind I was going to see him. I made up mind I wasn't going to prison without trying once more to see if he wouldn't do something for me."

"I don't know as you were wise, Jenness, to try to force yourself on him like that. Of course I've tried to get in touch with him myself, every way I could think of, and every way Joe and Waldo could think of. And I haven't succeeded . . . I hope you aren't sorry you went?"

"No, I'm not sorry I went. But I want to tell you now, Daddy, what really did happen . . . about the subversive literature, I mean."

Daniel found he could not instantly answer. He knew there must be no recriminations now, and no pedantic counsel either. Besides, his heart was so full of sympathy for this erring child of his, whose doom was close at hand, that he could not have uttered reproaches in any case. He waited a minute to steady himself, "studying," as he himself would have put it, what to say. Then he spoke slowly, weighing his words.

"Well you know I wanted all along you should do that, Jenness. I've never given up hope you would. I'm glad you're minded to do it now. Maybe this is as good a time

as any, while it's quiet here, like you say . . . You do
know Max Lentz, don't you?"

"Yes, Daddy. I've known him a long time. The first
time I saw him, Horace Vaughn brought him into the
private office and introduced him to me. Then he said,
'Jenness, this gentleman wants to send out some speeches
to the persons on our mailing list.' By that he meant the
list of the Stars and Stripes Forever Commission."

"Horace Vaughn hadn't said anything about this to you
before?"

"No, Daddy."

"And what did you say?"

"I said 'All right.' What else could I say? I was his
secretary. I had to do what he told me to do."

"I suppose you thought you had to, Jenness. It seems
to me, in a case like this, you could have refused."

"Then I'd have lost my job, Daddy."

"Yes. But it would have been better to lose your job
than——".

He could not finish. He could not say "than to be convicted of perjury . . . Than to go to prison." Again he
stopped, groping for words. "But of course it's too late
to think of that now," he said at last. "You did what
your boss told you to do, you thought you couldn't do
anything else, so you didn't ask any questions as to
whether it was right or wrong. That's the way it was,
isn't it, Jenness?"

"Yes, Daddy."

"And you're sure this was the first time you ever saw
Max Lentz?"

"Yes, Daddy. I'm very sure."

"You sound as if you had some special reason for being
sure, Jenness."

"I have, Daddy. Horace didn't stay in the office with
Max Lentz and me very long. He said he was late for
a committee meeting and he went off and left us together.
Mr. Lentz was very polite to me, and presently he said
he realized I would have to put a great deal of time and
trouble into preparing the mailing list, and that he'd like

to give me something in advance to show his appreciation."

"He offered you money and you accepted it?"

"Well, he handed me a sealed envelope. I didn't look inside it until after he had gone. We talked about the list quite a long while. When he left, I realized I didn't know how to reach him, and——"

"Couldn't you have found out, Jenness?"

"Yes, I suppose I could have found out. But after all, Daddy, I did put a lot of extra time and trouble into preparing that mailing list. It took about three weeks. I thought I was entitled to be paid extra for all that hard work. I was working hard enough anyway."

"If you were working overtime right along, didn't your regular employer ever take this into consideration?"

"Yes. He did. Of course my salary as a Congressman's secretary is fixed by law. He couldn't do anything about that. But he paid me extra himself. At least he gave me presents."

"I want you should tell me, Jenness, just how much money Max Lentz gave you for making out that mailing list and how much these presents from Vaughn came to. I aim to pay it all back."

"Horace didn't always give me presents of money, Daddy. Sometimes he gave me other things."

"Then you'll have to send them back, Jenness. Before tomorrow. I should think you'd want to. So's you can start with a clean slate."

No, that isn't what I ought to have said, he thought wretchedly. You don't talk about starting with a clean slate when a person's going to prison. It's when a person's coming out of prison that you do that. And Jenness won't be coming out of prison for a long, long time. Not for two years at least . . .

"I can't send clothes that I've worn back to Horace, Daddy. It would look ridiculous if I did that. Don't make me look ridiculous on top of everything else."

"No, Jenness, I won't do that. You'll have to figure, as close as you can, what those clothes cost. You must have a pretty fair idea about some of them, anyway. Then I'll send Vaughn a check, in a letter. I'll write on the check 'Reimbursement for advances.' I don't believe he'll refuse to accept it. And you can send back the jewelry."

Daniel had not previously voiced his suspicions about the jewelry. Now he quietly assumed that it was a gift from Vaughn.

"I'm afraid that'll be a wrench for you, daughter," he said gently. "I know that a girl as nice-looking as you are can't help but hanker after personal ornaments. But it can't be helped. You didn't come by those ornaments honestly. And now that you're starting in to be honest again . . ."

"I don't mind sending back the jewelry. At least I don't mind much. You see, when Horace gave it to me, I didn't think I was just a—sort of pastime. I thought he gave it to me because he cared for me. I thought he meant to marry me, by and by. If I hadn't believed Horace cared I wouldn't have taken it. I've always loved Horace Vaughn. If I hadn't, I'd have married Peter MacDonald."

"But you can't love Vaughn any longer, Jenness. A man like that, who used you and then deserted you in your hour of need!"

"No. I suppose I can't. But somehow I do. I haven't got used to not loving him yet. You see it was only this morning that I knew for sure. Until this morning I've kept on hoping. I thought perhaps he really was kept away by something important. I thought perhaps he didn't get the letters and the telephone messages. I thought perhaps——"

Jenness rose from the sofa and walked over to the window that led out on the little ornamental balcony. It was a mild day and she unfastened the French window and went out. For some moments she stood there looking out over the city with her back turned towards her father. He did not try to follow her, but after a long time he spoke to her.

"Come back here, Jenness. It makes me uneasy, trying to talk to you when I can't see your face and I want you should finish what you started out to tell me before your mother gets back. Was that piece of work you told me about the only one you did in Washington for Max Lentz?"

Jenness turned and came back into the room, leaving the French window unfastened. A little fresh air came stealing into the room, bringing refreshment with it. The unseasonable weather had made the steam-heated room uncomfortable.

"No. I sent out some other speeches," she said, sitting down on the sofa again. "The mailing list of the Stars and Stripes Forever Commission was just the first. I made lists of several other organizations."

"Did it take you as long to do that as it did to do the other?"

"Yes. Just about as long. About three weeks."

"And did Max Lentz give you something to repay you for your time and trouble then too?"

"Yes, Daddy."

"I want you should jot down all these sums, Jenness. I want you should let me know how much they all come to."

"All right, Daddy. I will."

There was no writing table in the living room, but there was a ridiculous ornamental desk beside her draped dressing table. She went into her bedroom and sat down at this. Daniel could see her scribbling on stray sheets of paper. He did not move or speak to her while she was doing it. But when she came back and silently handed him a slip of paper, he tucked it into his pocket without looking at it, putting his arm around her and kissing her.

"There," he said. "You're my girl, Jenness. You always have been. You always will be. I know you feel better now than you have in a long while too. Don't you, daughter?"

"Yes, Daddy."

"If you could only have told me sooner, you'd have felt better sooner. And maybe we could have helped you some —Mr. Waldo and Joe and me. We'd have studied on it together and I'm most sure we could have thought of something. Didn't you ever think before this that you'd better tell the truth, Jenness?"

"Yes. I've thought so lots of times. But I was frightened. I knew that if things went wrong, I'd be blamed and Horace might get into trouble. I didn't want Horace to get into trouble."

"There, there, I don't want you should talk about Horace Vaughn any more, Jenness, or think about him either, if you can help it. Except I do want you should tell me, if you can, how you happened to be meeting Lentz in the country too. That part of the story isn't clear to me yet."

"All right. I'll tell you about that by and by. But I don't want to talk any more now, Daddy, about anything. I can't." Suddenly she hid her face on his shoulder. "I can't stand it," she said. "I can't stand knowing that no one can help me, that Horace never meant to help me. I can't stand the thought of going to prison tomorrow. I can't do it, Daddy, I can't, I can't! Couldn't we—escape somehow? Couldn't you take me where no one would find me? Couldn't you, Daddy?"

It was still a sad saying but a true one, Daniel said later on to Serena, that there was no balm in Gilead for the hurt of the daughter of their people. Jenness had gone into her own room to take off her beautiful black dress and to lie down for a little while, after she had finished the task of putting her possessions in final order to leave. It was so still in there he thought she had gone to sleep. At least he hoped so. He suggested that Serena should not go in, at any rate, and risk disturbing her and Serena agreed with him.

"Were you able to say anything, Daniel, to give her comfort?"

"There isn't much I can say, is there, Mother? But she's told me what really happened, or a good share of what's happened. I think she will be more at peace with herself, now that she's done that."

"At peace with herself? In prison? You know as well as I do, Daniel, that she'll be beating against the bars, all the time."

They looked at each other, Daniel with a lump in his throat, Serena with overflowing eyes. Then Serena began to fumble in her handbag.

"I got a letter from Judith this morning," she said. "The clerk at the desk handed it to me as I went out. Judith's had leave and she's been over to Raeford to see Jerome and Alix. She's had a wonderful time, and she's just carried away with Alix. Maybe you'd like to see the letter yourself, Daniel."

"Thanks for thinking of it, Mother, but I don't know's I want to, right now."

"I thought it might make you feel better, knowing the others were all well and happy anyhow."

"No. Maybe it ought to. But it doesn't. It makes me feel worse."

He saw that Serena felt rebuffed, and because he did not want to add to her misery, he eventually asked for the letter and read it: *"Laura and I have just taken a trip to Fort Bragg, 130 m. from here, and we've had a wonderful time. The chief nurse gave us a 24 hr. pass so we left here Fri. at 2 and got back last night at 5. We got to Bragg about 8, had to stop five times, it rained so hard you couldn't see the headlights. When it rains it rains. Anyway we got there o.k. and of course, leave it to us, we went to the back gate and they wouldn't let us in, but finally they sent an M. P. with us to get a pass so we were o.k. then. It was nearly 9:30 so one of the M. Ps. at the gate took us to supper, then we asked for the 24th st. hospital. Six girls are there we wanted to see, but we couldn't find them anywhere, the hospital moves about every day I guess, so we gave up and drove back to the gate, and told the M. P. we were going on to Raeford and would be back in the morning. (We did and found the girls all right then.) Raeford is a small southern town but there are beautiful homes there and of course we had a swell time with Alix and Jerome. Alix has got the apartment fixed up just like nobody's business and she is the best looking thing you ever saw in your life besides being terribly nice. Jerome certainly drew a prize. Between Raeford and Fayetteville, the next town, the land is flat as a pancake with nothing but sand and pine trees as far as you can see. No, there are some peach trees too and fields of cotton and tobacco and rows and rows of sugar cane beyond the sand. We took a lot of pictures along the way. I'm going to send you a box, but don't laugh at it, will you, some cotton I picked myself,*

some pine needles, wait till you see them, so different from
ours, and leaves from a tree that grows down here, if you
put it in water it will grow into a plant and be beautiful."

Ordinarily these details about the North Carolina countryside and the town where his son was living would have
interested him, and as his wife suggested, it would have consoled him to know that Judith and Jerome were both doing
so well and that they were both enjoying themselves under
conditions into which Jerome's wife also fitted easily and
agreeably. But nothing consoled him now. He found it so
hard to concentrate on the letter that he read it three times
without fully grasping its contents. He was listening for
the sounds which did not come from the bedroom, and
the longer these were delayed the more troubled he became.

"Maybe you better peek in, Mother, after all. I can't
help but be uneasy."

"There isn't anything that could happen to her, in her
bedroom. I was uneasy myself, when she stole away this
morning so early, without a word to either of us. But I'm
not uneasy now."

"It isn't your way to worry, Mother, as much as it is
mine. I'm glad of it too. If both of us had worried all these
years, Farman Hill wouldn't have been a very peaceful
place to live in."

He tried hard to smile, but the effort was a rather feeble
one. His sense of impending disaster continued to increase.
At last he could stand it no longer. He himself went to
the door cautiously. Jenness was sitting at the silly little
desk, quietly writing. She had taken off the beautiful black
dress and had on a very simple gray one, which he had
never seen before. The room was in perfect order. Everything about its appearance, and Jenness' should have reassured him. But inexplicably, his feeling of catastrophe
persisted, though Jenness looked up with a more successful
attempt at a smile than he himself had achieved.

"It's way past dinner time, Daughter. And your mother's
put herself out considerable to be sure you had a tasty
meal."

"I'm coming right away. I didn't realize it was so late.

I found a lot to do at my desk, so I didn't lie down after all."

She rose and went into the living room with him, slipping her arm through his. Dinner was less of a strain than Daniel had feared. None of them ate heartily, but on the other hand none of them left Serena's excellent meal utterly untasted. Jenness helped her mother with the dishes, and before they had finished with these, Joe came in. He had a couple of hours to spare, he said; he thought perhaps they would like to go down to Waldo's boat for a little while. On the other hand, if he was in the way, and they would rather be left alone, all they needed to do was to tell him so; he would understand.

They were genuinely glad to see Joe, and they thought his idea about going to the boat was a good one. They were all still acting with control, but it was beginning to be like the false calmness of a well-behaved patient, who has been taken to the hospital the evening before a serious operation, or of a stricken family determined not to "give way" between a death and a funeral. The tension in the atmosphere seemed to lessen in Joe's presence, and the "couple of hours" which he had originally mentioned, doubled before anyone suggested starting back to the wharf. During the interval, he talked about everything under the sun, as he was so apt to do and so amply able to do. He thought there was a battle brewing in the Java Sea, he said, though as yet there was no official announcement of this; what he was telling them was all off the record. But after outlining the military aspects of the situation, with extreme clarity and comprehension, he went on to say that he had spent nearly a year in Java himself, and presently he had launched into a fascinating account of its sunsets and its volcanoes, its prehistoric ruins and its incomparable cuisine. It was not until they were back in the apartment that he made any reference to the impending imprisonment.

"Well, we've had a nice evening," he said cheerfully. "We'll be having a lot more too, just remember that. I'll be seeing you, Jenness, don't you think I won't—And don't *you* think so either," he added, turning momentarily from

Jenness to Daniel and Serena. "I'll be looking in on her, every now and then, and sending you bulletins. I don't know what the regulations are, but if I can't find some way of getting around them, I'm a hell of a reporter." He grinned, and put his arm around Jenness' shoulder. "You can get in touch with me too, if you need to," he said. "That's another thing to remember, and it might help. I'm not much to look at, but I usually show up when I'm needed. And when it comes to a show*down* . . ."

"Joe, please don't go. Please don't leave me. Don't let them put me in prison. They won't, as long as you stay with me. Daddy can't stop them and Horace won't, but you could. Please, Joe, please!"

Suddenly she was clinging to him, as she had clung to her father that morning, and she was trembling from head to foot. He looked beyond her, meeting Daniel's agonized eyes.

"I'm sorry, but I can't, Jenness," he said gently. "If I could have, I'd have done something to help you long before this. God knows I've tried. And God knows Peter tried, before he went away. If you'd only listened to him, if you'd only told the truth when he tried to make you, if you'd only realized whom you could trust and whom you couldn't . . . Lord, I'm not blaming you! Almost anyone would have done the same thing you did, under the same circumstances. But now that you've done it, we can't any of us save you from the consequences. You've got to work out your own salvation. Lots of people have done that in prison before this, Jenness, grand people too. You can do it if they could. Just keep saying that to yourself, instead of saying you can't stand it. Say that of course you can. Say that you're going to. Say that you'll make us all proud of you yet, as proud as we are of Peter. Give him something to come home to."

"Peter isn't like you, Joe. He'll never forgive me for lying. He'll never look at a girl who's been in prison."

"Of course he will. What do you want to bet? I'll bet you a hundred dollars he'll be racing after you so fast you'll be running away from him to keep from having him under foot. Only you mustn't run away. You mustn't run away from anything, you mustn't try to. It can't be done. Whatever you're trying to escape always catches up with you. The only time you can leave a difficulty is when you've licked it, when you've got it behind you that way. I ought to know. I've tried the other way often enough myself."

"I don't believe it. I won't believe it! I still think there's some way to escape. If you can't find one for me, I'll find one for myself. I *have* found one. I found it this morning. I thought it all out then. But I waited, hoping and hoping and hoping . . ."

She shook herself free. That was easy enough, for Joe had been holding her lightly. But how she eluded him afterwards, none of them ever knew. Joe was not lame and slow, like Dexter. He was quick as a cat. But he was not quick enough to stop Jenness as she rushed past him. He caught at her gray dress and grasped it as she reached the balcony. The dress tore, leaving a fragment in his hand. But Jenness herself had jumped. He could see her hurtling through the air and then lying quiet on the pavement beneath him.

8 mg."tar," 0.7 mg. nicotine
av. per cigarette by FTC Method.
© Lorillard 1976
NEW!
Low Tar & Nicotine Famous Micronite Filter
KENT
Golden
Lights
8 Mgs Tar. 0.7 Mgs. Nicotine
KENT GOLDEN LIGHTS
ONLY 8 MG TAR.
YET TASTES SO GOOD,
YOU WON'T BELIEVE THE NUMBERS.
Warning: The Surgeon General Has Determined
That Cigarette Smoking Is Dangerous to Your Health.

Of All Brands Sold: Lowest tar: 2 mg. "tar," 0.2 mg. nicotine
av. per cigarette, FTC Report Apr. 1976.
Kent Golden Lights: 8 mg. "tar,"
0.7 mg. nicotine av. per cigarette by FTC Method.

NEW!
KENT GOLDEN LIGHTS
LOWER IN TAR
THAN ALL THESE BRANDS.

Non-menthol Filter Brands	Tar	Nicotine	Non-menthol Filter Brands	Tar	Nicotine
KENT GOLDEN LIGHTS	**8 mg.**	**0.7 mg.** *	RALEIGH 100's	17 mg.	1.2 mg.
MERIT	9 mg.	0.7 mg. *	MARLBORO 100's	17 mg.	1.1 mg.
VANTAGE	11 mg.	0.7 mg.	BENSON & HEDGES 100's	18 mg.	1.1 mg.
MULTIFILTER	13 mg.	0.8 mg.	VICEROY 100's	18 mg.	1.2 mg.
WINSTON LIGHTS	13 mg.	0.9 mg.	MARLBORO KING SIZE	18 mg.	1.1 mg.
MARLBORO LIGHTS	13 mg.	0.8 mg.	LARK	18 mg.	1.2 mg.
RALEIGH EXTRA MILD	14 mg.	0.9 mg.	CAMEL FILTERS	18 mg.	1.2 mg.
VICEROY EXTRA MILD	14 mg.	0.9 mg.	EVE	18 mg.	1.2 mg.
PARLIAMENT BOX	14 mg.	0.8 mg.	WINSTON 100's	18 mg.	1.2 mg.
DORAL	15 mg.	1.0 mg.	WINSTON BOX	18 mg.	1.2 mg.
PARLIAMENT KING SIZE	16 mg.	0.9 mg.	CHESTERFIELD	19 mg.	1.2 mg.
VICEROY	16 mg.	1.1 mg.	LARK 100's	19 mg.	1.2 mg.
RALEIGH	16 mg.	1.1 mg.	L&M KING SIZE	19 mg.	1.2 mg.
VIRGINIA SLIMS	16 mg.	1.0 mg.	TAREYTON 100's	19 mg.	1.4 mg.
PARLIAMENT 100's	17 mg.	1.0 mg.	WINSTON KING SIZE	19 mg.	1.3 mg.
L&M BOX	17 mg.	1.1 mg.	L&M 100's	19 mg.	1.3 mg.
SILVA THINS	17 mg.	1.3 mg.	PALL MALL 100's	19 mg.	1.4 mg.
MARLBORO BOX	17 mg.	1.0 mg.	TAREYTON	21 mg.	1.4 mg.

Source: FTC Report Apr. 1976
*By FTC Method

PART III

Raeford, North Carolina

March 1942

CHAPTER 19

ALIX FARMAN, having put the finishing touches on the supper table, stood back to survey it with pride, before she went into the bedroom to change her dress. On Saturday nights, when Jerome came back from the post, she always made a little festival of his homecoming. There was a lace cloth on the table, and tall tapers in the crested candlesticks her Aunt Odilisse had sent her, and spring flowers rising from a bowl of actress glass. She had not forgotten, either, to set out the thin pointed spoons marked "Alma" which Jerome's father and mother had given her for a wedding present. Supper was ready and waiting: fricasseed chicken made from Mrs. Farman's recipe, but with rice to go with it, dry and fluffy as only a Creole could cook it, the "peas which looked like beans" which were still such a novelty to Jerome, green salad well mixed in a bowl rubbed with garlic, pecan pie prepared from nuts she had gathered herself in the yard. Jerome made the cocktails after he got there, and she did start the coffee dripping until she knew just when they would drink it. There was nothing more for her to do but make herself beautiful for her husband's coming.

While the water was running for her bubble bath, she laid out fresh clothes and slipped quickly from those she had been wearing all day. There was still plenty of time, she did not need to hurry; she could luxuriate in the scented water, in the soft towels with which she dried herself, and in the delicate powder which she dusted on afterwards. She wore, as her mother and grandmother and countless great-grandmothers had worn before, a chemise of fine linen, exquisitely made by hand and daintily bordered with lace, as her first garment. The others were more modern, but there was something about the way she put

them on that invested them all with quaint charm. Her
silk negligee was full-skirted and open-sleeved; when she
sat down in front of her dressing table, it spread out on
either side of her like a fan.

She leaned her elbows on the top of the table, and
cupping her face in her hands, gazed thoughtfully into the
mirror. The reflection was inevitably pleasing. She saw a
small oval face, the chin slightly dented with a dimple in
the center, lips which looked all the redder against the
whiteness of the surrounding skin, a straight nose, dark
eyes under still darker brows, and a smooth forehead
framed with hair that was darkest of all. It was a face that
had more than beauty in it, and it took its character from
the calm forehead and the generous mouth even more
than from the limpid eyes and the entrancing dimple. For
the brow and the lips did not belie each other; they com-
plemented each other. The one revealed an essential tranquility, an extraordinary capacity for composure; but the
other revealed supreme sensitivity and an infinite capacity
for loving and giving.

Looking at herself with quiet satisfaction, she unstopped
a flagon of perfume, sprinkled a few drops of this on her
tapering fingers, and rubbed it gently into her skin behind
her shell-pink ears and in the hollow between her white
breasts. She had noticed, in the past few days, that her
breasts were swelling a little, and they felt differently too,
when she touched them. She wondered if Jerome would
notice this, if he would miss the delicacy in which he had
so delighted, or if he would exult in the change because of
its prescience. There was as yet no other change in her
figure, and she could not help wishing, rather wistfully,
that there need not be, that in Jerome's eyes she might always remain the embodiment of loveliness and grace. He
had told her, over and over again, that he knew there had
never been such litheness and such pliancy in the body of
any other girl. And now the litheness and the pliancy
would soon be gone. She was not like a girl any more because she had become so wholly a wife. Would she be the
less beloved when she had lost that first freshness which

Jerome had so passionately loved, or would he also adore her ripening maternity?

Sighing a little, she replaced the flagon of perfume on her dressing table and began to unpin her hair. Next to her figure, her hair had always been her husband's greatest enthusiasm. Habitually, she wore it wound about her head in smooth braids which formed a coronal above the central part; but when it was unbound, it covered her like a soft black cloud. Jerome would never let her leave it braided at night. He wanted to see it the last thing before the lights went out, spread winglike over her white pillow or falling in dusky cascades over her breasts. Often he asked her to keep quiet while he arranged it to suit himself, first in one way and then in another, burying his fingers in its silky masses and drawing these out to their full length. On such occasions she lay very still, watching him with fond eyes and smiling lips, almost as she might have watched a child she was indulging. But all the time she knew in her heart that he was a man and not a child, and that the moment was coming when he would suddenly tire of this by-play, and take her suddenly in his arms and overwhelm her with his love. Then long afterwards, in the dark, he would move his hands towards her hair again and stroke it gently, telling her with renewed tenderness that he worshipped her . . .

Shaking her plaits free from their last pin, Alix sighed again; but this time it was less a sigh than a joyous intake of breath. She could bear the prospect of her coming disfigurement with tempered regret, because her hair would still remain her crowning glory. Usually she did not unbraid it until she went to bed; when she was dressing for dinner she merely rearranged and repinned it, so that it would lie becomingly above her brow, unruffled by the activities of the day which was past. But now she felt this was not enough; she wanted every strand to be as smooth and as shiny as satin. She took the braids apart and shook them free; then she began to brush her hair. In her absorption, she did not hear the turning of a latchkey in the outer door, or realize that her husband was at home until he strode across the room and imprisoned her in his embrace.

"Hello, beautiful!" he said fervently. "My, but it's good to see you! And good to get hold of you . . ." For the next few moments he said nothing more, and quite effectually he also deprived her of the power of speech. Then releasing her, he held her at arms' length, looking at her with utter gladness in his eyes. "You know you get *more* beautiful every time I go away," he said. "What do you do to yourself while I'm gone?"

"I try to prepare for your homecoming, *cher*."

She spoke with a slight and intriguing accent, which was a source of never-failing delight to Jerome, though he was apt to tease her playfully about it, and about the quaint, almost formal way in which she expressed herself. But this time there was no banter in his praise.

"And I'll tell the world you do a grand job . . . Say, I'm starving to death and I smelled all kinds of good things cooking as I came by the kitchen. But speaking of fragrance, you smell as sweet as a rose yourself. Is that a new scent you're using, or is it just you?"

"It *is* a new scent. But I hope it's partly me too."

He laughed, still joyously, and drew her towards him again, this time burying his face in the scented hollow. When he lifted it, he looked at her questioningly, and then put his hands gently under her bosom. She flushed a little.

"Yes. I wondered if you'd notice."

"How could I help noticing? I notice every least little thing about you. And this isn't a little thing."

"Do you mind?"

"Mind?"

"I mean, you—you liked me the way I was before. I was afraid you wouldn't want to see me change."

"I can't see any change yet. I can only feel one."

"I should have said, I was afraid you wouldn't want to *have* me change. I was afraid you'd always want me as I was—at first. Tell me truly, *cher*. Don't you?"

"You'll always be beautiful. You couldn't be anything else. I just told you that you grew more beautiful every time I went away."

"You're not answering me, dearest."

"I don't know just how to answer you. I think you'll go

on getting more and more beautiful. But I suppose it's true that I'll be a little sorry to see you change. Because you were so perfect just as you were. And because I've seen you such a short time. If I'd only had you a little longer——"

"But you wanted a baby, *cher.*"

"Yes. That's right. At least, I wanted to be sure you were going to have one, before I went away. I wanted to know there'd be another Jerome Farman on Farman Hill, whatever happened."

"But you're not going away yet and nothing is going to happen. Nothing to make us sad."

"Yes, that's right too. My number hasn't been called yet. I think an outfit's getting ready to push off the first of the week. But I'm not in it."

"Are you sure?"

"Of course I'm sure. If I were, I'd have been 'alerted' two or three weeks ago. You know that yourself."

He rose, lighted a cigarette, and began to move around the room. Alix sat still, watching him closely; but his restlessness did not disturb her. He was always eager, always impatient, always questing. His dark, mobile face, so different from those of his fair sisters, almost never wholly lost its haunted look, and lately this expression had become intensified. Alix knew that there were all sorts of reasons for this: he had never fully recovered from the strain of being up every night for a week, and in the field all that time, during the latest maneuvers. This strain was not caused by mere fatigue. Jerome was very strong. But he had been responsible for one company all the time and on the last day for five, as well as for a million dollars worth of property. This responsibility had told on him. And there were other matters which were troubling Jerome. The suicide of Jenness had been more than a source of profound sorrow to him; it had also been a horrible shock, and he was still oppressed by a sense of overwhelming tragedy. He had not been able to leave camp for the funeral, as this would have entailed an absence of several days at a time when he could not be spared; and during the mournful period which he would normally have spent with the rest of the bereaved family, he had shut himself away from Alix for the first time, and had sat moodily reading and rereading the letter Jenness had written him the day she killed herself. When he finally showed this letter to his bride, she understood why it had held him so sorrowfully spellbound.

"Dear Jerry"—Jenness had written, sitting at the ornate, inadequate little desk in her beruffled bedroom while her mother kept dinner warm and her father anxiously awaited her coming—

You and I have quarreled so many times these last few years that I'd like to tell you I'm sorry. Because you were right and I was wrong.

Besides, Daddy told me, just after he came to Washington, that you and I were both in this War but that we weren't fighting on the same side. He was right, too. So now that I've stopped fighting and you're just beginning, I'd like to write you one or two things that are directly or indirectly connected with that, too.

I've just told Daddy the truth about everything that happened here, but after I'd done that, I sort of gave out. I couldn't seem to go on and explain why Max Lentz met me on Farman Hill. Now I'll explain to you and later on you can tell Daddy.

One of the major activities in the propaganda ring Lentz belongs to has centered in acquiring properties that have strategic value from the military standpoint, and in 'planting' families of Axis sympathizers in key positions, so that they'd be all set to act when the time came. You probably know more about such values and such positions than I do. I still don't understand, for instance, why it should have seemed worthwhile to the Japanese Government to pay $250 a month to a Congregational minister in a little Vermont village like Peacham, which isn't even on a river or near a railroad. But it did, as I don't need to tell you, for there have been repercussions about that all over the country. So perhaps it's natural that a

*place like Farman should have seemed to have pos-
sibilities. After all it is near the river and on the railroad, it has fine timberland and look-offs, and enough
open pastureland to be under consideration for an
airport. Anyway I believe the families of German
extraction who have moved into town have found it
very easy to finance their purchases, and with one
exception, they all seem to see a good deal of each
other. The Hellmans, who are cousins of Max Lentz,
are undoubtedly the ringleaders. Just what they're up
to I don't know, but I do know they'll bear watching.
I think Dexter suspects this already, but if you agree
with me or know more than I do, you might tell him
so. I'd like to write to Dexter today too, but I don't
believe I'll have time. I don't believe I'll write but
one other letter. That's got to go to a man on the
other side of the world and it'll have just three lines
in it. They'll be the same as the first three lines in this
one, only they'll mean something different in this
case, and he'll know what it is.*

*Well anyway, whatever those people are up to in
Farman, they still haven't got the place they want for
headquarters, and they're trying to get our farm for
that. The Hellmans must have reported to Lentz that
it was just what they were looking for, because he
arranged to meet me there at Christmastime and go
over it with me. (I suppose he also took advantage
of the trip to confer with his henchmen, but I don't
know that for sure.) He was delighted with everything I showed him, and when we got on top of
Jerome's Hill, he kept muttering 'Kolossal! Kolossal!'
over and over again. And somehow he must have
found time, before he was arrested, to get in touch
with Gustav Meyer, for it was only a week after that
Daddy had such a fabulous offer for the place.*

*He turned this down, as he must have written you
himself, but it was an awful temptation and I can't
help feeling that someday he may be tempted again.
Not to sell it to anyone of whom he was suspicious*

*—he wouldn't do that, now that his suspicions are
aroused. But he might sell it if he thought the prospective purchaser was all right, to rid himself of
obligations. He has a horror of debt, you know that,
and he's spent a lot of money for me already and
means to spend a lot more. Don't let him sell it,
Jerome. It wouldn't be fair to have it go to make up
for what I've done. It's got to be kept for you. You've
earned the right to it that I've forfeited and I want
you to have it for your children. Please find the way
for Daddy to keep it.*

Goodbye. The best of everything to you.

Jenness

The impact of this letter had inevitably been terrific.
Ever since he began to brood over it, Jerome had been
attuned to catastrophe. Alix knew that it behooved her
not only to remain calm herself, but to create tranquility
for them both. She continued to sit still now, but after a
few moments, she drew her dressing gown around her
again, and quietly began to rebraid her hair. Jerome suddenly snuffed out his cigarette and came back to her.

"Don't do that," he said imperiously.

"Don't do what, *cher?*"

"Don't do anything to your hair. Leave it the way it is.
You know how I love to see it loose. And that hasn't
changed."

So I was right, she said to herself. He is going to mind
when I get clumsy and heavy; he dreads seeing me misshapen; he's rebellious because the time's coming when he
can't have me whenever he wants me. But he's comforted
by the thought of my hair, just as I was. My hair will be
beautiful through it all. And tonight, after he's had me,
he'll be happy again, he'll forget for a little while that the
time's coming when he can't. Then I must tell him the
other won't last long; only a few months. Afterwards I'll
be slim again—slim and supple and alluring. I've heard
that sometimes girls are lovelier after they've had their
babies than they were before. There are exquisite curves

that come, curves that younger girls don't have; and women learn how to be more seductive too, when they're a little older. They're not inexperienced in love or disconcerned by it. But after all it was the inexperience that fascinated Jerome first. He was captivated because I was so shy, it made his quick courtship seem more like a conquest; he wanted a virginal bride. He still wants me to seem virginal, but he wanted a baby too. I mustn't tell him he demands the impossible, I mustn't let him know he's hurt me a little, I must be very patient with him, very understanding, very generous because . . . She answered with continued tranquility.

"Dearest, please let me finish dressing. You go and make the cocktails and I'll be there in just a minute. You said you were starving and I have such a nice supper for you. I want you to eat it before it spoils."

"I don't care if it does spoil. I am starving, but not for food. I don't want any supper after all. I want you."

Once more he put his arms around her. "Before anything else changes," he said desperately, "before I begin to brood because anything's changed already. God, Alix, don't sit there looking at me so quietly when I want you so dreadfully! Don't keep me waiting like this!"

She raised her arms and put them around his neck. "Why, dearest," she said tenderly, "I was only quiet because I was waiting for you."

She was still undismayed when he decided, hours later, that he was hungry after all. She salvaged the supper, while he made the cocktails, and lighted the candles on the little lace-covered table. Lucky, lying beside the hearth where only embers remained, wagged his tail and looked up at her with adoring eyes, as she bent over to pat him when she fed the dying flames. Jerome, wearing the wine-colored dressing gown she had given him for a Christmas present, brought in the tray with the shaker and glasses and canapes, and they seated themselves near the rekindled fire to drink their cocktails. Jerome had emerged from the desperation that had threatened to engulf him, and he was

merrier than Alix had seen him in a long time, now that
he had escaped from its spell. The last few days at the
post had been unusually exciting, he told her eagerly, tossing off his first drink and pouring himself another. He had
been having a fine time learning to operate some of the
new power equipment, starting out with a big truck tractor
that pulled a trailer, and he had got so he could even run
one of the big Diesel caterpillar tractors after a fashion.
He had also been trying a power-driven road grader which
was a grand operating machine.

"Alix, you're not listening to me. Aren't you interested
in my machines?"

"Yes, dearest. I am interested, I am listening. But I
thought I heard a bell ringing."

"Nonsense, you can't have. Bells don't ring around here
at this time of night. You're forgetting how late it is." He
poured himself another cocktail, and went on. "We've still
got a street sweeper, a road roller and a big wrecking truck
I don't handle very well. When I've got the hang of those
I'll be able to operate everything we have on the field."

"Cher, I'm sorry to interrupt you, but I'm sure I do hear
a bell ringing. There must be someone at the front door. It
couldn't be the telephone, could it? I do know it's very
late."

"Of course it couldn't be the telephone. Or the doorbell
either. You must have imagined it, Alix."

"Listen! I hear it again."

They had no telephone of their own. The entire house
was serviced by one which stood in the front hall, downstairs. But as they opened the door of their apartment, they
knew Alix had not been mistaken, that a bell was ringing
insistently. Evidently the other occupants of the house
were all asleep, for no one else had answered it. Jerome,
still holding his cocktail glass and his cigarette, started
down the stairs in his wine-colored dressing gown. Alix
closed the living room door to keep out the draft which
swept in from the unheated hall and put another log on the
fire, so that if Jerome were chilled when he came back, he
would get warm more quickly. She could still hear the

sound of his voice, after she closed the door, though she could not hear the words he was saying. But she was not curious about the telephone call or alarmed about it. She only wanted to be sure that Jerome would not feel cold for long.

It was when she realized he had stopped talking but had not started up the stairs that she became conscious of impending calamity. She opened the door again, and went out into the cold hall herself. In the dim light she could barely see the outline of Jerome's figure, wrapped in the wine-colored dressing gown, and standing beside the telephone table. She called to him softly.

"Dearest, is anything the matter?"

He did not answer. She knotted her own dressing gown more closely around her waist and went quietly down the stairs. But a sharp pain shot suddenly through her swollen breasts and struck at her vitals when she looked at him.

"It's come after all," he said hoarsely. "My number *has* been called. An order's been sent from Washington substituting my name for another man's. He's probably made a fool of himself in some way. A man can be yanked out at the last moment if he has, and another one rushed in. I'm leaving Tuesday morning. You see now why I needed you so, why I told you I had to have you before anything else changed. It wasn't because I dreaded having you different. It was because I knew, somehow, that this was the last weekend we'd ever have together."

CHAPTER 20

"Look here, you mustn't lift that. It's too heavy."

"It doesn't feel heavy to me, *cher*. I can manage it all right."

"I said, don't try to lift it. If I see you lifting that, I'll keep thinking of you lifting other things. Then I'll start worrying for fear you'll lose the baby. You don't want me to do that, do you?"

"No, dearest. I promise you I will not do anything that will be bad for the baby. But I am very strong. There isn't any reason why I shouldn't work."

Alix had just finished packing a large metal-bound suitcase when Jerome spoke to her and, after locking it, she had instinctively started to carry it across the room and set it down in the same row with several others standing near the door. But now she relinquished it readily, looking up at him with a smile, as she brushed a little loose dust from her small white hands.

"That's just about the last anyway. Why don't we both sit down for a few minutes and rest? You need to, more than I do. You've worked ever so much harder. I'm going to make you some coffee. It will refresh you."

"No, just come and sit down beside me. I'd like that better than having you leave me to make the coffee. And there are still so many things I want to say to you."

"You know, *cher,* that it takes me only a moment to set the coffee to drip. Then I will come back and you shall tell me whatever you wish. We've plenty of time. You don't have to go for a long while yet."

He glanced at his wrist watch, biting his lips and wincing a little, but he did not contradict her or try to stop her from going out into the kitchen. He sat down beside the fireplace, stretching out his long legs, and throwing his arms over the back of the sofa. He was very tired, and as he reached for a cigarette, he winced again when he saw that the silver box in which Alix had formerly kept them, and the silver ash trays which went with the box, were all gone; there were only a package of Chesterfields and a cracked china saucer on the low coffee table where the silver had been. It was not that this in itself was important, but it was one more poignant reminder that the personal possessions which had given the room individuality and character were all packed: the framed family pictures, the fragile French ornaments, the crystal vases which had always been full of flowers, the silk bag in which Alix kept her fine sewing. The place was not cozy and intimate any more; it was bare and impersonal. It had ceased to be part of a home; it was just any rented room.

Alix came back and sat down beside him. She had washed her hands while she was gone and taken off the big apron in which she had been enveloped while she was packing. If she were tired, she did not show it. Her white forehead still had the serene look that emanated tranquility, her generous mouth was rosy and relaxed; even the freshness of the dress she was wearing, and which she had so carefully protected, intensified the impression she gave of being at leisure and at peace. She leaned back against Jerome outstretched arm and looked up at him lovingly.

"The coffee'll be ready presently. It will refresh you," she said again, as if nothing in the world mattered so much to her and his refreshment. "Let's just sit here for a few minutes, without talking, while we wait for it. After you've drunk it, you can tell me what's on your mind. There's no hurry."

"I've still got to write my folks. I haven't done that yet and I've got to have some leeway. I've got to tell them you're coming to Farman Hill, so they'll be looking for you."

"I can do that, after you're gone, if you'd like to have me."

"No, I want to tell them myself. I'm glad I can tell them that. But I've got to say good-bye too. That'll be harder."

His dark face had begun to work as it did in all moments of uncontrollable tensions. Alix slipped her hand into his.

"Yes, but you'll do it wonderfully. The way you do everything. So that you'll comfort and encourage them. I know."

"*You'll* comfort and encourage them. The way you've comforted and encouraged me. Alix, if it weren't for you——"

"*Voyons,* why should you say 'If it weren't for me?' because that's impossible now, isn't it? There is bound to be me, always. It's inevitable."

She laughed lightly, and carried the hand she was holding to her lips. Then, as she lowered it, she leaned back again, not against Jerome's oustretched arm but against his shoulder, as if she were inviting encirclement.

"There's a place where my head just fits," she said. "I've told you that before, haven't I, *cher*? I believe *le bon Dieu* arranged things in such a way that a wife's head should fit against her husband's shoulder, just as He arranged that a baby's head should fit against a mother's breast."

"And when you're holding our baby against your breast, I shan't see it."

"You'll think about it. You'll make it seem ever more beautiful than it really is, by thinking and dreaming. Often it's that way, isn't it, dearest? Aren't dreams beautiful realities?—But now we won't dream, we'll be very practical. I shall get the coffee and you shall tell me what is on your mind."

She disengaged herself gently and went without haste to the little kitchen. The savory smell of the coffee was already stealing through the dismantled living room, giving a last touch of homeliness to the atmosphere. When Alix came back, she was carrying a battered tin tray instead of a beautiful Sheffield one, and the coffee was in thick white cups instead of delicate porcelain. But its own excellence was unimpaired. Jerome drank it avidly, accepting a second serving with gratitude, and setting his cups down with obvious reluctance when the last drop was drained.

"I won't have any more coffee like that, Alix. There's no one who makes coffee like you."

"I can make you some more right away, if you want it."

"No. I want to talk to you now. We've got to be practical, as you said yourself. It just came over me, about an hour ago, that I hadn't said anything to you about money."

"It wasn't necessary that you should. It's not necessary now. I have plenty of money."

"What do you mean, plenty?"

"My mother left me a little. The de la Rondes have been wealthier than the St. Cyrs for a long time. They did not lose as much during the War Between the States, and they retrieved what they did lose faster. I think they have more resiliency of spirit, though they are not so strong physically."

"You never told me before about this money your mother left you, Alix."

"But, *cher,* we have had so little time together, as you say yourself, and so many things more important to talk about! Besides, you never asked me! You took it for granted that I was poor, because you found me working in a jewelry store. And I had been told American men liked to support their wives themselves. That they abhorred the dowry system. If we had needed my mother's money, I would have used it. But we didn't, living here in this simple way. I thought it better to let it go on piling up until we did."

"And how long has it been piling up already?"

"Why ever since my mother died, when I was a baby! My father paid all my convent expenses. Those were not heavy, and he had enough to do that, even in his most straitened days. Then afterwards, he was more prosperous. Not only because of his second marriage. He made some money himself. He left all of that to me. My stepmother wanted him to. She had enough for herself and her own children, more than enough. She can't begin to spend it all."

"Can you tell me, in round figures, how much you have?"

"Not exactly. It varies a little from year to year, though I am told the investments are all sound. But it is several thousand—the interest, that is. Of course the principal has never been touched."

"You have an income of several thousand a year?"

"Yes. I can spend that as I choose, now I'm twenty-one. The principal is held in trust till I am—twenty-five, I think it is. But if there were an emergency, I believe I could borrow on it, or use it in some other way. Arrangements like that can be made, can't they?"

"I think so. I don't know much about it myself. But you've knocked my breath away, Alix. I had no idea you were—an heiress. If I'd had any such idea——"

"You wouldn't have courted me so unceremoniously? You wouldn't have married me in such a rush? *Eh bien,* that was exactly what I was afraid of. It was one of the reasons I kept still. You will forgive me, won't you, *cher?* Because I wanted you to court me as you did and marry me as you did. I am very superstitious. I believe that something happens to rapture when you try to defer it. I believe it has a flood tide."

"Well, I guess you're right. And we caught it at the crest, didn't we?"

"Yes, in full."

She carried his hand to her lips again, and then she turned a little, so that she could look straight at him, while she spoke to him seriously.

"You see now it was best, don't you, *cher,* that I didn't tell you about the money before? But I should have told you tonight even if you hadn't asked me. Because I knew you wouldn't have very much to send me, and I wanted you to know that I could take care of myself and of our baby. I didn't want you to worry about us while you were gone, or fear we might be a burden to your parents. We shall have everything we need without asking them for anything but love and shelter. And I can save ahead too, for the baby's welfare and education. For everything you want him to have in the future."

"Can you do one thing more?"

"Of course. If it is something you want me to do. Tell me about it, dearest."

"I don't think I've any right to ask for it. But that hasn't stopped me before from asking for things. I—well, I can't help thinking what's going to happen to Mom and Dad as well as what's going to happen to you and the baby. It's on my mind a good deal. They've had a hard life, Alix. They've sacrificed everything for their children. And now Jenness has disgraced them and Judith has deserted them and I've got to go the other side of the world. So they haven't much left. Not even their own home. Farman Hill belongs to Dexter Abbott now. He won't claim it, but they'll always feel it's his, just the same. They'll never be able to pay back the money he loaned them."

"Shall I pay it back then? Is that what you want me to do?"

"I'm not sure. The idea did come to me while you were talking. About being able to use your principal after you're twenty-five, or perhaps before that, in an emergency. But it's too soon to tell yet how you can help them most. Maybe it'll be with money and maybe it won't. You'll have to feel your way along after you get there. And then do whatever you think's best, whatever you believe I'd do for them myself, if I could."

He rose slowly, drawing her up after him. When they were standing again, he tilted her face up and framed it with his hands, so that he could look straight into her eyes while he talked to her.

"You're not frightened, are you, Alix?"

"No."

"Not of anything?"

"No."

"You don't think I've asked too much of you?"

"You couldn't ask too much. You couldn't ask enough. I'd always wish I could give you more."

"And you know, don't you, that when I said the other night, this was the last weekend we'd ever have together, of course I meant the last weekend *just now*. Of course we'll have hundreds of other weekends."

"Of course."

"And listen, Alix—about your changing . . . I just wanted to tell you—it's been more wonderful since I came home Saturday than it ever was before. Of course there's a feeling about the first time—knowing you're doing something no one's ever done before to the girl you love—that means almost as much to you as the physical part. It doesn't seem to you anything could ever mean more in your relationship with her. You don't realize that is just the beginning—*in every way*. Now I know I'd have felt thwarted if I hadn't watched you changing because you were my wife, if I hadn't known I'd changed you. Does any of that make sense to you? Does it all sound unnatural and offensive?"

"It all makes sense, dearest, and none of it is unnatural or offensive. Everything you've said is normal and beautiful. It's what I'd rather have you say to me than anything in the world."

"And you're not going to say to yourself, are you, after I've gone, what you've never said to me? That I've been selfish and sensual? That we ought to have spent this last weekend differently?"

"How could I say anything to my self that I have not said to you? I have told you everything that is in my heart."

"Then you're not sorry for anything, Alix? If—if this *should* be the end, would it seem—perfect and complete?"

For a moment her lips quivered and she closed her eyes. Then she drew a deep breath and opened them again.

"No," she said. "I'm not sorry for anything. If this should be the end, it would seem perfect and complete."

She still insisted, after their supper, that she was not tired, that she did not need to rest. But Jerome knew better. There were dark circles under her eyes now and a telltale droop to her shoulders. He picked her up bodily and laid her on their bed. She kept very still, watching him with intent eyes, while he wrote the letter which was to be the harbinger of her advent at Farman Hill.

Dear Mom and Dad—

By the time you get this, I'll be gone. It came kind of quick when it did come. I had my orders Saturday night and I leave tomorrow morning. I've tried to call you twice, but both times the lines have been jammed and I couldn't get through. I am going half way around the world but I can't tell you where because our orders are secret.

I wish I could have got home, if only for a few days, but it's out of the question now. So I'm doing the next best thing: I'm sending Alix to you. I will not try to write you how I feel about her; you will know how I couldn't help feeling, the minute you look at her. She has given me three months of perfect happiness, and I suppose that is just as much as any man has a right to ask for, especially as it's all been on borrowed time. I knew when I married her that my number might be called at any moment. So I've had a lot more already than was really coming to me. Not that this makes it any easier to say goodbye to her. But after all, it isn't for long.

I know it will mean everything to you to have Alix with you, and I hope and believe it will mean a lot to her. As we've told you before, she hasn't any immediate family and she didn't raise any objections at all when I told her I wanted to have her stay on Farman Hill until I got back. In fact she seemed willing and glad to go to you, especially after I explained how I felt about having our baby born there, like all the other Farman babies. She said she felt just the same way, because all the St. Cyr babies had been born at their family home too, and that was the way it should be. She doesn't need or expect any special coddling on account of her condition, in fact she is very scornful of girls who do. So I know that she will not be a burden to you in that respect, and she will cheerfully make the best of whatever arrangements are possible for her confinement. I don't suppose they'll be ideal. But it ought to be feasible to give her reasonably good care, and she's very calm and courageous. Then afterwards you will all enjoy the baby together, and I will think of him sleeping in the first Jerome's cradle and later on using my high chair and drinking out of my mug. I hope Mom will tell him the same Bible stories she told me and that Dad will carry him out to the barn to visit the animals every Sunday afternoon, so that he will recognize them all and love them all even before he's old enough to talk. I know Dexter will be good to him too. It's a darned shame Dexter won't be having

*a child of his own just about the same age, and I'll
never forgive Judith for the way she's treated him.
But perhaps he'll take some comfort out of my child,
and I know I can count on him to stand by my wife
too, if anything should go wrong and she should need
a man's help. Not that it will, of course. But just the
same you might tell him I said so.*

*Alix will drive north, taking the trip by easy stages.
I have the car mostly loaded for her already and my
friends here will help her to finish. Of course she
shouldn't do heavy lifting, but she knows it and she's
promised to be careful, so I shan't worry about that
either.*

*I hope you will not mind having her bring her
dog, Lucky, with her. He is really a very nice dog,
though just now he is at that in-between-stage when
he is not much to look at. She is attached to him and
he will be company for her on the long drive, though
I am afraid she will have to stay at tourist camps
instead of hotels on his account, and it will be pretty
cold at this time of year as she gets further north.
But she says she doesn't mind that either. She says
that about everything. She's wonderful. You'll see.*

*I have a big job to do and the quicker the better.
That is about all there is to say except to tell you not
to worry, I'll be all right. That is, there is a lot more
to say but I don't know how to write it. So I'll just
send you all my love and tell you again not to worry.
Keep the old fire going and I'll be home before you'll
really have time to miss me, with a travel tale to tell
as good as a professional's. I will expect to see you
out on the porch waiting for me, Mom with her gray
shawl and Dad with his muffler.*

*Alix will tell you everything I haven't had time
for, and she will cheer you up if you should need it,
though there isn't any reason who you should. But
anyway she can do it. And I shall keep thinking of
you all together on Farman Hill and I shall know
that you are safe and well.*

Good-bye, and remember this is just a pleasure trip with a little work thrown in.

All my love—except what Alix has—

Jerome.

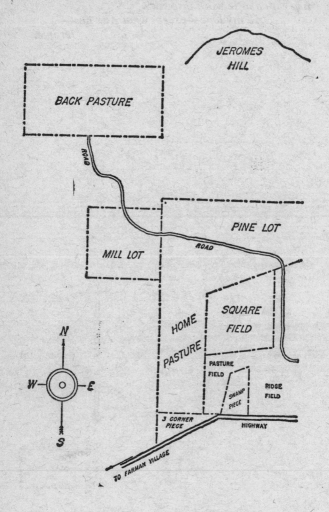

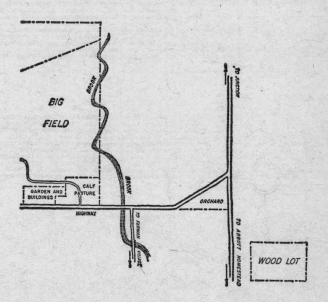

MAP OF FARMAN HILL

BIG

FIELD

BROOK

BROOK

GARDEN AND
BUILDINGS

CALF
PASTURE

HIGHWAY

TO FARMAN
VILLAGE

TO JUNCTION

ORCHARD

TO ABBOTT HOMESTEAD

WOOD LOT

PART IV

Farman Hill

March–September 1942

CHAPTER 21

MARCH, DEXTER had always thought, was the most dismal month of the year on Farman Hill. Daniel disagreed with him, saying November was; but Dexter pointed out that in November the sunsets did something to redeem the drabness of a countryside suddenly bereft of its multicolored fall foliage, whereas there was nothing to redeem the bleakness of March. Daniel admitted that now he thought of it, the November sunsets were much different from those at any other time of the year: deep yellow—well, golden, he supposed you'd call them, instead of bright pink, the way they usually were. You did sort of forget the ground was beginning to freeze in hard ruts, when you saw that peculiar gold color spreading over it, like a covering. Was that what Dexter meant?

"Yes, that's what I mean. And those golden sunsets last longer, too, than the pink ones. Of course the frozen ground, gilded that way, isn't as striking as the snowy mountains when they get rosy. But it has more meaning. At least it has to me."

"It doesn't mean a thing but deception. The gilt isn't real gold. And winter's right around the corner, snow and zero weather. Dearth and death. If it came in the spring now——"

"According to the Jews, the year begins in the fall."

Daniel looked at Dexter with passing wonderment. "You learned all sorts of things at college, or somewheres, that I never did, Dexter," he said, not without a touch of admiration. "Well, I don't know how we come to start on the subject of sunsets, let alone got around to the Jews. But now we are on it, I can't help saying it would take more than a strange-looking sunset to make me take comfort out of this spring. So it's all the same to me if there isn't anything special about them just now."

He nodded, and without saying anything more went on into the horse barn. Presently he reappeared, leading Gypsy. There was the characteristic prolonged pause while Gypsy contemplated the view, with even more deliberation than usual, it seemed to Dexter; then the old horse suffered himself to be led to the watering trough, where he drank indefinitely. After Gypsy's thirst had at last been slaked, Daniel took him back to the barn and brought out Nell. The mare had always lacked Gypsy's unique habits, and the process of getting her in and out of the barn had formerly not been a lengthy one. But now she was going blind. She had to be tenderly treated, and this took time too. It was growing dark when Daniel went back to the barn again to begin his milking. It was strange, as he had said, that he and Dexter had got onto the subject of sunsets just then, for there was no sunset of any kind, only a deepening of gray clouds and a rising of rough wind to signify the approach of evening. Dexter continued to stand in the yard, looking down from the barren hill to the dim valley beyond, his thoughts, even more cheerless than the scene before him, taking him far afield from the sombre sight . . .

He was thinking of Jenness as he had last seen her, with her bright hair arranged to hide the bruises on the still face which had once held the essence of vitality, and her white draperies disposed to conceal the shattered limbs which had once been so beautiful. With the closing of the coffin in which Jenness lay, a chapter of life itself had closed on Farman Hill, and no new chapter could ever be written that would make it the same . . .

He was thinking of Jerome, who had been promoted from Assistant Supply Officer, and when they last heard from him was Post Camp and Technical Supply Officer, in charge of all Air Corps property issued out around Hope Field. *"We have a large stock room with thousands of parts,"* Jerome had written his parents proudly. *"We have two immense refrigerators just to keep the film for the observation cameras and for the gun cameras. We have a*

*moth room for clothes and a special room for rubber
goods."* Jerome, who had been such a wild, feckless boy,
throve, inconsistently, on responsibility. That was why he
had done so well in the Boston bank; that was why he was
now doing so well at Fort Bragg; that was why, eventually,
he would do so well overseas. And what had Dexter, who
had left Jerome far behind in everything except sports,
when they were at school together, ever done well? What
did milking a few cows and feeding a few hogs and hauling
a few logs amount to? When it came to that, what good did
it do to stand by Daniel Farman while the older man did
the same things? Dexter knew that Daniel did not feel
these tasks had any meaning, now that Jenness was dead
and all hope and joy with her; and once work had lost its
meaning, it lost its value also.

Direct news from Jerome had not come through very
often of late. Occasionally one of his rare letters began,
*"I know I oughtn't to leave practically all the writing to
Alix, but I never seem to get around to it any more."*
Once, by way of explanation, he added, *"We have a new
C. O. and he is making a great many changes. I played
golf with him the other day. He's a gruff old Colonel, but
I think he will make a good C. O., because he knows
what he wants and gets it done."* It seemed natural to
Dexter that the new Commanding Officer at Fort Bragg
should have asked Jerome to play golf with him. Jerome
could make friends as easily as he could accept responsibility; that was another reason he was getting ahead so
fast—that and the fact he also knew what he wanted and
succeeded in getting it done. Everyone found Jerome likable and most persons found him lovable as well. *Lovable!*
That was why it had taken him only a week to persuade a
beautiful girl to marry him. And Dexter had not been able
to so persuade Judith, after courting her patiently for
years ...

Inevitably, his thoughts turned next to Judith. The
letters that came from her were addressed to him more
often than to her parents. Dexter did not answer them,
but he could not help reading them; he had to pass on
their contents to Daniel and Serena. Judith wrote about her

work too, but in a different vein from Jerome. *"We have a mental patient here in one of the wards, you should see him, a Negro, and what a riding I take from the Drs. and ward boys, because he told the Capt. he had fallen in love with me. It's funny, but I'm scared stiff of him. He asked for my picture and whether I'd take a ring from him, and he told me he didn't like it because some of the boys came over to see me at night. I hope they get rid of him soon, for he really is bad and there is no telling what he might do."* Dexter did not believe for a minute that Judith was actually afraid of the poor deranged Negro; she had never been afraid of anyone or anything, and would hardly begin to be now. He thought it was far more likely that she had written him about this patient because it gave her a chance to tell him, indirectly, about her male callers and prove she was not eating her heart out. Recently her manner of doing this had become less indirect: *"Last night all the Drs. and nurses here had a moonlight steak roast at a pond about 15 mi. from here. We had more darn fun, didn't get to bed until 1:30 and was I tired!"* . . . *"One of the pilots here has taken me up in his plane, we were up about 45 min. I'm going up again Mon. night too, if the weather clears. It's wonderful, those big bombers, the pilots are swell, they tell you all about it and everything. We were up nearly 5000 ft. at one time."* . . . *"Fri. night I went to a football game in Charlotte, it was a swell game, but a terrible crowd."* . . . *"I have just had a letter from a fellow in Ireland that I met on the way south, he sent me a handkerchief with a map of Ireland printed on it."* . . . *"After supper last night a fellow who's gone to Jackson (Miss.) now called me up from there, he's coming up to see me sometime next week."* . . *"Met a gent from Concord at Headquarters yesterday and one from Manchester the day before. I'll say the world is a small place."*

Judith's letters took their tenor from such passages as these; Dexter read them grimly, his heart hardening. He did not care whether or not they were written in this way from bravado; he was antagonized by the mere fact that they were so written. The final paragraph in the latest one he had received, though it sounded a different note, was especially annoying to him: *"Tell Pop to cheer up and not to feel too bad about Jenness, because after all I'm happy and intend to get home for a furlough soon. It only cost $15. from here to Boston by plane, all in 6 hrs. I wish you'd let me know when you get my letters. You're as silent as the grave. But anyway, I'll write soon again. Don't worry too much."*

"She knows I'm not worrying at all," he said to himself with increasing grimness. "At least, not about her. There's no earthly reason why I should. Why anyone should. She's having the time of her life. Except that she's irritated because I don't answer her letters, and she's made up her mind, if I don't pretty soon she'll come home and find out the reason. She ought to know the reason, without any more telling. But if she keeps on asking for punishment, as far as I'm concerned, she'll get it. I'll remind her too, when she gets to talking about silence and graves, she might think of Jenness. There isn't any reason why I should let her off easy. God knows she didn't let me off easy . . ." The grim lines around his mouth tightened. His eyes grew harder and harder as he looked out through the deepening dusk . . .

He was still standing in the yard and still wrapped in bitter melancholy, when a car turned in at the rough driveway and came to a stop beside him. Dazedly, he emerged from his meditation, with the realization that the car was unfamiliar to him, and that the driver was probably stopping to inquire the way. In the dusk, all he could see were the outlines of a slight, almost childish, figure at the wheel, and a small white face above it. The girl to whom these belonged lowered the window to speak to him.

"Is this Farman Hill?" she asked. The voice itself was soft, but an alien and very attractive accent gave it a piquant quality. As she spoke, a subdued, pleading little whine came from close by, and she turned to pat the head of a half-grown hound, which, Dexter belatedly observed, was curled up on the seat beside her. *"Tais toi,* Lucky," she said soothingly. "There is nothing to cry about. I'm only asking this gentleman where we are—My dog is generally very cheerful," she added, turning back to Dexter again.

"Half the time he looks as if he were laughing—you know that nice look some dogs have. But he's had a long ride, and he hasn't had a really good run in three days. He's tired. And I'm afraid he's hungry too. You mustn't misjudge him because he whined just now."

"I didn't misjudge him," Dexter answered. He did not think it was necessary to add that this was because he had not troubled to analyze the hound's probable temperament; but he was mildly astonished because this slight, pale girl, who looked very tired herself, seemed to take it for granted that he would be interested in her ungainly pet. "This *is* Farman Hill," he added. "Did you want to see someone here?"

"Why, I wanted to see all of you! Isn't this Dexter Abbott? And weren't you expecting me?"

"Yes, I'm Dexter Abbott. And of course you're very welcome," Dexter said, hoping that he was not betraying his perplexity. There was something about the girl which was dimly familiar, though he could have sworn he had never seen her before. "Come in and I'll call Mrs. Farman. I think you better take my arm if you don't mind. The ground's very rough and it's hard to see in this dim light."

"But of course I shall be very pleased to take your arm." The girl turned around, as he opened the door of the car, lightly accepting his outstretched hand. She did not start by sliding a little, as Jenness always had, in such a way that her skirts were drawn back above her knees; neither did she leap out as if she could not wait to begin doing something more purposeful than riding idly around the countryside, which was Judith's habit. Instead she stepped down slowly and rather carefully. She seemed so surprisingly lithe that Dexter was astonished to see her move in this way, almost as if she were afraid of hurting herself, and instinctively he sought to reassure her.

"Don't be afraid. I won't let you fall."

"I'm not afraid. But of course I don't want to fall. So it's very nice to have your help. Come, Lucky."

He felt her fingers tighten a little against his arm, and the confident touch was unexpectedly pleasant. He looked down at her, and saw that she was looking at him too, and that her smile was trustful and artless, almost like a child's, just as her figure had looked almost childish to him when he first saw her. Again, with a pang he could not repress, he thought of Jenness and her arch glances, of Judith and her firm lips.

"Mrs. Farman must have forgotten to tell me we were going to have company," he said, trying to dismiss these images. "Or else she did tell me and I forgot. I'm terribly sorry."

"But, Dexter, I am not company! Don't you know me from my picture? Didn't Mother Farman get Jerome's letter?"

Jerome's letter! We haven't heard from Jerome in days! Did Jerome write his mother a special letter about——"

"About me? Why, yes! To say he was going away, but that he was sending me to stay with you until he came back."

She stopped, drawing away from Dexter a little, and gazing at him with a bewilderment which now exceeded his own. *So that was it!* He had never seen this girl, but he had seen her picture, her picture as Jerome's bride! Only now she did not look like a bride any more. That was why he had not recognized her. There had been an extraordinary radiance about that bridal picture which was gone. But not the beauty that underlay it. He could not understand why he had not instantly seen what he saw now: that Alix St. Cyr, the fragile, exhausted girl, who had turned to him so trustfully in her weariness, was very beautiful.

"The letter should have been here two days ago, at least," Alix was saying in a puzzled voice. "Jerome wrote it before he left Raeford, Monday night. He's probably sailed by this time. He went very unexpectedly, taking the place of an officer who was withdrawn at the last moment. Of course I don't know what his port of embarkation is or where he's going. I haven't heard from him myself since he went away, and even if I had, he couldn't tell me anything. I left Raeford the morning after he did. I drove all day and got to Alexandria in the evening. I thought Father and Mother Farman would like to hear from Mrs. Porterfield and Joe Racina, who were so kind to them. They were very kind to me also, and I stayed over at Mrs. Porterfield's house for a day, partly because she seemed so glad to have me and partly because I didn't want to get too tired. Then I began to be afraid I was taking too much time, so I made the rest of the trip in two days. And now I *am* tired, just a little."

"Tired! You must be half dead! And then to get such a half-hearted welcome. It's all a darned shame! Come in, Alix, please, and sit down by the fire! Mrs. Farman must be in the kitchen getting supper, but I'll have her here in half a second!"

He flung open the door of the living room. It was still in darkness, except for the glow which came from the fire. Dexter drew the old rocker a little closer to the hearthstone, motioning towards this invitingly, and lighted the lamp standing on the gate-legged table. Then saying he would return at once, he disappeared abruptly. Alix, sinking wearily into the rocker, could hear his deep voice, and another, soft at first, but soon rising incredulously. The dialogue lasted only a minute. Almost immediately Dexter was back in the room accompanied by a full-figured woman who enfolded the tired traveler in an ample embrace before Alix could complete the little curtsy with which she tried to greet her mother-in-law.

"You poor child! You must be half dead!" she exclaimed, unconsciously repeating Dexter's words. "Now then, you sit right down again, and don't you try to say a thing until you've had a cup of hot tea. You can explain everything and tell us all about Jerome afterwards. I'm going to take one good look at you, and then I'm going straight back to make that tea for you. I've got the kettle boiling already, so I'll have it here in two shakes of a dead lamb's tail. Why, you look just the way I thought you would, Alix, only some prettier and a little mite more peaked. But of course you're all tuckered out. When you've had a good night's rest you'll be as fresh as a daisy. Dexter, I want you should go right out to the barn and tell Daniel our daughter-in-law's here."

"Yes, I'm going. But I think first I'd better start a fire in her room, don't you, so she won't freeze to death?"

"Why that's real thoughtful of you, Dexter! Yes, I guess you better. And fill a hot water bottle out of the kettle to put in the bed right away too. I'm afraid you're going to feel the cold here, Alix, seeing that you've never been accustomed to it, but we'll do everything we can . . ."

"Please don't worry, Mother Farman. I'm sure I shan't mind the cold. That is, not long. I'll get used to it."

She spoke simply and sincerely, as she had from the beginning. But she could not fully control her shivering; Dexter had seen the telltale shaking of her shoulders. He began to pile more wood on the fire in front of him.

"What fools we were, not to put a new furnace in this house when Jenness wanted us to!" he said almost savagely. He had insisted from the first that they must all go on talking as naturally as they could about Jenness; once they stopped, he said, it would be ten times harder to start again; there would always be a strain and a silence. But he was not thinking of Jenness now, or of Judith either, as he continued to pile wood on the fire. He was thinking of this poor little French bride, suddenly bereft of her beloved, who had come to take refuge among strangers, and who had been so inadequately received. Here she was half frozen as well as half dead and there was not even a room ready for her . . . "I suppose you're putting Alix in the East Chamber?" he went on. He had finished with the fire, and now he paused with his hand on the latch of the door leading into the closed hallway.

"Yes, I guess that'll be best, for tonight anyway. Of course you can choose for yourself, Alix, in the morning, between the East Chamber and the West. But in the East you get the morning sun, and then the sun from the South. It's bright all day."

"Jerome told me you'd give me the East Chamber because it was so sunny. I'm sure I'll love it—especially after Dexter has built a fire in it for me. I can see he has a hand for fires just as some people have a hand for gardens," Alix said gratefully. Then she added, with suppressed wistfulness, "The tea will taste good too."

"Are you sure you wouldn't rather have coffee?" Dexter inquired, his hand still on the latch.

"Now I presume you would. Jerome wrote us time and time again what wonderful coffee you made. Only I don't know how to make coffee in the French way. You'll have to teach me, soon as you're rested."

"Of course I will. And you'll teach me lots of other things. But now I'd really have the tea. But it was kind of you to think of the coffee, Dexter."

She was drinking the hot tea and eating thick slices of homemade bread and butter when Daniel came in from the barn. Her coat, made of some brown fur, less showy but more lustrous than those Jenness had worn, was still draped over her slim shoulders, almost concealing the cloth dress which matched it. But she had taken off her simple brown hat and laid it beside her gloves and bag on the gate-legged table. Between her own sips and mouthfuls, she was feeding Lucky, gently admonishing him not to get too close to the fire and reminding him of previous occasions when he had suffered from doing so. She did not rise to greet her father-in-law, or try to curtsy, as she had when Serena came in; but she held out her hand to him without timidity or constraint, and looked up at him with the same trustfulness in her smile which had so poignantly affected Dexter.

"This is Alix, Father Farman," she said. "Dexter told you I was here, didn't he? Jerome's letter must have been delayed. But it doesn't really matter, does it? You see I'm at home already . . . This is my dog, Lucky," she added. "I hope you don't mind because I brought him with me."

"We haven't had a dog around the house since Jerome was a youngster," Daniel answered. As he spoke, he realized that perhaps such a statement was a peculiar one with which to begin a greeting to a new daughter-in-law; but somehow it seemed natural for him to speak to Alix in this way and he went on, "It'll remind us of Jerome to have another . . . Jerome's all right, isn't he?"

"Yes, Father Farman. He's all right."

"He didn't take it too hard, did he, leaving the way he had to?"

"No, not too hard. It was just going away from me that he minded."

"Yes. Yes. Well, you can't hardly blame him for that." Daniel looked at Alix, more closely than before, and as he did so, he felt a pang of pity for his son, even greater than the pity he felt for her, though that was intense too. But he could not bring himself to put this deep feeling into words, and presently he leaned over and began to stroke Lucky, hoping that the gesture would rob his silence of its awkwardness. Instantly, the hound began to wag its tail, thumping excitedly against the hearthstone with it. "Why, Lucky's a real friendly dog, isn't he?" Daniel said, in gratified surprise. "Most generally dogs don't take to a stranger like that. I notice Pinkham hasn't got his back up either, and it's a rare thing when an old family cat doesn't spit at a strange dog. If you should ever want to get rid of him for a while, I'd just as lieve as not have him come out to the barn. Jerome's dog used to come out to the barn most every day."

"I could *bring* him out to the barn, couldn't I?" Alix asked. "Then we could both enjoy him. Together I mean. Jerome told me about the barn. And about the Cider Mill and the old Washroom. I can't wait to see them."

"Well now, you shall, the first thing in the morning," Daniel said heartily. He continued to stroke Lucky's head and to look down at the dog. It was just as well, he thought, that he had an excuse for doing this; not because he needed, any longer, to soften an awkward silence. It was easy, after all, to talk with Alix; but it was only by stroking her dog that he could restrain his impulse to stare at her. He could not understand why he found it so hard to take his eyes off her. Certainly she was very quietly dressed, and certainly she herself was quiet too, quiet and pale and small. Not—not dazzling, like Jenness. Jenness had always made him think of fresh roses and spun gold at the same time. But there was something else this girl made him think of, he was not sure yet just what, and he was trying to think. "About Jerome's letter," he said belatedly.

"Our rural delivery carrier's sick, he hasn't been up on the Hill in two days now, and there isn't anyone to take his place. Maybe it's different in the South, but it's almost impossible to find a man to do anything around here. Dexter and I are so driven we don't know how to make out. Of course Mother could have gotten the mail when she was out on the milk route. But I guess she didn't think of it. You see Jerome hasn't written much lately, and he'd always said, when he did get to go overseas, he'd probably have several weeks' warning. Before our daughter Jenness died, we used to watch for letters. It was different then. But lately it hasn't hardly seemed worth while."

"I know," Alix said, gently. "I know. Jenness used to write to me too. It was wonderful how she found time. And her letters were always so thrilling. She did so many things, she saw so many prominent people. I used to watch for her letters myself."

"Did you really?" Daniel asked huskily.

"Yes, really. And so did Jerome. He was awfully proud of Jenness, Father Farman. Of course he was proud of Judith too. But I think Jenness was his favorite, even if he did keep quarrelling with her. She had more charm, didn't she? And men like women to have charm, even when it's just their sisters, don't they? They admire capable women, but they love the charming ones, whether they're capable or not."

To his own amazement, Daniel chuckled. It was the first time he had chuckled since he lost Jenness.

"I don't know but what you're right," he said. This time he could not help looking at Alix, and then he realized that she herself had given him the word for which he had been groping. This wife of Jerome's had charm, to a greater degree than any woman, old or young, whom he had ever seen before; charm and refinement and distinction. That was why he could not help looking at her, in spite of her simple clothes and her pale face. That was why no man would ever be able to help looking at her. Neither Daniel himself, nor Daniel's son, Jerome, nor his neighbor Dexter nor any other male. Not because she would ever be wilfully or even consciously seductive, like Jenness, but because she was charming . . .

"I'm so glad Jenness could be my bridesmaid," Alix was saying softly, interrupting his portentous train of thought. "I never saw a girl look as pretty as she did on my wedding day. She looked just like a rose in her pink dress. And her hair was like the gold part in the middle of a rose, fine and soft and silky."

"Yes," Daniel said. He spoke laboriously, but there was astonishment in his voice too, and gratitude. "That's the way I always thought of Jenness myself. I was thinking of her that way just a few minutes ago, and wondering— It's sort of strange you should have thought the same thing."

"No, Father Farman, it isn't really. Anyone would naturally think of beauty and color and fragrance, thinking of Jenness, and then it would be natural to speak about it too. It's been wonderful to talk with you about Jenness this way. And please don't worry about the letter from Jerome. It was just to say he had to leave sooner than he'd expected, and that I was going to stay with you and Mother Farman until he got back, if you'd let me, and have my baby here, if that wouldn't make too much trouble for you. I know it wouldn't have meant to you what Jenness' letters did, it couldn't have. And anyway I'm sure you'll get it in the morning and then——"

"I'll get it this evening. Dexter has gone down to the post office after it," Daniel said. "Not but what we're just as glad as we can be to see you, Alix, without any letter, and to have you stay as long as you're a mind to. And about the baby—well, you'll talk to Mother, but I'm sure—" He stopped, suddenly remembering the old cradle, which had been so long empty, stored in the summer kitchen, and thinking— "I told Dexter I didn't want he should put himself out any," he went on, "but I said, if he'd just as lieve go to the village, he might as well. And he said he would. He said he wanted to see a man about a new furnace anyway. He's possessed that you're going to feel the cold and he wants to get right after a plumber. Dexter's real thoughtful when it comes to things like that, Alix."

"I'm sure he's thoughtful about everything. He was careful to see I didn't stumble, coming into the house. And then he went right upstairs to light a fire in my room. Mother Farman's up there now, doing lots of other things to make it comfortable. I think perhaps I ought to go and help her, don't you? Now that I'm so full of delicious tea and bread and butter and that I've had such a nice talk with you."

She rose, gathering her coat easily around her and picking up her hat and gloves. But she gave no effect of haste. Instead, she lingered a little, looking around her with thoughtful eyes, and then she turned to Daniel.

"I knew I was going to love this room," she said. "Jerome told me about it, you see. Only he didn't tell me half. Men are like that, aren't they, when it comes to describing rooms? Even very superior men like Jerome." She smiled, more gladly than she had before, and the dimple in the middle of her chin deepened. "He forgot to tell me about the flowers on the window sill. I was terribly afraid there wouldn't be any flowers, way up here, in wintertime. But women always manage to have flowers, don't they? Women like Mother Farman and me, I mean. And Jerome didn't tell me about the water-box either. It sounds just like the fountain in the patio of Tia Izola's house on Toulouse Street, in New Orleans. I used to go there every Sunday afternoon, when I was a little girl, to play in the patio. Tia Izola is my Spanish aunt and Tante Odilisse is my French aunt. Of course I am very fond of them both, but Tante Odilisse does not have a patio, only a gallery, so I always liked Tia Izola's house better. But I like this one best of all."

"Well now," said Daniel, clearing his throat. "Well now. I'm pleased to hear you say that, Alix. I'm real pleased. About the flower pots and the water-box too. It's nice you should feel that way. But you can look at all these things later on, after you've taken off your things and rested for a spell. You better let me show you up to your room now."

"It would be nice to have you come with me. But I know the way."

Still unhurriedly, and still holding her coat easily around

her shoulders, she moved across the room. Then she paused with her hand on the latch, where Dexter had paused, an hour earlier.

"When I open this door," she said, "I'll go into a hall with frescoes on the wall. There are frescoes in the rooms on either side of it too. But this one's the most beautiful of all, because there's a great, graceful tree in the center of it that extends from the lower part of the stairway to the ceiling in the upper hall. Jerome told me the frescoes were painted so long ago you don't know who did them, or exactly what they represent. But don't you think the artist may have had the Tree of Life in mind when he did that one, going all the way from the ground to the heights? Like the weavers who make the Persian rugs with the Tree of Life on them, you know. Tante Odilisse has one of those."

"Well now, I don't know," Daniel said doubtfully. "You mustn't get your hopes up about those frescoes. They're sort of crude, when you come right down to it. I don't suppose they were made by a professional. I suppose they were done by some fellow living around here, who'd never had any lessons. Or maybe by one of those itinerant artists who went from place to place on horseback and painted to pay for their board and lodging, the same as the itinerant cobblers made shoes and the itinerant tailors made coats."

"But, Father Farman, Tante Odilisse always says that rug-making is in some ways the most remarkable of all the arts, because rugs are made by uneducated persons and yet these people have such a great feeling for symbolism and beauty that they reveal it. I think the man who painted the frescoes may have had the same kind of a feeling. If he did, and could show it, then wasn't he a great artist whether he'd ever had any lessons or not?"

"I hadn't thought of it like that before. But maybe you're right."

"Tante Odilisse's mother used to have a great many Persian rugs and Gobelin tapestries that taught lessons and told stories," Alix went on. "But in the War Between the States most of them were cut up to make coverings for the wounded Confederate soldiers who took refuge on her plantation. She didn't have any blankets left to give them, but she still had her tapestries. It's nearly always possible to find something, in an emergency, isn't it, if you really want to? And from the one rug she had left, which she bequeathed to her daughter, Tante Odilisse could tell me the story about the Tree of Life, and what it meant. . . Well, after I have gone up the staircase that is sheltered by your frescoed tree, I will turn to the left and go into the East Chamber. It has a spool bed in it and a spool design around the old mirror over the dressing table. There's a beaded pincushion on the dresser and a cottage Bible in two volumes on a little table by the window. The prettiest picture in the room is called 'The Young Mother.' This mother and her little girl both have their hair done in a very charming way and are wearing charming dresses too, and the child is holding a doll——"

"Good land, Alix, I don't see how you remembered all that after you found it out! Not that I see how you got Jerome to tell you about it in the first place. You said yourself men don't tell more than half when they're describing a room and I never did know one who'd notice such things as beaded pincushions and the like."

"Jerome must have noticed them," persisted Alix. "Because he did tell me about them. He didn't skip when he talked about the East Chamber. Perhaps he associated it with his mother. Men notice more, when they're thinking about their mothers. Or perhaps he wanted me to know what a charming room we'd have on Farman Hill. Of course, when he first told me about it, he thought he'd bring me here himself, instead of sending me. He thought that was the room we'd have together. And I remembered what he told me because I was very much interested. I was more than interested, I was intrigued. And I think it's easier to remember about something that intrigues you, don't you, Father Farman?"

"I don't know's I ever thought of that either. You've said all kinds of things to me in this last hour, Alix, that I never thought of before."

"But they were nice things, weren't they? You didn't mind having me say them, did you?"

"No," he said slowly. "I didn't mind. They were nice things. I'll study them some, while you're resting. But I don't need to do that, to know they're nice. I'm— It's made me happier than I've been in a long time, Alix, just hearing you say them."

CHAPTER 22

IT WAS evident from her prompt reappearance that Alix had not rested. Jerome had told her supper was always early on Farman Hill, so she knew she had kept it waiting already, she said; the least she could do was not to delay it indefinitely, especially as she had not helped to get it. But she was grateful to Mother Farman for saying she might take time to "freshen up"; everything would taste better now she had washed and changed. The dress she had put on in place of the brown cloth was made of garnet-colored silk, and with it she wore an old-fashioned garnet locket. Serena, speaking to Daniel later about their daughter-in-law's costume, asked him if he had noticed that even her shoes matched the rest of it.

"They were made out of the same kind of silk as her dress—grosgrain we used to call it when I was young," Serena said. "And there were garnet buckles on them. I never saw such pretty little shoes in my whole life. Or such tiny feet either, on a grown girl. Didn't you notice, Daniel?"

"I noticed that she looked as pretty as a picture," he said. "And that everything she had on seemed to be about the same color of dark red. I couldn't have told you any of the details. But I did think of something else: those clothes of hers were becoming, same as the ones she had on when she came in, and I shouldn't be surprised but what they cost money. But still they didn't look anyways unsuitable for supper at a farmhouse, any more than the first ones looked too dressy for her to be wearing on a long trip. Sometimes city clothes do give a girl that look."

Serena knew what he meant. She remembered, not without a pang, the ice-blue satin which Jenness had worn on New Year's Eve, making every other woman at the little party look dowdy and shabby by contrast; but loyalty to her dead daughter prevented her from giving tongue to a comparison between Jenness and Alix. She contented herself by expressing still further her admiration of her daughter-in-law's equipment.

"Everything she took out of her bags has that same look," she said. "Simple and suitable and yet—well, I don't know—elegant is as good a word as any I guess: handmade nightgowns and chemises, sort of old-fashioned looking, and fine as anything you'd use for a baby; cashmere wrappers, cut so they had some shape to them; wool suits that seemed made a-purpose for walks in the country, and cotton dresses for house-wear, different from any I ever saw, and handsome silks for best. I wouldn't let her unpack much, because I could see how tired she was. But she had padded hangers to put her dresses on, and trees for all her shoes, and little perfumed pads to lay in her bureau drawers where she keeps her underwear. I can see she's just as tidy as she can be, Daniel. But it's different from our kind of tidiness. Now no one would think of calling Alix poison neat, the way they do Rhoda."

Daniel readily agreed that this was so, and he listened politely to Serena's enthusiastic comments about their daughter-in-law's apparel, after the manner of patient and considerate men when clothes are under discussion by their wives and daughters. Personally, he was much more concerned about Alix' health than about her wardrobe. She had said, several times, how good everything tasted, but she had actually eaten very little supper, finally excusing herself, when Serena tried to "tempt her," with the pretext that she had "made" too big a tea. She had talked readily about Jerome's letter, which Dexter had brought home with him, but it was obviously an effort for her to introduce other topics; and although she had insisted on helping to clear away and do the dishes, she had lapsed into silence when the family was grouped around the fire afterwards. Finally she confessed, apologetically, that she thought Mother Farman was right, that she had better go to bed and have a good night's sleep, so she could wake up fresh as a daisy in the morning; and then she had left them, saying goodnight to each one in turn somewhat ceremoniously, as if she were combining the careful courtesy of a well-trained child with the grace of an accomplished guest.

When morning came, however, she was far from being as fresh as a daisy. There had still been neither sound nor sign from her when Serena returned to Farman Hill after making the rounds on her milk route; and genuinely disturbed, Serena went upstairs and rapped lightly on her daughter-in-law's door. A pleading whine from Lucky was the only response, so Serena opened the door cautiously, and called to him in a low voice, knowing he should be aired and fed. But he would not stay out in the yard, and he took only a few hasty gulps of the food she set before him; presently, he went bounding up the stairs again. Serena followed him as he nosed his way back into his mistress's room and padded across to her bedside, where he laid his head on the counterpane, gazing at her anxiously and making little plaintive sounds. Alix, who was lying on her side, with the bedclothes almost covering her dark head, remained perfectly still, breathing so softly that Serena, with increasing alarm, bent over to listen, drawing back the covering a little. Gentle as the movement was, it served to rouse the sleeper. She nestled still deeper down in the bed, put her hand to her hair as if to shake it free, and then stretched out her arms. It was their unaccustomed emptiness which actually awakened her. She turned slowly from one side of the bed to the other and then lay blinking up at her mother-in-law with her great dark eyes. Finally, realizing where she was and who was with her, she sat bolt upright and burst into apologetic speech.

"Oh, I'm so sorry! I must have overslept! *Ten o'clock!* Why, it can't be!"

"Don't you worry about that. And don't you sit up in

bed either, without anything around your shoulders. This room's colder than charity. You cuddle down again under the bedclothes while I get a fire going, and then I'll bring you up some breakfast. I did feel concerned, not hearing a sound from you when it was getting on towards the middle of the morning, and I thought I better have a look at you. But I don't want you should get up. I want you should stay right where you are."

"But, Mother Farman, you mustn't build fires and get breakfast for me! That's the sort of thing I ought to do for you."

"You lie right down again this minute, Alix Farman. There's someone else you've got to think about now besides yourself, but it isn't your mother-in-law! You're all tuckered out and you need to rest. You need to keep warm too. I'm not going to have you catching pneumonia, not while I'm here to help it."

It was seldom that Serena spoke so severely to anyone, and she had hardly done so when she regretted it, fearing she had been too harsh. But Alix did not seem to resent the reproof. She lay down again obediently, drawing the covers close around her chin, and watching her mother-in-law attentively while Serena busied herself at the hearth.

"There!" Serena said heartily, when the fire had begun to blaze with briskness. "That's got a good start now, and when I come back, I'll put another log on it. I've got some coffee on the back of the stove, and I've made it double strength. I'll have it here in two shakes of a dead lamb's tail, and some fresh sugared doughnuts with it."

Her return was, indeed, surprisingly swift, but Alix was already half asleep again when she re-entered the room with her appetizing tray. It took will power on the girl's part and coaxing on her mother-in-law's part to make her sit up long enough to drink the coffee and eat one of the doughnuts. She said nothing more, when she had finished, about getting up; instead she slid wearily down on the pillows and closed her eyes.

"You don't feel sick, do you, Alix?" Serena inquired anxiously. "You haven't got any little sharp pains, or anything like that?"

"No—no. I'm just terribly tired. I'm so tired I don't feel as if I'd ever be rested again."

Her words ended in a sigh, which apparently she regretted instantly. She reopened her eyes and tried to smile.

"I'm sorry to be such a nuisance," she said, "but I never was as tired as this before, never in my life. I think I will have to lie still until I get rested. Don't bother about me, please, Mother Farman. Just let me sleep. And don't worry about the baby. Nothing is going to happen to him. I promise I'll tell you if I have a single little sharp pain. Only I won't. And you won't have to scold me again, to make me behave. I know how important that is for us all . . . There's one thing I'd like to speak to you about though, before you go away. In Louisiana we don't talk about in-laws, the way people do in other places. We talk about fathers and mothers and brothers and sisters, when they're connected to us by marriage, just the same way we do as if they were connected to us by birth. And we talk *to* those people the same way. Did you know that?"

"No, it's the first time I ever heard tell of it. But seems to me it's a real nice thing to do."

"Then you wouldn't mind, would you, if I called you Mother instead of Mother Farman? And Father Farman— you don't suppose he'd mind either, do you, if I called him Father? Because you see it would seem more natural to me, coming from Louisiana. That's what I'd have done if I'd stayed at home. But now this is going to be my home. And my own father and mother are dead and so altogether——"

"She had me crying," Serena told Dexter half an hour later. She was standing by the table in the winter kitchen, making an apple pie, but every now and then she lifted one of her floury hands and surreptitiously wiped the corners of her eyes with it. "She put up her face and kissed me, just like a little girl, and said 'Thank you, Mother,' when I told her I'd be pleased to have her call me that. Then she lay down again and went right off to sleep while I was still standing there looking at her. I never saw such long lashes before, not on any human being.

Or so much hair. She doesn't wear it braided in bed. It all floats out, over her pillow. I certainly would admire to have a picture of her, the way she looked lying there. It put me in mind of an illustration in the gift book Daniel gave me when I graduated from high school. We were keeping company then and he sent to Boston for it. Tennyson's 'Idylls of the King,' that's what it was, and the pictures in it were by Gustave Doré. There was a line under this special picture I'm thinking of that said—well, I don't remember exactly but———"

Dexter helped her out. " 'Elaine the fair, Elaine the lovable, Elaine the lily maid of Astolat,' " he said with a slight smile. "There are all sorts of things wrong with that picture, Mother Farman, as far as Alix is concerned. In the first place, Elaine wasted away from unrequited love, as I recall it, and that's the last thing Alix would ever do—you can bet your bottom dollar good old Lancelot, or any other man, would have been hot on her heels, if Elaine had been anything like Alix. In the second place, Alix would never lie down on any job she'd started. She wouldn't get on a raft and go floating down the river to get away from it. She'd fight the thing through. Just the same, I follow you. I've seen that gift book— It's the big blue one you keep under the family Bible in the East Parlor, isn't it? And if Alix hasn't any more on her and over her at this point than Elaine has in that Gustave Doré picture you're talking about, I'm afraid she'll freeze to death before you can get a photograph taken."

"You put it in a sort of droll way. I'm pleased to hear you joking, Dexter. I can't remember when I've heard you talk that way before. But just the same I'm worrying some myself about Alix being cold. You could see your breath in her room when I went into it. Of course there are lots of quilts on the bed, and I made Alix put on one of her cute little sacques when she sat up. But even when she's covered real good———"

"I talked to Melvin West when I went to the village last night," Dexter broke in. "He said he could get us a big coal-burning furnace that would heat this whole house. But of course he couldn't install it in weather like this. He'd

have to wait till summer. He suggested a couple of oil
heaters, one for the entrance hall and one for the upper
hall as a temporary arrangement. He said if the doors
were left open into the parlors and chambers, these oil
heaters would take the curse off the cold, with the fireplaces going too. I believe he's right. Anyway, I think the
experiment's worth trying. The heaters would set right on
the floor and wouldn't necessitate tearing up anything. I
told him I'd go down again this evening and let him know
what you and Father Farman thought."

"Have you spoken to Daniel?"

"No, not yet. I'm going to, but I thought I'd speak to
you first. About the heaters and about an upstairs bathroom too. Do you think you'd miss the middle room if it
were made into one? Melvin says that would be the most
practical place to put it. Of course you could get in one
across the front of the upper hall. But it seems too bad to
disturb the frescoes, and I thought maybe you could get
along all right with one less bedroom. Of course after
Rhoda gets back in the spring I'll be gone, and then you
could turn the whole upper story over to Alix. It would
give her more of a sense of privacy and of having a place
of her own than if she had to be downstairs most of the
time, whether she felt like it or not."

"You must have studied on this considerable, Dexter. I
don't see when you had the time."

"Well, I thought of the furnace and the bathroom before
Alix had been in the house five minutes. And I thought of
the rest of it during the night. Don't you think I've had
some pretty sound ideas?"

Without answering immediately, Serena began to trim
the dough from the edges of her pie. She had experienced
an unexpected thrill of joy when Dexter called her Mother
Farman; it was the first time he had done so since his
parting with Judith, and though she had never referred to
his abrupt change in addressing her at that time, it had
been one of the many small hurts which, consciously or
unconsciously, he had inflicted. Now he had either realized
how moved she was by the suggestion Alix had made, or
he had instinctively began to act like his old self again

because the mere presence of Alix had eased a strained situation. The result in either case was the same, and it put new heart into her. She was also touched by the thoughtfulness he evinced through his suggestions about creature comforts for Alix and by his realization of her daughter-in-law's sensitivity. But still she was disturbed. If improvements were made on Farman Hill, the cost of these must be met by money that was not hers nor her husband's. So far Dexter had foreborne from any comments which would remind them of their great indebtedness to him; but this did not relieve their minds of its existence and a further outlay would increase it. What was more, the mere fact that Dexter was taking the initiative in proposing changes might give Daniel the feeling the younger man considered that he now had the first right to do so. Greatly as Serena desired to safeguard her daughter-in-law's well-being, she had a still greater desire to protect her husband's pride. She procrastinated, pressing down the edges of the dough to make a fluted border, while she considered the proposition Dexter had made. She was still silent and still pensive when he came and put his arm around her.

"I know just what you're thinking about, Mother Farman," he said. "I knew beforehand how you would feel too. That's why I spoke to you before I spoke to Father Farman. But maybe there's something you haven't thought of, and that's Alix' side. I don't mean she couldn't take it, whatever conditions were. She'd never admit she was uncomfortable any more than she'd ever admit she was unhappy. It would be part of her code not to. You know what Jerome wrote in his letter: 'She says she doesn't mind the cold. She says that about everything. She's wonderful.'"

"Yes—I've been thinking considerable about Jerome's letter, Dexter."

"I guess we all have," Dexter said briefly He did not enlarge on the statement. But Serena knew Jerome's letter by heart now. She knew the part that Dexter had been thinking over just as well as she knew the part she and Daniel had been thinking over. She had already gone to the old bookcase in the West Parlor and found the bat-

tered book of Bible stories from which she had read to
her own children; she had spent an hour, before she went
to bed, leafing over the yellowed pages and mending the
ones that were torn. And she had caught Daniel in the
act of drawing the hooded cradle from the hiding place
where it had been shoved after Peter's abortive plan to
take "human interest" pictures centering around it. Well,
there would be plenty of human interest centering around
it now. For Dexter was thinking of the baby also. He was
remembering that Jerome had written: *"I know Dexter
will be good to him too. It's a darned shame that he won't
be having a child of his own about the same age, and I'll
never forgive Judith for the way she's treated him. But
perhaps he'll take some comfort out of my child, and I
know I can count on him to stand by my wife too, if anything should go wrong and she should need a man's help.
Not that it will, of course. But just the same you might tell
him I said so."* She and Daniel had handed the letter over
to Dexter after they had finished reading it themselves,
and Serena had seen him stop when he came to that part
and reread it. It had not been necessary for them to tell
him anything. He had begun to plan, at that moment, how
he could best stand by Alix. He would have done so, being
Dexter, even if she had been plain and dull, for Jerome's
sake. But now he was planning to do it for her sake . . .

"I don't know that she'd be any the worse physically,
in the long run, if she did put up with a few hardships,"
Dexter was saying, breaking in on Serena's train of
thought. "Of course she's terribly tired now, but I have
an idea she's a good deal stronger than she looks. I think
that after she's had her sleep out and got warmed up, you
won't be able to hold her down. But she's been—well,
I don't know how you look at it, but the way I do, she's
been pretty generous. I know what Jerome meant when
he said Alix would make up to you for almost everything
you've lost. She's a natural giver. I can't make out that
she's thought about herself at all. As far as I can see,
she's been thinking what Jerome wanted her to do, and
how she could help you and Father Farman bridge over
his absence, and whether the presence of someone else,

young and feminine, in the house, would keep you from thinking all the time about Jenness and Judith. Don't you believe I'm right, Mother Farman?"

"Well, maybe you are. About her being generous anyway. I don't know whether she's as strong as you say. I'm worrying some about her losing her baby."

"She won't lose her baby. She'll give you a great big bouncing grandson that you'll be crazy about. He'll be ruling the roost a year from now."

"I hope so, Dexter. I hope so. But when a girl's in the family way for the first time there's lots of things she doesn't think of, especially if she doesn't have morning sickness. I'd really feel easier about Alix if she had; a girl who can't keep anything on her stomach just naturally loses some of her spirit, and that's quite a safeguard. I think Alix had got lots of spirit, same as you say, and it might bring on a miscarriage, if it wasn't curbed. I spoke to her sort of sharp about taking care of herself while I was upstairs. I'm worrying about that too. I'm afraid I may have hurt her feelings. I'm afraid she doesn't know I did it for her own good."

"Of course she does. She won't think for a moment you meant to be unkind. She'll only think you spoke to her with authority. And she'll like that. She'll feel it's a sign you've really taken her into the family. Where she comes from, mothers and mothers-in-law are supposed to show authority. Husbands too for that matter. They're not considered worth their salt if they don't. I guess most of them do it in a nice way. I hope so anyhow. And I don't see how anyone could help being nice to a girl like Alix. But just the same, I think one of the reasons she fell so fast for Jerome was because he dominated her from the moment they met, and that was the sort of courtship she understood and admired. I think he's dominated her ever since. I think he's worshipped her too, but that's beyond the point. And when he had to leave, I don't believe he even asked her whether she would be willing to come here. Of course she was willing because she adores him too, but that's also beyond the point. I think he just told her he wanted her to come and she came."

"Maybe that was the way of it. So you think——"

"I think the least we can do for her, on Jerome's account and on hers too, is to let her know we appreciate her attitude and her actions, and that we want to do what we can for her too, even if it does mean putting our pride in our pockets. It's little enough, compared to what she's doing for us. But we can give her a few creature comforts, though they'll be pretty elemental, compared to what she grew up with, unless I'm missing another guess. And we can give her the idea we'd like to make her happy too, at least as happy as we can. We've got to keep that in mind all the time. We mustn't forget she's a stranger in a strange land. We mustn't forget the man she loves has gone to war. We mustn't forget she's facing the ordeal of childbirth."

"Why, Dexter!" Serena exclaimed. She put down her pie and looked at him searchingly. "Dexter Abbott, what's come over you? I've never heard you make a speech like that before, never in your life."

"You never saw anyone like Alix, ever in your life, either did you, Mother Farman?" he inquired, and bending over, kissed her on the cheek before he went out of the kitchen. Then he crossed the living room and went into the front hall, either neglecting or forgetting to close the door after him. Serena heard him calling to Lucky with an inviting whistle, and she heard Alix speaking coaxingly too: "Go along, Lucky, go with Dexter. He'll give you a good run. And I can go to sleep again." Then she heard Dexter calling back.

"So you're a sleepyhead today?"

"Yes, I am. I'm terribly ashamed of myself. And I'm terribly grateful to you for thinking of Lucky."

"I'll be glad to have him around. But I'd be happier still if you'd promise me, before I went out, that you wouldn't try to put one over on Mother Farman while she isn't there to watch you. She's worried about you. She wants you to stay in bed till you're really rested."

There was no immediate reply. In the silence Lucky came padding down the stairs, slowly and a little hesitantly; but he kept on coming. Dexter spoke to him encouragingly, first in dog talk and then in man talk, while he did so. Dexter himself seemed to be waiting without impatience for his answer from Alix and to be standing still until it came. Serena waited for it too.

"I don't want her to worry. If it'll make her any happier, and you too, of course I'll stay in bed."

"Right. And next week, when you're rested, I'll take you to a sugaring-off, if you'd like to see one."

"I'm sure I'd love to. But what is it, a sugaring-off?"

"That's what I'm going to show you. So long, Alix."

"*Au revoir,* Dexter."

The man and the dog went into the yard together. This time Lucky did not try to force his way back into the house; he circled about, barking excitely but happily. Dexter was still whistling to him when they disappeared together beyond the Big Barn. Not that this was peculiar, Serena said to herself; a man had to whistle to a dog, especially a dog who was in strange surroundings and did not know how to follow readily; it had nothing to do with a man's spirits. But Dexter was still whistling, an hour later, when Lucky had gone back upstairs and he himself was down cellar getting wood for the fireplace in the East Chamber. Serena paused to listen to the cheerful sound, in the act of taking the completed pie from the oven, and Daniel, coming in from the barn, heard it too. He looked at his wife with a slight smile.

"The wind's shifted," he said a little drily. "I shouldn't be surprised but what we'd have a thaw."

CHAPTER 23

WHEN THE doors were left open into the East and West Parlors and the East and West Chambers so that the new oil heaters could "take the curse off the cold," it seemed logical to leave the living room doors which led into the lower hall and both parlors open also. The change came about so naturally that nobody spoke about it until long after it was an accomplished fact. Then Serena mentioned it one day, rather wistfully, to Dexter.

"I won't deny but what those heaters are a considerable improvement. And now that the family's larger, and going to keep on growing, it's nice not to be cramped for space. But I can't help thinking all the time, Dexter, that Jenness wanted we should make changes too and we wouldn't listen to her. Maybe if we had——"

"I was afraid you'd say that someday, Mother Farman. But you're not thinking things through. Jenness wanted to throw the whole house open, but she didn't want to lift a finger to keep it in order after she'd done it. And she didn't want to spend a cent of her own money on making it more habitable. She didn't even want to stay here long enough to get the benefit of the innovations she kept teasing for. She just wanted to bask in them for a few days, knowing she'd had the satisfaction of getting her own way, and then go off and brag about her excellent background. The more impressive it was the better story she could tell."

"It isn't becoming of you, Dexter, to speak ill of the dead."

"I'm not speaking ill of the dead. You know I loved Jenness. I loved her almost as much as I loved Judith. I'd like to choke any outsider who disparaged her memory, and I hope the men who left her in the lurch will get all that's coming to them someday. But among ourselves we've got to look at things straight. We can't distort what Jenness did and what she wanted to do just because she's dead. Especially if that means taking any of the credit away from Alix for what she's done and what she wants to do."

Dexter paused for a moment, so that she could retort if she cared to. But though Serena looked at him thoughtfully, she said nothing, and he went on.

"The night Pearl Harbor was attacked, when Judith and I were sitting in the living room before supper, I told her that all those closed doors on the north side gave

it a secret look. And I said something else: I said I felt
as if it were a house divided against itself. It seemed that
way too. It *looked* that way. I was right. It was. Jenness
had divided it. There's something in the Bible, isn't
there, about a house divided against itself? That it can't
stand? Well, this house couldn't have stood much longer,
the way things were going, Mother Farman; it was being
undermined. You know that as well as I do. I don't mean
physically. I suppose it could have stood up for another
fifty years or so, with some patching, though it did need
a lot of repair—that is, if our German friends hadn't torn
it down. But I wasn't thinking of that. I meant it couldn't
have stood up much longer spiritually. And now it will.
It'll last as long as our country. And the family'll last with
it. There'll always be Farmans on the Hill."

"You have some real nice thoughts, Dexter. Sometimes
you talk most like a minister. But I still think you take
too much for granted. The baby isn't born yet and we
don't know as it'll be a boy."

"I do. I know it the same way I knew about the house.
But we can let that pass for a while if you like. We can
just be fair and say we know Jenness would never have
taken away that sense of secretiveness, no matter how
many living room doors she'd opened. There'd still have
been the feeling in the house that there was something
to hide. Because the feeling was based on fact. There *was*
somthing to hide. There isn't any more. And it *was* divided. It isn't any longer. It's united. I might almost say
it's resurrected. There's an atmosphere of rebirth around
it. And I don't mean just because of the baby—or perhaps I ought to say babies. There are a lot of baby animals
on the place, you know. You really ought to get out to
see them, every day or so, the way Alix does. Then you'd
follow me more easily. But I also mean because of all
the discarded utensils that have been put back to creative
use, and all the flowers that have been planted to relieve
the bareness, and all the wasted ground that is going to be
fertile again."

Again Serena looked at him thoughtfully but without
replying. There was no abashment in the way Dexter

returned her searching glance. Instead of looking embarrassed, he looked increasingly content.

"And we might add, it's not only united, it's solvent," he said cheerfully, "which always helps. Well, I must be getting along. If Alix should ask for me, tell her I've gone out to the Mill Lot, will you? She might like to come out there herself. It's a nice day and she's interested in that experiment we're making with buckwheat."

"She's resting right now, same as she always does for a little while after the dinner dishes are done. But I'll tell her, soon as she comes downstairs."

Dexter nodded, and went out into the yard. He no longer needed to call Lucky. The dog was waiting for him, alertly, and bounded after him the instant he appeared on the porch. Serena picked up the baby blanket she was knitting, and moved instinctively towards the old rocker beside the hearth. But owing to the mildness of the weather the fire had been allowed to die down in the middle of the day and, after a moment's hesitation, she walked through the open door into the West Parlor, and sat down by one of the south windows where the sun was streaming in. She could see the front yard from there, with the new shrubs on either side of the cleared cobblestones which formed the once-neglected walk. She could see the new rose bushes banked against the clapboards in big, earthy beds and the new hedge that divided the lawn from the road and that was just beginning to put out its first shoots. She could see the road too, and the valley beyond it, and the church steeple rising among the low white houses in the distant village. She could see the foothills and the mountains. It was amazing, how many things a farm woman could see, just by looking out of her own front windows. Serena had never realized it, all those years when she had looked no further than her own backyard. Yet the hills and the valley and the village had been there all the time, and there was no reason why the greenery and the flowers should not have been there too.

The flowers and greenery, of course, were due to Alix. But they had not been embraced by her first idea. It was the house itself which had commanded her primary attention. She had wanted to explore every nook and corner of it as soon as she had recovered from the devastating weariness that followed her long, lonely trip. Of course she had loved the little apartment where she and Jerome had lived in Raeford, bceause they had been so happy together in it; but there was nothing like a house, especially an old house, when it came to having a permanent home. Jerome had told her a great deal about this one, especially about the summer kitchen, where he had always liked to eat when he came home for his vacation. Wouldn't Mother take her out to the summer kitchen?

"Well, we use it mostly to store things in nowadays," Serena told her. "I hardly ever go there myself, except to get something. The last time I stayed there for any length of time was when Peter MacDonald was here." She had told Alix all about Peter's visit while her daughter-in-law was still in bed and had found Alix a ready listener, because Joe Racina had talked to her about Peter too, saying there wasn't a foreign correspondent who could touch him. As a result of these conversations, Alix had suggested a subscription to the *Bulletin,* and the Farmans were now following Peter's progress around the world. They knew he had left Hawaii and gone to the Philippines, that he had been on Bataan when it fell, that at present he was on Corregidor. Alix generally read his pieces aloud to the rest of the family in the evenings after supper, and now she looked up with eager interest when her mother-in-law mentioned him in connection with the summer kitchen.

"Peter wanted to see it so he could describe it in that piece he wrote for the *Bulletin* about Jenness and get pictures for illustrations," Serena went on. "I showed you the ones he did take. But land! It was so cold we couldn't stay out here more'n a few minutes. Our breath froze, pretty near. But thank goodness, there's been a thaw at last, same as Daniel said there would be. I was beginning to be afraid the weather'd never break. There's been years when we had real good sleighing here in April, and I thought this was going to be another of 'em. But you can sort of feel the spring in the air today. I don't

know as there'd be a better time to go out to the summer
kitchen if you're sure you want to see it. It really isn't
much of a sight."

Alix was very sure, and when they reached it she took
in, almost at a glance, the various features which Serena
had enumerated in talking to Peter. Her gaze rested with
appreciation on the blackened beams and the prodigious
hearthstone, the handhewn doorway and the wooden peg
fastenings. But it was at the open cheese cupboard, where
battered pots and pans were jumbled together in heterogeneous piles, and at the empty wooden buckets cluttering
the floor that she looked the longest. Serena found it hard
to believe that the lingering gaze was caused entirely by
admiration. At last, regarding her daughter-in-law curiously, she made an inquiry.

"You keep looking at that cupboard and at those kettles,
Alix, as if there was something peculiar about them. Have
you got anything special on your mind?"

"Yes, Mother. I couldn't help wondering why they
weren't being used."

"Well, you see the Farmans stopped making cheese
about the same time they stopped raising horses, like I
told Peter, and———"

"I know. But why did they stop?"

"I guess because they didn't have as much gumption as
their forefathers did. I said that to Peter too. I said it
looked like those first settlers could turn their hands to anything. But afterwards they kind of lost the knack."

"Don't you believe they could get it back again?"

"Why, I don't know. I never thought much about it,
to tell you the truth. I know I'm not half the hustler my
mother was, let alone my grandmothers, but just the same
I've always thought my hands were pretty full, as it was."

"Of course they have been, because you've had to work
alone for a long while. But now I'm here to help you. I
can make very good cheese. At least I have made it, a
number of times. I'd like to try making it again, if you'd
let me."

"*Let you!* Why, I'd be tickled to pieces, and so would

Daniel. But I don't want you working beyond your strength, Alix. I don't——"

"I shan't work beyond my strength. You haven't found out yet how strong I am. Anyway, it's very easy to make cheese and cheese is very convenient to have on hand. It makes such a nice dessert. Tante Odilisse always has cheese and fruit for lunch, instead of a sweet, the way they do in France. And now that sugar's going to be rationed . . . Of course we're not going to feel that so much as some people, with all the maple sugar we've got. But oughn't we to be filling those wooden buckets? They're meant to keep maple sugar in, aren't they?"

"Yes," said Serena. "They are. But we haven't tapped many of our trees, not in a long time, until this year. So we haven't needed many buckets. But after Dexter took you to that sugaring-off at Wendells', he seemed possessed to strike right off to the maple groves and stay there until he squeezed out the last drop of sap. I'm sure I don't know what got into him. But it might be a good plan to use those buckets again. I heard him say something about being short of big pails."

"I think it would be a wonderful idea to use the buckets," Alix said, disregarding the reference to the possible source of Dexter's industry. "I couldn't help thinking, when I first looked at them, that if my great-grandmother had had as many things as you have, after the War Between the States, the St. Cyrs needn't have lost Bellefontaine. But their utensils had all been destroyed, while yours have only been disused. And I was brought up to think Yankees were so painfully thrifty. Now I see that was just another Southern slander!"

Alix smiled, almost mischievously. The elfin look was curiously becoming to her usually grave little face, Serena thought, watching the girl as she seated herself, resting her elbows on a large rectangular table which bore the scars of much hard usage. "I don't wonder Jerome liked to eat here," Alix went on thoughtfully. "It would make a wonderful dining room, with those beams and that hearth and all those beautiful cupboards. It has so much character and so much space. It gives you the feeling there'd always be plenty of room for a family, no matter how large it became, and for all their friends too, no matter how many they had. And everyone would be happy in it. It's that kind of a room. In summertime that handhewn door could stand open, too, couldn't it, all the time? So that everyone would have the feeling that it was all right to come straight in. And the door would make a frame for the fields. I can see how they'd look from it, just like a picture."

"Yes," said Serena, a little doubtfully. "Yes, that's the way Jerome felt about the summer kitchen, only he couldn't put it into words as well as you do, Alix. I'm sorry now I didn't humor him more, letting him use it. Same as I'm sorry I didn't humor Jenness more with the things she wanted to."

"It's too late to humor Jenness, but it isn't too late to humor Jerome. We could tell him when we wrote, that we were going to use the summer kitchen as soon as it got warm enough. We could use it as a dining room for ourselves, and we could use it as a Red Cross workroom for the neighborhood. It's plenty large enough. There must be a great many women living around the Hill who can't get into the village very easily. They could make this their center. We could keep the surgical supplies in one of the cupboards, if we consolidated the contents in the others —I think the red cupboard would be best, don't you? And this table's plenty big enough to roll bandages on——"

"Why, Alix, how did you ever come to have such an idea!" Serena exclaimed, brightening visibly. "It would be so fitting, using the room Jerome loved for the Red Cross! And I've heard I don't know how many women say that what with not being able to drive cars themselves, and the menfolks so busy and all, they couldn't get to the village. But they could walk to come here. I'd be proud to think we'd provided for them, on Farman Hill."

"Yes, so would I. And we could send Jerome little sketches of the summer kitchen, showing him how we were planning to arrange it for ourselves and how we were planning to adapt it for the Red Cross. We could ask his advice and see if he could think of any improvements."

"That's so," Serena said, brightening still more. "We could, Alix. We could tell him you were planning to use the West Chamber for a nursery——"

"That you kindly offered it to me for a nursery," Alix interposed softly.

"—So of course we were going to take the old cradle up there and two or three of the old easy chairs and——"

"And the old sofa to put at the foot of the bed, so I could rest in the daytime——"

"—And that by the time we'd taken all those out and——"

"—And put the spinning wheel over by the hearth, we'd have all kinds of space. So then we'd put this big table in the middle of the room and arrange the Windsor chairs around it——"

"Why, Alix, I can see it all just as plain as day! I don't know why I never thought of it before! The summer kitchen's just the room for a community center! And leading right out of the winter kitchen the way it does, it'll be just as handy as the living room to eat in. And next year with the new furnace heating the whole house, we can bring the baby right out here with us, and he'll be warm as toast, same as all the rest of us!"

She was so happy that she could hardly be restrained from starting in immediately on the indicated housecleaning and furniture moving. The same night, after supper, they all gathered around the gate-legged table and watched Alix draw her first sketch which was to go to Jerome. They had heard from him only once, so far, in a letter written at his port of embarkation, but held up, apparently, for safety's sake. In it he had written Alix much the same sort of thing he had said to his parents in his last letter before leaving Raeford, but with a few additions: *We are just about to sail so you won't hear from me again in a long while. Don't worry about me, Alix, for I'll be all right. Just remember I'm doing my duty, as I know you want me to and as I want to, hard as it is to be separated from you, dearest. What has to be has to be and I'm*

*going to do my part as I should. So good-bye for just a
little while now. Be sure to take care of yourself for that's
what matters most and remember I'll be with you again
soon. All the love in the world to you, dear darling Alix,
but lots to Mom and Dad too and my best to Dexter.
Ever yours, Jerome. P.S. If Mom thinks it's too much
trouble to have the family eat in the summer kitchen this
year, do take your own small blacks out there sometimes,
and sit in the old doorway and look out at the fields, while
you're drinking your coffee. That's the view I like best of
any at Farman Hill. And when the baby's big enough, let
him sit there beside you, with a bowl of bread and milk
for his supper. That's where I always liked to eat my own
bread and milk."*

"It is, and that's a fact," Serena said a little tremulous-
ly. "So of course it's natural he should want his son should
do the same. But you tell Jerome, in this letter you're
writing now, Alix, that I see at last it won't be a mite
of trouble to have the family meals in the summer kitchen
all the time, like he's been plaguing me for years to do.
Tell him when he comes home he'll find the table all set
there. I'll get it ready before I put on my gray shawl and
go out on the porch to meet him. Tell him about our plans
for the Red Cross too, and for clearing out the cupboards
and giving the old pots and pans we can't use any more
to the scrap drive."

"I'll tell him everything, Mother. But just let me finish
this drawing first. That's the way the summer kitchen's
going to look after we get it fixed up, isn't it?"

She shoved the little sketch forward and they passed
it around the table, scrutinizing it carefully, one by one,
first Serena, then Daniel, then Dexter. Daniel made the
initial observation regarding it.

"If you're going to start in using that battered old furniture it ought to be repaired anyway and maybe it ought
to be rubbed down some too. My Uncle Elkanah was a
great hand to mend old things and rub 'em down afterwards. He had a knack of making things too. I guess he'd
have been a fair cabinet-maker, if he'd a chance. He loved
building materials and tools the same way I love land.

I used to hang around his shop considerable when I was
a youngster, rainy days, and he taught me some of his
own tricks of getting a junk heap to look like a million
dollars. I'm afraid I've forgotten a good share of what he
showed me, but it might come back to me gradually, with
practice. You can put in your letter to Jerome, Alix, that
I'm aiming to see what I can do to improve the looks of
that old furniture."

"I will. I'll tell him the summer kitchen's going to be
one of the most beautiful rooms in the house before we get
through with it. Of course they're all beautiful, but there's
going to be something special about this one, because
there's something special about Jerome. And this is his
room, isn't it?"

"Yes. That's another nice thought of yours, Alix. This
is Jerome's room, the one we're fixing up on purpose for
him. And the best part of it all is, we're going to do it
with just what we have on hand. We're not buying anything new to go in it. We're not running into debt."

"There's no reason why we should. Later on, we might
like to have a rug for it, but perhaps we could make a big
braided one ourselves out of scraps, next winter, evenings.
Then all we would need to buy would be material for curtains. Shantung would be nice, and I could block a pattern
on it that would go well with the rug, if you like the idea."

"I like all your ideas, Alix. And of course that would
save expense, if you blocked plain material yourself. But
the fact is——"

Alix had been busily completing her letter to Jerome
while the conversation about the summer kitchen continued. Now she folded the sketch which had been returned to her in with the scribbled sheets and closed the
flap of the envelope.

"The fact is," she said quietly, "there's something I've
been meaning to speak to you about, some evening when
we were all together they way we are now. But we've had
so many other things to talk about, and we've been so
busy reading Peter MacDonald's pieces, that I never seem
to get around to it. It was the same way with Jerome and
me. We never got around to it until just as he was leaving.

And then he said something about money, about not having as much as he'd like, to provide for me, and I told him that didn't matter at all, because I had plenty to provide for myself. More than plenty. More than I know what to do with."

Alix paused. None of the others spoke. A strange hush had stealthily descended on the living room while she was talking, and now that she had stopped, it deepened. They did not know how to cope with it. But Alix looked across the table at Dexter, above the letter she had finished addressing to Jerome.

"Jerome was surprised, just as you are. But after he understood, he was pleased. He was relieved. Money hadn't mattered to either of us—it doesn't, at first, to the husband and wife, in a marriage like ours. But it would have, by and by. It does, in any marriage. In any household. In any—partnership. I could have told him that in the beginning, if he'd asked me. I'm wise about money, because I'm French. The French understand these things and they're very practical. Of course they're very romantic too, but they know it's easier to be romantic if you're not worrying about money all the time. Or quarrelling about it. It's better to have these things settled. That's why French parents or other mature relatives often settle these things before a marriage or even before a definite engagement. So there won't be any question about them afterwards, marring romantic moments for the *jeunes mariés*—the young couple—themselves."

Daniel managed to clear his throat. "I see what you mean, Alix," he said. "Seems to me like I've heard tell about this custom among the French and I don't deny but what it might have some merit. I've seen lots of young couples start their first wrangling over money, when, up to the time they didn't see eye to eye about that, they'd been billing and cooing like a couple of turtle-doves. Not wrangling over how much there was, or how little either. But about how it ought to be parcelled out. I'm glad to say Mother and I never had words over money. Not what you'd really call words. But there's no woman living who's got gumption that likes to stand by and wait for a man to take money out of his pocket and give it to her. Especially if he's forgotten to do it until she's asked him to. Mother did start her milk route partly because———"

"Now, Daniel, we don't need to go into all that, before Dexter and Alix," Serena said hastily, finding her voice too. "You've always been a good provider—anyway as good as your means would allow. And Jerome would have been one too, if he'd stayed on at the bank. It was only because he had to go into the Army . . ."

"Yes, but he is in the Army. Getting ready to risk his life for the rest of us. Isn't that enough for him to be doing without having to worry about who's going to provide for me and our baby? I think it is. I'm thankful he doesn't need to. And I'm thankful he doesn't need to feel we'll be a burden to his father and mother either."

The remarks Alix was making were obviously in answer to Serena's. But she had not once taken her eyes off Dexter while she went on talking. She did not do so now.

"We must make up a budget," she said calmly. "We must see just how much it's fair that I should pay for the running expenses of the house. Food and heat and repairs that are part of ordinary upkeep. A fourth of whatever they are, I should think, shouldn't you, for the present? And more after the baby's born. Of course I ought to bear all the cost of supplementary improvements that are made on purpose for my comfort. Like the heaters and the upstairs bathroom, for instance. Will you please let me know how much those cost, Dexter?"

"I've paid for them already. I've forgotten just how much they were," Dexter said abruptly.

"But you must have the receipted bills then. If you'll give them to me in the morning, I'll make out a check."

"Of course I shan't give them to you in the morning. Of course you won't make out any checks payable to me, now or ever."

"Yes, I shall. I'm very eager to please you, Dexter, and very willing to try, as far as little things are concerned. But as far as big things are concerned, it seems to me more important to do what Jerome wants than what you want me to do. Let's not have any mistake about that now and then we won't ever have to discuss it again. And this is what Jerome wants me to do: he wants me to pay for everything he'd have paid for himself if he hadn't gone into the Army and then all his government checks can go straight into war bonds. He wants me to pay my share of the running expenses here all the time, and he wants me to bear the entire cost of extraordinary expenses, just as I said a minute ago. He wants me to do more than that, Dexter. He wants me to improve the looks of the place so that he can think of it as getting more and more beautiful all the time he's away; it will help him, while he's surrounded by the ugliness of war, to know he's going to have something beautiful to come back to. And he wants me to help make it more productive so that it can supply a real contribution to the home front while he's on the battle front. A rundown farm can't contribute nearly as much as one that's in good condition. I don't need to tell you that, Dexter, because you're a farmer and an able one. And I'm sure Father and Mother will forgive me for saying Farman Hill is rundown . . ."

"It isn't easy hearing," Daniel said quietly. "But I know it isn't easy saying either, for a girl like you, Alix, who's naturally soft-spoken. And it was time someone said it. I admire you for telling such a hard truth."

"Thank you, Father. It's helpful for me to know that you understand my position so well. Jerome wants me to put money into the property so that its value can first be restored and then increased. He thinks it's a patriotic duty and a family duty too. He feels it's important that his parents should have both peace of mind and material comfort in their advancing years, that his wife should have a suitable home and that his son's inheritance should be protected. And of course none of that can be done without a clear title to this place. So he wants me to pay back every cent Father and Mother Farman borrowed to help Jenness, Dexter."

"If you think I'm going to take money from a woman!"

The exclamation was an angry one. As he voiced it, Dexter tried to rise, as abruptly as he had spoken. Alix leaned across the table and laid a small white hand lightly on his arm. There was no coquetry in the gesture, but there was an appeal. Daniel, whose vision was unobscured by the turmoil seething in Dexter, knew it took courage for her to defy him, that such an action, on the part of a gentlewoman, was contrary to her every tradition and all her training. But she persisted.

"I'm Jerome's wife, Dexter. I'm his son's mother. I'm his parents' daughter. He feels I'm the proper person to represent him in the family while he's away. He feels it's more proper than I should do this than that you should. He'd accept the money from you if there wasn't anyone else to supply it. He has accepted a great deal of help in other ways and he's ready to accept a great deal more. He thought you'd be my partner here on Farman Hill, that you'd do the things I couldn't. I can't do manual labor. I can't take responsibility for the land. But Jerome thought I ought to do my share too. Part of my share was coming here in the first place. Part of it's having the baby. Part of it's supplying the funds. You're his best friend and he hoped you'd be my best friend too. But there isn't a friend in the world, Dexter, who means as much to a man as his wife, if he loves her the way Jerome loves me. You're not going to prevent me from doing what Jerome wants me to just because you're a man and I'm a woman, are you? You're not going to make it impossible for us to be friends and—and partners?"

"Seems like Mother told me, the day after Alix got here, that you said we ought to be able to put our pride in our pockets, Dexter," Daniel said drily. He saw that the white hand, which looked so small and fragile, was still resting lightly on Dexter's sleeve as he spoke and he looked down at it fondly. Then he found that his eyes were blurring. He took off his spectacles and wiped them slowly before he went on. But no one tried to interrupt him. He was speaking as the head of the house. "Of course maybe you didn't mean what you said. But Mother and I thought you did when we let you put those heaters and the upstairs bathroom into our house. I hope you aren't going to make us sorry we've been so beholden to you, instead of being grateful that you were such a friend in need when we didn't have any other. Because it's like Alix says. Dexter. She ought to safeguard this property for her son in the absence of her husband, so's he can carry on when we have to leave off. And she ought to develop it for the home front as her contribution to the war effort, seeing that she had the means to do it. It's her right and her duty. I'm gratified she sees it that way. And I'll take it very ill myself if you make it hard for her to exercise her right and do her duty."

The evening when all this had been discussed and decided had marked a turning point on Farman Hill. Serena had realized it at the time, and she had become increasingly aware of it in the weeks that followed, as one improvement after another was unobtrusively made in the property, and as the habitual forms of daily living became gradually more and more gracious and pleasant. Alix never again took issue with Dexter, and the extreme gentleness and deference of her subsequent manner towards him soothed the sting of her one triumphant tilt. His own manner was slightly constrained for a few days, but the girl's own ease and friendliness were so disarming that it was hard for him to remain indefinitely aloof. Serena well remembered the first time she had seen him in a softened mood.

It was the first warm day of spring, and Alix had taken the "small black" which she drank regularly when she came downstairs after her nap, and seated herself in the handhewn doorway facing the fields, as Jerome had suggested in his letter that she should do. She did not gulp her coffee down; she drank it slowly, humming as she sipped, and presently she set down her cup and began to sing:

> Brother, whar is you gwine?
> It's gwine home to glory.
> I's been travelin' a long hard road,
> I's been totin' a heavy load,
> But I's always done de bes' I knowed,
> Now I's gwine home to glory.

Serena, who was rearranging the red cupboard, listened to her with delight. The tune was catchy, and presently she began to hum herself. Then she happened to glance out of the north window and saw that Dexter was crossing the Square Field on his homeward way. Alix, apparently oblivious of this, went on with her singing:

> Sister, whar is you gwine?
> I's gwine home to glory.
> I's been blind but now I see,
> I's been bound but now I's free,
> De Lawd said, Sister, I's heared yo' plea.
> Now I's gwine home to glory.

Dexter had entered the Ridge Field. He was in plain sight now and also within easy earshot. Alix glanced up and saw him. Then she called to him.

"Hello, there! Wouldn't you like a cup of coffee too? You don't know how good it tastes at this time of day."

Dexter looked towards her and smiled. He was swift to see the significance of the place which she had chosen for her coffee-drinking. He quickened his pace and there was no longer any trace of resentment in his manner as he answered her.

"No, I don't, because I've never drunk any in the middle of the afternoon. But I'm willing to find out, if you think it's an important part of my education."

"Yes, I do. I'll bring the coffee pot and another cup."

Alix rose and went through the summer kitchen on her way to fetch these, stopping long enough to kiss Serena as she passed the red cupboard. Then she disappeared, still singing. Dexter, as well as Serena, was humming by this time:

> Parson, whar is you gwine?
> I's gwine home to glory,
> I's been hones' an' I's been fair,
> I's been leadin' a life of prayer,
> Been talkin' 'bout heaven, now I's gwine there,
> I's-a gwine home to glory.

Alix returned, carefully carrying the coffee service. She was wearing a quaint dress made of shepherd's plaid taffeta trimmed with little frills, and small strap slippers. She looked very sweet and rather picturesque. She placed the service on the sill beside her, and sitting down again, began to pour out the coffee. Dexter, accepting his cup from her, looked rather shamefacedly at his grimy hands and moved to the lower step so that her fresh skirt would not brush against his earth-stained overalls. Serena could see them plainly from where she was working and hear what they were saying to each other.

"Mother thinks it's warm enough for me to start some outdoor work, Dexter. But she thought I better consult you before I began to plant and I agreed with her."

"I'm very much flattered. But haven't you enough work to do in the house? It seems to me every day I hear you've started to make another kind of cheese. And I believe you lie awake nights thinking of new ways to use hackels and piggins. What did you think of planting? Don't you feel your father and I have that branch of activity pretty well in hand?"

"Dexter, if you ask me so many questions all at once, how can I answer them? *Bien,* I do not have enough work to do in the house, because Mother does nearly all of it, and now that we are getting so many nice electric machines and gadgets of all kinds it will be easier to do than ever. I have only made three kinds of cheese so far and I am not thinking of doing anything with hackels at the present time except using them for ornaments. A piggin is just a wooden bucket, you know that, and the piggins are all full of maple sugar. But I was thinking I might plant some flowers. Certainly, I suppose you and Father have planted plenty of potatoes and cabbages and onions, but if you have planted any pansies and roses and lilies, I have not seen them."

"I'm afraid I'll have to plead guilty. Did you want pansies and roses and lilies?"

"Yes. And Mother understands how I feel. She has been very sweet about it. You see, she has had flowers on

the window sill, during the wintertime, but she's never had
a real flower garden outdoors. Just a row of sweetpeas and
another of nasturtiums and another of candytuft, she says.
And a clump of golden glow in the back yard and the
one red rose bush by the door rock in the front yard.
And of course the lilac bushes. But I have explained to
her that in the South we think a real flower garden, planted
after a design, makes a place seem more homelike outdoors, just as the right arrangement of furniture around
a fireplace makes it seem more homelike indoors, than
stiff chairs in a senseless row. I have told her about the
old garden at Bellefontaine."

"Would you tell me about it if I had another cup of
coffee?"

"Yes, of course I will. It surrounds the house on every
side, beyond green lawns sloping in all directions. In the
rear there are walks that wind past beds of verbena and
petunia, and completely shut off from the rest of the flowers there is a rock garden. This is spread over a broad
hillside and enclosed with rhododendrons planted at random beyond the ferns and the low-growing plants which
nestle among the rocks, that are washed by a trickling
stream of water. It sounds something like the water trickling in our living room. There is a great deal of cress
growing on the banks of this little stream, and where it
widens into a pool there are waterlilies and lotus flowers.
Then on the right, there is a large fountain from which
water foams up like a sparkling arrow. This fountain is a
memorial. It was erected to the memory of Mammy Lou
who served for seventy-five years in the St. Cyr family,
and it is surrounded by pansies in huge clusters and a
diamond-shaped bed of violets that smell very sweet. There
are rows and rows of crepe myrtle beyond the fountain
with magnolias and sweet olive and camellias and gar-
denias scattered among them; and of course there are roses
everywhere: the Louis Philippe roses that you find in
every Louisiana garden, no matter how small it is, and
Lady Banksias and white Cherokee roses and gorgeous
red ramblers. The red ramblers are mingled with Virginia

bower and Confederate jasmine on the latticed walls of the three summerhouses, which are at the back of the house near the scuppernong arbor. The arbor and the summerhouses have always been favorite retreats for lovers . . . Are you getting tired of hearing about this garden, Dexter?"

"No, of course I'm not. I'm just as interested in hearing about the garden at Bellefontaine as I am in learning that coffee tastes good in the middle of the afternoon. Well, so these bowers are a favorite retreat for lovers? I should think they might be!"

"Yes, and close by, where the lovers can see them if they choose to stroll a little, there are fuchsias and tulips that came from Holland. And there are passion flowers too."

"Very appropriate, I should say, for a lovers' retreat."

"I see you do not know about passion flowers, Dexter. They were so named because their unique formation and deep purple color caused them to be associated with the Passion of Our Lord."

"I'm sorry, Alix. I didn't know. You must forgive me."

"There was no reason why you should have known before . . . Of course there is amaryllis in the garden too, and hibiscus, and there are oleanders in many different colors. There is boxwood in hedges and honeysuckle too. And then there are all the wonderful fruits, which have such gorgeous colorings and such stimulating fragrance—persimmons and pomegranates and peaches——"

"It sounds like a fairy tale to me."

"There are lots of things about Louisiana that sound like fairy tales, Dexter. And the best part about them is that they all happen to be true."

"I'm afraid they don't come true in New England. Those flowers and fruits you've been telling me about wouldn't thrive here, Alix. They'd all winter-kill."

"Yes, but there are hardier ones that wouldn't winter-kill. There is that one red rose by the door rock and I've seen some other bushes that I think are briar roses growing wild by the roadside. If they can thrive here, there must be other kinds of roses that can too. And there are lots of northern flowers—phlox and zinnias and dahlias and larkspur and cosmos and——"

"Good Lord, Alix! I never knew there were so many different kinds of flowers."

"Didn't your sister ever have a garden either?"

"No. It would have interfered with her schedule."

"But that's sad, isn't it, to have a schedule that interferes with flowers? I should so much rather have flowers that interfered with a schedule. Will you have another cup of coffee, Dexter?"

"Not today. But I'll have one or two tomorrow about this same time, if you'll fix them for me and give them to me here in this doorway. Coffee does taste good at this time in the afternoon. I've learned that much. Now you better come out and show me where you want to plant this northern garden of yours. I'll try to get the ground plowed for you early in the morning, if it's a good day."

"Why that would be wonderful, Dexter! But you wouldn't need to plow up the front yard, would you? I believe I'll start there, because Mother thought that was a good idea too—just with a little hedge to divide it from the road, and some rose bushes up against the clapboards, and a border for the cobblestone walk. We'll be having visitors pretty soon, won't we, now that it isn't cold any more? And it's so nice to greet a visitor in a pretty yard. It gives sense of welcome right away. But my mint I'll put in back. I'll need mint, Dexter, for juleps."

Alix and Dexter had gone around the house from the back yard to the front yard, talking earnestly as they started. Serena stopped arranging the red cupboard and watched them go. Dexter had apparently forgotten about his grimy hands and earth-stained overalls as completely as he had forgotten his resentment about the money. At all events, when the fresh silken skirts Alix was wearing brushed against him, he did not draw away. And when Alix began to sing again, he sang with her; and again Serena picked up the tune:

Sister, whar is you gwine?
I's gwine home to glory.
I's been blind but now I see,
I's been bound but now I's free,
De Lawd said, Sister, I's heared yo' plea.
Now I's gwine home to glory.

It was at the transfigured front yard that Serena kept
glancing now, as she went on with her knitting. Alix was
right; flowers did make a difference, they did give a place
a homelike look out-of-doors and that was what Farman
Hill had always lacked. (Of course the fresh paint helped
too; the house itself was so white and shiny, the shutters
so green and glossy, and out beyond, the barn so warmly
red. But after all, it was the flowers that mattered most.)
What was it Jenness used to say? That Farman Hill, like
the Farmans themselves, was pretty grim until you got
beneath the surface. Well, it was not grim any more. It
was gracious and inviting. All the neighbors had commented on this, when they came to call. For they had
come in large numbers, as Alix had predicted, first out
of curiosity and then out of kindliness. The isolation which
disgrace had brought upon the house had been of brief
duration; the warm and vital presence of Alix was far
stronger than the shameful shadow of Jenness. Visitors had
come straight up the front walk, just as naturally as could
be, and had sat in the East Parlor or the West Parlor,
according to their fancy. Indeed they were now doing it
with more ease than they had ever shown when they were
restricted to the living room, and they were eating and
drinking with relish the frosted cakes and strong coffee
which Alix offered them at all hours. It was no trouble
for Alix to receive company at any time; she always
seemed to have hot coffee and fresh cakes ready at the
right moment, and she seemed very glad to see these
neighborly callers and to accept the invitations which they
extended, at first rather timidly but gradually more boldly,
that she should come and pass the afternoon with them
too. These social visits paved the way for her suggestion
that they should work together as well as chat together,

and soon the summer kitchen was humming with neighborhood activity in behalf of the Red Cross. But there was one caller whom Alix apparently had expected, and on whose absence she eventually commented to her mother-in-law.

"I can't understand why Father Boudreau hasn't been to see me, Mother. Now your minister, Mr. Litchfield, has been very friendly. Don't priests go to see their parishioners in New England?"

"Why I don't know, Alix. Like I told you, I never was in a Catholic church in my life, except that one time Joe Racina took Daniel and me in Alexandria. Likely as not this Father Boudreau goes to see the Junction people who attend his church. Canucks they are mostly—Canucks and some Poles and Eyetalians."

"What's a Canuck?"

"A French Canadian."

"You say that in the same tone of voice that outsiders use when they come to Louisiana and talk about Cajuns— and sometimes when they talk about Creoles. Is there anything the matter with the French Canadians who live around here? I've been hoping I'd meet some of them. It would seem good to me to talk French once in a while."

"Why I suppose it might, Alix. I hadn't thought of that. I don't know whether you could understand these Can—these French Canadians though. I hear they talk some queer kind of a dialect and——"

"That's another thing that outsiders say about Cajuns," murmured Alix, glancing away.

"What's that, Alix? I don't think I quite caught what you said. But anyway these Can—these French Canadians are mostly men who work on the railroads and their families. The Eyetalians keep the fruit stalls and the cobbler shops and the Poles——"

"I think I'll speak to Father Boudreau next Sunday after church. I think I'll ask him if he won't come and have supper with us some night next week . . . that is, if you and Father wouldn't mind."

"Land sakes, Alix, Daniel and I wouldn't know what

to do with a Catholic priest in the house! Not but what we want you should feel free to ask anyone you've a mind to and not but what we'd do our best to make a friend of yours welcome. But a priest on Farman Hill—well, it would be sort of awkward and unnatural, Alix, and that's a fact."

"Perhaps the reason Father Boudreau hasn't been to call is because he's afraid you'd feel that way about his coming. But it wouldn' be, Mother. You'd see. And anyway, even if it were, we've got to make a beginning. Because of course if I were ill, or the baby, he'd have to come here. Not that I think either of us will be, but we should think of those things and speak of them. It's something like the money. If you consider everything calmly and prepare beforehand there's not half so apt to be awkwardness. Or if there is, you can meet it better."

For the first time since Alix had recoverd from the period of prostration which Serena had found so alarming, she looked at her daughter-in-law in a troubled way. Alix had been both unobstrusive and matter of fact in regard to her church-going. The first Sunday after her recovery she had come downstairs wearing the lustrous fur coat, and had asked Dexter to show her where he had put her car and to tell her the way to the Junction. He was still in his working clothes, having just returned from doing the chores at the Abbott Homestead, and he was truly sorry to learn that it was already too late for him to change and take her to church himself. But she said that she would really rather go alone; by and by, when it was no longer best for her to drive much, she would be very grateful for his cooperation. At the present time, however . . .

The way she said this had sounded so simple and sincere that Dexter had not importunated her then and the subject had never been broached again. With no previous discussion of her plans, and only a last-minute word to Serena—"I'm off to church, Mother. Anything I can do for you at the Junction?"—she drove away every Sunday morning, and occasionally she also went on weekdays—"I'm going to Confession this afternoon. I won't be long. I've tried hard to remember but I can't seem to think of anything very wicked I've done since I went the last time"— "Tomorrow's Ascension. That's a Holy Day of Obligation, like Sunday and the other Great Feasts, so I'm going to early Mass. I'll back for breakfast." These brief comings and goings of hers had neither upset the Farman household routine nor caused its members any mental disturbance, and Serena had been so agreeably surprised on both these points that she had made them a matter of comment to Daniel: she had always heard that Catholics made a great fuss about what they did and didn't do, no matter how much this upset everyone else, and about what they ate and didn't eat. She could see now that must have been just talk. This comfortable feeling had persisted until Alix mentioned the matter of the baby and its possible illness. Then she had a queer qualm. But Alix continued to talk quite cheerfully.

"And we must plan for the baptism," she said. "Of course the day you will go to a Catholic Church, Mother . . . I'll still be in bed and you'll take the baby for me— you and Father and Dexter. Dexter will have got used to it by that time, because the last month or so before the baby is due he's going to drive me to the Junction and it will be simpler if he comes in the Church than if he waits outside, because then there won't be any complications about meeting afterwards. I've asked him already if he doesn't think so and he agrees with me . . . Then we must begin to think about godparents. Perhaps my step-mother would come up for the baptism, or one of my aunts. And I have several available cousins. So before any of them arrives, it would seem to me very wise as well as very pleasant if we should have Father Boudreau to supper some night quite soon now."

"Would he eat the same as the rest of us?" Serena asked doubtfully. "I don't mean fish, if it was Friday he came. I understand about that. I mean, everything. I wouldn't know his tastes." The anxiety in her voice reflected more than her concern about the proposed supper; this was also the first time she had realized that there was a Catholic baptism in the offing or the question of godparents and impending visits of total strangers to consider.

"Well, he'd probably like a good highball first. Perhaps we ought to enlarge our private stock a little—I've been thinking about that too. I'll be needing Bourbon and brandy for juleps. And of course we'll want champagne for the christening, so we ought to sample one or two brands beforehand, and I think it would be nice to have some red wine too—a good sound Burgundy. That's so good with chicken and your fricassees are so wonderful. I think certainly we should give Father Boudreau one of your fricassees—we won't ask him on a Friday. And currant jelly and dandelion greens and rhubarb pie. And of course your marvelous Parker House rolls and mashed potatoes. And don't you think we might have some soup too?"

"I don't know but what we could, Alix, if you'd make it. I never was much of a hand to have soup, except a cream of tomato now and again. But that onion soup you make is just as tasty as it can be. And it beats me the way you take a few scraps of almost anything and throw them all together helterskelter into an iron pot with some water and a few hours later ladle out a fine broth. Well, the way you make it sound, I could get up a supper for Father Boudreau in two shakes of a dead lamb's tail with what we've got right here on the place. And maybe while we were sitting around the table things wouldn't be so awkward after all. But when we'd finished——"

"He'd probably like to play bridge. Dexter does; he says he played quite a lot of bridge in college. And Mrs. Barnes can play too. We could have a foursome."

"I don't see how you come to find out people's tastes and habits the way you do, Alix. Here you've hardly stirred off Farman Hill since you got to the country, but you know more about a good many of them than I do, living here all my life. Who was it told you the Catholic priest at the Junction played a good game of bridge?"

"I think it was Mr. Franchini. Mr. Franchini keeps his store open until noon on Sundays so I started going in there to buy oranges and somehow we got to talking. Mrs.

Franchini's expecting a baby about the same time that I
am, and one of his cousins is an Ursuline nun, so altogether——"

"You don't want to ask the Franchinis to supper too,
do you, Alix?"

"Not just now. But perhaps later on——"

"Let's see how we get along with the Catholic priest
first. The things you think of to do! Starting him off with
a highball and getting up a bridge game for him! But then
I never would have thought of using the summer kitchen
for a Red Cross workroom and that turned out all right,
so maybe——"

"It will, Mother. You'll see. We'll have a lovely party
and before it's over we'll all be fast friends."

Alix had been right about that too, Serena reflected,
again glancing from her lengthening baby blanket to the
burgeoning yard, where the one rose bush by the door
rock which so long had been its only ornament was
flanked by so much fresh bloom. Father Boudreau had
accepted the invitation from Alix with alacrity, and he and
Daniel and Dexter had all got along together like a house
afire, as Dexter himself said afterwards. He proved to be
a Canuck himself, born just "over the line" in Stanstead;
now that Serena saw one of these legendary figures at
close quarters, she was disposed to revise her estimate of
them. For Father Boudreau was jolly and shrewd and
homely. He ate and drank with relish, he cocked one eye
a little and told droll stories with gusto, he discussed the
questions of the day with acumen and wisdom; and when
the bridge game was finished, he chuckled over a score
which revealed that he was several hundred points ahead
of anyone else. But a more serious note crept into his voice
as he was saying goodbye, and friendly words of admonition accompanied his expressions of appreciation.

"I noticed the road was a bit rough in places as I came
up the hill tonight, Mrs. Jerome. My advice to you is that
you take it slowly now when you come to Mass, or Dr.
Barnes will be having something to say to you as well as
myself. Wouldn't Mr. Abbott be driving to the Junction

perhaps on an errand about church time now and then? I
thought so, I thought so! And maybe bringing you to the
rectory afterwards for a cup of coffee with my sister and
me. Yes, I've got my sister at the rectory, and a good
housekeeper she is to my way of thinking, though I never
knew her to make a fricassee that could compare with the
one I've had tonight. But be that as it may, you ought not
to be fasting too long mornings now, young lady, so don't
forget about the coffee that'll be ready for you after Mass
. . . Mrs. Farman, I can't thank you enough for the fine
supper and the pleasant evening you've given me. It isn't
often I've been asked out to a private home since I came
to the Junction . . . I thank you too, Sir, for your hospitality. I'd like to talk to you again, if I could, about plans for
another bond drive. We're not doing as much as we should
for a town of this size; we must all get together and do
more . . . Mrs. Barnes, can I take you to the village, or do
you have a car of your own here? Anything a poor priest
can do for a grand doctor——"

The village had not yet accustomed itself to giving Mrs.
Barnes a title, and the priest's praise of her was actually
the first that had been heard on Farman Hill. Shortly after
Judith's departure, the doctor with whom she had worked
so long had applied for a commission, reminding his patients that his wife had been a prosperous physician in
Winchester up to the time of their recent marriage and
that there was no reason why she should not practice
again, in his place. In no time at all he had been whisked
away, speedily achieving the rank of captain; now he was
already serving overseas. The village, which had been disposed to regard him as reliable but plodding and unremarkable, was electrified by this comet-like procedure; it
had considered him as much of a fixture as the church
steeple, and as indispensable. When it recovered from its
shock, it expressed its resentment in no uncertain terms:
it was vehemently opposed to lady doctors; henceforth it
would patronize the Junction. But the Junction itself was
depleted. Of the three doctors it had formerly possessed,
two were now gone, one like Doctor Barnes, to serve overseas, and the other to accept a profitable appointment at a

city hospital. The remaining incumbent was well over seventy and could not add to the burdens of a profession which he felt were already too heavy for him. Besides, there was not always time to send to the Junction in an emergency: the village had found itself forced to permit "Mrs." Barnes to minister to a child with croup, to another who swallowed a safety pin, and to a third who playfully opened a vein in his arm with a penknife. A sudden and severe fall which, but for "Mrs." Barnes' prompt action, might have resulted in a miscarriage for a woman who had long hoped in vain for a baby, represented her next triumph; and it was at this juncture that Alix had startled the Farmans by calmly announcing that personally she was very pleased at the prospect of having "Mrs." Barnes care for her.

"Both the de la Rondes and the St. Cyrs have always had midwives, until very recently, when their babies were born," she said. "My stepmother did not, but after all, she was only a Creole by marriage. Neither Tante Odilisse nor Tia Izola would have dreamed of having a gentleman for their confinement. I am sure they will be delighted when I write them about Mrs. Barnes. I shall do so immediately."

The news that Alix Farman was not only reconciled to having "Mrs." Barnes for her doctor, but supremely satisfied that this was so, spread like wildfire, and by the time the supper party at Farman Hill took place, the general mistrust of her adequacy was so far quieted that she already had more than she could do. She thanked Father Boudreau for his offer of a lift, but said she did have her own car. She had to go still further "out back" before she returned to the village; and heavens, she must hurry! She hadn't realized it was so late. But it had been such a delightful evening——

Alix accompanied the priest and the doctor to the front door. The entrance hall was illumined with candles and the light of these shone softly over the frescoes. She detained her guests to call their attention to these.

"You were admiring the murals in the East Parlor, Father, and Dr. Barnes said she liked the ones in the West Parlor better still. But I like this one best of all. It's the

Tree of Life. At least I call it that. I think it's appropriate
that the Tree of Life should be represented by a tall, graceful elm at Farman Hill, just as you might represent it by
a glossy live oak draped with violet moss, in Louisiana.
Tante Odilisse says the story of grass is the story of mankind, and when I told Dexter that, he agreed with me.
But trees reach closer to heaven. Perhaps the story of
mankind's in both of them—the strong roots imbedded in
the fertile soil, the nourishing crops, the lofty branches—it
makes a kind of trinity, doesn't it, Father?"

Yes, my daughter, it does. Well, take good care of this
Tree of Life on Farman Hill. And don't forget that Dr.
Barnes and I will be coming in every now and then to
have a look at it too."

"Thank you, Father. Goodnight, goodnight."

"I don't know as we've ever passed a pleasanter company evening on Farman Hill," Serena said to Daniel
afterwards. "I did feel real bad though to think we'd never
asked Father Boudreau here before, when he said it wasn't
often he'd been invited out to a private house since he
came to the Junction. I'm sorry we didn't include his sister
too—somehow I never thought of a priest having a sister.
And I feel easier now to think of Mrs. Barnes looking after
Alix than I did at first. Just the same, I wish Judith was
going to nurse her. If Judith hadn't gone away, she could
have taken care of Jerome's baby, and there isn't a nurse
anywhere around that can touch her when it comes to baby
cases. Dr. Barnes used to say so himself."

"If Judith hadn't gone away, she'd most likely be near-
ing her own time, in September," Daniel reminded his wife.
"There might have been two little cousins on Farman Hill,
not more'n a few months apart. And then two little youngsters running around the place again. It would have seemed
like old times, wouldn't it, Mother? But I guess it just
wasn't to be. We ought to be thankful for one."

"Maybe there'll be more, by-and-by. Do you know,
Daniel, every time Alix says something about the Tree of
Life, it gives me a kind of teary feeling, yet one that's
hopeful too? I've looked at those wall paintings day after

day for nearly thirty years, but I never would have thought of them in connection with the Tree of Life if Alix hadn't mentioned it. I thought they were just a parcel of crude pictures of ships and houses and water and land. More'n once I've been on the point of suggesting you should wash 'en over with some nice fresh-colored paint. But now that Alix has put this notion into my head, I feel they're a sort of symbol of permanence at Farman Hill."

"Yes," agreed Daniel. "I feel that way myself. I have, ever since Alix first spoke to me about 'em, the day she came here."

Serena recalled this conversation now. She gathered up the fleecy folds of her knitting and went out into the hall, where she stood for several minutes looking intently at the picture of the elm which Alix called the Tree of Life. Finally she put out a finger, and softly began to trace the outline of the sturdy trunk up to the feathery branches, as far as she could reach. She continued to do this for several moments, with a growing feeling of contentment and reassurance. Then, hearing the soft opening and shutting of an upstairs door, she scurried back into the West Parlor, rather shamefacedly, and resumed her interrupted work. When Alix came into the room, she was rocking back and forth in a settled way, her needles clicking in a steady rhythm.

"Well, Alix," she said, in a matter-of-fact voice, which was rather like her husband's. She hoped it would not betray her abashment in regard to her recent sentimental action, but she could suppress a slight fear that it might. "You look nice and rested. Did you have a good sleep?"

"Yes, Mother. I slept over an hour. And I do feel rested. If there's nothing you need me for, I think I'll go out for a walk."

"Dexter wanted I should tell you he's over in the Mill Lot this afternoon. He said maybe you'd like to come out there. He's planting buckwheat. He said you were interested in the experiment."

"Yes, I am. I'll go pretty soon. But there's no hurry. I'd like to sit here with you for a few minutes first. It's so pleasant in a quiet country parlor in the middle of a spring afternoon, isn't it?"

"Why, yes, it is. I've been enjoying myself this past hour, sitting all alone here, knitting, looking around the room and out into the yard and down towards the village. It's been real pleasant and real restful. I won't be half so tired, when I start to get supper, as if I hadn't taken this time out. I can work later in the evening and put more heart into my work. Just the same, the parlor seems a sight pleasanter to me now that you're here than it did before."

She looked fondly down at her daughter-in-law as she spoke. Alix had drawn up a low stool and seated herself by her mother-in-law's rocking chair, leaning her dark head against Serena's knees. She still moved easily and gracefully, and though her figure was fuller than when she had come to Farman Hill, she was not misshapen. Instead, each week seemed to add to the serenity of her bearing and the beauty of her bloom. There was a lustre about her looks, not only about her glossy hair and limpid eyes, but about her alabaster skin. The dress she had on was finished with old lace at the neck and elbows, and her rounded forearms and swelling breasts were soft and creamy against this. Serena had been schooled from childhood to make no "personal remarks" and to be chary of demonstration; but she could no more help complimenting and caressing Alix than she could have helped admiring and cuddling a baby.

"There's about one woman in twenty that gets better looking, when she's in the family way, than she's ever been before, and you're one of them. I declare I can't keep my eyes off you. I wish Jerome could see you."

"I wish I could see *him*. But perhaps it's just as well he can't see me. I am getting bigger—it shows more when I'm undressed and pretty soon it'll show all the time. Of course a lot can be done by wearing clothes that are cut just right, and having them spotless, and paying lots of attention to your hair and hands. And most of all bearing yourself erectly and looking at everyone straight in the face as if you were proud and pleased, instead of casting down your eyes as if you were self-conscious and ashamed. But just the same, I think Jerome would have looked in vain for allure, the last two months. He liked me the way I was. He dreaded to have me change. When he was saying good-bye, he tried to pretend he didn't, but I knew better. I knew he wanted to keep his image of romance unaltered."

"But land, Alix, a man doesn't expect his wife to be an image of romance when she's carrying his child!"

"It depends on the man, doesn't it, Mother? Now Father wouldn't. I don't believe Dexter would either. They think in terms of fruitfulness, like all farmers. They glory in every phase of its development because they never lose sight of its meaning. But Jerome is different. His great passion is for beauty. It isn't for symbolism."

Serena looked away from her daughter-in-law, gazing again at the verdant valley and the hills beyond. She knew that what Alix said was true. But unlike Alix she was not willing to admit it.

"I don't know as Daniel and Dexter think so much about symbolism either," she remarked defensively. "I never heard 'em say so. And Jerome will come down to earth after a while. If you should have two or three children, so's he gets accustomed to having you look the way you've go to if you're going to do it ——"

"Why of course I'm going to do it! I hope I'll have at least six—two girls and four boys. I think that would be a fine family, don't you, Mother? Or maybe seven—one lots younger that the others, when we'd almost forgotten there could be any more, and just before there really couldn't. Another boy, who'd be about the same age as the eldest daughter's first child. They'd seem more like cousins than aunt and niece or uncle and nephew or whatever it turned out to be. Then there'd always be a baby in the old cradle, because presently the eldest daughter would be having another, and a baby in a cradle does give a place such a homelike look. There wouldn't be any labor shortage on Farman Hill either. Even if half of the sons and daughters wanted to go away, the other half would probably want to stay, and with their families and all—Can't you just see it happening, Mother?"

"Well," said Serena smiling, "I can see a good share of

it anyway. You do put things in a nice cheerful light, Alix.
I'm pleased as punch to know you feel the way you do
about children. And Dexter says you take an interest in
all the animals too. He says you go out to see the calves
and colts every day or so."

"Yes. Because in a way I feel responsible for making
so much more work for him and Father. It isn't as if I
were doing anything to take care of the animals myself. I
know I can't this year. The least I can do is to show an
interest in them."

"You put up the money to buy the new stock, Alix.
You talked Daniel into raising colts again on Farman Hill.
And you took on so, when he said he was thinking of getting rid of his herd, same as Hite Wetherill and two or
three others have done around here, that he went to work
and doubled it instead!"

Serena gave a little chuckling laugh. Alix smiled and
nestled a little closer to her. But she answered without
visible excitement.

"I didn't know any better way to invest my money,
Mother, except in war bonds, and after all, I'm buying
those regularly too. I've got to do something with it, and
I'm certainly not spending much on living expenses. Besides, haven't we got to have more horses again on the
farm, if we can't have gasoline? Nellie and Gypsy are getting awfully old, and Dexter is saying already he doesn't
know how on earth he's going to get back and forth between Farman Hill and the Abbott Homestead, as much
as he ought to, if there are any more restrictions. And
next year there are bound to be more. We've got to look
ahead."

"I suppose we have, Alix. I suppose we have."

"Then there was a special reason why I 'took on so'
about the herd," Alix continued. "There was a very
sad example once, in Louisiana, of what could happen
if a man sold a herd to which he was attached. Didn't I
ever tell you about Mr. Pierre Estrade, who lived on the
next plantation to Bellefontaine?"

"No, but I wish you would. That is, if you've got the

time. I kind of think Dexter is waiting for you. But I do declare you tell interesting stories, Alix."

"Dexter doesn't mind waiting for me," Alir said serenely. "It was this way: Mr. Pierre Estrade owned a herd of Jersey cattle of the purest strain which were his great joy and pride. But he was very extravagant, not only in the way he handled this herd and in the quarters he supplied for them but about everything else connected with them. For instance, he had a special refrigerator to hold fresh milk placed in silver goblets, each with a silver top that was fastened down securely over it. The milk was left in these until a rich cream formed on the top, and then these goblets were set beside everyone's place at table. They were very much like the silver goblets I have for mint juleps. We'll be able to have juleps before long now, Mother."

"Yes," said Serena a little absent-mindedly. "You were telling me, Alix, about this Mr. Estrade and his herd. I was real interested——"

"Well the time came when his creditors began to press him for payment. He must have been very deeply in debt before that happened, because creditors are apt to be quite lenient in Louisiana, and then of course there are always the banks. So at last he decided that the Jersey cattle would have to go on the block, though it almost broke his heart to think of it. On the day of the sale, which was attended by people from all the surrounding parishes, Mr. Estrade rode into town to bid his cattle good-bye. His attachment to them was so great that he felt he could not let them go without this final farewell. And what do you suppose happened? At the sight of him, all the cows began to low in a mournful chorus, as if they were overwhelmed at saying good-bye to him too, and presently there was not a dry eyed spectator left. So then someone in the crowd said there was just one thing to do, and they passed around the hat, and got enough money to give the herd back to Mr. Pierre Estrade. He rode home at the head of his herd, all the way up the levee, and the cows lowed again as they went, but this time with joy, and presently they were all back in their own luxurious stalls, never again to leave them."

"Well, that is a real touching story. I'm almost crying myself," Serena said, wiping away one or two obstreperous tears. Then she added more practically, "Besides having the banks so lenient, I presume Mr. Estrade didn't have any shortage of help to complicate things for him, down there on the Mississippi. It's all very well for you to say there won't be any labor problems on Farman Hill, after your seven children grow up and get married and have families of their own. But that's looking farther ahead than I can manage. Daniel and Dexter are both working longer hours now than either of them ever did in their lives before, and that's saying plenty. What they'll do when haying and thrashing time comes I don't know."

"I don't either—yet. But I'm sure we'll find out before it does come. I think some of the men in the village who aren't farmers—the ones who keep stores and do things like that—are going to try to help, after hours. And the younger boys, who hadn't begun to take work seriously before. Of course it won't be skilled labor, but it'll be better than nothing. And next year it ought to be good. Besides, next year Dexter isn't going to run for selectman. He says older men can do things like that just as well as he can. He's going to put all his time into farming."

"Land sakes, Alix, Dexter oughtn't to give up a position like that! It gives him standing in the community."

"Does he need to have any extra standing given to him, Mother? He's got so much anyway."

Serena shook out her knitting thoughtfully.

"Take a look at this blanket, Alix," she said. "I've got it pretty near done. I've always liked that old basket stitch and I never saw anyone but my mother do it . . . Well, I don't know as he does. I guess he has got a kind of standing of his own. That's another thing I never thought much about—a farmer's standing. I've always thought ministers and teachers and bankers and such had more. But I don't know . . . Are you fixing to go out to the Mill Lot now, Alix? Maybe you'd take the mail along, if you are. It came in while you were asleep. I noticed there was a letter for Dexter from Judith."

"I'll be glad to take it, Mother. Is it on the secretary in the living room?"

"Yes. I'm sorry there wasn't one for you from Jerome, Alix. A long time's gone by since you've heard from him."

"I expected that. I'll be having a letter in a month or so now. That isn't long to wait."

She smiled again, and rising, put the stool on which she had been sitting back in its proper place before the hearthstone. Then she bent over to kiss her mother-in-law and murmur a few words of admiration about the new blanket before she went through the open door into the living room and picked up Judith's letter. She stood still for a moment, holding it in her hand and listening to the trickling water in the old waterbox; it was a sound that still intrigued her; she enjoyed it, consciously, whenever she heard it. But she went on, contentedly, for she enjoyed the silence in the winter kitchen too, and the mid-afternoon order which reigned there: the fragrant loaves of homemade bread, loosened from their pans and turned upside down to cool; the neat rows of rhubarb preserves at the side of the new range, the wide new sink cleared and empty. Most of all she enjoyed the beauty of the transfigured summer kitchen: the harmony of its ancient beams and handhewn portal, of the spacious cupboards which lined its walls and the wide planks which formed its floor. Everything was in readiness for the Red Cross workers who would gather there that evening. But now it was still and mellow in the afternoon sunshine. She ran her hand over the smooth surface of the long trestled table and began to sing:

> Way down on the ol' bayou
> Beneath a cypress tree,
> Miss Liza met her Sunday beau
> And sat upon his knee.
> De moon was shinin' high above,
> He whispered low, sweet words of love.
> O—h, Miss Liza an' her beau.

Still singing, she went through the handhewn door into the back yard, with Lucky gamboling along beside her. She first stopped to inspect her mint bed, which seemed promising, and afterwards a small clump of sweet clover and a Painted Beauty rose bush. When she had first talked of a flower garden, Serena had spoken, rather wistfully, of some sweet clover which had once grown to shrub size and from which she had been accustomed to cull the sweet white flowers to dry and place in dresser drawers. Alix had been enchanted with the idea, because she had always placed vetivert in her own dresser drawers; so she had been disappointed when Serena told her that the sweet clover had almost disappeared, through neglect, and she had been trying to nurture the remnants of it which she had found, and bring them back to life. There were some incipient signs that her efforts had not been in vain, and she was very pleased. She was also pleased to see that the Painted Beauty rose had not suffered through transplanting. This rose was Dexter's contribution to her horticultural efforts. He had dug it up, and brought it from the Abbott Homestead to Farman Hill. No one ever saw it any more, he said, down by the old wooden well, long since disused; perhaps it would help to brighten the back yard, until they could get other things growing. He had acted rather shy about this offering, just as he had been when he had brought in the first trailing arbutus from the woods and the first cowslips that bordered the spring in the Calf Pasture; he had cut Alix short when she tried to thank him for these; but she herself had been deeply touched by his thoughtfulness, and now she was eagerly awaiting the first revelation of the Painted Beauties. Dexter had told her that the blossoms would be white, but that each petal would be stencilled in crimson, and that before the buds unfolded these would be wholly crimson. He had added that the buds would form a striking contrast to the full blooms, for there were usually some of both on the bush at the same time.

"You don't mean a Lancaster and York rose, do you?" she asked excitedly. "Why that's one of the rarest varieties in the world! It's very valuable."

"I don't know anything about that and I never heard it called a Lancaster and York."

"You remember about the War of the Roses, don't you? You can see how the name would be applicable?"

"Yes, now that you speak of it. And I get the idea—But I'd rather think of my mother's rose in terms of sentiment than of value—I'm giving it to you because it was hers, not because it may be worth money. And I hope it will represent peace and not war between two factions."

"It will, Dexter. Peace and contentment and—mutual understanding. We'll forget that it's rare, and only remember that it's beautiful. And we'll always call it the Painted Beauty."

They had never spoken of it again, but for weeks Alix had felt that she could hardly wait to see the strange striped radiance of this rose. There was no sign of it yet, but the purple lilacs were already beginning to bud, and beyond the vegetable garden, where the peas, corn and lettuce were already up, the fringe of apple trees were faintly rosy. Alix was happy to see that this was so. If the apple blossoms were coming out there, more of them would be blooming in the main orchard, over by the Wood Lot. She and Dexter could go and gather them for her mother to take to the cemetery on Decoration Day. Serena had been afraid that there would be no flowers, except such "boughten" ones as Alix might provide; now, obviously, between the lilacs and the apple blossoms, there would be plenty from Farman Hill itself; and though Alix would gladly have bought out the florist at the Junction, to cover the new grave in which Jenness lay, and the old ones where Farmans long dead and gone were entombed, she knew this would not have seemed the same to Serena.

For a moment she hesitated between the two routes which would take her to the Mill Lot. It was much quicker, of course, to go by the old wood road; but she was in no hurry, and the longer way was the more appealing. She pulled open the gate leading into the Ridge Field and crossed this, carefully skirting the Swamp Piece. Dexter had told her that once, years before, a pair of steers had

floundered in the mud there, according to legend, and
sunk before they could be rescued. He said he could not
vouch for the truth of the story, but at the same time he
had warned her not to get too close to the water; as soon
as she struck spongy ground, he had said, she should retreat. She did so, cautiously, now. But when her footing
was firm, she stopped long enough to gaze with admiration
at the wild blue flag which edged the swamp and the
velvety cat-o'-nine tails which rose from it, while she listened to the merry twittering of the bobolinks. The sound
was so cheerful that it moved her to go on with her own
song:

Way down on de ol' bayou
About three miles from town,
Where de sweet magnolias bloom,
Lives ol' parson Brown.
Dey wandered down dere side by side,
An' soon de weddin' knot was tied.
O—h, Miss Liza an' her beau.

Besides the bobolinks, there were other birds in the
swamp land, goldfinches and red-winged blackbirds. Alix
watched several of them sweeping by and for a moment
her fascinated gaze followed their swift, brilliant flight.
Then as they darted away, taking with them some element
of vividness from the landscape, she saw that a stately
blue heron, which she had not previously noticed, was
standing close to her. She kept still, fearful of frightening
it away. But it continued to stand in motionless solemnity
so long that eventually she decided to take the risk of disturbing it and went on, as noiselessly as she could. Several
times, as she skirted the swamp, she turned back to look
at it; but when she reached the Pasture Field, its immobil-
ity was still complete.

She let down the bars leading into the Home Pasture
and carefully replaced these. She was no more afraid of
the cows feeding beyond than she was of the rabbits which
went scampering away at her approach, or the red chip-
munks and gray squirrels which frolicked around the trees.

Indeed there was no reason why she should be. The cows
looked up, mildly, at her approach, and stared at her
with soft mournful eyes. But they did not move, and
presently they bent their fawn-colored heads again, and
went on with the crunching which made such a crisp
rhythmic sound. Alix thought their fodder must taste very
good, to judge from its looks. The grass over which she
was walking was studded with bluets and wild strawberry
blossoms, and here and there she could see some clamber-
ing honeysuckle and some little clusters of tiny short-
stemmed violets, not only purple ones, but yellow ones and
white ones too. She stopped to pick some of the violets
and was amazed at their freshness and fragrance. The
great heart-shaped violet bed at Bellefontaine, beautiful
as it was, had lacked something that these casual clusters
possessed. She considered carefully what it might be . . .
Bien, it must be that the heart-shaped bed was artificial
and that these clumps were natural, that the bed was
walled-in and the clumps unconfined. She thought of the
garden at Bellefontaine with tenderness but without regret.
Wandering freely in the springtime, it was good to find
flowers that were free too, so good that again she was
impelled to burst into song:

> Way down on de ol' bayou
> Miss Liza an' her beau
> Built a little cabin home
> Wid roses 'roun' de do'.
> Now picaninnies, three or fo'
> Is playin' on dat cabin flo'
> An' ain't nobody happy as Miss Liza an' her beau.

Along the stone wall enclosing the Square Field and
dividing it from the Home Pasture was a fringe of maple
and white birch with tiny leaves still only half uncurled
and green as jade. Among them an occasional vagrant
apple tree, which had sprung into life from seed, straying
out of the tidy orchard, branched forth rosily. These in
turn were bordered with a profusion of wild cherry bushes,
already in full bloom, white and fluffy as cotton in the

South. There were occasional pines scattered all through the pasture, and at the north end, where the land sloped gently, a growth of hard wood enclosing a grove of evergreens which separated it from the Mill Lot. Among these evergreens were quantities of fir balsams, and Alix had heard her father-in-law say that everyone in the neighborhood came here to cut their Christmas trees. There were more than enough trees for the neighborhood, Alix reflected, looking at them thoughtfully from afar; and when she reached the grove, instead of going straight through it, she wandered about in it, observing how much dead wood there was, and how much new growth, and viewing each with a practical eye. The grove, like the pasture, was a pleasant place in which to linger. She thought so, even more, when she caught sight of three beautiful young deer. They stopped in their tracks and looked at her with gentle eyes, more startled than the cows, before they went leaping gracefully away. It was some time before she left it and came out on open ground again . . .

She was still a long way off when Dexter called to her, and she instantly knew that he must have been watching for her. It was true that he did not mind waiting; but he liked to know she was coming, and this time he had not been sure. She did not know, she had told him after dinner, whether it would be best for her to leave Mother that afternoon. As Decoration Day approached, Mother was thinking more and more about Jenness. Alix knew how that was; it was the same with Tante Odilisse and Tia Izola as All Saints' Day approached.

"So you did come, after all!" Dexter exclaimed. His voice was joyous as he called. He stopped planting and hurried forward to meet her.

"Yes. It was all right. Mother's happy today. She's been sitting in the West Parlor, knitting a baby blanket and looking out of the front windows. She's found it all very pleasant."

"I should think she might."

"I did too. I sat with her nearly an hour. But when I

was glad I could get outdoors. It's a beautiful day. When you have to wait a long time for spring, the way you do in New England, it seems very precious when it does come, doesn't it? You can't take it casually, the way you do in the South. You want to treasure it, to make the most of every bit of it, because it doesn't last long."

"Yes," Dexter said slowly. "You do."

"I think I'm beginning to understand why Mother never missed having a flower garden. Not that I wouldn't always want one myself, because a patterned garden is an integral part of my heritage. But it isn't of hers; the land takes the place of it. The whole farm is gardenlike at this time of year. It has seemed, all the way up here, as if I were walking through a garden. There was something about the violets, especially—" She told him how she had considered the question of the heart-shaped bed at Bellefontaine and the clumps in the Home Pasture, and then she held out the little bunch of short-stemmed, sweet-smelling violets she had gathered. "You've brought me flowers lots of times, Dexter, so I brought you these. Could you stick them in a buttonhole somewhere?"

"Of course I could. Thanks a lot, Alix—for bringing me the violets and for telling me how you feel about them too. You're right about the whole place being a garden at this time of year. And you haven't seen it all yet, either. I want to take you into the woods on Jerome's Hill and show you the flowers there . . . the wake-robins and the lady-slippers, the Solomon's seal and the Indian pipes that are coming out now. Of course I could pick them and bring them to you, but those wood flowers are so much prettier in their natural surroundings. Besides, you'd love the woods at this time of year—they're so sweet and still. Don't you think we could go up on Jerome's Hill Sunday after dinner?"

"I don't see why not . . . I did stop in the evergreen grove as I came through, Dexter—that's one of the reasons I was so late. I saw three deer."

"You might see them any time. Or a fox. Or even a bear. Once I picked up some wild apples that were windfalls from one of those trees by the stone wall, and when I went back to get them, with a bushel basket, the apples were gone, but there were bear tracks all around. Another time I saw a mother skunk with three baby skunks following in Indian file. They were just as pretty as they could be, but I kept very still!"

"I should think so! I'm satisfied, Dexter, to have seen the deer."

"Wouldn't you like to see some partridges and some golden pheasants? You may in the fall—usually a cock pheasant and two or three hens together. The cocks keep regular seraglios and they're very beautiful."

"Yes, I'd like to see them, too. I'll come back in the fall, Dexter. It's thrilling to think that we have our own private deer park and our own special game preserve, isn't it?

"Very thrilling. But you'll see sights that are even more thrilling in the fall, Alix—all the hillsides flaming with color when the leaves turn gold and scarlet, and one in a while the Northern Lights streaming across the sky at night."

"Do you really have Northern Lights here?"

"Yes, really. Sometimes they're silvery and still, and sometimes they're rainbow colored, but moving as no rainbow ever does. They dart and leap and flicker and flash, and every now and then they soar up to the very summit of the heavens. I've often stood and watched them all night long."

"If you do that this year, I'll watch them with you, Dexter. I'd never thought I'd see the Northern Lights streaming across the horizon and soaring to the heights of the heavens." She seemed to be turning this over in her mind, with eagerness and wonder and awe, and for a moment she did not speak at all. Then, in a more practical tone of voice, she said, "By the way, Father tells me that everyone in the neighborhood goes up to that grove to get Christmas trees."

"Yes, I guess that's true. I know our Christmas tree at the Abbott Homestead always came from Farman Hill."

"But, Dexter, it's pleasant to be generous, and still it's prudent to make a profit too, isn't it, when that's possible? Couldn't some of the fir balsams be marketed? If people around Farman like to use them for Christmas trees, other people might too. And there are any number of trees that could be cut without injuring either the value or the looks of the grove."

"I guess you're right about that too. You're a pretty hard-headed little business-woman, aren't you, Alix? The catch is, you don't look enough like one."

"I'm French," said Alix, as if that explained everything. "Oh—I almost forgot! I've brought you a letter, Dexter, from Judith. It came with the carrier, after you left. Mother thought you'd like to have it now, without waiting until you came in at milking time."

"Yes," Dexter said again. "Yes, of course. Do you know, Alix, I think there must really have been a mill on this piece of land once? I think that must have been the way it got its name. I asked Father Farman, and he said he didn't know, but that it sounded reasonable. So then we started looking, and we think we've found some old foundations. Anyway, we've found some traces of what might have been foundations. It's so long since the Mill Lot has been all dug up the way it's had to be this year, that Father Farman had forgotten all about them. But he's going to look through some of his old papers tonight and see if he can find some specifications . . . Would you care to come and look at what we did discover, Alix? It's up at the other end of the lot by the road to the Back Pasture. That's not too far for you to walk, is it?"

"No," said Alix. "It isn't too far for me to walk. I'd like to go there. Some old foundations! Why then we could build a new mill someday, couldn't we, on the same spot?"

"I knew that's what you'd say right off. I was sure you'd want to build something new on the old foundations. That's what you're doing all the time, isn't it, Alix?"

"I hope so. I'm trying to. Am I succeeding, Dexter?"

"I'll say so."

They walked on together through the freshly planted field towards the road leading to the Back Pasture. Neither of them remembered the unopened letter from Judith which Dexter had put in his pocket.

CHAPTER 24

DEXTER HAD agreed with Rhoda that for her short spring vacation it was not worth while to open the Abbott Homestead. It was complicated, as well as expensive, to turn the water and the heat on and off; besides, Rhoda added, there would have been so much cleaning to do, first to get the house ready to live in for a week and then to leave it in good shape before it was closed again. So she had stayed on Farman Hill, occupying the West Chamber which was now destined for a nursery and finding, in this adjacency to the one occupied by Alix, a ready excuse for running in on her frequently. The strong attraction Rhoda had felt for the girl, merely from looking at her picture, had been intensified from the moment she actually saw her in the flesh; and the generous responsiveness Alix revealed to her first timid advances, encouraged her to seek closer and closer communion with Jerome's young wife. Never in her starved and thwarted life, as far as Rhoda could remember, had she talked with anyone freely and intimately as she now found it possible to talk with Alix; never had she been able to offer a spontaneous caress, or known the joy of having one tendered to her. Before she left to return to her school, she had already asked if she might spend the weekend of Memorial Day on Farman Hill. She gave as her reasons, first, her desire to see for herself that the Abbott lot in the cemetery was decorated just as she would like to have it; and second, the practicality of utilizing this occasion to set in motion the domestic wheels at the Abbott Homestead, where she would be returning for the summer three weeks later.

The two reasons seemed sufficiently sound, both to herself and to her prospective hosts. But deep down in her own heart, she knew that these plausible pretexts veiled her real motive: to be with Alix again, to occupy a chamber close to hers, to rejoice in her companionship, and to talk, far into the night, of her own plans and of her own hopes. After everyone else had gone to bed, after the house was hushed and the deep tranquility of night lay over the countryside like a veil, she was still sure of a welcome in the East Chamber. She could sit on a low stool beside the bed where Alix lay at ease, her braids black against her white pillows, her fine laces soft over her breast; she could hold the girl's hand and pour out the confidences she could share with no one else.

Memorial Day fell on a Saturday, and Rhoda was fortunate in getting a ride from St. Johnsbury to Farman Hill on Friday evening. But the Red Cross unit was working in the summer kitchen that night, and it was already so late when the meeting got under way, that she did not need a word of caution from Dexter to remind her that Alix was very tired, and that if they were going to the graveyard early next morning, the girl ought to have her sleep. Rhoda did not mean to be selfish or inconsiderate about this precious friendship which had come to her so late, and her delight in the prospect of a baby on Farman Hill was almost as great as Serena's; not for worlds would she have had Alix overtax her strength. Nevertheless, Dexter, who was himself on duty at the lookout station that night, took his sister aside to voice the unnecessary warning before he left the house.

"We all impose on Alix, Rhoda. You're no worse than any of the rest of us. But I know you kept her awake till all hours, when you were here in April. Yes, I also know she was comfortably settled in bed, so that she was getting a certain amount of rest while you talked to her, and I know she kept telling you she loved having you, and all that. But it doesn't alter the fact that she couldn't have got much sleep. Suppose you let up a little on the midnight heart-to-heart talks, this visit. Whatever do you find to say to her anyhow?"

"Why I don't know. All sorts of things that wouldn't interest a man. I suppose they're not very important, when you come right down to it. But somehow it seems natural for me to talk to Alix. And I feel better after I've done it too. It gives me the sort of feeling that told hymn 'Sweet Hour of Prayer' tells about:

> In moments of regret and grief,
> My soul has often found relief.

I don't mean to be sacrilegious, Dexter, but———"

Rhoda was blushing so painfully that Dexter was almost sorry he had raised the subject. He knew how long it had taken this submerged sister of his to batter down the bars of repression, how shy she still felt about speaking of the deep significance which her friendship with Alix had for her. But it mattered more that Alix should be protected than whether Rhoda was hurt.

"I don't think you're sacrilegious," he said kindly. "I know myself exactly how you feel. It *is* easy to talk with Alix, and there is a sense of relief afterwards. But see if you can't talk to her in the daytime. There ought to be a chance tomorrow. After all you and she are going to the graveyard together."

Yes, they were, Rhoda said; she did not attempt to argue with her brother, who left for his observation post immediately afterwards. She went on into the summer kitchen and joined the other women who were working around the trestled table, with Alix at one end of it and Serena at the other. She knew she could not explain to Dexter that talking was not the same in the daytime, when you were doing other things more or less simultaneously and when you were subject to constant interruption from outsiders. It was in the blessed unshattered quietude of night that the secret places of the heart could be laid bare. She thought she was beginning to understand, for the first time, why married persons should share a room. Not that she permitted herself to dwell, even now, on the thought of their physical need for each other; but she had begun to grasp the meaning of their spiritual need, and to see that only when they were safe from intrusion could they fully unburden their souls to each other, and afterwards realize the fullness of comfort and support.

"Maybe if Dexter had been married, he'd understand too," she said to herself. "It's a sin and a shame that he isn't. That girl Judith!" She would not give Judith credit for anything, not even for the time she was planning to take the brief leave that was coming to her. Judith had received several invitations to go to the beach and otherwise divert herself over Labor Day, according to Serena; but she had declined them all in favor of coming to Farman Hill, because it was then that Jerome's baby was due. Secretly, Serena herself entertained certain qualms about this impending visit; she could not help feeling that there would be awkwardness between Dexter and Judith, no matter how adeptly Alix handled the situation. After all, Alix would probably be in bed most of the time Judith was at home, and therefore automatically prevented from spreading oil on troubled waters which might overflow anywhere and at any moment. But Serena did not admit these fears to anyone, not even to Daniel, and she kept telling everybody how much she was looking forward to Judith's homecoming, and what a relief it was to know that Alix would have expert care during her confinement. She mentioned all this at the Red Cross meeting, and her friends agreed with her, saying it certainly was a problem to find a nurse anywhere and that if Judith hadn't been coming . . .

"It certainly is as much as your life is worth to be took sick nowadays," Mrs. Johnson said, seating herself at the trestled table and reaching for the gauze. "But then, when it comes to a question of help, you're druv into a corner, sick or well. I don't know a living soul, on the Hill or in the village either, except Elvira Wendell, who goes out to work or takes in any these days. If it hadn't been for her, I'd of just had to let my spring housecleaning go. And I've never done that, not once since I was married. But I'm not so spry as I was once, and of course you can't get a hired girl for love or money. When it comes to that, you can't get a hired man. I don't know how the men-folks are going to get in their crops."

"There was farmerettes in the last war," Mrs. Merrill said doubtfully. "Not that we ever got any of 'em around here, or that I think they'd have been much good to us if we had. Mostly they seemed to be posing for their pictures with rakes over their shoulders and I don't need to tell any of you there's a lot more to farming than that —Pass me them scissors, will you, Sue? Thanks kindly— But maybe we could find some city girls who'd like to get out into the country for a spell and who would do their share. I don't know though—Looks like they was all rushing to join them new WAACS right now—10,000 of 'em just these last two days, according to the paper. . . . Well, maybe some of us could work outside ourselves. Women work outside right along, in Hawaii, according to the letters I got from the boys."

"Land sakes, Maime, how do you think we're going to find time to work outside when we don't know which way to turn so's to get our housework done, like Kate says?"

"I dunno, but I guess we'll have to study on it," Mrs. Merrill replied stubbornly. "I know I could dig potatoes, if I had to, same as I can pull up weeds. I guess maybe we better see the potatoes get in this fall, even if we do let dirt roll up in some of the corners."

"If I could figure out how to get my canning done, I wouldn't worry so much about the potatoes," Mrs. Hawkins interposed. "Here we'll be having wild strawberries in no time and raspberries right after that, and there isn't an extra ounce of sugar in my pantry. I'm making out real well with my cooking. Ed says he can't hardly tell the difference when I use honey and maple syrup, and he's got a real sweet tooth, so that's considerable of a compliment, coming from him. But it's different with canning berries. I don't think the outlook's so good for meat either. We've got a beef critter we could slaughter, but I don't know just how I'd manage afterwards. If I only had one of those pressure cookers——"

"We've got one," Alix said reassuringly. "I think Mrs.

Childs has too. Perhaps we could have a canning group,
just the way we have this Red Cross Unit, and do the
work here. What do you think, Mother?"

"Why I don't know," Serena answered pleasantly. "I
don't know but what we could. I think maybe you've got
another good idea there, Alix. . . . Oh, good evening, Elvira. I'm pleased to see you. It was getting along so late
in the evening I was afraid you couldn't get over."

"I've done five big washings," Mrs. Wendell announced
with pardonable pride. "The last one Mrs. Barnes sent
was simply immense. That's what delayed me. That and
listening to the radio. I've been real strong-minded about
keeping it off through the day, but Hite turned it on after
he got in from the barn, and then I just couldn't tear myself away from it. I don't know how the rest of you feel,
but I'm real worried about what's going to happen to that
little village where the people rose up against Heydrick
the Hangman. I can't pronounce it, every news commen-
tator does it a different way——"

"Lid—i'—che," Alix said slowly.

"Li—di'—che, that's it. It seems Heydrick's life is hanging by a thread right now. And the Germans are saying
that if he dies, they're going to wipe the village of Lidice
right out of existence, for a reprisal. Seems so I couldn't
bear to think of it. A village like Farman, where people
was living along same as we are, till this war come! And
maybe tomorrow, while we're celebrating Decoration Day,
there won't be any village left there!"

The thought was so sobering that for a few minutes the
women worked on in silence. Eventually, however, Mrs.
Carleton turned to Mrs. Merrill.

"You spoke of the twins awhile back, Anna. I hope you
keep right on having good news from them?"

"Yes, I'm thankful to say I do. "They're certainly seeing the world, like the Navy posters say you can, and
they're still together too. What about your boys? I heard
they'd left Camp Devons."

"Yes, that's so. I don't know just where they are right
now, but I kind of suspicion it might be New Guinea, or
maybe Caledonia. Hank started keeping regular company

with a girl in Ayer, before he went overseas, and she sends me her letters too. But she doesn't know any more than I do at the present time. Of course Bill's going to come in under the new draft. He can't hardly wait. But that means I won't have any of 'em left at home."

"You must be awfully proud, Mrs. Carleton, to think of having all three of your sons fighting for their country."

"Yes. Yes, I am proud, Alix. But I can't help thinking, that out of that number———"

Mrs. Carleton's lips were trembling visibly, and her voice was shaking. Alix changed the subject, with quiet skill. The scrap drive was on, she reminded her guests, and the need for old metal urgent. They must all begin to look through their attics and their sheds. Perhaps it would be a good plan to form a committee then and there. Wouldn't Mrs. Carleton be the chairman? They couldn't possible have a better one. Mrs. Carleton demurred a little, but she was overpersuaded by a rising vote in her favor. After this, there was intermittent grumbling about the way Civilian Defense was being handled, coupled with the expressed wish that Mr. La Guardia and Mr. Landis would stop their "name calling" and get down to the business of providing proper equipment. There was also some whispering about a local war bride whose baby had been born surprisingly soon after her nuptials. But for the most part conversation continued to center on the scrap drive. . . .

When the neighbors left after their evening's work was finished, Alix and Rhoda went upstairs together, but Rhoda, mindful of Dexter's admonition, did not ask Alix if she could come into the East Chamber, and Alix herself did not suggest it, as Rhoda had hoped against hope that she might. After all, if Alix invited her, it would be rude to decline altogether. She could go for just a few minutes, no matter what Dexter said. But Alix only paused with her hand on the latch and checked their plans for the next morning, to be sure they understood each other.

"We'll meet at six and go out and pick the lilacs and the apple blossoms, as many as can be spared from the

back yard and the Garden Orchard. Dexter put the apple
blossoms he and I picked this afternoon in some big stone
crocks out in the Old Washroom, so that they'd keep cool
overnight. We got quite a lot. The buds are further out
in the Wood Lot Orchard than they are in the Garden
Orchard. And Dexter said he'd ride over to the cemetery
at the same time we did, so that he could lift the crocks
out of the cars for us and place them wherever we wanted
them to go. They're too heavy for us to move. He's going
to take his car and I'll take mine. Then we'll all be independent. He can come straight back to the farm and go
on with his work and you and I can stay in the cemetery
as long as we like. Mother'll join us when she gets back
from her milk route and see whether she approves of what
we've done. I hope we can please her, especially with the
flowers we put on Jenness' grave. That matters most this
year."

"Yes, I suppose it does," Rhoda tried not to speak
grudgingly, and to keep the scorn out of her voice; but
she could not pretend that she had ever loved Jenness, or
that she did not keenly feel the disgrace this vain and
wayward girl had brought on them all. "Well you seem
to have everything nicely planned, Alix, same as usual. Do
you want I should call you?"

"I think I'll wake up anyway. I'm nearly always awake
by six. But you might call me, just to make sure. I'd like
to have you. Good night, *chère.*"

"Good night, Alix."

They kissed and parted. It was a long time before
Rhoda went to sleep. She lay under the canopy of the
tent bed in the West Chamber, thinking of all the things
she had hoped to say to Alix that evening, and which
there had been no chance to tell, because Alix was tired
and could not squander her strength for her friend, when
she needed to conserve it for her baby. She wondered
whether Alix would be less tired the next evning, and she
did not see how this would be possible, for they would be
a long time in the graveyard, arranging the flowers, and
afterwards there would still be all the usual daily tasks
at Farman Hill awaiting attention. Besides, she herself

would have to go to the Abbott Homestead to open and
air it and start the cleaning there. She had only Saturday
in which to work, for of course she must go to church
on Sunday morning and Sunday afternoon she must start
back to St. Johnsbury. She worried and her worries kept
her from enjoying unbroken slumber even after she fell
asleep; she dreamed and tossed restlessly about and looked
at her watch half a dozen times to make sure it was not
six o'clock yet. But when she went into the East Chamber
she found Alix looking refreshed and rosy. The girl was
awake, but it was easy to see, from her appearance, that
she had rested well. She was telling her beads, but she
laid down her jewelled rosary and greeted Rhoda with
a smile.

"I'm just finishing the last decade. I'll be up in two
minutes. And I'll meet you at the back door in twenty,
shall I?"

Dexter was already piling the tall crocks filled with
apple blossoms into his car when they went down, and
he said he would be glad to help them pick the lilacs too.
These had come out wonderfully in the unprecedented
warmth of the last few days and now their tight little buds
were bursting into fragrant bloom; they were soft and full
as feathers. Dexter had happened to see some white ones
on the untrimmed bush back of the corn barn at the Abbott
Homestead, so he had picked those that morning too, and
some iris—silver and gold both—in twin overgrown clumps
between the icehouse and the hen house. He had forgotten
all about the white lilacs and the iris clumps until lately;
then he had remembered that his mother had been fond
of flowers, and had gone poking around to see what might
have survived. He had found a bed of lilies of the valley
too, and some peonies which would also be blooming
presently; he guessed Alix had made him flower conscious;
he must have passed right by all these blooming bushes
and flower beds for years without even seeing them, and
now here they were staring him in the face. He grinned
as he said all this, and proudly held up the white lilacs
and the gold silver iris, which were really very beautiful,
for Alix to see. He was no longer self-conscious about his

offerings, as he had been when he transplanted the Painted Beauty and brought in the arbutus from the woods and the cowslips from the Calf Pasture.

"Are you riding over to the cemetery with me or with Rhoda?" he asked, still grinning.

With Rhoda, of course, Alix said, getting into her own car. Had he forgotten that Rhoda couldn't drive? Apparently he had, momentarily, for a look of mingled annoyance and disappointment crossed his face, and he muttered something intended to remind Alix that she was not supposed to do much driving herself anymore. She was not supposed to take *long* drives, Alix said, correcting him calmly; but after all, it was only three miles to the cemetery. She'd see him there, she added, nodding to indicate that he was to start off first. Rhoda felt unhappy again; she knew Dexter had wanted to talk to Alix himself, and though she could not imagine what he might have to say, she remembered that he had felt the same way about her the night before and tried, magnanimously, to be more understanding than he had shown himself. It was inconceivable that Dexter and Alix should be sharing secrets of any kind, in the sense that they could have anything to say to each other which the whole world might not hear; but Rhoda had learned how much the mere sense of privacy could mean. She was sorry she could not drive a car herself, since that would have meant Dexter and Alix could have gone to the cemetery together, and she said so, apologetically, to Alix.

"Why, *chère,* it doesn't matter at all!" Alix exclaimed. "Dexter and I can go out for a ride together whenever we like—at least we can until gasoline is rationed and then we still have Gypsy and Nell to fall back on! And by the time they have gone to the horses' heaven, we'll have the new colts broken, if everything goes well . . . But wouldn't you enjoy driving a car? I should think you'd like to learn. I'm sure I could teach you, very easily, and you could borrow mine, whenever you liked, until you could get one of your own."

"Do—do you really think I could learn to drive a car? You don't think I'm too old?"

"Of course you could learn to drive a car! *Too old!* You're not old at all—in fact I think you look younger that you did when you were home in April. I'm going to start teaching you this minute—we've got a nice straight road ahead of us and not another car in sight. Wait a second—I'll stop and get out and you can slide over into my seat. Now then! That's the clutch and you must push down on it; and that's the gearshift, and you change speeds this way——"

Rhoda was still at the wheel, her cheeks pink with excitement and mild fright, her eyes glued on the wholly unobstructed highway, when they turned in at the creaking iron gate of the cemetery. It was still so early that hardly anyone else was there yet, and they went slowly along the uneven road towards the rear, where the Abbotts' lot was situated. Like most of the others this was rather bare, its plain tombstones and unimaginative monument unrelieved by softening shrubbery, except for two or three hydrangeas. But further back a triangular piece of land, enclosed by pines and birches, pointed out towards the river, and it was here that the Farmans and all their folk were buried. Dexter was already filing vases from the pipeline that ended with the Abbotts' lot, and under the direction of Alix and Rhoda put the heavier ones in place. Then he left them, again with visible reluctance.

"Are you going to Confession this afternoon, Alix?"

"No, I don't think so. Why?"

"I've got two or three errands to do at the Junction. I could take you there, just as well as not."

"Couldn't the errands wait until Monday, Dexter? I think Rhoda's depending on your help, down at your house, this afternoon."

"All right. We'll go Monday then."

Alix waved to him in a friendly way as he started off, but her mind seemed to be already preoccupied. She put the white lilacs and the whites iris together, arranging them and rearranging them several times before she was satisfied with them. Then she massed the graceful clusters together on Jenness' grave. For a time Rhoda watched her in tight-lipped silence. Finally she spoke with more disapproval in her voice than she had ever betrayed to Alix before.

"You're not going to put all those handsome flowers Dexter picked for you in one place, are you, Alix?"

"Yes, I thought I would . . . all except the golden iris. I want you to put that on your parents' graves, so they'll be decorated with something that came from the Abbott Homestead. Don't you like the way I've fixed the white flowers?"

"You couldn't have made them look any prettier if you'd been an undertaker. But just the same it seems to me they ought to be divided."

"Why? There are flags on all the soldiers' graves, and it detracts from those if you put on too much else. And we've plenty of apple blossoms and lilacs for all the other Farman graves. And the golden iris for the Abbotts'."

Rhoda did not feel she could discuss the subject of Jenness again. It was very peaceful on the point of land which seemed so detached from the rest of the cemetery, and which, unlike the bare stretch beyond, was so shaded and lovely. There was a fragrance about it too, which came from the pines, and the breeze which stirred their branches made soft flickering shadows on the green grass and on the tombstones, old and gray except for the new white one engraved with the name of Jenness. The valley was visible from this enclosure, the winding river, and beyond them the Vermont hills. Little by little, the severity of Rhoda's mood softened in the tranquil atmosphere. Alix, too, seemed perfectly at peace. When her work was finished she seated herself on a slight slope near the apex of the traingle, where by turning in one direction she could look over the valley, and by turning in the other, at the decorated graves. Rhoda remembered now that she had said she intended to wait in the cemetery for her mother-in-law, and evidently her surroundings caused her no constraint. Rhoda had never before seen anyone reveal such evident contentment in a graveyard; apparently Alix was not oppressed by the omnipresence of the dead.

"Do you celebrate Decoration Day in Louisiana, same

as we do here?" she asked, for the sake of saying something.

"Yes. That is, the soldiers' graves are decorated. But among the Stars and Stripes, you see the Stars and Bars for the men who died in the War Between the States. And we do not think so much of decorating civilians' graves at this time. All Saints' is the time for that. On All Saints' Eve, we light lamps before the tombs and they flicker and gleam in the darkness throughout the night. In the country many of us still have our own little family cemeteries, and often we stay in them, watching the lights to be sure they do not go out, until very late. Sometimes different members of a family take turns in keeping a vigil, so that the tombs are not left at all. But no matter how little sleep we have had, we are back with our flowers early in the morning of All Saints'. And sometimes we stay all day, both in the small country cemeteries and in the big city cemeteries. We carry our lunch and our needlework and our prayer books, and even playthings for the children. Because the children go, too, and have their games. Everyone goes—the very young and the very old, the happy and the sorrowful. You see cripples in wheel chairs, and boys and girls rolling hoops and jumping rope and lovers with their arms around each other. It is a day of reunion for families, for the members of the family that are dead and for those who are still living. We all feel very close together on that day. But the feeling does not make us sad; it makes us happy, even those of us who have gone out grieving in the first place. By night our sorrow has been assuaged by this communion with our dead. I have been wishing that Mother could have some of that feeling, when she comes here today."

"I'm afraid she won't. I'm afraid she's going to break down. But it'll comfort her, in a way, Alix, to see how beautiful you've made Jenness' grave look. I guess you were right to put all those white flowers together after all."

"Yes. I think I was. I hoped it might comfort her to see them like that. And I shall try to think of something to say to her, *chère*, that will also be of comfort."

For a few moments Alix said nothing more to Rhoda.
She seemed to be pondering on the words of comfort that
she meant to speak to Serena. She sat very still, with her
hands folded in her lap; the moving pine trees cast their
flickering shadows on her thoughtful face and on her white
dress. Rhoda sat still too, watching her and thinking how
lovely she looked as she sat there, almost like a statue
herself. Rhoda was beginning to be less burdened by the
dead, just as she was less burdened by the thought of
Jenness, because Alix seemed so at home among the
tombs and yet so little bound by them.

"Tell me about the soldiers who are buried here,
Rhoda," Alix said at last. "Most of the Farmans have been
fighting men, haven't they?"

"Yes. The first Jerome was a captain in the French and
Italian Wars. His son was a colonel in the American Revolution and his grandson was a commodore in the War
of 1812. One of the Farmans was killed at Monterey, one
died of starvation in Danville Prison, and another of yellow fewer in Cuba."

"But they were all brought back here to be buried?"

"Yes, of course. All the Farmans have been born on
the Hill and buried on the Point."

"I see . . . And they all had good records?"

"Yes, they all had good records. You can read about
those on their tombstones."

"I'm going to by and by. But I like just sitting here,
right now. There's plenty of time. I doubt if Mother gets
here for another hour, and she might like to point out
the inscriptions to me herself, explaining them and helping
me to read between the lines . . . Has there been a Farman in every war?"

"All except the last one. Daniel didn't go to the First
World War. You see Jerome wasn't quite two years old
when the United States got in and Jenness was a baby.
I don't know for sure, but I think Serena persuaded Daniel
that his duty was at home, and that they've both been
sorry ever since. That's one reason why they're so proud
of Jerome. I think they'd be proud of Judith too, if it
weren't for the way she behaved to Dexter."

"Yes. She must have made Dexter very unhappy. But I can see her side. She made me see it when she came to stay with Jerome and me, in Raeford. She says nobody else can see it, but I do. I believe Dexter will too someday. Then he won't be unhappy about it any more."

"Seeing her side, if she has one, won't give him his wife, Alix. Dexter ought to have a wife and a home and children. The way things are now he lives about the same as any hired man who's single, except that he's better fixed than most."

"Yes. I think he feels that way himself sometimes. Of course every man wants a wife and a home and children eventually. Of course he wants and needs the experience of love."

The brooding look had not left Alix' face while she talked of the fighting Farmans and of Judith. But now she looked up with a smile.

"Just as every woman wants and needs it," she said. *"Le bon Dieu* must have thought all that out very carefully. Men and women aren't complete without each other. They can't be. They're dependent on each other—on union. I'm sorry you've never had that experience, *chère*. You'd have made some man such a wonderful wife. And you'd have been so happy yourself, in marriage. There's nothing on earth comparable to its rapture."

Rhoda turned away, scarlet to the roots of her hair. She had never heard anyone speak like this before. She would never have supposed that any woman of refinement would reason like this. But Alix was not only a woman of refinement, she was a great lady, a devout Christian, a tender and gentle spirit . . .

"I know you sacrificed your own life for Dexter," she was now saying. "I know that was real consecration to duty. Judith believes she's consecrated to duty and I have hope and confidence that someday she really will be. But she isn't yet. You were. You always have been. Didn't the man you loved care enough to wait for you, Rhoda? I'm not asking out of curiosity. I'm asking because I'm fond of you, because you and I seem to have come so close to each other."

"Alix, I'm—I'm so thankful that you're fond of me. I'm so thankful that you feel we're close to each other. Because I'm fond of you, I feel close to you. And I never had a friend, not a real friend like you, before." She bent her head, weeping with mingled sorrow and joy. "I never loved a man either," she managed to say at last. "Not the way— not like you have. There never was a man loved me the way Jerome loves you. I didn't know anything about that kind of love when I was young. The girls I knew kept company with boys or they didn't. The girls who did looked down on the others and made fun of them. They clubbed together and told each other secrets. I guess some of the secrets were pretty smutty too. Anyway I got the feeling they were. I was left out at first, and afterwards, if a boy so much as looked at me, I sort of froze up. I think I've stayed frozen up, pretty near ever since. It was being left out by the other girls that did it to me first, and then being passed over by the boys, and then losing my father and mother and having Dexter on my hands—well, it did seem as if one thing led to another. But I've been happier this winter than I've ever been in my life. It began when I got my old school back. I was so touched the family I used to board with wanted me again, and so pleased at finding such an improvement in the old schoolhouse, that I felt different almost as soon as I left home. I knew I wouldn't have got the position if there hadn't been such a scarcity of teachers, but my pride wasn't hurt about that because the rest mattered so much more. Then the children took to me right away and I had good discipline, but I gave them good times too, and evenings I read books that I got out of the library. I hadn't allowed myself to read much for a long time because once I get started it's hard for me to stop and I was afraid I'd neglect my work. Saturdays I most generally went into St. Johnsbury, and I got a lot of pleasure out of that too; there's so much you can do in a place of that size. And then I came home for my spring vacation and found you on Farman Hill and you were willing to be friends with me——"

"Yes," said Alix. "Yes, chère." She reached out and took Rhoda's hand, and then she continued to hold it in her own, stroking it gently. "Tell me more, Rhoda. Tell me everything you feel like saying. I know that you wanted to talk with me last night, but I had promised Dexter I would go straight to bed, because he thought that I was very tired, and he reminded me that I must not get too tired on account of the baby. I try to do what he wants in little ways, because he has been very kind about doing what I want in big ways. We made a bargain at the beginning of our partnership and it has worked out very well. That is greatly to Dexter's credit, as it is very hard for a man and a woman to work successfully together as partners when the woman has most of the money. The only credit that is due to me is that I have not disputed with Dexter when he thought I was tired, whether I really was or not. It helps a man to forget about money if he thinks he is taking good care of a woman. So this morning he was in very good humor because he was convinced I was rested on account of having taken his advice, and now you and I are here in this quiet place where he will not interfere with us any more and no one else can disturb us. Don't cry, Rhoda. There's nothing to cry about. You said you'd never been so happy in your life and you made me see how this might be. But haven't you been, really?"

"Yes I have, really. But I've got a problem, Alix, just the same. I don't know how to deal with it."

"Won't you tell me about it? I don't know that I could help, but sometimes it is helpful just to tell a friend about a problem."

"I've—I've got attached to a little boy."

Alix stopped stroking Rhoda's hand and instead gripped it hard, to steady her.

"Yes? But why is that a problem? I should think an attachment for a little boy might give you a great deal of companionship and comfort, and of course you could probably do a great deal for him too. Is this little boy one of your pupils, Rhoda? Is he an orphan?"

"No, he isn't one of my pupils. Of course I'm very fond of all my pupils—they're wonderful children. But there isn't one of them who can compare with this little boy. He lives in St. Johnsbury. I don't know whether he's an orphan or not."

"I'm afraid I don't understand very well, Rhoda. How can you help knowing whether he's an orphan or not?"

"Because he's a little refugee. He was smuggled out of Germany some way to England and by and by friends managed to get him to this country. But his mother and father didn't get out. He's never heard from them since he went over the frontier. His father's probably in a concentration camp. He lives with his uncle in St. Johnsbury."

"I see," Alix said, speaking more and more gently. "You know the uncle and through him you met this charming child."

"I didn't exactly meet the uncle, Alix. Not—not the way we usually mean when we speak of meeting anyone. The uncle keeps a clothing store, and when I started off to teach school last winter, Dexter gave me a hundred dollars to spend on clothes. So I went into this store to buy clothes and——"

"Why that is a wonderful way to meet anyone, Rhoda! That is the way Jerome and I met each other! I was working in a jewelry store in Fayetteville, and Jerome came in to buy a service pin for his mother and——"

Rhoda looked up, astonishment and relief mingling in the expression of her tear-stained face.

"Why so it *was!*" she exclaimed. "I never thought of that, Alix! And—and Daniel and Serena didn't mind because you and Jerome met that way either, did they, Alix?"

"I suppose they did at first," Alix said calmly. "But that was before they understood. They understand now though. And I should have understood anyway, about you . . . So you went into this store to buy clothes, and you and the proprietor got into conversation. You told him that you were a teacher and that you wanted a new outfit which would be suitable for your profession. He helped you to choose this outfit, and then he told you that since you were a teacher perhaps you might be interested in hearing about the little nephew who had just come to live with him—the smartest child he'd ever seen, leading every one of his classes."

"Why, Alix, that is exactly the way it was! You see it just as plain as day! And I hadn't any more than started to tell you."

"Oh, yes, you had, *chère*. You'd made it all clear to me. Mr.——"

"Mr. Cohen."

"Mr. Cohen told you about his little nephew, who was leading all his classes. Mr. Cohen was terribly proud of——"

"Of Benny."

"Of Benny, but just the same he was worried about him, because there was such a terrible background of tragedy in this child's life that he didn't know how to surmount. Especially without anyone to help him. Because Mr. Cohen himself is a——"

"Widower."

"A widower, without anyone to run his house properly or help him bring up his own——"

"Little daughter. Little Rachel."

"Little daughter, Rachel. So he asked your advice about the children, just as you had asked his about your clothes. You and he talked a long while, and the next time you went to St. Johnsbury you found you needed——"

"Some more stockings."

"Some more stockings. So you went into Mr. Cohen's store again, hoping that perhaps this time you might see Benny too, because it was Saturday. And sure enough, there was Benny, and you asked him if he wouldn't like to go to the movies because you had no one to go with you——"

"Yes. Yes. Yes. That was just the way it started, Alix. But it didn't stop there. And now I don't know what to do."

Rhoda bent her head and her tears began to flow again. Alix went on in her quiet way.

"What do you want to do, Rhoda? Whatever you want to do is probably the thing you ought to do."

"I want to bring Benny home with me when I come back next time. I want to have him with me at the Abbott Homestead. I want to keep him there. I—I love him. I

don't see how I could love him any more if he were my
own child."

"Perhaps you couldn't. Doesn't his uncle want him to
come to the Abbott Homestead with you, Rhoda?"

"Yes, he'd be glad to have Benny come home with me.
But——"

"Is there any other reason, Rhoda, why you couldn't
bring him?"

"Maybe you didn't understand, Alix. You seemed to,
but maybe you didn't. Benny—Benny's a little Jew boy."

"Why of course I understood. He wouldn't have been a
refugee from Germany unless he had been a little Jewish
boy, would he?"

"But, Alix, there's—there's never been a Jew at the
Abbott Homestead."

"No, I suppose not. And there's never been a Catholic
on Farman Hill before either. But there is now. And in
the future there always will be. Because my children will be
Catholics, Rhoda. And *they'll* be the inheritors of Farman
Hill!"

Again she pressed the hand she had been holding. This
time Rhoda felt there was more than tenderness in the
pressure. There was strength too, and purpose.

"There's always been friendship between Farman Hill
and the Abbott Homestead, hasn't there?" she asked. "I
believe there always will be. I'm sure I hope so. I'd like to
think the old tie could continue in a new way, that Catholic
children on Farman Hill and Jewish children at the Abbott
Homestead would be friends. Perhaps more than friends
sometime. Perhaps lovers. That's as it should be, Rhoda.
There isn't a strain on earth so strong that it isn't the better
for new blood every now and then. Any breeder will tell
you that. There isn't any culture so ancient that another
can't contribute to it. There isn't any religion without rites
which have kinship with another. We've been slow in finding this out, we've done things separately a long time. But
we've all had a part in making this country what it is—
the Farmans and the Abbotts and the St. Cyrs and the
Cohens—and the time's coming when we're going to make

it a greater country than it ever was before because we're
all going to work for it *together!"*

Alix rose, and as she did so, the breeze which had blown
so softly over her, causing the pines to make shadows on
her face, caught her dress in a sudden gust and whipped
it closely around her. Her figure, no longer artfully dis-
guised, was revealed by the clinging folds, in all the fullness
of its burden and its promise. Her face, no longer shaded,
shone with joy and light. In this place, sacred to the past
and to the dead, she had become a symbol of the future
and of the living. She stretched out her arms as if to welcome these.

"Come," she said. "Come. Let's walk out to meet
Mother. She'd be glad to have us. It won't be so hard for
her to come here if she doesn't have to do it alone. Nothing
is so hard if you don't have to do it alone. But you and
I have talked enough for now. Or almost enough. There's
only one thing you need to tell me, one thing that I'm
not sure I have straight, though I believe I have. Was
it your idea that Benny should come to the Abbott Homestead alone, Rhoda? Or was it your idea that Mr. Cohen
and Rachel would come too?"

CHAPTER 25

THERE HAD not been a single day all summer that Dexter
had not risen by four, or when he had gone to bed earlier
than ten. The basic routine was the same, day after day.
First he fed the horses and the young calves. Then he
milked the cows. After milking, he fed the herd, giving
the milk-producing cows grain on top of their grass silage,
green fodder or hay, and also making another round to
give grain to the horses, who had not received this at their
first feeding. By this time, unmistakable sounds from the
pigsty and the hen house revealed the impatience for

feed in those quarters, and this impatience was assuaged before Dexter went in for his own breakfast.

After breakfast, he drove the cows to pasture, returning to the barn to clean it. His standards of cleanliness for his work were almost as high as his sister's for hers; but even if they had not been, the necessity of meeting those of the official milk inspector would have maintained them. When the horses were curried, the routine daily tasks were finished until evening, when they began again in reverse order with the additional task of setting the milk to cool; but meanwhile the seasonal work went on: the hauling and scattering of fertilizer in the early spring; the plowing and harrowing of enough land to receive crops necessary to carry all the livestock through the coming winter. By the time the last of the harrowing was done, the corn, potatoes and beans already required cultivating. Then came the long hot days of haying, the cutting of the green crops like millet and sudan grass, and also oats, if any of the latter were to be cut before they ripened. Next came the harvesting of barley, ripe oats and the reaping of the rowen. From spring till fall the vegetable garden also required constant attention; in and out of season fences had to be made and repaired, sheep shielded from destructive dogs, cows kept from straying out of pasture land where they could harmlessly graze into corn fields which they could ruthlessly trample. Even in mid-winter there was logging and ice-cutting, and at the end of winter tree-tapping.

There was nothing new about any of this for Dexter. He had been filling the wood boxes, feeding the hens, and driving the cows to and from the pasture by the time he was seven years old; by the time he was fourteen, he was regularly doing a man's work outside of school hours; by the time he was twenty-one, he was regularly doing two men's work, despite his lameness. In addition, besides following the usual communal custom of cooperating with his neighbors during the period of harvest and ensiling, he had spent a great deal of time on Farman Hill, even before recent events had indicated a special reason for doing so. He belonged to the comparatively small group of young men who had never seriously considered leaving his

native village, and who neither sought nor desired more
diversion or excitement than the countryside afforded. His
first, and almost his only rebellion against his manifest lot
in life had occurred when he was rejected by the draft
board. The consciousness of the vast amount of work to
be done on a farm, and the knowledge that he must generally reckon on doing it single-handed because of the
perennial shortage of farm labor, as a rule acted like a spur
and a stimulant. But like most spurs, this one occasionally
lost its sharpness; like most stimulants, this one gradually
became less and less intoxicating.

Since the coming of Alix, he had achieved a greater
realization of both the essentiality and the significance of
farming, not only in its relation to the war effort but to the
universe at large; and this realization had also upheld him.
But the element of personal incentive was lacking. No
matter how hard he worked, his reward was vicarious.
Farman Hill did not belong to him, and it never would;
there was no longer even the prospect that someday it
might belong to his children, as there had been when he
believed that Judith's heirs would be his also. He and
Rhoda owned the Abbott Homestead jointly, and now that
it was she and not he who was considering the foundation
of a family, his share in that place had less and less meaning. If he could only have felt that his labors were maintaining or creating something which he loved because it was
his own, and that someone he loved was maintaining or
creating it with him, his outlook would have been one of
hope instead of discouragement, no matter how greatly it
was affected by weariness. But now, after months of inten-
sive endeavor, his labors still seemed unrewarding. He was
depressed not only because his brain and body was weary,
but because his spirit was subdued. He had only one
thought and one desire when evening came, and that was
for rest and refreshment. He found these in the quiet companionship of Alix, and he did not want or seek any other.

She still turned out a surprising amount of work every
day: her garden was a mass of bloom as a result of her
fostering care, and she had made an instantaneous success
of her cheeses. Serena was marketing these on her milk

route and there were always more orders than could be
filled. Alix also kept all the running accounts and did it
with meticulous care. It was just as important, she said,
that the farm books should be balanced as that the town
books should be; she and Dexter checked each other's
figures, and her ledgers were always quite as accurate as his
and far neater in appearance. The arts of fine penmanship
and exquisite spacing which she had acquired at the convent stood her in good stead now; she took infinite pains
with her books and they were beautiful to behold. But one
of her chief charms, at least in Dexter's eyes, was that, unlike a bustling New England housewife, she did all this
without any appearance of haste or flurry, and that when
the stints she had set herself were finished, she did not immediately begin searching for more through an excess of
conscientiousness; she enjoyed her hours of leisure and
made them enjoyable for others. He did not realize that
this repose was one of spirit as well as manner, learned,
like the fine needlework and the exquisite penmanship,
from nuns whose rule provided for six hours of daily
prayer, though theirs was also the most venerable teaching
order on the continent. But little by little, Dexter had come
to resent any intrusion on the time which he shared with
her. When Serena reminded him that Judith's arrival was
imminent, with the obvious assumption that he would meet
the Express at the Junction, his reaction to her inoffensive
remarks was one of acute if unreasonable annoyance.

"Gosh, Mother Farman, I can't take time to go to the
Junction Saturday night! We'll have to work in the Big
Field as long as it's light enough to see! If we should happen to have a hard rain on Sunday, we might lose the
greater part of our oat crop. All the neighbors said that
we'd bitten off more than we could chew, planting such a
big one in the first place. I'm darned if I'll give them the
satisfaction of crowing that they were right and we were
wrong when we've come along so well this far."

"I think Judith would take it very hard if you didn't go
to meet her, Dexter. After all——"

"After all, I took it very hard when she wouldn't marry
me! And I've got over that. I guess she can get over it if

I'm not standing at the station waiting to see her train pull in!"

He flung out of the winter kitchen, where Serena was mixing bread, and walked through the house, looking for Alix. Sometimes, after the supper dishes were done, she went to sit on the door rock, where she could watch the sunset and the moonrise, and the mist rising from the river to cover the twin meadows on either side of it. She called this mist "the gauzy veil which concealed the valley bride," and it had a great fascination for her, especially when it hung so low that the hills and sky were visible and clear above it. He found her on the door rock now, though it was a night when there was neither light in the sky nor mist in the valley. Instead there was a strange sultriness in the air. He let the screen door slam after him, instead of closing it carefully and quietly and dropped down beside her without speaking. For some moments she did not speak either, but continued to sit with her chin in her hand, looking out over the sombre valley. At last she turned and regarded him in the same thoughtful way that she had considered the landscape.

"What's the matter, Dexter?" she asked.

"It seems Mother Farman's expecting me to meet Judith Saturday night."

"Well, that is a reasonable expectation, isn't it? Why should you be upset about that?"

"It might be a reasonable expectation if we weren't harvesting oats just now, trying to finish before the weather breaks. It looks as if it were going to rain tonight and, if it does, that'll do enough damage, without inviting any more through unnecessary delay."

"And are the oats, and the weather, the only factors in your disinclination to meet Judith?"

"You must know that they're not. You must know I don't want to see her anyway."

"But you've got to see her. She's going to be here for a number of days. She's made a great effort to get leave so she could be home at a time when I needed her."

"She's made a great effort to be here at a time when

you'd be in bed, so that she can say what she pleases and do what she pleases without interference."

"Without interference? Do you feel that I have interfered with anything or anybody on Farman Hill, Dexter?"

"No, of course not. You've been its salvation. But Judith likes to manage in her own way. She likes to criticize and lecture. She's always been ungracious and now she'll be disagreeable. Besides she'll be jealous."

"Jealous?"

"Yes. Because she might have done and been so much like what you've done and been, Alix. A comfort and a help to her parents. A partner and an inspiration to me. A leader and a creator in the neighborhood. And she wouldn't. She didn't think that role was big enough for her."

"I think, Dexter, that you are very unjust. I must ask you not to talk in the way that you are doing now. It is most unbecoming."

"Unbecoming!" Dexter exclaimed angrily, echoing a word in his turn.

"Yes. You should not speak to me in this way of Judith. You knew her and loved her long before you ever heard of me. You shouldn't underestimate the importance of such a lifelong tie, you shouldn't remark on it disparagingly to a comparative outsider. That is what I meant by saying your conversation was unbecoming. And I will also repeat that your comments are unjust. Judith didn't leave because she felt the role she could play here was too small for her. Probably it was. Probably Judith can play a much larger role elsewhere than she could have here. But that is beyond the point. The reason she left was because she felt it was not *her* role. I know it is mine. We all have our own."

Dexter muttered something unintelligible under his breath. In the distance there was a low rumble of thunder, and momentarily, the gloom of the valley was severed by lightning. But no wind came with it. The sultriness of the air was increasingly oppressive.

"I am not capable of taking any public part in the war or of qualifying for an important profession," Alix went on with her customary calm. "I was not even a success as a salesgirl, working in a jewelry store. If I had been, possibly I should not have been so delighted to leave it. The only sort of thing I can do is the simple sort you see me doing here, which you praise far too highly, by the way. It is the only sort of thing I want to do. I am very happy here. I was contented at the convent with the nuns, and my relatives were always very kind to me when I visited them. But I always wanted a real home and a father and mother and now I have them. I am also happy because I am going to have a baby. I am not dreading the time that is so near now. I understand that I shall suffer, but that seems to me incidental, a means to an end. There are not many things worth having that are easy to get, Dexter."

"I suppose you're right," Dexter said resentfully. "Just the same I don't see how you can take all this the way you do."

"But, Dexter, how else can I take it? I have always wanted to have children and now that desire, like the desire for a home, is about to be fulfilled. At least in part. I shall have my first one. And eventually I shall have others. I would not be sincere in saying that I am wholly happy here unless I believed that, for children are not only precious in themselves but for what they represent. You must understand that, Dexter, because you wanted the complete experience of love so much yourself. I do not have to explain its necessity to you as I had to explain it to Rhoda. I do not have to tell you how horribly I have missed Jerome in that sense as in every other."

"No, Alix, you don't," Dexter said in a low voice.

"I was sure you would understand. I was overwhelmed by love at first, Dexter. But before Jerome left I had become like Eve—my desire was to my husband, that he should rule over me. That desire has kept getting stronger and stronger. And he has been gone so long already."

"Yes, Alix, I know."

Again a fork of lightning quivered through the gloom. When it was gone, the darkness was more complete than before.

"If I did not know it was hard for Jerome too, I would

not mind so much," Alix went on. "But every time he writes he tells me."

Letters from Jerome had been coming through for over two months now. The first one, arriving after a cable sent from Karachi, contained a vivid account of his long trip around the Cape of Good Hope: since then others had drifted in irregularly, describing his first experience in India. Alix had read aloud from all of these, and Dexter had listened to these extracts with Daniel and Serena: *"We didn't get off the ship at Freetown, but sat in the harbor and sweated, for it is very hot there. It isn't a very big place, only a few hundred white people; all the rest are black. The blacks are just like children. They would come out to the ship with their little boats and circle around, hoping we would throw things to them. We used to shoot into the water near them to scare them away, and would they paddle when that happened! I saw one who had on a white collar and tie, but that was all."* . . . *"Capetown is a nice place, it lies in a half circle next to the sea with mountains rising behind it. I went up on the mountain twice at night and the view was wonderful. I have never met people who tried to do more for a group of strangers than the ones we met in South Africa. They drove us around in their cars, took us to their homes for dinner and did everything they could to make our stay pleasant. The night before we left they gave a party for us at a country club called Kelley Grove and had in all the local belles for us to dance with."* . . . *"We are going where I told you I thought we would, but we don't know what part yet. I hope it will be a little cooler there, but they say it won't be. I don't like this heat at all. I'm wet all the time. I put on a clean shirt, if I have one, and in ten minutes it's soaked through."* . . . *"We have lots of camels here. I enclose my picture taken on one. They pull the carts and carry loads in camel caravans along the sides of the road. Our meat is very tough and sometimes the boys say we must be getting the camels' harness to eat instead of the camels."* . . . *"We have cows running all around the city, but they are sacred, so you can't touch them. They are especially thick in the native section. The beggars are terrible. They run after us saying, 'Bricksu, Sahib,' which means 'Alms for the poor' and try to shine our shoes. They also say 'Get the hell out of here,' like parrots, because they have heard us say it so much."* . . . *"We have had the first rain that has fallen here in five years. We got flooded out three times."* . . .

The interest Dexter had shown in these passages had been genuine, though it had been tinged with envy. Sometimes Alix read trivial, homely items aloud too: Jerome had learned to drink tea, which he had always detested. Jerome was having a hard time sewing on his own buttons and checking his own laundry. But he was also getting accustomed to eight-course dinners, with a corresponding number of wines, served at nine-thirty in the evening by barefoot native bearers *"all dressed up in white, even to white gloves, and red turbans and sashes."* Apparently the British officers who entertained the young Americans at their mess did so with considerable style. Jerome had closed one letter by saying: *"I guess you'll find me a good deal changed, darling, when I finally get home. This world traveling is a great experience for anyone."* It would have been a great experience for Dexter, one from which he would have wrung knowledge as well as excitement. If he could have had such an experience, perhaps he would have changed too. He would not always have been a plodding farmer, going on with a ceaseless round of drudgery, unvaried except by season, and so dulled by weariness that he lacked the initiative to observe the niceties of life. With release and incentive, he might have been a man whom women would have loved, as Alix loved Jerome and as Judith had failed to love him. He would gladly have given ten years of his life if Judith had ever spoken as Alix had been speaking when that forked lightning quivered through the darkness.

The thunder still rumbled intermittently in the distance, but the darkness was unillumined now, and under cloak of it Alix was talking again, telling him about the parts of Jerome's letters which she had skipped before. Of course he had always known they must contain such parts, but that was different from hearing them. "He says he's living for the time when his ship sails into the home port and he finds me waiting on the dock for him. He says he keeps wondering what we'll say to each other first. Of course we won't say anything at first, because we'll be in each other's arms. He says he misses me more than I will ever know. But I do know, because I miss him the same way. He says he feels that I'm so far off. Of course I feel that he is. He says he wants to come home. Oh, dear Lord, how I want to have him! He says to keep my chin up, to say a little prayer for him when I go to church. When I go to church! As if I weren't praying for him every hour of the day, every hour of the night when I'm awake. But wanting him too. And I don't know—whether I can keep my chin up always, Dexter—whether——"

"Alix, don't—don't let it get you down like this now. You have kept your chin up. You have done everything just as Jerome would have wanted it done. You've been brave and faithful and patient—everything a man would want his wife to be. Not just Jerome—any man."

Suddenly he could not say any more, even to comfort Alix. He did not dare to touch her. He heard the thunder rumbling again, more loudly now, and felt the first big drops of rain splashing down on his face. Still he did not stir, because he could not. But Alix put out her hand and felt for his shoulder. It had grown so very dark that she could not see him, though they were so close to each other, and she needed support in order to rise. She was great with child now, and she moved with difficulty, but his shoulder steadied her; she leaned on it heavily and gratefully.

"It has done me good to talk to you like this," she said softly. "There is no one but you to whom I could have said all this, Dexter. But in these last months you and I have suffered in the same way and that has given us kinship. So we could say much things to each other. I must not stay here talking to you any longer. It is beginning to rain. But I want you to know how much you have comforted me."

"You have comforted me more often than you know," he said. "So I am very glad if I have comforted you." He did not say she had comforted him that night, but if she noticed this lack, she gave no sign of it.

"Speaking of Judith," she said, as naturally as if they had never stopped doing so, "I am sure David Cohen would be delighted to get her at the Junction on his way down from St. Johnsbury Saturday night. He could time his coming in such a way as to do it very easily. It might be a good way for him and Judith to meet. There would not be any awkwardness if they met in that way. And I know it is important that you should stay late in the Big Field, Dexter. Only I do not like to have you give that as a reason for not meeting Judith, when it is not the real one. I like to have you truthful, in thought and speech both. I am trying to achieve that sort of truth. It will help me if you do it too."

She felt for the screen in the darkness, found it, and swung it open. The electric switch was just inside the door, and she snapped it on. The fresco that she loved formed a background for her full figure, and she turned to look at the painting before she started upstairs.

"There's another Bible verse I love that fits in with the one I quoted to you when we first began to talk," she said. " 'When desire cometh, it is a tree of life.' It was the coming of desire, to Jerome and to me, that has kept alive the Tree of Life on Farman Hill, wasn't it? That is a lovely thought for me to take with me as I go to my room, knowing that the child of our love is so near to birth now."

"Yes. It is. Good night, Alix. And—thanks for everything. I'll get in touch with David and find out if it would be convenient for him to meet Judith, because I am needed in the fields. But you're right. That wasn't the real reason I didn't want to meet her. And I will tell you the truth in the first place next time."

He watched her out of sight, and then he latched and bolted the front door, switched off the light, and went through the front hall to the living room. This was dark and empty, so he concluded that Daniel and Serena had already gone to bed, and proceeded to the porch, locking up from outside, with his own key. The rain was now coming down in sheets, and he made a quick dash for his car,

which was parked in the yard. Nowadays he drove back
and forth from the Abbott Homestead to save both time
and strength. He had returned there as soon as Rhoda
came home for her summer vacation. Only the fact that
he had been so hard-pressed by work and that he had
turned instinctively to Alix at the end of each day, had
prevented him from taking more pleasure in his sister's
companionship than ever before. She had brought Benny
with her when she came, and the week after that, Rachel
had joined them; both children had now been at the house
all summer, and their presence had completely transformed
it. After the first week, Rhoda had confessed that she
would either have to stop worrying about the dirt that was
tracked in, or succumb to a nervous breakdown; but she
had said it smilingly, and she had hugged Benny while she
was saying it. Dirt was not her only problem by any means:
tight little bunches of wilting flowers which required vases;
fledgeling birds which had fallen from undiscovered nests
that had to be found again; a cosset lamb, which could
be fed only from a bottle; unkempt and noisy children
who were the offspring of the least respectable families
in the neighborhood—all these found their way into
Rhoda's erstwhile immaculate kitchen. Her schedule had
become a thing of the past too; she was forever finding
that the cookie jar was empty, that some new pets had
been added to the fast-growing collection, that Benny had
cut a gash in his knee, that Rachel did not have a clean
dress left to her name. By the time all this had been set
to rights, the poor schedule was completely shot to pieces.
Rhoda said this herself, laughing as she said it. Dexter had
never known before that his sister had such a pleasant
laugh.

It was now generally accepted that Rhoda had an "understanding" with David Cohen, though they themselves
did not fully understand just how they were to work this
out. It had seemed best to them both for Rhoda to stay
at the Homestead that summer with Dexter, keeping the
children with her, and for David to pay weekend visits
there. They were both also agreed that she should go
back to her school in the fall, since the need for teachers

was still so great. But they had practically decided that they might get married just before school opened, and that Rhoda could commute back and forth from St. Johnsbury to the near-by village where she taught. She was not in the least appalled at "managing" in the modest apartment over the store which was all David could offer her as a home at the moment. Certainly, she said, it would be more sensible for them to stay there for the present than to buy a house, only to find that was more than she could swing, together with her school teaching. Besides, David might feel later on that he would like to give up storekeeping and live on the farm; it was too soon to decide all that yet. But it was not too soon to decide that they would be happy together and that at their age it would be foolish to enter into a long engagement. Of course there were plenty of people who thought they were foolish, to say the least, to enter into an engagement at all. But as long as they had concluded they could afford to disregard such adverse opinions, there was no reason why they should not go quietly ahead with their plans.

It was inevitable that any autumnal romance should be the talk of the town, and the circumstances surrounding Rhoda's made it especially adaptable for wagging tongues. But it had never been customary for the village to close its doors to an outsider if those on Farman Hill stood open, and the Farmans' attitude in this instance was unmistakable: they had always known Rhoda would make a good wife for someone and they were glad she had found a man who would make her such a good husband. Dexter was equally definite and equally outspoken; he made David Cohen welcome, in every sense of the word, and his cordiality to the children was spontaneous and genuine. Rhoda did not ask how much impetus Alix had given to this attitude; she was so thankful that it existed, so happy in her tardy promise of a fuller and richer life, that she was ready to accept her brother's position without probing.

Dexter found her in the sitting room with the two children when he reached home, dripping wet, after his talk with Alix on the door rock. Rhoda no longer sat in a straight-backed kitchen chair knitting endless gray socks during the evening; she read aloud, sharing with her eager young listeners the books she loved so much and which she had so long denied herself. Rachel, like Alix, loved needle-work, and the shared taste had been an immediate bond between them; the young girl took a great interest in her clothes, and she was now putting the finishing touches on a new dress, while Rhoda read aloud. It was a fine white dress, with inserts of lace, made entirely by hand, after a convent pattern Alix had given her. She held it up with pride for Dexter to admire. Though she was just then at her least attractive age, it was easy to guess that in a year or two she would be extremely handsome. Her thick black hair bushed out around her face, her smooth cheeks glowed with crimson under their tan, and her luscious lips parted in a merry smile. Her figure was developing fast, and her breasts and hips were temporarily too full for her height. But she was growing tall too; before long she would be Junoesque. Benny was entirely different; he sat quietly making a cat's cradle, his lean dark little face bent over it, his slim brown fingers intertwined with the string. He was a small child, almost shrivelled-looking, and he sat with his shoulders hunched and his pitiful, thin legs drawn up underneath him; he had gained nearly ten pounds that summer, but the shadow of suffering and starvation still seemed to hover over him. He paid no attention to Dexter's entrance. But when Rhoda closed the book from which she was reading, putting a mark carefully in the place where she had left off, he looked up with an expression akin to pain.

"Oh, Aunt Rhoda, please don't stop! That's such an interesting place. Please go on!"

"Benny, you never want me to stop. You always say it's an interesting place . . . I'm reading this new biography of Haym Solomon to them," she said to Dexter. "When I've finished that, I'm going to read one I've found about Judah P. Benjamin. I think it's a good idea——"

She did not complete her sentence, but Dexter nodded, understanding, as he shed his dripping slicker. She thought it was a good idea to teach them something about the prominent part Jews had played in American history. He knew very well that the idea had not originated with Rhoda, but after all that did not matter. She had digested it and was putting it to good use.

"Do you think David would mind stopping at the Junction on his way down here Saturday, and picking up Judith?" he inquired, running his fingers through Benny's tousled hair.

"Why, of course not. I'll telephone him about it right away, so there won't be any mistake." She rose, eagerly. Dexter could see that she was delighted to have an excuse to telephone David Cohen. "But don't you want to meet Judith yourself, Dexter?" she added in a tone which betrayed her surprise.

"No," Dexter said bluntly. "I don't." This time he did not mention the oats that needed harvesting. "Come on, Benny. Hard-working men like you and me need our sleep."

"But if Aunt Rhoda's going to telephone Uncle David, I want to speak to him too."

"Well, I suppose you do. Just the same I'd like to see if you can't beat me to bed. I'm going to take a hot shower, so you've got some leeway."

"All right, Uncle Dexter. Just as soon as I've spoken to Uncle David."

"How's Alix?" Rhoda inquired solicitously, pausing on her way to the telephone. "It's been a hot day. I've been afraid she'd feel it."

"It has been hot. But this thunderstorm will clear the air. And she seems to be all right."

"Has she heard from Jerome lately?"

"Yes. She's had two letters this week. He's all right too."

"What does he say?"

Dexter did not feel like discussing Jerome's letters any more that night. But he knew he had no right to leave Rhoda's affectionate and natural curiosity unsatisfied.

"He's up in the country now. I mean he was when he wrote—among the ride paddies and the tea plantations. He wrote a long account of rice gathering as it's done on

an Indian plantation. It seems the coolies take the rice
home and put it on a clean piece of ground. Then they
hitch up three or four oxen and walk them around on this
to separate the rice from the plant. Alix was very interested, because of course she'd seen rice harvested so differently in Louisiana. Jerome has a basha hut for an office,
made of bamboo with a thatched roof. He said the neigh-
boring planters had been very friendly, and that he was
going to dinner with one of them the next evening. But
he spoke of the jackals too. He says they howl all night,
and that this noise, mingled with the beating of the native
tomtoms, makes a very weird sound."

"My goodness, I should think it would," Rhoda said,
shuddering a little. "It must be hard for Alix, Dexter, to
keep thinking of Jerome in a place where jackals howl at
night."

"Of course it's hard," he answered, so harshly that
Rhoda looked at him with increased surprise. She could
not divine the turmoil which the evening had roused in his
breast, but neither could she believe that she had offended
him. He saw her flush, and added, more gently, "I'm sorry,
Rhoda—I've got a grouch tonight. Well, at least Jerome's
out of that awful place where the sand blew all the time,
getting into his eyes and his food and his bed. I think he
minded the sand more than he does the jackals really. He
says the green grass and the green trees look awfully good
to him."

"Well, naturally," Rhoda said. There was relief in her
voice now, not only on account of Jerome, but on account
of Dexter. "There isn't any special reason, is there, Dexter,
why you should have a grouch? I mean, nothing has upset
you?"

"Well, a stone got into the grain separator and broke
some of the teeth in the cylinder. We had to stop work and
wait for two hours while Hite Wendell went to the Junction
to get new parts. The only ones he could find weren't satisfactory—I don't need to tell you how hard it is to replace
machinery nowadays. Meanwhile we lost those two hours
in the field and we needed them. This happened just about

dinnertime, so Mother Farman and Alix had to give Hite
his dinner after he got back. They didn't complain—of
course they wouldn't. But I feel they have about enough
to do, nowadays, without serving two dinners."

"They've got more than enough. I ought to have gone
over to help them."

"Well, after all, you've got the children here, and next
week you'll have the corn cutters to feed yourself. Something else will probably go wrong then. I never knew it to
fail, when a man had more on his hands already than he
knew how to manage. A few days ago, when we were
hurrying to get in the last of the rowen, so we could start
on the oats, the old hay fork rope went to pieces. As I just
said, it's one darn thing after another."

"You wouldn't be happy doing any other kind of work,
Dexter."

"I'd be happy if I were in the fight, like Jerome, right
now," he said almost savagely. Then, after a minute, he
added more gently, "But you're right. I'm a congenial
countryman. It's just the endless grind of a farm that gets
me down every once in a while. But I guess I can stand the
grind here if Jerome can stand it in India. He seems to be
pretty busy—says he has four different jobs going that all
have to be looked after at once. Of course he couldn't say
what they were or his letter wouldn't have passed the
censor. But he's had a chance to buy Alix some presents.
He wrote her about those too, and she's very pleased. I'm
not sure I can remember what all of them were, but I know
there were some things made of ivory on the list—an
inlaid table and a powder box. And some velvet bags and
cushions. And several jackets—one made of wool and one
made of silk and one made of tapestry."

"I shouldn't think Alix could wait to get them."

"She's looking forward to getting them. But she won't
be impatient about it. After all she didn't get any letters for
months, and she never complained about that."

"I don't think I could have so much self-control, Dexter,
if—if it was David that was gone. I'm afraid I'd take on.
Alix never takes on."

"No," he said. "Well, good night, Rhoda. Benny, remember what I told you about beating me to bed."

Benny, who was less interested in showers than he was in books, beat Dexter to bed by five minutes and to sleep by fully five hours. The storm had subsided and the rain fell gently and rhythmically on the roof. But its steady sound did not soothe the man who lay and listened to it; neither did the realization that its fall tonight lessened the likelihood of another storm which might mean ruin to the oat crop. And when he finally drowsed, towards morning, he was startled into wakefulness by a vision so vivid that he was not sure at first whether it was a dream or an image.

He saw Alix standing under the Tree of Life with her arms outstretched. That much was clear. But the face of the man to whom she was appealing was in shadow and he was escaping her. When Dexter saw this, he knew he was dreaming. For no real man would try to elude Alix.

CHAPTER 26

DAVID COHEN was very pleased to have the opportunity of meeting Judith at the Junction. She had sometimes been in his store, during the course of shopping trips to St. Johnsbury, but she had never entered into conversation with him, as Rhoda had done on the fateful day when she bought the hundred-dollar outfit. He did not feel at all sure Judith would know him by sight, though he was certain he would have recognized her, even if he had not been looking for a personable young woman in uniform. The same porter whom Jenness had so lavishly over-tipped was still on duty, but apparently Judith's largesse was less bountiful, for he made no move to carry her bags down the platform after she descended from the train. Actually this did not make much difference, as she had only two, which she would have been quite capable of handling herself if David had not been there. But he advanced deferentially to help her.

"I'm David Cohen, Miss Farman. I think probably you know that I'm a friend of Rhoda Abbott's."

"Yes, I did—Is Dexter sick?"

"No, he's quite well, I'm glad to say. But he's right in the midst of harvesting a very fine crop of oats. And then we have to be careful about conserving gasoline. I'm on my way to spend the Labor Day weekend at the Abbott Homestead so I had to come straight through the Junction anyway."

"I'm sure it's very kind of you to meet me. But it does seem like an imposition to ask an outsider to do this when——"

"Your family has been so kind to me that I don't feel like an outsider any longer, Miss Farman. I hope you won't feel that way about me either. This is my car, right here. May I help you in?"

Judith was accustomed to getting in and out of cars without assistance, and told David Cohen so. She answered his pleasant questions about her trip rather curtly too. She had been disappointed because she had not been able to fly all the way. It would have been much quicker by air. But the connection in Boston was poor, so it had been better to take a train from there. She was glad to get out of North Carolina. Was that ever hot! She did not ask any questions in return for David's, and the last part of the drive was somewhat silent. But as he began to slow down, before they reached the house on Farman Hill, she spoke rather sharply.

"We always go around to the side door. Perhaps you didn't know."

"But see, the lights are all on in front! Every time I have been here with Rhoda we've gone up the cobblestone walk and in at the front door."

"Well, perhaps *visitors* do now. But the *family* never would."

Obligingly, David turned in at the side yard. When it was too late to stop him, Judith saw that her father and mother were waiting at the front door. David lifted out the two bags and set them on the porch, asking Judith where she would like to have them taken next.

"Oh, don't trouble! I'll carry them upstairs myself later on. I'm used to carrying bags. Thank you for meeting me. Goodnight."

She opened the porch door and went into the living room with a curiously letdown feeling. Daniel and Serena, who had seen the car swing around to the side and heard it stop, now hastened back to welcome her. But they were disappointed because she had not made the indicated entrance when the stage had been so carefully set. There was a slight awkwardness in their greetings.

"Well, well, Judith! It is good to see you! How well you're looking! We were waiting for you at the front door because we've sort of got the habit now— . . . Wouldn't David stop? I suppose he was in a hurry to see Rhoda and the children but we'd have been pleased if he'd come in for just a minute."

"I didn't ask him to stop. I thought this was a family home-coming. I didn't know I was supposed to be received formally, like company, or to bring anyone with me."

"Well, you see David's getting to be almost one of the family. The children are here off and on almost all the time, tagging around at Dexter's heels and playing with Lucky, so it's natural . . . But of course we want you should do just as you've a mind to. I do want you should come out and see the summer kitchen though, the first thing. You won't hardly believe your eyes."

"I can hardly believe them now. What have you *done* to everything?"

"Why we've just opened up the house more and put it all to use. And your father's waxed the floors and rubbed down the old furniture. We haven't bought a thing new, Judith, except the kitchen and heating equipment, and we were lucky about getting under the wire on those, before everything was frozen. But we've thrown away a lot of junk that was cluttering up space and that was no good any more. We made the biggest contribution to the scrap drive,

Judith, of anyone around the Hill. And you've no idea the amount of work we turn out in our Red Cross unit."

Serena was already proudly leading the way into the summer kitchen. She was so happy she did not even notice that Judith was looking about her with the compressed lips which, with her, always presaged a storm. Unconscious of the impending outburst, Serena prattled on.

"When I brought Peter MacDonald out here last winter, Judith, I told him about the little chest I found just after I was first married, with a baby's shoe in it, half made, and some scraps of leather. I said I'd always wondered why that shoe was never finished. I've been kind of afraid the baby might have died. Well, Peter took some notes and said he was going to write a story with a happy ending about that little shoe. I never heard from him on the subject again, but I didn't think that was strange, because of course he started off around the world, right after that . . . Do you see his pieces, Judith, in the *Bulletin?* I declare the latest one, about the Dieppe raid, is the most exciting thing I ever read."

"I don't have time to read the papers," Judith said shortly. "Mom, this old pie safe's been out on the side porch with a lot of other junk, ever since I can remember. Whatever possessed you to make an *ornament* out of it?"

"Why, Judith, it isn't an ornament! We've got a lot of our Red Cross supplies in it. And we all think it looks real nice, now that the dirty white paint's been scraped off, and you can see the grain of the wood and the design on the tin, and all . . . Well, I started to tell you about this piece Peter meant to do. We got a letter from Joe Racina the other day—he writes us every now and again—and he said Peter handed those notes over to him just before sailing, and told Joe to see what *he* could do with them. So Joe wrote a story, and he's sold it to the *Saturday Evening Post!* It's the first time he's ever made it. He's tickled most to pieces, and of course we can't hardly wait till it comes out. Joe says when he gets a vacation, if he ever does, he's going to take part of the money he got for his piece and come up here to make us a visit. He certainly would be real welcome. He certainly——"

"Mom, perhaps you didn't know it, but I took a great dislike to Joe Racina. There was every reason why I should. I know he was kind to you and Dad but he behaved like a perfect bear to me. I'd rather not talk about him, if you don't mind. I would like to hear about Dexter though. I've been expecting he'd come in at any moment. Where on earth is he?"

"Why he went home early tonight. He and your father harvested the last of the oats just about half an hour ago. It's the biggest crop, Judith, that anyone——"

"Well, where's Alix?"

"She's upstairs. She's been going to bed early this last week. I'm afraid she gets real tired, though she hasn't said so. I think she's very close to her time, Judith. But she wants you should come right in to see her."

"Naturally I'm going right in to see her, since I'm going to take care of her. I hope Dr. Barnes hasn't let her put on too much weight. And I hope everything's properly prepared. There are quite a number of questions I want to ask her and——"

"Well, so you shall, Judith, so you shall. But do stop in just a minute as you go by and look at the parlors. Would you ever have thought they could be so pretty? And then this old wall painting in the hall, that's been here ever since the house was built, what do you suppose Alix calls it? 'The Tree of Life'! She's told us some stories, Judith, about——"

"Oh, Mom, I don't want to hear any of that tonight! I want to go to bed, as soon as I look Alix over. I'm tired myself. You haven't fixed up my room to look like a magazine illustration, have you?"

"No, Judith, it's just the same as ever. Dexter slept there all winter of course, but I must say he was careful not to disturb anything. And now there's a bathroom leading out of it, the one we made out of the middle room. I think you'll find it real convenient. And the West Chamber's going to be the nicest nursery—Come upstairs, Judith, do ... Have you taken the bags up already, Daniel?"

"Yes, Mother. I figured you and Judith wouldn't miss me for a minute and I was right. You were so busy showing off the house, and Judith was so busy criticising it, you didn't either of you see when I went out of the room."

Daniel spoke with unwonted dryness. He had been more alert than his wife to the danger signals Judith was flying. Now, remarking that he was all tuckered out after hustling so to harvest the last of the oats, he bade his daughter an undemonstrative good night. He added, rather tritely, that he would be seeing her in the morning; then he disappeared into his own room with a final comment to the effect that the wind had shifted, and that they might be getting another storm; it was just as well the oats were in. Serena, still resolutely cheerful, preceded Judith up the stairs. Before they reached the top, Alix called to them.

"Come in, Mother. Come in, Judith. I'm so glad you're here, *chère.*"

She put up her arms and drew Judith's face down to her own. The caress was so childlike and loving that Judith could not help returning it. But after she freed herself, she did not sit down in one of the easy chairs which Alix had thoughtfully placed beside the bed. Instead she looked around her with an appraising rather than an approving eye.

"It really would have been much better if you'd gone to a hospital, Alix. This room isn't suited for a delivery. That big bed, for instance."

"Why, Judith, don't you see the day bed at the foot of it? It matches so perfectly perhaps you didn't notice it. Mother says that small spool beds are rare, that we're fortunate to have found this one, when we cleaned out the summer kitchen. And Father mended it and polished it so beautifully that now it's one of the prettiest pieces of furniture we have in the house. Dr. Barnes was pleased that we found it too. She says it will be ever so convenient. And of course I'm delighted, because it's so much like the accouchement beds we have in Louisiana. Tante Odilisse——"

"I want to check over your supplies tonight, Alix. And I think I better telephone Dr. Barnes. When did she examine you last? Mother, perhaps you might go downstairs. I've got to ask Alix some pretty plain questions . . ."

"She thought I couldn't stand hearing her ask some pretty plain questions!" Serena told Daniel indignantly, when she rejoined him. Daniel was half asleep already, or at least appeared to be, so Serena got no satisfaction out of him, and certainly she had got none out of Judith. "Here that girl hasn't been home in eight months, and instead of sitting down and visiting with us, or saying anything pleasant about what we've accomplished in her absence, short-handed like we've been——"

"I guess that's part of the trouble, Mother. Judith would rather accomplish things herself than to have someone else do it. I bet she's lying in her bed now—that is, if she's through asking Alix plain questions—cursing herself because she didn't think of fixing up the summer kitchen, and wondering why she let another woman step into her shoes in so many ways. That is, the shoes she might have worn. Not that she ever did."

Unconsciously, Daniel had said almost the same thing to Serena that Dexter had said to Alix and unfortunately they had both come very close to telling the truth. Judith had not expected her homecoming to be exactly joyous, in view of the fact that Jenness had died and that Jerome had gone to war since she left there; but she had expected it to be triumphant. And none of the triumph she saw about her was due in any way to herself; indeed some of it had been achieved in spite of her. Her father and mother were secure and contended in a home which had been almost miraculously transformed. They were awaiting with eager anticipation a grandson who would not be her child. Rhoda, whom she had scornfully designated, over and over again, as a "congenital old maid," had an earnest and devoted suitor. Dexter had just garnered his largest crop and was too tired to come and meet her . . .

Her eventual meeting with Dexter, which did not take place until Sunday at midday, did nothing to soothe her outraged feelings. She overslept, an almost unprecedented thing for her to do, and went downstairs to find a completely deserted house. A place was laid for her on the trestled table in the summer kitchen, which seemed to her almost like insult added to injury; and on a small sheet of ruled paper lying beside it was a pencilled note from her mother.

> *Dear Daughter—*
>
> *Your father and I hoped you would go to divine service with us in the village this morning, but we know you must be tired and need to have your sleep out, so think it best not to wake you but to start without you. I have left the coffee pot on the back of the stove, or if you prefer fresh coffee, of course there is the new percolator. I have squeezed some orange juice for you already which is in the new refrigerator. There are doughnuts in the jar and some rolls in the covered pan beside it. Dexter has taken Alix to Mass at the Junction and we're all going to meet at the Abbott's for dinner. Rhoda said if you would telephone what time you would like to go over David would come and get you.*
>
> *Love*
Mom
>
> *P.S. Please bring Lucky with you when you come, as he gets real lonesome if he is left by himself all day, and besides, the children enjoy playing with him."*

Judith reheated the coffee that was already made, disdaining the new percolator, though she did condescend to take the orange juice out of the new refrigerator. After she had eaten her breakfast and washed the dishes, she went through the house again, room by room, observing the details of the spaciousness and dignity which now characterized it. Then, in turn, she went into the transformed front yard, the new flower garden, and the enlarged vegetable patch. Lucky followed her, sniffing rather doubtfully at her heels. She did not encourage him, for she was not fond of dogs, but when he took the lead himself, trotting along towards the barn and turning back hopefully, as if he expected her to catch up with him now, she did so. Apparently she had hit upon a route that he was accustomed to pursuing with someone else; it occurred to her that perhaps Alix regularly covered the same ground in the same way, and without knowing why, she lost interest in doing so herself. But because she had started, she went on to the empty and orderly barn. The cattle were all turned out to pasture now and its vacancy, like its dimness, was oppressive. One broad shaft of light streamed from a small high window over the loft, and where its rays struck the beam, this shone like a bar of gold. She turned away from it, shuddering, and as he did so, a sharp, whirring sound pierced the stillness. It came so suddenly and so eerily, and it startled her so, that she cried out. Almost instantly she realized that it was caused by the swallows who fluttered back and forth in the barn throughout the summer, and had always done so. She had been as accustomed to them, from childhood, as to the bluebirds who perennially built their nests in the trunk hollow of the old crab apple tree flanking the side yard, and the robins who built theirs amongst the branches of the poplars in the front yard. Birds had always come closer to the house on Farman Hill than to most houses, because they were never molested there: Baltimore Orioles, chipping sparrows and song sparrows, red-headed woodpeckers and downy woodpeckers—all these and many other birds frequented the place. Pinkham, the old family cat who had taken so kindly to Lucky, had never been known to catch one. Even when they flew straight over his head, he only blinked his big yellow eyes and stretched his velvety paws a little more widely in the sunshine, composing himself once more to slumber.

Judith was instantly chagrined at her senseless fright over the swallows, and was thankful that no one had witnessed it. Nevertheless, she hurried out into the yard again, involuntarily still thinking of Jenness. Well, at least her mother had not insisted that she should go to the cemetery. That was something. But she recoiled from the prospect of dinner at the Homestead in company with a miscellaneous crew. The Puritan Abbotts who were dead and gone would turn over in their graves if they knew that Dexter and Rhoda were flinging open its doors to a

Catholic Creole like Alix and to German Jews like the Cohens.

The more she thought about this desecration, the more indignant she became. She decided not to telephone Rhoda, which would possibly serve as a hint that she was not enthusiastic about driving with David again. So she walked over to the Homestead along the highway which was now bordered by Bouncing Bet and Queen Anne's Lace, early goldenrod and late milkweed. Because of the unseasonable heat which prevented her from hurrying, this walk took her longer than she had expected. She was a little late, and when she arrived, there was no one in sight but two strange children, unmistakably Jewish: a thin, wretched-looking little boy who was sitting on the grass, bent over a book, and a rather blowsy girl who was playing with some rabbits. The boy went on reading, as if unaware of the newcomer's approach. The girl looked up laughingly.

"Hello!" she said. "You're Miss Judith Farman, aren't you? Auntie said to tell you everyone was out back of the house."

"Back of the house!"

"Yes. Didn't you ever go there? It's nice. I'll show you."

The little girl jumped up and bounded off, scattering rabbits in every direction as she did so. Judith followed slowly and disapprovingly. She found all the adults seated under the maples in the rear, where there was a spacious spread of shade, instead of being crowded together on the small front porch. They had tall frosted silver goblets in their hands, from which they were sipping something in a leisurely way, and Judith observed that besides the Abbotts and the Farmans and the Cohens, Dr. Barnes was also there, and two strangers, a ruddy-faced priest, and his feminine counterpart, unmistakably his sister. When Dexter and Rhoda came forward to greet Judith, which they did together, goblets in hand, she saw that these goblets contained mint juleps. Apparently there was no end to the innovations which had been introduced on the long-static countryside.

"Hello, Judith," Dexter said pleasantly. He was still holding his mint julep in one hand, but he extended the other and took her fingers in a firm brief grip. "Nice to see you back after all this time. I was sorry to hear from David that you didn't have such a good trip. You know everyone here, don't you? Or haven't you met Father Boudreau and Miss Boudreau before? Or, I'm sorry! Well, you do now so that's all right . . . Alix made a julep for you too. She's a great believer in mint juleps. She says there's an old saying in Louisiana that they melt the icicles in the blood of the aged and make the tropic blood of youth run roses. We'll have to see if she's right in your case," he added, starting towards the house while Rhoda in turn greeted their guest. "Your goblet's still in the refrigerator, so it would stay frosted. I'll get it."

"No, Uncle Dexter, let me!"

"It's my turn this time, Rachel. You got Uncle Daniel's for him."

The thin little boy still held his book, his brown fingers marking his place, but he had come out of his trance and was looking at Dexter eagerly and devotedly. His cousin had already bounded off again, and in a minute he ran after her, with Lucky at his heels, barking lustily. Rhoda excused herself, saying that she had finished her julep and that she was going into the house to get dinner on the table. No, she didn't want any help, she had everything all ready—except that perhaps David would fill the glasses for her. She had on a white dress, which retained a few traces of the primness which had long characterized her clothes, but it was easy to see that these were gradually being eliminated. Her cheeks were flushed, partly from her one julep perhaps, but mostly from pride and happiness, and where her hair had loosened a little, it waved becomingly. Presently she called everyone in to a dinner which would have done credit to any cook. Well, it was just a family meal, she kept saying as everyone praised it: her own broilers, her own beans and beets and green corn, her own mustard pickle and apple jelly. She did think the cucumbers and the summer squash, which were the contribution from Farman Hill, were unusually good that year, but this was no credit to her. And the rice had come from Louisiana. Alix had sent to Crowley on purpose for it; it

was a very special kind called Blue Rose. Alix had shown
her how to cook it too, so it would be light and fluffy
instead of heavy and soggy. And Alix had made the coffee.
They were going back under the trees to drink that. But
not until they had some peach ice cream and some gold
and silver cake—or green apple pie, if they would prefer
that. Serena had brought the green apple pie too—she
knew Rhoda favored these, and so she always made the
first one of the year for Rhoda's birthday, which was just
past, and then kept on making them, one a week, as long
as the green apples lasted. No, they must not give a
thought to the dishes. The children were going to help her
with those after the company had gone. Benny was the
best little dishwasher she had ever seen. He could wash
faster than she and Rachel together could dry, and that
was plenty fast. Rhoda beamed proudly at the children and
Rachel beamed back. But Benny got up from his seat and
went over to Rhoda and rubbed his cheek against hers
for a minute. Then he returned to his own chair and his
heaped plate of ice cream.

Those children! Judith said to herself. Those strange
dark intense Jewish children, at the Abbott Homestead!
And those equally strange French Canadians, a Catholic
priest and his sister, stocky, jocular, ruddy. Strangest of
all, in a way, Alix St. Cyr, Jerome Farman's wife, with
her black braids wound sleekly around her small head, and
a fine old lace fichu falling over her full figure, and great
jewelled rings on her tiny white hands. Alix had mixed the
mint juleps, Alix had cooked the rice and prepared the
coffee, as Judith had already been reminded; now Alix was
telling some fantastic story about Louisiana, and everyone was listening as if she were Ruth Draper or Cornelia
Otis Skinner. Lucky was lying at her feet, panting ecstati-
cally, his wide pink mouth open in a doggy grin, and
Benny had stolen up to her and was leaning over the arm
of her chair in rapt fascination. Dexter was sitting on one
side of her, puffing contentedly at a pipe, and Father
Boudreau was on the other, with a fresh drink in his hand,
though they had hardly finished coffee.

"My grandfather met my grandmother at a valentine party," Alix was saying, "and the next year they were married on St. Valentine's Day. From then until her death he sent her a beautiful valentine every year, making it an event and searching through all the shops where valentines were sold, in order to purchase those which were most appropriate. He did not confine himself to those made with lace paper and sentimental pictures; he bought her beautiful porcelain cupids and other ornaments of that type, and heart-shaped pendant earrings and lockets. I still have the entire collection. The paper valentines are pasted in an album that has his initials and hers entwined on the cover and I often wear the jewelry. The porcelain ornaments are put away, but sometime I am going to gather them together in a cabinet. Perhaps twin cabinets would look well on either side of the fireplace in the West Parlor, against the panelling. What do you think, Mother?"

"I think they'd give that room just the finishing touch," Serena said enthusiastically. "You could amuse yourself arranging them, while you're getting your strength back. What did you have in mind putting in the other one?"

"I have several old memory chains. Every girl wore those in my grandmother's day; friends gave them to each other as a token of friendship and every link represented some beautiful association. They could be arranged to encircle the Nautch embroidery which was brought from Persia, together with some enamel vases—*blue de roi* interlaced with flowers of gold."

Judith looked at her father to see if she could not discover something in his face which would indicate a protest at bringing such baubles to Farman Hill; but Daniel, like Dexter, was contentedly smoking a pipe, sitting beside Serena, who was rocking back and forth, wielding a palm leaf fan, and looking positively smug over the prospect of enshrining porcelain cupids and Nautch embroidery in the West Parlor. Some other children, whom Judith mentally dismissed as "riffraff," had come to play with Rachel and Benny, and they went capering around in the circle, chanting in a singsong as they pranced.

Oats, beans, peas, and barley grows
'Tis you nor I nor nobody knows,
How oats, beans, peas, and barley grows
'Tis you nor I nor nobody knows.

The children stopped capering and began to make other fantastic gestures as they stood still and went on with their song:

"First the farmer sows his seed"—they chanted, swinging their arms back and forth——

"Then he stands to take his ease"—their hands were all on their hips now——

"Nods his head and claps his hands"—a lot of silly bobbing, a hearty sound like applause——

"And turns around to view his lands"—they were all spinning like tops.

A-waiting for a partner
A-waiting for a partner
Open the ring and let her in,
And kiss her when you get her in.

It was Rachel who was taken into the ring this time and who was left in the middle of it when the chanting and the capering began again. The stanzas were repeated as they had been sung the first time, except that at the end the injunction was to open the ring and let *him* in and kiss *him* when you got *him* in. Rachel looked past the circle of children to the elders seated beneath the trees.

"I choose Uncle Dexter," she said brightly.

"Say, that's a fine idea! Come on, Dexter, and kiss Rachel."

Dexter rose good humoredly and sauntered over to where the children were playing.

"I'm very much flattered," he said. "But what'll I do when it comes my turn to choose? I'd have to ask Rachel to come into the ring with me, and then we'd go on and on the same way. There's no grownup girl who wants to help me with my oats, beans, peas, and barley, not to mention the heavier work. As I recall it, there's another verse that goes into that."

"Yes, there is. But we can't sing it until you're in the ring with Rachel. We can decide afterward what to do next. Oh, come on, Dexter, just this once!"

"All right, just this once."

The children closed in around Dexter and Rachel. She lifted up her gay, rosy face and Dexter kissed her while the other children sang:

> Now you're married you must obey,
> You must be true to all you say,
> You must be kind, you must be good,
> And help your husband chop the wood.

It was ridiculous, it was revolting, Judith said to herself. She never would have believed that Dexter would let himself be drawn into a fantastic game like that, closing her mind to the memory of all the times she and he had played it together when they were children. What was more, she never would have believed that he would say, in that pointed manner, that no grownup girl wanted to help him plant his oats and chop his wood, or that he would publicly kiss a forward little adolescent like Rachel. Why the girl must be thirteen or so, and Judith had always heard that Jewesses matured early. In another two or three years, Rachel might very well be throwing herself at Dexter's head, with disastrous results. After all, he was only twenty-seven now. When he was thirty and Rachel was seventeen . . .

The picture was so appalling that Judith longed to escape from this crowd and retreat to some quiet place where she could consider it without further provocation. But no one except the children suggested stirring, and when they were tired of their game, they came and made a ring around Alix, teasing her to sing to them. At first she protested, saying laughingly that she never sang and told stories the same day and that she had already told stories. But they gave her no peace.

"Just one song, Alix. Well, just one verse then. One verse of 'Going Home To Glory.'"

"All right, we'll sing the second verse of 'Going Home To Glory.' That's the verse Dexter likes best:

> Sister, whar is you gwine?
> I's gwine home to glory.
> I's been blind but now I see,
> I's been bound but now I's free,
> De Lawd said, Sister, I's heared yo' plea.
> Now I's gwine home to glory.

Judith looked down at the ground, a queer drumming in her ears which seemed to come from the reverberations of the song in which everyone was now joining. "I's been blind but now I see, I's been bound but now I's free." *So that was Dexter's favorite song, was it?* And now the children were clamoring for another song, and in spite of her protests, Alix was humoring them.

"All right! What about a new one for a change? I've sung all the old ones so often."

"Oh, goodie, goodie! What's the name of the new one, Alix?"

" 'Ol' Man Noah.' Listen and then sing it with me:

> Ol' man Noah, he built de ark,
> Built de ark, he built de ark,
> Ol' man Noah, he built de ark
> Kase de Lawd done told him to.

> Ol' man Noah, he sawed an' nailed,
> De sinners, dey hee-hawed an' railed,
> But ol' man Noah, he sawed an' nailed
> Kase de Lawd done told him to.

> Ol' man Noah, he filled de ark,
> Filled de ark, he filled de ark,
> Ol' man Noah, he filled de ark
> Wid critters two by two.

Two lions an' two kangaroo,
Two leopards an' two tigers, too,
He filled de ark, yes, two by two,
Kase de Lawd done told him to.

Two by two! Two by two! That was even worse than
hearing about Dexter's favorite verse. Rhoda was looking
at David, Alix was obviously thinking about Jerome. But
this song apparently had no significance for Dexter at all,
as far as the "two by two" connotation went. He had Benny on his lap now, and his arms around two of the "riffraff" children who had come to play. And apparently this
song was not new to him, in any case, for he was going
on with it not only lustily but without guidance:

De lions dey got mad an' roared,
Ol' Mis' Noah was sad an' bored,
But ol' man Noah, he slep' an' snored
For de whole long deluge through.

Ol' man Noah, he sent a dove,
Sent a dove, he sent a dove,
Ol' man Noah, he sent a dove
For to see was de rainin' through,

De dove, she brought a green leaf back,
De Good Book says, an' dat's a fack,
So ol' man Noah says 'Le's unpack,
Kase de rainin' now is through.

Evidently everyone but Judith was enjoying all this very
much, for it was not until late in the afternoon that anyone made a move toward departure. Then Father Boudreau said he must get back to the Junction for Benediction
and Dr. Barnes said she must go to see a patient with a
broken leg and Dexter said it was high time he got out to
the barn. Almost without formal leave-taking, the group
began to disintegrate. But Dexter leaned over Alix and
spoke to her before he went in to change from gray flan-
nels to overalls.

"Do you have to go home now, with Father and Mother Farman, or can you wait until I come up to the Hill and ride over with me?"

"I think perhaps I better go now, Dexter. Dr. Barnes is coming in to see me after she's been to the Merrills'."

"Well, in that case . . . But I'll see you later, won't I?"

"If you don't today, you will some other day soon, you know."

She turned to speak to David who had taken the seat vacated by the priest on her other side and Dexter started for the house. Judith rose deliberately and joined him.

"I want very much to have a confidential talk with you, Dexter, about the possibility of going overseas."

"It sounds exciting. But as you know, I'm a hard-pressed farmer, and this is milking time."

"You're coming up to Farman Hill after you've finished milking here, aren't you? I overheard what you said to Alix."

"Yes, I thought you did. But from what she said to me, which you doubtless overheard also, I don't believe I'll be there long this evening. You'll be busy too, won't you, if Dr. Barnes is there?"

"Not necessarily. Dr. Barnes will be making just a routine call. There are one or two things I want to talk over with her, but when I've done that——"

"Well, we'll see how it works out. I'm sorry, Judith, but I do have to go now."

Unless she actually stepped in front of him, she had no way of stopping him. She turned away with flaming cheeks. Her mother was already in the nice-looking car which Judith assumed belonged to Alix, and her father was carefully helping his daughter-in-law to get in beside his wife. Rhoda, reluctant to let them go, was standing nearby, still talking to them.

"Remember, Alix, I can take care of your folks at the Homestead just as well as not. Your stepmother and your Aunt Odilisse and your Cousin Prosper and anyone else who might feel like coming. We can double up. Rachel can sleep in my room." Rachel, who had again boisterously thrust herself forward, gave a whoop of joy at this announcement and Rhoda silenced her gently. "I want you should tell them so, Alix, when you write."

"Thank you, *chère*. I will. I don't know yet whether Maman and Tante Odilisse will both come. But Prosper'll come anyway. Or I might ask Mr. Franchini to serve as a godfather. I have an idea he'd be delighted."

"Mr. Franchini! The man who keeps the fruit store at the Junction?"

"Yes, Judith. He and I have grown to be very good friends. He's asked me to be his baby's godmother. It seems to me turn about might be fair play."

"And who are all these other people you're discussing?"

"They're my Creole relatives. They're coming up for the baby's baptism. You see there have to be two sponsors, a godmother and a godfather. I guess Prosper ought to get in on it anyway. He is the *beau cousin* I was supposed to marry, according to the best laid family plans. I'm very fond of him, but I didn't want him for a husband. That was the main reason I went to Fayetteville. I was tired of being importuned. And then everything turned out for the best, because I met Jerome. But Prosper is very attractive. Perhaps you'd like to consider him for yourself, Judith."

"I shouldn't dream of getting married until after the war. And I wouldn't marry a Creole in any case."

"I'd forgotten for the moment you had such a prejudice against us. I do remember now, Mother said you took an immediate dislike to Joe Racina. Was that because you thought he was a Creole too? He isn't really, you know, so don't condemn him by putting him in that category. I was surprised to learn you had such an aversion for him. I found him delightful company, that day I stopped in Alexandria on my way north. He put himself out to be nice to me. Are you sure you didn't misunderstand his attitude towards you?"

Judith made no direct reply, but nobody seemed to notice it. They were now on their way back to Farman Hill and she was secretly raging. She had not contrived to get in a single word alone with Dexter and she was amazed that the others did not seem to realize what an affront she considered this. They were talking about the nice time they had had, the good dinner, the congenial company; they were commenting on Rhoda's improved looks, on David's pleasant ways, on the extraordinary adaptability of the two children. Judith could think of nothing to contribute to this conversation, and her father and mother and Alix were all apparently quite unconscious of the lack. But when they were almost to Farman Hill, Alix gave her a small swift sign, and Judith understood that her sister-in-law wished to speak with her privately. She followed her upstairs.

"I think I've started, Judith."

"Oh for heaven's sake! Then why did you sit there like that under the trees all the afternoon as if you hadn't a care in the world? Why did you let Dr. Barnes take that other call?"

"Why I thought it was very pleasant under the trees, didn't you? And I thought Dr. Barnes would have plenty of time to make her other call and that then she'd be all the freer to stay with me. It takes quite a while for the first baby, doesn't it? You're not annoyed with me, are you, Judith?"

"Annoyed! Of course I'm annoyed. This isn't the way to act when you're in labor, Alix! As if it didn't amount to anything at all!"—

"It's the way the St. Cyrs always act," Alix said. Her voice, which was usually so quiet, had a ring of pride, almost of defiance in it. "I'm sorry if you don't like it, Judith. But I shan't change, just to suit you. It doesn't amount to to anything at all, if you mean the pain. I'm not afraid of a little pain. You'll never get me to say I am. But just the same, I don't understand why you seem to be actually hoping I'll have a hard time."

It was very quiet, except for the song of a whippoorwill, and it was very dark, except for occasional flashes of heat lightning beyond the hills. For a moment after she went outside, Judith could see nothing. But she knew that Dexter was there. Apparently he had formed the habit of sitting on this door rock, looking out into the darkness, for Judith had seen him there the night before too, when Alix had still been having pains intermittently, and she herself had slipped downstairs for some supper, leaving her mother and Dr. Barnes in charge. She had stopped briefly to speak to him then. Now she sank down beside him.

"I couldn't come before," she said. "It hasn't been possible for me to leave her again, all this time. But she's resting quietly now. I think she'll sleep, off and on, for the next twenty-four hours, more on than off. I wish I could myself. I feel as if I'd been through the wars. She wore me out completely—that little frail-looking girl! And that huge boy! *No one* has babies that size any more!"

"Apparently Alix does," Dexter said. He moved away a little and spoke dully, rather coldly. His voice sounded oddly harsh above the sweet notes of the whippoorwill. "There's no reason why you can't get some sleep now yourself, is there? According to Dr. Barnes, everything's well in hand at last. She spoke to me, from the window in the upper hall, a few minutes ago. And Mother's been out, crying with joy; Father too, pretty well choked up himself with pride at the thought the name's going on. I don't believe he's thinking of anything else. I remember he said to me once, that if Jerome's wife had a child, he'd be sorry if she had a hard travail, but he wouldn't grieve over it; he'd feel it ought to be worth it to her, to bear Jerome's son. I know it was. But God, when I think of the hell Alix must have gone through! And you talk about her having worn *you* out!"

"It needn't have been so long, if the case had been handled differently," Judith said defensively. "I said all the time she ought to go to a hospital. I said she ought to have a specialist. I said she ought to have a small baby."

"Yes, that's what *you* said. But after all, lots of other people are saying that women had better go back to having their babies at home because the hospitals are so overcrowded, and in some cases so inaccessible. You seem to overlook the fact that the nearest hospital is thirty miles away, that we haven't enough gasoline to go back and forth there, and that it hasn't a nurse available for private duty. You also seem to overlook the fact that the specialists have all gone into the Service. I can't say anything about the size of the baby; I don't know anything about that. But I do know that quite aside from these other aspects of the case, which I have just mentioned, Jerome said that he wanted the baby born here, like all the other Farmans. And it was what Jerome said that counted with Alix. What Jerome said and what he let her see without saying. I'm not blaming him. He didn't realize he was making things hard for her any more than those Creoles Alix told us about: they employed midwives instead of doctors rather than let any strange man into a lady's room! His mother and grandmother got on all right too—Jerome's heard that over and over again. They took childbirth in their stride, without any whimpering, and had great husky children. So he assumed Alix would too. And she has!"

"You talk as if that were praiseworthy. She could have left Farman Hill and gone to a big city to have her baby if she couldn't get adequate care around here. I call what she did sheer foolhardiness."

"Yes, you would. You wouldn't understand it was Jerome's heart's desire that mattered to Alix, whatever she went through to give it to him. You don't know what it means to love a man like that, you selfish shirker!"

Judith sprang to her feet. If Dexter had suddenly struck her, she could not have been angrier or more amazed. But before she could lash out at him in her turn, Dexter raged on.

"Why your sister Jenness had twice the guts you have! She didn't have the sense to pick a real man or the strength to fight through to a hard end, like Alix. But she did have the sand to take the rap for whoever was really responsible. I'll give her that much credit. And if you have any credit coming to you, for anything, I don't know what it is!"

He stopped, momentarily speechless with anger. Judith seized upon the opening.

"Don't you dare talk to me like that! Do you suppose I don't know why you're acting the way you do? Leaving my letters unanswered all these months! Avoiding me ever since I came home! Mocking and insulting me now! You're in love with Alix! You're not contented with letting your silly old sister make a fool of herself over a Jewish storekeeper; you won't be satisfied until you've done something much worse yourself! I wouldn't put it past you to get involved with that bold little piece you were fooling around with today. She's certainly asking for trouble, and you seem to be an easy mark. But that would be just an incident. While your best friend's off fighting for his country, you're waiting for a chance to step into his shoes. You've had to bide your time till the baby was born. But now you'll take Alix as soon as you can get her. You're hoping to hear Jerome's been killed, so you can marry her and get her money too. But if he isn't you'll try to take her anyway!"

PART V

Arzeu, North Africa

December 1942–January 1943

CHAPTER 27

IT WAS very dark on deck. But this darkness was not impenetrable, except in the cove where the ship rode at anchor. Every now and then it was illumined by the flare of bursting bombs and roaring guns. When this happened, the outline of the hills which rose in tiers beyond the town sprang into sharp relief against the sky. Momentarily, they looked as if heat lightning were playing over them. They reminded Judith of the hills encircling her own home, as these had intermittently appeared on the dark night after Jerome's son was born, when she had sat on the door rock at Farman Hill with Dexter.

The sight was uncannily the same. But the profound stillness of the New England countryside was wholly lacking here. Not that the noise was continuous. It came at intervals so irregular that Judith ceased to await it, breathlessly; she found that when she did that, it did not come until she had ceased to brace herself against this, and then the shock was all the more intense. While she was scanning the shore, she learned to distinguish between the different kinds of signs: the bombs *thudded;* the rifles *cracked;* the shells whistled; and after the whistle came still another sound, as if a stake were being driven into the ground. At first there had been a bombing too, but the big guns which theoretically protected the harbor of Arzeu had been silenced almost immediately. The cove was quiet. Only the distant hills reverberated.

One of the straps on Judith's life belt seemed to bind a little, and she shifted it to adjust it better over her blue shirt. She had learned to call the life belt a Mae West, like the other nurses in her unit, and to joke about it, though she knew well enough that the underlying reasons for its constant wear were far from funny. She had never grown

503

really accustomed to the Mae West, but she was thoroughly
at home now in her shirt and slacks, her short anklets and
flat shoes. It was just as well, she reflected, because she
would probably be wearing those for a long time. But if
everything went all right, she should be rid of the Mae West
within twenty-four hours now.

When she finished adjusting the strap, Judith turned to
see who was near her, and felt relieved, rather than otherwise, because none of her special friends was anywhere in
sight. Almost everyone was on deck, yet everyone seemed
withdrawn. The earlier part of the evening had been gay.
Dinner, as usual, had been a merry meal and an excellent
one. The transport was a Dutch freighter, now operating
under the British Merchant Marine, which had formerly
plied between the East Indian Islands; its standards of
cuisine were high and it clung to its indigenous ceremonials.
Judith relished the fine foreign food to the full, and still
found it intriguing to be served by Javanese stewards whose
heads were covered by turbans twisted into rabbits' ears,
and whose sarongs were made of oddly figured batik. She
lingered in the mess hall until certain preliminary sounds
presaged the imminence of the program; then she picked up
her menu, so that she could paste it later in her memory
book, folded it into her shirt pocket, and went into the
lounge.

The enlisted men were giving an entertainment. "Got the
hut—two—three—four—blues" the men yodelled over
and over again; this ditty had become their theme song.
Afterwards they switched to the tunes of the First World
War—"Over There"—"The Long Long Trail"—"Keep the
Home Fires Burning"—which produced such a sensation
of nostalgia that the next selections were frankly sentimental. Judith noticed several pairs of eyes turned appealingly
in her direction while their owners vociferated "Let me call
you sweetheart, I'm in love with you." The concert ended
with hymns, and several songsters came so close to tears,
in the course of these, that it seemed best to enliven the
atmosphere with a complete change. Card tables were ac-
cordingly set up, and bridge, rummy and black jack were
soon in full swing, to radio accompaniment. There was a

good deal of interference, but in spite of this, news flashes were coming through from the United States:

The War Department announced tonight that United States Army, Navy and Air Forces had started landing operations during the hours of darkness at numerous points on the shores of French North Africa. The operation was made necessary by the increasing Axis menace to this territory. Steps have been taken to give the French people, by radio and leaflets, early information of the landings. These combined operations of the United States forces were supported by units of the Royal Navy and of the Royal Air Force . . . Lieutenant General Dwight D. Eisenhower of the United States Army is Commander-in-Chief of its Allied Forces . . ."

The White House announced tonight that a powerful American force was landing on the Mediterranean and Atlantic Coasts of the French Colonies in Africa to forestall the invasion of Africa by Germany and Italy, which if successful would constitute a direct thrust to America across the comparatively narrow sea from West Africa. A powerful American force equipped with adequate weapons of modern warfare and under American command is attacking today . . ."

Here is a communication from the American General Eisenhower, Commander-in-Chief of the forces now disembarking in French North Africa. This is one of the General Staff Officers speaking to you. This communication is of the highest importance and is addressed to the French armies on land, sea and air in North Africa: "Frenchmen of North Africa—The forces which I have the honor of commanding come to you as friends to make war against your enemies. This is a military operation directed against the Italian-German military forces in North Africa. Our only objective is to defeat the enemy and free France. I need not tell you that we have no designs either on North Africa or on any part of the French Empire. We count on your friendship and ask for your aid. I

*have given formal orders that no offensive action be
taken against you on condition that for your part you
take the same attitude . . ."*

"Well, I guess the folks at home know we're in it by
now," Laura remarked briefly, looking across the table at
Judith.

"I guess they do," Judith answered, still more briefly.

"It seems kind of queer, doesn't it, to hear that way
about a battle you're in yourself?"

"Yes, it does."

Judith had been winning steadily all evening and her
luck was still holding. But suddenly her feeling of pleasurable excitement deserted her. She laid down her cards.

"I don't like to break up the game, but if you can find
someone to take my place, I believe I'll go on deck."

"That's all right. I guess we'll be coming along pretty
soon too. Unless we go to bed. Of course we can go to bed
if we like, so long as we don't undress and keep on the
alert for final orders."

"Yes. But I don't feel like going to bed any more than I
feel like playing cards."

She had tried to avoid the appearance of abruptness in
her departure, but her companions sensed her sudden
yearning for solitude, probably because many of them had
the same feeling. So none of them tried to rejoin her, and
she remained solitary in the midst of the crowd. The flaring
lights above the tiers of hills, and their accompaniment of
thudding, crackling and whistling, had long since ceased to
startle her. Eventually they did not even distract her from
her thoughts of Farman Hill . . .

The horror of her last days at home was still a vivid
memory. It took far less than the chance resemblance between intermittent gunfire glare and heat lightning to recall
it. Judith lived in its nightmare much of the time. There
had been no retort to the outrageous charge she had made
that night on the door rock. Before Dexter could hurl one
at her, almost before her own accusations were out of her
mouth, Dr. Barnes had called her impellingly. The summons was so imperative that she knew, as she turned and

rushed up the stairs, that it meant disaster. Alix was not asleep after all; she was having a hemorrhage. For the next few hours Judith fought not only the unforeseen catastrophe, but her own overwhelming panic. She had never lost her head or mistrusted her own capacities on a case before, not even in her first fumbling inexperienced days of nursing; her efficiency in an emergency and her faith in herself had been the twin sources of her success. But now she was overwhelmed with the terror that this sudden calamity was due, directly or indirectly, to her; either there had been some flaw in her manipulations, some oversight in her watchfulness, or else Alix had suffered some kind of a shock before she had rallied sufficiently to stand it. Was it possible that Judith's own angry voice, raised far above its normal level, had been the enraged carrier of injury through the open windows?

There was no time and no way to answer the dreadful question. Both Judith and the doctor had their hands full. Through an oversight which seemed to Judith inexcusable, Alix had not previously had her blood typed; neither had anyone else who might supply her in such an emergency. This was hurriedly done now. David took samples to the Junction for analysis by the aged physician there, while Dr. Barnes and Judith awaited a report. Meanwhile Alix sank lower and lower; Judith was sure she would die before the essential word could come. But somehow she was sustained, and when the message finally came through, this told them that it was Dexter's blood which matched. Dr. Barnes' only equipment was for the old-fashioned type of transfusion. Dexter stretched out on the big bed beside Alix, who had been moved back into this after her delivery, and she received his blood through the glass cylinders in which its flow was regulated by petcocks, to prevent it from clotting. They lay so close together that her black braids mingled with his fair hair and his powerful shoulders touched her slim, sloping ones. Alix was intermittently submerged in waves of complete unconsciousness and Judith did not think at any time she was fully aware of what was happening. But when the transfusion was over, her lips and fingers both moved slightly, and Dexter knew before Judith did that Alix was signalling to him.

"Thank you. But please don't leave me yet. I still need you."

The words were almost soundless, but their appeal was unmistakable. Dexter spoke brusquely to the doctor.

"I suppose I can stay."

"You must keep quiet yourself. But you may stay if you lie still. There's nothing more you can do for her, though."

"She seems to think there is."

He took one of the tiny white hands which lay so limply on the smooth sheet and enfolded it with a big brown one. It fluttered for a moment in his, then grew quiescent. Judith had the strange feeling that strength was still flowing from Dexter to Alix and she believed they shared the sensation. Eventually Alix went to sleep and this time her slumber was healing and profound. But it was not until morning that Judith and Dr. Barnes were fully reassured and it was this same morning that the telegram came which was addressed to Alix, but which Judith was the first to receive:

"SECRETARY OF WAR DESIRES THAT I TENDER HIS DEEP SYMPATHY TO YOU IN THE LOSS OF YOUR HUS-BAND CAPTAIN JEROME FARMAN. REPORT JUST RE-CEIVED THAT HE WAS KILLED IN ACTION IN THE FAR EASTERN AREA. LETTER FOLLOWS.

ULIO
ADJUTANT GENERAL.

The letter came before it was safe to show Alix the telegram. Judith discussed the matter with her parents and with Dexter; they were all of the opinion that they had no right to open the letter, that it belonged to Alix. They would have to wait until she was well enough to read it before they learned its contents themselves. Alix was convalescing satisfactorily at last; but her milk, though abundant now, had been slow in coming, and for the baby's sake, as well as her own, it would be most unwise to risk a second upset. It was not until Judith was back in Charlotte, on the point of departure for the port of embarkation, that she received a typewritten copy which Dexter had made for her of the letter from the War Department.

This stated, briefly, that nine United States airmen had been killed in Southeast India when a plane crashed, for unknown causes, as it was about to take off to attack the Japanese Navy. Among the victims of the accident were two ground officers, who had sacrificed their own lives in a vain attempt to rescue the flyers. One of these ground officers was Captain Farman. Major General Martin S. Burnham had cited all nine for the decoration of the Purple Heart. These awards would be made posthumously and Captain Farman's widow would receive his medal in due time . . .

The letter from Dexter which contained this communication had been courteous but impersonal. Judith still kept it in her brief case.

Dear Judith—

Enclosed is the news which was unavailable when you left. I hope when you have read it that your grief over Jerome's death will be swallowed up in pride for the way he met it. Personally I believe this is just the way he'd have asked to go, if he could have chosen. He was always reaching out for new adventure before he could quite catch up with it. Now he's off on the greatest one of all.

"Naturally you are very much in our thoughts these days, as you start off on a great adventure of your own while we stay here, plodding along in our usual dull way on Farman Hill. We all hope your new experience will bring you the rich reward of a sense of service, and that you will find the fulfillment you have sought so long in vain. Personally I should like to add that I hope you will not dwell with unhappiness or regret on anything that happened while you were at home. I am very sorry that I spoke to you in anger and I realize I deserved an angry retort. Neither of us meant what we said and the sooner we put it out of our minds, the better. With all the years of friendship that we have to remember, surely we can afford to

forget the few unpleasant episodes that have marred it, especially at a time when we are both saddened by a common loss.

Faithfully yours,
Dexter Abbott.

That was all. Not a word about her parents, or Alix or the baby. Except for the objective reference to their long friendship, the letter might have been written to a woman Dexter had only just met, and with whom further meetings were immaterial, one way or the other, as far as he was concerned. Not until she received this letter, had Judith faced the finality of her break with Dexter. But she had been facing it ever since, and she faced it now, looking out at the bursting bombs which so greatly resembled the heat lightning she had watched with him . . .

"Judith, are you in a trance or something? I've spoken to you three times!"

"I'm terribly sorry! Is anything the matter, Laura? Are there any new orders?"

"No, nothing's the matter—at least nothing special. I suppose you might call a battle like the one that's going on over there a slight disturbance! And there aren't any new orders, or even any new rumors—I've been nosing around a little, but nothing doing. And my drinks seemed to have died on me—not that I've had any drinks, but you know what I mean. So I've decided I'll go to bed. I came to see if by chance you'd had any such thought."

"No, I've been thinking about home. My mind was about four thousand miles away when you spoke to me— that's why it took me a minute to jerk in back again. I was thinking about my sister-in-law, Alix, my brother's widow, and her baby."

"Why she was all right, wasn't she, the last you heard?"

"Oh, yes! She's very well again now. She must have great recuperative powers. Mom wrote me that the way she took the news of Jerome's death was simply wonderful. It set an example of fortitude to all the rest of them. Since then some of her Creole relatives have been north to visit her. I guess they created quite a sensation in Farman. Mom wrote that her Aunt Odilisse was a perfect picture of elegance, and that her Cousin Prosper was the handsomest man you'd see in a month of Sundays. They tried to persuade Alix to go back to Louisiana with them, and Mom said she wouldn't have blamed the girl if she had. It looks as if they might have a hard winter on Farman Hill, without enough gasoline to get back and forth between there and the Abbott Homestead, let alone get to the Junction, and not enough fuel oil to do any real heating. That's tough on someone who's grown up in the South, let alone how it affects a young baby. But Alix insists Farman Hill was the place where Jerome wanted his son to grow up, and that she's going to stay there, whatever happens."

"It sounds as if she had sand herself."

"Sand! I should think she did! I've had lots of confinement cases, but I never saw a woman in labor take her pains the way Alix did . . . I'll be along in a little while, Laura. I still don't feel like going to bed. But you better snatch some sleep while you can."

She looked at Laura fondly and gave her friend's hand a little squeeze, before she turned away again. The two girls had become greatly attached to each other. When the chance had come for Judith to leave Morris Field and join the medical outfit organized in Charlotte itself, Laura had asked for permission to join her too and this had been granted. Now they both belonged to the evacuation unit. They had gone from the United States to England together and had been there for almost a month. Like the other nurses, they had been kindly received in a number of pleasant private English homes, and had done quite a little sightseeing together; both of these shared experiences had given the girls additional interests in common and had helped to cement their friendship. They had finally left England for an unannounced destination, spending a seemingly endless period zigzagging back and forth across the sea, until they began to wonder if they were on their way to America again. Then late one starless night they suddenly realized that the freighter was slipping silently through then Straits of Gibraltar, and knew they must be on their way to Africa. Now here they were in the harbor of Arzeu, watching the battle that was raging beyond the hills.

Laura was already sleeping peacefully when Judith went below decks. Most of the nurses occupied four-berth cabins, but Judith and Laura had been fortunate in their assignment to one which they had to themselves. It was tiny, hardly more than a cavity in the side of the ship, with only the width of a small washstand between their bunks and the further wall. They hung their clothing on the pipes which ran along this wall, and learned to dodge each other as they dressed and undressed. Judith very often went to bed after Laura, for her energy was more inexhaustible she was also generally up first, partly because she had been used to early rising all her life, and partly because she liked to listen to the first broadcasts from England, coming in over the BBC. She was especially eager to hear these the following morning, in order to compare them with those to which she had listened with such a feeling of unreality the night before. So she went to the lounge, where the officially controlled radio was located on the wall. But apparently very little news was given out from Great Britain, for the items were vague and brief and presently she left the lounge and went up on deck to stay until the time came for the church services conducted by the Army Chaplain.

Again, as in the case of the broadcast, she was unexpectedly disappointed. The scene was less exciting than she had anticipated. It was actually harder to follow the battle in the daylight than it had been in the darkness, when the flashes of flame had revealed the position of the troops. But the harbor was swarming with activity. Close to the Dutch freighter, a French luxury liner rode surprisingly at anchor. She had been peacefully following her regular run between Algiers and Casablanca, uninformed that a battle was in progress, when she had been tracked down by destroyers and seized as a prisoner of war. But she was wholly unmolested. Her multi-colored pennants, strung from stem to stern, were still fluttering gaily in the brisk breeze; her red and brown paint gleamed in the sunshine, amidst the sober gray with which she was surrounded; her passengers were crowding her decks and exchanging pleasantries with each other. From nearby troop ships, soldiers and sailors were pouring off, while tanks and jeeps were being lowered into barges by cranes. The deep blue waves were very rough, and every now and then, in this unloading process, a man lost his footing and plunged into the water, yelling for help and struggling from his equipment as he slid towards the sea. This equipment was still loosely worn, with straps untied; in most cases the men could shake it off before it weighted them down in the water. But there was always a moment of peril for them and of suspense for the rescuers and onlookers, before the victim were hauled back to safety, dripping and sputtering.

While this multitudinous moving was going on, doctors who had been variously transported from England, were assembling to join their own unit on the Dutch freighter, and about mid-afternoon, the naval personnel left it for the dock. Laura, joining Judith to observe the departure, glanced at her wrist watch.

"It's four o'clock already. I don't believe we'll be ordered off as late as this. If we're not that'll mean another night on board."

"Yes. We can't shake Mae West after all . . . I wish we'd been able to get more news on the radio today."

"If we had, we might have a better idea of how things are going over there." Laura glanced towards the hills, which were now beginning to shade into the sky. "I can't help wondering how many of the boys are getting hurt and how soon we can do something for them."

"I'm thinking about them, but I'm thinking about my family too. Mother especially. As we said yesterday, the folks at home know by this time we're in it and she'll be thinking that I'm not any safer than Jerome was, any longer."

Silence came between them again, and though they continued to stand side by side, neither of them found it easy to break; after a few desultory attempts they gave up the effort. As they started down to dinner, however, their attention was arrested by a poster on the bulletin board which stood at the head of the stairway leading to the mess hall. This notice was brief and to the point:

GENERAL MEETING TO BE CALLED IN MESS HALL BY
COMMANDING OFFICERS OF EACH UNIT
AT POSTED TIME:

AIR CORPS	19 O'CLOCK
EVACUATION	20 O'CLOCK
~~NAVAL UNIT~~	~~21 O'CLOCK~~"

The final item had been crossed out. The girls gathered that the Naval Unit had left earlier than had originally been planned, either without attending a general meeting or following attendance at one called after the posting of the notice. Without too much interest, they speculated on this while they ate their dinner which as usual was ample, excellent and well served; but they had ceased to find food and service stimulating; their minds were on the general meeting which was about to begin.

They took their places for it almost casually, sitting down, without formality, wherever they felt inclined, and rising to attention only when their commanding officer, Colonel Weiner, came in. He was a Pennsylvania Dutchman, ruddy, stocky and habitually brusque. He barked out his order "At ease!" and without preamble began his address.

"You will go to your cabins and put your belongings in order. Your suitcases are to be left locked. They will be brought to you later on shore. The officers will be in field dress, wearing the leggings and field uniform. The nurses will be in regulation slacks, blue shirts and sweaters. You will all pack your musette bags with three days' rations, clothing for three days and toilet articles, checking to see that water-purifying pills are included. You will check first aid pac and make sure it is on your pistol belt. When you leave the ship you will carry your musette bag on your back, have your gas mask on the left side, and the pistol belt around your waist. You will carry the heavy coat and nothing more than that over your arm. The flag which will be issued to you is to be pinned on the left outer sleeve. At no time will anyone purposely detach himself from his group. But if in the confusion of landing, accidental detachment takes place, you will resort to the password . . . Is that clear to everyone? If not, questions should be asked now."

Colonel Weiner paused appreciably. No one spoke. To most of his hearers, his instructions were wholly comprehensible, and those who were slightly confused were uncertain whether this confusion was due to the orders or to the general situation, so a slight embarrassment kept them silent. Oddly enough, Colonel Weiner seemed somewhat embarrassed himself. His next remarks were still rather roughly voiced, but somehow the habitual element of brusqueness seemed lacking from them.

"I do not need to remind you that you are about to go under fire. For most of you it will be the first time. For some of you it may be the last time. You know the reasons why it is ncessary that you should go. If you did not, none of you would be here now. But I think it may be helpful to you if you will concentrate on just one of these reasons. Keep saying to yourselves tomorrow, 'I am doing this for the folks at home. It is something they could not do for themselves, but that I can do for them and must do for them.' I believe it was Lincoln who said, 'I am doing the best I can, the very best I know how, and I mean to keep on doing it to the very end.' You might keep saying this to yourselves too. That is all. The meeting is dismissed."

The girls were awakened the next morning by the sound of light tapping. They heard it on the door next to theirs before they heard it on their own and it was followed by a low murmur. The chief nurse was making the rounds of the cabins, personally informing every nurse in the unit that she must be ready for disembarkation at ten and that immediately after breakfast she must come to the mess hall for final inspection. Again the meeting was apparently informal. The nurses assembled without any set formation, and sat down where they pleased. The chief

nurse walked among them making slight adjustments and
brief remarks, her manner brisk, her figure taut, her face
expressionless. They were to be divided alphabetically, she
informed them. The nurses whose names fell within the
first half of the alphabet would file to the side of the ship
first; the nurses whose names fell within the second half
would await their turn.

"Well, I'm gladder than ever my name's Hurlburt,"
Laura whispered to Judith. "Aren't you glad yours is Farman? And that F and H come so close together?"

"Yes, I'm very glad."

When the nurses filed up on deck again, they saw that
the enlisted personnel, which had still been gathered
around the companionway when they themselves had been
summoned to the mess hall, had now gone—ambulance
drivers, staff corps, corpsmen and technicians. The deck
was clearing fast, and an atmosphere of emptiness had
begun to permeate the upper regions of the ship, while
below conditions became more and more tumultuous.
The sea was even rougher than the day before; it was
hard enough to get down the swinging gangway in orderly
single file, and it was almost impossible to board the
heaving, sputtering barges. These rose with the waves,
banging down again on the surface of the water as it
swept away. A long time elapsed before a laden barge
could shove off and the process preceding departure had
been so hazardous and unpleasant that there was not
much talking or joking among the doctors and nurses on
the half-hour run to the rocky platform which served the
town as a dock. Then the hard scramble to land on this
was followed by a tedious wait which, Laura finally muttered to Judith, was about as lengthy as the trip from
England to Africa. She had been briefly intrigued by the
experience of passing under the shadowy bows of other
ships on the way to shore, and both amazed and amused
to find how much smaller the once mighty freighter seemed,
now they were off it. She had also found some diversion
in watching the unloading of jeeps and half-tracks which
was still going on. But after all, she had seen the same

thing yesterday. Enough was enough. She was tired and hot and hungry and thirsty . . .

The musette bags were growing heavier by the minute. Some of the nurses were already buckled down by them before they reached the shore; others, who had managed to keep erect during the difficult crossing, instinctively tried to shift the weight from one shoulder to the other while they sat on the rock. Judith was almost the only one who not drooping visibly before they were half through their march across town. The order had finally come to fall in, and they had started in formation, the enlisted men marching first, four abreast, then the officers, two abreast, then the nurses, also two abreast, and led by the head nurse. The midday heat was intense, the sky brassy, the dust smothering. The streets were crowded with goats and donkeys, cats and dogs, and choked with Arabs and halfbreeds in filthy flowing robes: garrulous old men displaying their festering sores, whining children who thrust their grimy hands into the nurse's faces, demanding gum and chocolate. Beyond the mob, the girls could catch occasional glimpses of a sidewalk café, with little tin chairs and tables set out in front of an open doorway, or of the portals and domes of a mosque; but for the most part the low, sand-colored adobe buildings were too nondescript to attract their attention.

The clear sound of ringing bells, cleaving musically through the heavy air, came gratefully to their ears. They were approaching a large sprawling structure, mustard-yellow in color, and built with a high flat roof, which seemed to be a Christian church of some sort. It stood in a courtyard, surmounted by a square belfry and surrounded with a high blank wall intersected by an iron gate, through which a stream of people was passing to and fro. For a moment it looked to the members of the unit as if this incongruous edifice might be their strange destination. Then they saw that opposite it was a double row of long dilapidated huts, set down in a bare enclosure fenced in by wire. The place was deserted, but there was something barrack-like in its forlorn appearance, and presently they were given to understand that it was a former French garrison, already captured by American troops, and that temporarily it was to serve the unit as a shelter.

Viewed from within, the huts proved even more depressing than they had from without. They each consisted of a single large room, with open apertures for windows and a door at either end, and contained nothing except frames made of two long and two short sticks over which wire had been stretched by way of bedsprings. On top of the wire lay burlap bags and bundles of straw, which the girls lifted up gingerly, and hastily flung outside, making bonfires of them with the least possible delay. The bags hardly needed carrying, Laura remarked with disgust; they were crawling on their own impetus already. Big beetles dropped from the walls, their shells crackling when they were trodden under foot, their broken bellies smearing the clay floors; these carcasses added to the cultch which had to be cleared away before the girls could spread out their issued coats for makeshift beds. At one end of the barracks, a mess hall and kitchen were located, equipped with a long flat iron stove thickly covered with grease, a motley collection of odd-shaped pots and pans which were also filthy, and long tables for cutting meat and serving food. The head nurse, after one swift glance at the condition of these quarters, closed the doors and told her charges to keep out. They would have to lunch on bar chocolate, she said. By suppertime, perhaps they could heat up something. There was a little driftwood lying about, which could be salvaged for an outdoor fire. Of course the complete lack of water was a handicap, but in one respect at least, she hoped the nurses would soon be more comfortable: some enlisted men had been set to work to dig slit-trenches to supplement the square sieve-like sewer, surrounded by wilted reeds, which had so far constituted the sole sanitary equipment of the garrison.

"If they hadn't done something to supplement it pretty soon, we'd have all burst," Laura remarked in an undertone to Judith as the head nurse went on her way. "Do you realize how many hours it was between the time we left the ship and the time these luxurious accommodations were available?"

"It was a pretty long time. But we didn't come to Africa for the sake of the porcelain plumbing, Laura."

"Weren't you uncomfortable?"

"Yes, I was uncomfortable. But I was so amused by those cute little Arabs, I forgot about it after a while. How do you suppose they ever learned to say gum and chocolate so soon? You wouldn't think they'd have even found out what those are by this time."

"Well it would have taken more than a few filthy Arab kids to divert my thoughts at that point. My sweater was killing me too. I tried to inch out of it but I couldn't. And I kept wondering what we'd do if we got the curse, on top of everything else."

"We'll have to get it sooner or later. It probably wouldn't be any worse to have it here than where we're going next."

"Where are we going next?"

"Well naturally I don't know any more than you do. But I don't imagine it's furnished with private bathrooms, wherever it is. Listen, Laura, you're not going to let this get you down, the very first day, are you? Remember what Colonel Weiner told us last night we better keep saying over and over to ourselves—'I'm here to do something for the folks at home that they couldn't do for themselves. But I can do it for them and I must.' "

"Oh, Judith, don't *preach!*"

"I'm not preaching. But I do think that was a grand slogan he gave us. I've been saying it to myself all day. Come on, let's see what we can do about that driftwood. It'll be fun to get a fire going. You won't have such a gloomy outlook on life after you get something in your stomach besides bar chocolate and lukewarm water out of a canteen. The fire'll feel good too. It's funny, isn't it, the way it starts getting cold here the minute the sun goes down, when it's so hot in the middle of the day?"

The fire did feel good and the picnic supper worked wonders for Laura. She was ashamed that she had been such a sissy, she whispered to Judith as they lay down on the coats they had spread out on the floor, and the next day she was a good sport about everything. The nurses had been told to keep as close as possible to the walls, when it was necessary for them to move around the enclosure, as a good many snipers were still abroad; and stray shots resounded with sufficient frequency to prove that the warning was not an empty one. But Laura joked about the snipers with Judith and the other nurses who were passing the time by making a Red Cross flag out of some scraps of cloth they had found. When the flag was finished, they played cards until it was time for another picnic supper, and after supper they lay down, grateful for the folding cots which a detail had brought up from the docks. The second night was far more comfortable than the first. Really, the day had been sort of fun, Laura said drowsily as she drifted off, and Judith, who was still wide awake, answered that she thought it had been grand; she really felt right at home in the old garrison now and would be sorry to leave it.

She expressed no regrets, however, when the order to do so came through the next morning. On fifteen minutes' notice, the nurses were piled into Army trucks which came charging into the garrison and quickly charged forth again, bearing the girls out to a flat clay-like countryside, where close-clipped vineyards edged the one rutty road. They passed through a forlorn and empty village on their way to their unknown destination, and Laura, seeing that Judith was looking around her with fascination, quickly evinced similar interest herself.

"Do you know the name of this burg?"

"I heard someone say it was St. Cloud. It's probably named for the one in France. Isn't there a St. Cloud just outside of Paris?"

"I don't know. I've never heard of it and I've never been there. But if it's anything like its namesake, I guess I don't need to shed any tears over my loss."

The truck swerved sharply in order to skirt a dead mule which blocked the center of the thoroughfare, and in doing so struck some shattered fragments of artillery which were strewn helter-skelter along the roadside. An unseen

rifle cracked sharply, and a bullet whizzed by, searing a
tip of Judith's ear as she quickly ducked. She put her
hand to it, instinctively, and rubbed it for a moment. But
she shook her head when Laura asked her if it hurt, and
leaned forward to ask an eager question of the truck
driver.

"Have we much further to go, Corporal?"

"Naw, just a few kilometers. Maybe you ain't heard
about these little short-changed miles they have around
here."

"Tell me about them."

"Well, I never passed no arithmetic test in my life,
so I don't know as I can. The best way I can figure though,
you take five kilometers and get three miles out of 'em.
If you got less than five kilometers to work with, you're
out of luck, that's all, unless your specialty was mathe-
matics before the Army nabbed you."

"Don't they have speed limits in Africa?" Judith inquired, without complete irrelevance.

"Naw," said the Corporal again. "Leastwise if they do,
I don't know nothing about 'em. I just told you I never
was no scholar. If the Ayrabs or the Frenchies either one
wants me to slow down to sixty, they gotta put up signs
in the King's English."

"But supposing your commanding officer——"

"Oh, he's a swell guy. Likes to get there himself . . .
Do you see them tents out there in that oat field right
ahead of us? Well, that's what we're slowly aiming for.
The latest in hospitals. Latest is right too. It's so late it
ain't built yet. But I guess when you girls get to work it
will be. Better had, I'll say, if you ask me. When a scrap
like this one's on, somebody's liable to get hurt. And I
don't mean no singed ear neither."

He brought his truck to a stop with a jerk, and Judith,
thanking him for the good time he had given her, jumped
out and again looked around her with an experssion of
fascination. Above the matted stubble which covered the
ground, four large tents were rising; beyond these, a number of pup tents were already scattered about; and everywhere there were signs that the building was just beginning.

The oat field itself, like the vine-covered countryside through which she had just passed, was completely flat; but beyond it, a great purple mountain loomed against the sky, casting a long cool shadow which darkened and softened the drab ground, and turned the dingy green of the canvas tents to luminous black.

"I'm so glad we've got a mountain," she said, turning to Laura. She spoke almost as if a lost and precious personal possession had suddenly been restored to her. "I like the sea, but it isn't the same as having a mountain, not to anyone that was raised on a hill, with bigger hills all around it. Well, I suppose now we find out which tent is ours, and get our bedding rolls from wherever they are and have a snack of supper. If we get organized ourselves, that's probably all we can do tonight. It gets dark so terribly early."

Judith's assumption proved correct; by the time their quarters were assigned and their equipment in place, it was too late for the nurses to do anything more that night. But the next morning the first sound they heard was one of steady rhythmic pounding which went on and on. It came from hammers hitting stakes as the latter were driven into the ground; and as fast as tents were fastened to these stakes, the nurses went inside, helping corpsmen to set up cots on the bare ground. Soon there were twenty-two beds in each tent, with a few bedside tables scattered among them and some boxes for charts. There were two sheets for each bed, one blanket, one pillow and one pillowcase and on top of these one face cloth and one towel neatly folded. The tent was no longer a mere canvas covering, set out in a stubble field; it was a hospital and a hospital which was filling fast.

Laden ambulances and trucks were tearing up to the oat field now. Corpsmen were bringing stretcher cases straight to the cots, while soldiers still able to hobble were helping each other. In the receiving tent the uniforms of the wounded men had already been exchanged for pajamas, which like the bedclothing and towels, had come from the medical supply tent, now also up. At the same time this change was taking place, the corpsmen had made out the patients' "field jackets" from their "dog tags," afterwards folding and clipping the small squares of paper which bore so misleading a name to the pockets of their pajamas, or tying the papers around the men's wrists. Only the worst wounded had been washed, and even this bathing had been scanty and superficial, for water was at a premium; but they had all been nourished. Big cans of chocolate and coffee were already heating, and there was an ample supply of condensed milk and granulated sugar to go with these, besides plenty of Spam. One of the officers had bargained, locally and successfully, for some tangarines, and every patient had been given one of these to suck. For the most part, the men ate and drank readily, even eagerly. They had all received first aid at battalion stations, whence those in a critical condition had been sent straight to the city hospital in Oran. The men who were left were the ones with shell shock, with broken legs and arms, with burns caused by exploding hand grenades and unexploded shells. By evening the nurses, who had been hurriedly assigned to general duty that morning, were given detailed duty, and Judith was placed in the tent which was set aside for shellshocked patients. Some of these men were deafened, some dazed. A few were crying, helplessly and hysterically. Others were swearing, using the "man's language" which had long since ceased to seem an insult to Judith. Many of them, utterly oblivious of their changed surroundings, were shouting and screaming—"Look out, here comes a shell!"—"Everybody in a fox hole, boys!"—"Damn you, that one's mine!" Only one man was completely unconscious. Such light as there was in the tent came from three small lanterns which swung from the ridgepole, one at either end and one in the middle. It happened that the unconscious man's cot was almost midway between two of these lanterns, and, in the dimness, Judith found it difficult to decipher the inscription on his "field jacket." She unclipped the small folded piece of paper from his pocket, and walking quietly to the center of the tent, held it up to the light.

"*Peter MacDonald*"—she read—"*Correspondent, Washington* Bulletin, *Washington, D. C. Protestant. Blood type*

O. By stretcher. Unconscious. Shell shock and shrapnel wounds."

For a moment she stood perfectly still, looking at the paper she held with a gaze as unbelieving as it was captivated. Then she started slowly back to the cot she had left. She had already realized that this man was badly injured, but now she began to examine him more closely. He was unshaven and his face was still smeared with dust, though apparently it had been superficially washed. There was a deep shrapnel wound in his left shoulder and another in the calf of his right leg; there were also several lesser ones scattered through his thighs. There was a hot water bottle at his feet and another beside his body, but they were only lukewarm. She sent a corpsman to the mess hall for hot water, trying not to worry because there were no additional bottles for so serious a case. After putting those which had been refilled back in place, and taking Peter's pulse, which was very slow, she went back to the improvised desk where the nurses who had been on duty during the day had left their reports, and from one of these found that blood plasma had already been administered, that dressings had twice been applied, and that the pulse condition in itself was not alarming. There seemed to be nothing she could do in the way of more personal service at the moment, so she conscientiously began to check her other patients. But involuntarily she returned to Peter MacDonald, bending over him with a solicitude which no matter how hard she tried, she could not feel towards any of the others. She straightened up to see the chief nurse standing beside her, and hastened to rise herself, words coming with a rush.

"Lieutenant Arnold, I've come across a friend of the family, who's also quite a well-known person. This is Peter MacDonald, the war correspondent for the Washington *Bulletin.* I haven't read many of his articles myself, but I understand they've caused quite a stir."

"Yes, I should imagine they would. I happened to see the one he wrote on the Dieppe raid and I'll never forget it. It was the most thrilling piece of descriptive writing I ever ran into. As a matter of fact, I was just trying to locate Mr. MacDonald. An officer who's in one of the other tents with a broken arm said he thought MacDonald must be here somewhere, as they've been together right along. They were both on the same ship in the Battle of Oran Harbor and it was one of those sunk by the French. According to this Captain Briggs, MacDonald was wounded early in the engagement, but he remained at his post on the vessel that picked them up and took them ashore. He went right on sending out dispatches, in the face of enemy fire. After being ordered to abandon ship, he swam ashore, and filed another story right away." The head nurse paused, and looked down at Peter with increased attention and admiration. "Apparently he kept right on covering and filing stories. After all, the Battle of Oran Harbor took place four days ago and it's a long way from here . . . So he's a friend of yours, Lieutenant Farman?"

"No, I never saw him before myself. He came to our house on Farman Hill once, on an assignment, but I was away on a case at the time. My father and mother liked him a lot, though. And later on, when they went to Washington, he arranged to have another staff writer on the *Bulletin* look after them. . . . He'd already started around the world himself, then. But my parents got to know him, indirectly, that way too, because this friend of his did so much for them." Judith hesitated a minute and then she added, "I believe he was very much in love with my sister Jenness. She—she died last spring. I am afraid her death was a terrible blow to him."

"It must have been. And it's very natural you should feel a great interest in Mr. MacDonald. I'll try to see that you're relieved in other ways as much as possible, so that you can give most of your time to him for the present. He needs special attention in any case. I hope we can get all of that shrapnel out of him tomorrow. You may stay here, Lieutenant Farman, unless and until otherwise ordered."

Judith pulled up a packing case and sat down. There was still nothing definite that she could do, but she was thankful to remain temporarily where she was, if only to collect her thoughts. These continued to be distracted by the shouts and screams of other men, and when there seemed to be a chance that she might quiet one of these, she rose and went to him. But she kept going back to Peter, working on her report in the intervals of watching him, and also going on with the rest of her routine. The dressings on the two deep wounds needed changing again before long, and she removed the bloodstained bandages and adroitly replaced them with fresh ones; there was not enough gauze to do this more than once, but she reinforced them several times. About one o'clock, Peter began to move and moan; she straightened his bed clothing, and bent closer to see if she could catch any words, but his mutterings were unintelligible. The night went on and on.

It was just as dawn was breaking that he opened his eyes. At first he looked unseeingly ahead of him. Then gradually his gaze focussed and cleared in semi-recognition. Something resembling a smile twisted his pale lips and he tried to stretch out his hand.

"Jenness," he whispered hoarsely. "Why, Jenness! What-are-you-doing-on-this-damn-battlefield?"

Judith took his groping fingers gently in hers. "There, there!" she said soothingly. "You're not on the battle-field any longer. You're in a nice safe hospital. And I'm not Jenness. I'm just a nurse."

"You-needn't-try-to-put-anything-like-that-over-on-me," he retorted. His voice was still shaky, but there was re-turning spirit in it already. "Don't-you-suppose-I-know-my-own-girl? Two-don't-come-this-much-alike——" He gripped her fingers, as if to test their reality and looked at her more fixedly, but still smiling. "If you're not on that damn field, what am I doing where you went? Did the bloody bastards get me after all?"

CHAPTER 28

COMPARED TO the tents in the oat field, the city hospital in Oran, where convalescent patients as well as those in critical condition were cared for, seemed almost painfully clean, spacious and airy, especially after the glare and noise of the crowded street on which it stood. Judith had come in from Arzeu on an Army truck, which had deposited her at the Continental Hotel; from there she had threaded her way through the usual motley crowd of Arabs and animals, hoping against hope that nothing would happen to her blue uniform before she escaped from the dirty crew. After weeks of living in shirts and slacks, it seemed good to have on a well-tailored skirt and blouse again, and to feel that her hair was neatly confined by her overseas cap. She went rapidly up the steps of the hospital, which was flanked on either side by apartment houses, and entered a large open foyer, suggestive of an adequate but barren hotel lounge, with long corridors branching from it in every direction. Then she stepped up to the desk and spoke to the non-commissioned officer on duty.

"Good morning, Sergeant. This is Lieutenant Farman. I've come to see Mr. MacDonald."

"Yes, Lieutenant. He's expecting you. Turn down there to the right and take the self-operating elevator to the seventh floor. Perhaps you didn't know that this is Oran's skyscraper. When you get to the top, the floor nurse will show you the way to Mr. MacDonald's room."

Like the foyer, the corridor which Judith eventually reached had a white tiled floor, high whitewashed walls, and long French windows opening down the middle. Judith regarded it with admiration as she went on, and finally voiced this high approval to the floor nurse who was acting as her guide. This nurse shrugged her shoulders slightly.

"You should have seen it when we moved in. We did nothing but scrub for three days. We haven't routed out all the sources of filth yet. But it does look all right now, and actually it is a lot better . . . . This is Mr. MacDonald's room, Lieutenant Farman. You'll find him alone. His roommate's almost well and is out on pass."

There was a frame screen in front of the open door, and Judith entered so quietly that Peter was not instantly aware of her presence. Judith was glad of this, because it gave her a moment of grace in which to take in his appearance. He was sitting up in bed, looking remarkably healthy and preternaturally clean. His bed linen was immaculate, and so were his white pajamas. His skin had the fresh clarity indicative of frequent bathing, and even his fingernails ended in snowy arcs. A pleasant breeze was blowing through the room, ruffling his well-washed hair around his temples.

Judith had a momentary pang at the thought of her own unkempt patients, whom she could not even attempt to keep looking like this, and suddenly she felt drab and dingy herself. She had not been able to take a tub bath or to get a shampoo since she left the Dutch freighter . . . Peter had a cigarette in one hand and a fountain pen in the other. In front of him was a large wooden lap board, littered with sheets of yellow paper already partially covered with notes to which he was rapidly and intently adding. But after a moment, he sensed the fact that he was not alone and glanced up. Instantly his face lightened with his agreeable grin and he put down the pen and moved the lap board aside.

"Well, see who's here!" he said heartily. "Looking like a million dollars too! Come over here, where I can really take in all this swank." As he spoke he held out his free hand with a welcoming gesture. Then he put down the cigarette too, and held out both hands. "I like you a lot, in skirts," he said. "But someday I hope I'll see you without a jacket and cap too. You've got a figure and a mop of hair just like your sister's, haven't you? Of course you must have been told that a thousand times."

"No, I haven't. Jenness was always the glamour girl of the family. I don't think it ever occurred to most people that we looked alike."

"Well the resemblance would never escape the reportorial eye. I probably should have called you Jenness instinctively, wherever I'd come face to face with you, even if I hadn't been shellshocked when I first saw you . . . How about a nice kiss for the wounded here?"

"Peter, you don't need to be told that Army nurses don't kiss their male patients."

"I bet some of them do," Peter retorted. "They may have to sneak it in, but I bet they do it. Not that it matters. We could start the custom, if it doesn't exist. Anyway, I'm not your patient any more. I've escaped from your clutches. But I'm still an imprisoned convalescent, who needs cheering. Do you really have to be so professional? There, that's lots better . . . Now sit down and tell me how you manage to pass the time since my lamented departure from tent city."

"There's no difficulty about passing the time," Judith answered, seating herself, with somewhat heightened color, in the small white chair by the bed. "We're getting new patients all the time. The Arabs have started to bring in their children. Most of them are suffering from malnutrition, but there have been victims from accidents too. Besides, most of the soldiers don't stage such quick comebacks as you did. When I think of the state you were in that first night! All that shrapnel still inside of you, when it ought have been out days before, and that awful concussion! And there you'd been filing stories right along, wounds or no wounds, shell shock or no shell shock! It was a good thing the surgery tent started to function the next morning."

Peter lighted another cigarette and waved it airily. "The *Bulletin* sent me abroad with the fixed idea that I was going to file stories right along," he said. "You don't know Sheppard as well as I do. If you did, you'd realize he'd think a little shrapnel and a slight shock were just all in the day's work, and that the guy who let them hold up a piece had better get himself a new job, selling ribbons, or moving lawns or something of that sort. Just the same he's sent me a swell cable, saying my stuff isn't going over so bad at that. I'll show it to you if I can ever find it. It's here somewhere among my notes. I had it in my hand just before you came in, gloating over it for about the 'steenth time. No, not that one—That one's from Joe. He cabled too. Gosh, you don't need to drop it like that! It won't burn you. . . . Well, so you're looking after young Arabs? How do you like it?"

"Very much. I like it all."

"Not wearing you down, now that the novelty's worn off?"

"No, I like it better and better all the time."

"Then I bet you've got a beau, you fickle flirt. Just when I thought I was getting you nicely broken in for myself too."

"No, Peter, I haven't. Honestly I haven't. I haven't got a beau and I don't want one. I'm too interested in my work. I—I love it."

"The hell you do!" Peter exclaimed irreverently. Then, scrutinizing her more carefully, he added in a different tone, "I guess you do at that. But you're not so wedded to it, are you, that you won't go out on the town with men when I'm up and around again?"

"Of course not. I'd be delighted to go out with you, Peter, any time you want me to, when I can get leave. Not that I believe there's much to do in Oran, though I don't know from personal experience. This is the first time I've been away from tent city."

"High time too!" Again he studied her, noticing that the flush which had come into her cheeks when she spoke of her work still colored them, though the flush that had come when he kissed her had lasted only a minute. Her lashes were wet too, and she had not looked him full in the face again yet. Her voice was unsteady when she spoke. She probably was dead on her feet, for one thing. He'd seen something of the hours she kept, and the conditions under which her work was done; and evidently there hadn't been a day's let-up. But even so . . . "We'll find something to do," he went on. "There must be shows, of a sort, at the cafés. Probably pretty bum, but any show's a pastime. And then there are dances. My roommate's been raving about the dances at the Continental and at the Casino. He says there are patios and swimming pools and everything that it take. He hasn't much above the ears, so perhaps it's not all as hot as he indicates. However, a dance is a dance for all that. And then there are shops, quote exotic, colorful, mysterious shops end quote. Don't tell me you're not interested in dancing and shows and shopping? You must have some human weaknesses."

"I have any number of them. And I am interested. I'm interested in everything. Some of the other girls have been to those dances and they've had a grand time. They've bought some lovely curios too—embroidered scarfs and wood carvings and handmade jewelry. I thought I might get a little ornament of some kind for my sister-in-law. I don't suppose she'd wear it, while she's in mourning. But she's very fond of jewelry under normal conditions. The women in her family always have been. She told me once that at their ancestral home, Bellefontaine, there was a secret drawer for jewels, equipped with a golden key, at the head of every bed."

"Those poor planters stinted themselves in every way, didn't they?"

"Now you're teasing me again. I'm serious. I really would like to get a ring or something for her."

"I'd like to get a ring, or something for you," suggested Peter. "Look, it won't be long before you get leave again, will it?"

According to him it was eons. He was quite cross about it, saying he would probably be in Berlin by the time Judith tore herself away from her Arab kids long enough to pay him any attention. As a matter of fact, she came to the hospital several more times before Peter was pronounced sufficiently convalescent to "go out on the town," and accompanied him on his first excursion, which took him as far as a sidewalk café. They settled themselves at one of the little tin tables, unhurriedly sipping diluted sauterne and listening to a third-rate accordion player; and eventually they went inside, and "assisted" at a review, in which some rather dilapidated dancers who reeked of perspiration and cheap perfume gave a tawdry leg show. Before it was over, Peter glanced rather fearfully, several times, at Judith; he did not feel at all sure that she might not find parts of it almost insufferably offensive. But her expression betrayed no distaste and, when she caught him looking at her, she returned his glance with a pleasant smile.

"You're not getting too tired, are you?" she asked solicitously. "We can leave any time, you know. I wouldn't be disappointed if we didn't stay to the end, I've had such a nice evening already."

"I'm not at all tired. I wasn't sure how well you could take this sort of thing, that's all. But you seem to be bearing up under it nobly."

"I've enjoyed it. Everything's so different here, Peter, and so exciting. Then I like being with you too."

She spoke without a trace of coquetry, and a few minutes later she said that even if Peter did not feel tired, it was high time he was getting back to bed: she was not going to have his nurse on her neck, and she would get on another nurse's neck in a minute, herself, if some such careless creature let one of her patients get overtired. Peter grumbled that he was being browbeaten and bullied, but eventually he consented to being dragged away from the review, only to break into fresh complaints over Judith's casual manner of leave-taking when they reached the city hospital. This time Judith spoke to him more curtly.

"You must be even crazier than I thought you were, if you think I'm going into a clinch with you here."

"I didn't say anything about a clinch—not what you'd call a real clinch. But it can't do any harm to give a poor sick fellow a nice little good-night kiss."

"This is a public street and I'm in uniform. I'm not just a girl out for a good time; I'm a member of the armed forces of the United States. It was all right that—that once in your room, just to show you I was glad to see you again, and to find you were getting along so well. But I'm not going to be guilty of conduct unbecoming an officer and—and a lady. If we're going to keep having arguments about this, Peter, I'm not going out with you any more."

She left him so abruptly that he could not have stopped her without doing so forcibly, and he neither saw her nor heard from her for a week. During the interval, he wrote her several notes, all of which went unanswered, and finally he got hold of a press car and went out to tent city himself. The head nurse, whom he approached first, was disposed to regard his plea with leniency: Lieutenant Farman had been working very hard, she said, and had some leave coming to her; it would readily be granted. But Judith, when he finally found her, declined to ask for it.

She was standing beside the great canvas pouch, suspended on a tripod between the tents, which he had learned was a "Lister bag," filling an enamel basin with water from one of its four small spigots. She shook her head and went on with her work, almost without looking at him.

"We're terribly shorthanded, Peter. Three of the nurses are flat on their backs with dysentery this minute. Someone's got to do their work."

"Have they been flat on their backs all this last week?"

"No. But it's true they are now. I'm not stringing you."

"Not slapping me on the wrist either, by any chance, are you?"

"Yes. I warned you and you wouldn't listen. So there was nothing I could do except keep out of your way."

"But I have listened. I am now a changed man. I shall not so much as lift the hem of your snowy skirt to my unworthy lips." He glanced with twinkling eyes, at her dingy slacks, and grinned; but his tone was more serious than his words or his manner. "I thought we'd go shopping today. I've found a place where they sell carved bookends and salad bowls. I thought you'd find those useful for the fine library to which you are constantly adding, and for those dainty dishes you are so skilled in preparing and which all the most eminent medical authorities assure us should form a prominent part of the daily diet."

In spite of herself, Judith laughed. Greatly encouraged, Peter continued his recital.

"And I found another place where they have great wide bracelets that look just like handcuffs except that they are made of gold and silver. This store sells nice colored stones too—blue stones and green stones and red stones and everything. You said something about wanting to get an ornament for your sister-in-law. I don't like to hurry you, but there's a rumor going around that all jewelry's about to be frozen. The unscrupulous Yankees have been taking advantages of the poor innocent natives, so the authorities have stepped in."

"Peter, your paper just wastes money paying you to write stories. You'd do it anyway. You'd rather get off a good story than eat or sleep. It's as natural to you as breathing."

"I'm glad you appreciate my talents. But I'd also like a word to the effects that your appreciate my company."

"Peter, I haven't time to go into Oran with you today, no matter what the head nurse says. Honestly, I haven't. But I'll tell you what I will do, if you'll behave yourself."

"All right. Go ahead and tell me."

"I'll take a walk with you after I get off duty tonight. Of course, if you don't care about hanging around tent city that long, it's perfectly all right with me. On the other hand, you might do some snooping and get a story. You wouldn't have to snoop very hard at that. There are any number of stories staring me in the face. The only trouble is I don't know how to write them and I haven't the time anyway."

"Don't let that worry you. I think you've got something there. You tell me these stories that are staring you in the face and I'll find the time to write them down. I've got more time than anything else just now. I don't know how these damn doctors think I'm going to stay on the payroll, if they won't let me get back to my job. But we'll let that pass for the moment. You tell me the stories, just the way you're talking to me now. That's all you have to do. You don't need to know how to write them. I know how to write them. And you'll be making a substantial contribution to the noble cause of bigger and better journalism."

"Do you mean it? Or are you still raving on?"

"I never was raving on. You can start right in telling me stories while we take this walk you began to bait me with. I'll see what I can dig up for myself in the meantime. But I'd like to know when we meet again and where we're going, if both those items aren't military secrets."

"I'll meet you right here at seven-thirty. And we'll walk out to that olive grove on the south side of the field. You can see it now, if you look hard. There's an old stone well there we can sit on. It's a lovely place."

"It sounds so. Also sounds as if you'd been there before."

"For heaven's sake! Of course I've been there before! It isn't a quarter of a mile away. But I haven't been there for a—for a——"

"For a date?"

"No."

"And it's clearly understood that this is a date?"

"Yes. That is, if——"

"If I promise there'll be no improper advances?"

"Peter, you're the absolute limit! If you're going to talk that way——"

"Isn't it all right if I don't act that way? And I won't. Cross my heart and hope to die. As I said before, I shall not so much as lift the hem of your snowy skirt to my——"

"Oh, do stop talking about *hems!* Do stop making an ass of yourself! Do let me get back to my *job!*"

She was off again, but there was no real indignation in her departure this time, as there had been the time before. She was laughing when she disappeared and waving a gay hand, and she was back on the dot of the appointed time. Somehow she had created the chance to get cleaned up and change her clothes. Her golden head was bare, but she had on the uniform which Peter liked. Everything

about her was attractive. She did not walk as-if she were
weary, but with the same swinging grace which had always characterized Jenness. It seemed to Peter, as he
looked at her, that there had been a change in Judith's
walk in the brief time since he had first met her. She had
always carried herself sturdily and erectly, but there had
not always been this freedom in her progress; she moved
now like one released. The way in which she addressed
the stray Arabs they met after they crossed the field and
came to the road which skirted it, was also characteristic
of this new freedom. These people came and went to the
hospital now to see their relatives who were patients, and
they also kept their fruit stands on the adjacent road; so it
was natural that by this time Judith should act towards
them without constraint. But it was evident that the feeling
was more positive than this, that actual friendliness existed
between her and the nomads. They smiled when they saw
her coming, and she stopped and spoke a few words of
Arabic with a rising inflection, as if she were questioning
their accuracy, yet without much embarrassment or hesitation. Her hearers were obviously delighted at her efforts,
and the colloquy which ensued caused a slight delay, which
Peter accepted with thinly veiled impatience.

"You seem to have the desert population feeding out
of your hand," he observed, as Judith finally detached herself pleasantly from her admirers and continued her interrupted walk towards the grove at Peter's side.

"Well, after all, I feed out of theirs!" she answered gaily.
"I don't know what we'd do without their tangerines. Those
have been a godsend from the beginning."

"I'll say that something seems to keep up your strength.
Don't you ever get tired? You don't act as if you did."

"Of course I do. But it doesn't get me down, the way it
does some of the girls. I'm stronger than most of them to
start with. And then there's always the thrill of the work,
for a stimulant. I don't need to explain that to you, because you've got the same feeling about your own job. Any
man who will go plunging around for three days, full of
shrapnel, before he drops in his tracks——"

"Well we won't go into all that again. Look, I think

you've really delivered the goods, with this grove of yours. I thought you might be merely telling me a tall tale. But I can see already it's quite a swell spot."

"A swell spot! What an expression! It's beautiful, Peter. It's—well, it's sort of Biblical. Don't you see what I mean?"

Ungrudgingly, he admitted that he did. Before coming to Africa he had been to Palestine and Syria, and there he had been entranced by the silvery effect of the olive trees on the misty plains below the hills and in the orchards beside the springs. The same delicate gauzy radiance enveloped this grove and its deep cool well. Judith sat down on the limestone rim and looked down at the dark patterns which the moonlight was making with the olive branches on the pale ground. Peter stood and looked at Judith.

"There's a nice Bible story, too, that began at a well," he said finally, breaking in on the companionable silence. "About a girl named Rebekah and a fellow named Isaac, as I recall it. We could start a story of our own at this well, Judith."

"Yes. I've been thinking about what you said. I believe I've got one for you that you'll like. It's about a sergeant. He has the same cot you were in when you were at tent city and he's got a bad case of shell shock too. He——"

"Did he come out of his trance calling you pet names too?"

"No. That is, not exactly. But——"

"Judith, when I said we might start a story here, I wasn't thinking of what I said this afternoon. I didn't mean a story about a sergeant either. The idea of starting a story about a sergeant on a beautiful moonlight night like this! It makes me shudder to consider such a sacrilege. I meant a story about us."

"What sort of a story?"

"A story like Isaac's and Rebekah's. He took her in a tent and——"

"Peter, you promised you wouldn't!"

"I promised I wouldn't make any improper advances. This isn't an improper advance. It's an honorable proposal of marriage. As you'd know if you'd let me finish my quotation. I'm surprised you didn't remember the story better yourself. Isaac took Rebekah into his tent—his mother Sarah's tent to be exact—and 'she became his wife and he loved her.' Do you remember now?"

"Yes, I remember now."

"Well——"

Judith was still studying the dark patterns on the pale ground. She sat silent for so long that at last Peter leaned over and put his hand gently on hers. Still she did not look up and he was appalled to feel a warm wet teardrop on his hand.

"Why, Judith!" he exclaimed. "What have I said? What have I done? I didn't mean to be crude or clumsy. I didn't realize I was. Of course I'm an incurable clown, but just the same——"

"No, no. It isn't that. The story's beautiful, Peter, beautiful and symbolic and—and appropriate. I'm touched that you told it, that you thought of telling it, in this place and in—in such a connection. It gives me an insight into your character that I didn't have before. Of course I knew you were brave and brilliant but——"

"Now, now! If I'm such a paragon as all that I must be a great catch too. What are you crying about, if I haven't offended you and if I'm not obnoxious to you?"

"I'm not crying. That is, I've almost stopped. Crying, I mean. I ought to have stopped all the rest of this long ago."

"Why, if you like me?"

"Because I don't love you. At least, I'm not in love with you. I've grown very much attached to you, but I don't want to make the same mistake twice."

"What do you mean, make the same mistake twice?"

"I loved Dexter Abbott. I've told you about him. I loved him from the time I was a little girl. I thought I was in love with him too. If I hadn't thought so, I never would have got engaged to him. But I finally found out I'd never wanted to be his wife, not really. If I had, I couldn't have left him the way I did. It took me a long time to understand that; I was awfully angry when I found he didn't want me any more. But that was really just hurt pride. I think it was while I was coming over in the convoy, that I began to understand. And while I was watching the battle from the harbor, I suddenly understood everything. There's something about danger that makes you see more clearly than you can in safety."

"Well I'll grant you that. But I won't grant that just because you finally found out you never were in love with Dexter Abbott it's any sign that you couldn't fall for me. I'd say it was all to the good. I'd say——"

"You've said a lot already, Peter. Please let me say one or two things now. You see it didn't take me so long to realize I wasn't in love with you as it took me to realize I'd never been in love with Dexter. I recognize the symptoms better now. I knew, before you left tent city for the Oran hospital that I cared for you a lot, that I wanted you for my friend. And I thought it was all right to go along with things the way they were, because I didn't believe you'd fall in love with me. I thought you might like a little light diversion, but that's different. I thought I could look out for myself all right, if that was what you wanted. I didn't think you'd get out of hand. Then when you began to——"

"Then when I began to, you froze up and ran off. But that wasn't because you didn't like me, Judith. It was because you didn't like my technique. I'll admit I made a mistake. I ought to have known you weren't an easy necker. Just the same, you ought not to have taken me too seriously. You ought to have known I really wasn't up to mischief."

"I did. That is, I thought you were experimenting, like most men. Because of course there was always the off chance that you were mistaken, that you might find out I was an easy necker after all."

"Well suppose now that we've both got that off our chests, we drop the subject. Because that's very much in the past tense anyway. And what counts right now——"

"I don't believe you'd be quite so eager to put it in the past tense if your conscience weren't hurting you a little. But what counts right now isn't that you've asked me to marry you. It's also whether you're in love with me."

"You know damn well I'm in love with you. So if you wouldn't mind, I'd appreciate it if we could have a little

less talking and a little more action for a while. I don't
want to seem to hurry you, and I don't want to call forth
any more remarks about conduct unbecoming an officer
and a lady. But after all, even officers and ladies must
succumb to the inevitable sooner or later, or the race
wouldn't go on. And we're not on a public street now.
We're in a beautiful olive grove beside an ancient stone
well, and the moon is shining softly overhead. It's the sort
of setting for a love scene you couldn't find once in a
million years, if you started out to hunt for it. And here
we just stumbled on it."

"Yes, but the trouble is you stumbled on it with *me*. If
you'd stumbled on it with Jenness, that would have been
different."

He had already put his arm around her. Now, instead of
trying to draw her closer, he slackened his hold. The
movement was involuntary, and so slight that he instantly
hoped she had not noticed it. But his hope was unfounded.

"You were in love with Jenness," Judith said, "terribly
in love with her. It was an awful blow to you when she
betrayed you. I don't mean in the physical sense. Of course
she didn't do that, because she'd never belonged to you.
She wasn't even as close to you as I was to Dexter. But
she betrayed you in a spiritual sense. You like to talk as if
you were as tough as they come, and you like to act that
way too, off and on. But that kind of talk and behavior
isn't the real you. It was the real you that loved Jenness,
and you haven't got over loving her. The main reason you
think you're in love with me is because you think I look
like her. You've made up your mind that I'm enough like
her so that you could forget about her if you had me."

Again Peter involuntarily loosened the hold he had on
Judith. Again she drove her advantage home.

"But that wasn't all you decided. You decided that in
the ways we weren't alike, you'd gain. You told yourself
that Jenness was a weakling, but that I was a tower of
strength, that she was a wastrel, but I was a savior. And
so on. You compared us, and I came out ahead. But I
didn't deserve to. I've got just as many faults as Jenness

had, Peter. They don't happen to be the same ones, but I've got them. Dexter found that out eventually and told me so, in the plainest language I ever heard. No, I take that back. Another man told me the same things, even more plainly, the second time he saw me."

"Well I hope you told *him* to go straight to hell! Of all the damn impertinence——"

"It was Joe Racina, Peter."

Peter laughed. The laugh was not especially hearty, because the events of the past hour had shaken him beyond the point of merriment. Nevertheless it sounded a note of relief.

"Joe Racina!" he exclaimed. "Oh, that's different! I told you a few minutes ago you ought not to have taken my harmless little passes so seriously. Well you ought not to have taken Joe's jeremiads seriously either. He's always shooting off his mouth about something. He's a good reporter, one of the best. He's a darn good friend too, if you come down to that. But he can be brutally frank when he feels like it, and he feels like it fairly often, especially when he's driving himself too hard. He works around forty-eight hours out of the twenty-four. Half the time he doesn't stop to eat or sleep for days on end. Probably you rubbed him the wrong way about some little thing when he was all fagged out."

"I did rub him the wrong way. But it wasn't about some little thing. It was about a lot of big things. And he may have been tired or out of sorts. But he was right too. He was dead right. I deserved everything he said to me."

She turned her head away, but not before Peter had seen that she was biting her lips to keep them from trembling. The moonlight had grown more and more radiant as the night advanced. He could see Judith as plainly as if it had been midday; but no sunshine would have revealed her in such mystic glory; her fine spun hair, that shone with almost silvery lustre; her fresh face which was transfigured with strange splendor; her soft white throat, visibly merging with the still softer and whiter breast which was invisible; the flowing lines of her strong slender limbs and body . . . Seeing her so, inevitably he drew her closer to him again, but tenderly rather than urgently. Then, finding that she neither rebuked nor resisted him, he tried again to plead his cause.

"Listen, darling," he said. "You had me frightened there, for a minute. It's true that you do make me think of Jenness. It's true that I was terribly in love with her and that the reason you—attracted me so much at first was because you reminded me of her. But that isn't the reason you attract me now. It hasn't been for a long long time. I'm in love with you for yourself now, Judith. Not because you're like Jenness in some ways, or unlike her in others, but because you're you. Jenness has been dead nearly a year. I felt as if she were dead long before that. I never wanted to bring her back into my life after she lied to me. Surely you don't want me to be bound by a tragic buried past. You can't. You must want me to be happy in the present."

"Yes, Peter, of course I want you to be happy. That's why I won't marry you. Because you wouldn't be happy with me. Not for long."

"The hell I wouldn't! What makes you think so?"

"I've told you, I'm not in love with you."

"All right, I'll take a chance that I can make you fall in love with me. I won't shilly-shally around for years like Dexter Abbott. I'll marry you tomorrow. And we'll begin our honeymoon right away. There couldn't be a better time and place. If you'll just turn your face around, Judith, and relax a little and act your age, I'll show you."

"Peter—I—I can't."

"For God's sake, why not?"

"Because it isn't just that I'm not in love with you. It's that I'm in love with someone else. I'm in love with Joe Racina."

"You're stark raving crazy, that's what you are! *In love with Joe Racina!* Why, you hate him like a rattlesnake!"

"No, I'm not. Yes, I am. No, I don't."

"You sound more like a lunatic every minute! Hell, you never saw Joe Racina but twice in your life!"

"It isn't the number of times you see a man that counts. It's what happens when you do see him."

"Well Christ, what *did* happen? You don't mean to tell me that Joe——"

"No, *no*, NO! Of course not! Nothing happened. That is, nothing special. What I meant was, it's the way a man makes you *feel*."

"I still don't see what you're driving at. I didn't realize Joe roused any tender or ardent feelings, as far as you were concerned, or any sensation except aversion. In fact I've heard you say yourself that you took an immediate dislike to him."

"Yes, that's what I *said*. How could I say anything else? Can't you understand that it's terribly humiliating to a girl to fall in love with a man who thinks she's the scum of the earth? Let alone having to confess that she has? And you've made me! There wasn't any other way to stop you."

"I've got to stop *you*, that's what I've got to do. If I could get my hands on Joe, I'd strangle him before he did any more damage, acting like a damn fool. He must have sized you up wrong from start to finish if——"

"No, he didn't. I've told you already, everything he said was true. And it wasn't all a jeremiad. He did say he thought if I'd cut out all the nonsense I was going in for, and settle down to being a real nurse, I might get to be quite a girl after all. But I could see he didn't believe I ever would cut out the nonsense or settle down. I didn't either, until after I'd done all sorts of dreadful things. I can't tell you about them now, but you'll have to take my word for it I did them. Since then I've been sorry, since then I have tried. But I know it's too late. I know Joe would never believe that I have . . . Please, Peter, don't look at me like that! Please let me go!"

"But see here——"

"Peter, don't you realize I've had all I can stand for one night?"

Her words ended in one single dreadful sob. Then she bent her shining head. Suddenly he saw that the strength which had seemed to him so inexhaustible was streaming away from her, that in another moment it would be utterly spent unless he could save it for her.

"There," he said soothingly. "You'll feel a lot better,

now that you've got that out of your system. Not that there's anything to be ashamed of. A feeling like what you've got—well it makes almost anyone into a grand person. And when someone like you gets it, she's tops, that's what. I'll say you're quite a girl, and then some. And as for being a real nurse—why, Judith, there isn't another in the unit who can touch you! Don't you believe for a moment Joe Racina thinks you're the scum of the earth. He couldn't! He was just shooting off his mouth, that's all, like I told you he did, every once in so often. If he knew you—you cared like this, he'd be so proud he couldn't see straight. I think he's always had an idea no girl was going to care for him, really. If you'd only tell him what you've told me, after you go home, without waiting for him to say anything——"

"I couldn't do that, Peter."

"Well, no, I suppose you couldn't. But I'm glad you've told me. I'm proud that you've confided in me. Besides, all this must have been bottled up inside of you for months and months and that always hurts. I'm sorry I wrung it out of you the way I did though. If I'd had any sense at all, I'd have stopped badgering you when you first tried to call me off. Of course I haven't much sense, not enough to go in when it rains. But enough to know it's time to take you in now. Come along, Judith. And don't you think for a moment we're not going to be pals, the way you planned it. Pals and maybe collaborators too. Because I want to hear that story about the sergeant after all. You tell it to me while we're walking back to the hospital."

They went slowly out of the grove and down the road towards the oat field. In the distance, the dark outline of the tents was clear against the brilliant sky. Less distantly, a few Arabs were still loitering, their robes fluttering around them. Apparently they were waiting to speak to Judith again, and as she saw this, she quickened her pace a little. But when she and Peter came close to the Arabs, it was to Peter that one of them held out his hand, offering some tangerines that clustered among green leaves on a short stem.

Peter accepted the offering somewhat abstractedly. His mind, at the moment, did not adjust itself readily to Arabs and tangerines, any more than it had adjusted itself to the story of the sergeant. The gift seemed to fit, in a general way, with Judith's remarks about her reliance on this particular fruit, but more than that he did not grasp or try to grasp. He saw her glance from the giver to the gift, and then he saw her look at the tangerines more closely, before he heard her cry out and felt her clutch for the tangerines herself. At least he thought he had heard her cry out, he told Joe Racina, in writing about it afterwards. But he was never sure. He was only sure that she had snatched the cluster from his hand and run like the wind towards the grove, holding it until she was a long way off from the others before she threw it still further away.

Of course it would be a so-called crack correspondent who would never have heard about these cute little fancy bombs. The Germans had dropped them long before and the Arabs were still finding them and picking them up unguardedly. Of course it would be a mere nurse who would instantly recognize one for what it was, and reach for it and run with it . . .

No, he wasn't even singed, or any of the Arabs. But Judith . . . Well, they were going to take Judith on a bomber to the Gold Coast and from there to Miami via Brazil on a stratoliner. She was conscious most of the time, which made it hard as hell. Not just because the suffering from the burns was so bad. She could take suffering, if anyone ever could. But because she knew it would be a long, long time before she could go back to active duty again. Probably it would be so long that the war would be over by that time. And Judith was an Army nurse, above all else. It was hard for her to know that the Army would go on without her.

And something else. She also knew that no one would ever mistake her for Jenness again.

PART VI

"The Red Pavilion"

January–July 1943

CHAPTER 29

THE BOMBER was flying very high, and after the heat of Arzeu, the cold bit into the very bones. Laura fastened her coat more closely around her, but still she shivered as she went down the narrow aisle separating the bunks; she bent over her patients to make sure they were warm enough, hoping that none of them would hear her teeth chattering.

There were five of these patients altogether, so that with the flight surgeon and the nurse on duty, quarters were pretty cramped. Two of the patients were ambulatory cases: a man who had been blinded, and a man who had already lost one arm through bombing and now seemed in danger of losing the other through an inexplicable cancerous sore. The others were all stretcher cases: one man was in a body-cast with a broken back. Another had paralysis, not infantile as the diagnosticians had originally believed, but a newer and still more insidious type, caused by a vitamin deficiency. The third was Judith, who was mutilated and burned.

Every time that Laura loked down at Judith, she was overwhelmed with fresh compassion. She could look at her without worrying lest Judith should see her expression, for there was a light bandage over Judith's eye, in addition to the thick, heavy bandages which swathed her head and neck and her shoulders and arms as well as part of her body. She had not lost her eye-sight, like the poor bereft creature who sat bolt upright, hour after hour, in one of the stiff straight chairs placed in front of the narrow bunks swung in tiers from the skeleton ribs on the rounded sides of the bomber; but it had been injured, and in order that the injury might be repaired as rapidly as possible, her eyes were shielded, and she was advised to keep them closed most of the time. She had not rebelled against the light bandage, or asked how soon it would be feasible to remove it so that she could look around, at least. In fact she had rebelled only once, and that was when she found that Laura had been assigned to duty on the bomber, to care for the patients who were being sent back to the United States by plane, because their condition was too critical to permit the long trip by boat.

"I know you asked for it. I know you didn't need to take it. You asked for it so you could stay with me. And now you probably won't get another chance to serve overseas."

"Well we've both said, lots of times, that there was plenty for nurses to do in the United States."

"Yes, but what we both *wanted* was overseas duty. We both moved heaven and earth to get it. And just because I have to go home, there isn't any reason why you should. I'm going to protest. I'm going to say I won't stand for it. I'm going to say it sends my temperature up just to think of it."

"It won't do you any good. The orders have come through already. Can't you understand, Judith? I didn't want overseas duty so much for itself, the way you did. I wanted it because you got it, and I was hellbent to do everything you did. I was a copycat. I'm still a copycat. If you're going home, I want to go home too."

"You're saying that to cheer me up. But it doesn't cheer me up. It makes me perfectly miserable."

"I'm not saying it to cheer you up. I'm saying it because it's true. I'm a copycat and I'm a clinging vine. I can't get along without clinging to you, Judith. I'm lost without you, and that's all there is to it. I don't care where you're going to be, I'd rather have duty in that place, wherever it is, than anywhere else. I'm not being Polly Annaish. *I mean* it."

Laura said this so emphatically that there was no doubting her sincerity; and she had stoutly continued to affirm the same thing, over and over again. Even after they were aboard the bomber, she had found occasion to remark several times, in a general way, that she thought it was much the most exciting duty she had got so far; much more exciting than tent city. She said so now, buttoning her coat more closely around her and trying to keep her teeth from chattering.

"I never supposed, when I was strolling down Main Street in Winchester, Mass., that I'd be flying over Africa in an Army bomber," she shouted, to the group as a whole. It was necessary to shout, because the bomber made a great deal of noise, and otherwise she could not be heard above it. "Did you ever think you would, when you were coasting on Farman Hill?" she shouted at Judith.

"No," Judith said, smiling. She did not shout, because shouting represented too much of an effort, but Laura heard her, partly because she was standing very close to her and partly because Judith had the kind of a voice which carried well, even above noise. Laura thought, for the thousandth time, how thankful she was that nothing had happened to Judith's mouth, not only because it would have been so hideous to hear that clear voice muffled, but because the mouth itself was so lovely to look at, with firm curving lips and even white teeth. To a surprising degree, Judith's lips had kept their color too. Laura glanced from Judith to the man with the broken back, in the body-cast, whose bunk was swung on the opposite side of the aisle, and saw the difference between his white drawn lips, which seemed to epitomize all his suffering, and Judith's full rosy ones, which seemed to epitomize all her courage. Then for the first time since the accident, instead of being over-whelmed with compassion in looking at Judith, Laura felt uplifted by hope.

The flight surgeon, Captain Spaulding, who was lean and agile, with hawklike features, tanned skin and crisp, close-cropped hair, nodded meaningly at Laura, and then twisted his head slightly to one side and nodded again. She understood this meant they would be coming down present-ly, and that she must prepare her patients for the descent, so that they would not be startled or shaken when the bomber began its downward glide. But all in all, the land-ing was made with surprising ease, and two ambulances were waiting, drawn up at the hangar, to which the patients were transferred without delay or difficulty, Captain Spaulding riding with those who went in one and Laura with those who went in the other. The evening air was clear and cool and refreshing, and the roads over which they went wound smoothly across the clean sand. As they approached the low rectangular building which served as an evacuation hospital, Laura could see nurses wearing white dresses and white shoes, waiting in the doorway to receive the newcomers. She had almost forgotten that nurses were ever dressed in that way. She could not remember, either, when she had felt so happy as she did when she saw Judith being wheeled into a pleasant little room where there was a white iron bed with clean white sheets on it, and learned that she was to be bathed and fed, and that she would have time to rest, before she was transferred to a stratoliner. In a way, Laura would have liked to do everything for Judith herself. But she needed a bath and some supper too, and she knew Judith was in good hands. She sat down at the table covered with a white cloth, and ate two broiled lamb chops and a big baked potato and some creamed spinach and drank glass after glass of iced tea. She had almost forgotten that there was food and drink like that, too.

The sudden darkness of the desert had descended before the ambulances drew up at the door again, and there was no moon, only the thickly strewn stars which always made Laura think of daisies in an upside-down field which was just over her head instead of just under her feet, they seemed so close, and she never could restrain the impulse of stretching out her hands from time to time, as if to gather them. She knew it was trite to feel about the desert stars in this way, that hundreds of travelers had done so before; yet their brightness and their nearness were like a fresh miracle to her every time she saw them, and she could not help reaching towards them any more than she coulld help gazing at them. She knew it would probably be a long time before she saw stars which looked like these again, if she ever did, and her last look at them was more intent than her first look at the camouflaged stratoliner, which she did not even see until she was alongside it. However, when she saw the Pullman berths within, she promptly forgot about the stars, in her relief because all her patients could be properly put to bed now; the blind man and the man with the cancerous arm would not have to sit up on stiff straight chairs any longer; the man with the broken back and the man with paralysis and Judith could all be made much more comfortable than in the hard, narrow bunks which swung in tiers against the skeleton frame of the bomber. She lay down herself, after all her patients were settled for the night, and slept soundly for several hours before the flight surgeon, who had taken over while she rested, wakened her to tell her they were coming down again pretty soon now. They would be making only a short stop this time, he said; but there was a small dispensary at their landing place, and she would have a chance to take her patients there. It wouldn't be as palatial as the evacuation hospital, he added, with a grin; he didn't know that they'd serve roasted peacock tongues and chilled nectar there; but there might be a jug of wine and a loaf of bread. Maybe after all she'd been through, she might think that was paradise enow.

The classical allusion was lost on Laura, who was agreeably puzzled by the flight surgeon's pleasantries; but she was none the less appreciative of the dispensary's benefits, both for herself and for her patients. They were standing the trip very well, she thought, except for the man with the broken back, whose lips were more white and drawn every time she looked at him, though nothing in the nature of a complaint came from them. She had never heard a wounded man complain, not once, all the time she had been in Africa, and she supposed she never would, no matter how badly he was hurt. Then suddenly she gave a little stifled laugh, realizing that she was not where she was, except that she knew she was somewhere in the Western Hemisphere. The stratoliner had made several brief stops, at out of the way places which all looked very much alike and which all had small dispensaries. She was used to these, and to flat stretches of sandy beach where airplanes seemed to be coming and going but which otherwise seemed to be very much detached from the world. Then they came down at a place which looked different. It seemed to be very much part of the world, full of bustle and confusion and activity and people, and she glanced up and saw an American flag flying.

"Why where *are* we?" she asked breathlessly, turning to the flight surgeon, who was unexpectedly standing beside her, looking at the flag too.

"Didn't you know? We're in Miami. We've got them all back on American soil. Now all we've got to do is to get them to Washington. I think we'll just about make it, Lieutenant."

She knew that he was thinking of the man with the broken back, just as she was. But neither of them said so. They saluted the flag and then they went back to their patients.

After they reached Walter Reed Hospital, Judith was permitted to leave the light bandage off her eyes for a little while. The shades were drawn in her room, and the light was soft and dim, so Colonel Witherspoon, who had charge of her case, told her that she might see how it felt to have them uncovered. She promised to tell, right away, if they began to hurt. But they did not. She blinked a little, because it was so long since she had used them, and then she looked around, wonderingly and admiringly, at everything in the small, shadowy quiet room. But she kept looking back, over and over again, at the large crystal vases, filled with yellow roses, which almost covered the white enamelled bureau.

"I thought nobody knew when we were getting in," she said at last, to the hovering nurse. Laura had been temporarily taken off duty, for a check-up and a rest, after reporting in, and had not yet been reassigned anywhere; so Lieutenant Webster, the nurse with Judith now, was a stranger.

"Nobody did. At least nobody was supposed to. But someone must have had a pretty good general idea. Someone who was determined there'd be flowers in your room, whenever you got here. Because a big box of yellow roses, addressed to you, has been delivered every day for a week. I've had to throw the first ones away. Those on the bureau are the ones that came yesterday and to-day."

"Were there any cards?"

"Yes. I've saved the cards, of course. They're all addressed in the same handwriting. Do you want me to give them to you now? Oh—I'm terribly sorry, Lieutenant Farman."

The nurse was even sorrier than she sounded. Her voice, like the voice of most nurses on duty, was precise and dispassionate. But her feelings were under less complete control. She was stricken that she should have made a slip of the tongue like that. Of course she could not give the cards to her patient, because Lieutenant Farman could not take them, or open them or hold them. Both her hands were bandaged and both her arms, all the way to the shoulder; in fact the bandaging on her arms joined the bandaging on her head and neck. It was a wicked shame. Eeveryone said she had been a fine nurse, one of the best; and not only that: judging from her mouth and nose and eyes, she must have been a lovely looking girl too. Of course, it was nothing short of miraculous, what could be done with plastic surgery nowadays. Lieutenant Webster had herself seen several of these miracles performed. Nevertheless there was always a great change . . . She had often wondered if the patients who were so changed in appearance did not feel changed inside too, and she realized that personally she would never have been happy to look like a different woman, not even to become a handsomer one, because then it would not have seemed as if she were the same woman. Somehow she thought this maimed, helpless, bandaged girl who lay looking up at her with trustful eyes would feel the same way.

"I'm terribly sorry," she said again. "Shall I open the envelopes and read the cards to you now, Lieutenant Farman?"

"Yes, please. And don't worry about what you said. Anyone would have said that. It was a perfectly natural thing to say."

"I have the cards marked, in the order they came. I'll begin with the first one, shall I?"

"Yes, please."

The nurse laid six of the envelopes down on the bedside table and opened the seventh one. She was aware of her patient's eyes, fixed intently upon her.

"It says—'To a real nurse who is quite a girl. Congratulations to the United States Army and love to her. Joe.'"

The nurse replaced the card in the envelope and put it carefully down besides the others. Then she opened the second one.

"It says—'To a real nurse who is—' It says the same thing as the other one, Lieutenant Farman."

"That's all right. There wasn't anything else to say. You needn't open any of the others. I'm sure they all say the same thing. But I'd like to have you leave them here beside me, if that's allowed. Perhaps you'd prop one of them up on something, so I could look at it once in a while."

"I can prop it up against this tumbler. There! Is that the way you wanted it?"

"Yes. Just the way."

Judith turned her eyes to look at it without saying anything more and then she closed them. The nurse was aware that the patient was no longer gazing at her intently.

"Do your eyes pain you, Lieutenant Farman? Do you think perhaps I had better put the light bandage back on again?"

"No, my eyes don't pain me. And I don't need the light bandage. But if there isn't any special treatment I'm supposed to have, right now, I'd like to be alone for a little while."

"Well, there is no special treatment ordered for the moment. But it is almost time for you to have some nourishment and——"

"I've had it. Please——"

When the nurse came back, half an hour later, the patient's eyes were open again and she was looking at the card. The nurse brought her two messages.

"Colonel Witherspoon has decided to operate in the

morning, Lieutenant Farman. At first he thought it might be better to wait a day or two, until you'd recovered from the fatigue of your trip. But you seem to have stood that very well, all things considered. And every day counts, in a case like yours."

"Yes, I know."

"Colonel Witherspoon's coming in to see you himself, to talk to you about it, a little later on. He believes you'd rather be told, beforehand, just what he thinks can be done, just what the results will probably be. Usually we don't discuss these details with a patient, but Colonel Witherspoon thought, in your case——"

"Yes, he's quite right. I'd rather know."

"And of course I must prepare you for the operation. I don't need to explain these preparations to you. Of course you've made them hundreds of times for other patients yourself."

"Yes, of course."

"But before I start, you're to be allowed a visitor. For just five minutes. I'm sure you understand it couldn't be longer than that. It's most unusual, in fact it's highly irregular, to permit anything of the sort. However, this visitor has been waiting a long time and somehow he's succeeded in persuading Colonel Witherspoon——"

"I understand perfectly. I won't let him stay any longer than that. And I'm very grateful to Colonel Witherspoon for making an exception to the rule. Please tell him I said so."

The nurse went out. Judith heard the sound of her discreet footsteps, gradually being swallowed up by distance. Then she heard them approaching again, to a less even muffled accompaniment, and the nurse's precise dispassionate voice in the doorway.

"This is Lieutenant Farman's room, Mr. Racina. Remember, it is for just five minutes."

"It won't take me two," Joe retorted, putting her in her place.

He swung into the room, instantly filling its barren whiteness with his hugeness and his vitality and his kindliness. He had on the same clothes he had been wearing when

Judith last saw him, shabbier now for a year's hard usage, and they were still unpressed and still flecked with cigarette ashes. But his clothes did not matter; it was his magnetism that counted, and his understanding. He walked straight over to the bed and looked down at Judith with his queer, crooked smile. She could not say anything. But she looked up at him with her unbound eyes, and instinctively she tried to stretch out one of her bandaged hands before she remembered that she could not. Joe put his own immense hands down on the bandages, not only on the ones she had tried to move, but on those which covered the other hand too, leaning over her as he did so.

"Gosh, what a break for me!" he said heartily. "If a lady can't shake hands with a guy, there's only one alternative left to the poor, unresourceful creature. Besides, you've had this kiss coming to you for quite a long time. Remember, Judith? I made a great mistake when I let you get away without it before. But you can bet your bottom dollar I'm never going to make a mistake like that again."

He kissed her. Judith was sure there had never been a kiss like it in the world before.

"You hurry up and get well, because you and I are going to do things and go places together," Joe went on. "If you think I mind because you're scratched up a little, you've got to think again, that's all there is to it. And don't you try to start talking back to me, because I can talk back to *you*, a hell of a lot faster. I don't propose to let a few bumps and bruises interfere with my plans. I've known from the first minute I looked at you that you were my girl, even if I did act like such a damn fool."

He let go her bandaged hands and slipped his strong arms under her injured shoulders. He kissed her again, and this time the kiss was a longer one. Judith realized, in the course of it, that she still had a great deal to learn about kissing.

"And don't you believe for a moment that it was because you looked like your sister I knew you were my girl," Joe said at last. "Jenness was grand for a date, God rest her poor soul, but I never wanted her for a wife. I never wanted anyone but you for that. Of course I did my share of hell-raising when I was a youngster. I acted like a dman fool then, too. But now I'm all through acting like a damn fool and ready to act like a good husband. Fact."

CHAPTER 30

JOE RACINA'S wire, addressed to both Daniel and Serena, and asking if he could make them a flying visit caused a pleasurable stir on Farman Hill. A wire, answering in the affirmative, was immediately dispatched. But after it had gone, Serena began to express doubts as to the worthiness of the reception they could give him.

"We haven't got a real spare room any more, not what you could rightly call one," she said to Daniel, taking pains to speak when Dexter and Alix were both out of earshot, so that neither one's feelings could possibly be hurt. "With Dexter in the back room and Alix in the East Chamber and the West Chamber turned into a nursery . . . Of course we could put up a bed in one of the parlors. But somehow Joe doesn't seem like the kind of a man that would fit into a parlor any time, as well as he would into a homelier place, let alone sleeping easy in one."

"Alix'll move the baby's things into her own room, without anyone saying a word to her, Mother. You'll see. After all the tent bed's still up in the West Chamber. It'll look like a regular spare room again, in two shakes of a dead lamb's tail, as you'd say yourself."

"Well, maybe. But I'm afraid we can't feed him right either. Joe's a hearty eater, and he likes to drink coffee at all hours, same as Alix does. And we haven't got enough coffee for her, let alone an extra person. I think it's a considerable cross to her, Daniel, not to offer it to company all the time, like she used to—even more than going without it herself, though heaven knows she used to drink two or three of those small blacks, as she called them, every time she sat down for a spell. It's a mercy Dexter doesn't like coffee. I don't know what we'd have done if we hadn't had his coupons to fall back on."

"For a man who's sort of set in some of his ways, considering how young he still is, the dislike Dexter took to coffee seemed real sudden to me," Daniel remarked drily. "Many's the time I've seen him drink down three or four cupfuls. But you're right, Mother, his coupons have come in handy. I like my coffee as well as anyone," he added thoughtfully. "But I haven't had any trouble, resigning myself to doing without it, because I know it has to come here in ships and that those are needed for other purposes. I feel different about the things we can raise ourselves. It makes my gorge rise every time I think about the wheat that was plowed under and the pigs that were slaughtered and the sugar that was burned. I can't help but feel the men who gave orders for all that to be done weren't practical farmers, or students of history either. Why way back in Bible times, the Lord told the children of Israel they'd got to provide for seven lean years when they were having seven fat years. And they weren't aiming to feed anyone outside their own tribe either."

Serena raised a finger as a signal of warning, and the next moment Daniel, whose hearing was not quite as acute as his wife's, though his eyesight was sharper, heard the light step of their daughter-in-law approaching. Daniel had never ceased to wonder how anyone who came into a room as quietly and unobtrusively as Alix always did, could not only make her own presence felt so poignantly, but also apparently transform her surroundings. In the plain black dresses, with close-fitting, buttoned basques and full skirts, which she was wearing this winter, she looked more than ever as if she had stepped out of a daguerreotype. The black onyx brooch fastening her white turnover collar at the throat, the fine white cuffs folded back from her wrists, and the dainty embroidered handkerchief which she carried, added to the general effect; so did her simply parted hair, braided and wreathed around her small head, and the lines of her figure, curving from the full breast of a nursing mother to a trim and tiny waist. She pulled out one of the stools by the fireplace and sat down on it, picking up the little wicker sewing basket which she always kept within easy reach.

"Are you worrying about feeding Joe Racina?" she inquired calmly. "I thought I heard something as I came through the hall . . . You mustn't. He'll think one of your dinners is a feast, Mother. Of course it really will be, but even if it weren't, we could make it seem that way, by the way we carried it off. I think my favorite story is the one Tante Odilisse tell about a very old butler of her mother's. Her mother had unexpected callers one very warm day, when there wasn't even any ice in the house. When we worry about rationing, we don't stop to think that in those days there wasn't anything left to ration in the South. Well, this butler put some silver napkin rings in the bottom of the silver pitcher he filled with shrub, and came into the drawing room, rattling them around. He filled and refilled the goblets himself, never letting the pitcher out of his hand and going right on with his rattling. Everyone exclaimed about what a delicious cooling drink he had prepared and went away refreshed."

"That's a good story, Alix, like all your stories are. Just the same, I'm afraid it would take more than some silver napkin rings, rattling around in a pitcher, to fool Joe Racina. He's a pretty shrewd observer. There's not much gets past him."

"It's just because he's shrewd that he appreciates values," Alix replied. "True ones and false ones. He'd know the napkin rings, or their equivalent, represented a true value. But I guess we won't have any trouble giving him ice, at least, in this weather. . . . By the way, I have his room all fixed for him. That is, I think it looks nice, and it's just as warm as toast. Dexter brought up some extra wood this morning and I've had an open fire going there all day. Do you want to come and see it, Mother?"

"No," Serena answered, avoiding a direct glance from her husband. "I'm willing to take your word for it that it looks nice. If you're satisfied with its looks, anyone would be. I think I better get started on that feast you're talking about though. It wouldn't surprise me but what Joe got here some sooner than we expect him."

"It would surprise me if he didn't. I think he probably sent his wire from the airport, after he'd started. Of course he knew you'd wire back you'd be glad to see him. He wouldn't wait for an answer, if he were in a hurry, and he usually is, isn't he? He'd take its contents for granted."

"Maybe you've guessed right again. But what I haven't figured out yet, is what started him up here, at a moment's notice, in the dead of winter."

"Don't you think he's coming to bring us news of Judith?"

"So soon?" Serena looked at her daughter-in-law with startled eyes. "Why we haven't had a word from the War Department yet, not even about the accident!"

"No. Apparently the War Department doesn't advise families about accidents unless those are fatal." For a moment Alix paused, looking away; but only for a moment. It was almost miraculous that her mother-in-law had not broken under the double bereavement she had already suffered that year; if she were forced to endure another, a collapse would be almost inevitable. Alix had long since learned to suppress her own sorrow, in order that it might not overwhelm Jerome's parents also; she did not dwell on it now. "Please keep on trying to believe that the very fact you haven't heard from the War Department means everything's all right," she said gently.

"After all, Peter's letter was definite, even if it wasn't official, and it came through very quickly, thanks to his press privileges. I imagine he wrote to Joe at the same time he wrote to us. He'd realize Joe would be in a position to get in touch with Judith faster than we could, and that he'd want to."

"But we don't know that she's left Africa yet, either," Serena persisted.

"No, we don't *know*. Of course all such movements have to be kept secret, for the sake of future movements. But I believe she has and I believe that Joe's fully informed. He's probably got friends in the Air Transport Operations

Division at Miami, or in the Medical Unit there. I imagine Joe's got friends almost everywhere. But even if he doesn't actually have personal acquaintances in Miami, you may be sure he has some kind of indirect contacts or that he'll establish them. He'll let someone know that he's eagerly watching for the arrival of Lieutenant Farman and he'll get someone to tip him off about the approximate dates when the next hospital planes will be arriving. If the Farmans were only gamblers, like the St. Cyrs, I'd ask you to make a wager with me."

"Well, I might take you up, at that," Daniel announced unexpectedly. He had been relieved, rather than otherwise, to find Serena worrying over the adequacy of Joe Racina's entertainment. Since the loss of Jerome, she had given little thought to trivialities, and it was a good sign if she could at last, despite her anxiety about Judith. Moreover, he was not unmindful of the effort Alix was making; if a delicate girl could show so much fortitude, certainly a strong man could. "What was it you wanted to bet, Alix?" he asked.

"That Joe'll see Judith before she's been in Washington twenty-four hours."

"I guess I won't bet with you after all. I haven't a mind to throw away money and I shouldn't be a mite surprised but what he did. If Peter wrote to him, and that seems likely too, Joe'll keep a sharp lookout for her. It's as you say, he'll know that we'll be worrying, and he's got means at his disposal of finding out things that we haven't."

"But he could telephone us or telegraph us."

"He did telegraph you, Mother."

"Yes, to say he was coming. You'd think he could put anything he needed to say into a letter, without going to all that trouble."

"It would depend a little, wouldn't it, on what he wanted to say? I should think so anyhow. You remember when Jerome had something important to say, he didn't try to put it all in a letter. He sent me to say it for him, because he couldn't come himself. Well, Joe can come himself. And I'm sure you're safe in assuming he's bringing good news. If Judith's condition had been critical, he'd have sent for you to come to Washington, so that you could have seen her as soon as possible, instead of taking the time to come here. He's coming to bring you tidings that are joyful as well as important. You wait and see."

"It still seems like quite a trip for a busy man to take in the dead of winter, just to say a girl he hardly knows is all right," Serena said doubtfully. "You haven't got me convinced yet, Alix. I expected to see Joe in the spring-time. He planned to make us a visit then. But spring's a long way off yet. I'll feel better when this mystery's cleared up."

"Spring does seem a long way off today," Alix admitted. "But there's a famous poem, isn't there, with a question in it—'If winter comes, can spring be far behind?'—Perhaps Joe feels, for some reason, that there's spring in the air already. Perhaps he'll bring a breath of it with him." She looked up from her needlework to the window, where the snow was drifting against the panes. As it drifted, it made a sound like sugar, running through a sieve, but a little louder; the noise of it was distinct above the trickling in the water box. It looked something like sugar too, as she had seen this glistening in great piles before it was shoveled into burlap bags in the mills, and for a moment a wave of almost uncontrollable nostalgia swept over her. Spring really was near in Louisiana, and the bayous the water was running freely towards the Gulf between lush, green shores, while here the icebound river was flanked with frozen fields, and still the snow continued to descend. "Dexter must have got caught in the storm," she said thoughtfully. "It'll be a bad day in the woods. And a bad day in the air, too. But I think he and Joe will both be here in time for supper. I believe I'll make a hot Tom and Jerry for them. It'll taste good to them when they come in out of the cold."

"If we only knew what train Joe was taking we'd squeeze out the gasoline to meet him," Daniel said, rising. It was such a bad day that he had permitted himself the relaxa-tion of a brief respite from work during the early part of the afternoon, but now it was time for him to go back to the barn and begin the chores. He had to start a little early, for he was doing Dexter's as well as his own, while Dexter was logging. "I presume Jerry's asleep, Alix?" he added, a little wistfully. He had rather counted on playing with the baby, during his unusual period of leisure, and he was unable to leave the living room without indirectly voicing his disappointment.

"Yes. He didn't take much of a nap this morning, and he reeled off as if he were drunk when he finished his afternoon feeding. But he'll be waiting for you when you get in, Father—and I shall too," she added, rising to give him the caress which was so spontaneous with her and so difficult for a New Englander to achieve, and walking over to the side door with him.

"Oh, look!" she said, nodding in the direction of the yard. "Our variegated guests are here again!"

"Why, so they are, Alix, so they are," he said, following her glance. On the snow-covered ground some kernels of corn gleamed like small gold nuggets on a silver surface, and a gray squirrel, two blue jays, and three golden pheasants were picking avidly at these, the gorgeousness of their coloring and the grace of their movements enhanced by the whiteness and stillness of their surroundings. "All those creatures are natural enemies," he said slowly. "I never saw them come together peacefully in a group before, much less feed together."

"Did you ever scatter corn out there before, Father, to see what would happen?"

"No," he said still more slowly, "I never did. None of us thought of it, Alix, till you suggested it. Well, I guess we're learning, right in our own yard, that hunger can force a truce. It isn't a bad thing for a farmer to study on, a year like this."

"You don't know, either, do you, that once there is a truce there couldn't be friendship?"

"No, I don't know that either. We've made friends with lots of people, Alix, since you came here that we never would have known except for you. And we're the better for knowing them, too." She knew that he was thinking of the Boudreaus and the Cohens, but she said nothing, and he went on, "Well now, it looks as if even strange animals were getting to be friendly under your guidance."

"It may be my guidance, Father, but it's your place. I couldn't do anything unless you stood back of me. . . . Well, I could stay here all the afternoon, watching those guests, but I must get ready for others. And don't you worry about Joe, any more than you're worrying about Dexter. Joe won't expect you to meet him and he'll turn up safe and sound. He'll find a car for himself. Probably you'll find him sitting here in front of the fire with Pinkham on one side of him and Lucky on the other, when you get in from the barn."

Like so many predictions that Alix made, this one proved correct. When Daniel returned to the living room, he found this pleasantly filled. The baby, who had been so big to begin with, and who had continued to gain with complete disregard for charts and statistics, had long since outgrown the hooded cradle, as far as stretching out to sleep in it was concerned; but he sat in it to play, late every afternoon. It was regularly drawn up beside the old rocker which his grandparents alternately used, and near one of the twin stool which his mother liked to move about. He was sitting up in it now, with two or three small, soft pillows behind his sturdy little back, and a strong band of belting across his plump little middle. In one chubby fist he held a rattle, which he alternately chewed and banged against the edge of the cradle, and he was making gurgling sounds, indicative of great contentment, which formed a running accompaniment to his elders' conversation. Normally, Jerry was a very jolly baby, though he was capable of showing extreme rage if things did not go to suit him, and the vigor with which he howled, when angry, was comparable to the apparently inexhaustible energy with which he bounced up and down when he was happy.

At this moment, everything seemed to suit him in his small world. His grandmother was sitting in the armchair, surreptitiously rocking the cradle with one foot, and the baby was swaying delightedly back and forth in rhythm to this accompaniment. When he caught sight of his grandfather, the gurgling sounds he was making became loud crows of joy, and he beat about with his arms and legs. Alix was sitting quietly on his other side, silently watching not only her child and her needlework, but the two men who now made up the group, and who both had their legs stretched out in front of the fire and steaming glasses of Tom and Jerry in their hands. Dexter still had on the high boots and heavy reefer he had worn in the woods; his coonskin coat lay over the back of the chair, his fur cap and mittens beside him. His face and hands had the red chapped look which characterizes a countryman's exposure to weather which is rigorous but endurable; Joe's dark countenance, on the other hand, had the drawn appearance of the Latin to whom a northerly climate must, from the very nature of things, be almost unendurable. But he seemed to be bearing up well, in spite of this handicap. Daniel had never seen the journalist's grin when it was more cheery than as he rose to greet his host, glass in hand. The New Englander instantly knew that there was no need of asking for Judith, until Joe told them about her in his own time and in his own way. If all had not been well with her, Joe would not have looked like that.

"Just see me, will you, right in the bosom of the family!" Joe explained jovially. "I was getting quite a little attention from this young world-beater of yours too, until you came in and cut me out. I believe I told you once the lady St. Cyrs might look as if a breath of wind would blow them away, but that they always had big bouncing babies. Perhaps by this time you believe me."

"Yes, I believe you. I've found you're a pretty reliable fellow, Joe," Daniel replied. He had picked up the delighted baby, and was tossing him high in the air, while the child gurgled and crowed more loudly than ever. Daniel was smiling himself, broadly, as he spoke, for there was something about the sight of his sturdy little grandson which never failed to bring fresh joy to his heart, and he was pleased through and through to find Joe Racina beside his hearthstone "in the bosom of the family." But somewhere within him there was a still small murmur reminding him that Joe had said something more when he spoke of the big bouncing babies produced by the female St. Cyrs, who looked as if a breath of air might blow them away, but who ran their plantations themselves when their husbands were not there to do it. "Probably you'll have half a dozen young Farmans to help you carry on, before you get through," Joe had said. "I never knew a St. Cyr yet who didn't have a lot of children. There was one who had five in three years . . ."

There would never be half a dozen young Farmans now, because Jerome, who alone could have begotten them, had been killed in India; and Alix, who would have conceived them, was a widow at twenty-two. Daniel glanced down at Alix now, sitting quietly on the low stool, with her needlework in her hand, wearing her quaint black dress and her black hair done in a quaint way. Daniel could not have imagined a more circumspect and correct picture of young widowhood, and he knew that with her there had been no question of assuming a virtue she did not have. Her grief over Jerome's death, though controlled, had been profound, and she had not yet regained the blitheness which formerly had been coupled with her courage. She did not sing, except for an occasional lullaby to her baby; she did not speak with the delicate archness which had so charmed Daniel at the beginning; there was no merriment in her rare, elusive smile, and no buoyancy in her manner. She was mindful of her baby, as she sat there before the fire, but her innermost thoughts were about Jerome, and there was room for no one else in these except in so far as she directed them towards the happiness and well-being of her family and her friends. Yet deep within his own heart he knew that her dignified behavior and grave bearing no more altered her essential fecundity than her widow's weeds concealed the curves of her full breast and tapering waist. He remembered fields which he had seen lying fallow, not because of negligence or infertility, but through prudent design, to conserve their potential productiveness. Something about Alix suggested to him the same powerful dormancy. He felt that she could not fail to fulfil the traditions of her family, that she too would inevitably experience abundant maternity. And with this foreknowledge came dread lest this fulfilment should wrest her from him, now that he loved her as if she had been his own daughter. Her cousin, Prosper St. Cyr, had not returned to Farman Hill since the baby's baptism. But Daniel knew that the handsome Creole was only biding his time with characteristic respect for a mourning period. To him the marriage of Alix with an outsider represented only an interlude in an otherwise unbroken family cycle, and he believed and intended that sooner or later the cycle would be completed. . . .

As Daniel tossed the beloved baby into the air and talked with his welcome guest, he realized that he was not alone in his careful appraisal of Alix. Dexter was watching her too, as he sat silently sipping the hot drink she had made for him, and slowly losing his chilled, stiffened look. And Joe was watching her, as he drained one glass of Tom and Jerry after another and smoked his interminable cigarettes. Daniel made up his mind that, before Joe went back to Washington, he would create an occasion to talk with his visitor about Alix. He hoped and believed that such a conference might relieve his mind to a certain extent. But for the moment, he waited with the same eagerness as the others for the explanation of Joe's precipitate visit.

Joe did not try his patience. "I was just starting to tell the rest of the family some good news, when you came in," he said genially. "Judith got into Washington last Wednesday. She stood the trip remarkably well—so well that Colonel Witherspoon, who's in charge of her case, decided to operate the next day. There wouldn't have been time for any of you to get there before the operation, so we decided not to tell you about it until it was over. Of course it wasn't a life or death proposition, or we would have. It was just a question of how much he'd be able to do for her—and how much she'd be able to do for herself. He's a damn good fellow and a damn good surgeon too, but a lot depended on her. If she hadn't been able to put herself unreservedly in his hands, with lots of faith and without any resistance, he couldn't have helped her nearly as much as he has. The best doctor in the world can't buck a patient's opposition or antipathy. Well, Colonel Witherspoon didn't have any to buck. Judith said he couldn't get started quick enough to suit her. She didn't fight anesthesia, she didn't fight anything. And she's been as quiet as a lamb right along. The result is that she's coming on now like a house afire."

"I've got a high opinion of your powers of observation, Joe, like I said before," Daniel remarked drily. "But if anyone else had told me Judith was acting like a lamb, sick or well, I'd have laughed in his face. If I'd got around, myself, to comparing my daughter to any of the domestic animals, I'd have said she was like a handsome, headstrong filly that was bound to take the bit in her own teeth—not but what she's a fine girl, you understand."

"Oh, I understand all right," Joe said, almost airily. "But when you get a filly like that, it makes a difference, doesn't it, sometimes, who handles her and how? Not that I know anything about horses, and I've always hated that term "breaking' like hell . . . Well anyway," he continued, rather hastily, as if aware that he was treading on somewhat delicate ground, "it doesn't matter whether you call her a lamb or a filly or a damn fine girl, or anything else that comes into your head. What matters is that she's going to come out of this accident and this operation almost as good as new. She'll have to wear her hair down over the sides of her forehead and the tops of her ears, but I should think it would be becoming to her that way. And she won't be wearing low-necked dresses for a long while, though I think they can be cut out a little in the front— heart-shaped, that's what you call them, isn't it. Alix?"

"Yes," Alix answered, looking up at Joe with the first spontaneous smile that Daniel could remember seeing on her face.

"Well, then, she'll have a hair-do that'll make her look like a saint who's stepped out of one of the best canvases produced by the Siennese School," Joe said cheerfully. "And a heart-shaped neckline that will do credit to Valentina, or whatever that dressmaker's name is. I think she'll look like a million dollars, myself. Especially with her African Campaign ribbon pinned on her chest."

"We haven't seen the African Campaign ribbon here. What's it like?" Dexter inquired, speaking for almost the first time.

"It's green with brown bindings. It has the American colors in bars down the center, and the enemy colors in bars down the sides. It's just as snappy as it can be."

"I'm proud as Punch that she's earned the right to wear it," said Serena, finding her voice too. "But, Joe, will— will she be able to *do* anything?"

"Oh, sure!" Joe said, still cheerfully, holding out his drained glass as he spoke. "Alix, I never could fly with one wing—Thanks, that'll keep me fluttering anyway for the next few minutes . . . She'll be able to do lots of things in time. We don't know yet just how much use she'll have of her hands, but some. She hasn't lost any of her fingers, which is a minor miracle. I'm afraid they won't all flex easily or grip firmly, but we'll see. I think she'll be able to hold a book and do a little knitting, after awhile. I don't suppose she'll sit up, without support, for a good many months, but there'll be no reason eventually why she can't be moved back and forth between a bed and a sofa, and get a change that way. I think——"

"But, Joe, that wasn't what I meant when I asked if she'd be able to do anything! I meant, would she be able to go back to her nursing. And from what you tell us——"

Serena was vainly trying to keep her voice under control. Joe interrupted her before the attempt became any vainer than it was already.

"No, Mrs. Farman, she won't," he said. "I don't see that it would help to pretend that she might, so I'm not going to string you along. But she's *been* a nurse. She's done what she'd set her heart on doing, and she's done it magnificently. Don't you think that counts for more than *how long* she could do it? I hope you do, because Judith does herself. She's happy with the prospect of doing something else now."

"I can't believe it. You don't know Judith like we do, Joe. You haven't seen her but a few times. That's what Daniel meant, when he spoke about her being more like a high-strung filly than a gentle lamb. Judith's our daughter and it's natural——"

"I'd like to hear the rest of what Joe started to tell us, wouldn't you, Mother?" Alix inquired. She had taken the baby from his grandfather now, and held him cradled in her arms as she nursed him without ado or self-consciousness. His downy head was pressed against her bosom, his small fists kneaded it as he suckled, and every now and then he stopped long enough to draw a deep contented breath and look trustfully up at his mother before he attacked his source of supply again. "What is Judith planning to do next, Joe?" Alix inquired.

"Well, we've got a plan worked out for her to help me. We've talked it over. We've got Peter to thank for it really. You see, when the accident occurred, he'd just persuaded Judith to tell him about some of her impressions and experiences, with the idea of shaping them into stories himself. Then he found he wouldn't be able to do it, because Judith was coming home and he was going on to Tunisia. So he gave the tip to me. Just the way he did about the little old unfinished shoe. And day before yesterday I spoke to Judith about it. That was the first time she'd been able to talk much, but she fell right in with the idea. She started in and told me a story about a man who was a medical aide, up in the front lines—that's where the M. A.'s are most of the time, of course, because that's where they're most needed. But this one was very comfortably settled in quite a nice foxhole, when a man in another foxhole called out that he had a headache and wanted an aspirin tablet. The aspirin was in a kit wagon way back at the rear, so our hero climbed out of his foxhole and crawled back to the wagon. He got the aspirin and gave it to the man with the headache. Then he crawled back to the wagon a second time to replace the medical kit, and had one leg up, just ready to crawl in, when a shell came along and got his leg. He was taken to tent city and Judith was his nurse. She thought the headache came pretty high."

"You're going to make a story out of that!"

"You thought it was interesting just the way I told it

then, didn't you? After I get it dressed up, you won't know it. If I can't sell it to the *Post,* I can sell it to some other magazine. There are lots of other magazines, and they all have to print stories. You wouldn't think so sometimes, from the way the editors act, but they do. So Judith and I are going to cater to them. She's going to tell the stories to me and I'm going to write them down. We're going half and half on the proceeds."

"Well, that's generous of you Joe, and thoughtful. You've shown a kind spirit, like you always do. But Judith won't be contented, month after month, just lying in a hospital bed, doing a bit of reading and a bit of knitting and waiting for you to come and see her once in a while, so she can tell you a story. I don't see how you ever came to think she could be. We've got to think of something else for her to do. We've got———"

"Oh, I have thought of something else! I've given it a hell of a lot of thought, really I have, Mrs. Farman. I figured myself the hospital would wear her down after a while, not just Walter Reed either. I knew that in the natural course of events she'd be sent from there to Forest Glen, which the Army uses for a convalescents' home now. I was damned if I was going to let poor Judith go to Forest Glen, after everything else she's been through. On top of North Africa, it would be just too much. If you could see it once, you'd understand how I feel. It used to be a girl's finishing school, and I should think it would finish almost any girl. It pretty nearly finished me. It's all up hill and down dale, with rocks and rills and woods and temple hills—Well, I don't know as there are any temples, but there are medieval fortress and Chinese pagodas and Swiss chalets and Spanish haciendas and moated castles. I believe these were the former sorority houses, but they look like something you might dream about when you'd eaten fried oysters and mince pie just before you went to bed. Or when you were coming out of a long siege of D. T.'s. I'd just polished off a pretty good meal, the first time I went there, with a couple of drinks, or it might have been three, along with it. It was coming on dusk when I got up to the main building, and all I could see, no matter what direction I looked in, were row and rows of stucco maidens, upholding the brick arches of the porticos. I decided I must have forgotten to put any water in my whiskey, so I staggered off to sober up before I went to the desk, but every place I stumbled into, here was another virgin. Every one of them made of stone. Of course that was the worst of it. So finally——"

No one had interrupted Joe. He had interrupted himself to look at Alix. She was laughing so heartily that she had amazed even her baby, who abruptly stopped nursing to stare at her, and then burst into roars of infantile glee himself. Daniel was laughing too, in a quiet way he had which shook him without making any sound, and Dexter had lost the strained sober look which had become almost as habitual with him as Alix' expression of sadness had with her. Only Serena's face was still unrelaxed, and she glanced with bewilderment from one to the other.

"I must have missed the joke somewhere," she said. "I don't quite understand what this peculiar place you're talking about has to do with Judith. And I still don't feel easy about her, Joe, whatever you say. I keep on thinking of her lying helpless in that hospital room, month after month."

"But I'm trying to tell you that she won't be, Mrs. Farman. I'm telling you very badly and I'd be sorry, except that I am pleased because I made Alix laugh . . . Were you ever in Forest Glen, Alix?"

"Yes," Alix said, wiping her eyes with her delicate handkerchief. "I went there once while it was still a girls' school, to visit a friend. And you made me see it all over again. I felt just the way you do about the stucco virgins. And the fountain that looked like a birthday cake. And the urns. Did you ever see so many urns, Joe, in all your life?"

"Did I ever?" said Joe excitedly. "Well, that was it, Mrs. Farman. I didn't think Judith would ever make a satisfactory convalescence among all those rocks and rills and fountains and urns. And I didn't think the example of the stone virgins would be good for her either. I thought that was the last sort of thing a girl like Judith

ought to look at." Again he paused for an instant, as he
had before when he seemed to be treading on delicate
ground, and this time he shot a quick glance at Dexter.
To his infinite relief, Dexter glanced back at him, and he
saw that there was no resentment in the New Englander's
eyes, but amusement and understanding and something
akin to friendliness. "I had the male convalescents in
mind too," Joe went on, with renewed buoyancy. "They all
wear maroon jumpers, which don't appeal to me personally, but you never can tell what will take a girl's eye. So
I asked Mrs. Porterfield if it wouldn't be all right to
bring Judith out to Alexandria as soon as the little matter
of Army regulations regarding discharge had been fixed up
and I could pry her loose from Walter Reed. A C. D. D.,
that's what Judith will have to have, and of course it will
take time to get it. But I thought that in the meanwhile
it would be helpful if Judith had something to look forward to. And Mrs. Porterfield was delighted. She took a
liking to all the girls who came there together and slept
in her attic. Which reminds me, have any of you heard
from Gracie lately? You remember Gracie, don't you,
Mrs. Farman, that cute little piece who did the night clubs
with me? I had a letter from her just the other day. She's
engaged to three men. One of them is in Texas and one's
in Iceland and one's in Aberdeen, so with everything arranged so well, geographically speaking, there aren't any
complications for her. But her correspondence must be
quite a burden to the censors."

Alix laughed again. Joe did not interrupt himself this
time because of her laugh. It encouraged him to go on.

"Of course Mrs. Porterfield's house is full up, as usual,"
Joe said. "She's gone right on using the attic for a dormitory,
it worked out so well for those five nurses. She's got five
WAVES in it now. A new Mid-Western Congressman has
the Victorian room you slept in, Mrs. Farman. Gundesen,
his name is—a good fellow too. Not that he and I agree
about anything. But that makes the meals more interesting.
. . . Well, so I couldn't get the Victorian room for Judith
and that has moved me to make a really heroic sacrifice.
I have told Mrs. Porterfield she could have my room

cleaned. Under my personal supervision, naturally. I've arranged with the *Bulletin* to take three days away from the
office for this supervision. Mrs. Porterfield agreed with
me that we ought to be able to get off the first few layers
of dirt in that length of time. Of course Judith will want
to do a lot more than that, herself, as soon as she's able.
It's taking a mean advantage of her, isn't it, to put her
down in the midst of such a mess, when she can't do anything about it? I know her fingers will be simply itching
to scrub the floor and the woodwork, not to speak of
sifting and sorting all my papers and throwing away half
my good clothes. But I'm safe for a while anyway. And
it really will be a nice place for her. You remember it,
don't you, Mrs. Farman? It runs both the length and
breadth of the ell, so it's a great long room. It has a
little gallery at the end of it, and windows on three sides,
so there's sunshine there all day. It has a private bathroom and three big closets—I think one of those could
be made into a kitchenette, or at least a little gallery. Mrs.
Porterfield's perfectly willing to see what can be done. Not
that she doesn't always provide plenty to eat, as you
know, but sometimes it's fun to fix up a little private snack,
and then there's always the question of drinks. A regular
apartment would have been better, in a way, but then it
would have cost more, and of course I haven't any money,
never expect to; and then besides, there just aren't any
apartments in Washington or environs, that's all there is
to it. Only the other day we carried a piece in a box about
a Chicago woman who was suing her husband for a di-
vorce because he left her the day after the wedding to
hunt up an apartment in Washington and she hasn't heard
from him since. That was two years and a half ago, and
she's getting impatient. She doesn't know the situation as
well as I do, or she wouldn't. If I were the judge, I'd tell
her to give her poor bridegroom a break."

Everyone was smiling now, even Serena. Nevertheless,
though her anxiety was somewhat assuaged, her bewilderment still persisted.

"I can see where Judith could be made real comfortable

in that room of yours, if it really did get a good thorough cleaning, Joe," she said. "It is spacious and sunny, same as you say. Quiet too, at the back of the house like it is. There wouldn't anything disturb Judith there. I don't know how you feel about it, but every hospital I was ever in, you couldn't try to take forty winks without a nurse coming in to wash your face or take your temperature or give you nourishment. I should think most anyone would need a rest cure, after coming out of a hospital. . . . That room of yours has a pleasant outlook too, right over Mrs. Porterfield's yard, with those handsome magnolia trees in it. The gallery'd be pleasant too in the springtime. Judith could be rolled right out there, and have a change and get the air, even if she couldn't sit up much. Why, I think it would be real nice for her! And she could go on having treatments from this doctor who understands her case so well, if she needed to, near him like she'd still be. I know we couldn't do for her what she ought to have up here. Maybe we can get down to visit her. I'm dying to see her, but I don't know . . ."

"Of course you'll go down to visit her, Mother. You'll go back with Joe. I'll look after Father and Dexter while you're gone."

"That's what I wanted to suggest, Alix, if it wouldn't be too much for you."

"Of course it wouldn't be too much for me, Joe. I'm very strong."

"I guess you are at that."

Joe's scrutinizing gaze rested on her again, with increasing appreciation. The baby had gone to sleep now, replete with milk. Alix had fastened her dress again without disturbing him, but she had made no move which suggested she was thinking of carrying him off to bed. It was evident to Joe that she did not intend to stir until she had heard him out, and that she did not believe he had yet come to the end of his story.

"Besides, we Louisianians have got to stand together, you know, in this hotbed of New Englanders," she said. "Perhaps you'll do as much for me someday."

"You bet your life I will," Joe replied heartily. "All right then, Mrs. Farman, it's settled that you're taking the next plane back to Washington with me."

"The next plane! Now, Joe, I didn't say anything about taking any plane. I said I was dying to see Judith, but I guess I can wait until a train can get me to Washington, you've relieved my mind so much about her. We'll talk about ways and means later. If you'll excuse me now, I think I'll go and have a look at the kitchen fire. I could sit here forever listening to you, but the time's coming when you'll be wanting your supper. I do take it very kindly, Joe, that you made the trip up here on purpose to tell us all about Judith at first hand. And you certainly have looked out for her welfare, better'n anyone I know of could have done it. Just the same, it seems too bad that you should be turned out of your room when you've had it so long and like it so much; I know you've got used to having your things there. There aren't many men would be so unselfish, I realize that. It's kind of imposing on your good nature to let you do it though."

"You must have misunderstood me, Mrs. Farman. I'm not that good-natured, not by a damn sight. I've made all the concession I'm going to, saying I'd have the room cleaned up. But I haven't the least idea of getting out of it. After all, I don't think I'll be much in Judith's way. It's a great big room, and I have to leave for the office every morning around six and altogether . . ."

Alix sat very still. Again Daniel realized that her quietude was also her force. Dexter was very quiet too, and for a moment the smile left his lips. Then he looked at Alix; she returned his glance with a smile of her own, and his smile came back. Joe got up and lumbered over to Serena, putting his arm around her.

"Oh, hell," he said, "I came here on purpose to tell you that Judith and I are married, and then I left that part out somewhere along the line. I married her the night she got back. The doctor said I could see her for five minutes and that was enough." Joe cleared his throat a little and then he bent over and kissed his mother-in-law. "I hope you don't mind because that was the way I did it," he said. "It seemed to be the only way I could do it. And we're both so happy we can't see straight. So I guess myself it was meant to be that way."

CHAPTER 31

THEY DECIDED to have supper in the kitchen, because Joe's visit marked a great occasion. They had compromised about the use of this room since the cold weather began: it was kept in perfect order, and Alix assiduously fostered its open and useful character, determined that it should not again deteriorate into a closed and chilly catch-all. The Red Cross Unit still continued to meet there, three times a week, and on those evenings a roaring fire was built on the great stone hearth to supplement the furnace heat, which was kept carefully in check. Alix also continued to care for her cheeses in this room, finding that when she was moving actively about, she could generally keep comfortable, even if it was not warm enough for sedentary work; when she could not, she built a small open fire or pushed up the furnace temporarily. But the family habitually ate in the living room again, for the winter was the severest in many years, and the fuel situation presented complications. Coal had so far been available, but it had to be hauled all the way from the Junction, and the query as to how much longer there would be gasoline enough to do this constantly arose; there was not space enough in the cellar to store large quantities at a time, and it was so expensive that even small quantities made a considerable dent in the budget Alix had carefully worked out. The oil heaters in the hallways, set up as a temporary expedient when Alix first came, had been cautiously kept where they were after the installation of the coal furnace; but the amount of oil allowed by the rationing board hardly sufficed to take the chill off the air. The parlors had been regretfully but resolutely shut off; however, the door between the entrance hall and the living room was kept open, because it was necessary for Alix to use this passageway to get to and from her bedroom, and it was not safe to expose either her or the baby to extreme cold or sudden changes of temperature. Privately, Dexter rejoiced at this necessity; it kept the front of the house from having the secret look which he had formerly found so sinister. And he was pleased now when he saw her flinging open the parlor doors and passing back and forth into the summer kitchen setting the table. Without any admonition from her, he brought in great armfuls of wood and started huge fires in all these rooms. Firewood, fortunately, was still abundant on the place, though time and labor for cutting it and getting it in were lacking. But he felt, as she did, that this was an occasion for prodigality, not for prudence; and she paused beside him, with a duster in her hand, as he was brushing up the hearth in the West Parlor, there was nothing forced about the smile with which he returned her pleased glance.

"Thanks, Dexter. You've helped a lot. I did want this to seem like a party, and now it will. You like Joe Racina, don't you?"

"I don't see how anyone could help liking him. He's a thoroughly likable fellow. You don't realize that he's homely as a hedge fence, as we say around here, because he's got such a way with him, as we also say around here."

"They're both good expressions. I'll adopt them. And I know just what you mean about Joe, because in a different way, the same thing's true about you. I didn't notice you were lame, until I'd been here for weeks and weeks. You give a general impression of such strength that it's hard to realize you're handicapped in any way. And then of course you're so good-looking that nobody who can see your face thinks of glancing down at your feet."

Alix was dusting the ruby glass vases on the mantelpiece. She put down the one which was decorated with the golden deer and picked up the one which was decorated with the golden bird as she spoke. She did not look around while she continued the pleasant task of "redding up" for company the room which had been closed, and her voice, like her manner, was impersonal. She could not see the deep flush which overspread Dexter's face, and she was apparently oblivious of the strained note in his speech when, rather belatedly, he answered her.

"Didn't Jerome tell you?"

"Why, no, he never mentioned it. Probably it didn't seem noticeable to him either. Noteworthy rather. I don't believe he felt it was important enough for special mention."

"But, Alix, if I hadn't been lame I'd have gone to war. Jerome must have realized that and you must have realized it too."

"Jerome may have realized it. I'm not saying he didn't. I'm only saying he didn't think it was important enough for special mention. And I'm sure he thought that what you're doing here *is* important. You know I've always felt that it was. It never occurred to me that you ought to be doing something else, so I never gave any thought to the reason either."

The fire was burning brightly now behind the polished andirons and the hearth was swept and garnished. Dexter straightened up.

"Are you paying me all these compliments to help save my pride?" he asked almost harshly. Usually he was gentleness itself in speaking to Alix. She stopped dusting and turned to look at him.

"I wasn't paying you compliments," she said quietly. "I was telling you the truth. It seemed natural to say what I did to you, Dexter, after what you said about Joe Racina. I'm sorry if I offended you. I keep forgetting how averse you New Englanders are to what you call 'personal remarks.' We Creoles feel honored when anyone pays us a sincere tribute. And I didn't realize your pride needed saving—either because you're a farmer instead of a soldier or because a girl you don't love any more has married a man who does love her. Of course I understand that you might feel slightly chagrined because he won her so easily when you couldn't win her no matter how hard you tried. But that would be a very superficial viewpoint, wouldn't it? A feeling like that couldn't cut deep, or at all events it shouldn't. You ought to know by now that love must be mutual to be triumphant. And Judith didn't love you as much as you loved her. She wanted to be a nurse more than she wanted to be your wife. But she'd rather be Joe's wife than the reincarnation of Florence Nightingale."

"You've taken all the wind out of my sails, haven't you? As completely as when you told me you were going to clear the mortgage on this place and keep Farman Hill for your son?"

"I don't want to take the wind out of your sails and I'm not trying to. But when the wind fails, from causes beyond your control or mine, I'd like to see you fall to on the emergency oars and keep the boat going somehow, just the same."

"You'e not suggesting I'm lying down on the job, are you?"

"Not in the physical sense. You're the hardest worker I've ever known, Dexter. And you've got one of the best minds. It's just as good as Joe Racina's. But you don't use yours as well as he uses his. And after all, a mind is just a kind of tool."

"All in all I don't seem to stand comparison with him very well."

"When I did compare you with him, very favorably, you didn't like that either. You're not consistent, Dexter—I don't think there's anything to be gained by an argument, do you? Anyway I don't believe we ought to take time to go on discussing this. The room's in order now and it will warm up presently. That's what we came here to see to. I want to go upstairs to change into a party dress and take one more look at the baby, and then I'm going to put on an apron and help Mother get supper on the table. It must be almost ready."

She did not dally over her dusting any longer. She opened the door and went out into the hall. Dexter followed her, still defiantly, still determined to have the last word. But in the hall they found Joe Racina. For once he was not smoking. He was standing with his hands behind his back, intently scrutinizing the frescoes. Dexter had an uncomfortable feeling that Joe might have overheard the conversation which had just taken place—not that he suspected Joe of intentional eavesdropping, but that he recognized the journalist's unerring instinct for following whatever was going on. However, neither Joe nor Alix seemed in the least uncomfortable. They looked at each other with friendliness and understanding.

"Judith says you call this fresco the tree of life."

"Yes, I do. Don't you think that's a good name for it?"

"Excellent. . . . I suppose you know all the Biblical quotations about that special arboreal growth?"

"I know the one about 'Hope deferred maketh the heart sick. But when desire cometh, it is a tree of life.' I quoted it to Dexter once. Do you remember, Dexter?"

"Yes, I remember," he said curtly.

"It's a good one. And doubtless it was very apt as you used it," Joe remarked casually. "But there are some other good ones too. First that description of the Garden of Eden—'And out of the ground made the Lord God to grow every tree that is pleasant to the sight, and good for food; the *tree of life* also in the midst of the garden and the tree of knowledge of good and evil.' I've always wondered why Adam and Eve bothered with the forbidden tree, when the tree of life was there too, and why hardly anyone ever mentions the fact that it was."

"I never thought of it before, but it's a good point. Tell me more, Joe. There are more, aren't there? You asked me if I knew them *all*."

"Oh, there are lots more. The one I just quoted is in the second chapter of Genesis and the final one is in the last chapter of Revelations, so you see they go all the way from Alpha to Omega. The tree of life must have loomed pretty large on the horizon of the men who penned Holy Writ."

"Yes, it must have. But how did you happen to know so much about it, Joe?"

"Oh, I taught Biblical history for a while, in the course of my checkered career."

"Biblical history!"

"Yes. That wasn't what I started out to teach. I started

out to teach English. At a little freshwater college, the year after I got through college myself. I wanted to go on, you see, and get a Master's Degree, and I didn't have any money. Well, anyway, I started out to teach English, as I said—English I and English III—there wasn't any English II. And then the President discovered I could speak Italian, so he added that to the curriculum. He had a very fancy curriculum, according to the catalogue. Harvard couldn't begin to compete with it. There was even a course in china painting featured on it. Fact."

"Joe, you're making this up as you go along."

"It's the gospel truth. Next I began to teach economics. Economics was the only subject I ever flunked myself— your baby knows more about money than I do. But that didn't make any difference to this bastard."

"Which bastard?"

"The president of the college. He wanted a course in economics and I was the only teacher he could bulldoze into giving one. Agriculture came next. Most of my students were right off the nearest farms, and I'd never been further from New Orleans than Thibodaux until I landed in this institution, but that didn't make any difference. Agriculture I taught, out of a book, keeping one chapter ahead of the horny-handed sons of toil who sat gaping at me. And finally Biblical history was added to the list. I don't know whether my pupils got anything out of that, but I did. I always did like literature."

"Well, please go on about the tree of life."

"I didn't know you wanted me to do it indefinitely. And I don't feel so sure I can give you all those quotations word for word. But I've always thought the most significant of all was the one with the promise, 'To him that overcometh I will give to eat of the tree of life which is in the midst of the paradise of God.' "

"Yes, I think perhaps it is. What's the last of all, the one that marks Omega?"

"Well, it goes something like this: 'He showed me a pure river of water of life, crystal clear, proceeding from the throne of God. On either side of the river was the tree of life which bear twelve kinds of fruit and the leaves of the tree were for the healing of nations.' "

"Do you believe the nations can ever be healed again, Joe, after this war?"

"Yes, if women like you will go on nurturing the tree of life so that it will bear fruit in every month."

Dexter left them in the hall, still looking at the frescoes and still talking about the tree of life. He could not remember when he had been so tired, not even during the long hot summer, when he had sought Alix out night after night on the door rock. Yet in spite of his weariness, his thoughts were tumultuous. He wanted to seek Alix out again now, to tell her he was sorry he had been so churlish, and to claim the same quiet companionship which had formerly assuaged his spirit. But he was afraid there would be no chance tonight. Alix was preoccupied with Joe's visit and its meaning and with Joe himself. She would have neither the time nor the temper for anything or anyone else. Dexter went on to his own room with resentment and rebellion in his heart. Joe and Alix did not seem to notice his departure.

When he came downstairs again, the others were already assembled for supper, waiting for him. But he was not sorry he had taken time to shower and shave and change. Daniel and Serena had both put on their best clothes, and Alix was all in white, with pearls around her throat and wrists. Joe was saying something to her about *La Reine Blanche* and Dexter remembered, vaguely, that it had long been the custom, among certain queens, to wear white instead of black for mourning. He had once read a description of Mary Queen of Scots garmented in this way after the death of the boy king who was her first husband, and he thought it might be the same passage which Joe, who seemed to have read everything, had in mind as he spoke. At all events, Alix did look queenly in her white clothes, with her black braids for a crown, and Dexter felt there was a queenly element about her too, quite apart from her looks: she always had dignity, but she seemed suddenly to have acquired a strange new stateliness which

made her less approachable than before. Very often, when
he was a little late like this, she said persuasively, quoting
her Aunt Odilisse, "If you don't come quickly, the rolls
won't hold the butter!" But this time she did not speak to
him or look at him at all, and he felt that she was perhaps
keeping herself purposely aloof from him because he had
so boorishly rebuffed the graciousness and delicacy with
which she had tried to soften the affront which his pride
had suffered through Judith's marriage. This impression
was intensified by the fact that no one else seemed to find
her unapproachable. Joe, while obviously appreciating her
charm, felt no awe of her; he was rattling gaily on, as they
moved towards the candlelighted supper table, apparently
in answer to some questions which had been put to him
while Dexter was absent.

"Well, I knew if she came out of the operation disfigured, I'd never be able to convince her I wanted her
anyway. So I couldn't take any chances. I had to marry her
first, and to do that I had to work fast. That chaplain at
the hospital is an awfully good scout. He saw my side. In
fact everyone was swell, even the old Colonel. Laura got
a great thrill out of it all. She's always getting vicarious
thrills out of what Judith does. Incidentally, she's back on
the job, taking care of Judith again, or I wouldn't be here.
. . . Well, Laura was bridesmaid and the old Colonel was
best man and there was great regard for all the proper
ceremonial. Believe it or not, I even went to Confession
beforehand. I wore out three priests . . ."

"Joe!" exclaimed Alix, laughing again, though not in the
same way she had laughed when he spoke of the stone
virgins.

"Fact. I started in before Judith got back, because
naturally I'd made up my mind I was going to marry her
as soon as I heard she was coming home. I confessed to
one priest and then after I got out of the church, I remembered a lot more sins I'd committed, so I went back
and a different man was on duty; I knew because I read the
little sign outside the confessional that has the officiating
priest's name on it. Of course I concluded that I'd exhausted the first one, but I persevered. Then I went away

again and I remembered some more sins. Newspapermen
are a bad lot, you must have heard that over and over. But
I was determined to do a thorough job once I'd started. I
went back a third time and——"

"Don't let Joe deceive you," Alix said, laughing again
and linking her arm through her father-in-law's. "It's a
good sign when a Catholic takes his marriage to a girl
who's non-Catholic so seriously, especially when he admits
he's 'wandered a long way from the fold.' . . . Having said
that in your defense, Joe, I'm going to ask you to keep
quiet for a few minutes now, if you can. We always have
grace before meat in this house. It's Father's turn to talk."

They gathered around the candlelighted table, Daniel
taking his place at the foot of it and resting his hands on
the back of his chair. "Lord, for what we are about to
receive, make us duly thankful," he said, as usual. But this
time he did not need a signal from Serena to make him go
on. "Bless this food to our use and us to Thy service—
whatever that service may be. Help us to do our share in
keeping our country safe, and give us understanding so
that we may know Thy will in this regard. Accept our
thanks that the daughter of this house who has been
through danger on a foreign shore among strangers is now
safe in her own land and in her husband's keeping. Let
the new member of our family find favor in Thy sight, as
he has in ours. For Jesus' sake. Amen."

They all continued to stand for a moment with bowed
heads after Daniel had finished. Serena and Dexter echoed
the *Amen* under their breath. Alix quietly crossed herself.
Then Joe coughed a little, turning his face away, before he
pulled out first Serena's chair and afterwards Alix'. They
both looked up at him cordially as they sat down, and Joe
seemed completely at ease in taking his place between
them. But he did not begin to talk again. He waited for
Daniel to speak first.

"The wind's shifted. I wouldn't be surprised but what it
stopped snowing," Daniel remarked, starting to ladle out
soup from the giant tureen. It was one of the soups Alix
made by "taking a few scraps of almost anything and
throwing them helter-skelter into an old iron pot," as her

mother-in-law said; and after he had swallowed the first spoonful, Joe turned again, this time to face Alix, smacking his lips slightly and running his tongue to one corner of his mouth and then to the other, as a further sign of appreciation. Next he picked up a roll, and went through the motions of trying to weigh it, as if to signify that it had no weight at all, before he began to fold butter inside it. But he remained respectfully silent, waiting for Daniel to go on. "I'd like you to see something of the place, Joe," Daniel continued eventually, savoring his own soup. "Of course I can't take you out on the land, not a night like this. But you could look over the outbuildings and the stock, if you're a mind to. You can pass right from the piazza to the woodshed and from there through the wagon house and the cider mill to the horse stable. You can keep under cover all the way. We provide for that in this neck of the woods."

"I'd say you better. But I'd like very much to see the outbuildings and the stock. Do you make cider here? That's something Judith didn't tell me."

"Well, we hadn't for a long time. But we started the old press going again last fall. Alix kept saying she couldn't think of anything that would taste quite so good to her as a nice cool drink of cider, and we felt we had to humor her. I never was given to understand that cider was the best drink for nursing mothers; but then on the other hand, I had heard it was a good thing to humor 'em all you could," Daniel said drily. He looked at Alix fondly as he spoke, and instantly she stretched out her hand and squeezed his. "We got quite a lot of juice, first and last," Daniel went on. "The wild apples that grow along the stone wall out by the Square Field have quite a tang of their own. That cider brought a good price—what we didn't keep ourselves, for drinking and vinegar . . . Dexter, I wouldn't be surprised but what Joe'd relish a glass of cider with his supper. Don't you want to go down cellar and draw some?"

"Yes, I'd be glad to."

"Could I help?"

"No thanks, Joe. I know just where it is. I can manage all right alone."

Dexter was not sorry to leave the firelight and candlelight in the summer kitchen for the darkness of the cellar. For some undefinable reason, he was increasingly apprehensive. He had told Alix the truth when he said he found Joe thoroughly likable, and Alix had driven another truth home in challenging him to admit that his pride did not really need saving because a girl he no longer loved had married another man. But he was baffled by Alix himself. He realized that she and Joe shared a culture and spoke a language which were alien to him, and the realization was disturbing to him. But he did not divine that the most disturbing element in the strain which had arisen was actually his failure to recognize those essential qualities of hers which Daniel saw all too clearly. The lonely wife, the grieving widow, the expectant and later the nursing mother —in such roles as these she was a familiar and friendly figure to Dexter; no matter how much she differed from other women he had known, or vastly she seemed their superior, she was still his close companion. But now that she had become a white queen, he felt she was eluding him. His outlook became hopeless, his world empty at the thought . . .

He drew the cider slowly, and brought it up from the cellar with care. It was cold and clear, a beautiful russet color, and it foamed like champagne as it flowed into the hobnail glasses. It formed a perfect complement to the roast pork, roast potatoes, roast onions, winter squash, hot apple sauce and cold slaw marinated in boiled dressing which now loaded the table. Everyone drank a toast to Judith, draining the hobnail glasses, and Joe immediately reached for the bubble-brimmed pitcher again. Daniel was immensely satisfied at the results of his idea.

"I don't know but what you'd like to stop long enough to look over the old press, while we're going through the cider mill," he suggested. "You can still see the four wooden screws that were put in when it was first set up, along about 1815. They're around six inches across and five feet long. It must have been quite a job to make them. Of course there wasn't any machinery in those days."

"No, of course not. I'd like very much to see them. And anything else you'll be good enough to show me."

"Well, we might go up to the old carpenter shop while we're about it, too. That's over the cider mill. I've got some pieces of furniture there I'm fixing over. When Alix coaxed us into putting this room to use, we had to find some place for the junk that was piled up here. I've got a good share of it mended now, but not all of it. Maybe you might take a notion to have me send you and Judith a few pieces for that big room of yours. Not but what Mrs. Porterfield's house is well furnished. But as long as your father-in-law's handy at cabinet-making . . ."

"That's a darn good idea. I'll look over the available supply tonight and decide what I want most. Then I'll consult Judith and send for what she wants most. That's the way it generally works out, isn't it?"

The prevailing geniality seemed intensified as the meal progressed. The roast pork and its accessories were followed by a creamy rice pudding. The rice had come from Crowley, where Alix had a kinsman who kept her regularly supplied; but the pudding had been made from a recipe of Serena's. You put the uncooked rice into the milk, she explained to Joe, seeing he was really interested in this too. You had to use a deep baking dish, and the oven had to be just right—an even, moderate oven. Then every now and then you opened the oven door and stirred the rice around in the milk and gradually——

"I'd have sworn nothing would have persuaded me to eat a pudding made out of rice," Joe said, passing his plate for another helping. "The library paste usually seems to be the principal ingredient. As a matter of fact, I don't know how Alix ever weakened to the extent of letting you put Crowley rice into a pudding—rice is a *vegetable*, a gift of God to gravy. Good rice takes on the flavor of any meat it's served with and it really shouldn't be served with anything else. But this pudding's the exception that proves the rule. Does Judith know how to make it?"

"Why of course she does! Judith's a real good cook. She's a capable girl, Joe. She can turn a hand to anything."

Serena stopped short. The meal had been so pleasant that temporarily she had been enabled to forget that it would be a long time before Judith could turn her hand to anything, if indeed she could ever turn it easily again. Joe helped out his mother-in-law.

"She can teach me then. I like to cook myself. I'm surer every minute that it'll be a good plan to turn one of those closets into a kitchenette . . . Is this some of your cheese, Alix? And some of your coffee? Well, that was all I needed to polish off the best meal I ever ate. It really *is* the best meal I ever ate. Fact."

By common unspoken consent they lingered on at the table. Joe reached instinctively for an ash tray just as Alix slipped a small glass saucer under his falling ashes. Again he looked at her with appreciation.

"Service with a smile," he observed under his breath. " 'Good? Hell, it's perfect!' . . . I think perhaps it's just as well I can't see the whole place tonight," he added. "I'd never be able to tear myself away, not even to return to my beautiful bride, if I liked it all as much as I like what I've seen so far. Besides, I need an excuse to make that spring visit we planned. I hope you haven't forgotten we did plan it, because I haven't. I think perhaps it may be a summer visit though instead of a spring visit. Say around the Fourth of July. Would that suit you just as well?"

"Yes," Daniel said, looking at Serena, who nodded her assent. "Yes, around the Fourth will be a real good time. We're almost sure to be getting pleasant weather by then."

"Fine! Because I'd like to take Judith to see my mother as soon as she gets her C. D. D. I think I can manage both visits all right because I didn't have my vacation at all last year or the year before that, so I deserve double time and I'm going to try for it. Naturally, I want Mother and Judith to meet. And anyway Judith ought to see Louisiana in the spring, when the water hyacinths are coming into bloom on the bayous and the levees are covered with clover."

"We have quantities of clover on Farman Hill," Serena

said quickly. "The fields are a beautiful sight in clover time. Didn't you notice them, Alix, days when you walked up to the Mill Lot?"

"No. Spring was very late last year, you remember. By the time the clover finally came out, I wasn't walking as far as the Mill Lot."

"That's so. I'd forgotten it was near July before it bloomed."

"In Louisiana, it's in full bloom in April," Joe said. "So are the roses—the shell-pink kind and the butter-colored kind that climb over everything. And the chinaberry trees break out into spiked balls, like rockets. And the sweet olive begins to smell good . . . I should think you might like to go to Louisiana yourself this spring, Alix."

"Yes, I should. I've been thinking of almost the same sort of things that you have. I'd like to take Jerry to visit my aunts just as you'd like to take Judith to visit your mother. And I don't believe there's a sight like the water hyacinths anywhere in the world—amethyst and emerald carpets floating on the top of still waters between lush banks. Last year, when May came, and it was still cold and bleak here, I believe I was more homesick for the hyacinths than I was for anything else. I was thinking of them today too, when I looked out at the snow, sifting against the windowpanes."

Alix was homesick for hyacinths! She had never given the least sign that she was homesick for anything; indeed, she had said repeatedly that Farman Hill was now her home. But she had been thinking of them for months and months, of hyacinths and all that they represented—verdure and fertility and warmth, at a time when Farman Hill was still barren of beauty and bitten by frosts. And now that Joe had spoken of these attributes, her tongue had been unloosed and she had done so too. She wanted to take her baby and go to her own people, when the hyacinths were in bloom! Suddenly Dexter knew that was what she was going to do, that his feeling of foreboding was based upon this knowledge quite as much as it was on the knowledge that his behavior had brought about an estrangement. Or was it because he had created an estrangement that she was going?

"I hadn't made up my mind about the best time for the visit," Alix went on. "I thought it would be better to go while I was still nursing the baby, because I wouldn't want to run the risk of having him upset by a change of food; of course I don't know how much longer I can keep on. Not that there's any sign yet that I can't, but sometimes milk gives out suddenly . . . On the other hand, there's the question of climate. Jerry's a pretty husky specimen, you've seen that for yourself, Joe. But I wouldn't want to take the chance of bringing him back into the cold, after he grew accustomed to a milder temperature. I'd have to keep him in the South until it was warm here too."

"But, Alix, you never said a word before about going south to see your folks! I didn't know you so much as thought of such a thing!"

"I haven't said anything before, Mother, because I wasn't sure what I'd better say. You know I don't usually say anything until I've come to some kind of a decision. But that doesn't mean I haven't been thinking it over. When I promised Jerome I'd raise Jerry here, I didn't mean I'd never take him anywhere else. Jerome wouldn't have expected me to promise that, or wanted me to. He'd have wanted Jerry to know my people also. After all, Jerry's half Creole."

"I never thought of that, Alix, I declare I never did! But you wouldn't stay long if you went, would you? I don't hardly know how we'd get along without you, if you did!"

"Why, Mother, of course you do! You'd get along just the way you did before I came."

"No, we wouldn't, Alix. It was different before you came. We didn't know then what we'd missed, not having you. But now that we do know, we couldn't stand it if you should stay away for long."

She's saying everything I can't say, Dexter told himself, getting up and going to the great hearth. He put another log on the fire, and shifted those which were already there about with the tongs; but when he had done this, he did not return to the group at the table; he stood still, looking down into the flames. He felt as if a heavy weight had suddenly descended on his shoulders, bending them to the breaking point, and as if there were iron bands around his heart, such as the faithful servitor in the old fairy tale had burst asunder. But he could not burst his asunder; they grew tighter every moment, constricting him. He glanced over towards Daniel, and saw that the older man's watchful gaze was already upon him, measuring his misery, and he realized that a burden had descended on Daniel too, and that there were bands around his heart also; but these were easier for him to bear because he had braced himself and breathed deeply when he knew they were inevitable, and he had known this for some time. They had not oppressed him without warning, as they had Dexter, and they were not as heavy or as close in his case. Suddenly Dexter knew all this, and knew also that Daniel understood and shared his suffering . . .

"Well then, I won't stay away for long," Alix was saying. The words should have cheered and released him, Dexter thought, coming slowly back to the table because it was not seemly that he should stay away from it any longer while the others continued to sit there. But they did not. What was it Joe had said about Judith? Joe was not talking any more, he was sitting still and listening intently, while he smoked and smoked; but before enveloping himself in this deep silence he had shot one bolt after another. He had said that Judith had done what she had her heart set on doing and had done it magnificently, and that this counted for far more than how long she she had done it. Well, it mattered less how long Alix stayed in Louisiana than how glad she found she was to get back there and how great a share Prosper St. Cyr had in this gladness . . .

". . . and of course I won't go until you and Father have both been to see Judith," Alix was saying now. "It seems too bad that you both shouldn't go back with Joe, so that you can both see her right away, and together. But I know you think it would 'cause talk,' if you left Dexter and me here on Farman Hill without either of you, so you'll have to make your visits on the installment plan, and I'll keep house until you've finished." This time it was Alix instead of Serena who was saying the words no one else could pronounce, and she did it with delicate archness, in the way Daniel had delighted to hear her speak when she first came to Farman Hill, but which had been so long subdued. The coming of Joe had meant a great deal to Alix; she was cheered and released, even though Dexter was not. Hadn't you better begin to pack now, Mother, while Father and Dexter take Joe out to the barn?" she asked. "I suppose Joe wants to catch the two o'clock train from the Junction, so that he can get the first plane out of New York in the morning, if it clears. He never could get to Montpelier in this storm, even if we had gasoline enough to take him; and I'm sure the planes are grounded there anyway . . . You did mean to take the two o'clock from the Junction, did't you, Joe?"

"Yes, I did, Evangeline Adams. And I expect my mother-in-law to be ready to go with me too. Now that she's got a newspaperman in the family, she'll have to get into his stride. He can't slacken his for her, no matter how much he'd like to—And in this case," Joe concluded, tipping up his cup to get the last drop of coffee, "he wouldn't like to at all. He's in a hell of a hurry to get back to his wife."

She'd had so many different things sprung on her, all the same evening, that she couldn't see straight or think straight, Serena protested; she was so stirred up, she didn't know as she'd be able to manage the packing. Of course she wasn't put out because Joe and Judith had got married the way they did; likely as not it was the only way they could do it, if they were to see anything of each other. She knew what a hospital was like, any hospital, when it came to rules, and she supposed military hospitals were even stricter than others. If Joe and Judith hadn't been man and wife, he never could have got to go there, whenever he wanted to see her. But it was sudden just the same. For her part, she liked time to get ready for a wedding, and this was the second sudden marriage they had had in the family in a little over a year. Serena said this before she thought how it would sound to Alix and was instantly sorry. To cover her confusion, she began to talk about the trip Alix was figuring on taking. Why it would last days and days, coming and going both. Alix would get all tuckered out, and then something would happen to her milk. And Jerry might catch something. Measles. Whooping cough. Even scarlet fever. Serena kept coming from her bedroom, where she was theoretically packing, to the kitchen, where Alix, with a large apron pinned over her beautiful white dress, was unhurriedly washing the dishes. She lamented and protested to such an extent that it took all her daughter-in-law's powers of persuasion to calm her and fortify her for her journey.

"I'll take a compartment straight through from New York, Mother, and Jerry and I'll have just as much privacy and comfort as we would if we stayed at home," Alix told her. "I think I'm justified in doing it, even if it is expensive. Of course it's an expensive trip anyway. But still . . ."

"But still it's your own money. Now don't you get the idea I begrudge you the expense, Alix. You've a right to spend your own money as you see fit. I'd be the last to say you squandered it or that you were selfish about it. You're naturally real saving, and when you do start spending, it's always for someone else."

Serena had reason to speak with sincerity and feeling on this subject. Alix' initial action in clearing the title to the farm to protect it for her son, and in restoring and restocking the property to safeguard its value for him and make it more generally productive, had been followed by other gestures equally generous, wise and patriotic. Scrupulously, she had put a tenth of Jerome's life insurance money into war bonds, since she knew that after six months she would not be able to draw on his salary for that, and she was planning to put all of the small pension she would have after this into them also. The rest of the insurance money had been put aside for Jerry's education, and Alix continued to insist that the major part of her own income must be used for the maintenance and development of Farman Hill. The amount she apportioned for personal expenditures was negligible; her mother-in-law was mystified at the illusion of elegance with which she managed to imbue her wardrobe, considering how little she spent on it; the sums that went to her Church were much larger. With her realization of all this, Serena was genuinely distressed that Alix might think her concern over her daughter-in-law's proposed departure was caused by financial considerations.

"You know I don't begrudge you the money you spend, whatever 'tis, and I'm not asking, don't you, Alix?" she said anxiously.

"Yes, Mother. And I wasn't thinking of the money either, that is not primarily, when I said I thought I was justified in taking the trip. I meant it really wasn't a pleasure trip, or I wouldn't make it in wartime. It's a journey of discovery."

"Now you've got me more puzzled than ever, Alix! How can you make a journey of discovery to a place you've lived in all your life, until this last year?"

"Well, I can. I'll have to explain to you later, or there won't be any time left for you to get packed. But Jerry won't catch anything and I won't lose my milk. You wait and see. We'll both be back here, hale and hearty, in the summertime."

"You *promise,* don't you, Alix?"

"Do you really need to have me promise you, Mother, when you know what I promised to Jerome? Besides, I've told you over and over again I feel this is my home now. But I promised Tante Odilisse too . . ."

"What was it you promised your aunt, Alix? If it isn't prying into your affairs to ask . . ."

"I'll tell you by and by . . . Now let's see—hose, hankerchiefs, bed slippers, face cloth, dressing gown—Is there anything else you want to put in your overnight case, Mother?"

As Alix had suggested, Daniel and Dexter took Joe to see the barn while she did the dishes and Serena packed— or rather, Daniel conducted Joe, and Dexter rather diffidently accompanied them. He knew it would seem surly if he did not go, and he had no wish to do that. But after all it would have been unbecoming of him to take any initiative, as he would have been glad to do if Joe had been disposed to visit the Abbott Homestead or had had the time to do so. This was not his stock, these were not his buildings which Joe was inspecting. They epitomized the stronghold and the granary which Farman Hill had been from generation to generation, together with the new vitality and prosperity realized through the advent of Alix. His only claim of kinship to them lay in the love and labor he had lavished upon them. You could not care for a colt or a calf or even a lesser or an older animal, day after day, he had discovered to his cost, without becoming attached to it, whether it belonged to you or not; and familiar buildings, like familiar beings, had their own meaning and their own appeal. As a child he had played in these places they were going over; as a man he had worked in them. He had a feeling for them which Joe could never approach or fathom. But it was Joe, not he, who was a member of the Farman family now, Daniel's son-in-law, Judith's husband . . .

They passed from the old wagon-house and the old cider mill to the horse stable and milk room and cow barn. Joe's attentiveness was not merely perfunctory. He asked intelligent questions, and it was evident that these were not prompted merely by surface civility, with which—Dexter had already gathered—Joe was not overconcerned at any time. He was really interested both in the rugged attributes of the old buildings, and in the modern improvements which had been recently added to them. He stopped to admire an ancient ox-bow suspended over one of the beams, and a long battered work bench that stood beneath one of the windows; he admired the practicability and cleanliness of the steel stanchions and feeding troughs. Nor was he as totally uninformed about agricultural implements and usages as Dexter had anticipated; he recognized the identity of the straw-cutter, and dipped a questing and capable hand into several meal bags, determining their contents without coaching. But a place like this would never have the significance to him that it did to Dexter; it was not really his province. Instinctively, before long, he found a way of returning to his own.

"Do you ever see anything of your neighbors, the Hellmans, these days?" he asked his father-in-law, as they began retracing their steps.

"No, almost nothing. They're still on the place they bought and improved. And of course they go to the village and the Junction to do errands. Aside from that they don't seem to stir around much of any. Dexter and I have spoken of it more than once."

"How do you figure that out?" Joe inquired, bringing Dexter into the conversation without apparent effort.

"I don't. That is, I can't. It isn't because I haven't tried. Of course we've never found out just what they meant to do here, if anything. I've always thought they wanted to use Jerome's Hill for a signal station, and I know that's what Jenness thought too, from the farewell letter she wrote Jerome. But I've never caught anyone trespassing there, though I've kept a close watch."

"There aren't any similar hills, are there, on the Hellman property, or any other property that's been sold within this last year?"

"Well, of course, this whole countryside's hilly—you've seen that for yourself. But Jerome's Hill is the only one that really stands out, until you get three or four miles south of here, and the elevation there is on property that's been in the same family for as long as Jerome's Hill has belonged to the Farmans. The others are only what I suppose you'd call hillocks. There are two of those on Hellman's place, with a scrubby little pasture between them. And another one on Becker's land, half a mile away."

"The scrubby little pasture isn't big enough for a landing field, it is?"

"Gosh, no! In the first place, if there were ever any lights in it, we'd have seen them long before this, just as we'd have seen any towers on the hillocks and found any kind of machinery."

"Don't you have heavy fogs rising from the river here, a good part of the time? It seems to me Judith told me that even when there's bright starlight overhead, often you can hardly see your hand before your face, on the road. What's true of a road would be true of a pasture."

"Yes, that's so. And we do have those fogs, practically all the year around, except in midwinter. But if there isn't enough light for us to see through the mist, there wouldn't be enough light for a plane to come down, either. You couldn't make a landing in the pasture I'm talking about without killing all concerned twice over—getting in and getting out. There *was* some talk of establishing an airfield here, as you may have heard—there's a plateau that's very well suited for the purpose down by the village. But the project seems to have fallen through. And I can't make out that anything is being done with timberland either. It's as much as your life is worth to get any help with lumbering, let alone finding people who want to go in for it on a large scale . . . No, I think the Hellmans have decided not to go on with whatever they started, or else they're biding their time. I'd give a good deal to know which."

"You're damn right you would . . . And what about all their little playmates?"

"They're all very quiet too. In fact they're intermittently out of town a lot. I think they're getting tired of this quiet place. Incidentally, though, in the lot I first set down as their playmates, there's one family that never was. I found out more about them while my sister was home last summer."

"Yes? What?"

"I don't know that you'd be especially interested. But my sister Rhoda married a Jew last fall—a darn nice fellow named David Cohen, a widower who kept a clothing store in St. Johnsbury for years. I think he was naturalized along about 1920. His young daughter, Rachel, and his little nephew, Benny, spent the summer with Rhoda and me. Rachel was born and brought up in St. Johnsbury, but Benny'd been there only about a year. He was a refugee. Well, the children in the neighborhood began to drift in to play with Rachel and Benny, the way children do, you know. There were two boys and a girl from one of those families I'd been watching, the Lippmans."

"Yes? Well? Of course I'm interested."

Joe swung himself up into an empty hayrack that was backed into the rear of the barn, and dangled his legs over the edge. He did not notice the powdery dust that coated it or the lacy cobwebs that overhung it. He was absorbed in Dexter's story.

"Well, I found out that they are refugees, too."

Dexter leaned against the side of the wall, folding his arms and bracing himself with one foot against the beam which paralleled the floor. He was determined not to betray his impatience to return to the house. Daniel had begun to chew a straw reflectively, and there was a companionable sound of cows stirring in their stanchions and horses moving about in their stalls.

"You've got Jewish refugees farming in this township?"

"Yes. It's really a very arresting family. There's an old lady, over eighty, but still very active and alert. She looks after the poultry, says she'll have more than a thousand pullets in the spring. I gather that her son, August, who owns the farm, was the youngest of her children, and that she's—shall we say, lost?—all the others. He used to be a designer of machinery, the kind used for making labels, if that means anything to you—it doesn't to me. Now he seems to be familiar with every type of machinery and construction on a farm. His wife's a wonder too. She can do papering and painting better than Hite Wendell, our regular man—in fact she's taken over most of his work to free him for farming. But she excels in canning too. I never saw anything equal to what she did with our wild strawberries and Rhoda says the same. She's going out this next summer to demonstrate to farm groups, under the auspices of the County Home Economics Bureau. Meanwhile, she's acting as co-chairman with Mrs. Farman at the Red Cross Unit that has its headquarters in the summer kitchen, where we ate our supper."

"And they have three kids? All smart as steel traps, too, I suppose?"

"They have four. But you're right about the steel traps. The eldest son is about sixteen—he's better at the actual work on the farm than his father. I might add that he's a senior in the village high school and that he's leading his class. But that's almost a racial characteristic, isn't it? His younger brothers and sister all lead theirs, and incidentally

so do Rachel and Benny. The whole family plays various
sorts of musical instruments—I couldn't say offhand how
many, but I believe they want to organize a town band, or
something of the sort, in their odd moments. They've
come out of their shell a good deal lately. At first, they
practically stayed in hiding. It was the younger kids coming over to our house that first turned the trick. And I'm
hoping that sooner or later they'll do us an awfully good
turn with Benny too."

"How?"

"He has something locked up inside of him we can't get
at—not even my sister, who adores him and whom he
adores. When he was smuggled out of Germany to England, his mother had to act so fast that she didn't try to
teach him but three sentences in English—'I am cold'—'I
am hungry'—and 'I feel sick.' She was afraid that if she
taught him more than that he might get confused. Well,
when he landed in New York, David went to meet him,
and welcomed him with great affection and solicitude—in
German. Benny looked at him with a perfectly blank stare
and said in beautiful English, 'I am sorry, Sir, but I do not
understand what you are saying to me.' "

"Gosh! And how long had the kid been in England?"

"Three or four months."

"And he's never admitted since that he knew any
German?"

"Never. David's tried everything he could think of to
make the child talk—spoke to him in German when he was
half asleep at night, coaxed him adding up long columns
of figures, all that sort of thing. None of it has worked.
Neither have letters. Of course not very many of those
have slipped through. But when one does come in, and
David hands it to Benny, Benny gives it straight back, saying very politely, 'Would you mind reading it to me, Sir,
if it's something you think would interest me?' It was
months before he called David uncle, and then he did it as
a mark of affection and not as an admission of relationship."

"And he never refers to his home either?"

"No. The same blank look comes over his face when

Germany is mentioned that appears when anyone speaks to him in German. Of course, his attitude prevents David from finding out anything about the conditions the child lived under and escaped from and how much danger his parents seem to be in."

"Cripes, what a story! And you're hoping it will be the children's game that will finally do the trick?"

"Yes. There's a simple old game they're all very fond of called 'Oats, peas, beans, and barley grows.' Hugo, the little Lippman boy, who's Benny's special friend, is very interested in it, but he can't follow it, even yet. And strangely enough, his brothers and sisters can't seem to make him understand it, though they do themselves, well enough. One day Hugo broke down and cried because he thought he was being stupid. So then Benny put his arm around Hugo, and we thought he was going to explain what it was all about, in German. But at the last moment, after he'd actually opend his lips and made a little sympathetic sound, he closed them again, and the old blank look came over his face. But it was a close shave. We're convinced that someday——"

Joe coughed a little, as he had when Daniel asked grace before meat. "I smoke too much," he said, shaking another cigarette out of the package. "Oh, I forgot—I ought not to be doing this in a barn anyway. Why didn't you remind me?—Well, I'd like to meet the Lippmans the next time I come up—and your sister and brother-in-law too, of course."

"Rhoda and David will be very pleased to welcome you at the Abbott Homestead. They're coming to stay for good as soon as Rhoda's school year is up. She's a teacher, and she thought she ought to finish out the spring term, because teachers are so scarce. But she's been fortunate in finding someone to take her place—through the Lippmans, I believe. She can't go on herself, anyway. She's expecting a baby. She's very happy about it. She was afraid she might be too old."

"Well, that's fine! And your brother-in-law's giving up his business to settle on the farm?"

"Yes. Rhoda didn't urge it at all. But of course he knew

that was what would make her happiest. As far as that goes, I think he's happy about it too, not just for her sake but for his own. And naturally the children are delighted."

"Naturally—Well, I'm afraid I've got to be on my way now. Do you suppose my mother-in-law will be packed by this time?"

They found her in the living room, already dressed in her traveling clothes. She was murmuring that she still could not understand why Alix should be planning to leave in the spring, after sticking it out all winter, and she had also begun to express her concern over the new cheeses— whoever would look after those while Alix was away? No one else had the knack of making them that Alix had . . . But she was ready. Her small, neat suitcase and her small, neat overnight bag were placed side by side near the door. The snowstorm had subsided. The drive to the Junction would not be a bad one, Daniel said, but he added that he thought they should get started in good season, on the chance that there might be trouble of some sort. It was hard to keep the engine from freezing in this weather; besides, his tires were in bad shape and he had not been able to get any new ones. Joe seconded the suggestion of an early start; even if they had no trouble, he thought his father-in-law ought to wedge in forty winks before milking time, and he wouldn't have a prayer, if he didn't start back from the Junction at a fairly reasonable hour. If he and his mother-in-law had time to kill, Joe said, he would take her to a midnight show. No midnight shows at the Junction? Nonsense! Bound to be. Some kind of a midnight show . .

"Goodbye, Alix," Joe said heartily. He kissed her in a brotherly way, without hesitation or self-consciousness. Apparently it did not occur to him, or to her, that he would take leave of her otherwise. "Perhaps we can arrange to meet in Louisiana. I think you've got a good idea about going. Nothing like finding out for sure, you know . . . Goodbye, Dexter. I'm afraid I won't be seeing you in Louisiana, but I'll be seeing you here in July. Keep your eye on those quiet neighbors of yours. I've an idea they'll still stand watching. I'll take your love to Judith, shall I? I'm sure she'd like to know you sent it."

"Yes, of course."

"Well, so long. Take good care of Lucky. Every dog has his day, doesn't he?"

The door closed after him. Daniel was already in the car, arguing with the reluctant engine, and Serena was seated beside him, a look of mingled anxiety and anticipation on her face. Dexter bolted the door carefully and stood watching the car till it lurched out of sight through the snow. Then he turned back towards the house.

The room was very still. The shifting of snow on the windowpanes had ceased with the storm, for there was no wind. Even the tinkling of the old water box seemed to have become a mere murmur. In the fireplace, the flames licked the logs noiselessly, for the well-dried wood did not crackle after it had really begun to burn. Lucky was sound asleep, his legs stretched out, his belly turned toward the warmth. Pinkham was slumbering so deeply that he had ceased to purr. A hush so profound must also be prescient, Dexter thought. Then he realized it came partly from isolation. A house filled with the comings and goings of many persons were never silent like this. But now he and Alix were alone, except for the sleeping baby upstairs. Never had he been conscious, in quite this way, of shared solitude. But Alix was no longer to be seen. The small stool where she had been sitting, with her face cupped in her hands, had been shoved back against the panelling. For a moment, Dexter was afraid that she had gone to bed, that he would not be able to talk with her. The fear mounted as he walked through to the summer kitchen and found that this was empty too, and almost dark. Only the last embers still glowed on the great hearth. He went back into the living room again, and then he noticed for the first time that the door leading into the West Parlor was slightly ajar, and that a glimmer of light shone through it. He pulled open the door and walked in.

Alix was standing by one of the cabinets which had come from Louisiana. She was gazing intently at the precious ornaments which her grandfather had given her grandmother, and the memory chain which was a token of friendship was now wound around her wrist above the pearl bracelet. Dexter walked over to her and put his hand on her shoulder. He had never done anything of the sort before. And at no time had it occurred to him to kiss her, affectionately but dispassionately, as Joe had just kissed her. It did not occur to him now. It meant so much to him to touch her that he could not do it casually. But he felt now that unless he could actually feel her flesh beneath his fingers he could not summon courage to shatter this strange stillness with words.

"Alix," he said. "Alix."

She did not move away from him when he put his hand on her shoulder, yet he felt again, as he had felt earlier in the evening, that some inner withdrawal was taking place, that she was no longer approachable, but aloof. He spoke to her beseechingly.

"Alix, don't go to Louisiana."

"Why not, Dexter?"

She asked the question gently, almost tenderly, and yet Dexter knew that she was not swerved from her purpose. He answered with increasing desperation.

"Because I can't bear to have you go. It's as Mother Farman told you: before you came, we don't know what we'd missed in not having you—how much wisdom, how much grace. There was knowledge at Farman Hill before, but it hadn't mellowed. And there was goodness, but it hadn't flowered. Now we've felt the warmth of your wisdom and seen the bloom of your grace."

"That's a beautiful tribute for a man to pay to a woman, Dexter. I'm grateful for it. I hope I deserve it."

There was nothing in her voice to indicate that she wanted to reproach him because he had shown himself so surly when she tried to pay him a similar tribute. But he knew that the memory of his surliness was still in her mind, just as he knew that nothing he had said had served to divert her from her aim. Doggedly he repeated his petition.

"Don't go, Alix. I couldn't stand it if you left me."

"I haven't said anything about leaving. I promised Jerome his son should be brought up on Farman Hill."

"You didn't say anything about a visit to Louisiana until tonight. If you didn't say anything about a visit, you might not say anything about going for good either. You didn't promise Jerome you'd stay on Farman Hill forever, yourself."

"No, Dexter, I didn't. Jerome wouldn't have asked me to make such a promise."

"Then I'm asking you."

"You mustn't."

"Why not?"

"Because I have to go."

"Why?"

"Don't you know?"

"I think so. But I'm not sure."

"You may be sure I wouldn't go if I didn't believe it was best."

"You're going back to Louisiana to marry your cousin."

"No, Dexter, I'm not. Prosper wouldn't ask me to marry him now."

"Then you're going back to decide whether you'll marry him when he does ask you."

Alix always moved so quietly that Dexter would not have believed there could be more tranquility in her progress than he had observed hundreds of times already. But she had freed herself from his fingers and glided away from him before he realized what had happened. He stepped in front of her.

"Aren't you?" he challenged her.

"No, not primarily. I haven't begun to give serious thought to marriage, Dexter. I was in love with my husband. And he's been dead less than six months."

"But he is dead. You can't live with a memory all your life. You realize that yourself or you wouldn't say you hadn't *begun* to think about marriage. The very way you say that shows you believe you will begin by and by, that you will think of it seriously sometimes."

"Yes, Dexter, I believe I shall."

The complete candor of the statement was disconcerting. Momentarily Dexter was too dumbfounded to retort.

"I really don't know much about marriage yet," Alix

went on, still speaking with the same disconcerning candor. "Of course there is the prearranged alliance, such as Tante Odilisse favors, but from which I shrank because I was unconsciously seeking for romance and I had not found it then. Now that I have had it, I can see that a family arrangement may sometimes be very wise, provided the romantic experience has preceded it. I still feel that without this it would be dangerous, because the yearning for romance might come at any time, and unless it were already satisfied, the consequences might be very awkward for everybody. There should not be any awkwardness about marriage, especially about one which is presumably well organized."

"I think you're putting it very mildly," Dexter remarked ironically.

"Well, I can put it vehemently too. So far I have been referring, indirectly, to Prosper and myself, as you must have guessed. But I can talk about Jerome and myself too, if you insist. Of course Jerome and I were passionately in love with each other, and because this was so, he was eager for the consummation of our love and I was eager that every desire of his should be fulfilled. Later, when I learned the whole meaning of love like his, of course our desires were the same. I have tried to tell you before that such desires must be mutual if there is to be harmony in union. Jerome and I were joyously united, and because he was an honorable man and I was *jeune fille sérieuse,* we were legally united first. But I am not at all sure that is all there is to marriage, and I did not have a chance to find out, because Jerome was obliged to leave me before we had emerged from our first rapture."

"It sounds to me as if you were thinking a good deal about marriage after all. If you're not, what are you thinking of?"

"I can't help feeling it is rather presumptuous of you to ask, Dexter, especially in that way. But I will tell you, if it will comfort you or clarify things for you. I'm thinking of the whole pattern."

"The whole pattern?"

"Yes. What some dramatist has called the design for living. I haven't drawn mine yet. Not because I haven't tried. But because something keeps happening to it. I thought I was drawing it when I left Louisiana and went to work in a store. Then I met Jerome, so I gave that up. I married him and started another pattern, a pattern that came to include another person—a little child. Then Jerome went to war and I began here, weaving along with several other persons. Then Jerome died. I thought perhaps I could go on weaving with the other persons, just the same, even if he were dead. But now I've found out that I can't."

"When did you find that out?"

"Not all at once. Just little by little. Perhaps, if you must ask questions, it would be better to ask me how than when."

"All right. How?"

"By seeing the snow drifting against the windowpanes. By realizing you couldn't rise above your lameness and your defeat. By hearing Joe talk about the tree of life."

"All today!"

"It only crystallized today. But it must have been coming for a long time. I've got to straighten out the pattern, Dexter, and I can't do it here. I've lost my sense of perspective. I've got to regain it. I've got to go away so that I can."

"You're deserting us when we need you most!"

"No, I'm not. I'm leaving you for a little while so I can be sure how to help you best in the end."

Suddenly she held out her hand. The gesture was generous rather than impulsive. But Dexter did not respond to it and she let her hand fall slowly to her side again.

"Cher," she said softly. She had never called him that before and he did not grasp the implication. She saw that this was so, and she went on speaking with increased gentleness. "You must not think, Dexter, that I shall leave here without a wrench. It is true that I have longed to see a southern spring again. But I found spring very beautiful here, when it finally came. Don't you remember what I said to you last year—that it seemed doubly precious because we waited so long for it and lost it so soon?"

"Yes, I remember."

"And it is also true that I shall be glad to see my own people—the people who were mine before I married," she said, correcting herself, "and to live as they do again, at least for a short time. While I'm pondering on the pattern, Dexter. Thinking how to make it beautiful—and permanent. Besides, I'm not going yet, you know. Probably not for a couple of months. We'll see a great deal of each other in those two months."

"And what good will that do me, if afterwards you're going?"

"I don't know. But you do. You must. If you didn't, you wouldn't have asked me not to go away at all. If I am wise and—and gracious, as you were kind enough to say, won't my wisdom and my graciousness mean something to you, in these next months?"

"No. Not enough. Not any longer. Not unless I can have your love too. I've got to have that to survive."

They were out at last, the words he had vowed never to utter. Before they were out of his mouth he was horror-stricken. He was sure Alix would flee from him now, as soon as she had rebuked him according to his deserts. But she only stood still, looking at him very gravely.

"There is a time and a season for all things, Dexter," she said. "And this is not the time or the season for you to speak to me of love. I wish I might have left before you did so. You are strong enough to survive by yourself. I am very sure of this. But we will speak of it again—at some other time and season."

CHAPTER 32

NONE OF THEM was ever quite sure who first mentioned the suitability of having a Fourth of July party at Farman Hill, or what was given as the primary reason why it should be considered timely and appropriate.

At Christmastime, no one had suggested that the neighbors should be bidden, as usual, to drink a New Year's toast in the first Jerome's punch. Neither Daniel nor Serena could have borne the thought of reviving the memories of the preceding New Year's Eve, when Peter had helped Dexter to brew the punch and Jenness had fluttered to and fro in her ice-blue finery; and during the grim months which followed, the fleeting visit of Joe Racina was the only one which broke the gruelling monotony. Somehow, the women who formed the Red Cross unit managed to meet more or less regularly, though there were some nights when they had to knit alone at home instead of going out to roll bandages together, because the depth of the snow made the roads utterly impassable, or the arctic cold both prevented them from leaving the pipes in their houses unguarded and from rashly risking exposure to the weather themselves; but except for these faithful workers, no one even tried to be neighborly, in the old sense of the word. Even if so-called "pleasure driving" had not been officially banned, actual lack of gasoline in the vicinity would have effectually precluded any but the most essential movements at all times; and periodically, when the source of supply was completely paralyzed, these were prevented too. Inevitably, the fuel-starved region hibernated.

Besides, a blight had fallen on Farman Hill itself. To a great degree, Alix had been resourceful enough and strong enough to counteract the effects of the disgrace and death of Jenness, and her steadfastness and self-control acted as a challenge to the others after the loss of Jerome. But the consternation roused by her resolve to leave for Louisiana, and the restraint which Dexter had caused by his confession of despair and yearning gradually corroded the atmosphere. Alix herself could not cope with this change because her very efforts to restore harmony and good cheer were a constant reminder that during her impending absence there would be no one to bolster the flagging courage of the household. Even the contagious joviality of the baby lost its effect as one terrible day of cutting cold relentlessly succeeded another and still no sign of deliverance came, while the problem of provisions grew more and more acute. There was no meat coming into the village, and there were few immediate means of augmenting the local supply, which had gradually become more and more inadequate as the community had mistakenly learned to depend more and more on outside sources. Other standard foodstuffs were equally scarce. The Farmans, and their neighbors were all planning to keep more cattle and hogs and hens in the spring, and the Farmans did not add, as many others did, "If we can get the help to take care of them and pay for the grain to feed them." They were undaunted by the prospect of harder and harder work, and thanks to Alix, they were "better fixed" financially than most. But meanwhile, even women who had prided themselves on always setting a good table, though they had but little to do with, were fretting, and the men who had always considered that they were good providers were fuming, and both groups were worrying.

Alix alone seemed to have escaped the vicious contagion. She worked longer and longer hours without visible signs of fatigue, and when she sat down to rest, holding her baby in her arms, she sang a spiritual into which she tried to infuse the same encouragement which she animated "Goin' Home to Glory":

" 'Ol' 'Lijah was a prophet which was favored by de Lawd,
    He passed so many miracles dat all de folks was awed.
    Ol' 'Lijah worked on orders dat he got straight from
        de Lawd.
    Glory halleluia!

    De ravens fed ol' 'Lijah in de lonesome desert lan'.
    De Lawd He sont de ravens kase dere was no grub
        at han',
    Dey brought ol' 'Lijah bread an' meat dere in de
        desert lan'.
    Glory halleluia!"

Intrinsically, the tune of "Ol' 'Lijah" was as catchy as any she had sung; but somehow the magic had filtered away from her music. One evening when Dexter came in and found her sitting in front of the fire with Jerry, he spoke to her almost harshly.

"If you don't mind very much, I wish you wouldn't stress such an optimistic note, tonight."

She stopped singing instantly and regarded him with mild wonder, but without either anger or protest.

"Of course I won't sing, if you don't want me to," she said quietly. "I didn't realize it annoyed you."

"You know darn well it doesn't usually annoy me. But I don't think I could stand any kind of a song tonight . . . I'm afraid Gypsy's dying, Alix."

"Why, he whinnied to me, the way he always does, when I went out to the barn this morning! I took him some apple parings."

"Yes. But I've noticed that he's been getting steadily weaker this last month. And just now, when I backed him out of his stall to take him to the watering trough, he collapsed on the floor. I've put a lot of hay under him, especially under his head. He keeps trying to raise his head. But there's no strength left in his neck."

"Have you told Father?"

"No, not yet. You know how he grieved when he found Nell dead in her stall. And Gypsy's the last of this race."

"The new colts are coming along finely, Dexter."

"Yes. But it's a different strain. It won't make up to Father Farman for the loss of Nell and Gypsy. He's still milking. I thought I wouldn't say anything to him until he'd finished."

"I'll come with you, Dexter, right away."

She always kept some heavy wraps in the entry, handy to slip into herself and to button around Jerry. She did not put her baby down, but carried him in her arms as she went quickly out to the barn beside Dexter, with Lucky at her heels. They opened the door of the horse stable softly, as if it had led into the death chamber of some beloved relative. Gypsy's great body, extended on the barn floor, almost blocked their passage; but Alix walked quietly around him and sat down on the lower of the two steps which led up to the floor of the main barn, looking about her for the best place to install Jerry. As usual, there was some loose hay lying about, and she shoved stray wisps of this together until she had assembled enough for a little nest in which she could place Jerry. The baby had just begun to sit up unsupported, and he did so now, without objection, in the small snug nest made by hay; but instead of laughing and crowing, as he usually did, he looked about him with large eyes which were still trustful, but which wonder and solemnity had darkened for the first time. Lucky crouched down beside Jerry, his dog-smile gone too; his head, instead of being held high, as usually, was laid sideways on his paws, and small whining sounds came from his throat. Having settled the baby and soothed the dog, Alix went over to Gypsy and knelt down beside him, tucking more straw under the heavy head which he was still ineffectually trying to raise.

"Is there anything more we can do for him?" she whispered to Dexter, who was leaning against the grain chest which flanked the steps, looking miserably towards the dying horse. He shook his head.

"No. If there were, I'd be trying to do it, instead of just standing here."

"You don't think he's suffering, do you?"

"No. He's just breathing his life away."

"Will it last long?"

"I don't think so."

Dexter crossed over and knelt down beside Alix. She spoke again, very softly.

"Can you guess what I'm thinking of, Dexter."

"No. How could I?"

"I'm thinking of the time I lay breathing my life away, and you saved me. It makes me wish that together we could save Gypsy now."

He made a small sound of disparagement. He had never permitted her to thank him for the transfusion which had saved her life, or even to suggest that she owed this to him. Now he made a gesture which was almost contemptuous.

"Why are you always angry, Dexter, when I thank you?"

"I'm not angry. But there isn't anything to thank me for. I wish you wouldn't talk about it."

"I won't, if it displeases you, I only wondered whether you could guess my thoughts. Sometimes, in moments like these, two persons can be even closer together mentally than they are physically. You and I were, that other time. You knew I wanted you to stay with me. You told Dr. Barnes so."

Again he made a small sound, but this time it was indeterminate. He could not shut her off, curtly, when what she said was so true. They had been mentally very close together, that dreadful night after Jerry's birth, and they had been physically very close too. They had lain side by side on her bed, with hands clasped and shoulders touching. They were kneeling shoulder to shoulder now, and presently, though inadvertently, their hands touched. Neither one drew away. Watching together beside the dying horse, they recaptured some of the lost chords in the harmony which had so long eluded them. They were still kneeling shoulder to shoulder when Daniel swung open the gate beside the stanchions and came in from the cow barn. He saw, before they did, that Gypsy was dead, and lifted Jerry from his nest of straw, to take the baby away.

Daniel took the horse's death very hard, as Dexter had predicted he would. He had never been able to bring himself to shoot any kind of an animal which had to be put out of its misery. He had always hired a veterinary to come and do this, even when times were hardest, leaving the farm long enough to be sure that he would not hear the shot when it came. It was also always understood that when one of the old horses died a natural death, he could call on Hite Wendell to come and drag it away and bury it. But the intense cold precluded burial now. Hite could only drag Gypsy to a secluded part of the woods and leave his body there. They all kept thinking of him in that way. . . .

Though the strain between Dexter and Alix had perceptibly slackened under their shared sorrow, this did not prevent her from carrying out her purpose of going south, and she departed with Jerry late in February, leaving Lucky behind her. The dog drooped wretchedly after she went, reflecting the spirits of everyone in the household. To make

matters worse, Serena and Daniel successively returned
from Washington so appalled by the state in which they
had found Judith that they could not conceal this dismay,
though Daniel's efforts to do so were slightly more successful than Serena's; they could not understand Joe's
optimistic attitude or the doctor's matter-of-fact acceptance
of the almost imperceptible change in her condition. With
nothing to lighten it, either in evidence or in prospect, the
overhanging depression descended further and further.

A long time elapsed before the pall lifted again, but at
last it was penetrated, little by little, so that here and there
a gleam of light shone through it. The first glimmer came
with a letter from Judith, in her own handwriting. It was
only a note, to be sure, painstakingly achieved in pencil,
but it gave proof-positive that she was beginning equally
unmistakable assurance of her happiness. She was "home,"
she said, and though her parents experienced a temporary
pang that "home" now meant to her a rented room at Mrs.
Porterfield's instead of Farman Hill, they were able to
suppress this. There was nothing wanting in the apartment
—she called it an apartment: the sun streamed through it
from morning until night, making it bright and cheerful.
It seemed so spacious, after the cramped quarters of tent
city and a hospital room that she was almost lost in it,
when Joe was out of it; but when he came home, late in
the afternoon, he filled it for her, in all senses of the word.
He had thought of everything to make it convenient and
comfortable for her, and it was spick and span too, except
for his closet and his desk, both of which she had promised
never to touch; but then, those would not seem like Joe's
if they were orderly, and she would not want any possession of his to lack the look of belonging to him. Justin
wheeled her out on the gallery every pleasant morning,
and she lay there, mostly just basking, but sometimes knitting a little too. She could hold needles very nicely now.
She and Joe had sold one story to the *Post* already—it
was to be published under their joint names, because Joe
insisted it was her story just as much as it was his. They
were drafting another now, a longer one. It might even
turn out to be a serial. She was going to have her picture

taken pretty soon, so they could see her new hair-do. She was almost sure they would like it . . .

The first letter from Judith was followed by numerous others, more and more encouraging in vein, and when she wrote from Louisiana, she did so with a joyousness which permeated every line. They had stayed first with Joe's grandfather and grandmother at the little double-barreled shotgun house on Erato Street, where Joe had grown up. Then they had gone "over the Lake" to visit his parents. Joe's father had now established a bakery of his own at Bay St. Louis. During the depression, there had not been enough revenue for the whole family to live on, under the original arrangement, but now Joe's father was very prosperous. The shop was in the front of the building he occupied and the bakery in the back, with the living quarters upstairs; Joe and Judith had been given the large front room for theirs, and it was always permeated with the faint fragrant odors that drifted up from the bakery. Lying in bed, Judith could look across the Bay, past the spidery walks leading up to the weather-beaten bathhouses, and the shrimp-luggers plying back and forth through the fringe of trees that outlined Cat Island. There were still a few yachts, too, tied up at the wharf, as yet unrequisitioned by the government; they were more or less like Mr. Waldo's yacht, as far as he could judge. But the luggers interested her more, now. The water was warm and still and shiny. It was unlike any water she had ever seen before; the sight of it did something queer to her. She understood now why Alix had said when she first caught sight of the Sound from the train window, that a lump had come into her throat and tears into her eyes. You came to feel about these southern waters very deeply and very soon, whether they were part of the Bay or part of the River or part of a bayou . . .

Speaking of Alix, they had seen quite a good deal of her, though Joe had said beforehand that they might not and Judith could understand what he meant. Both of the aunts Alix had come to visit had huge houses in the old French Quarter, and her stepmother had one in the Garden District. Judith had never seen anything like these houses either, or the scale on which they were run. With intermingled rapture and awe, she described paved patios, spiral stairways, "wing-rooms," ancestral portraits, crystal chandeliers, gilt-framed mirrors and other features of a luxurious way of living as strange as it was fascinating to her. Alix and all her relatives had been very hospitable, so she and Joe had seen a good deal of it, after all. Daniel and Serena devoured these details with avidity, for Alix herself had said very little about them. She wrote conscientiously and regularly, but briefly, and her letters were largely confined to descriptions of Jerry's progress. As the weeks went on, she seemed to become less and less communicative, and it was Judith's letters, rather than hers, which broke the monotony and enlivened the atmosphere at Farman Hill. They did for her parents what letters from Jenness had once done.

Meanwhile Dexter had taken an unpremeditated step which seemed to cause him contentment out of all proportion to any apparent benefits which might accrue to him from it: one day as he was coming home from the village, he noticed that the front door had blown open in one of the small abandoned houses on the lonely stretch of road leading to Farman Hill. It was banging back and forth in the wind, allowing the snow to drift over the desolate threshold and revealing the emptiness within. The natural instinct of the New Englander for preservation of property prevented Dexter from leaving the door like that; presently the wind would wrench it completely from its hinges, and then the snow would sweep, unimpeded, all through the deserted dwelling, doing untold damage. He plowed his way to the blocked door and went through the house, looking for something with which he could barricade the entrance from within; he could always let himself out through a window, and leave this unlocked for the time being, returning later to make everything properly fast.

He passed through several rooms, in his search for something to serve his purpose; it was not until he reached the shed, where some battered blocks of wood were lying about, that he was successful; and meanwhile he had been amazed at the amount of space in the house, which, from the road, looked so small, and also at the number of conveniences it contained. The place, and those which adjoined it, had been bought when he was a little boy by some "summer people" who had "fixed up" this one and had intended to restore and rent the others; but they had soon wearied of their experiment with the "simple life" because this proved so much more complicated than expected by those unversed in the ways of the countryside. They had not made friends with their neighbors, to whom they always referred, condescendingly, as the "natives," and before long they had retreated to their urban ease again, with bitterness in their hearts. But they had never offered the property for sale, and no one had ever tried to persuade them to part with it. Only a little land went with the houses, and this was "sour" through long disuse; no practical farmer would bother with it. The location was too far from the village for the convenience of a man with business or professional interests, and besides, there were very few of these in the township; and there was nothing about the houses themselves, calculated to attract the average outsider. But strangely enough, Dexter was attracted by what he saw of the one which he covered in part, and when he returned to it, later in the day, with a hammer and nails, he went through it thoroughly and thoughtfully. The partition originally dividing the two small rooms on one side of the front door had been knocked out, so that these now formed one large one. On the other side was a dining room, and, at the rear, one large and one small bedroom and a bathroom. The kitchen was in the ell, and there were three dormer bedrooms and another bathroom upstairs. A huge central chimney opened out into adequate fireplaces on every side, there was a good cellar with a furnace, and the foundations seemed firm. The roof was too heavily covered with snow to permit inspection, but there was no evidence of leaks in the house. Before he went to bed that night, Dexter wrote a portentous letter, and a few weeks later he broke a surprising piece of news to the Farmans.

"I've become a property owner," he said, with a touch of whimsicality which he had not shown in a long time.

"A property owner! Land sakes, haven't you always

been one? I don't know what the Abbott Homestead is, if it isn't property."

"Oh, it's property all right! And I know Rhoda and David would always do everything they could to prevent me from feeling I was in the way there. But after all, a new baby can use up a lot of space, as you found out for yourself here this winter, if you didn't find it out before, when your own children were babies, and I suppose you did. Then there's the ready-made Cohen family besides. Rachel and Benny have got to have room for themselves and for their friends. And last but not least Rhoda and David ought to have their own home, without a third person chiseling in on the scene."

"Chiseling! I'd like to know if it isn't your own home! Before I'd let a parcel of outsiders, like the Cohens, drive me off my own place——"

Daniel raised a warning hand. "The Cohens haven't driven Dexter off, Mother," he said. "You wouldn't find a milder mannered man than David Cohen, not in a month of Sundays, or two better behaved youngsters than Benny and Rachel. It was a happy day for Rhoda when she first stepped into David's store, and you know it as well as I do. Why she's been like a different woman ever since!"

"Yes," Serena admitted, "she has. Especially since she found out she was in the family way. At first she was so afraid it wasn't anything but change of life that she wasn't easy in her mind, not for a minute. But now that the quickening's begun . . . Just the same though, I think she's left Dexter holding the small end of the horn."

"Judith did that before Rhoda did, you know." Dexter reminded her. But he did not say it bitterly or reproachfully, and almost immediately he added, "But you must know I don't begrudge Judith her happiness, or Rhoda either. I guess some men are just naturally meant to hold the small end of the horn and that I'm one of them."

"Maybe the end won't be so small as you think for," Daniel remarked. He did not look at Dexter as he spoke, and his voice, as usual, was matter-of-fact, so that there seemed to be no special significance to his words. "In the meantime, before you get there, I'd like to know what his property is you've acquired, if you'd just as lieve tell us."

"I've bought the strip of land that runs along the highway to the village, just beyond the turn, and the three little old houses on it."

"Why, Dexter, you never!" Serena exclaimed. "A saving man like you! Those houses are all tumbling to pieces and it would be as much as your life was worth to raise anything on that land but rocks."

"Two of the houses are badly in need of repair, but they're not tumbling to pieces, by any means. I've been all through them so I know. And the third one's in pretty good shape, as you'd say yourself. After Mrs. Wendell has given it a good scrubbing and Mrs. Lippman has papered and painted it, you won't know it. Of course the land'll have to be reclaimed, but as far as looks go, it won't seem like the same place when the grass has been mowed and the bushes cut back. Incidentally your brook runs through the pasture in the rear. I shouldn't be a bit surprised to find I could get some good fishing there."

"What on earth do you want with a house, Dexter, let alone three of them?"

"Well, I thought I might live in one of them—the one that could easily be made livable. Of course the repairs on the others would have to be done gradually because of wartime restrictions and scarcity of materials and labor. But I think they could be fixed eventually and that they might turn out to be a good investment. I can't help feeling that some day more people are going to find out the country's a good place to live in. If that day ever comes, I could rent or sell the two extra houses. If it doesn't, I still would have had fun fiddling with them."

"But, Dexter," Serena said again. "It makes me feel bad to think of your leaving us to go and live in a house all by yourself when you're so welcome here. There hasn't anything happened, has there, to make you feel you aren't welcome? Because Daniel and I, both of us, would bite out our tongues rather than have you think——"

"I know you would, Mother Farman, and neither of you

has said anything. Neither of you has *done* anything either to make me feel I wasn't welcome. But just the same . . ."

"Well, has *anyone* done something or said something?"

"Now, Mother, we don't want to go prying too closely into Dexter's affairs," Daniel cautioned her. This time he did look at Dexter, and there was kindliness in his glance, and understanding. "Besides, you talk as if he was going clear down to the village. It isn't more than a stone's throw from our front yard to the first of those houses, and one that's in good shape. You could stand right on our door rock and spit to it."

"Daniel Farman, I don't throw stones and I don't spit, and you know it! And as if Dexter didn't have enough to do, with his farm work, without cooking victuals and cleaning house!"

"I thought perhaps you'd still cook my victuals for me, Mother Farman. As Father Farman says, this little place is only a stone's throw away. I planned to keep on coming over here for my meals, or having them with Rhoda and David, if I were nearer the Abbott Homestead than I was to Farman Hill, when mealtime came. I know I wouldn't fare badly, whichever I did. You both set a pretty good table." He grinned, speaking more cheerfully than at any time since Alix had gone away. "Probably I shan't do much housecleaning," he went on. "Men don't, you know, when they're left to themselves. But perhaps Mrs. Wendell will come in once a week or so to clean for me. Or something. Anyway I'd like to try it. I've kept thinking lately that I'd like to lie in bed, listening to the rain on the roof and knowing it was my own roof. And getting up to put wood on the fire and knowing it was my own fuel and my own hearthstone. And fishing in a brook and knowing it was my own stream. And sweetening sourly and knowing I'd restored my own acres to fertility. And I thought maybe David and Rhoda might lend me Benny part of the time. After all, they'll be having a child of their own soon. Benny's nose might be at least bit out of joint at the Abbott Homestead. And he and I get along together better and better all the time. I taught him to swim last summer, you know, and we went fishing quite a few times. Besides, he's getting more and more interested in soil and crops. He asks me questions about them, and I like having him. I like having him with me. It's not unnatural, is it, that we should feel drawn to each other? After all, we're both outliers———"

"But I thought it was Rhoda Benny clung to."

"Yes, he's very attached to her. But after all, Rhoda's a woman and she's got a lot more to fill her life now than she had when she first found Benny. Not that she'd ever have taught him to swim or taken him fishing, in any case. And a boy needs a man to do these things with him, just as a man needs a boy to feel he's projecting his own pursuits and his own pleasures into the future."

Serena continued to look sceptical and troubled. It was outlandish, she said, for a bachelor to talk about looking after a ten-year-old child, without anyone to help him. Just when Benny was beginning to fill out and act human, too! Dexter tried to soothe her.

"Of course I'd come to you all the time for advice," he said tactfully. "And you'd be feeding him, most of the time, so I believe he'll keep on filling out. Of course, none of it may work. But if it doesn't, you wouldn't refuse to take me back, would you?"

"I know just what Dexter has in mind, Mother," Daniel told Serena. "You let him be. It will work out."

When Rhoda heard of her brother's rash purpose, she was even more upset than Serena had been, because she felt, still more strongly than Serena, that she was responsible for driving him out of his own home. She fretted about it so continually that David was obliged to remind her, speaking to her with more firmness than ever before, that it was bad for the baby, as well as for herself, to "take on so." But when she returned to Farman, and saw for herself how much pleasure her brother was already deriving from his purchase, her anxiety was allayed. A little mowing and pruning and plowing, a little scrubbing and papering and painting, had done wonders, as he had predicted himself. The only furniture that he had put in the house had come from Daniel's carpenter shop and from the Abbott and Farman attics. It was scattered some-what sparsely about in the living room and in the smaller of the two downstairs bedrooms; beyond that he had not tried to go at all. He did not try to do any cooking either, and Mrs. Wendell came in, as he had suggested, to clean for him once a week. She did this somewhat defiantly, stating, to anyone who listened, that she had never in all her born days heard such plumb foolishness as it was for Dexter Abbott to go and live all by himself in a tumbled-down old shanty, when he owned, or as good as owned, two nice houses. But she did the cleaning thoroughly, just the same, and Dexter noticed that little by little she was doing other things too.

She gathered up his laundry and took it home with her, returning it, when she came the next time, not only well-washed and smoothly ironed, but neatly mended. There was no sense, she snorted, in having Serena running over apurpose to change the bed and pick up soiled clothes and lay out fresh ones, when she herself had to go there any-way, to clean. Presently some muslin curtains appeared at the many-paned windows which had long presented such a forlorn, blank look. These curtains, Mrs. Wendell explained with another snort, when questioned as to their source, were some old ones she had found cluttering up a chest in her shed chamber. She had been minded to throw them out, and then she had decided that, after all, they would look better than nothing; it was getting on her nerves to see nothing hanging in those windows. Next an occasional pie, or a few hermits, began to make their appearance; she said nothing about them beforehand, but she left them on the living-room table when she went away at night, and upon further questioning, she said, still defiantly, that she knew a man liked a snack sometimes, just before he went to bed, and that she had got it into her head Dexter might be hungry. The climax came when he opened the door one evening to find the small dark house filled with the scent of lilacs. Mrs. Wendell had picked them that afternoon, when she finished her clean-ing, and had put some in a large crock on the hearthstone and others in a Mason jar on the desk. They were full and fluffy and fragrant, and they came from his own bushes.

It was after he saw the lilacs that Dexter insisted the house was really in order now, that there was no reason why Benny could not come to stay with him there at any time.

He encountered bitter opposition on this score from both Serena and Rhoda—so bitter that he decided not to press the point until after Serena had become more accustomed to the idea and Rhoda was preoccupied with her new baby. After all, he would not have long to wait, and it was better to achieve his ends harmoniously than hurriedly, if he could not do both. But he effected a compromise: The Cohens were already spending the weekends at the Abbott Homestead, getting it ready for the summer, and Dexter's first idea was that he and Benny might spend every Sunday fishing. During the period when he had been driving Alix to the Junction so that she could go to Mass, he himself had grown away from the habit of regular attendance at the village church, and he had not resumed it; neither could he see any reason, he observed rather tartly, why Rhoda should try to make Benny into a good little Congregationalist, and in this viewpoint he had his brother-in-law's firm, though gentle backing. Thus aided and abetted, he succeeded in making good his own escape and the boy's, the morning after the subject was first discussed, and almost defiantly took the road to his own little house while the church bells were still ringing, with Benny trudging in triumph beside him. But Benny's face fell when instead of making straight for the brook, Dexter stopped in the shed and took an old tire casing from the corner where it was concealed behind some kegs, afterwards rolling it carefully to a smooth spot in the small pasture at the rear. Then he laid his bandana in the center of the circle thus enclosed and stood back.

"I thought you said we were going fishing, Uncle Dexter," Benny protested, impatiently.

"We are going fishing," Dexter chuckled. "Not to catch fish, you understand."

"Aw, gee whiz——"

"One of these days you'll realize the big thing is to fish, not necessarily to catch them. Look now!"

He slipped off the cap of his aluminum rod case, and affectionately drew from their cloth folder the three sections of his fly-rod. Benny watched, his querulous pout gradually changing to an expression of less and less grudging interest. Dexter jointed the three sections, first rubbing the ferrules along the pits of his nostrils, then sighting carefully to align the guides, and finally making the slender rod—rapier-thin and rapier-tempered—sing in fluid grace by an almost imperceptible flicking of his wrist. The reel was affixed below the cork hand-grip, the line run through the guides, a section of leader cunningly knotted to its free end, while Benny watched more and more raptly.

"Why did you rub those ends by your nose?" he finally burst out.

Dexter scratched his head. "Well, Sir," he replied, "the regulation answer to that one is that the oil your skin leaves between your nostril and your cheek is exactly the right thing to lubricate the two pieces, so as to slide them together and yet form a seal so that they can't pull apart. But I guess the real reason is that the first man who ever used a jointed fly-rod liked to do it and taught the next fellow to do it that way. Now stop asking questions and keep your eyes on your Uncle Dexter."

Waving the tip of the rod back and forth in a slow and singing rhythm with a light movement of his right wrist, Dexter stripped line from the reel with his left hand. Steadily the length of line beyond the flexing rod-tip increased, an elongating S-curve extending the slender filament first before and then behind. A downward pressure of the right hand suddenly shot the line straight forward toward the target of the old tire, and when it came to rest the tip of the gleaming leader lay just across the rubber and within the ring.

"Gee!" breathed Benny. "That was keen."

"Not so musty, at that," admitted Dexter. "And when you learn how to do it, so you can place the fly about where you want it, then it'll be time for us to go to the brook. And you're not a bit more anxious to have a big one smash at it when it lands than I am to be where I can see you when it happens. Now you take the rod, Mister, and see what you can do . . . just to keep the line away from you, not feeding it out or anything."

Benny's hands trembled with eagerness as Dexter passed him the rod, after reeling in all but fifteen feet or so of line. Strangely enough, he found he did not know what to do with it after he held it though. It had looked so easy and effortless when Dexter waved it. He tried to switch it and Dexter laughed.

"No, no. Not like a ballbat or a tennis racket. Like a . . . like a . . . well, like a fly-rod. Here!"

Swiftly he knelt half beside and half behind the boy, took his small, soft hand, rod-grip and all, into his sinewy brown paw, and deftly made the rod-tip sing once more.

"Now try it by yourself, Big Mister."

Benny tried valiantly, but the smooth action in which rod and line and wrist became all part of one lovely curve continued to elude him.

"That's all right," Dexter reassured him with affectionate patience. "Look, the back-cast—I mean the part where the line runs out behind you before you cast ahead—is just as important as the cast itself. More. You can't make a good cast without a perfect back-cast, and you can't help making a good cast if your back-cast is perfect. See? Now when you bring the rod back—and not too far, remember—kind of wait till you feel the pull of the line on the rod and then sort of twitch it forward . . . There you are. That was a dandy. Now just keep on trying. First thing you know you won't have to think about any of this. It will just be part of you."

There they stood, in the green and gold meadow, through the long afternoon, until Dexter decided the small wrist had taken all the punishment it could for one afternoon.

"You did finely, Benny. I'm proud of you," he said as he pulled the rod sections apart with a sound like a cork being drawn from a bottle, rubbed the rod lovingly with his handkerchief and then restored it to its case. "Little by little the something-or-other said . . ."

"And one of these days we really will cast in the brook?"

"Positively. . . ."

It was soon evident that the plan for Sunday fishing was one of mutual benefit and mutual joy, as far as Dexter and Benny were concerned. But it continued to trouble Rhoda, and to a lesser degree, Serena also. It would cause talk, they both insisted, if such a leader of the community as Dexter Abbott spent every Sabbath in such a godless way, not to speak of setting such a bad example to a child. Again Dexter, reluctant to stir up harassing scenes, effected a compromise: Instead of fishing all day Sunday, he and Benny would have a picnic every Saturday night. Surely there was no reason why Benny could not walk over Saturday afternoons and go fishing with Dexter for an hour after his chores were done; nor was there any reason why he should not stay long enough afterwards to help Dexter clean and eat the fish. The boy could go home all right by himself, later on. Well, gosh, *why not?* Dexter himself had tramped around, all over the hills, before he was half as old as Benny, and Rhoda had never said a word. It was time Benny got away from her apron strings. It was also time he got his nose out of a book, once in a while. Pretty soon the nose and the book would be growing together, if Rhoda let him go on reading and reading and reading. . . .

Benny himself entered so eagerly into the plan for the fishing and the picnic suppers that Rhoda finally capitulated, though not without some murmuring about the hours they entailed. It was all very well for Dexter to say he had gone ranging all around when he was half the size of Benny. He had not done it in the dead of night. Now he worked so late that it was not until dusk that he and Benny started for the brook with their rods. This was true enough, every Saturday. But the evening when Dexter put a small hook on the end of the leader, and Benny finally snagged the handkerchief, called for a special celebration. And the evening when Benny finally had a "big one smash at the fly when it landed" and Dexter *was* there to see it happen was such a great occasion for them both that they made a ceremonial of cooking the fish afterwards and it was later than ever when they were through. If he had not known that Rhoda would have worried herself sick over the child's non-appearance, Dexter would have been tempted to keep Benny overnight. But he had no telephone in the little old house yet, and a survey of Farman Hill revealed that its lights were all out; he would wake Serena and Daniel if he went there to telephone. He walked up to the turn of the road with Benny, half-minded to go along to the Abbott Homestead himself; however, after his cutting remarks about apron strings, he felt he could not consistently do so, but neither could he resist the impulse to put his arm around the little boy's shoulders. He was very reluctant to let Benny go. A word would have sufficed to keep them together still.

"Sure you can find your way all right, Benny? It's a pretty dark night and the fog's heavy too."

"I don't mind the dark. And I think the mist's pretty."

"Well. . . . we had a good time together, didn't we?"

"You bet. I wish Aunt Rhoda would let me stay with you all the time. Then we *could* go fishing every Sunday."

"Well, we'll have to work up to that gradually. We don't want to hurt her feelings. But maybe she will let you stay by-and-by. Of course she will. You're going to live with me all the time, Benny, as soon as I get the place really fixed up. Then we'll do as we please."

"If I lived with you now, I could help you fix it up. We could do lots of other things together, besides fish."

"Yes, we could. We'll try talking it over with Aunt Rhoda tomorrow. Good night, Benny."

"Good night, Uncle Dexter."

Dexter stood still, at the turn of the road. It was not a case of watching Benny out of sight, for he was immediately swallowed up in the density of the fog; it was simply another instinctive revelation of Dexter's reluctance to be separated from the child. For a few moments, he could hear Benny whistling, and hoped this was not akin to the proverbial reaction of a small boy passing a graveyard. Well, Benny must be halfway up the first hollow by now and well on his way to the second slope. And after all, there were houses all along the road. He turned back to his own house, hugging this thought, and sat down in front of the dying fire to smoke a pipe before going to bed. But instead of dwelling contentedly on the picnic they just had, as he puffed away, or visualizing other aspects of their growing intimacy, his concern about Benny continued to deepen. He did not relish the idea of having Benny seek shelter with the Hellmanns or ask help from them, though Germans were traditionally kind to children, whatever their other failings might be. Kind to children? What about the thousands of Jewish children, orphaned through their cruelty, homeless and starving themselves? And Benny was a Jewish child. . . .

Dexter could not stand it any longer. He knew that what he was doing was irrational. There was no reason whatsoever why Benny should need to ask for help or seek for shelter. By this time, he would probably be over the second slope, down the other small hill, and halfway across the long level stretch that led to the Abbott Homestead. But Dexter could not help that. Cursing under his breath because his lameness made his progress so slow, even without the added handicap of the fog, he started back in the direction of the Hellmann's house.

There was an eerie quality to the night. Its uncanny atmosphere alone might well have frightened a child, even if no extraordinary sights or sounds penetrated the mists and the silence, and presently Dexter heard an extraordinary sound. At first, he could not identify it; then he thought it was like the noise of scampering feet. Some sort of a creature was coming towards him, for the footsteps were growing louder. He stopped and listened with increasing intentness and alarm. Then he realized that the noises were not like those made by an animal, but like those made by a human being. At the moment that this realization crystallized into a certainty, he felt the impact of a small body hurled against his. His arms shot out and the next instant he had Benny locked against his heart.

"There," he heard himself saying. "There, Benny. There —son. What a darn fool I was to let you start off! But everything's all right now. Don't be frightened."

"I'm not frightened," Benny panted. "I didn't come back because I was scared. I came back because I heard something."

"You can hear almost everything, Benny, in the country, on a night like this. You'll get used to these country sounds. It's just because it's so dark that they seem strange. They're friendly sounds, really."

"No, Uncle Dexter, you don't understand. It was just people talking."

"People talking! What people?"

"Mr. Hellmann and his friends."

Dexter felt his heart turn over. He waited, steadying himself before answering Benny.

"How did you happen to hear Mr. Hellmann and his friends, Benny? They weren't talking on the road, were they, on a night like this?"

"Gosh, no! They were talking in Mr. Hellmann's house. Drinking beer and talking."

"But how could you see them from the road in this fog? How could you *hear* them? They weren't shouting, were they?"

"No, they weren't shouting. And I couldn't see them from the road. It was Mrs. Hellmann I first heard. She was playing the piano and—and singing. She was singing a song I hadn't heard in a long time. A song I used to like a lot."

Again Dexter felt his heart turn over.

"What song, Benny?" he asked, hoping his voice did not betray his inner tumult.

" '*Röslein, Röslein, Röslein rot, Röslein auf der Haide.*" My mother used to sing it to me."

" '*Röslein rot.*' But, Benny——"

Dexter caught himself just in time. In another second he would have said, "But, Benny, you've told us, over and over again, that you didn't understand German!" Here was the long-awaited miracle of liberated speech finally released by forces even stronger than those which had suppressed it. But it was hesitant still. The response to it must be wary as well as tender, or it might be silenced again, perhaps forever.

"I think perhaps we'd better walk along towards the Abbott Homestead, Benny, while you tell me about this," he said gently. "I'm very eager to hear it. But we don't want to have your Aunt Rhoda too much disturbed because you're late, do we?"

"No, Uncle Dexter."

Benny had stopped panting. He had slipped his hand inside Dexter's and was trotting easily along beside him.

"So you went and stood under the window to hear Mrs. Hellmann sing this song you used to be so fond of?"

"Yes, under one of the parlor windows. She was all alone in the parlor, singing. And then, pretty soon, she closed the piano and turned out the lights and went upstairs. And after that I heard what the men were saying. They were drinking beer in the dining room."

"And what were they saying, Benny?"

"Mr. Hellmann said, *'Die Marke war heute am Brief.'* He was the first one I heard, especially."

"You'll have to translate for me, Benny. I studied a little German in college, but that was a long time ago."

He was still so startled that he was not sure how to chart his course. But he tried to speak casually, as if it were the most natural thing in the world for Benny to translate for him, a trifling and customary service which the child might perform at any time. Apparently his procedure was wise, for Benny answered naturally, too.

" 'The stamp was on the letter today.' "

"The stamp was on the letter today! And what next?"

"Mr. Wagner said, *'Also Mittwoch dann, wie gewöhnlich'*—Wednesday, then, as usual!' "

"*As usual!* They were talking about something they'd been doing for a long time, then."

"Yes, Uncle Dexter, I'm sure they were. Because after that Mr. Wagner began to laugh, in a funny kind of a way. A—a——"

"A guffaw?"

"Yes, I . . . I guess so. Like he had too much beer. And Mr. Becker kind of giggled, and said, *'Wenn das dumme Amerikanische Mistvieh nur wüsste, was die Ernte*

unserer schönen Wiese ist, da wirde es wirklich Maula-
ffen——' "

"Please, Benny——"

" 'If the stupid American cattle only would know what
sort of a harvest we get in our lovely little pasture, then
they really would be surprised.' "

"Did he say *lovely* little pasture?"

"Well, it means pretty, like a pretty girl. *You* know.
But Mr. Hellmann's pasture isn't really pretty, Uncle Dexter. It's sort of——"

"Sort of scrubby? I've called it that myself, Benny, before."

"Yes, it is scrubby, Uncle Dexter. But Mr. Becker called
it pretty. I think he was joking, though. And Mr Hellmann didn't like the joke. He tried to shut Mr. Becker
up. He snapped at him. *'Halts Maul, Heu—ochs!'* That's
just a real tough way of saying 'Shut up.' Do you understand, Uncle Dexter?"

"Yes, I think I do. At least, I think I might, if I could
hear some more. That wasn't all, was it, Benny?"

"Oh, no, there was a lot more. They kept on talking
mean at each other. After Mr. Hellmann told Mr. Becker
in that tough way to shut up, he said, the same way, that
you never could tell who might be listening. Mr. Wagner
began to—to—guffaw again, like it was a big joke to
pretend somebody could be listening in such a place and
at such a time, or like anybody outside could make heads
or tails out of what they were saying. But Mr. Hellmann
didn't talk like he thought it was funny. He said Mr.
Wagner was getting so he was drinking too much beer,
like tonight, and that pretty soon nobody could trust him
any more, because when he drank too much, he talked
too much. For all he knew, Mr. Hellmann said, Mr.
Wagner might get pally with the first government agent
he met, and let on what he was carrying."

"Did you think he was carrying something, Benny?"

"No, not tonight. But I think he was going to. I think
he wanted to. Because he said, 'What about letting me
take the next trip?' And Mr. Hellmann said no, he was
going to send Mr. Krauss on the next trip. The others

didn't like that, but Mr. Krauss did, a lot—He never talked much up to then, but after that he began to brag about how he was trustworthy, and Mr. Hellmann backed him up and said Krauss was the only one of the whole lot who could keep his mouth shut, drunk or sober, and that he was the only one who had any real sense of time. He said the others weren't any too early when the plane last landed."

"When *what* plane last landed? and *where,* for God's sake?"

In his excitement, Dexter forgot to keep his voice quiet and his question casual, and this time he did not catch himself quickly enough. He instantly had reason to rue his mistake.

"I don't know, Uncle Dexter. How could I know what plane they were talking about or where it landed? They didn't say. I can't tell you any more than I heard."

"Of course you can't, Benny. I'm sorry I barked at you like that. But you're telling me such a thrilling story that I'm very much excited."

"Well, I'm excited too, Uncle Dexter. That's why I hurried back. Anyway, I hurried partly on account of that and partly because I thought it could be important, maybe."

"I think it might be, Benny. . . . You didn't hear anything more, did you, after Mr. Hellmann complained because Mr. Becker and Mr. Wagner weren't any too early the last time the plane landed?"

"Yes, a little. They talked back to him. They said once he found fault because they were *too* early. And he said sure, did they want you to catch them going to their posts?"

"Oh, so they have posts too, do they?"

"I guess so. Because almost the last thing I heard was that they'd go to their hilltops on the dot of 11:15. And Mr. Hellmann said that he'd be in the pasture at 11:15 too. Mr. Becker asked him what he was going to give Mr. Ellis this time, but he didn't get any answer. Mr. Hellmann just growled and pretty soon they began saying good night to each other. I didn't dare listen after that. I crawled back across the lawn as fast as I could. And when I got to the road, I began to run. I ran back to find you. I didn't expect to find you so soon. Of course I didn't know you were coming to find *me*. But I guess we just had to find *each other* tonight, don't you think so?"

Dexter could feel Benny's fingers, no longer slipped quietly inside his own, but gripping them hard. He gripped them hard in return.

"Yes, Benny," he said, "I guess we did. And we won't let anyone separate us again, either. That is, of course we must go on to Aunt Rhoda's now—look, we're almost there! I can see the picket fence, even through the fog. But I'm going to ask her again if she won't let you live with me all the time, after school closes. I'm going to try to persuade her that I need you more than she does. Because, after all, she has David and Rachel already, and presently she'll have the new baby, and they'll all keep her company. I haven't anyone but you to keep me company, or to help me fix up my house, or to tell me exciting things, the way you have tonight. I *depend* on you. It's a great thing, Benny, when a man has a boy he can depend on, the way I can on you, to help him when there's something important to be done."

They agreed that what Benny had heard was their secret, that they would not share it with anyone else in Farman, not even Aunt Rhoda. They would keep still as mice about it, at least until Dexter had had a chance to think it over. After he had done that, he might want to tell someone else, he said. But he would let Benny know. . . .

Benny agreed with him, gravely, and they both remained unabashed over Rhoda's reproaches because Dexter had brought Benny back so late. They knew she was not really very angry. Rachel had already gone to bed, and Rhoda and David were comfortably ensconced in the living room when Dexter and Benny came in. Rhoda was knitting and David was reading aloud to her, and they were obviously very much absorbed in each other. Secretely, Dexter wondered whether she had really worried about

Benny at all until she glanced up at the clock. Nothing
about her appearance indicated that she was harassed.
She presented a picture of utter contentment.

Dexter stayed with Benny until the child was undressed,
defending him against Rhoda's urgent suggestion of a
bath, and clasping him hard around the shoulders again
when they parted. David looked up from his book as Dexter came downstairs again, first urging him to stay all
night and then offering to run him home. If there was a
slight incongruity about his remarks, neither man noticed
it; Dexter knew that David was not consciously trying
to pre-empt the role of host, or to infer that the Abbott
Homestead was no longer his brother-in-law's home. But
the very fact that the remarks had been made spontaneously, revealed the tacit understanding that the little old house
which had so long been abandoned was now Dexter's
natural habitat. Thanks a lot, he said easily, but he needed
to be on Farman Hill the first thing in the morning, so
he really thought he had better be getting back there, and
he honestly liked the walk. However, he was going out
to his office in the barn for a few minutes first. There
were some papers he wanted to glance through.

He had been in the office almost daily, but this was
the first time in a long while that he had lingered there.
He sat down in front of his old-fashioned roll top desk,
and for some moments sat staring at the photograph of
Judith in her ruffled graduation dress. More than once,
during the past winter, when there was a fire in the Franklin stove, he had been on the point of tearing up the picture and consigning it to the flames. But at the last moment he had always refrained, because it seemed like a
puerile as well as a melodramatic gesture, and, in the final
analysis, he was not sure that he desired to destroy it.
After all, the picture represented an idyllic period which
was wholly past, and which he and Judith had shared
as schoolmates as well as sweethearts. With lessening pain
he was beginning to detach this period from the tem-
pestuous episodes which had preceded the rupture of their
relationship, and to regard it with almost affectionate
nostalgia. But he no longer wanted Judith's photograph to

dominate its surroundings in solitary supremacy. He must get a picture of Benny to put on the desk too, a picture taken by a fine photographer, one who would be able to interpret and reproduce the sensitivity and brilliance back of Benny's unremarkable features and thin, pointed little face. And he wished, desperately, that he might also have a picture of Alix. He could have asked her for one, before the break caused by his own boorishness and presumption, without seeming bold or offensive, and quite conceivably, she might have granted his request. It would have heartened and inspired him to look at her likeness while she was away. Yet even now, when the question was wholly academic and he was preoccupied in other ways, he asked himself what form this likeness could have taken. Certainly he would not have wished to contemplate the image of Jerome's bride in a lace veil, or Jerome's widow in her mourning crepe. He remembered how she had looked when he first saw her serving coffee in the old doorway, wearing her quaint little checked dress with the small pleated ruffles. This was a pleasing memory, yet when it came to that, it was Jerome who had first suggested that she should drink her "small blacks" looking out over the fields. Perhaps it was better, after all, that he himself still had no picture of her. Someday he might have one which represented a new vision, all his own. . . .

He set down the picture of Judith, and opened the safe where he kept his account books. A certain page was still marked by the piece of scratch paper on which he had first jotted down, in accidental and startling juxtaposition, the names of Hellmann, Lippman, Krauss, Wagner and Becker. He stood staring at them again now, and as he did so, the questions Joe had asked, the night they had gone out to the barn together, reechoed across his stimulating consciousness: "There aren't any hills similar to Jerome's, are there, on the Hellmann property?" . . . "The scrubby little pasture isn't big enough for a landing field, is it?" . . . Don't you have heavy fogs, rising from the river here, a good part of the year?" That strange sixth sense of the born reporter, sharpened and strengthened by training and experience, had inspired these ques-

tions; and now the conference at which Benny had been
an unpremeditating eavesdropper seemed to supply partial
answers to them: The following Wednesday evening, at
11:15 on the dot, Mr. Hellmann would be in some near-
by pasture, and Messrs. Becker, Wagner and Krauss would
simultaneously be stationed on near-by hills, apparently to
await the arrival of a plane. And evidently the purpose of
all this was to receive or present some mysterious but
valuable object, the nature of which, if disclosed, would
be of immense interest to the first government agent in
whom Mr. Wagner might tipsily confide, at an unguarded
moment. And obviously all this had been going on for
some time, since there had been a reference to meeting
"as usual." . . .

Dexter had no sixth reportorial sense, no training and
experience along the lines which Joe possessed in such
abundant measure. But Alix herself had said that he had
just as good a mind as Joe's, if he would only use it as
well, and she had told him, too, that his work was, or
could be, no less important than Jerome's. He needed no
picture of her to see her in the guise of the White Queen,
and to hear the challenge of the words she had spoken
when she so appeared. He had become increasingly conscious that this was the time appointed for taking up her
challenge. Because of Benny, he was at last beginning to
see how he might do it. The fact that he could see only
through a glass, darkly, must not deter him. He could,
if he would, still see face to face. . . .

On the wall, under the loudly ticking clock, hung a
large calendar issued by an insurance company. On this,
Sundays and holidays and the phases of the moon stood
out in scarlet from the rest of the type, which was in bold-
face. With this calendar confronting him, it was almost
inevitable that he should check on the accuracy of his
impression the following Wednesday would be a moonless
night. He applied the significance of this further fact to
the many now in his possession, all of which seemed to
be growing less and less vague with every passing minute.
And the minutes were not dragging any longer, they were
racing on towards midnight. Presently, the big cheap wall

clock struck twelve, in the same noisy strident way that it ticked. Deliberately, Dexter waited for another five minutes, listening to this ticking. Then he picked up the telephone. At midnight the local exchange closed, and the infrequent calls which still occurred were handled until morning through the Junction, where the eldest Franchini girl was the night operator.

"Hello," he said. "Hello, Teresina, is that you? I want you to put through a long distance call for me. I've waited a long time on purpose to give it to you, because I know you'll keep it confidential. I want you to get me Mr. James Thirkell, at the Federal Bureau of Investigation in Washington."

CHAPTER 33

"I'M SORRY I can't make you more comfortable, but this house has been empty a long while. I only bought it a couple of months ago, and I haven't done much yet about fixing it up. I sleep here, but I don't eat here, except on Saturday nights, when Benny, the little boy I told you about, comes for a picnic with me. It happens I just raised a howl about having him stay here all the time, so I was able to get in a little extra furniture and food on Sunday, without rousing any suspicions. But I didn't dare do too much. There aren't enough beds to go around, but I think there's enough bedding for some extra shakedowns, and I don't believe you'll go hungry."

"Well, under all the circumstances, Mr. Abbott, you don't need to apologize for lack of luxury. But I would like to have a little talk with you. Perhaps this would be as good a time for it as any. We've had quite a trip and we're about ready to turn in, but then, we've got all day tomorrow to sleep in—we can't do anything else, since we've got to stay in hiding. Incidentally, I don't see how you could have planned a better place for that than a semi-abandoned house, if you'd tried."

"Thanks. Well, I generally start milking about five, but that still gives us several hours leeway, and it wouldn't hurt if I were a little late for once."

Both men spoke with slight formality and with a surface lightness which neither felt. The midnight call which Dexter had put through to Washington on Saturday had been productive of prompt results. It was now late Tuesday evening, and Thirkell, his right-hand man, Bates, and three able lieutenants, were seated in Dexter's sparsely-furnished living room with a big plate of sandwiches in front of them and tall drinks in their hands. No one had noticed their unobstrusive arrival and the cars in which they had come from the Montpelier airport were backed into the small dilapidated side shed which wholly concealed them. The shed was still unregenerated into a garage, but this did not prevent it from serving as an effective hiding place.

"If I understand you correctly, your little nephew——"

"Benny isn't my little nephew—I wish he were! He's a little Jewish refugee, the nephew of a man my sister's recently married—a darned nice fellow named David Cohen. Benny's stubbornly insisted, ever since he got to this country, that he didn't remember a single word of German—it's been a queer psychological case that's had us completely foxed and a good deal worried. But he overheard this conversation I told you about at the Hellmanns' house on his way back to my sister's after his picnic supper here with me, and he came tearing back to tell me about it and translate it for me. He's only ten years old, but the protective secrecy in which he's shrouded himself for so long was completely shattered, so he must have instinctively grasped the tremendous potential significance of what he'd overheard. You really think he's stumbled on something important, don't you?"

"I'd put it a good deal stronger than that, Mr. Abbott. I think he's supplied the missing link that may help us first to strengthen and then to uncoil a venomous and deadly chain."

James Thirkell looked up from his sandwich with a smile. He had a pleasant, almost ingenuous face, and he spoke agreeably and cordially, the first formality of his manner gradually fading as he went on.

"I seem to be getting a little mixed in my metaphors," he said. "Tangled up in my own links, rather. But what I'd like to make clear to you is the Bureau already feels tremendously indebted to Benny Cohen and Dexter Abbott for their effective and intelligent assistance, and that I honestly believe the whole country will have reason to be grateful to them both in the course of time."

"I haven't done anything. Benny did it all. Benny and Joe Racina. I believe you know him already. He was here in January, and he asked some questions which aroused my suspicions so that when Benny———"

"Yes, I know Racina, and he's a good fellow, too. Let's not quarrel about the credit, Mr. Abbott. There's enough for everybody. But here's the situation: For some time we've been vainly trying to locate the transit route by which valuable information is getting through to the enemy. We've suspected where it started, and we've found some of the places which it eventually reached; but in between the two there was a blank. However, we felt we had reason to watch a certain Damon Ellis in regard to the transactions. Does the name mean anything to you?"

"No, not a thing."

"Well, he's a metallurgist with an international reputation in his specialty, who's frequently called into consultation with some of the biggest contractors of war supplies. He was born and brought up in Burlington, and he still makes his home and maintains an office there. But he's constantly being summoned to various parts of the New England and New Jersey manufacturing areas, and he always makes these trips by air to save time—in fact he was one of the first men in his line to travel regularly in his own plane. Our suspicions about him were first roused when a photostat of a confidential drawing known to have been in Ellis' possession at one time was found among the papers of a suspect already under observation. None of us could figure out how it got there, but we began watching Ellis as he landed and searching his baggage without his knowledge. Nothing phony developed. He was carrying just the usual stuff, and he went directly from the field to his clients and from there back to the airport, seeing no one who could have acted as a go-between or who was not above suspicion. Of course his flight reports have always been completely in order too—he never could have got off the ground if they hadn't been. And it didn't seem possible to us that he could make a stop so short that it wouldn't be detected. He couldn't have, either, unless he had some extremely able confederates working with him."

"But how could these confederates have worked with him?"

"Well, the drawings for the devices could have been sent to him by courier in Burlington from his clients, and he could have made photostatic copies of them there. Then he could have turned over these copies to your industrious acquaintance, Mr. Hellmann, in the course of his flight. No one could suspect that such stuff could *originate* in a dump like Farman Hill, so Hellmann could almost mail out the stuff that was slipped him, if it wasn't convenient to send it in any other way. As a matter of fact, it apparently has been taken out by hand sometimes, as there's been all this talk about trips. On the other hand it could be sent on in an order for groceries, or anything of that sort. Doesn't Wagner keep one of the local stores? Isn't he dealing with wholesalers all the time?"

"Why, yes, I suppose he must be. But how in the name of heaven would it be physically possible for Ellis to land the stuff here? I can see how it might have been done if this gang had got hold of the Farman place, as they tried to last year—Jerome's Hill could have served as a signal station, and the Big Field would have been fine for landing. But just wait until you see the place the conversation at the Hellmanns' seems to point to. It's just a scrubby little hollow between two hillocks."

"Exactly. Of course, possession of the Farman place would have made everything much simpler for these birds, but that doesn't mean they couldn't manage without it if they had to. Theoretically, it's even possible for invading airplanes to make landings in scrubby little pastures like the one you've been describing, if they fly by the Great Circle, which, as you know, couldn't be more conveniently located—that is, if they weren't intercepted. However, this case hasn't anything to do with invading airplanes, unless I'm very much mistaken. It's a case of receiving packages containing information in regard to devices used by the Allied Army."

"But I still don't see how it's physically possible——"

"You've got three or four families of German origin here in town besides the Hellmanns, according to your own report. In fact Benny Cohen heard representatives of all those families talking together in Hellmann's house. Now of course we haven't got all the pieces fitted together yet. But I think we'll find out tonight that Mr. Krauss and Mr. Becker and Mr. Wagner are all standing alertly on those three insignificant little hillocks which surround the pasture, and which serve as radio masts."

"But *how?*"

"Well, let's say that each of the three men in question has a little radio-sending apparatus like the army walkie-talkies—something that can send a signal from the tops of those hills that's too weak to be heard far, but that's strong enough to give a plane an accurate three-point fix, to that it could land on instruments alone, regardless of a fog or anything else."

"You mean like the soldiers in the movies carry on their backs?"

"Why they even have them small enough now to hold in one hand! And let's assume that some time ago, Messrs. Krauss, Becker, and Wagner were all supplied with these little hand-held radio gadgets that don't require any installation. We don't need to assume that every once and so often, Mr. Hellmann gets some insignificant little missive in the mail—a catalogue, or a circular, or something like that—which, incidentally, has a stamp put on it in some queer, catty-cornered way. We know this for a fact. And when that happens, which is always in the dark of the moon, Messrs. Krauss, Becker, and Wagner know that four nights later, they are to be on their little hillocks with their little walkie-talkies firmly in hand."

James Thirkell finished his sandwich in a meditative bite, and drained his tall glass as if he were enjoying his drink to the last drop. "I believe there'll be more to say tomorrow," he remarked, pensively, though still pleasantly, "but that seems to be about all for the moment, except to tell you again how grateful I am to you and Benny. . . . Oh, and to say in passing that I was as pleased as you must have been to learn that Pete MacDonld got the Pulitzer Prize for his account of the Dieppe raid. I'd like to see him back in Washington, but I suppose there's no hope of that until the war's over . . . Look, I've been taking a mean advantage of you, talking to you most of the night, when I can sleep all day and you can't." He glanced around the room, his agreeable smile widening as he saw that among his lieutenants, only the faithful Bates had managed to stay alertly awake through the long colloquy, in which, as subordinates, they had taken no part. The others were all drowsing in their chairs, two in attitudes of complete relaxation, the third, though still sitting bolt upright, betraying his somnolent state by unmistakable sounds. "I meant to suggest that we should flip a coin to see who would get the beds," he went on. "But I really think Bates and I had better take them. It would be a pity to disturb these slumberers, now."

It was not until late the next afternoon that Dexter saw anything more of his five guests. The "shake-downs" he had supplied were in the dormer rooms, and when he came back to his own house, after eating breakfast, as usual, with the Farmans, he found that the three men whom he had left sleeping by the fireside had apparently discovered these, for they had disappeared. He did not disturb them, or waken Thirkell and Bates, who were in the big downstairs bedroom, beside the small one he had taken for his own. He would change things around, he decided, now that Benny was coming to live with him, giving the boy the small bedroom, and taking the large one for himself. He did not see why he had not done that in the beginning. A grown man needed space to move around in, even a man who was using a room alone; and if, eventually, he were no longer alone, the space should be ready to share.. . . .

He had taken advantage of Serena's absence on her milk route, and Daniel's in the barn, to bring down some more provisions surreptitiously. Now he left in his kitchen two thermos bottles full of hot coffee, a dozen fresh eggs, and some bread sliced ready for toasting. Oranges and dry cereal, butter and cream, sugar and doughnuts were already there, so he decided there should be no trouble about breakfast, if the men waked before he came back the next time. Serena had a meat loaf, which she served hot, for dinner that day, and after Dexter had sung its praises, he was in a position to ask, easily enough, if he might take some home with him. Well, she was going to have it cold for supper, Serena said, but after that he was welcome to any that was left over. She guessed Mrs. Wendell was getting him in the habit of midnight snacks, and though she did not hold with eating late at night, herself, she had no mind to have Dexter beholden to the neighbors, when she could feed him herself; that was what she had kept saying right along. When Dexter finally returned to his house again, he carried a covered basket containing fully half of the meat loaf in question, and a big bowl of greens to go with it. His house was still in darkness, but when he turned on the lights, he found that the men were all foregathered in the big bedroom at the rear, and that they had been playing poker, as long as they could see. They had all had a fine sleep, and had found about five times as much food as they could eat. Thirkell told him. Good Lord, had he brought still more? Now that he had come home, around his customary hour, there was no reason why there should not be lights in the house, if the shades were drawn; anyone passing by would assume, correctly enough, that he had turned them on himself. They could continue their game where they had left off. Only, they hoped that now he would join them. Perhaps he could do something with Bates, who so far had been breaking the bank.. . . .

The evening was unexpectedly pleasant. In the course of conversation, which for the most part was general and unprofessional now, Dexter made the discovery that one of his own college classmates was a friend of Thirkell; later they drifted from a discussion of mutual interests to the wider field of national politics. It was the first time Dexter had ever had a chance to discuss the latter subject with persons who were actually a living part of it, and he seldom came into contact, even indirectly, with former friends who were outside his persent immediate circle. This new-found male companionship, at one and the same time cultured and vigorous, was satisfying and stimulating. Dexter found himself consulting Thirkell about the best possible preparatory school for Benny, and the advisability of picking up his own lost threads, so that when Benny went to college—his college—there would be some sort of a background for the boy. Thirkell thought it would be a good plan, too, if Dexter and Benny could get down to Washington sometime. If they could, Thirkell would see to it that they met some of the personages around whom the conversation had been centering. Nonsense, of course it wouldn't be a bother; they'd have the keys to the city handed to them on a silver salver. . . .

Unobtrusively, Thirkell glanced at his wrist watch and with his friendly smile, lifted his hand, so that Dexter could see it too. The small silvery hands on the dark dial were pointing to half-past ten. Dexter nodded, smiling also.

"Yes, I think we've timed it just about right. As I understand it, we're all going to the Hellmann pasture first, or rather, we're going to surround it, after giving Mr. Hellmann a chance to get in there before we do. Then, if everything goes off according to schedule, I'll guide three of you to the three hillocks afterwards, to make the acquaintance of Messrs. Becker, Wagner and Krauss. But our primary concern is with Hellmann and Ellis. We don't need to hurry, but we ought to be getting along. I never saw the fog thicker, so we'll have to feel our way. And I can't go as fast as the rest of you, I'm afraid."

Somewhat self-consciously, he glanced down at his

bad leg, and then back at his guests. Except for Thirkell's, all their faces were politely blank. But suddenly he knew that these experssions did not veil sympathy, or contempt, but surprise. Until he had called attention to it himself, only one man out of five had realized that he was lame. Perhaps, after all, Alix had been right when she said that no one who saw his face would think of looking at his feet. He rose triumphantly, an acknowledged leader among men.

"If you'll just follow me," he said, with authority, "I'm sure everything will go off without a hitch. We've got a long hard walk ahead of us, but of course I know every inch of this countryside as well as I know the back of my own hand. These are my hills."

It was coming. In the summer silence, broken only by the distant croaking of frogs and the monotone of the cuckoo, the steady hum of a motor became louder and louder. In the white mist, no outline was visible, even after the hum had become a roar. Then, as it circled the pasture, the plane was detached from the density, becoming a dim shape. It made a second circle, and the next instant, without showing a single light, it had landed in the very center of the pasture.

Hellmann's timing had been uncannily accurate. The plane had scarcely shuddered into stillness when he was beside it. Now that Dexter's eyes had become accustomed to the darkness, he could see from the clump of bushes where he was hiding, the stocky figure and square head of the German plainly. Hellmann was carrying a hooded flashlight in one hand, and as the door of the plane opened a few inches, he extended the other, and a package was instantly dropped into it. In the same second, Thirkell, who had quietly crept up behind him, put his hand gently on Hellmann's shoulder.

"Don't bother about that any more," he said, still very pleasantly. "I'll take charge of it from now on."

Bates had crept across the pasture, too, and Dexter could see him diving into the plane, presumably pinioning the pilot. He could also hear the clink of handcuffs, as

Thirkell went on talking pleasantly, now addressing himself to his approaching host.

"Very satisfactory in every respect, Mr. Abbott. Mr. Bates and I will take these two gentlemen along in our car. Don't worry about the plane. It can stay right here until it's convenient for us to send for it. And now, if you'll just lead on to those hills. . . ."

CHAPTER 34

DEXTER HAD not been writing to Alix himself. She had not suggested that she would like to have him, and he had wisely decided against taking the initiative. After his precipitate purchase he had said, rather diffidently, first to his sister and then to the Farmans, that he hoped they would not mention it in the course of their own correspondence. Rhoda, as it happened, had no inclination to do so; she was still so greatly bewildered and deeply hurt when he made his request, that she felt the longer she could conceal from Alix the lengths to which she had driven her brother, the better. Serena, on the other hand, had been eager to lay the whole question of Dexter's peculiar conduct before her daughter-in-law and ask for an opinion. It was with great reluctance that she finally promised to say nothing either to Alix or to Judith, since the latter might also conceivably pass the news along; and after she and Daniel were in bed that night, she voiced her disappointment.

"I set a lot of store by Alix' views," she complained. "If I could have heard them, it would have helped to ease my mind."

"You'll hear them when she gets home."

"She hasn't breathed a syllable yet about coming home."

"No, but she will. She'll come for this summer anyhow. I don't feel so certain she won't go away again in the fall, but it's sure as shooting she'll come back for the summer."

"I'd give a good deal if I felt as certain of it as you do, Daniel. I know she made her promise to Jerome in good faith. But when she gets down among all those relatives of hers . . ."

"There's only one relative we need to worry about and I don't believe he'll say anything to her yet. If he does, I think she'll shut him up in short order, same as she did Dexter."

"Daniel Farman, what on earth are you talking about?"

In her excitement, Serena sat up in bed and switched on the light. She reached for the little crocheted shawl which she always kept handy, both night and day, and wrapped it closely around her, over her long-sleeved nightgown. Then she plumped up her pillow and placed it in the small of her back.

"I want you should tell me this minute what you're talking about, Daniel."

Daniel blinked a little, and drew up the bedclothes to indicate that he was loath to begin a dissertation at this hour. But he knew there was no escape. After a moment he groaned slightly and turned over, facing his wife.

"Why I'm just saying that the only relative Alix has got who's liable to make trouble for us is that good-looking cousin of hers, Prosper St. Cyr. And I don't think he'll make her an out and out proposal, not until she's been a widow for at least a year. Those Creoles set a lot of store by mourning. You could tell that from the way he and his mother talked when they were here for the baby's baptism, let alone what Alix has said to us herself. Of course it's plain as a pikestaff that he wants to marry her. But then, he always has, and she ran away from him once before. If he pushes her too hard, she'll run away from him again."

"Yes, but what's this you're saying about Dexter?"

"Don't you know how Dexter feels about Alix?"

"I know he's an honorable man," Serena said, in the same spirited way in which she had spoken of him to Jenness. "He's not one to covet his neighbor's wife, no, nor to make up to her when his best friend's off fighting for his country and he's safe at home. I'm surprised you should suggest such a thing, Daniel Farman. I'd take my Bible oath on it Dexter never looked at Alix to lust after her or——"

"Easy there, Mother, easy there. I know Dexter pretty well myself, and I don't need you nor anybody else to tell me about his moral character. But he's human, like the rest of us. And Alix isn't his neighbor's wife any more; she's his neighbor's widow. And his best friend isn't fighting for his country any more; his friend's dead, and Dexter is carrying on the fight, as well as he can, himself. There isn't anything in scripture or elsewhere as I know of that says an honorable man can't ask a widow to marry him."

"Daniel, I don't see how you can speak of it like that, as if it didn't matter much one way or another, as if it was someone that wasn't any relation to us who had died. Jerome was our son, our only son. He was killed in action, when he wasn't hardly more than a boy, when he hadn't been married but a few months. He never even saw his own son. It was a terrible tragedy, and Alix felt it just as much as we did. She didn't give way, but she grieved. You can't tell me she'd so much as think of putting anyone else in Jerome's place. It's an injustice to her to say that she might. Even if Dexter should forget himself—and mind you I'm still saying I think that's unlikely—she wouldn't."

"Mother, I knowed she grieved. Alix isn't one to put on, not about anything. She mourned our son sincerely. And she wouldn't ever put anyone else in his place. He had a place in her life no one else could fill. But it was his own place. After awhile there might be another place, a vacant one, in her life, that someone else could fill. I don't mind telling you I'm sort of hoping it might be Dexter."

"It's beyond me, Daniel Farman, how you can lie there and tell me you hope you'll see your son's young widow marry again. Before he's hardly cold in his grave! Why just think of the talk it would cause if Dexter Abbott should try to step into Jerome's shoes!"

"Easy there, Mother, easy there—I guess I'll have to keep right on saying that to you. I told you awhile back that if Prosper St. Cyr or Dexter Abbott or any other man should speak to Alix about marriage too soon, Alix would make short shift of him. And I'll tell you too, seeing you've driven me into doing it, that I've suspicioned for some time Dexter did speak to her too soon and that this was one of the reasons she thought best to go away. I'll admit I'm some surprised Dexter forgot himself, as you call it—he may not set so much store by crepe veils and black edges on writing paper as Prosper St. Cyr does, but he's got a proper respect for death himself. He wouldn't set out to woo a widow before her first husband was cold in his grave. But I guess he couldn't help himself, Mother, and that's all there is to it. When a woman's got charm like Alix has, men just naturally want to marry her. They can't leave her alone, not with the best will in the world. It don't seem to matter whether she's young or old or rich or poor; if she's got charm they want her. And they don't want to carry on with her either. They want to marry her. So you mustn't be too hard on Dexter if he told Alix how it was with him, like I suspicion he did, a mite too soon. Not but what she knew it anyway. Women like that know such things; it's kind of a sixth sense with them. But they know how to handle such things too."

"Seems to me you flatter yourself you know an awful lot about women, Daniel, for a respectable man who married young and who's always lived a quiet life in the country."

"Well maybe I flatter myself too much, but I'm going to tell you one more thing about women like that, and then I'm going to turn over and go to sleep, if you'll let me. They don't kick over any traces and they don't do any bragging. They don't have to act wild to attract attention because they get more notice than they want anyway, and they don't have to keep telling how fetching they are because any fool can see that for himself, with one swift glance. But they do get married. If their husband live,

they're faithful to 'em, and I guess most generally they're
happy with 'em—anyways I know Alix was happy with
Jerome. But if their husbands die, they wait a decent interval, and then they get married again. It's as natural to
'em as breathing. Why I remember an old lady who lived
in White Falls when I was a boy who'd been married five
times. She was seventeen the first time and seventy the
last time. She used to say, when anyone tried to argue
her out of this habit of hers, that as long as the Lord took
'em, she would. She was a mighty attractive old lady too.
She had charm right in her coffin. I bet all the male angels
sat up and took notice when she got to heaven!"

Daniel drew up the bedclothes again, and closed his
eyes as if to indicate that he had now shot his bolt and
that he proposed to go to sleep; Serena could continue
to sit up, with her gray shawl around her, or lie down too,
just as she pleased. But he softened to the extent of making one more remark, in considerably more serious vein
than his previous one.

"Alix is going to marry someone sooner or later, and
don't you forget it," he said warningly. "If she marries
Prosper St. Cyr, she'll live in Louisiana, and we'll be
lucky if we see her once in awhile, summers—I think she'd
still try to come here summers, and I think she'd bring up
Jerry to think this was his home. I don't believe she'd ever
forget her promise to Jerome, and I think she'd keep it
as well as she could, no matter who she married. But if
she marries Dexter, she'll stay right here, and we'll have
her and Jerry both with us or near us all the time. That
would suit me right down to the ground and I guess it
would you, too, Mother. But there's another reason I hope
it'll be Dexter she'll choose, and it isn't selfish one like the
other. It's something I hope for her own good and his.
I believe that down deep in their hearts they both want
the same thing out of marriage, and I'd like to see them
get it. Dexter and Judith didn't want the same thing, and
they'd never have been happy together, like Joe and Judith
are. And unless I miss my guess, Jerome and Alix wouldn't
have wanted the same thing either, in the long run. Maybe
it's a mercy they weren't married time enough to spoil

anything. He must have gone to his death with a perfect memory and she'll go to hers with one too. . . . But Alix can't live with a memory," Daniel added unconsciously repeating Dexter's words. "She's got to live with a man. If you find out that man's going to be Dexter, you'd better get right down on your knees and thank your Maker."

Daniel never spoke to his wife again about Alix and Dexter, and Serena was still "studying" on what he had said to her when the Farmans and all their neighbors were dumbfounded to discover that their quiet village was again featured in the headlines streaming across every newspaper in the country:

> ## FBI TRAPS AGENT WHO GAVE NAZIS DATA ON U.S. ARMS—

they read with amazement—

> ### METALLURGIST ADMITS CONFEDER-ATES IN FARMAN, N. H., AIDED HIM
>
> ### LANDED PLANE IN OBSCURE PASTURE
>
> #### War Contracts Consultant
> #### Had Access to Secrets
>
> ### SOLD PLANS FOR FANTASTIC SUMS

In addition to these breath-taking announcements the local small-town dailies carried a top lead which was still more thrilling as far as the community was concerned:

> DEXTER ABBOTT OF FARMAN HILL AND BENJAMIN COHEN OF ST. JOHNSBURY INSTRUMENTAL IN HELPING GOVERNMENT AGENTS TO EFFECT ARREST

For the next few days, the countryside seethed with excitement. Joe made a hurried trip up from Washington, bringing Marcy Heath with him, and the *Bulletin* was only one of many metropolitan papers to feature the story. The village swarmed with reporters and photographers arriving from far and wide. Only one topic arose for discussion at the meeting of the Red Cross, and the Ladies' Aid. Benny became the hero of every small boy within a radius of fifty miles, and Dexter was hailed as Farman's leading citizen. While this turmoil still seethed, the town taxi turned in at the side yard of Farman Hill, one afternoon the latter part of June, and Alix got out of it, holding Jerry in her arms.

Her mother-in-law rushed out to meet her, overwhelmed by delight and surprise. Alix set down the baby while she paid the driver, and he staggered uncertainly towards the piazza, his plump pink face wreathed in proud smiles. His grandmother picked him up and hugged him hard.

"Walking!" she gasped unbelievingly. "Walking already! We've got to stop him though, a big baby like that, trying to walk before he's ten months old. If we don't, he'll get bow-legged. Well, I declare, Alix, you've given me such a turn, I don't know what to say."

"Won't you say you're glad to see me?"

"*Glad to see you!* I'm so glad I can't see straight! But why didn't you let us know, so's we could meet you at the depot?"

"Right in the middle of a beautiful June day, when Father and Dexter are both busy in the fields? Now, Mother! You know me better than that! But haven't you a kiss for me too?"

She had a dozen, Serena said excitedly, enveloping Alix as well as Jerry in her ample embrace. Once within her mother-in-law's arms, it took Alix some minutes to extricate herself and her son, who had caught the contagion of rejoicing, and was gurgling and shouting too. The driver—the same one who had once been ungratefully labeled by Peter as a dumb yokel—obligingly carried out bags and set them down in the East and West Chambers. The rooms were all open, in a welcoming sort of way, and they were in beautiful order. Alix walked from one to another, exclaiming with admiration and delight.

"How could you do so much, Mother, all alone! I can see you don't need my help, not the least bit in the world."

"Now don't you dare say that, Alix Farman. I need you the worst way and I've missed you every minute, more'n you'll ever know. Well, I wanted to have everything nice, so's if you did come back———"

"*If* I came back! Why, Mother, you knew that I was coming back!"

"Well, I hoped so anyways. Maybe I should have said I wanted you should find everything the way you'd want it *when* you came back. It seemed like we'd never get warm weather, but after all, you can't stop the coming of spring, same as you said yourself, and when we let all the fires out, of course we opened up all the doors again. Not but what we still have a fire in the living room, now and again, in the evening. You don't feel any chill in the air, do you, Alix? Because if you do, I can start up a fire now, in two shakes of a dead lamb's tail———"

"No, I don't feel any chill in the air. . . . The roses look lovely in the front yard, beside the door rock, don't they?"

"Yes, they do. But just you wait until you see the Painted Beauty in your garden. It's half in bud and half in bloom, and it's the *handsomest* rose———"

"I'm going out to see it in just a minute . . . You don't mean to tell me you've taken care of my garden for me too, do you, Mother?"

"No, Dexter has done that. Of course Benny has helped him some, since school let out. Benny's as handy a child as I ever saw, in a garden. But all the same, I honestly don't see how Dexter has had the time, especially since———"

Serena stopped short, blushing painfully. She had almost let the cat out of the bag.

"Especially since what, Mother?"

"Especially since there's been all this commotion about Hellmann and his gang," Serena continued, glibly if guiltily. "You've read about that in the papers, haven't you, Alix?"

"I couldn't very well help it, if I read the papers at all, could I? I've eaten up every word of it, and I've never been so excited in my life! But the commotion's beginning to die down now, isn't it?"

"Well, some. But then Dexter's got big crops and a lot of stock on his hands, and he had to neglect those for a few days while he was all taken up with the FBI. That couldn't be helped, and since then he's been trying to make up for lost time. You'll want to see the calves and the colts yourself, Alix, same as you used to last year. Daniel's pretty proud of them, I can tell you. I believe he's out in the barn now. You could go and surprise him, like you did me. And the clover! The clover's all in bloom now— most generally the clover and the roses come together, on Farman Hill. They're late but they're out at last. I don't want you should miss seeing the clover this year, Alix."

"I won't. I'll see it today before sunset. I'll put Jerry down for his nap, and then I'll go out to the barn and surprise Father, then afterwards I'll go to see the clover . . . Where's Dexter working this afternoon, Mother?"

"Why he's up in the Mill Lot cultivating. The Mill Lot's planted with corn this year."

"You haven't done anything yet about building on those old foundations, have you?"

"No, but the menfolks are still talking about putting something up there. Maybe not a mill, but an extra farm building of some sort. I guess they're waiting for you to make suggestions."

"Oh, I'll make suggestions . . . But what's happened to the little old abandoned houses on the road to the village?"

"Why—they—they were sold. Just recently."

"Have we got some nice new neighbors?"

"Well, nothing's settled, but I think maybe we will have . . . Alix, don't you believe the baby would let me put him down for his nap? I do want you should get out and see that clover with the afternoon light on it. It's like a great sea of color."

"We can try. He's a very friendly baby. He always was, you know."

Jerry was still friendly, but not quite friendly enough to satisfy his grandmother's fondest hopes. He regarded her amicably, as long as his mother also remained in attendance, but as soon as Alix tried slipping out of his sight he set up a scream that testified to the strength of his lung power as well as the strength of his will power. It was not until he was fast asleep that she could leave him. Then she still had to stop to admire the Painted Beauty and see how well the rest of the garden was going, before Serena was satisfied. Now that the little abandoned houses were no longer under embarrassing discussion, she did not want Alix to leave her. When her mother-in-law finally released her, Alix hesitated for a moment. She was tempted to go straight to the Mill Lot without stopping first at the barn. But she knew that was not the way it should be, and she went through the house a second time and across the side yard.

The great door of the big barn stood open to admit the summer air. Dusty shafts of sunshine streamed through it, falling from a tiny window in the gable and illuminating its darkness. They had the length, and the splendor, of similar shafts, streaming from high stained glass windows in old churches, and like these, they patterned the floor with lozenges of light. The mingled scents of grain and milk and hay filled her nostrils as she went forward, and she thought, not irreverently but reflectively, that though in church the fragrance would have been that of incense instead, these too had their deep significance. The stillness was like that of a church also, and the vastness. Without premeditation, Alix felt it would be natural and fitting to say a little prayer, and in spite of her haste she was impelled to kneel down and cross herself.

"Hail Mary, full of grace, the Lord's is with thee," she murmured instinctively; but she did not go on with the Ave. Instead a prayer that was new and spontaneous came to her lips: "Dear Lord, who by Thy birth didst glorify a humble stable and all the creatures in it, give grace to this stable, to the men who work in it and to the animals that are sheltered by it. Let it be a storehouse not only of crops but of goodness. Help us to fill it and to make it secure, so that it may be both a fortress for this farm and a stronghold for the whole land. From it, let us send forth food to share with those who have less than ourselves. And let us all rejoice in the harvest which Thou wilt send in Thine own good time."

She was so wrapped in reverence, so lost in petition, that she did not hear her father-in-law as he came towards her. When he saw her, he stopped short, and stood looking down at her with joy in his heart, but with a lump in his throat. He did not want her to be startled by seeing him, as he had been startled by seeing her, so he waited until she rose and turned towards the milk room, looking for him. Then he spoke to her.

"Daughter," he said gently. "Daughter, I'm thankful you're home. We've missed you very much. We've needed you . . ."

It was he who asked if she were not going to seek Dexter out too, before she had shown any restiveness or expressed any intention of leaving him. She'd see a change in Dexter, he said, a change for the better. After Judith left, the winter before, Dexter had sort of gone to pieces for a while. But after Alix left, this last winter, it had been just the opposite; he had not only pulled himself together, he had forged ahead considerable. You wouldn't hardly believe the same man could act so different, two winters running, unless you suspicioned that maybe it made a difference what sort of a woman it was went away and how she did it. Alix made no direct reply to this comment, but she said yes, she was going out to find Dexter. Mother had told her that she would find him cultivating in the Mill Lot, and had told her, too, that the clover was in full bloom now, and that it was a beautiful sight. She did not want to miss that sight on Farman Hill this year, as she had the year before. He smiled.

"Did you see the clover on the levees that Joe talked about?"

"Yes, I saw it, in April. That was beautiful too."

"And the water hyacinths that we don't have here, either in April or in June? Did you see those too?"

"Yes, Father. I saw those too."

"And weren't they as lovely as you expected, after all?"

"Yes. But after I'd seen them, I was satisfied. I could

leave them. I knew I could go and see them again some day. That satisfied me. I didn't feel I had to live beside them all the time."

"And there wasn't anyone in Louisiana you felt you had to live with either?"

"No, Father, I felt I had to come back and live here."

"You're sure now?"

"Yes, I'm very sure. I had to find out, but now I know."

He lifted one of his horny hands and smoothed back her hair from her white brow. Her face had changed since he last saw her. It was still calm, but it no longer had only the calmness of control; it had the calmness of assured and happy expectancy. He bent over and kissed her forehead gravely, as once in a great while he had kissed his own daughters'. He had never done this before to Alix, unless she first proffered a caress. As she stood quietly, accepting his, he noticed how greatly her figure had changed, too. It had lost the full-breasted look of the nursing mother; its contours, though still curved, were more delicate and gracile than they had been. He knew how readily and fittingly they would lend themselves to love again. He asked her a question, gravely, as he had kissed her, but gently, too.

"You've weaned Jerry, Alix?"

"Yes, I had to, last month. I don't think it was the journey south—we both stood that very well. I think it was just that it was time anyway."

"Yes, I think so too. He thrives, doesn't he, on the food he has now?"

"Oh, yes. You'll see. He's even trying to walk. Mother says it's too soon. She says he'll be bowlegged if I don't stop him."

"You can't stop a child after he's once started to walk— or anything else that's a natural human development. You understand that, don't you, Alix?"

"Yes, Father. I think so."

"You can't shirk these other things either and you mustn't shrink from them. You understand that too, don't you?"

"Yes, Father."

"Well, you haven't a father of your own to speak to you,

or a mother either, and sometimes there are things that need saying. If I thought Serena'd say them to you, I wouldn't. But I know she won't."

"What was it you wanted to say, Father?"

"I don't know's it's necessary after all. I've got considerable respect for your judgment, Alix, not to mention your character and your courage. But I just wanted to remind you of something I thought might have been put into Holy Writ alongside of the place where it says it isn't good for a man to live alone: it isn't good for a woman either. And I wanted to tell you too, just in case you didn't know it, it isn't often a young woman has as hard a time with her second child as she does with her first."

"I did know. Not that it would have mattered anyway, the hard time I mean. Don't worry about me, Father. I do understand and everything will be all right. But thank you for talking to me as you have anyway. I hope we'll have lots of such talks together."

"I hope so, daughter."

He watched her out of sight. There was no question, this time, that she might take the long leisurely route past the Swamp Piece and through the two pastures. She struck straight for the old wood road. The fields on either side of it, as far as she could see, were covered with clover, spreading out in vast shimmering sheets of fresh fragrance and variegated color. Bands of yellow bordered the road itself; beyond were patches of pink and stretches of white; and intermingled with all these, was the red clover, the richest and brightest of all. The breeze stirred the grasses in such a way that they rose and fell in ripples, like waves, and the sun gave them a gloss like the sheen of silk. Bees hummed in the blossoms and birds fluttered over them— the beautiful black and orange songsters which Alix had learned to call golden robins instead of Baltimore orioles, since she came to Farman Hill. Along the old stone wall, clusters of fruit, hard and green as jade, were already beginning to form on the wild apple trees, and in the grove the fresh shoots pointed like bayberry candles from the fir balsams. A scurrying woodchuck dove into his hole, and some tiny field mice scampered away and were swallowed up by the clover. But Alix saw no other animals. For a long time the solitude was supreme.

She had almost reached the foundations of the Old Mill before she saw Dexter. Evidently he had sat down to rest for a few minutes, for he was partially hidden by a section of the crumbling wall which cast a long shadow over the sturdy growth of corn with which the Mill Lot was planted this year. The corn rustled a little in the same breeze that rippled the clover, so that he did not hear her light step, and he did not see her either, until she was almost beside him. Then he sprang up and reached her in a single stride, stretching out his arms so spontaneously that they were around her before he realized that he had caught her to him.

"Alix!" he exclaimed. And again, "Alix!"

He did not ask her when she had come or how or why. Only one thing mattered, and this was that she was there. Apparently it was the only thing which mattered to her too, for she did not say anything at all. She was a little breathless, and it was unlike Alix to be breathless, because neither haste nor excitement was characteristic of her. But today she had hastened and she was excited. She stood with her face close to his breast until she was quiet again, and all the time she was conscious of his heart's steady beating. Finally she looked up at him.

"I came home," she said. "This time I've come to stay."

CHAPTER 35

IT WAS while they were all sitting around the fire after supper, as nearly as any of them could remember later on, that the question of the Fourth of July party came up for the first time; but still none of them remembered whether it was Serena who spoke of it first or Daniel or Alix or

Dexter. But somehow they found themselves saying that presently Judith and Joe would be there too, that Joe hadn't met any of the neighbors and of course he ought to, that no gathering would be complete without Rhoda and she was getting pretty near her time. So perhaps while Joe and Judith were at Farman Hill, before Rhoda's time actually came, it might be a good plan to ask their friends in. Then someone said that the Fourth of July fell on Sunday, so that was a good day for the menfolks; and presently they were agreeing there ought to be green peas, as usual, for the Fourth, and that salmon wasn't rationed so there was no reason why they shouldn't get some; and what with the recent easing upon the regulations about coffee, if everyone would bring a little, they could get by. Raspberries would be starting to ripen too, and there were always more of those in the Home Pasture than any one family could eat; and nobody could ask for a better cake than one with a good thick maple sugar frosting. Why they could have a real nice supper, Serena said, warming to her subject; good enough for anyone. They could ask the Litchfields and the Haywoods and the Childs, same as they always had; maybe they had better ask the Wendells and the Merrills and the Haskins too; after all, these were all neighbors; and the Brents and Mrs. Barnes——

"You'd ask all the women who work in the Red Cross Unit, wouldn't you, Mother, whether they've ever been here to a party before or not?" Alix asked. "And the Boudreaus and the Franchinis and the Lippmans?"

"Why, yes, I presume so, if you want I should, Alix. Yes, of course, we would—Wouldn't we, Daniel?"

"Yes, Mother, of course."

They sat for some time planning the Fourth of July party. Then Serena remembered that perhaps Judith might be sensitive about her scars. Alix did not think so.

"Why don't you write and ask her, Mother, if you're afraid? But I feel sure she'll say no. Why should she be sensitive about those, instead of being proud of them, the way she is of her African service ribbon? Aren't they in the same category?"

"Well now, Alix, I suppose they are, if you think of it that way. But Judith used to be such a fine-looking girl."

"She's fine-looking now too. Remember you haven't seen her since she left the hospital. I saw her several times in Louisiana. She reminds me more of Jenness than she ever did—she doesn't look like Jenness any longer, of course, but she has more and more of her grace—and more and more of her own too. Her hair's very becoming to her, drawn down over her brow and ears and gathered into a knot at the nape of her neck. It softens her face. Her face has softened a lot anyhow, but the way she does her hair adds to the effect. Her clothes are becoming too. She and Joe design them together. Joe's very interested in Judith's clothes."

"I wish she'd get him to take a little more interest in his own." Serena said feelingly. "But I guess she likes him just the way he is—Well, I'll drop her a line the first thing in the morning and that'll relieve my mind. I guess it's all right to go ahead and plan though. Rhoda won't hesitate to come for fear of being conspicuous, will she, Dexter?"

"I'd get the surprise of my life if she did. She taught school all those last weeks in a smock, and gave her pupils a straight-from-the-shoulder talk, so I understand, that they'll never forget. If we could have had a few speeches like that when I was going to a district school, it would have done away with a lot of spying and sneaking and smut."

"Dexter is right, Mother," Daniel said, rising. "Well now that we've got everything nicely settled, or practically settled, about this party we're going to have, I think maybe you and I better be starting for bed. I've had a pretty hard day and I'm all tuckered out——"

"Dexter and I are going for a walk," Alix announced unexpected. "He says he has something he wants to show me. I'm going upstairs to have a look at Jerry and get a wrap—It's never hot here in the evening, even in June, is it?—You go ahead to bed if you feel like it, Father," she added archly. "But if you're just doing it on our account, you might as well keep on sitting here, by the nice warm fire."

"What on earth are you going to take a walk for, at this
time of night?" Serena remonstrated. "We are going to bed,
same as Daniel says. But even if we weren't———"

"Even if you weren't, there are still the East Parlor and
the West Parlor and the summer kitchen," Alix said, still
archly. "But we really are going for a walk, Mother. I'm
not sure I know why, but I have my suspicions. And I
think you do know. You answered very guiltily and self-
consciously this afternoon, when I asked you a perfectly
simple question. I should think you'd be ashamed of yourself, a church member in good standing!—Well, sit up for
us or not, just as you feel you'd like to."

She sauntered out of the room, singing as she went up
the stairs. They recognized the words of the song they had
not heard in so long:

> Way down on de ol' bayou
> Beneath a cypress tree,
> Miss Liza met her Sunday beau
> And sat upon his knee.
> De moon was shinin' high above,
> He whispered low, sweet words of love.
> O———h, Miss Liza an' her beau.

Alix came donwstairs again with a loose velvet coat
over her white dress. The coat was crimson, almost the
same color as the buds on the Painted Beauty rosebush before these unfolded. Apparently she had thought of this
herself, for as she sauntered back into the living room she
said she was going out into the garden for a minute, and
did Dexter want to come with her or would that take him
out of his way? She didn't want to make this walk of his
too long for him, after a hard day's work . . .

He laughed and said he guessed he could stand that
much more of walk, and then he stood beside her, watching
her delightedly while she plucked two roses from the
Painted Beauty bush and tucked them into her braids, just
above her left ear.

"There was a Marechal Neil rosebush at Bellefontaine

that grew to be as large as a tree," she told him. "This variety was originally brought to Louisiana by the Count of Clausel, one of Napoleon's favorite officers. Some years later, another French Count happened to be strolling through Clausel's garden on the evening preceding a duel he had engaged to fight in defense of a beautiful woman's honor. He asked for a cutting, and brought it to my great-grandmother, who was an old friend of his, with the petition to plant it himself in her garden. But he gave her full directions for its care, saying jestingly that if he were killed the next day, he was sure the roses would bloom forever, as a memorial to him. Within a few hours he lay dead on the field of honor. And sure enough! Before a year had past the little cutting had grown into a big bush. Later on, experts from near and far came to see it, pronouncing it the largest and most fragrant rose they had ever seen. Now the root from the mother stem is noted throughout the South for its glorious flowers. But they are not half so gorgeous, to my way of thinking, as these Painted Beauties."

Dexter tried to listen to the story, but he only half heard it, because he was looking so fixedly at Alix and his mind was on what he saw, instead of on what he heard. The starlight was very bright, so that it was easy for him to see her.

"I've never seen you with flowers in your hair before," he said. "I wish I could have a picture of you."

"Well, you can, of course. . . . "You've never seen me when I was so happy before. It's as natural as breathing for Creoles to put flowers in their hair when they're happy."

"Are you really very happy?"

"Yes, really. Very happy. Aren't you?"

"What do you think? Come, let's get started on our walk."

They skirted the garden and went down the highway to the point where the road to the village branched off. Then they turned and followed this for a few hundred feet. As they went up the walk to the little house that had been deserted for so long, Dexter paused for a moment.

"If I'd known you were coming, I'd have tried to make some special preparation. But I didn't have a chance."

"I'm glad you didn't. I'd rather see it just as you're living in it—That's what you are doing, isn't it?"

"Yes. At least I sleep here. And once in a while Mrs. Wendell leaves me a pie or something like that so I can have a snack late at night. But I'd like to really live here and to have Benny here with me. It's a nice little house. That is, I think it is. And I think it might be made very homelike. Let's see what you think."

He turned a switch and radiance flooded the dark living room. Mrs. Wendell had been there that day; the place smelled of scrubbing and strawberries and roses. There was a big bowl of the berries on the table, and beside them some hermits folded in a clean darned napkin. The roses, like the lilacs which had preceded them, were in a stone crock and a glass preserving jar. But they were very red and very fragrant. Alix reached for one and added it to the Painted Beauties which were in her braids already.

"Are you hungry? What about feasting on strawberries, sugar and cream? They're more or less classically linked, aren't they, with the fine seams you like to sew?"

"Yes . . . As a matter of fact I don't mind washing the dishes. But I'd enjoy the strawberries too."

"I hoped you would. We'll have a party of our own, without waiting for the Fourth of July. And what about a little fire?"

"Well, it's June, but after all, speaking of classical illusions, what is so rare as a day in June—without a fire, if you live in New Hampshire?"

They kindled it together, and when it began to burn brightly, sat down in front of it. A small bench, which had evidently once served a cobbler, was among the objects Dexter had brought down from the old carpenter shop over the cider mill, and they drew it up in front of the hearth, where a cricket was chirping merrily. Alix said this was a sign of good luck, and Dexter agreed with her when she added, parenthetically, that the bench was big enough for both of them.

"Tell me about this nice little house, Dexter. How you happened to think of buying it, and all."

He told her: about the rain on the roof and the wood in the shed and the fish in the brook; about the unexpected and increasing poignancy of his feeling for Benny. He did not refer to the discovery of the subversive activities and she did not raise the question herself. There would be time to discuss all that later on when more intimate matters were settled. But she listened intently, her eyes never leaving his face, while he told her of those things which were nearest to his heart. He talked for a long time, and when he finally stopped explaining his feeling for the place and for the child, he asked her a question.

"Now tell me something."

"I wish I could tell you something as thrilling and touching and full of meaning as what you've just told me. You've proved to me that in spite of what you've said, you can survive and build a life for yourself, without any woman to shape it for you. A man ought to do that first."

"What do you mean by 'first,' Alix?"

"I mean before he asks a woman to share it. She should do that, if she cares for him, but she shouldn't ever shape it. Now that you've shaped your own . . ."

She did not finish the sentence, but it was not necessary for either one that she should. Dexter went on again where he had left off before.

"If you say what I hope you may, without any right or reason to hope for it, there will be a lot more meaning to it than what I've told you."

"What is it, Dexter, that you think you haven't any right or reason to hope for?"

"That some day you might feel the same way about the place that I do."

She did not answer instantly, but neither did she withdraw from him, as she had on that dreadful day which had marked their estrangement. She seemed to be pondering what he had said to her, sitting, as he had so often seen her sit before, with her chin cupped in her hand and her eyes fixed on the fire. He did not disturb her, and at last she spoke, thoughtfully but understandingly.

"It would take some adjustment, wouldn't it, Dexter? After all, I've told Father and Mother that I feel Farman Hill is my home, and I do."

"Yes. But sometimes people have more than one home, don't they? A summer home and a winter home, like the former owners of this house. Or a northern home and a southern home. And what I'm suggesting wouldn't involve as much difference of time and space as either of those arrangements. It would apply to any time of year and it would only involve crossing the road. I don't see why you couldn't feel that you belonged in both places—that it, supposing all the other factors were favorable."

"Perhaps I could . . . I'll think over that aspect. But I must think about Jerry too."

"I don't see why he should be any more of a problem than Benny. He'd run back and forth between the two places, Alix, every day, and he couldn't have done that if you'd kept him in Louisiana part of every year. And he'll still inherit Farman Hill, whether he stays there all the time or not. At least, he'll be one of the heirs to it. We mustn't forget that Judith and Joe may have children some day too. Probably they'd never be as much attached to it as Jerry will, because he'll live on it or near it all the year around, and they'd be in Washington most of the time, or even further away, if Joe should get transferred somewhere else—I have an idea that sooner or later he and Judith will get overseas together, in some capacity. But their children would have an equal right to share in Farman Hill if they wanted it or if their parents wanted them to have it. Perhaps this is as good a time as any to say I wouldn't want my children to have it. I've considered the possibility of buying the Hellmann farm for Benny—After all, the Hellmanns won't be needing it any more, and it seems to me the gesture might be appropriate, all things considered." He paused, smiling, and again Alix returned his smile. Then he went on, more thoughtfully. "That doesn't need to be settled right now. But while I'm about it, I might add that I'd want to pay all the expenses of running my own place too."

"Yes. I can understand how you'd feel about all those

questions. And it is just as well to have them settled now. I wouldn't make any difficulty for you, Dexter, about those. It was different when we disagreed about Farman Hill."

Spontaneously she looked up with another smile, and spontaneously slid her hand into his. He pressed it and again the knowledge that there was harmony and understanding between them filled him with happiness. He went on without making any further reference to the last point he had raise.

"But otherwise, except for this matter of inheritance, I'd never make any difference between Jerry and Benny and my own children, Alix. You know that too, don't you? And I don't think Jerry'd ever feel any difference either. Of course we'll tell him about his own father, we'll teach him to honor Jerome's memory. But I think Jerome will be an ideal to him rather than a personality, don't you? Whatever you do? Even if you shouldn't ever marry again."

"Yes, inevitably. I've thought of that already. And I've thought that perhaps ever before he left Raeford, Jerome had a presentiment of how it would all end. I believe when he wrote that letter, saying it was a shame you wouldn't be having a son of your own about the same time that Jerry was born, he was thinking ahead. It wasn't just by chance that he said he knew you'd be good to my baby and that he hoped the baby would be some comfort to you too. I believe he was seeing then everything we're facing now. Perhaps more clearly than I see it myself yet."

"Perhaps he was, Alix . . . Is there anything else you feel needs adjustment?"

"No. I think everything else is adjusted already. Except perhaps the element of time. Are you in a hurry, Dexter?"

"No, I'm not in a hurry. You've taught me, very effectually, that it doesn't pay to be in a hurry, as far as you're concerned. That is, it doesn't pay as far as I'm concerned. There doesn't seem to be any set rule about these things. A year and a half ago, I'd come to a different decision, and Joe Racina proved I was right in that case. But this is something else again and I'm mighty glad of it."

There was no hint of rancor or regret in his voice. He rose, still holding her hand and drawing her gently up too.

"Would you care to see the rest of the house? I'd like to have you, if you would. But I know you've had a long journey and a hard one. You ought to rest. I ought to see that you do. So presently I must take you back to Farman Hill."

"All right. But what is it, Dexter, that journeys proverbially end in?"

Their plans were still in this pleasant but indefinite stage when Joe and Judith arrived at Farman Hill, and neither of them had said anything to Daniel or Serena. They did not say anything to Joe or Judith either. But Joe spoke of it to Judith on his own initiative, when they went to their room the night after their arrival. Judith had declined the use of the East Chamber, though Alix had meticulously removed all Jerry's belongings from it, so that it again had the tidy and slightly formal aspect suitable for a spare room, according to Serena's views. But that was just the trouble with it, Judith said. She didn't want to sleep in a spare room when she came home. She wanted to sleep in the room where she felt she belonged, and this was the little back chamber over the winter kitchen, where she had always slept. Yes, it was rather small for a big man like Joe to squeeze into. But they could manage. She didn't take up much room herself. She had learned not to. That was one good thing about being a nurse; you learned to fold yourself up into practically no space at all.

They had all enjoyed a very pleasant evening in the summer kitchen, and they had talked a good deal about the Fourth of July party, which was now only a few days off. Judith was delighted at the prospect of seeing all her old friends in this way, and of having Joe meet them. Joe said he was delighted too, and everyone knew by this time that when Joe said he was delighted, he really meant it. Judith thought there was quite a good deal she could do to help get ready for the party. She could go raspberrying and she was almost sure she could shell peas too, she said, glancing down at her hands. They did not look much the way Judith's hands used to look, Serena thought, with a pang of pity. Judith's hands had been so strong and square and brown once; now they were very thin and very lax and translucent in their whiteness, except where the fine scars ran across them, like threads. But they had a new beauty of their own, and presently Serena realized this and was comforted in the realization. She could see how Judith's white fingers would look, reaching for red raspberries and dropping them into a silvery pail, and she could see how Judith's white hands would look with the green peas running through them into a yellow bowl. She knew that both would be a lovely sight. Alix had been right in saying that Judith now had much of Jenness' grace, and much of her own besides. . . .

All right, Judith could shell the peas, Joe said, stretching out his long legs and arms, and he would do anything Mother Farman would like to have him in the way of helping; but he thought for a fact he could be most useful if he went fishing for a day, or perhaps two days. Oh yes, he understood that Alix was sending to Boston for salmon, all very swish too. But personally he always believed in patronizing local products. Dexter had told him there were trout in the brook, not to mention bass and pickerel and pike in the river. He had always had an idea that if he brought a bass bug north, and showed it to some of those New England trout, he'd open a lot of eyes. Now he was going to try it out. He'd be very busy. . . .

The group broke up early. Dexter and Alix went over to the little house, which she was gradually helping him to furnish. He was free from his farm work only after it was dark, so by common consent they regularly gave up most evenings to the little house now, and they invited Joe and Judith to go over with them, to see how they were getting along. Well, perhaps the next night, Joe said. They'd like to see it very much. But tonight Judith was pretty tired. He was going to tuck her in under that nice old patchwork quilt with the Rose of Sharon design on it. He did not consult her when he said this; he simply made the statement, looking at her with his queer crooked grin. Then they said good night to everyone else and went upstairs together.

It was still difficult for her to dress and undress and he helped her get ready for bed. So he had done nothing about preparing for it himself when she actually was tucked in under the old patchwork quilt; he was still puttering around the small room, bumping his head occasionally against the low slanting roof, swearing a little when he did so, and filling the room with cigarette smoke. It was then that he spoke to her about Dexter and Alix.

"It looks as if that were going to work out pretty well."

"Do you really think it will?"

"Hell, I don't see any reason why it shouldn't! Do you?"

"She's giving up an awful lot. Think of those magnificent houses we saw in New Orleans, Joe, that belong to her aunts and her stepmother! She could live in luxury, in any of those; she could have wealth and ease and position, and pleasure of every sort."

"Do you really think frills of that kind are important?"

"I should think they might be, to a girl like Alix."

Not when she's convinced she's gaining so much by giving them up. And Alix has got a pretty good sense of values. Dexter's stock mounted in my estimation the minute I knew she was considering him. She's discovered something or brought out something the rest of you missed. But if it hadn't been there in the first place, she couldn't have brought it out or discovered it . . . You gave up an awful lot yourself, didn't you? And you seem to be bearing up all right, so far."

"What are you talking about, Joe Racina? I didn't give up anything at all."

"That's what you say now—Damn white of you, too! But how about that career which meant more than anything else in the world once? Wasn't that more important to you than the position and the pleasures, et cetera, et cetera, ever could have been to Alix?" He came and sat down beside Judith, on the bed, swinging his long legs over the side and holding his cigarette between his fingers. "And what about Dexter's sister, Rhoda what's-her-name? Wasn't she all wrapped up in her school teaching? She gave up a lot too, didn't she, when she married that meek little shopkeeper?"

"Rhoda? Why she didn't even begin to live, before she met David!"

"All right. If you didn't give up anything, and Rhoda didn't give up anything, I don't believe Alix has either. It depends on the way a woman looks at it all—or perhaps I might venture to flatter my much maligned sex and say it depends upon the way a man persuades her to look at it all . . . Did you ever read 'The Red Pavilion,' Judith?"

"No, I never did. I never read anything, that is, not enough to count, until I married you. And you seem to have read everything under the light of the sun. Tell me about the red pavilion, Joe."

"I'll do better than that. I'll quote the poem to you."

He leaned over and put his arms under her shoulders, as he had that first day when she came back from Africa, and so many times since. Judith loved to have him hold her in this way:

"Leave thy father, leave thy mother and thy brother;"
Joe said—
"Leave the black tents of thy tribe apart.
Am I not thy father and thy brother, and thy mother?
And thou—what needst with thy tribe's black tents
Who hast the red pavilion of my heart?"

He stopped reciting but he continued to hold her. Judith looked up at him with adoring eyes.

"I don't need *anything* else, now I have it," she said softly. "You're right, Joe. If Dexter has given Alix her red pavilion, she doesn't need her tribe's black tents. No woman does, when she has that red pavilion."

They all got to church the morning of the Fourth of July. Serena said at first she didn't see how they were going to manage it, with such immense crowds piling in on them, that very afternoon; in the same breath, however, she said she wouldn't feel right if they didn't. This was a different Fourth from the other Fourths. The kids wouldn't be setting off firecrackers under her feet, all the time she was trying to make the rounds of her milk route, and scaring her half out of her senses. There wouldn't be a rally either, that they would have to go to, right out in the blazing sun, with someone from the Fisheries Department in Concord reading a great long prepared speech about how Thomas Jefferson came to write the Declaration of Independence. She thought it was sort of significant, too, that this Fourth came on a Sunday and she'd like to say so to the Lord in prayer. But still she didn't see how she could manage it . . .

Alix told her mother-in-law that she felt the same way about this particular Fourth, adding she was sure that somehow they could manage church, and they did. She and Dexter went to the Junction, taking Jerry with them, and Dexter sat in the car, amusing Jerry, while she went to Mass. Serena and Daniel went to the village, as usual, and Judith and Joe went with them. When they all met for their pickup lunch afterwards, Alix reported that Father Boudreau had told her he and his sister would be along early, bringing the Franchinis with them, in order to take advantage of their "C" card and save gas, and Serena was able to make a similar report: Mr. and Mrs. Litchfield were coming early too, and they were going to bring Grandma Lippman with them, because she would be more comfortable riding in their car than she would be wedged in among all the musical instruments. The Lippmans had succeeded in organizing the band on which they had set their hearts, and it was to play on Farman Hill that afternoon for the first time in public.

It was a beautiful day, warm, as New England interprets warmth, but with enough breeze to make the flags flutter, and that was always a good sign, Serena said, on the Fourth of July. There were two tall flag poles in the front yard, one on either side of the cobblestone walk, and from these American flags were waving. Then there was a row of standards, all the way across the front of the house, back of the rose bushes, and these standards upheld the flags of the United Nations. Flags had been fastened in clusters, too, on the pillars of the porch and against the lintels of the doors. It was the first time that so many flags of so many different countries, had ever been displayed on Farman Hill, or anywhere else in the neighborhood, and the guests were loud in their expressions of admiration over the spectacle these flags presented.

A good many of the womenfolk came fairly early, so that they could enjoy passing the afternoon with Serena and Judith and Alix and Rhoda, while they helped with the final preparations. Most of them came on foot or behind some old family horse which had fortunately survived the machinery era, and many of them brought small supplementary offerings besides the sugar and coffee which represented their rightful contribution. ("Well, I didn't know but what you could find use for an extra pound of butter. I churned yesterday" . . . "I think that recipe of mine for butternut bread's as good as any I ever tasted, if I do say so myself.") Some of the menfolk came early too—All those, in fact, who were not farmers, and who were therefore unhandicapped by the problem of chores. Joe had said he was sure he could look after these male guests all right, while Daniel and Dexter were busy in the barn; and he not only succeeded in doing this, but in making them at ease with their fellow visitors, in the cases where acquaintance was being made for the first time. Alix had set the trestled table in the summer kitchen for a buffet, and Rhoda and Judith had orders to sit quietly at either end of it, Rhoda serving the salmon and peas, Judith the raspberries and the coffee. Mrs. Wendell was stationed with Serena in the winter kitchen. Benny and Rachel were passing plates, swelling with self-importance.

Everyone who had a settee had loaned this for the occasion, so there were plenty of seats scattered about in the flower garden and through the back yard. As the additional guests arrived, at suppertime, they took their places on these settees, drawing up the miscellaneous folding tables which had also been loaned, and eating heartily and comfortably. There had been a blessing before they began, asked by Mr. Litchfield, who stood in the old handhewn doorway, where he could be seen and heard both by those who were in the two kitchens, and those who were in the garden and yard. (" 'I will lift up mine eyes unto the hills,' he had begun, "from whence cometh my help. My help cometh from the Lord, who made heaven and earth' . . . Help us now, O Lord, as we ask this of Thee surrounded by our hills which are Thine also.") During supper, the

Lippman band played proudly—regional songs and war songs and patriotic medleys. ("Dixie" to compliment Alix and Joe; "The Caissons Go Rolling Along" to compliment Judith; "The Long Long Trail" because it had been written by a New Hampshire man; "Yankee Doodle" because it merged so easily in "Columbia the Gem of the Ocean.") When all had eaten their fill, Father Boudreau offered the evening prayer. ("Visit, we beseech Thee, O Lord, this habitation, and drive far from it all snares of the enemy. Let Thy holy angels dwell herein, to preserve us in peace; and may Thy blessing be always upon us.") Then Daniel himself took his place in the handhewn doorway, and raised his hand.

"Friends," he said simply. It was the way he had always begun his greeting to his guests, and he saw no reason for changing now to a more elaborate preamble, though never before had he felt moved to say as much as was in his heart now. "Friends, since we had our last gathering here, there's been a good many changes on Farman Hill, and in our village, and all over the world. Most of you joined with me and my wife in drinking our New Year's toasts, when Pearl Harbor wasn't more'n a few weeks behind us. Most of you but not all of you. We weren't acquainted then with Father Boudreau, who's the pastor of the church our daughter-in-law attends, or his sister, or the Franchinis, who go to St. Theresa's too. We weren't acquainted with David Cohen, who's married our neighbor, Rhoda Abbott, and his daughter Rachel and his nephew Benny. We weren't acquainted with the Lippmans' who are furnishing us with our music this afternoon, and who've brought so much general culture into our farming community. We weren't acquainted with Alix St. Cyr, who married our son Jerome, or with Joe Racina, who's married our daughter Judith. Mother and I feel we've gained considerable, this last year and a half, adding all these people to our circle of friends. We're sure the rest of you who didn't know them before either will agree with us it's a better circle as well as a bigger one because of them. We won't ask them to rise and take bows, one by one. This isn't a banquet or a rally or the like of that. It's just a friendly Sunday night supper on a national holiday that seems different to us from any Fourth of July we ever celebrated before. But I will ask the rest of the old-timers to join with Mother and me in giving these new-comers a hand, to show them how glad we are to have them here in our home town and on Farman Hill."

The applause was immediate and vociferous. Its beneficiaries responded to it variously, some rather bashfully and blushingly, others with unconcealed gratification. The clapping continued so long that Daniel was obliged to raise his hand again, in order to command silence to go on.

"I began by saying we'd seen changes on Farman Hill since the last friendly gathering we had here. I don't need to tell you the first of these changes was wrought by death, and that it was the sort of death that's pretty hard to speak of, even after time's got in its work of healing. But I'm going to speak to you about the death of my daughter Jenness today, though I've never done it before and don't know's I ever shall do it again. I'm going to speak of it for a special reason. I've a notion some of you may have been saying among yourselves, 'If Jenness Farman hadn't gone to Washington and taken the kind of job she did, she would be alive and well today.' She might, friends she might. But then again, there's nothing certain about it. We've got to be careful where we put the blame, even when we're bowed down by grief. Mother and I always tried to give our children a good Christian home and a good Christian example. But maybe we didn't succeed as well as we might have, or maybe Jenness herself didn't try to follow our teachings as carefully as she could have. Anyway, we're not going to let the loss of our daughter keep us from looking towards Washington with hopefulness and trust. It's the capital of our country; it comes mighty close to being the capital of the world today; we can't afford to have our faith in it undermined by a personal tragedy. It's the same with men in public office. Human nature being what it is, you can't get away from the fact that take any large group, there's bound to be some men in it who aren't worthy of their office. There's been bad presidents and bad popes and bad

lawyers and bad farmers. But that wasn't because they were
presidents and popes and lawyers and farmers; it was because they were bad anyway; and there's been lots of 'em
blamed for being bad who were doing the best they
could, and it turned out to be pretty good. If you read
back some and study over the history of our country,
you'll find there hasn't been a war yet but what the
people have blamed the President and his associates and
the duly elected members of Congress and the officers at
the head of the Army and Navy for the way things were
going. They started right in with Washington and they
were still at it strong with Wilson. But when all's said and
done, we've won every war we ever got into, and none
of these leaders were more'n cold in their graves than the
same people who'd been vilifying them were calling them
heroes and martyrs. I've got faith to believe we're going
to win this war too, and to think that twenty years from
now we'll look back and say, 'Well, our leaders in World
War Number Two had their faults and made their mis-
takes, but just the same they did take us on to victory!' "

Daniel paused and looked around him, as if daring any
of his listeners to challenge his prophecy. There was
some applause, and though it was not as hearty or as
prolonged as it had been when he spoke of the old-timers
and the newcomers, it was sincere and respectful. There
were also two or three shouts of "Hear, hear!" and several
low murmurs of approbation. "I tell you it takes gumption for a man who's lost his daughter, like Daniel lost
Jenness, to stand up before a crowd and make a statement
like that," Hite Wendell muttered to Mr. Litchfield, "Yes,
and it takes belief in God's everlasting mercy," Mr. Litchfield murmured in reply . . .'

"The second change that's come to Farman Hill since
we last gathered here came by death too, as you all know,"
Daniel was continuing. "I don't need to say quite so
much about the loss of my son Jerome as I did about
the death of my daughter Jenness. It isn't so hard in
that case to look past the loss to the lesson. Not that it
wasn't a bitter blow to my wife and me when we heard
he'd been taken from us, and how. Our only son, and a

son we were proud of through and through, like we had every reason to be. I guess there isn't anything that can make up to grieving parents for the loss of their only son, and Mother and I aren't the only ones in this group who know that either." Daniel looked towards Mrs. Haskins, who was surreptitiously wiping her eyes on the corner of her best hankerchief: Chet, her only son, who had joined the Marines, had gone from New River to Guadalcanal, and she had received a telegram like the one which had come for Alix. Nor was the community loss limited to only sons: the Wests had lost one of theirs in the raid over Tokyo, the Carletons one of theirs in the Aleutians. The Merrill twins who were so devoted to each other and who had succeeded in staying together, as far as anyone knew, had both been missing for months. But Daniel realized he must not speak of all this. There were other things to say and he must get on with them.

"Whenever we go to the graveyard and see the memorial that's been raised to our son, Mother and I say to each other, 'This is the first time a Farman hasn't been buried at the Point.' We can't help it. We can't help thinking that he's lying in a lonely grave somewhere in India instead of right here among his own folks. But then we cheer each other up. We tell each other that the other part of the Farman tradition still holds, that there's been another boy born on the Hill." Daniel looked around to see Alix standing close to him with Jerry in her arms. He took the baby from her and held him on high for everyone to see.

"The Farmans are going on," he said solemnly. "That's one respect in which there hasn't been any change on the Hill and there won't be. Jenness is dead and Jerome's dead, but Jerome's son is alive, and he'll go forward, where I have to leave off. That isn't all either. My other daughter's been spared, my daughter Judith. She's here with us today, she and her husband whom you've helped me to welcome. She's had considerable to tell her mother and me about her experiences as a nurse over in Africa, and maybe it'll be so she can tell some of these stories to you too. I hope so, because they're real interesting, all of

them. But the one I like the best is about the speech the
commanding officer made to the unit she was in, the night
before they disembarked for Oran. He gave them their
instructions about their equipment and all such and then
he said, 'Keep saying to yourselves tomorrow, "*I am doing this for the folks at home. It is something they could
not do for themselves but that I could do for them and
that I must do for them.*" ' They did keep saying this to
themselves as they went under fire. Some of them for the
first time. Some of them for the last time. But every one
of them who heard that man talk kept saying it."

Daniel looked over at Judith and the men and women
who had been listening to him with increasing intentness
followed his glance. She was sitting with her shining
head bent, the soft hair drawn down on either side of her
brow and over her ears, so that the scars on her face did
not show much, and her slight transparent hands were
folded in her lap. The African Campaign ribbon was
pinned on the dress made with the long sleeves and the
carefully cut neckline. She flushed a little, when she
realized that everyone was looking at her, but then she
herself looked at Joe, and saw that there was pride as
well as love in his eyes and this steadied her.

"That speech put something into my head," Daniel
went on. "It gave me an idea for a slogan we could have
ourselves, right here in Farman. I've said to most of you
before that the time was past when we could say the world
had kind of gone by us here and that we were real glad
of it. I've said we'd got to wake up and realize we were
part of a world story after all. Yes, and we're part of a
world struggle—at least the struggle of that share of the
world that wants to see right prevail over might. So I think
we better say to ourselves every day when we go out
into our barns and our kitchens and our gardens and our
fields, '*I am doing this for the men and the girls overseas. It is something they could not do for themselves, but
that I could do for them and must do for them. I can
keep a herd, and hens, and hogs. I can make butter and
cheese. I can preserve fruits and vegetables. I can feed my*

family so that they won't have to use food that's needed for some other family that can't feed itself, and I can help to feed other families too. This is my work. It's war work, just as much as if I were in a fox hole or on a bomber or under fire. I can work a little harder and a little longer than I ever have before.' I won't say 'Well, I've always worked from four in the morning till nine or ten at night, right through the times other men have been belly aching about overtime after an eight hour day, and howling for more pay.' It won't help any to say that because some other men won't carry their share of a load, I won't carry mine either. The only thing that will help will be for me to carry all I can as long as there's a call for it. Maybe those other men don't feel about their country the way I do. But whether they do or not I've got to keep faith with myself. I've got to fight to the last ditch to make the Farman Hill of the future worthy of the Farman Hill of the past, so that when my son's son gets ready to carry on after me he won't be ashamed of what I've done or afraid the heritage his father died to save will be taken from him by the enemies of freedom and the powers of darkness."

The same spontaneous applause resounded that had broken out when Daniel had asked his old friends and neighbors to welcome the newcomers in their midst. But this time he responded more solemnly.

"When Father Boudreau was offering prayer he asked that the snares of the enemy might be driven from this habitation and that holy angels might dwell therein and preserve us in peace," Daniel reminded his hearers. "I feel that prayer's been answered in one way already and I hope it'll continue to be answered in every way. We mustn't forget that we've had enemies of freedom and powers of darkness right here in our midst, and the third change that's come to Farman Hill since we last met here is that they've been rooted out. We've got Dexter Abbott and Benny Cohen to thank for that—at least they were the Lord's instruments this time. But another time there might be other dangers and the Lord might choose other instruments. We've all got to be watchful and ready to do His will."

Daniel gave Jerry back to Alix and again raised his hand. "There's just one more thing, friends, I want to say, and then I'll be through. I didn't set out to make a speech. I told you this wasn't a banquet or a rally or anything of that sort. But listen: it isn't enough just to raise food. There isn't a truer line in the whole Bible than the one that says, *'Men does not live by bread alone, but by every word that proceedeth out of the mouth of God.'* We've got to keep on living by that word ourselves, and we've got to help spread it to the four corners of the earth along with the four freedoms we hear so much about nowadays. It's real easy to slip into the way of thinking that well-being's something that belongs only to the body and that peace is something that belongs only to the mind. But they're not. They're fruits of the spirit. They're part of the spirit of America."

The shadows were beginning to come down from the higher hills; their quiet light covered the fertile fields spreading out from the handhewn doorway. Daniel stepped down and walked over to the Painted Beauty rose bush. The various members of the Lippman family had grouped themselves and their musical instruments around this. No one in the gathering had listened to his words with more rapt attention, and though they rose at his approach, they did not try to speak to him. A hush had fallen on them, as it had on everyone else. Daniel put his hand on the eldest boy's shoulder.

"It's been a fine thing for us to have your band at our party," he said. "Every one of you can play better'n all the musicians we ever had on Farman Hill before, put together. The Lord's given you a great talent that none of us has here on this place. But I'll tell you what: there's a little old melodeon in my parlor that my grandfather and his womenfolk used to take around with them when they went to funerals, doing the best they could to furnish music when there wasn't any other. That melodeon folds up real easy. If you'd help Dexter and Joe to get it and bring it out here in the garden, I think Mother would like to sit down alongside of you boys and play the last selection we have with you. Generally when we have a party at Farman Hill we end up with 'Blest Be the Tie That Binds.' But I think maybe there's something else that would be even more appropriate this evening."

It took only a minute to bring the melodeon out. Dexter and Joe, with the help of the two eldest Lippman boys, did it with the utmost ease. Serena seated herself at it, her worn fingers on the yellowing keys, and looked up at her husband. His own glance traveled slowly from Judith and Joe to Alix and Dexter and finally rested on Jerry. Then he gave the signal. Together Serena and the Lippmans began to play and everyone joined in the singing:

> My country, 'tis of thee,
> Sweet land of liberty,
>   Of thee I sing;
> Land where my fathers died,
> Land of the pilgrims' pride,
> From every mountain side
>   Let freedom ring.
>
> My native country, thee,
> Land of the noble free,
>   Thy name I love;
> I love thy rocks and rills,
> Thy woods and templed hills;
> My heart with rapture thrills
>   Like that above.
>
> Let music swell the breeze,
> And ring from all the trees
>   Sweet freedom's song:
> Let mortal tongues awake;
> Let all that breathe partake;
> Let rocks their silence break,
>   The sound prolong.

Our fathers' God, to thee,
Author of liberty,
　　To thee we sing:
Long may our land be bright
With freedom's holy light;
Protect us by thy might,
　　Great God, our King.

AUTHOR'S NOTE

I HAVE had occasion to remark before that books are conceived and created in strange and devious ways.

The lore of Louisiana proved so fascinating to me that I was very loath to leave New Orleans when *Crescent Carnival* was finished. It took a grim reminder from an inexorable publisher of my promise that the southern sojourn should be only an interlude to bring me back to my natural habitat; and still I could not see Washington as the setting for another story. In writing *All That Glitters*, I had described the end of one era, and I knew we would not come to the end of another until the War itself was ended. It seemed to me dangerous to use the Capital as a major theme, because, owing to its kaleidoscopic qualities, it changes so fast that what might be a well-proportioned picture when a book was written could be entirely out of perspective by the time this was published; nevertheless I could see that, used incidentally, it might well have a logical place in a diversified pattern. I was giving a good deal of anxious thought as to how best to weave the pattern and find the place, when late one night I picked up a copy of the *New York Times*, and turned, as is my habit, to the editorial page, where the daily poem, variously authored, never fails to add a touch of grace to the graver contributions. There, tucked away in the lower right-hand corner, were the delightful verses entitled *New England Village, 1942*, by Milton Bracker, who is now serving with distinction as a foreign correspondent. Immediately I realized that therein lay the theme of my erstwhile elusive story—the story of a typical family, living in a New England village like one of those I have known and loved all my life: a village still unchanged in its outward attributes, yet taking a major part in the war effort, both through its sons and daughters who have joined the Armed Forces and through its less privileged citizens who have had the quiet courage to carry on at home.

What Milton Bracker's poem *New England Village, 1942*, published in the *New York Times*, did for me in one way, Egon Glesinger's article *Nazis in the Woodpile*, published in the *Saturday Evening Post*, did for me in another. The latter clarified various alien activities and pointed the way to fictionizing these. So did some clippings and comments furnished me by Mr. Arthur Dow, State Editor of the *Burlington Free Press*. Mr. and Mrs. Everett Sawyer of North Haverhill, New Hampshire, and Mrs. Daniel Carr, Jr., of West Roxbury, Massachusetts, also furnished me with invaluable source material relative to other phases of the war.

The story of the medical aide who lost a leg in supplying an aspirin table was originally written by Mr. Dale Harrison of the *Chicago Sun*, who has kindly permitted me to adapt this. The account given by Jenness to her parents of a wartime cocktail party in Washington and the description of the costume which she herself wore to this were both inspired through an article by Malvina Lindsay, who all too wisely and wittily reveals, in the pages of the *Washington Post*, the foibles of the *Gentler Sex*. I first saw the delightful verses, "Nurses! Curses!" quoted from the Fort Banks *Digest* in Hope Ridings Miller's column in the same newspaper; and Dillard Stokes, who has temporarily deserted journalism to serve in the Armed Forces, is still another *Post* writer to whom I wish to acknowledge my indebtedness.

Many of the Southern stories which are interspersed in the text were told me by Miss Frances Clark of Meridian, Mississippi, though one or two came from Miss Naomi Deutsch, a staff member of the Pan-American Sanitary Bureau. Miss Teckla Holilngsworth, the distinguished author of many charming Southern spirituals, wrote all the lyrics which are similarly interspersed. Incidentally, I should perhaps again remind the gentle reader, as I did in the foreword of *Crescent Carnival*, that the term Creole is under no circumstances used in the Southern States to denote a person with any colored blood, though this is sometimes done in the West Indies. Webster's definition of a Creole—in the United States—is "a white person descended from the French and Spanish settlers of Louisiana and the Gulf States and preserving their characteristic speech and culture." Mr. Lionel Durel, Professor of French at Tulane University, goes a step further and includes the white descendant of any Continental colonizer in the region. Either of these interpretations may be accepted as correct and both should be carefully borne in mind.

Dr. Hugo Schiff, Rabbi of Temple Beth El in Alexandria, Virginia, and Mrs. Edith Deutsch Lashman of New Orleans have furnished me with valuable data about Jewish refugees, and I have fictionized some of the experiences which came under this same category. Mr. and Mrs. Daniel Carr of North Haverhill, New Hampshire, Mr. and Mrs. Haines H. Johnson of Newbury, Vermont, and Judge and Mrs. Frank N. Brock, also of Newbury, have all given me invaluable assistance in my endeavor to interpret the rural scene. Miss Betsy Jager of the *Wichita Beacon,* a brilliant journalist who specializes in covering trials, and numerous members of the Bar have been of equal assistance in helping me to interpret the process of the law and in checking the accuracy of legal procedure as I have described it and legal idiom as I have used it. Lieutenant Bernice Carroll, who was a member of the Charlotte Evacuation Unit, has checked in the same way on the accuracy of the African descriptions. Father H. Joseph Jacobi, Director of the Associated Catholic Charities in New Orleans, Miss Katharine McKiever of the N. C. W. C. News Service, and Miss Nancy Lee Tackett of Alexandria, Virginia, are others that have been most cooperative in regard to source material, of miscellaneous character.

I was unfamiliar with the beautiful poem by Francis Thompson entitled "The Red Pavilion" until I ran across it in May Morrill Miller's delightful novel, *First the Blade,* published by Alfred A. Knopf. Mrs. Miller quotes this poem at the beginning of one of her chapters and also uses it as a chapter title. Had I not found it in this way, I should not have been able to use it as the title for the last part of my own story, for which it seems so perfectly suited.

The airplane accident resulting in the death of nine officers, all of whom were decorated with the Order of the Purple Heart, which suggested the fictional use of a similar episode in my story, actually took place in May, 1942, not in August, 1942. The Medical Unit from Charlotte, North Carolina, officially known as the Evacuation Unit, actually left for Africa via England earlier in the summer of 1942 than I have indicated. These variations have their counterpart in other episodes unrelated to military operations, which have been directly or indirectly suggested by actual events. But nothing in this book is intended as a description of these, or of any other actual events, and there are no conscious portrayals of any persons connected with them, as all characters are entirely imaginary. By a curious coincidence, three of these characters, christened completely at random, were found to possess the names of real persons—though these persons in no way resembled their fictitious godchildren!—and these names were changed after the novel was actually in galley. I have had similar experiences before and probably shall again, for the number of possible name combinations, like the number of possible card combinations, has no limit! But if anything of this sort occurs unrectified, I can only hope that the gentle reader will view it with indulgence and understanding, knowing it to be accidental.

In order to get the script into shape within the stipulated time, Harriet Whitford Kintner and Virginia Allen, both of whom gave up their former secretarial work with me to marry members of the Armed Forces and bring up war babies, returned to form a "day shift" and a "night shift," wedged in somehow amidst the exigencies of their new duties. Between them, they managed to type the script as I read it aloud to them from the penciled draft which still represents my own wearisome way of writing a story. Meanwhile my equally faithful housekeeper, Clara E. Wilson, fed all three of us—and many of the other individuals who, like my "shifting" secretaries, had to come to "Tradition" when and as they could—plentifully and well at all sorts of odd hours. She has uncomplainingly and continually waited for us to give form and finish to elusive ideas and to take advantage of precious daylight without interrupting our prolonged labors, and when we ourselves signified a break in these she has refreshed and rewarded us. Through this pleasant and cooperative attitude she too has had a share in the writing of this book.

The greatest incentive of all, however, has come from persons who will allow no public acknowledgment of this, who will not even admit that their opinions have been a mainstay, their admonitions a challenge and their encouragement an inspiration. If I have not been able to meet their standards of sincerity, of perseverance and of workmanship, at least I have tried. The effort has meant a great deal to me, both as a writer and as a woman. I hope it will mean something to them.

F. P. K.

"Pine Grove Farm," North Haverhill, New Hampshire, December, 1942.

"Tradition," Alexandria, Virginia, January-February, 1943.

Orleans Club, New Orleans, Louisiana, March, 1943.

"Tradition," Alexandria, Virginia, April-June, 1943.

Orleans Club, New Orleans, Louisiana, July, 1943.

St. Regis Hotel, New York City, August, 1943.

"Pine Grove Farm," North Haverhill, New Hampshire, September, 1943.